A Portrait of the Artist as a Young Man

BY JAMES JOYCE

FICTION

*Dubliners
*A Portrait of the Artist as a Young Man
 Ulysses
*Finnegans Wake

OTHER WORKS

*Exiles (*play*)
 Giacomo Joyce (*notebook*)

COLLECTIONS

*Collected Poems
 Letters of James Joyce (*three volumes*)
*The Critical Writings of James Joyce
*Selected Letters
 The Portable James Joyce

VIKING CRITICAL EDITIONS

A Portrait of the Artist as a Young Man (*edited by Chester G. Anderson*)
Dubliners (*edited by Robert Scholes and A. Walton Litz*)

RELATED WORKS

*A Skeleton Key to *Finnegans Wake*
 By Joseph Campbell and Henry Morton Robinson
*Fabulous Voyager: James Joyce's *Ulysses*
 By Richard Kain
*My Brother's Keeper: James Joyce's Early Years
 By Stanislaus Joyce
*A Shorter Finnegans Wake
 Edited by Anthony Burgess
 James Joyce
 By John Gross (Modern Masters)

* *Available in Viking Compass edition.*

A Portrait of the Artist

as a Young Man

by

James Joyce

New York: The Viking Press

Twenty-sixth printing April 1974

Originally published in 1916

The definitive text, corrected from the Dublin holograph by Chester G.
Anderson and reviewed by Richard Ellmann, first published in 1964 by
The Viking Press, Inc.
625 Madison Avenue, New York, N.Y. 10022

VIKING COMPASS EDITION

A note on the text will be found on page 255.

Distributed in Canada by
The Macmillan Company of Canada Limited

SBN 670-56682-9 (hardbound)
SBN 670-00009-4 (paperbound)

Library of Congress catalog card number: 64-20678

Printed in U.S.A.

A Portrait of the Artist as a Young Man

Et ignotas animum dimittit in artes.
—Ovid, *Metamorphoses,* VIII, 188.

I

O<small>NCE</small> upon a time and a very good time it was there was a moocow coming down along the road and this moocow that was coming down along the road met a nicens little boy named baby tuckoo. . . .

His father told him that story: his father looked at him through a glass: he had a hairy face.

He was baby tuckoo. The moocow came down the road where Betty Byrne lived: she sold lemon platt.

> *O, the wild rose blossoms*
> *On the little green place.*

He sang that song. That was his song.

> *O, the green wothe botheth.*

When you wet the bed first it is warm then it gets cold. His mother put on the oilsheet. That had the queer smell.

His mother had a nicer smell than his father. She played on the piano the sailor's hornpipe for him to dance. He danced:

> *Tralala lala*
> *Tralala tralaladdy*
> *Tralala lala*
> *Tralala lala.*

Uncle Charles and Dante clapped. They were older than his father and mother but uncle Charles was older than Dante.

Dante had two brushes in her press. The brush with the maroon velvet back was for Michael Davitt and the brush with the green velvet back was for Parnell. Dante gave him a cachou every time he brought her a piece of tissue paper.

7

The Vances lived in number seven. They had a different father and mother. They were Eileen's father and mother. When they were grown up he was going to marry Eileen. He hid under the table. His mother said:

—O, Stephen will apologise.

Dante said:

—O, if not, the eagles will come and pull out his eyes.

> *Pull out his eyes,*
> *Apologise,*
> *Apologise,*
> *Pull out his eyes.*
>
> *Apologise,*
> *Pull out his eyes,*
> *Pull out his eyes,*
> *Apologise.*

*   *   *

The wide playgrounds were swarming with boys. All were shouting and the prefects urged them on with strong cries. The evening air was pale and chilly and after every charge and thud of the footballers the greasy leather orb flew like a heavy bird through the grey light. He kept on the fringe of his line, out of sight of his prefect, out of the reach of the rude feet, feigning to run now and then. He felt his body small and weak amid the throng of players and his eyes were weak and watery. Rody Kickham was not like that: he would be captain of the third line all the fellows said.

Rody Kickham was a decent fellow but Nasty Roche was a stink. Rody Kickham had greaves in his number and a hamper in the refectory. Nasty Roche had big hands. He called the Friday pudding dog-in-the-blanket. And one day he had asked:

—What is your name?

Stephen had answered:

—Stephen Dedalus.

Then Nasty Roche had said:

—What kind of a name is that?

And when Stephen had not been able to answer Nasty Roche had asked:

—What is your father?

Stephen had answered:

—A gentleman.

Then Nasty Roche had asked:

—Is he a magistrate?

He crept about from point to point on the fringe of his line, making little runs now and then. But his hands were bluish with cold. He kept his hands in the sidepockets of his belted grey suit. That was a belt round his pocket. And belt was also to give a fellow a belt. One day a fellow had said to Cantwell:

—I'd give you such a belt in a second.

Cantwell had answered:

—Go and fight your match. Give Cecil Thunder a belt. I'd like to see you. He'd give you a toe in the rump for yourself.

That was not a nice expression. His mother had told him not to speak with the rough boys in the college. Nice mother! The first day in the hall of the castle when she had said goodbye she had put up her veil double to her nose to kiss him: and her nose and eyes were red. But he had pretended not to see that she was going to cry. She was a nice mother but she was not so nice when she cried. And his father had given him two fiveshilling pieces for pocket money. And his father had told him if he wanted anything to write home to him and, whatever he did, never to peach on a fellow. Then at the door of the castle the rector had shaken hands with his father and mother, his soutane fluttering in the breeze, and the car had driven off with his father and mother on it. They had cried to him from the car, waving their hands:

—Goodbye, Stephen, goodbye!

—Goodbye, Stephen, goodbye!

He was caught in the whirl of a scrimmage and, fearful of the flashing eyes and muddy boots, bent down to look through the legs. The fellows were struggling and groaning and their legs were rubbing and kicking and stamping. Then Jack Lawton's yellow boots dodged out the ball and all the other boots and legs ran after. He ran after them a little way and then stopped. It was useless to run on. Soon they would be going home for the holidays. After supper in the studyhall he would change the number pasted up inside his desk from seventyseven to seventysix.

It would be better to be in the studyhall than out there in the cold. The sky was pale and cold but there were lights in the castle. He wondered from which window Hamilton Rowan had thrown his hat on the haha and had there been flowerbeds at that time under the windows. One day when he had been called to the castle the butler had shown him the marks of the soldiers' slugs in the wood of the door and had given him a piece of shortbread that the community ate. It was nice and warm to see the lights in the castle. It was like something in a book. Perhaps Leicester Abbey was like that. And there were nice sentences in Doctor Cornwell's Spelling Book. They were like poetry but they were only sentences to learn the spelling from.

> *Wolsey died in Leicester Abbey*
> *Where the abbots buried him.*
> *Canker is a disease of plants,*
> *Cancer one of animals.*

It would be nice to lie on the hearthrug before the fire, leaning his head upon his hands, and think on those sentences. He shivered as if he had cold slimy water next his skin. That was mean of Wells to shoulder him into the square ditch because he would not swop his little snuffbox for Wells's seasoned hacking chestnut, the conqueror of forty. How cold and slimy the water had been! A fellow had once seen a big rat jump into the scum. Mother was sitting at the fire with Dante waiting for Brigid to bring in the tea. She had her feet on the fender and her jewelly slippers were so hot and they had such a lovely warm smell! Dante knew a lot of things. She had taught him where the Mozambique Channel was and what was the longest river in America and what was the name of the highest mountain in the moon. Father Arnall knew more than Dante because he was a priest but both his father and uncle Charles said that Dante was a clever woman and a wellread woman. And when Dante made that noise after dinner and then put up her hand to her mouth: that was heartburn.

A voice cried far out on the playground:

—All in!

Then other voices cried from the lower and third lines:

—All in! All in!

The players closed around, flushed and muddy, and he went among them, glad to go in. Rody Kickham held the ball by its greasy lace. A fellow asked him to give it one last: but he walked on without even answering the fellow. Simon Moonan told him not to because the prefect was looking. The fellow turned to Simon Moonan and said:

—We all know why you speak. You are McGlade's suck.

Suck was a queer word. The fellow called Simon Moonan that name because Simon Moonan used to tie the prefect's false sleeves behind his back and the prefect used to let on to be angry. But the sound was ugly. Once he had washed his hands in the lavatory of the Wicklow Hotel and his father pulled the stopper up by the chain after and the dirty water went down through the hole in the basin. And when it had all gone down slowly the hole in the basin had made a sound like that: suck. Only louder.

To remember that and the white look of the lavatory made him feel cold and then hot. There were two cocks that you turned and water came out: cold and hot. He felt cold and then a little hot: and he could see the names printed on the cocks. That was a very queer thing.

And the air in the corridor chilled him too. It was queer and wettish. But soon the gas would be lit and in burning it made a light noise like a little song. Always the same: and when the fellows stopped talking in the playroom you could hear it.

It was the hour for sums. Father Arnall wrote a hard sum on the board and then said:

—Now then, who will win? Go ahead, York! Go ahead, Lancaster!

Stephen tried his best but the sum was too hard and he felt confused. The little silk badge with the white rose on it that was pinned on the breast of his jacket began to flutter. He was no good at sums but he tried his best so that York might not lose. Father Arnall's face looked very black but he was not in a wax: he was laughing. Then Jack Lawton cracked his fingers and Father Arnall looked at his copybook and said:

—Right. Bravo Lancaster! The red rose wins. Come on now, York! Forge ahead!

Jack Lawton looked over from his side. The little silk badge with the red rose on it looked very rich because he had a blue sailor top on. Stephen felt his own face red too, thinking of all the bets about who would get first place in elements, Jack Lawton or he. Some weeks Jack Lawton got the card for first and some weeks he got the card for first. His white silk badge fluttered and fluttered as he worked at the next sum and heard Father Arnall's voice. Then all his eagerness passed away and he felt his face quite cool. He thought his face must be white because it felt so cool. He could not get out the answer for the sum but it did not matter. White roses and red roses: those were beautiful colours to think of. And the cards for first place and second place and third place were beautiful colours too: pink and cream and lavender. Lavender and cream and pink roses were beautiful to think of. Perhaps a wild rose might be like those colours and he remembered the song about the wild rose blossoms on the little green place. But you could not have a green rose. But perhaps somewhere in the world you could.

The bell rang and then the classes began to file out of the rooms and along the corridors towards the refectory. He sat looking at the two prints of butter on his plate but could not eat the damp bread. The tablecloth was damp and limp. But he drank off the hot weak tea which the clumsy scullion, girt with a white apron, poured into his cup. He wondered whether the scullion's apron was damp too or whether all white things were cold and damp. Nasty Roche and Saurin drank cocoa that their people sent them in tins. They said they could not drink the tea; that it was hogwash. Their fathers were magistrates, the fellows said.

All the boys seemed to him very strange. They had all fathers and mothers and different clothes and voices. He longed to be at home and lay his head on his mother's lap. But he could not: and so he longed for the play and study and prayers to be over and to be in bed.

He drank another cup of hot tea and Fleming said:

—What's up? Have you a pain or what's up with you?

—I don't know, Stephen said.

—Sick in your breadbasket, Fleming said, because your face looks white. It will go away.

—O yes, Stephen said.

But he was not sick there. He thought that he was sick in his heart if you could be sick in that place. Fleming was very decent to ask him. He wanted to cry. He leaned his elbows on the table and shut and opened the flaps of his ears. Then he heard the noise of the refectory every time he opened the flaps of his ears. It made a roar like a train at night. And when he closed the flaps the roar was shut off like a train going into a tunnel. That night at Dalkey the train had roared like that and then, when it went into the tunnel, the roar stopped. He closed his eyes and the train went on, roaring and then stopping; roaring again, stopping. It was nice to hear it roar and stop and then roar out of the tunnel again and then stop.

Then the higher line fellows began to come down along the matting in the middle of the refectory, Paddy Rath and Jimmy Magee and the Spaniard who was allowed to smoke cigars and the little Portuguese who wore the woolly cap. And then the lower line tables and the tables of the third line. And every single fellow had a different way of walking.

He sat in a corner of the playroom pretending to watch a

game of dominos and once or twice he was able to hear for an instant the little song of the gas. The prefect was at the door with some boys and Simon Moonan was knotting his false sleeves. He was telling them something about Tullabeg.

Then he went away from the door and Wells came over to Stephen and said:

—Tell us, Dedalus, do you kiss your mother before you go to bed?

Stephen answered:

—I do.

Wells turned to the other fellows and said:

—O, I say, here's a fellow says he kisses his mother every night before he goes to bed.

The other fellows stopped their game and turned round, laughing. Stephen blushed under their eyes and said:

—I do not.

Wells said:

—O, I say, here's a fellow says he doesn't kiss his mother before he goes to bed.

They all laughed again. Stephen tried to laugh with them. He felt his whole body hot and confused in a moment. What was the right answer to the question? He had given two and still Wells laughed. But Wells must know the right answer for he was in third of grammar. He tried to think of Wells's mother but he did not dare to raise his eyes to Wells's face. He did not like Wells's face. It was Wells who had shouldered him into the square ditch the day before because he would not swop his little snuffbox for Wells's seasoned hacking chestnut, the conqueror of forty. It was a mean thing to do; all the fellows said it was. And how cold and slimy the water had been! And a fellow had once seen a big rat jump plop into the scum.

The cold slime of the ditch covered his whole body; and, when the bell rang for study and the lines filed out of the playrooms, he felt the cold air of the corridor and staircase inside his clothes. He still tried to think what was the right answer. Was it right to kiss his mother or wrong to kiss his mother? What did that mean, to kiss? You put your face up like that to say goodnight and then his mother put her face down. That was to kiss. His mother put her lips on his cheek; her lips were soft and they wetted his cheek; and they made a tiny little noise: kiss. Why did people do that with their two faces?

Sitting in the studyhall he opened the lid of his desk and changed the number pasted up inside from seventyseven to seventysix. But the Christmas vacation was very far away: but one time it would come because the earth moved round always.

There was a picture of the earth on the first page of his geography: a big ball in the middle of clouds. Fleming had a box of crayons and one night during free study he had coloured the earth green and the clouds maroon. That was like the two brushes in Dante's press, the brush with the green velvet back for Parnell and the brush with the maroon velvet back for Michael Davitt. But he had not told Fleming to colour them those colours. Fleming had done it himself.

He opened the geography to study the lesson; but he could not learn the names of places in America. Still they were all different places that had those different names. They were all in different countries and the countries were in continents and the continents were in the world and the world was in the universe.

He turned to the flyleaf of the geography and read what he had written there: himself, his name and where he was.

> *Stephen Dedalus*
> *Class of Elements*
> *Clongowes Wood College*
> *Sallins*
> *County Kildare*
> *Ireland*
> *Europe*
> *The World*
> *The Universe*

That was in his writing: and Fleming one night for a cod had written on the opposite page:

> *Stephen Dedalus is my name,*
> *Ireland is my nation.*
> *Clongowes is my dwellingplace*
> *And heaven my expectation.*

He read the verses backwards but then they were not poetry. Then he read the flyleaf from the bottom to the top till he came to his own name. That was he: and he read down the page again. What was after the universe? Nothing. But was there anything round the universe to show where it stopped before the nothing place began? It could not be a wall but there could be a thin thin line there all round everything. It was very big to think about everything and everywhere. Only God could do that. He tried to think what a big thought that must be but he could think only of God. God was God's name just as his name was Stephen. *Dieu* was the French for God and that was God's name too; and when anyone prayed to God and said *Dieu* then God knew at once that it was a French person that was praying. But though there were different names for God in all the different languages in the world and God understood what all the people who prayed said in their different languages still God remained always the same God and God's real name was God.

It made him very tired to think that way. It made him feel his head very big. He turned over the flyleaf and looked wearily at the green round earth in the middle of the maroon clouds. He wondered which was right, to be for the green or for the maroon, because Dante had ripped the green velvet back off the brush that was for Parnell one day with her scissors and had told him that Parnell was a bad man. He wondered if they were arguing at home about that. That was called politics. There were two sides in it: Dante was on one side and his father and Mr Casey were on the other side but his mother and uncle Charles were on no side. Every day there was something in the paper about it.

It pained him that he did not know well what politics meant and that he did not know where the universe ended. He felt small and weak. When would he be like the fellows in poetry and rhetoric? They had big voices and big boots and they studied trigonometry. That was very far away. First came the vacation and then the next term and then vacation again and then again another term and then again the vacation. It was like a train going in and out of tunnels and that was like the noise of the boys eating in the refectory when you opened and closed the flaps of the ears. Term, vacation; tunnel, out; noise, stop. How far away it was! It was better to go to bed to sleep. Only prayers in the chapel and then bed. He shivered and yawned. It would be lovely in bed after the sheets got a bit hot. First they were so cold to get into. He shivered to think how cold they were first. But then they got hot and then he could sleep. It was lovely to be tired. He yawned again. Night prayers and then bed: he shivered and wanted to yawn. It would be lovely in a few minutes. He felt a warm glow creeping up from the cold shivering sheets, warmer and warmer till he felt warm all over, ever so warm; ever so warm and yet he shivered a little and still wanted to yawn.

The bell rang for night prayers and he filed out of the study-hall after the others and down the staircase and along the corridors to the chapel. The corridors were darkly lit and the chapel was darkly lit. Soon all would be dark and sleeping. There was cold night air in the chapel and the marbles were the colour the sea was at night. The sea was cold day and night: but it was colder at night. It was cold and dark under the seawall beside his father's house. But the kettle would be on the hob to make punch.

The prefect of the chapel prayed above his head and his memory knew the responses:

> *O Lord, open our lips*
> *And our mouth shall announce Thy praise.*
> *Incline unto our aid, O God!*
> *O Lord, make haste to help us!*

There was a cold night smell in the chapel. But it was a holy smell. It was not like the smell of the old peasants who knelt at the back of the chapel at Sunday mass. That was a smell of air and rain and turf and corduroy. But they were very holy peasants. They breathed behind him on his neck and sighed as they prayed. They lived in Clane, a fellow said: there were little cottages there and he had seen a woman standing at the halfdoor of a cottage with a child in her arms, as the cars had come past from Sallins. It would be lovely to sleep for one night in that cottage before the fire of smoking turf, in the dark lit by the fire, in the warm dark, breathing the smell of the peasants, air and rain and turf and corduroy. But, O, the road there between the trees was dark! You would be lost in the dark. It made him afraid to think of how it was.

He heard the voice of the prefect of the chapel saying the last prayer. He prayed it too against the dark outside under the trees.

> *Visit, we beseech Thee, O Lord, this habitation and drive away from it all the snares of the enemy. May Thy holy angels dwell herein to preserve us in peace and may Thy blessing be always upon us through Christ, Our Lord. Amen.*

His fingers trembled as he undressed himself in the dormitory. He told his fingers to hurry up. He had to undress and then kneel and say his own prayers and be in bed before the gas was lowered so that he might not go to hell when he died. He rolled his stockings off and put on his nightshirt quickly and knelt trembling at his bedside and repeated his prayers quickly quickly, fearing that the gas would go down. He felt his shoulders shaking as he murmured:

> *God bless my father and my mother and spare them to me!*
>
> *God bless my little brothers and sisters and spare them to me!*
>
> *God bless Dante and uncle Charles and spare them to me!*

He blessed himself and climbed quickly into bed and, tucking the end of the nightshirt under his feet, curled himself together under the cold white sheets, shaking and trembling. But he would not go to hell when he died; and the shaking would stop. A voice bade the boys in the dormitory goodnight. He peered out for an instant over the coverlet and saw the yellow curtains round and before his bed that shut him off on all sides. The light was lowered quietly.

The prefect's shoes went away. Where? Down the staircase and along the corridors or to his room at the end? He saw the dark. Was it true about the black dog that walked there at night with eyes as big as carriagelamps? They said it was the ghost of a murderer. A long shiver of fear flowed over his body. He saw the dark entrance hall of the castle. Old servants in old dress were in the ironingroom above the staircase. It was long ago. The old servants were quiet. There was a fire there but the hall was still dark. A figure came up the staircase from the hall. He wore the white cloak of a marshal; his face was pale and strange; he held his hand pressed to his side. He looked out of strange eyes at the old servants. They looked at him and saw their master's face and cloak and knew that he had received his deathwound. But only the dark was where they looked: only dark silent air. Their master had received his deathwound on the battlefield of Prague far away over the sea. He was standing on the field; his hand was pressed to his side; his face was pale and strange and he wore the white cloak of a marshal.

O how cold and strange it was to think of that! All the dark was cold and strange. There were pale strange faces there, great eyes like carriagelamps. They were the ghosts of murderers, the figures of marshals who had received their deathwound on battlefields far away over the sea. What did they wish to say that their faces were so strange?

Visit, we beseech Thee, O Lord, this habitation and drive away from it all . . .

Going home for the holidays! That would be lovely: the fellows had told him. Getting up on the cars in the early wintry morning outside the door of the castle. The cars were rolling on the gravel. Cheers for the rector!

Hurray! Hurray! Hurray!

The cars drove past the chapel and all caps were raised. They drove merrily along the country roads. The drivers pointed with their whips to Bodenstown. The fellows cheered. They passed the farmhouse of the Jolly Farmer. Cheer after cheer after cheer. Through Clane they drove, cheering and cheered. The peasant women stood at the halfdoors, the men stood here and there. The lovely smell there was in the wintry air: the smell of Clane: rain and wintry air and turf smouldering and corduroy.

The train was full of fellows: a long long chocolate train with cream facings. The guards went to and fro opening, closing, locking, unlocking the doors. They were men in dark blue and silver; they had silvery whistles and their keys made a quick music: click, click: click, click.

And the train raced on over the flat lands and past the Hill of Allen. The telegraphpoles were passing, passing. The train went on and on. It knew. There were coloured lanterns in the hall of his father's house and ropes of green branches. There were holly and ivy round the pierglass and holly and ivy, green and red, twined round the chandeliers. There were red holly and green ivy round the old portraits on the walls. Holly and ivy for him and for Christmas.

Lovely . . .

All the people. Welcome home, Stephen! Noises of welcome. His mother kissed him. Was that right? His father was a marshal now: higher than a magistrate. Welcome home, Stephen!

Noises . . .

There was a noise of curtainrings running back along the rods, of water being splashed in the basins. There was a noise of rising and dressing and washing in the dormitory: a noise of clapping of hands as the prefect went up and down telling the fellows to look sharp. A pale sunlight showed the yellow curtains drawn back, the tossed beds. His bed was very hot and his face and body were very hot.

He got up and sat on the side of his bed. He was weak. He tried to pull on his stocking. It had a horrid rough feel. The sunlight was queer and cold.

Fleming said:

—Are you not well?

He did not know; and Fleming said:

—Get back into bed. I'll tell McGlade you're not well.

—He's sick.

—Who is?

—Tell McGlade.

—Get back into bed.

—Is he sick?

A fellow held his arms while he loosened the stocking clinging to his foot and climbed back into the hot bed.

He crouched down between the sheets, glad of their tepid glow. He heard the fellows talk among themselves about him as they dressed for mass. It was a mean thing to do, to shoulder him into the square ditch, they were saying.

Then their voices ceased; they had gone. A voice at his bed said:

—Dedalus, don't spy on us, sure you won't?

Wells's face was there. He looked at it and saw that Wells was afraid.

—I didn't mean to. Sure you won't?

His father had told him, whatever he did, never to peach on a fellow. He shook his head and answered no and felt glad. Wells said:

—I didn't mean to, honour bright. It was only for cod. I'm sorry.

The face and the voice went away. Sorry because he was afraid. Afraid that it was some disease. Canker was a disease of plants and cancer one of animals: or another different. That was a long time ago then out on the playgrounds in the evening light, creeping from point to point on the fringe of his line, a heavy bird flying low through the grey light. Leicester Abbey lit up. Wolsey died there. The abbots buried him themselves.

It was not Wells's face, it was the prefect's. He was not foxing. No, no: he was sick really. He was not foxing. And he felt the prefect's hand on his forehead; and he felt his forehead warm and damp against the prefect's cold damp hand. That was the way a rat felt, slimy and damp and cold. Every rat had two eyes to look out of. Sleek slimy coats, little little feet tucked up to jump, black shiny eyes to look out of. They could understand how to jump. But the minds of rats could not understand trigonometry. When they were dead they lay on their sides. Their coats dried then. They were only dead things.

The prefect was there again and it was his voice that was saying that he was to get up, that Father Minister had said he was to get up and dress and go to the infirmary. And while he was dressing himself as quickly as he could the prefect said:

—We must pack off to Brother Michael because we have the collywobbles! Terrible thing to have the collywobbles! How we wobble when we have the collywobbles!

He was very decent to say that. That was all to make him laugh. But he could not laugh because his cheeks and lips were all shivery: and then the prefect had to laugh by himself.

The prefect cried:

—Quick march! Hayfoot! Strawfoot!

They went together down the staircase and along the corridor and past the bath. As he passed the door he remembered with a vague fear the warm turfcoloured bogwater, the warm moist air, the noise of plunges, the smell of the towels, like medicine.

Brother Michael was standing at the door of the infirmary and from the door of the dark cabinet on his right came a smell like medicine. That came from the bottles on the shelves. The prefect spoke to Brother Michael and Brother

Michael answered and called the prefect sir. He had reddish hair mixed with grey and a queer look. It was queer that he would always be a brother. It was queer too that you could not call him sir because he was a brother and had a different kind of look. Was he not holy enough or why could he not catch up on the others?

There were two beds in the room and in one bed there was a fellow: and when they went in he called out:

—Hello! It's young Dedalus! What's up?

—The sky is up, Brother Michael said.

He was a fellow out of the third of grammar and, while Stephen was undressing, he asked Brother Michael to bring him a round of buttered toast.

—Ah, do! he said.

—Butter you up! said Brother Michael. You'll get your walking papers in the morning when the doctor comes.

—Will I? the fellow said. I'm not well yet.

Brother Michael repeated:

—You'll get your walking papers, I tell you.

He bent down to rake the fire. He had a long back like the long back of a tramhorse. He shook the poker gravely and nodded his head at the fellow out of third of grammar.

Then Brother Michael went away and after a while the fellow out of third of grammar turned in towards the wall and fell asleep.

That was the infirmary. He was sick then. Had they written home to tell his mother and father? But it would be quicker for one of the priests to go himself to tell them. Or he would write a letter for the priest to bring.

Dear Mother

I am sick. I want to go home. Please come and take me home. I am in the infirmary.

Your fond son,
Stephen

How far away they were! There was cold sunlight outside the window. He wondered if he would die. You could die just the same on a sunny day. He might die before his mother came. Then he would have a dead mass in the chapel like the way the fellows had told him it was when Little had died. All the fellows would be at the mass, dressed in black, all with sad faces. Wells too would be there but no fellow would look at him. The rector would be there in a cope of black and gold and there would be tall yellow candles on the altar and round the catafalque. And they would carry the coffin out of the chapel slowly and he would be buried in the little graveyard of the community off the main avenue of limes. And Wells would be sorry then for what he had done. And the bell would toll slowly.

He could hear the tolling. He said over to himself the song that Brigid had taught him.

> *Dingdong! The castle bell!*
> *Farewell, my mother!*
> *Bury me in the old churchyard*
> *Beside my eldest brother.*
> *My coffin shall be black,*
> *Six angels at my back,*
> *Two to sing and two to pray*
> *And two to carry my soul away.*

How beautiful and sad that was! How beautiful the words were where they said *Bury me in the old churchyard!* A tremor passed over his body. How sad and how beautiful! He wanted to cry quietly but not for himself: for the words, so beautiful and sad, like music. The bell! The bell! Farewell! O farewell!

The cold sunlight was weaker and Brother Michael was standing at his bedside with a bowl of beeftea. He was glad for his mouth was hot and dry. He could hear them playing on the playgrounds. And the day was going on in the college just as if he were there.

Then Brother Michael was going away and the fellow out of third of grammar told him to be sure and come back and tell him all the news in the paper. He told Stephen that his name was Athy and that his father kept a lot of racehorses that were spiffing jumpers and that his father would give a good tip to Brother Michael any time he wanted it because Brother Michael was very decent and always told him the news out of the paper they got every day up in the castle. There was every kind of news in the paper: accidents, shipwrecks, sports and politics.

—Now it is all about politics in the paper, he said. Do your people talk about that too?

—Yes, Stephen said.

—Mine too, he said.

Then he thought for a moment and said:

—You have a queer name, Dedalus, and I have a queer name too, Athy. My name is the name of a town. Your name is like Latin.

Then he asked:

—Are you good at riddles?

Stephen answered:

—Not very good.

Then he said:

—Can you answer me this one? Why is the county Kildare like the leg of a fellow's breeches?

Stephen thought what could be the answer and then said:

—I give it up.

—Because there is a thigh in it, he said. Do you see the joke? Athy is the town in the county Kildare and a thigh is the other thigh.

—O, I see, Stephen said.

—That's an old riddle, he said.

After a moment he said:

—I say!

—What? asked Stephen.

—You know, he said, you can ask that riddle another way?

—Can you? said Stephen.

—The same riddle, he said. Do you know the other way to ask it?

—No, said Stephen.

—Can you not think of the other way? he said.

He looked at Stephen over the bedclothes as he spoke. Then he lay back on the pillow and said:

—There is another way but I won't tell you what it is.

Why did he not tell it? His father, who kept the racehorses, must be a magistrate too like Saurin's father and Nasty Roche's father. He thought of his own father, of how he sang songs while his mother played and of how he always gave him a shilling when he asked for sixpence and he felt sorry for him that he was not a magistrate like the other boys' fathers. Then why was he sent to that place with them? But his father had told him that he would be no stranger there because his grand-uncle had presented an address to the liberator there fifty years before. You could know the people of that time by their old dress. It seemed to him a solemn time: and he wondered if that was the time when the fellows in Clongowes wore blue coats with brass buttons and yellow waistcoats and caps of rabbitskin and drank beer like grownup people and kept greyhounds of their own to course the hares with.

He looked at the window and saw that the daylight had grown weaker. There would be cloudy grey light over the playgrounds. There was no noise on the playgrounds. The class must be doing the themes or perhaps Father Arnall was reading a legend out of the book.

It was queer that they had not given him any medicine. Perhaps Brother Michael would bring it back when he came. They said you got stinking stuff to drink when you were in the infirmary. But he felt better now than before. It would be nice getting better slowly. You could get a book then. There was a book in the library about Holland. There were lovely foreign names in it and pictures of strangelooking cities and ships. It made you feel so happy.

How pale the light was at the window! But that was nice. The fire rose and fell on the wall. It was like waves. Someone had put coal on and he heard voices. They were talking. It was the noise of the waves. Or the waves were talking among themselves as they rose and fell.

He saw the sea of waves, long dark waves rising and falling, dark under the moonless night. A tiny light twinkled at the pierhead where the ship was entering: and he saw a multitude of people gathered by the waters' edge to see the ship that was entering their harbour. A tall man stood on the deck, looking out towards the flat dark land: and by the light at the pierhead he saw his face, the sorrowful face of Brother Michael.

He saw him lift his hand towards the people and heard him say in a loud voice of sorrow over the waters:

—He is dead. We saw him lying upon the catafalque.

A wail of sorrow went up from the people.

—Parnell! Parnell! He is dead!

They fell upon their knees, moaning in sorrow.

And he saw Dante in a maroon velvet dress and with a green velvet mantle hanging from her shoulders walking proudly and silently past the people who knelt by the waters' edge.

*   *   *

A great fire, banked high and red, flamed in the grate and under the ivytwined branches of the chandelier the Christmas table was spread. They had come home a little late and still dinner was not ready: but it would be ready in a jiffy, his mother had said. They were waiting for the door to open and for the servants to come in, holding the big dishes covered with their heavy metal covers.

All were waiting: uncle Charles, who sat far away in the shadow of the window, Dante and Mr Casey, who sat in the easychairs at either side of the hearth, Stephen, seated on a chair between them, his feet resting on the toasted boss. Mr Dedalus looked at himself in the pierglass above the mantel-piece, waxed out his moustache-ends and then, parting his coattails, stood with his back to the glowing fire: and still, from time to time, he withdrew a hand from his coattail to wax out one of his moustache-ends. Mr Casey leaned his head to one side and, smiling, tapped the gland of his neck with his fingers. And Stephen smiled too for he knew now that it was not true that Mr Casey had a purse of silver in his throat. He smiled to think how the silvery noise which Mr Casey used to make had deceived him. And when he had tried to open Mr Casey's hand to see if the purse of silver was hidden there he had seen that the fingers could not be straightened out: and Mr Casey had told him that he had got those three cramped fingers making a birthday present for Queen Victoria.

Mr Casey tapped the gland of his neck and smiled at Stephen with sleepy eyes: and Mr Dedalus said to him:

—Yes. Well now, that's all right. O, we had a good walk, hadn't we, John? Yes . . . I wonder if there's any likelihood of dinner this evening. Yes. . . . O, well now, we got a good breath of ozone round the Head today. Ay, bedad.

He turned to Dante and said:

—You didn't stir out at all, Mrs Riordan?

Dante frowned and said shortly:

—No.

Mr Dedalus dropped his coattails and went over to the sideboard. He brought forth a great stone jar of whisky from the locker and filled the decanter slowly, bending now and then to see how much he had poured in. Then replacing the jar in the locker he poured a little of the whisky into two glasses, added a little water and came back with them to the fireplace.

—A thimbleful, John, he said, just to whet your appetite.

Mr Casey took the glass, drank, and placed it near him on the mantelpiece. Then he said:

—Well, I can't help thinking of our friend Christopher manufacturing . . .

He broke into a fit of laughter and coughing and added:

—. . . manufacturing that champagne for those fellows.

Mr Dedalus laughed loudly.

—Is it Christy? he said. There's more cunning in one of those warts on his bald head than in a pack of jack foxes.

He inclined his head, closed his eyes, and, licking his lips profusely, began to speak with the voice of the hotelkeeper.

—And he has such a soft mouth when he's speaking to you, don't you know. He's very moist and watery about the dewlaps, God bless him.

Mr Casey was still struggling through his fit of coughing and laughter. Stephen, seeing and hearing the hotelkeeper through his father's face and voice, laughed.

Mr Dedalus put up his eyeglass and, staring down at him, said quietly and kindly:

—What are you laughing at, you little puppy, you?

The servants entered and placed the dishes on the table. Mrs Dedalus followed and the places were arranged.

—Sit over, she said.

Mr Dedalus went to the end of the table and said:

—Now, Mrs Riordan, sit over. John, sit you down, my hearty.

He looked round to where uncle Charles sat and said:

—Now then, sir, there's a bird here waiting for you.

When all had taken their seats he laid his hand on the cover and then said quickly, withdrawing it:

—Now, Stephen.

Stephen stood up in his place to say the grace before meals:

Bless us, O Lord, and these Thy gifts which through Thy bounty we are about to receive through Christ Our Lord. Amen.

All blessed themselves and Mr Dedalus with a sigh of pleasure lifted from the dish the heavy cover pearled around the edge with glistening drops.

Stephen looked at the plump turkey which had lain, trussed and skewered, on the kitchen table. He knew that his father had paid a guinea for it in Dunn's of D'Olier Street and that the man had prodded it often at the breastbone to show how good it was: and he remembered the man's voice when he had said:

—Take that one, sir. That's the real Ally Daly.

Why did Mr Barrett in Clongowes call his pandybat a turkey? But Clongowes was far away: and the warm heavy smell of turkey and ham and celery rose from the plates and dishes and the great fire was banked high and red in the grate and the green ivy and red holly made you feel so happy and when dinner was ended the big plumpudding would be carried in, studded with peeled almonds and sprigs of holly, with bluish fire running around it and a little green flag flying from the top.

It was his first Christmas dinner and he thought of his little brothers and sisters who were waiting in the nursery, as he had often waited, till the pudding came. The deep low collar and the Eton jacket made him feel queer and oldish: and that morning when his mother had brought him down to the parlour, dressed for mass, his father had cried. That was because he was thinking of his own father. And uncle Charles had said so too.

Mr Dedalus covered the dish and began to eat hungrily. Then he said:

—Poor old Christy, he's nearly lopsided now with roguery.

—Simon, said Mrs Dedalus, you haven't given Mrs Riordan any sauce.

Mr Dedalus seized the sauceboat.

—Haven't I? he cried. Mrs Riordan, pity the poor blind.

Dante covered her plate with her hands and said:

—No, thanks.

Mr Dedalus turned to uncle Charles.

—How are you off, sir?

—Right as the mail, Simon.

—You, John?

—I'm all right. Go on yourself.

—Mary? Here, Stephen, here's something to make your hair curl.

He poured sauce freely over Stephen's plate and set the boat again on the table. Then he asked uncle Charles was it tender. Uncle Charles could not speak because his mouth was full but he nodded that it was.

—That was a good answer our friend made to the canon. What? said Mr Dedalus.

—I didn't think he had that much in him, said Mr Casey.

—*I'll pay you your dues, father, when you cease turning the house of God into a pollingbooth.*

—A nice answer, said Dante, for any man calling himself a catholic to give to his priest.

—They have only themselves to blame, said Mr Dedalus suavely. If they took a fool's advice they would confine their attention to religion.

—It is religion, Dante said. They are doing their duty in warning the people.

—We go to the house of God, Mr Casey said, in all humility to pray to our Maker and not to hear election addresses.

—It is religion, Dante said again. They are right. They must direct their flocks.

—And preach politics from the altar, is it? asked Mr Dedalus.

—Certainly, said Dante. It is a question of public morality. A priest would not be a priest if he did not tell his flock what is right and what is wrong.

Mrs Dedalus laid down her knife and fork, saying:

—For pity's sake and for pity sake let us have no political discussion on this day of all days in the year.

—Quite right, ma'am, said uncle Charles. Now, Simon, that's quite enough now. Not another word now.

—Yes, yes, said Mr Dedalus quickly.

He uncovered the dish boldly and said:

—Now then, who's for more turkey?

Nobody answered. Dante said:

—Nice language for any catholic to use!

—Mrs Riordan, I appeal to you, said Mrs Dedalus, to let the matter drop now.

Dante turned on her and said:

—And am I to sit here and listen to the pastors of my church being flouted?

—Nobody is saying a word against them, said Mr Dedalus, so long as they don't meddle in politics.

—The bishops and priests of Ireland have spoken, said Dante, and they must be obeyed.

—Let them leave politics alone, said Mr Casey, or the people may leave their church alone.

—You hear? said Dante turning to Mrs Dedalus.

—Mr Casey! Simon! said Mrs Dedalus. Let it end now.

—Too bad! Too bad! said uncle Charles.

—What? cried Mr Dedalus. Were we to desert him at the bidding of the English people?

—He was no longer worthy to lead, said Dante. He was a public sinner.

—We are all sinners and black sinners, said Mr Casey coldly.

—*Woe be to the man by whom the scandal cometh!* said Mrs Riordan. *It would be better for him that a millstone were tied about his neck and that he were cast into the depth of the sea rather than that he should scandalise one of these, my least little ones.* That is the language of the Holy Ghost.

—And very bad language if you ask me, said Mr Dedalus coolly.

—Simon! Simon! said uncle Charles. The boy.

—Yes, yes, said Mr Dedalus. I meant about the . . . I was thinking about the bad language of that railway porter. Well now, that's all right. Here, Stephen, show me your plate, old chap. Eat away now. Here.

He heaped up the food on Stephen's plate and served uncle Charles and Mr Casey to large pieces of turkey and splashes of sauce. Mrs Dedalus was eating little and Dante sat with her hands in her lap. She was red in the face. Mr Dedalus rooted with the carvers at the end of the dish and said:

—There's a tasty bit here we call the pope's nose. If any lady or gentleman . . .

He held a piece of fowl up on the prong of the carvingfork. Nobody spoke. He put it on his own plate, saying:

—Well, you can't say but you were asked. I think I had better eat it myself because I'm not well in my health lately.

He winked at Stephen and, replacing the dishcover, began to eat again.

There was a silence while he ate. Then he said:

—Well now, the day kept up fine after all. There were plenty of strangers down too.

Nobody spoke. He said again:

—I think there were more strangers down than last Christmas.

He looked round at the others whose faces were bent towards their plates and, receiving no reply, waited for a moment and said bitterly:

—Well, my Christmas dinner has been spoiled anyhow.

—There could be neither luck nor grace, Dante said, in a house where there is no respect for the pastors of the church.

Mr Dedalus threw his knife and fork noisily on his plate.

—Respect! he said. Is it for Billy with the lip or for the tub of guts up in Armagh? Respect!

—Princes of the church, said Mr Casey with slow scorn.

—Lord Leitrim's coachman, yes, said Mr Dedalus.

—They are the Lord's anointed, Dante said. They are an honour to their country.

—Tub of guts, said Mr Dedalus coarsely. He has a handsome face, mind you, in repose. You should see that fellow lapping up his bacon and cabbage of a cold winter's day. O Johnny!

He twisted his features into a grimace of heavy bestiality and made a lapping noise with his lips.

—Really, Simon, said Mrs Dedalus, you should not speak that way before Stephen. It's not right.

—O, he'll remember all this when he grows up, said Dante hotly—the language he heard against God and religion and priests in his own home.

—Let him remember too, cried Mr Casey to her from across the table, the language with which the priests and the priests' pawns broke Parnell's heart and hounded him into his grave. Let him remember that too when he grows up.

—Sons of bitches! cried Mr Dedalus. When he was down they turned on him to betray him and rend him like rats in a sewer. Lowlived dogs! And they look it! By Christ, they look it!

—They behaved rightly, cried Dante. They obeyed their bishops and their priests. Honour to them!

—Well, it is perfectly dreadful to say that not even for one day in the year, said Mrs Dedalus, can we be free from these dreadful disputes!

Uncle Charles raised his hands mildly and said:

—Come now, come now, come now! Can we not have our opinions whatever they are without this bad temper and this bad language? It is too bad surely.

Mrs Dedalus spoke to Dante in a low voice but Dante said loudly:

—I will not say nothing. I will defend my church and my religion when it is insulted and spit on by renegade catholics.

Mr Casey pushed his plate rudely into the middle of the table and, resting his elbows before him, said in a hoarse voice to his host:

—Tell me, did I tell you that story about a very famous spit?

—You did not, John, said Mr Dedalus.

—Why then, said Mr Casey, it is a most instructive story. It happened not long ago in the county Wicklow where we are now.

He broke off and, turning towards Dante, said with quiet indignation:

—And I may tell you, ma'am, that I, if you mean me, am no renegade catholic. I am a catholic as my father was and his father before him and his father before him again when we gave up our lives rather than sell our faith.

—The more shame to you now, Dante said, to speak as you do.

—The story, John, said Mr Dedalus smiling. Let us have the story anyhow.

—Catholic indeed! repeated Dante ironically. The blackest protestant in the land would not speak the language I have heard this evening.

Mr Dedalus began to sway his head to and fro, crooning like a country singer.

—I am no protestant, I tell you again, said Mr Casey flushing.

Mr Dedalus, still crooning and swaying his head, began to sing in a grunting nasal tone:

> *O, come all you Roman catholics*
> *That never went to mass.*

He took up his knife and fork again in good humour and set to eating, saying to Mr Casey:

—Let us have the story, John. It will help us to digest.

Stephen looked with affection at Mr Casey's face which stared across the table over his joined hands. He liked to sit near him at the fire, looking up at his dark fierce face. But his dark eyes were never fierce and his slow voice was good to listen to. But why was he then against the priests? Because Dante must be right then. But he had heard his father say that she was a spoiled nun and that she had come out of the convent in the Alleghanies when her brother had got the money from the savages for the trinkets and the chainies. Perhaps that made her severe against Parnell. And she did not like him to play with Eileen because Eileen was a protestant and when she was young she knew children that used to play with protestants and the protestants used to make fun of the litany of the Blessed Virgin. *Tower of Ivory,* they used to say, *House of Gold!* How could a woman be a tower of ivory or a house of gold? Who was right then? And he remembered the evening in the infirmary in Clongowes, the dark waters, the light at the pierhead and the moan of sorrow from the people when they had heard.

Eileen had long white hands. One evening when playing tig she had put her hands over his eyes: long and white and thin and cold and soft. That was ivory: a cold white thing. That was the meaning of *Tower of Ivory*.

—The story is very short and sweet, Mr Casey said. It was one day down in Arklow, a cold bitter day, not long before the chief died. May God have mercy on him!

He closed his eyes wearily and paused. Mr Dedalus took a bone from his plate and tore some meat from it with his teeth, saying:

—Before he was killed, you mean.

Mr Casey opened his eyes, sighed and went on:

—It was down in Arklow one day. We were down there at a meeting and after the meeting was over we had to make our way to the railway station through the crowd. Such booing and baaing, man, you never heard. They called us all the names in the world. Well there was one old lady, and a drunken old harridan she was surely, that paid all her attention to me. She kept dancing along beside me in the mud bawling and screaming into my face: *Priesthunter! The Paris Funds! Mr Fox! Kitty O'Shea!*

—And what did you do, John? asked Mr Dedalus.

—I let her bawl away, said Mr Casey. It was a cold day and to keep up my heart I had (saving your presence, ma'am) a quid of Tullamore in my mouth and sure I couldn't say a word in any case because my mouth was full of tobacco juice.

—Well, John?

—Well. I let her bawl away, to her heart's content, *Kitty O'- Shea* and the rest of it till at last she called that lady a name that I won't sully this Christmas board nor your ears, ma'am, nor my own lips by repeating.

He paused. Mr Dedalus, lifting his head from the bone, asked:

—And what did you do, John?

—Do! said Mr Casey. She stuck her ugly old face up at me when she said it and I had my mouth full of tobacco juice. I bent down to her and *Phth!* says I to her like that.

He turned aside and made the act of spitting.

—*Phth!* says I to her like that, right into her eye.

He clapped a hand to his eye and gave a hoarse scream of pain.

—*O Jesus, Mary and Joseph!* says she. *I'm blinded! I'm blinded and drownded!*

He stopped in a fit of coughing and laughter, repeating:

—*I'm blinded entirely.*

Mr Dedalus laughed loudly and lay back in his chair while uncle Charles swayed his head to and fro.

Dante looked terribly angry and repeated while they laughed:

—Very nice! Ha! Very nice!

It was not nice about the spit in the woman's eye. But what was the name the woman had called Kitty O'Shea that Mr Casey would not repeat? He thought of Mr Casey walking through the crowds of people and making speeches from a wagonette. That was what he had been in prison for and he remembered that one night Sergeant O'Neill had come to the house and had stood in the hall, talking in a low voice with his father and chewing nervously at the chinstrap of his cap. And that night Mr Casey had not gone to Dublin by train but a car had come to the door and he had heard his father say something about the Cabinteely road.

He was for Ireland and Parnell and so was his father: and so was Dante too for one night at the band on the esplanade she had hit a gentleman on the head with her umbrella because he had taken off his hat when the band played *God save the Queen* at the end.

Mr Dedalus gave a snort of contempt.

—Ah, John, he said. It is true for them. We are an unfortunate priestridden race and always were and always will be till the end of the chapter.

Uncle Charles shook his head, saying:

—A bad business! A bad business!

Mr Dedalus repeated:

—A priestridden Godforsaken race!

He pointed to the portrait of his grandfather on the wall to his right.

—Do you see that old chap up there, John? he said. He was a good Irishman when there was no money in the job. He was condemned to death as a whiteboy. But he had a saying about our clerical friends, that he would never let one of them put his two feet under his mahogany.

Dante broke in angrily:

—If we are a priestridden race we ought to be proud of it! They are the apple of God's eye. *Touch them not,* says Christ, *for they are the apple of My eye.*

—And can we not love our country then? asked Mr Casey. Are we not to follow the man that was born to lead us?

—A traitor to his country! replied Dante. A traitor, an adulterer! The priests were right to abandon him. The priests were always the true friends of Ireland.

—Were they, faith? said Mr Casey.

He threw his fist on the table and, frowning angrily, protruded one finger after another.

—Didn't the bishops of Ireland betray us in the time of the union when bishop Lanigan presented an address of loyalty to the Marquess Cornwallis? Didn't the bishops and priests sell the aspirations of their country in 1829 in return for catholic emancipation? Didn't they denounce the fenian movement from the pulpit and in the confessionbox? And didn't they dishonour the ashes of Terence Bellew MacManus?

His face was glowing with anger and Stephen felt the glow rise to his own cheek as the spoken words thrilled him. Mr Dedalus uttered a guffaw of coarse scorn.

—O, by God, he cried, I forgot little old Paul Cullen! Another apple of God's eye!

Dante bent across the table and cried to Mr Casey:

—Right! Right! They were always right! God and morality and religion come first.

Mrs Dedalus, seeing her excitement, said to her:

—Mrs Riordan, don't excite yourself answering them.

—God and religion before everything! Dante cried. God and religion before the world!

Mr Casey raised his clenched fist and brought it down on the table with a crash.

—Very well, then, he shouted hoarsely, if it comes to that, no God for Ireland!

—John! John! cried Mr Dedalus, seizing his guest by the coatsleeve.

Dante stared across the table, her cheeks shaking. Mr Casey struggled up from his chair and bent across the table towards her, scraping the air from before his eyes with one hand as though he were tearing aside a cobweb.

—No God for Ireland! he cried. We have had too much God in Ireland. Away with God!

—Blasphemer! Devil! screamed Dante, starting to her feet and almost spitting in his face.

Uncle Charles and Mr Dedalus pulled Mr Casey back into his chair again, talking to him from both sides reasonably. He stared before him out of his dark flaming eyes, repeating:

—Away with God, I say!

Dante shoved her chair violently aside and left the table, upsetting her napkinring which rolled slowly along the carpet and came to rest against the foot of an easychair. Mrs Dedalus rose quickly and followed her towards the door. At the door Dante turned round violently and shouted down the room, her cheeks flushed and quivering with rage:

—Devil out of hell! We won! We crushed him to death! Fiend!

The door slammed behind her.

Mr Casey, freeing his arms from his holders, suddenly bowed his head on his hands with a sob of pain.

—Poor Parnell! he cried loudly. My dead king!

He sobbed loudly and bitterly.

Stephen, raising his terrorstricken face, saw that his father's eyes were full of tears.

*   *   *

The fellows talked together in little groups.

One fellow said:

—They were caught near the Hill of Lyons.

—Who caught them?

—Mr Gleeson and the minister. They were on a car.

The same fellow added:

—A fellow in the higher line told me.

Fleming asked:

—But why did they run away, tell us?

—I know why, Cecil Thunder said. Because they had fecked cash out of the rector's room.

—Who fecked it?

—Kickham's brother. And they all went shares in it.

But that was stealing. How could they have done that?

—A fat lot you know about it, Thunder! Wells said. I know why they scut.

—Tell us why.

—I was told not to, Wells said.

—O, go on, Wells, all said. You might tell us. We won't let it out.

Stephen bent forward his head to hear. Wells looked round to see if anyone was coming. Then he said secretly:

—You know the altar wine they keep in the press in the sacristy?

—Yes.

—Well, they drank that and it was found out who did it by the smell. And that's why they ran away, if you want to know.

And the fellow who had spoken first said:

—Yes, that's what I heard too from the fellow in the higher line.

The fellows were all silent. Stephen stood among them, afraid to speak, listening. A faint sickness of awe made him feel weak. How could they have done that? He thought of the dark silent sacristy. There were dark wooden presses there where the crimped surplices lay quietly folded. It was not the chapel but still you had to speak under your breath. It was a holy place. He remembered the summer evening he had been there to be dressed as boatbearer, the evening of the procession to the little altar in the wood. A strange and holy place. The boy that held the censer had swung it gently to and fro near the door with the silvery cap lifted by the middle chain to keep the coals lighting. That was called charcoal: and it had burned quietly as the fellow had swung it gently and had given off a weak sour smell. And then when all were vested he had stood holding out the boat to the rector and the rector had put a spoonful of incense in it and it had hissed on the red coals.

The fellows were talking together in little groups here and there on the playground. The fellows seemed to him to have grown smaller: that was because a sprinter had knocked him down the day before, a fellow out of second of grammar. He had been thrown by the fellow's machine lightly on the cinderpath and his spectacles had been broken in three pieces and some of the grit of the cinders had gone into his mouth.

That was why the fellows seemed to him smaller and farther away and the goalposts so thin and far and the soft grey sky so high up. But there was no play on the football grounds for cricket was coming: and some said that Barnes would be the prof and some said it would be Flowers. And all over the playgrounds they were playing rounders and bowling twisters and lobs. And from here and from there came the sounds of the cricketbats through the soft grey air. They said: pick, pack, pock, puck: like drops of water in a fountain slowly falling in the brimming bowl.

Athy, who had been silent, said quietly:

—You are all wrong.

All turned towards him eagerly.

—Why?

—Do you know?

—Who told you?

—Tell us, Athy.

Athy pointed across the playground to where Simon Moonan was walking by himself kicking a stone before him.

—Ask him, he said.

The fellows looked there and then said:

—Why him?

—Is he in it?

—Tell us, Athy. Go on. You might if you know.

Athy lowered his voice and said:

—Do you know why those fellows scut? I will tell you but you must not let on you know.

He paused for a moment and then said mysteriously:

—They were caught with Simon Moonan and Tusker Boyle in the square one night.

The fellows looked at him and asked:

—Caught?

—What doing?

Athy said:

—Smugging.

All the fellows were silent: and Athy said:

—And that's why.

Stephen looked at the faces of the fellows but they were all looking across the playground. He wanted to ask somebody about it. What did that mean about the smugging in the square? Why did the five fellows out of the higher line run away for that? It was a joke, he thought. Simon Moonan had nice clothes and one night he had shown him a ball of creamy sweets that the fellows of the football fifteen had rolled down to him along the carpet in the middle of the refectory when he was at the door. It was the night of the match against the Bective Rangers and the ball was made just like a red and green apple only it opened and it was full of the creamy sweets. And one day Boyle had said that an elephant had two tuskers instead of two tusks and that was why he was called Tusker Boyle but some fellows called him Lady Boyle because he was always at his nails, paring them.

Eileen had long thin cool white hands too because she was a girl. They were like ivory; only soft. That was the meaning of *Tower of Ivory* but protestants could not understand it and made fun of it. One day he had stood beside her looking into the hotel grounds. A waiter was running up a trail of bunting on the flagstaff and a fox terrier was scampering to and fro on the sunny lawn. She had put her hand into his pocket where his hand was and he had felt how cool and thin and soft her hand was. She had said that pockets were funny things to have: and then all of a sudden she had broken away and had run laughing down the sloping curve of the path. Her fair hair had streamed out behind her like gold in the sun. *Tower of Ivory. House of Gold.* By thinking of things you could understand them.

But why in the square? You went there when you wanted to do something. It was all thick slabs of slate and water trickled all day out of tiny pinholes and there was a queer smell of stale water there. And behind the door of one of the closets there was a drawing in red pencil of a bearded man in a Roman dress with a brick in each hand and underneath was the name of the drawing:

Balbus was building a wall.

Some fellows had drawn it there for a cod. It had a funny face but it was very like a man with a beard. And on the wall of another closet there was written in backhand in beautiful writing:

Julius Cæsar wrote The Calico Belly.

Perhaps that was why they were there because it was a place where some fellows wrote things for cod. But all the same it was queer what Athy said and the way he said it. It was not a cod because they had run away. He looked with the others in silence across the playground and began to feel afraid.

At last Fleming said:

—And we are all to be punished for what other fellows did?

—I won't come back, see if I do, Cecil Thunder said. Three days' silence in the refectory and sending us up for six and eight every minute.

—Yes, said Wells. And old Barrett has a new way of twisting the note so that you can't open it and fold it again to see how many ferulæ you are to get. I won't come back too.

—Yes, said Cecil Thunder, and the prefect of studies was in second of grammar this morning.

—Let us get up a rebellion, Fleming said. Will we?

All the fellows were silent. The air was very silent and you could hear the cricketbats but more slowly than before: pick, pock.

Wells asked:

—What is going to be done to them?

—Simon Moonan and Tusker are going to be flogged, Athy said, and the fellows in the higher line got their choice of flogging or being expelled.

—And which are they taking? asked the fellow who had spoken first.

—All are taking expulsion except Corrigan, Athy answered. He's going to be flogged by Mr Gleeson.

—Is it Corrigan that big fellow? said Fleming. Why, he'd be able for two of Gleeson!

—I know why, Cecil Thunder said. He is right and the other fellows are wrong because a flogging wears off after a bit but a fellow that has been expelled from college is known all his life on account of it. Besides Gleeson won't flog him hard.

—It's best of his play not to, Fleming said.

—I wouldn't like to be Simon Moonan and Tusker, Cecil Thunder said. But I don't believe they will be flogged. Perhaps they will be sent up for twice nine.

—No, no, said Athy. They'll both get it on the vital spot.

Wells rubbed himself and said in a crying voice:

—Please, sir, let me off!

Athy grinned and turned up the sleeves of his jacket, saying:

> *It can't be helped;*
> *It must be done.*
> *So down with your breeches*
> *And out with your bum.*

The fellows laughed; but he felt that they were a little afraid. In the silence of the soft grey air he heard the cricketbats from here and from there: pock. That was a sound to hear but if you were hit then you would feel a pain. The pandybat made a sound too but not like that. The fellows said it was made of whalebone and leather with lead inside: and he wondered what was the pain like. There were different kinds of pains for all the different kinds of sounds. A long thin cane would have a high whistling sound and he wondered what was that pain like. It made him shivery to think of it and cold: and what Athy said too. But what was there to laugh at in it? It made him shivery: but that was because you always felt like a shiver when you let down your trousers. It was the same in the bath when you undressed yourself. He wondered who had to let them down, the master or the boy himself. O how could they laugh about it that way?

He looked at Athy's rolledup sleeves and knuckly inky hands. He had rolled up his sleeves to show how Mr Gleeson would roll up his sleeves. But Mr Gleeson had round shiny cuffs and clean white wrists and fattish white hands and the nails of them were long and pointed. Perhaps he pared them too like Lady Boyle. But they were terribly long and pointed nails. So long and cruel they were though the white fattish hands were not cruel but gentle. And though he trembled with cold and fright to think of the cruel long nails and of the high whistling sound of the cane and of the chill you felt at the end of your shirt when you undressed yourself yet he felt a feeling of queer quiet pleasure inside him to think of the white fattish hands, clean and strong and gentle. And he thought of what Cecil Thunder had said; that Mr Gleeson would not flog Corrigan hard. And Fleming had said he would not because it was best of his play not to. But that was not why.

A voice from far out on the playground cried:

—All in!

And other voices cried:

—All in! All in!

During the writing lesson he sat with his arms folded, listening to the slow scraping of the pens. Mr Harford went to and fro making little signs in red pencil and sometimes sitting beside the boy to show him how to hold the pen. He had tried to spell out the headline for himself though he knew already what it was for it was the last of the book. *Zeal without prudence is like a ship adrift.* But the lines of the letters were like fine invisible threads and it was only by closing his right eye tight tight and staring out of the left eye that he could make out the full curves of the capital.

But Mr Harford was very decent and never got into a wax. All the other masters got into dreadful waxes. But why were they to suffer for what fellows in the higher line did? Wells had said that they had drunk some of the altar wine out of the press in the sacristy and that it had been found out who had done it by the smell. Perhaps they had stolen a monstrance to run away with it and sell it somewhere. That must have been a terrible sin, to go in there quietly at night, to open the dark press and steal the flashing gold thing into which God was put on the altar in the middle of flowers and candles at benediction while the incense went up in clouds at both sides as the fellow swung the censer and Dominic Kelly sang the first part by himself in the choir. But God was not in it of course when they stole it. But still it was a strange and a great sin even to touch it. He thought of it with deep awe; a terrible and strange sin: it thrilled him to think of it in the silence when the pens scraped lightly. But to drink the altar wine out of the press and be found out by the smell was a sin too: but it was not terrible and strange. It only made you feel a little sickish on account of the smell of the wine. Because on the day when he had made his first holy communion in the chapel he had shut his eyes and opened his mouth and put out his tongue a little: and when the rector had stooped down to give him the holy communion he had smelt a faint winy smell off the rector's breath after the wine of the mass. The word was beautiful: wine. It made you think of dark purple because the grapes were dark purple that grew in Greece outside houses like white temples. But the faint smell off the rector's breath had made him feel a sick feeling on the morning of his first communion. The day of your first communion was the happiest day of your life. And once a lot of generals had asked Napoleon what was the happiest day of his life. They thought he would say the day he won some great battle or the day he was made an emperor. But he said:

—Gentlemen, the happiest day of my life was the day on which I made my first holy communion.

Father Arnall came in and the Latin lesson began and he remained still, leaning on the desk with his arms folded. Father Arnall gave out the themebooks and he said that they were scandalous and that they were all to be written out again with the corrections at once. But the worst of all was Fleming's theme because the pages were stuck together by a blot: and Father Arnall held it up by a corner and said it was an insult to any master to send him up such a theme. Then he asked Jack Lawton to decline the noun *mare* and Jack Lawton stopped at the ablative singular and could not go on with the plural.

—You should be ashamed of yourself, said Father Arnall sternly. You, the leader of the class!

Then he asked the next boy and the next and the next. Nobody knew. Father Arnall became very quiet, more and more quiet as each boy tried to answer and could not. But his face was blacklooking and his eyes were staring though his voice was so quiet. Then he asked Fleming and Fleming said that that word had no plural. Father Arnall suddenly shut the book and shouted at him:

—Kneel out there in the middle of the class. You are one of the idlest boys I ever met. Copy out your themes again the rest of you.

Fleming moved heavily out of his place and knelt between the two last benches. The others boys bent over their themebooks and began to write. A silence filled the classroom and

Stephen, glancing timidly at Father Arnall's dark face, saw that it was a little red from the wax he was in.

Was that a sin for Father Arnall to be in a wax or was he allowed to get into a wax when the boys were idle because that made them study better or was he only letting on to be in a wax? It was because he was allowed because a priest would know what a sin was and would not do it. But if he did it one time by mistake what would he do to go to confession? Perhaps he would go to confession to the minister. And if the minister did it he would go to the rector: and the rector to the provincial: and the provincial to the general of the jesuits. That was called the order: and he had heard his father say that they were all clever men. They could all have become highup people in the world if they had not become jesuits. And he wondered what Father Arnall and Paddy Barrett would have become and what Mr McGlade and Mr Gleeson would have become if they had not become jesuits. It was hard to think what because you would have to think of them in a different way with different coloured coats and trousers and with beards and moustaches and different kinds of hats.

The door opened quietly and closed. A quick whisper ran through the class: the prefect of studies. There was an instant of dead silence and then the loud crack of a pandybat on the last desk. Stephen's heart leapt up in fear.

—Any boys want flogging here, Father Arnall? cried the prefect of studies. Any lazy idle loafers that want flogging in this class?

He came to the middle of the class and saw Fleming on his knees.

—Hoho! he cried. Who is this boy? Why is he on his knees? What is your name, boy?

—Fleming, sir.

—Hoho, Fleming! An idler of course. I can see it in your eye. Why is he on his knees, Father Arnall?

—He wrote a bad Latin theme, Father Arnall said, and he missed all the questions in grammar.

—Of course he did! cried the prefect of studies. Of course
he did! A born idler! I can see it in the corner of his eye.

He banged his pandybat down on the desk and cried:

—Up, Fleming! Up, my boy!

Fleming stood up slowly.

—Hold out! cried the prefect of studies.

Fleming held out his hand. The pandybat came down on it
with a loud smacking sound: one, two, three, four, five, six.

—Other hand!

The pandybat came down again in six loud quick smacks.

—Kneel down! cried the prefect of studies.

Fleming knelt down squeezing his hands under his armpits,
his face contorted with pain, but Stephen knew how hard his
hands were because Fleming was always rubbing rosin into
them. But perhaps he was in great pain for the noise of the
pandies was terrible. Stephen's heart was beating and fluttering.

—At your work, all of you! shouted the prefect of studies.
We want no lazy idle loafers here, lazy idle little schemers. At
your work, I tell you. Father Dolan will be in to see you every
day. Father Dolan will be in tomorrow.

He poked one of the boys in the side with the pandybat,
saying:

—You, boy! When will Father Dolan be in again?

—Tomorrow, sir, said Tom Furlong's voice.

—Tomorrow and tomorrow and tomorrow, said the prefect
of studies. Make up your minds for that. Every day Father
Dolan. Write away. You, boy, who are you?

Stephen's heart jumped suddenly.

—Dedalus, sir.

—Why are you not writing like the others?

—I . . . my . . .

He could not speak with fright.

—Why is he not writing, Father Arnall?

—He broke his glasses, said Father Arnall, and I exempted
him from work.

—Broke? What is this I hear? What is this your name is? said the prefect of studies.

—Dedalus, sir.

—Out here, Dedalus. Lazy little schemer. I see schemer in your face. Where did you break your glasses?

Stephen stumbled into the middle of the class, blinded by fear and haste.

—Where did you break your glasses? repeated the prefect of studies.

—The cinderpath, sir.

—Hoho! The cinderpath! cried the prefect of studies. I know that trick.

Stephen lifted his eyes in wonder and saw for a moment Father Dolan's whitegrey not young face, his baldy whitegrey head with fluff at the sides of it, the steel rims of his spectacles and his nocoloured eyes looking through the glasses. Why did he say he knew that trick?

—Lazy idle little loafer! cried the prefect of studies. Broke my glasses! An old schoolboy trick! Out with your hand this moment!

Stephen closed his eyes and held out in the air his trembling hand with the palm upwards. He felt the prefect of studies touch it for a moment at the fingers to straighten it and then the swish of the sleeve of the soutane as the pandybat was lifted to strike. A hot burning stinging tingling blow like the loud crack of a broken stick made his trembling hand crumple together like a leaf in the fire: and at the sound and the pain scalding tears were driven into his eyes. His whole body was shaking with fright, his arm was shaking and his crumpled burning livid hand shook like a loose leaf in the air. A cry sprang to his lips, a prayer to be let off. But though the tears scalded his eyes and his limbs quivered with pain and fright he held back the hot tears and the cry that scalded his throat.

—Other hand! shouted the prefect of studies.

Stephen drew back his maimed and quivering right arm and held out his left hand. The soutane sleeve swished again as the pandybat was lifted and a loud crashing sound and a fierce maddening tingling burning pain made his hand shrink together with the palms and fingers in a livid quivering mass. The scalding water burst forth from his eyes and, burning with shame and agony and fear, he drew back his shaking arm in terror and burst out into a whine of pain. His body shook with a palsy of fright and in shame and rage he felt the scalding cry come from his throat and the scalding tears falling out of his eyes and down his flaming cheeks.

—Kneel down! cried the prefect of studies.

Stephen knelt down quickly pressing his beaten hands to his sides. To think of them beaten and swollen with pain all in a moment made him feel so sorry for them as if they were not his own but someone else's that he felt sorry for. And as he knelt, calming the last sobs in his throat and feeling the burning tingling pain pressed in to his sides, he thought of the hands which he had held out in the air with the palms up and of the firm touch of the prefect of studies when he had steadied the shaking fingers and of the beaten swollen reddened mass of palm and fingers that shook helplessly in the air.

—Get at your work, all of you, cried the prefect of studies from the door. Father Dolan will be in every day to see if any boy, any lazy idle little loafer wants flogging. Every day. Every day.

The door closed behind him.

The hushed class continued to copy out the themes. Father Arnall rose from his seat and went among them, helping the boys with gentle words and telling them the mistakes they had made. His voice was very gentle and soft. Then he returned to his seat and said to Fleming and Stephen:

—You may return to your places, you two.

Fleming and Stephen rose and, walking to their seats, sat down. Stephen, scarlet with shame, opened a book quickly with one weak hand and bent down upon it, his face close to the page.

It was unfair and cruel because the doctor had told him not

to read without glasses and he had written home to his father that morning to send him a new pair. And Father Arnall had said that he need not study till the new glasses came. Then to be called a schemer before the class and to be pandied when he always got the card for first or second and was the leader of the Yorkists! How could the prefect of studies know that it was a trick? He felt the touch of the prefect's fingers as they had steadied his hand and at first he had thought he was going to shake hands with him because the fingers were soft and firm: but then in an instant he had heard the swish of the soutane sleeve and the crash. It was cruel and unfair to make him kneel in the middle of the class then: and Father Arnall had told them both that they might return to their places without making any difference between them. He listened to Father Arnall's low and gentle voice as he corrected the themes. Perhaps he was sorry now and wanted to be decent. But it was unfair and cruel. The prefect of studies was a priest but that was cruel and unfair. And his whitegrey face and the nocoloured eyes behind the steelrimmed spectacles were cruel looking because he had steadied the hand first with his firm soft fingers and that was to hit it better and louder.

—It's a stinking mean thing, that's what it is, said Fleming in the corridor as the classes were passing out in file to the refectory, to pandy a fellow for what is not his fault.

—You really broke your glasses by accident, didn't you? Nasty Roche asked.

Stephen felt his heart filled by Fleming's words and did not answer.

—Of course he did! said Fleming. I wouldn't stand it. I'd go up and tell the rector on him.

—Yes, said Cecil Thunder eagerly, and I saw him lift the pandybat over his shoulder and he's not allowed to do that.

—Did they hurt much? Nasty Roche asked.

—Very much, Stephen said.

—I wouldn't stand it, Fleming repeated, from Baldyhead or any other Baldyhead. It's a stinking mean low trick, that's what it is. I'd go straight up to the rector and tell him about it after dinner.

—Yes, do. Yes, do, said Cecil Thunder.

—Yes, do. Yes, go up and tell the rector on him, Dedalus, said Nasty Roche, because he said that he'd come in tomorrow again to pandy you.

—Yes, yes. Tell the rector, all said.

And there were some fellows out of second of grammar listening and one of them said:

—The senate and the Roman people declared that Dedalus had been wrongly punished.

It was wrong; it was unfair and cruel: and, as he sat in the refectory, he suffered time after time in memory the same humiliation until he began to wonder whether it might not really be that there was something in his face which made him look like a schemer and he wished he had a little mirror to see. But there could not be; and it was unjust and cruel and unfair.

He could not eat the blackish fish fritters they got on Wednesdays in Lent and one of his potatoes had the mark of the spade in it. Yes, he would do what the fellows had told him. He would go up and tell the rector that he had been wrongly punished. A thing like that had been done before by somebody in history, by some great person whose head was in the books of history. And the rector would declare that he had been wrongly punished because the senate and the Roman people always declared that the men who did that had been wrongly punished. Those were the great men whose names were in Richmal Magnall's Questions. History was all about those men and what they did and that was what Peter Parley's Tales about Greece and Rome were all about. Peter Parley himself was on the first page in a picture. There was a road over a heath with grass at the side and little bushes: and Peter Parley had a broad hat like a protestant minister and a big stick and he was walking fast along the road to Greece and Rome.

It was easy what he had to do. All he had to do was when the dinner was over and he came out in his turn to go on walking but not out to the corridor but up the staircase on the right that led to the castle. He had nothing to do but that: to turn to the right and walk fast up the staircase and in half a minute he would be in the low dark narrow corridor that led through the castle to the rector's room. And every fellow had said that it was unfair, even the fellow out of second of grammar who had said that about the senate and the Roman people.

What would happen? He heard the fellows of the higher line stand up at the top of the refectory and heard their steps as they came down the matting: Paddy Rath and Jimmy Magee and the Spaniard and the Portuguese and the fifth was big Corrigan who was going to be flogged by Mr Gleeson. That was why the prefect of studies had called him a schemer and pandied him for nothing: and, straining his weak eyes, tired with the tears, he watched big Corrigan's broad shoulders and big hanging black head passing in the file. But he had done something and besides Mr Gleeson would not flog him hard: and he remembered how big Corrigan looked in the bath. He had skin the same colour as the turfcoloured bogwater in the shallow end of the bath and when he walked along the side his feet slapped loudly on the wet tiles and at every step his thighs shook a little because he was fat.

The refectory was half empty and the fellows were still passing out in file. He could go up the staircase because there was never a priest or a prefect outside the refectory door. But he could not go. The rector would side with the prefect of studies and think it was a schoolboy trick and then the prefect of studies would come in every day the same only it would be worse because he would be dreadfully waxy at any fellow going up to the rector about him. The fellows had told him to go but they would not go themselves. They had forgotten all about it. No, it was best to forget all about it and perhaps the prefect of studies had only said he would come in. No, it was best to hide out of the way because when you were small and young you could often escape that way.

The fellows at his table stood up. He stood up and passed out among them in the file. He had to decide. He was coming near the door. If he went on with the fellows he could never go up to the rector because he could not leave the playground for that. And if he went and was pandied all the same all the fellows would make fun and talk about young Dedalus going up to the rector to tell on the prefect of studies.

He was walking down along the matting and he saw the door before him. It was impossible: he could not. He thought of the baldy head of the prefect of studies with the cruel nocoloured eyes looking at him and he heard the voice of the prefect of studies asking him twice what his name was. Why could he not remember the name when he was told the first time? Was he not listening the first time or was it to make fun out of the name? The great men in the history had names like that and nobody made fun of them. It was his own name that he should have made fun of if he wanted to make fun. Dolan: it was like the name of a woman that washed clothes.

He had reached the door and, turning quickly up to the right, walked up the stairs and, before he could make up his mind to come back, he had entered the low dark narrow corridor that led to the castle. And as he crossed the threshold of the door of the corridor he saw, without turning his head to look, that all the fellows were looking after him as they went filing by.

He passed along the narrow dark corridor, passing little doors that were the doors of the rooms of the community. He peered in front of him and right and left through the gloom and thought that those must be portraits. It was dark and silent and his eyes were weak and tired with tears so that he could not see. But he thought they were the portraits of the saints and great men of the order who were looking down on him silently as he passed: saint Ignatius Loyola holding an open book and pointing to the words *Ad Majorem Dei*

Gloriam in it, saint Francis Xavier pointing to his chest, Lorenzo Ricci with his berretta on his head like one of the prefects of the lines, the three patrons of holy youth, saint Stanislaus Kostka, saint Aloysius Gonzaga and blessed John Berchmans, all with young faces because they died when they were young, and Father Peter Kenny sitting in a chair wrapped in a big cloak.

He came out on the landing above the entrance hall and looked about him. That was where Hamilton Rowan had passed and the marks of the soldiers' slugs were there. And it was there that the old servants had seen the ghost in the white cloak of a marshal.

An old servant was sweeping at the end of the landing. He asked him where was the rector's room and the old servant pointed to the door at the far end and looked after him as he went on to it and knocked.

There was no answer. He knocked again more loudly and his heart jumped when he heard a muffled voice say:

—Come in!

He turned the handle and opened the door and fumbled for the handle of the green baize door inside. He found it and pushed it open and went in.

He saw the rector sitting at a desk writing. There was a skull on the desk and a strange solemn smell in the room like the old leather of chairs.

His heart was beating fast on account of the solemn place he was in and the silence of the room: and he looked at the skull and at the rector's kindlooking face.

—Well, my little man, said the rector, what is it?

Stephen swallowed down the thing in his throat and said:

—I broke my glasses, sir.

The rector opened his mouth and said:

—O!

Then he smiled and said:

—Well, if we broke our glasses we must write home for a new pair.

—I wrote home, sir, said Stephen, and Father Arnall said I am not to study till they come.

—Quite right! said the rector.

Stephen swallowed down the thing again and tried to keep his legs and his voice from shaking.

—But, sir . . .

—Yes?

—Father Dolan came in today and pandied me because I was not writing my theme.

The rector looked at him in silence and he could feel the blood rising to his face and the tears about to rise to his eyes.

The rector said:

—Your name is Dedalus, isn't it?

—Yes, sir.

—And where did you break your glasses?

—On the cinderpath, sir. A fellow was coming out of the bicycle house and I fell and they got broken. I don't know the fellow's name.

The rector looked at him again in silence. Then he smiled and said:

—O, well, it was a mistake; I am sure Father Dolan did not know.

—But I told him I broke them, sir, and he pandied me.

—Did you tell him that you had written home for a new pair? the rector asked.

—No, sir.

—O well then, said the rector, Father Dolan did not understand. You can say that I excuse you from your lessons for a few days.

Stephen said quickly for fear his trembling would prevent him:

—Yes, sir, but Father Dolan said he will come in tomorrow to pandy me again for it.

—Very well, the rector said, it is a mistake and I shall speak to Father Dolan myself. Will that do now?

Stephen felt the tears wetting his eyes and murmured:

—O yes sir, thanks.

The rector held his hand across the side of the desk where the skull was and Stephen, placing his hand in it for a moment, felt a cool moist palm.

—Good day now, said the rector, withdrawing his hand and bowing.

—Good day, sir, said Stephen.

He bowed and walked quietly out of the room, closing the doors carefully and slowly.

But when he had passed the old servant on the landing and was again in the low narrow dark corridor he began to walk faster and faster. Faster and faster he hurried on through the gloom excitedly. He bumped his elbow against the door at the end and, hurrying down the staircase, walked quickly through the two corridors and out into the air.

He could hear the cries of the fellows on the playgrounds. He broke into a run and, running quicker and quicker, ran across the cinderpath and reached the third line playground, panting.

The fellows had seen him running. They closed round him in a ring, pushing one against another to hear.

—Tell us! Tell us!

—What did he say?

—Did you go in?

—What did he say?

—Tell us! Tell us!

He told them what he had said and what the rector had said and, when he had told them, all the fellows flung their caps spinning up into the air and cried:

—Hurroo!

They caught their caps and sent them up again spinning skyhigh and cried again:

—Hurroo! Hurroo!

They made a cradle of their locked hands and hoisted him up among them and carried him along till he struggled to get free. And when he had escaped from them they broke away in all directions, flinging their caps again into the air and whistling as they went spinning up and crying:

—Hurroo!

And they gave three groans for Baldyhead Dolan and three cheers for Conmee and they said he was the decentest rector that was ever in Clongowes.

The cheers died away in the soft grey air. He was alone. He was happy and free: but he would not be anyway proud with Father Dolan. He would be very quiet and obedient: and he wished that he could do something kind for him to show him that he was not proud.

he is different

The air was soft and grey and mild and evening was coming. There was the smell of evening in the air, the smell of the fields in the country where they digged up turnips to peel them and eat them when they went out for a walk to Major Barton's, the smell there was in the little wood beyond the pavilion where the gallnuts were.

The fellows were practising long shies and bowing lobs and slow twisters. In the soft grey silence he could hear the bump of the balls: and from here and from there through the quiet air the sound of the cricket bats: pick, pack, pock, puck: like drops of water in a fountain falling softly in the brimming bowl.

II

UNCLE Charles smoked such black twist that at last his nephew suggested to him to enjoy his morning smoke in a little outhouse at the end of the garden.

—Very good, Simon. All serene, Simon, said the old man tranquilly. Anywhere you like. The outhouse will do me nicely: it will be more salubrious.

—Damn me, said Mr Dedalus frankly, if I know how you can smoke such villainous awful tobacco. It's like gunpowder, by God.

—It's very nice, Simon, replied the old man. Very cool and mollifying.

Every morning, therefore, uncle Charles repaired to his outhouse but not before he had creased and brushed scrupulously his back hair and brushed and put on his tall hat. While he smoked the brim of his tall hat and the bowl of his pipe were just visible beyond the jambs of the outhouse door. His arbour, as he called the reeking outhouse which he shared with the cat and the garden tools, served him also as a sounding-box: and every morning he hummed contentedly one of his favourite songs: *O, twine me a bower* or *Blue eyes and golden hair* or *The Groves of Blarney* while the grey and blue coils of smoke rose slowly from his pipe and vanished in the pure air.

During the first part of the summer in Blackrock uncle Charles was Stephen's constant companion. Uncle Charles was a hale old man with a welltanned skin, rugged features and white side whiskers. On week days he did messages between the house in Carysfort Avenue and those shops in the main street of the town with which the family dealt. Stephen was glad to go with him on these errands for uncle Charles helped him very liberally to handfuls of whatever was exposed in open boxes and barrels outside the counter. He would seize a handful of grapes and sawdust or three or four American apples and thrust them generously into his grand-nephew's hand while the shopman smiled uneasily; and, on Stephen's feigning reluctance to take them, he would frown and say:

—Take them, sir. Do you hear me, sir? They're good for your bowels.

When the order list had been booked the two would go on to the park where an old friend of Stephen's father, Mike Flynn, would be found seated on a bench, waiting for them. Then would begin Stephen's run round the park. Mike Flynn would stand at the gate near the railway station, watch in hand, while Stephen ran round the track in the style Mike Flynn favoured, his head high lifted, his knees well lifted and his hands held straight down by his sides. When the morning practice was over the trainer would make his comments and sometimes illustrate them by shuffling along for a yard or so comically in an old pair of blue canvas shoes. A small ring of wonderstruck children and nursemaids would gather to watch him and linger even when he and uncle Charles had sat down again and were talking athletics and politics. Though he had heard his father say that Mike Flynn had put some of the best runners of modern times through his hands Stephen often glanced with mistrust at his trainer's flabby stubblecovered face, as it bent over the long stained fingers through which he rolled his cigarette, and with pity at the mild lustreless blue eyes which would look up suddenly from the task and gaze vaguely into the blue distance while the long swollen fingers ceased their rolling and grains and fibres of tobacco fell back into the pouch.

On the way home uncle Charles would often pay a visit to the chapel and, as the font was above Stephen's reach, the old man would dip his hand and then sprinkle the water briskly about Stephen's clothes and on the floor of the porch. While he prayed he knelt on his red handkerchief and read above his breath from a thumbblackened prayerbook wherein catchwords were printed at the foot of every page. Stephen knelt at his side respecting, though he did not share, his piety. He often wondered what his granduncle prayed for so seriously. Perhaps he prayed for the souls in purgatory or for the grace of a happy death or perhaps he prayed that God might send him back a part of the big fortune he had squandered in Cork.

On Sundays Stephen with his father and his granduncle took their constitutional. The old man was a nimble walker in spite of his corns and often ten or twelve miles of the road were covered. The little village of Stillorgan was the parting of the ways. Either they went to the left towards the Dublin mountains or along the Goatstown road and thence into Dundrum, coming home by Sandyford. Trudging along the road or standing in some grimy wayside publichouse his elders spoke constantly of the subjects nearer their hearts, of Irish politics, of Munster and of the legends of their own family, to all of which Stephen lent an avid ear. Words which he did not understand he said over and over to himself till he had learned them by heart: and through them he had glimpses of the real world about him. The hour when he too would take part in the life of that world seemed drawing near and in secret he began to make ready for the great part which he felt awaited him the nature of which he only dimly apprehended.

His evenings were his own; and he pored over a ragged translation of *The Count of Monte Cristo*. The figure of that dark avenger stood forth in his mind for whatever he had heard or divined in childhood of the strange and terrible. At night he built up on the parlour table an image of the wonderful island cave out of transfers and paper flowers and coloured tissue paper and strips of the silver and golden paper in which chocolate is wrapped. When he had broken up this scenery, weary of its tinsel, there would come to his mind the bright picture of Marseilles, of sunny trellisses and of Mercedes. Outside Blackrock, on the road that led to the mountains,

stood a small whitewashed house in the garden of which grew
many rosebushes: and in this house, he told himself, another
Mercedes lived. Both on the outward and on the homeward
journey he measured distance by this landmark: and in his
imagination he lived through a long train of adventures, marvellous as those in the book itself, towards the close of which
there appeared an image of himself, grown older and sadder,
standing in a moonlit garden with Mercedes who had so many
years before slighted his love, and with a sadly proud gesture
of refusal, saying:

—Madam, I never eat muscatel grapes.

He became the ally of a boy named Aubrey Mills and
founded with him a gang of adventurers in the avenue. Aubrey
carried a whistle dangling from his buttonhole and a bicycle
lamp attached to his belt while the others had short sticks
thrust daggerwise through theirs. Stephen, who had read of
Napoleon's plain style of dress, chose to remain unadorned
and thereby heightened for himself the pleasure of taking
counsel with his lieutenant before giving orders. The gang
made forays into the gardens of old maids or went down to the
castle and fought a battle on the shaggy weedgrown rocks,
coming home after it weary stragglers with the stale odours of
the foreshore in their nostrils and the rank oils of the seawrack
upon their hands and in their hair.

Aubrey and Stephen had a common milkman and often
they drove out in the milkcar to Carrickmines where the cows
were at grass. While the men were milking the boys would
take turns in riding the tractable mare round the field. But
when autumn came the cows were driven home from the
grass: and the first sight of the filthy cowyard at Stradbrook
with its foul green puddles and clots of liquid dung and steam-
ing brantroughs sickened Stephen's heart. The cattle which
had seemed so beautiful in the country on sunny days revolted
him and he could not even look at the milk they yielded.

The coming of September did not trouble him this year for
he was not to be sent back to Clongowes. The practice in the

park came to an end when Mike Flynn went into hospital. Aubrey was at school and had only an hour or two free in the evening. The gang fell asunder and there were no more nightly forays or battles on the rocks. Stephen sometimes went round with the car which delivered the evening milk: and these chilly drives blew away his memory of the filth of the cowyard and he felt no repugnance at seeing the cowhairs and hayseeds on the milkman's coat. Whenever the car drew up before a house he waited to catch a glimpse of a wellscrubbed kitchen or of a softlylighted hall and to see how the servant would hold the jug and how she would close the door. He thought it should be a pleasant life enough, driving along the roads every evening to deliver milk, if he had warm gloves and a fat bag of ginger-nuts in his pocket to eat from. But the same foreknowledge which had sickened his heart and made his legs sag suddenly as he raced round the park, the same intuition which had made him glance with mistrust at his trainer's flabby stub-blecovered face as it bent heavily over his long stained fingers, dissipated any vision of the future. In a vague way he under-stood that his father was in trouble and that this was the reason why he himself had not been sent back to Clongowes. For some time he had felt the slight changes in his house; and these changes in what he had deemed unchangeable were so many slight shocks to his boyish conception of the world. The ambition which he felt astir at times in the darkness of his soul sought no outlet. A dusk like that of the outer world obscured his mind as he heard the mare's hoofs clattering along the tramtrack on the Rock Road and the great can swaying and rattling behind him.

He returned to Mercedes and, as he brooded upon her image, a strange unrest crept into his blood. Sometimes a fever gathered within him and led him to rove alone in the evening along the quiet avenue. The peace of the gardens and the kindly lights in the windows poured a tender influence into his restless heart. The noise of children at play annoyed him and their silly voices made him feel, even more keenly than he had

felt at Clongowes, that he was different from others. He did
not want to play. He wanted to meet in the real world the
unsubstantial image which his soul so constantly beheld. He
did not know where to seek it or how: but a premonition
which led him on told him that this image would, without any
overt act of his, encounter him. They would meet quietly as if
they had known each other and had made their tryst, perhaps
at one of the gates or in some more secret place. They would
be alone, surrounded by darkness and silence: and in that
moment of supreme tenderness he would be transfigured. He
would fade into something impalpable under her eyes and
then in a moment, he would be transfigured. Weakness and
timidity and inexperience would fall from him in that magic
moment.

*   *   *

Two great yellow caravans had halted one morning before
the door and men had come tramping into the house to
dismantle it. The furniture had been hustled out through the
front garden which was strewn with wisps of straw and rope
ends and into the huge vans at the gate. When all had been
safely stowed the vans had set off noisily down the avenue:
and from the window of the railway carriage, in which he had
sat with his redeyed mother, Stephen had seen them lumbering
heavily along the Merrion Road.

The parlour fire would not draw that evening and Mr Dedalus rested the poker against the bars of the grate to attract
the flame. Uncle Charles dozed in a corner of the half furnished uncarpeted room and near him the family portraits
leaned against the wall. The lamp on the table shed a weak
light over the boarded floor, muddied by the feet of the van-
men. Stephen sat on a footstool beside his father listening to a
long and incoherent monologue. He understood little or
nothing of it at first but he became slowly aware that his father
had enemies and that some fight was going to take place. He
felt too that he was being enlisted for the fight, that some duty

was being laid upon his shoulders. The sudden flight from the comfort and revery of Blackrock, the passage through the gloomy foggy city, the thought of the bare cheerless house in which they were now to live made his heart heavy: and again an intuition or foreknowledge of the future came to him. He understood also why the servants had often whispered together in the hall and why his father had often stood on the hearthrug, with his back to the fire, talking loudly to uncle Charles who urged him to sit down and eat his dinner.

—There's a crack of the whip left in me yet, Stephen, old chap, said Mr Dedalus, poking at the dull fire with fierce energy. We're not dead yet, sonny. No, by the Lord Jesus (God forgive me) nor half dead.

Dublin was a new and complex sensation. Uncle Charles had grown so witless that he could no longer be sent out on errands and the disorder in settling in the new house left Stephen freer than he had been in Blackrock. In the beginning he contented himself with circling timidly round the neighbouring square or, at most, going half way down one of the side streets: but when he had made a skeleton map of the city in his mind he followed boldly one of its central lines until he reached the customhouse. He passed unchallenged among the docks and along the quays wondering at the multitude of corks that lay bobbing on the surface of the water in a thick yellow scum, at the crowds of quay porters and the rumbling carts and the illdressed bearded policeman. The vastness and strangeness of the life suggested to him by the bales of merchandise stocked along the walls or swung aloft out of the holds of steamers wakened again in him the unrest which had sent him wandering in the evening from garden to garden in search of Mercedes. And amid this new bustling life he might have fancied himself in another Marseilles but that he missed the bright sky and the sunwarmed trellisses of the wineshops. A vague dissatisfaction grew up within him as he looked on the quays and on the river and on the lowering skies and yet he continued to wander up and down day after day as if he really sought someone that eluded him.

He went once or twice with his mother to visit their relatives: and, though they passed a jovial array of shops lit up and adorned for Christmas, his mood of embittered silence did not leave him. The causes of his embitterment were many, remote and near. He was angry with himself for being young and the prey of restless foolish impulses, angry also with the change of fortune which was reshaping the world about him into a vision of squalor and insincerity. Yet his anger lent nothing to the vision. He chronicled with patience what he saw, detaching himself from it and testing its mortifying flavour in secret.

He was sitting on the backless chair in his aunt's kitchen. A lamp with a reflector hung on the japanned wall of the fireplace and by its light his aunt was reading the evening paper that lay on her knees. She looked a long time at a smiling picture that was set in it and said musingly:

—The beautiful Mabel Hunter!

A ringletted girl stood on tiptoe to peer at the picture and said softly:

—What is she in, mud?

—In the pantomime, love.

The child leaned her ringletted head against her mother's sleeve, gazing on the picture, and murmured as if fascinated:

—The beautiful Mabel Hunter!

As if fascinated, her eyes rested long upon those demurely taunting eyes and she murmured again devotedly:

—Isn't she an exquisite creature?

And the boy who came in from the street, stamping crookedly under his stone of coal, heard her words. He dropped his load promptly on the floor and hurried to her side to see. But she did not raise her easeful head to let him see. He mauled the edges of the paper with his reddened and blackened hands, shouldering her aside and complaining that he could not see.

He was sitting in the narrow breakfast room high up in the old darkwindowed house. The firelight flickered on the wall and beyond the window a spectral dusk was gathering upon

the river. Before the fire an old woman was busy making tea
and, as she bustled at her task, she told in a low voice of what
the priest and the doctor had said. She told too of certain
changes she had seen in her of late and of her odd ways and
sayings. He sat listening to the words and following the ways
of adventure that lay open in the coals, arches and vaults and
winding galleries and jagged caverns.

Suddenly he became aware of something in the doorway. A
skull appeared suspended in the gloom of the doorway. A
feeble creature like a monkey was there, drawn thither by the
sound of voices at the fire. A whining voice came from the
door, asking:

—Is that Josephine?

The old bustling woman answered cheerily from the fireplace:

—No, Ellen. It's Stephen.

—O . . . O, good evening, Stephen.

He answered the greeting and saw a silly smile break over
the face in the doorway.

—Do you want anything, Ellen? asked the old woman at
the fire.

But she did not answer the question and said:

—I thought it was Josephine. I thought you were Josephine, Stephen.

And, repeating this several times, she fell to laughing fee-
bly.

He was sitting in the midst of a children's party at Harold's
Cross. His silent watchful manner had grown upon him and he
took little part in the games. The children, wearing the spoils
of their crackers, danced and romped noisily and, though he
tried to share their merriment, he felt himself a gloomy figure
amid the gay cocked hats and sunbonnets.

But when he had sung his song and withdrawn into a snug
corner of the room he began to taste the joy of his loneliness.
The mirth, which in the beginning of the evening had seemed
to him false and trivial, was like a soothing air to him, passing
gaily by his senses, hiding from other eyes the feverish agita-

tion of his blood while through the circling of the dancers and amid the music and laughter her glance travelled to his corner, flattering, taunting, searching, exciting his heart.

In the hall the children who had stayed latest were putting on their things: the party was over. She had thrown a shawl about her and, as they went together towards the tram, sprays of her fresh warm breath flew gaily above her cowled head and her shoes tapped blithely on the glassy road.

It was the last tram. The lank brown horses knew it and shook their bells to the clear night in admonition. The conductor talked with the driver, both nodding often in the green light of the lamp. On the empty seats of the tram were scattered a few coloured tickets. No sound of footsteps came up or down the road. No sound broke the peace of the night save when the lank brown horses rubbed their noses together and shook their bells.

They seemed to listen, he on the upper step and she on the lower. She came up to his step many times and went down to hers again between their phrases and once or twice stood close beside him for some moments on the upper step, forgetting to go down, and then went down. His heart danced upon her movements like a cork upon a tide. He heard what her eyes said to him from beneath their cowl and knew that in some dim past, whether in life or in revery, he had heard their tale before. He saw her urge her vanities, her fine dress and sash and long black stockings, and knew that he had yielded to them a thousand times. Yet a voice within him spoke above the noise of his dancing heart, asking him would he take her gift to which he had only to stretch out his hand. And he remembered the day when he and Eileen had stood looking into the hotel grounds, watching the waiters running up a trail of bunting on the flagstaff and the fox terrier scampering to and fro on the sunny lawn, and how, all of a sudden, she had broken out into a peal of laughter and had run down the sloping curve of the path. Now, as then, he stood listlessly in his place, seemingly a tranquil watcher of the scene before him.

—She too wants me to catch hold of her, he thought. That's why she came with me to the tram. I could easily catch hold of her when she comes up to my step: nobody is looking. I could hold her and kiss her.

But he did neither: and, when he was sitting alone in the deserted tram, he tore his ticket into shreds and stared gloomily at the corrugated footboard.

The next day he sat at his table in the bare upper room for many hours. Before him lay a new pen, a new bottle of ink and a new emerald exercise. From force of habit he had written at the top of the first page the initial letters of the jesuit motto: A.M.D.G. On the first line of the page appeared the title of the verses he was trying to write: To E—— C——. He knew it was right to begin so for he had seen similar titles in the collected poems of Lord Byron. When he had written this title and drawn an ornamental line underneath he fell into a daydream and began to draw diagrams on the cover of the book. He saw himself sitting at his table in Bray the morning after the discussion at the Christmas dinnertable, trying to write a poem about Parnell on the back of one of his father's second moiety notices. But his brain had then refused to grapple with the theme and, desisting, he had covered the page with the names and addresses of certain of his classmates:

Roderick Kickham
John Lawton
Anthony MacSwiney
Simon Moonan

Now it seemed as if he would fail again but, by dint of brooding on the incident, he thought himself into confidence. During this process all these elements which he deemed common and insignificant fell out of the scene. There remained no trace of the tram itself nor of the trammen nor of the horses: nor did he and she appear vividly. The verses told only of the night and the balmy breeze and the maiden lustre of the moon. Some undefined sorrow was hidden in the hearts of the protagonists as they stood in silence beneath the leafless trees and when the moment of farewell had come the kiss, which had been withheld by one, was given by both. After this the letters L.D.S. were written at the foot of the page and, having hidden the book, he went into his mother's bedroom and gazed at his face for a long time in the mirror of her dressingtable.

But his long spell of leisure and liberty was drawing to its end. One evening his father came home full of news which kept his tongue busy all through dinner. Stephen had been awaiting his father's return for there had been mutton hash that day and he knew that his father would make him dip his bread in the gravy. But he did not relish the hash for the mention of Clongowes had coated his palate with a scum of disgust.

—I walked bang into him, said Mr Dedalus for the fourth time, just at the corner of the square.

—Then I suppose, said Mrs Dedalus, he will be able to arrange it. I mean about Belvedere.

—Of course he will, said Mr Dedalus. Don't I tell you he's provincial of the order now?

—I never liked the idea of sending him to the christian brothers myself, said Mrs Dedalus.

—Christian brothers be damned! said Mr Dedalus. Is it with Paddy Stink and Mickey Mud? No, let him stick to the jesuits in God's name since he began with them. They'll be of service to him in after years. Those are the fellows that can get you a position.

—And they're a very rich order, aren't they, Simon?

—Rather. They live well, I tell you. You saw their table at Clongowes. Fed up, by God, like gamecocks.

Mr Dedalus pushed his plate over to Stephen and bade him finish what was on it.

—Now then, Stephen, he said, you must put your shoulder to the wheel, old chap. You've had a fine long holiday.

—O, I'm sure he'll work very hard now, said Mrs Dedalus, especially when he has Maurice with him.

—O, Holy Paul, I forgot about Maurice, said Mr Dedalus.

Here, Maurice! Come here, you thickheaded ruffian! Do you know I'm going to send you to a college where they'll teach you to spell c.a.t. cat. And I'll buy you a nice little penny handkerchief to keep your nose dry. Won't that be grand fun?

Maurice grinned at his father and then at his brother. Mr Dedalus screwed his glass into his eye and stared hard at both his sons. Stephen mumbled his bread without answering his father's gaze.

—By the bye, said Mr Dedalus at length, the rector, or provincial, rather, was telling me that story about you and Father Dolan. You're an impudent thief, he said.

—O, he didn't, Simon!

—Not he! said Mr Dedalus. But he gave me a great account of the whole affair. We were chatting, you know, and one word borrowed another. And, by the way, who do you think he told me will get that job in the corporation? But I'll tell you that after. Well, as I was saying, we were chatting away quite friendly and he asked me did our friend here wear glasses still and then he told me the whole story.

—And was he annoyed, Simon?

—Annoyed! Not he! *Manly little chap!* he said.

Mr Dedalus imitated the mincing nasal tone of the provincial.

—Father Dolan and I, when I told them all at dinner about it, Father Dolan and I had a great laugh over it. *You better mind yourself, Father Dolan,* said I, *or young Dedalus will send you up for twice nine.* We had a famous laugh together over it. Ha! Ha! Ha!

Mr Dedalus turned to his wife and interjected in his natural voice:

—Shows you the spirit in which they take the boys there. O, a jesuit for your life, for diplomacy!

He reassumed the provincial's voice and repeated:

—*I told them all at dinner about it and Father Dolan and I and all of us we had a hearty laugh together over it. Ha! Ha! Ha!*

*　　　*　　　*

The night of the Whitsuntide play had come and Stephen from the window of the dressingroom looked out on the small grassplot across which lines of Chinese lanterns were stretched. He watched the visitors come down the steps from the house and pass into the theatre. Stewards in evening dress, old Belvedereans, loitered in groups about the entrance to the theatre and ushered in the visitors with ceremony. Under the sudden glow of a lantern he could recognise the smiling face of a priest.

The Blessed Sacrament had been removed from the tabernacle and the first benches had been driven so as to leave the dais of the altar and the space before it free. Against the walls stood companies of barbells and Indian clubs; the dumbbells were piled in one corner: and in the midst of countless hillocks of gymnasium shoes and sweaters and singlets in untidy brown parcels there stood the stout leatherjacketed vaulting horse waiting its turn to be carried up on the stage. A large bronze shield, tipped with silver, leaned against the panel of the altar also waiting its turn to be carried up on the stage and set in the middle of the winning team at the end of the gymnastic display.

Stephen, though in deference to his reputation for essaywriting he had been elected secretary to the gymnasium, had had no part in the first section of the programme but in the play which formed the second section he had the chief part, that of a farcical pedagogue. He had been cast for it on account of his stature and grave manners for he was now at the end of his second year at Belvedere and in number two.

A score of the younger boys in white knickers and singlets came pattering down from the stage, through the vestry and into the chapel. The vestry and chapel were peopled with eager masters and boys. The plump bald sergeantmajor was testing with his foot the springboard of the vaulting horse. The lean young man in a long overcoat, who was to give a special display of intricate club swinging, stood near watching with interest, his silvercoated clubs peeping out of his deep sidepockets. The hollow rattle of the wooden dumbbells was heard as another team made ready to go up on the stage: and in another moment the excited prefect was hustling the boys through the vestry like a flock of geese, flapping the wings of his soutane nervously and crying to the laggards to make haste. A little troop of Neapolitan peasants were practising their steps at the end of the chapel, some circling their arms above their heads, some swaying their baskets of paper violets and curtseying. In a dark corner of the chapel at the gospel side of the altar a stout old lady knelt amid her copious black skirts. When she stood up a pinkdressed figure, wearing a curly golden wig and an oldfashioned straw sunbonnet, with black pencilled eyebrows and cheeks delicately rouged and powdered, was discovered. A low murmur of curiosity ran round the chapel at the discovery of this girlish figure. One of the prefects, smiling and nodding his head, approached the dark corner and, having bowed to the stout old lady, said pleasantly:

—Is this a beautiful young lady or a doll that you have here, Mrs Tallon?

Then, bending down to peer at the smiling painted face under the leaf of the bonnet, he exclaimed:

—No! Upon my word I believe it's little Bertie Tallon after all!

Stephen at his post by the window heard the old lady and the priest laugh together and heard the boys' murmur of admiration behind him as they passed forward to see the little boy who had to dance the sunbonnet dance by himself. A movement of impatience escaped him. He let the edge of the blind fall and, stepping down from the bench on which he had been standing, walked out of the chapel.

He passed out of the schoolhouse and halted under the shed that flanked the garden. From the theatre opposite came the muffled noise of the audience and sudden brazen clashes of the soldiers' band. The light spread upwards from the glass roof making the theatre seem a festive ark, anchored among the hulks of houses, her frail cables of lanterns looping her to her moorings. A sidedoor of the theatre opened suddenly and a shaft of light flew across the grassplots. A sudden burst of music issued from the ark, the prelude of a waltz: and when the sidedoor closed again the listener could hear the faint rhythm of the music. The sentiment of the opening bars, their languor and supple movement, evoked the incommunicable emotion which had been the cause of all his day's unrest and of his impatient movement of a moment before. His unrest issued from him like a wave of sound: and on the tide of flowing music the ark was journeying, trailing her cables of lanterns in her wake. Then a noise like dwarf artillery broke the movement. It was the clapping that greeted the entry of the dumbbell team on the stage.

At the far end of the shed near the street a speck of pink light showed in the darkness and as he walked towards it he became aware of a faint aromatic odour. Two boys were standing in the shelter of a doorway, smoking, and before he reached them he had recognised Heron by his voice.

—Here comes the noble Dedalus! cried a high throaty voice. Welcome to our trusty friend!

This welcome ended in a soft peal of mirthless laughter as Heron salaamed and then began to poke the ground with his cane.

—Here I am, said Stephen, halting and glancing from Heron to his friend.

The latter was a stranger to him but in the darkness, by the aid of the glowing cigarettetips, he could make out a pale dandyish face, over which a smile was travelling slowly, a tall overcoated figure and a hard hat. Heron did not trouble himself about an introduction but said instead:

—I was just telling my friend Wallis what a lark it would be tonight if you took off the rector in the part of the schoolmaster. It would be a ripping good joke.

Heron made a poor attempt to imitate for his friend Wallis the rector's pedantic bass and then, laughing at his failure, asked Stephen to do it.

—Go on, Dedalus, he urged, you can take him off rippingly. *He that will not hear the churcha let him be to theea as the heathena and the publicana.*

The imitation was prevented by a mild expression of anger from Wallis in whose mouthpiece the cigarette had become too tightly wedged.

—Damn this blankety blank holder, he said, taking it from his mouth and smiling and frowning upon it tolerantly. It's always getting stuck like that. Do you use a holder?

—I don't smoke, answered Stephen.

—No, said Heron, Dedalus is a model youth. He doesn't smoke and he doesn't go to bazaars and he doesn't flirt and he doesn't damn anything or damn all.

Stephen shook his head and smiled in his rival's flushed and mobile face, beaked like a bird's. He had often thought it strange that Vincent Heron had a bird's face as well as a bird's name. A shock of pale hair lay on the forehead like a ruffled crest: the forehead was narrow and bony and a thin hooked nose stood out between the closeset prominent eyes which were light and inexpressive. The rivals were school friends. They sat together in class, knelt together in the chapel, talked together after beads over their lunches. As the fellows in number one were undistinguished dullards Stephen and Heron had been during the year the virtual heads of the school. It was they who went up to the rector together to ask for a free day or to get a fellow off.

—O by the way, said Heron suddenly, I saw your governor going in.

The smile waned on Stephen's face. Any allusion made to his father by a fellow or by a master put his calm to rout in a moment. He waited in timorous silence to hear what Heron might say next. Heron, however, nudged him expressively with his elbow and said:

—You're a sly dog, Dedalus!

—Why so? said Stephen.

—You'd think butter wouldn't melt in your mouth, said Heron. But I'm afraid you're a sly dog.

—Might I ask you what you are talking about? said Stephen urbanely.

—Indeed you might, answered Heron. We saw her, Wallis, didn't we? And deucedly pretty she is too. And so inquisitive! *And what part does Stephen take, Mr Dedalus? And will Stephen not sing, Mr Dedalus?* Your governor was staring at her through that eyeglass of his for all he was worth so that I think the old man has found you out too. I wouldn't care a bit, by Jove. She's ripping, isn't she, Wallis?

—Not half bad, answered Wallis quietly as he placed his holder once more in the corner of his mouth.

A shaft of momentary anger flew through Stephen's mind at these indelicate allusions in the hearing of a stranger. For him there was nothing amusing in a girl's interest and regard. All day he had thought of nothing but their leavetaking on the steps of the tram at Harold's Cross, the stream of moody emotions it had made to course through him, and the poem he had written about it. All day he had imagined a new meeting with her for he knew that she was to come to the play. The old restless moodiness had again filled his breast as it had done on the night of the party but had not found an outlet in verse. The growth and knowledge of two years of boyhood stood between then and now, forbidding such an outlet: and all day the stream of gloomy tenderness within him had started forth and returned upon itself in dark courses and eddies, wearying him in the end until the pleasantry of the prefect and the painted little boy had drawn from him a movement of impatience.

—So you may as well admit, Heron went on, that we've fairly found you out this time. You can't play the saint on me any more, that's one sure five.

A soft peal of mirthless laughter escaped from his lips and, bending down as before, he struck Stephen lightly across the calf of the leg with his cane, as if in jesting reproof.

Stephen's movement of anger had already passed. He was neither flattered nor confused but simply wished the banter to end. He scarcely resented what had seemed to him at first a silly indelicateness for he knew that the adventure in his mind stood in no danger from their words: and his face mirrored his rival's false smile.

—Admit! repeated Heron, striking him again with his cane across the calf of the leg.

The stroke was playful but not so lightly given as the first one had been. Stephen felt the skin tingle and glow slightly and almost painlessly; and bowing submissively, as if to meet his companion's jesting mood, began to recite the *Confiteor*. The episode ended well for both Heron and Wallis laughed indulgently at the irreverence.

The confession came only from Stephen's lips and, while they spoke the words, a sudden memory had carried him to another scene called up, as if by magic, at the moment when he had noted the faint cruel dimples at the corners of Heron's smiling lips and had felt the familiar stroke of the cane against his calf and had heard the familiar word of admonition:

—Admit.

It was towards the close of his first term in the college when he was in number six. His sensitive nature was still smarting under the lashes of an undivined and squalid way of life. His soul was still disquieted and cast down by the dull phenomenon of Dublin. He had emerged from a two years' spell of revery to find himself in the midst of a new scene, every event and figure of which affected him intimately, disheartened him or allured and, whether alluring or disheartening, filled him always with unrest and bitter thoughts. All the leisure which his school life left him was passed in the company of subversive writers whose gibes and violence of speech set up a ferment in his brain before they passed out of it into his crude writings.

The essay was for him the chief labour of his week and every Tuesday, as he marched from home to the school, he read his fate in the incidents of the way, pitting himself against some figure ahead of him and quickening his pace to outstrip it before a certain goal was reached or planting his steps scrupulously in the spaces of the patchwork of the footpath and telling himself that he would be first and not first in the weekly essay.

On a certain Tuesday the course of his triumphs was rudely broken. Mr Tate, the English master, pointed his finger at him and said bluntly:

—This fellow has heresy in his essay.

A hush fell on the class. Mr Tate did not break it but dug with his hand between his crossed thighs while his heavily starched linen creaked about his neck and wrists. Stephen did not look up. It was a raw spring morning and his eyes were still smarting and weak. He was conscious of failure and of detection, of the squalor of his own mind and home, and felt against his neck the raw edge of his turned and jagged collar.

A short loud laugh from Mr Tate set the class more at ease.

—Perhaps you didn't know that, he said.

—Where? asked Stephen.

Mr Tate withdrew his delving hand and spread out the essay.

—Here. It's about the Creator and the soul. Rrm . . . rrm . . . rrm. . . . Ah! *without a possibility of ever approaching nearer*. That's heresy.

Stephen murmured:

—I meant *without a possibility of ever reaching*.

It was a submission and Mr Tate, appeased, folded up the essay and passed it across to him, saying:

—O . . . Ah! *ever reaching*. That's another story.

But the class was not so soon appeased. Though nobody spoke to him of the affair after class he could feel about him a vague general malignant joy.

A few nights after this public chiding he was walking with a letter along the Drumcondra Road when he heard a voice cry:

—Halt!

He turned and saw three boys of his own class coming towards him in the dusk. It was Heron who had called out and, as he marched forward between his two attendants, he cleft the air before him with a thin cane, in time to their steps. Boland, his friend, marched beside him, a large grin on his face, while Nash came on a few steps behind, blowing from the pace and wagging his great red head.

As soon as the boys had turned into Clonliffe Road together they began to speak about books and writers, saying what books they were reading and how many books there were in their fathers' bookcases at home. Stephen listened to them in some wonderment for Boland was the dunce and Nash the idler of the class. In fact after some talk about their favourite writers Nash declared for Captain Marryat who, he said, was the greatest writer.

—Fudge! said Heron. Ask Dedalus. Who is the greatest writer, Dedalus?

Stephen noted the mockery in the question and said:

—Of prose do you mean?

—Yes.

—Newman, I think.

—Is it Cardinal Newman? asked Boland.

—Yes, answered Stephen.

The grin broadened on Nash's freckled face as he turned to Stephen and said:

—And do you like Cardinal Newman, Dedalus?

—O, many say that Newman has the best prose style, Heron said to the other two in explanation. Of course he's not a poet.

—And who is the best poet, Heron? asked Boland.

—Lord Tennyson, of course, answered Heron.

—O, yes, Lord Tennyson, said Nash. We have all his poetry at home in a book.

At this Stephen forgot the silent vows he had been making and burst out:

—Tennyson a poet! Why, he's only a rhymester!

—O, get out! said Heron. Everyone knows that Tennyson is the greatest poet.

—And who do you think is the greatest poet? asked Boland, nudging his neighbour.

—Byron, of course, answered Stephen.

Heron gave the lead and all three joined in a scornful laugh.

—What are you laughing at? asked Stephen.

—You, said Heron. Byron the greatest poet! He's only a poet for uneducated people.

—He must be a fine poet! said Boland.

—You may keep your mouth shut, said Stephen, turning on him boldly. All you know about poetry is what you wrote up on the slates in the yard and were going to be sent to the loft for.

Boland, in fact, was said to have written on the slates in the yard a couplet about a classmate of his who often rode home from the college on a pony:

> *As Tyson was riding into Jerusalem*
> *He fell and hurt his Alec Kafoozelum.*

This thrust put the two lieutenants to silence but Heron went on:

—In any case Byron was a heretic and immoral too.

—I don't care what he was, cried Stephen hotly.

—You don't care whether he was a heretic or not? said Nash.

—What do you know about it? shouted Stephen. You never read a line of anything in your life except a trans or Boland either.

—I know that Byron was a bad man, said Boland.

—Here, catch hold of this heretic, Heron called out.

In a moment Stephen was a prisoner.

—Tate made you buck up the other day, Heron went on, about the heresy in your essay.

—I'll tell him tomorrow, said Boland.

—Will you? said Stephen. You'd be afraid to open your lips.

—Afraid?

—Ay. Afraid of your life.

—Behave yourself! cried Heron, cutting at Stephen's legs with his cane.

It was the signal for their onset. Nash pinioned his arms behind while Boland seized a long cabbage stump which was lying in the gutter. Struggling and kicking under the cuts of the cane and the blows of the knotty stump Stephen was borne back against a barbed wire fence.

—Admit that Byron was no good.

—No.

—Admit.

—No.

—Admit.

—No. No.

At last after a fury of plunges he wrenched himself free. His tormentors set off towards Jones's Road, laughing and jeering at him, while he, torn and flushed and panting, stumbled after them half blinded with tears, clenching his fists madly and sobbing.

While he was still repeating the *Confiteor* amid the indulgent laughter of his hearers and while the scenes of that malignant episode were still passing sharply and swiftly before his mind he wondered why he bore no malice now to those who had tormented him. He had not forgotten a whit of their cowardice and cruelty but the memory of it called forth no anger from him. All the descriptions of fierce love and hatred which he had met in books had seemed to him therefore unreal. Even that night as he stumbled homewards along Jones's Road he had felt that some power was divesting him of that suddenwoven anger as easily as a fruit is divested of its soft ripe peel.

He remained standing with his two companions at the end of the shed, listening idly to their talk or to the bursts of applause in the theatre. She was sitting there among the others perhaps waiting for him to appear. He tried to recall her appearance but could not. He could remember only that she had worn a shawl about her head like a cowl and that her dark eyes had invited and unnerved him. He wondered had he been in her thoughts as she had been in his. Then in the dark and unseen by the other two he rested the tips of the fingers of one hand upon the palm of the other hand, scarcely touching it and yet pressing upon it lightly. But the pressure of her fingers had been lighter and steadier: and suddenly the memory of their touch traversed his brain and body like an invisible warm wave.

A boy came towards them, running along under the shed. He was excited and breathless.

—O, Dedalus, he cried, Doyle is in a great bake about you. You're to go in at once and get dressed for the play. Hurry up, you better.

—He's coming now, said Heron to the messenger with a haughty drawl, when he wants to.

The boy turned to Heron and repeated:

—But Doyle is in an awful bake.

—Will you tell Doyle with my best compliments that I damned his eyes? answered Heron.

—Well, I must go now, said Stephen, who cared little for such points of honour.

—I wouldn't, said Heron, damn me if I would. That's no way to send for one of the senior boys. In a bake, indeed! I think it's quite enough that you're taking a part in his bally old play.

This spirit of quarrelsome comradeship which he had observed lately in his rival had not seduced Stephen from his habits of quiet obedience. He mistrusted the turbulence and doubted the sincerity of such comradeship which seemed to him a sorry anticipation of manhood. The question of honour here raised was, like all such questions, trivial to him. While his mind had been pursuing its intangible phantoms and turning in irresolution from such pursuit he had heard about him the constant voices of his father and of his masters, urging him to be a gentleman above all things and urging him to be a good catholic above all things. These voices had now come to be hollowsounding in his ears. When the gymnasium had been opened he had heard another voice urging him to be strong and manly and healthy and when the movement towards national revival had begun to be felt in the college yet another voice had bidden him be true to his country and help to raise up her fallen language and tradition. In the profane world, as he foresaw, a worldly voice would bid him raise up his father's fallen state by his labours and, meanwhile, the voice of his school comrades urged him to be a decent fellow, to shield others from blame or to beg them off and to do his best to get free days for the school. And it was the din of all these hollowsounding voices that made him halt irresolutely in the pursuit of phantoms. He gave them ear only for a time but he was happy only when he was far from them, beyond their call, alone or in the company of phantasmal comrades.

In the vestry a plump freshfaced jesuit and an elderly man, in shabby blue clothes, were dabbling in a case of paints and chalks. The boys who had been painted walked about or stood still awkwardly, touching their faces in a gingerly fashion with their furtive fingertips. In the middle of the vestry a young jesuit, who was then on a visit to the college, stood rocking himself rhythmically from the tips of his toes to his heels and back again, his hands thrust well forward into his sidepockets. His small head set off with glossy red curls and his newly shaven face agreed well with the spotless decency of his soutane and with his spotless shoes.

As he watched this swaying form and tried to read for himself the legend of the priest's mocking smile there came into Stephen's memory a saying which he had heard from his father before he had been sent to Clongowes, that you could always tell a jesuit by the style of his clothes. At the same moment he thought he saw a likeness between his father's mind and that of this smiling welldressed priest: and he was aware of some desecration of the priest's office or of the vestry itself, whose silence was now routed by loud talk and joking and its air pungent with the smells of the gasjets and the grease.

While his forehead was being wrinkled and his jaws painted

black and blue by the elderly man he listened distractedly to the voice of the plump young jesuit which bade him speak up and make his points clearly. He could hear the band playing *The Lily of Killarney* and knew that in a few moments the curtain would go up. He felt no stage fright but the thought of the part he had to play humiliated him. A remembrance of some of his lines made a sudden flush rise to his painted cheeks. He saw her serious alluring eyes watching him from among the audience and their image at once swept away his scruples, leaving his will compact. Another nature seemed to have been lent him: the infection of the excitement and youth about him entered into and transformed his moody mistrustfulness. For one rare moment he seemed to be clothed in the real apparel of boyhood: and, as he stood in the wings among the other players, he shared the common mirth amid which the drop scene was hauled upwards by two ablebodied priests with violent jerks and all awry.

A few moments after he found himself on the stage amid the garish gas and the dim scenery, acting before the innumerable faces of the void. It surprised him to see that the play which he had known at rehearsals for a disjointed lifeless thing had suddenly assumed a life of its own. It seemed now to play itself, he and his fellow actors aiding it with their parts. When the curtain fell on the last scene he heard the void filled with applause and, through a rift in the side scene, saw the simple body before which he had acted magically deformed, the void of faces breaking at all points and falling asunder into busy groups.

He left the stage quickly and rid himself of his mummery and passed out through the chapel into the college garden. Now that the play was over his nerves cried for some further adventure. He hurried onwards as if to overtake it. The doors of the theatre were all open and the audience had emptied out. On the lines which he had fancied the moorings of an ark a few lanterns swung in the night breeze, flickering cheerlessly. He mounted the steps from the garden in haste, eager that some prey should not elude him, and forced his way through the crowd in the hall and past the two jesuits who stood watching the exodus and bowing and shaking hands with the visitors. He pushed onward nervously, feigning a still greater haste and faintly conscious of the smiles and stares and nudges which his powdered head left in its wake.

When he came out on the steps he saw his family waiting for him at the first lamp. In a glance he noted that every figure of the group was familiar and ran down the steps angrily.

—I have to leave a message down in George's Street, he said to his father quickly. I'll be home after you.

Without waiting for his father's questions he ran across the road and began to walk at breakneck speed down the hill. He hardly knew where he was walking. Pride and hope and desire like crushed herbs in his heart sent up vapours of maddening incense before the eyes of his mind. He strode down the hill amid the tumult of suddenrisen vapours of wounded pride and fallen hope and baffled desire. They streamed upwards before his anguished eyes in dense and maddening fumes and passed away above him till at last the air was clear and cold again.

A film still veiled his eyes but they burned no longer. A power, akin to that which.had often made anger or resentment fall from him, brought his steps to rest. He stood still and gazed up at the sombre porch of the morgue and from that to the dark cobbled laneway at its side. He saw the word *Lotts* on the wall of the lane and breathed slowly the rank heavy air.

—That is horse piss and rotted straw, he thought. It is a good odour to breathe. It will calm my heart. My heart is quite calm now. I will go back.

*   *   *

Stephen was once again seated beside his father in the corner of a railway carriage at Kingsbridge. He was travelling with his father by the night mail to Cork. As the train steamed out of the station he recalled his childish wonder of years before and every event of his first day at Clongowes. But he felt no wonder now. He saw the darkening lands slipping past him, the silent telegraphpoles passing his window swiftly every four seconds, the little glimmering stations, manned by a few silent sentries, flung by the mail behind her and twinkling for a moment in the darkness like fiery grains flung backwards by a runner.

He listened without sympathy to his father's evocation of Cork and of scenes of his youth, a tale broken by sighs or draughts from his pocketflask whenever the image of some dead friend appeared in it or whenever the evoker remembered suddenly the purpose of his actual visit. Stephen heard but could feel no pity. The images of the dead were all strange to him save that of uncle Charles, an image which had lately been fading out of memory. He knew, however, that his father's property was going to be sold by auction and in the manner of his own dispossession he felt the world give the lie rudely to his phantasy.

At Maryborough he fell asleep. When he awoke the train had passed out of Mallow and his father was stretched asleep on the other seat. The cold light of the dawn lay over the country, over the unpeopled fields and the closed cottages. The terror of sleep fascinated his mind as he watched the silent country or heard from time to time his father's deep breath or sudden sleepy movement. The neighbourhood of unseen sleepers filled him with strange dread as though they could harm him; and he prayed that the day might come quickly. His prayer, addressed neither to God nor saint, began with a shiver, as the chilly morning breeze crept through the chink of the carriage door to his feet, and ended in a trail of foolish words which he made to fit the insistent rhythm of the train; and silently, at intervals of four seconds, the telegraphpoles held the galloping notes of the music between punctual bars. This furious music allayed his dread and, leaning against the windowledge, he let his eyelids close again.

They drove in a jingle across Cork while it was still early morning and Stephen finished his sleep in a bedroom of the

Victoria Hotel. The bright warm sunlight was streaming through the window and he could hear the din of traffic. His father was standing before the dressingtable, examining his hair and face and moustache with great care, craning his neck across the waterjug and drawing it back sideways to see the better. While he did so he sang softly to himself with quaint accent and phrasing:

> *'Tis youth and folly*
> *Makes young men marry,*
> *So here, my love, I'll*
> *   No longer stay.*
> *What can't be cured, sure,*
> *Must be injured, sure,*
> *   So I'll go to*
> *   Amerikay.*
>
> *My love she's handsome,*
> *My love she's bonny:*
> *She's like good whisky*
> *   When it is new;*
> *But when 'tis old*
> *And growing cold*
> *It fades and dies like*
> *   The mountain dew.*

The consciousness of the warm sunny city outside his window and the tender tremors with which his father's voice festooned the strange sad happy air, drove off all the mists of the night's ill humour from Stephen's brain. He got up quickly to dress and, when the song had ended, said:

—That's much prettier than any of your other *come-all-yous.*

—Do you think so? asked Mr Dedalus.

—I like it, said Stephen.

—It's a pretty old air, said Mr Dedalus, twirling the points of his moustache. Ah, but you should have heard Mick Lacy sing it! Poor Mick Lacy! He had little turns for it, grace notes he used to put in that I haven't got. That was the boy who could sing a *come-all-you,* if you like.

Mr Dedalus had ordered drisheens for breakfast and during the meal he crossexamined the waiter for local news. For the most part they spoke at crosspurposes when a name was mentioned, the waiter having in mind the present holder and Mr Dedalus his father or perhaps his grandfather.

—Well, I hope they haven't moved the Queen's College anyhow, said Mr Dedalus, for I want to show it to this youngster of mine.

Along the Mardyke the trees were in bloom. They entered the grounds of the college and were led by the garrulous porter across the quadrangle. But their progress across the gravel was brought to a halt after every dozen or so paces by some reply of the porter's.

—Ah, do you tell me so? And is poor Pottlebelly dead?

—Yes, sir. Dead, sir.

During these halts Stephen stood awkwardly behind the two men, weary of the subject and waiting restlessly for the slow march to begin again. By the time they had crossed the quadrangle his restlessness had risen to fever. He wondered how his father, whom he knew for a shrewd suspicious man, could be duped by the servile manners of the porter; and the lively southern speech which had entertained him all the morning now irritated his ears.

They passed into the anatomy theatre where Mr Dedalus, the porter aiding him, searched the desks for his initials. Stephen remained in the background, depressed more than ever by the darkness and silence of the theatre and by the air it wore of jaded and formal study. On the desk before him he read the word *Fœtus* cut several times in the dark stained wood. The sudden legend startled his blood: he seemed to feel the absent students of the college about him and to shrink from their company. A vision of their life, which his father's words had been powerless to evoke, sprang up before him out of the word cut in the desk. A broadshouldered student with a moustache was cutting in the letters with a jackknife, seriously. Other students stood or sat near him laughing at his handiwork. One jogged his elbow. The big student turned on him, frowning. He was dressed in loose grey clothes and had tan boots.

Stephen's name was called. He hurried down the steps of the theatre so as to be as far away from the vision as he could be and, peering closely at his father's initials, hid his flushed face.

But the word and the vision capered before his eyes as he walked back across the quadrangle and towards the college gate. It shocked him to find in the outer world a trace of what he had deemed till then a brutish and individual malady of his own mind. His recent monstrous reveries came thronging into his memory. They too had sprung up before him, suddenly and furiously, out of mere words. He had soon given in to them and allowed them to sweep across and abase his intellect, wondering always where they came from, from what den of monstrous images, and always weak and humble towards others, restless and sickened of himself when they had swept over him.

—Ay, bedad! And there's the Groceries sure enough! cried Mr Dedalus. You often heard me speak of the Groceries, didn't you, Stephen. Many's the time we went down there when our names had been marked, a crowd of us, Harry Peard and little Jack Mountain and Bob Dyas and Maurice Moriarty, the Frenchman, and Tom O'Grady and Mick Lacy that I told you of this morning and Joey Corbet and poor little good hearted Johnny Keevers of the Tantiles.

The leaves of the trees along the Mardyke were astir and whispering in the sunlight. A team of cricketers passed, agile young men in flannels and blazers, one of them carrying the long green wicketbag. In a quiet bystreet a German band of five players in faded uniforms and with battered brass instruments was playing to an audience of street arabs and leisurely messenger boys. A maid in a white cap and apron was watering a box of plants on a sill which shone like a slab of limestone in the warm glare. From another window open to the air came the sound of a piano, scale after scale rising into the treble.

Stephen walked on at his father's side, listening to stories he had heard before, hearing again the names of the scattered and dead revellers who had been the companions of his father's youth. And a faint sickness sighed in his heart. He recalled his own equivocal position in Belvedere, a free boy, a leader afraid of his own authority, proud and sensitive and suspicious, battling against the squalor of his life and against the riot of his mind. The letters cut in the stained wood of the desk stared upon him, mocking his bodily weakness and futile enthusiasms and making him loathe himself for his own mad and filthy orgies. The spittle in his throat grew bitter and foul to swallow and the faint sickness climbed to his brain so that for a moment he closed his eyes and walked on in darkness.

He could still hear his father's voice.

—When you kick out for yourself, Stephen—as I daresay you will one of those days—remember, whatever you do, to mix with gentlemen. When I was a young fellow I tell you I enjoyed myself. I mixed with fine decent fellows. Everyone of us could do something. One fellow had a good voice, another fellow was a good actor, another could sing a good comic song, another was a good oarsman or a good racketplayer, another could tell a good story and so on. We kept the ball rolling anyhow and enjoyed ourselves and saw a bit of life and we were none the worse of it either. But we were all gentlemen, Stephen—at least I hope we were—and bloody good honest Irishmen too. That's the kind of fellows I want you to associate with, fellows of the right kidney. I'm talking to you as a friend, Stephen. I don't believe in playing the stern father. I don't believe a son should be afraid of his father. No, I treat you as your grandfather treated me when I was a young chap. We were more like brothers than father and son. I'll never forget the first day he caught me smoking. I was standing at the end of the South Terrace one day with some maneens like myself and sure we thought we were grand fellows because we had pipes stuck in the corners of our mouths. Suddenly the governor passed. He didn't say a word, or stop even. But the next day, Sunday, we were out for a walk together and when we were coming home he took out his cigar case and said: *By the bye, Simon, I didn't know you smoked:* or something like that. Of course I tried to carry it off as best I could. *If you want a good smoke,* he said, *try one of these cigars. An American captain made me a present of them last night in Queenstown.*

Stephen heard his father's voice break into a laugh which was almost a sob.

—He was the handsomest man in Cork at that time, by God he was! The women used to stand to look after him in the street.

He heard the sob passing loudly down his father's throat and opened his eyes with a nervous impulse. The sunlight breaking suddenly on his sight turned the sky and clouds into a fantastic world of sombre masses with lakelike spaces of dark rosy light. His very brain was sick and powerless. He could scarcely interpret the letters of the signboards of the shops. By his monstrous way of life he seemed to have put himself beyond the limits of reality. Nothing moved him or spoke to him from the real world unless he heard in it an echo of the infuriated cries within him. He could respond to no earthly or human appeal, dumb and insensible to the call of summer and gladness and companionship, wearied and dejected by his father's voice. He could scarcely recognise as his his own thoughts, and repeated slowly to himself:

—I am Stephen Dedalus. I am walking beside my father whose name is Simon Dedalus. We are in Cork, in Ireland. Cork is a city. Our room is in the Victoria Hotel. Victoria and Stephen and Simon. Simon and Stephen and Victoria. Names.

The memory of his childhood suddenly grew dim. He tried

to call forth some of its vivid moments but could not. He recalled only names: Dante, Parnell, Clane, Clongowes. A little boy had been taught geography by an old woman who kept two brushes in her wardrobe. Then he had been sent away from home to a college. In the college he had made his first communion and eaten slim jim out of his cricketcap and watched the firelight leaping and dancing on the wall of a little bedroom in the infirmary and dreamed of being dead, of mass being said for him by the rector in a black and gold cope, of being buried then in the little graveyard of the community off the main avenue of limes. But he had not died then. Parnell had died. There had been no mass for the dead in the chapel and no procession. He had not died but he had faded out like a film in the sun. He had been lost or had wandered out of existence for he no longer existed. How strange to think of him passing out of existence in such a way, not by death but by fading out in the sun or by being lost and forgotten somewhere in the universe! It was strange to see his small body appear again for a moment: a little boy in a grey belted suit. His hands were in his sidepockets and his trousers were tucked in at the knees by elastic bands.

On the evening of the day on which the property was sold Stephen followed his father meekly about the city from bar to bar. To the sellers in the market, to the barmen and barmaids, to the beggars who importuned him for a lob Mr Dedalus told the same tale, that he was an old Corkonian, that he had been trying for thirty years to get rid of his Cork accent up in Dublin and that Peter Pickackafax beside him was his eldest son but that he was only a Dublin jackeen.

They had set out early in the morning from Newcombe's coffeehouse where Mr Dedalus' cup had rattled noisily against its saucer, and Stephen had tried to cover that shameful sign of his father's drinkingbout of the night before by moving his chair and coughing. One humiliation had succeeded another: the false smiles of the market sellers, the curvettings and oglings of the barmaids with whom his father flirted, the compliments and encouraging words of his father's friends. They had told him that he had a great look of his grandfather and Mr Dedalus had agreed that he was an ugly likeness. They had unearthed traces of a Cork accent in his speech and made him admit that the Lee was a much finer river than the Liffey. One of them in order to put his Latin to the proof had made him translate short passages from Dilectus and asked him whether it was correct to say: *Tempora mutantur nos et mutamur in illis* or *Tempora mutantur et nos mutamur in illis.* Another, a brisk old man, whom Mr Dedalus called Johnny Cashman, had covered him with confusion by asking him to say which were prettier, the Dublin girls or the Cork girls.

—He's not that way built, said Mr Dedalus. Leave him alone. He's a levelheaded thinking boy who doesn't bother his head about that kind of nonsense.

—Then he's not his father's son, said the little old man.

—I don't know, I'm sure, said Mr Dedalus, smiling complacently.

—Your father, said the little old man to Stephen, was the boldest flirt in the city of Cork in his day. Do you know that?

Stephen looked down and studied the tiled floor of the bar into which they had drifted.

—Now don't be putting ideas into his head, said Mr Dedalus. Leave him to his Maker.

—Yerra, sure I wouldn't put any ideas into his head. I'm old enough to be his grandfather. And I am a grandfather, said the little old man to Stephen. Do you know that?

—Are you? asked Stephen.

—Bedad I am, said the little old man. I have two bouncing grandchildren out at Sunday's Well. Now then! What age do you think I am? And I remember seeing your grandfather in his red coat riding out to hounds. That was before you were born.

—Ay, or thought of, said Mr Dedalus.

—Bedad I did, repeated the little old man. And, more than that, I can remember even your greatgrandfather, old John

Stephen Dedalus, and a fierce old fireeater he was. Now then! There's a memory for you!

—That's three generations—four generations, said another of the company. Why, Johnny Cashman, you must be nearing the century.

—Well, I'll tell you the truth, said the little old man. I'm just twentyseven years of age.

—We're as old as we feel, Johnny, said Mr Dedalus. And just finish what you have there, and we'll have another. Here, Tim or Tom or whatever your name is, give us the same again here. By God, I don't feel more than eighteen myself. There's that son of mine there not half my age and I'm a better man than he is any day of the week.

—Draw it mild now, Dedalus. I think it's time for you to take a back seat, said the gentleman who had spoken before.

—No, by God! asserted Mr Dedalus. I'll sing a tenor song against him or I'll vault a fivebarred gate against him or I'll run with him after the hounds across the country as I did thirty years ago along with the Kerry Boy and the best man for it.

—But he'll beat you here, said the little old man, tapping his forehead and raising his glass to drain it.

—Well, I hope he'll be as good a man as his father. That's all I can say, said Mr Dedalus.

—If he is, he'll do, said the little old man.

—And thanks be to God, Johnny, said Mr Dedalus, that we lived so long and did so little harm.

—But did so much good, Simon, said the little old man gravely. Thanks be to God we lived so long and did so much good.

Stephen watched the three glasses being raised from the counter as his father and his two cronies drank to the memory of their past. An abyss of fortune or of temperament sundered him from them. His mind seemed older than theirs: it shone coldly on their strifes and happiness and regrets like a moon upon a younger earth. No life or youth stirred in him as it had stirred in them. He had known neither the pleasure of companionship with others nor the vigour of rude male health nor filial piety. Nothing stirred within his soul but a cold and cruel and loveless lust. His childhood was dead or lost and with it his soul capable of simple joys, and he was drifting amid life like the barren shell of the moon.

> *Art thou pale for weariness*
> *Of climbing heaven and gazing on the earth,*
> *Wandering companionless . . . ?*

He repeated to himself the lines of Shelley's fragment. Its alternation of sad human ineffectualness with vast inhuman cycles of activity chilled him, and he forgot his own human and ineffectual grieving.

*   *   *

Stephen's mother and his brother and one of his cousins waited at the corner of quiet Foster Place while he and his father went up the steps and along the colonnade where the highland sentry was parading. When they had passed into the great hall and stood at the counter Stephen drew forth his orders on the governor of the bank of Ireland for thirty and three pounds; and these sums, the moneys of his exhibition and essay prize, were paid over to him rapidly by the teller in notes and in coin respectively. He bestowed them in his pockets with feigned composure and suffered the friendly teller, to whom his father chatted, to take his hand across the broad counter and wish him a brilliant career in after life. He was impatient of their voices and could not keep his feet at rest. But the teller still deferred the serving of others to say he was living in changed times and that there was nothing like giving a boy the best education that money could buy. Mr Dedalus lingered in the hall gazing about him and up at the roof and telling Stephen, who urged him to come out, that they were standing in the house of commons of the old Irish parliament.

—God help us! he said piously, to think of the men of those times, Stephen, Hely Hutchinson and Flood and Henry Grattan and Charles Kendal Bushe, and the noblemen we have now, leaders of the Irish people at home and abroad. Why, by God, they wouldn't be seen dead in a tenacre field with them. No, Stephen, old chap, I'm sorry to say that they are only as I roved out one fine May morning in the merry month of sweet July.

A keen October wind was blowing round the bank. The three figures standing at the edge of the muddy path had pinched cheeks and watery eyes. Stephen looked at his thinly clad mother and remembered that a few days before he had seen a mantle priced at twenty guineas in the windows of Barnardo's.

—Well that's done, said Mr Dedalus.

—We had better go to dinner, said Stephen. Where?

—Dinner? said Mr Dedalus. Well, I suppose we had better, what?

—Some place that's not too dear, said Mrs Dedalus.

—Underdone's?

—Yes. Some quiet place.

—Come along, said Stephen quickly. It doesn't matter about the dearness.

He walked on before them with short nervous steps, smiling. They tried to keep up with him, smiling also at his eagerness.

—Take it easy like a good young fellow, said his father. We're not out for the half mile, are we?

For a swift season of merrymaking the money of his prizes ran through Stephen's fingers. Great parcels of groceries and delicacies and dried fruits arrived from the city. Every day he drew up a bill of fare for the family and every night led a party of three or four to the theatre to see *Ingomar* or *The Lady of Lyons*. In his coat pockets he carried squares of Vienna chocolate for his guests while his trousers' pockets bulged with masses of silver and copper coins. He bought presents for everyone, overhauled his room, wrote out resolutions, marshalled his books up and down their shelves, pored upon all kinds of price lists, drew up a form of commonwealth for the household by which every member of it held some office, opened a loan bank for his family and pressed loans on willing borrowers so that he might have the pleasure of making out receipts and reckoning the interests on the sums lent. When he could do no more he drove up and down the city in trams. Then the season of pleasure came to an end. The pot of pink enamel paint gave out and the wainscot of his bedroom remained with its unfinished and illplastered coat.

His household returned to its usual way of life. His mother had no further occasion to upbraid him for squandering his money. He too returned to his old life at school and all his novel enterprises fell to pieces. The commonwealth fell, the loan bank closed its coffers and its books on a sensible loss, the rules of life which he had drawn about himself fell into desuetude.

How foolish his aim had been! He had tried to build a breakwater of order and elegance against the sordid tide of life without him and to dam up, by rules of conduct and active interests and new filial relations, the powerful recurrence of the tides within him. Useless. From without as from within the water had flowed over his barriers: their tides began once more to jostle fiercely above the crumbled mole.

He saw clearly too his own futile isolation. He had not gone one step nearer the lives he had sought to approach nor bridged the restless shame and rancour that divided him from mother and brother and sister. He felt that he was hardly of the one blood with them but stood to them rather in the mystical kinship of fosterage, fosterchild and fosterbrother.

He burned to appease the fierce longings of his heart before which everything else was idle and alien. He cared little that he was in mortal sin, that his life had grown to be a tissue of subterfuge and falsehood. Beside the savage desire within him to realise the enormities which he brooded on nothing was sacred. He bore cynically with the shameful details of his secret riots in which he exulted to defile with patience whatever image had attracted his eyes. By day and by night he moved among distorted images of the outer world. A figure that had seemed to him by day demure and innocent came towards him by night through the winding darkness of sleep, her face transfigured by a lecherous cunning, her eyes bright with brutish joy. Only the morning pained him with its dim memory of dark orgiastic riot, its keen and humiliating sense of transgression.

He returned to his wanderings. The veiled autumnal evenings led him from street to street as they had led him years before along the quiet avenues of Blackrock. But no vision of trim front gardens or of kindly lights in the windows poured a tender influence upon him now. Only at times, in the pauses of his desire, when the luxury that was wasting him gave room to a softer languor, the image of Mercedes traversed the background of his memory. He saw again the small white house and the garden of rosebushes on the road that led to the mountains and he remembered the sadly proud gesture of refusal which he was to make there, standing with her in the moonlit garden after years of estrangement and adventure. At those moments the soft speeches of Claude Melnotte rose to his lips and eased his unrest. A tender premonition touched him of the tryst he had then looked forward to and, in spite of the horrible reality which lay between his hope of then and now, of the holy encounter he had then imagined at which weakness and timidity and inexperience were to fall from him.

Such moments passed and the wasting fires of lust sprang up again. The verses passed from his lips and the inarticulate cries and the unspoken brutal words rushed forth from his brain to force a passage. His blood was in revolt. He wandered up and down the dark slimy streets peering into the gloom of lanes and doorways, listening eagerly for any sound. He moaned to himself like some baffled prowling beast. He wanted to sin with another of his kind, to force another being to sin with him and to exult with her in sin. He felt some dark presence moving irresistibly upon him from the darkness, a presence subtle and murmurous as a flood filling him wholly with itself. Its murmur besieged his ears like the murmur of some multitude in sleep; its subtle streams penetrated his being. His hands clenched convulsively and his teeth set together as he suffered the agony of its penetration. He stretched out his arms in the street to hold fast the frail swooning form that eluded him and incited him: and the cry that he had strangled for so long in his throat issued from his lips. It broke from him like a wail of despair from a hell of sufferers and died in a wail of furious entreaty, a cry for an iniquitous abandonment, a cry which was but the echo of an obscene scrawl which he had read on the oozing wall of a urinal.

He had wandered into a maze of narrow and dirty streets. From the foul laneways he heard bursts of hoarse riot and wrangling and the drawling of drunken singers. He walked onward, undismayed, wondering whether he had strayed into the quarter of the jews. Women and girls dressed in long vivid gowns traversed the street from house to house. They were leisurely and perfumed. A trembling seized him and his eyes grew dim. The yellow gasflames arose before his troubled vision against the vapoury sky, burning as if before an altar. Before the doors and in the lighted halls groups were gathered arrayed as for some rite. He was in another world: he had awakened from a slumber of centuries.

He stood still in the middle of the roadway, his heart clamouring against his bosom in a tumult. A young woman dressed in a long pink gown laid her hand on his arm to detain him and gazed into his face. She said gaily:

—Good night, Willie dear!

Her room was warm and lightsome. A huge doll sat with her legs apart in the copious easychair beside the bed. He tried to bid his tongue speak that he might seem at ease, watching her as she undid her gown, noting the proud conscious movements of her perfumed head.

As he stood silent in the middle of the room she came over to him and embraced him gaily and gravely. Her round arms held him firmly to her and he, seeing her face lifted to him in serious calm and feeling the warm calm rise and fall of her breast, all but burst into hysterical weeping. Tears of joy and relief shone in his delighted eyes and his lips parted though they would not speak.

She passed her tinkling hand through his hair, calling him a little rascal.

—Give me a kiss, she said.

His lips would not bend to kiss her. He wanted to be held firmly in her arms, to be caressed slowly, slowly, slowly. In her arms he felt that he had suddenly become strong and fearless and sure of himself. But his lips would not bend to kiss her.

With a sudden movement she bowed his head and joined her lips to his and he read the meaning of her movements in her frank uplifted eyes. It was too much for him. He closed his eyes, surrendering himself to her, body and mind, conscious of nothing in the world but the dark pressure of her softly parting lips. They pressed upon his brain as upon his lips as though they were the vehicle of a vague speech; and between them he felt an unknown and timid pressure, darker than the swoon of sin, softer than sound or odour.

III

THE swift December dusk had come tumbling clown-
ishly after its dull day and, as he stared through the dull
square of the window of the schoolroom, he felt his belly crave
for its food. He hoped there would be stew for dinner, turnips
and carrots and bruised potatoes and fat mutton pieces to be
ladled out in thick peppered flourfattened sauce. Stuff it into
you, his belly counselled him.

It would be a gloomy secret night. After early nightfall the
yellow lamps would light up, here and there, the squalid
quarter of the brothels. He would follow a devious course up
and down the streets, circling always nearer and nearer in a
tremor of fear and joy, until his feet led him suddenly round a
dark corner. The whores would be just coming out of their
houses making ready for the night, yawning lazily after their
sleep and settling the hairpins in their clusters of hair. He
would pass by them calmly waiting for a sudden movement of
his own will or a sudden call to his sinloving soul from their
soft perfumed flesh. Yet as he prowled in quest of that call, his
senses, stultified only by his desire, would note keenly all that
wounded or shamed them; his eyes, a ring of porter froth on a
clothless table or a photograph of two soldiers standing to
attention or a gaudy playbill; his ears, the drawling jargon of
greeting:

—Hello, Bertie, any good in your mind?
—Is that you, pigeon?
—Number ten. Fresh Nelly is waiting on you.
—Goodnight, husband! Coming in to have a short time?

The equation on the page of his scribbler began to spread

out a widening tail, eyed and starred like a peacock's; and, when the eyes and stars of its indices had been eliminated, began slowly to fold itself together again. The indices appearing and disappearing were eyes opening and closing; the eyes opening and closing were stars being born and being quenched. The vast cycle of starry life bore his weary mind outward to its verge and inward to its centre, a distant music accompanying him outward and inward. What music? The music came nearer and he recalled the words, the words of Shelley's fragment upon the moon wandering companionless, pale for weariness. The stars began to crumble and a cloud of fine stardust fell through space.

The dull light fell more faintly upon the page whereon another equation began to unfold itself slowly and to spread abroad its widening tail. It was his own soul going forth to experience, unfolding itself sin by sin, spreading abroad the balefire of its burning stars and folding back upon itself, fading slowly, quenching its own lights and fires. They were quenched: and the cold darkness filled chaos.

A cold lucid indifference reigned in his soul. At his first violent sin he had felt a wave of vitality pass out of him and had feared to find his body or his soul maimed by the excess. Instead the vital wave had carried him on its bosom out of himself and back again when it receded: and no part of body or soul had been maimed but a dark peace had been established between them. The chaos in which his ardour extinguished itself was a cold indifferent knowledge of himself. He had sinned mortally not once but many times and he knew that, while he stood in danger of eternal damnation for the first sin alone, by every succeeding sin he multiplied his guilt and his punishment. His days and works and thoughts could make no atonement for him, the fountains of sanctifying grace having ceased to refresh his soul. At most, by an alms given to a beggar whose blessing he fled from, he might hope wearily to win for himself some measure of actual grace. Devotion had gone by the board. What did it avail to pray when he

knew that his soul lusted after its own destruction? A certain
pride, a certain awe, withheld him from offering to God even
one prayer at night though he knew it was in God's power to
take away his life while he slept and hurl his soul hellward ere
he could beg for mercy. His pride in his own sin, his loveless
awe of God, told him that his offence was too grievous to be
atoned for in whole or in part by a false homage to the Allsee-
ing and Allknowing.

—Well now, Ennis, I declare you have a head and so has
my stick! Do you mean to say that you are not able to tell
me what a surd is?

The blundering answer stirred the embers of his contempt
of his fellows. Towards others he felt neither shame nor fear.
On Sunday mornings as he passed the churchdoor he glanced
coldly at the worshippers who stood bareheaded, four deep,
outside the church, morally present at the mass which they
could neither see nor hear. Their dull piety and the sickly smell
of the cheap hairoil with which they had anointed their heads
repelled him from the altar they prayed at. He stooped to the
evil of hypocrisy with others, sceptical of their innocence
which he could cajole so easily.

On the wall of his bedroom hung an illuminated scroll, the
certificate of his prefecture in the college of the sodality of the
Blessed Virgin Mary. On Saturday mornings when the sodality met in the chapel to recite the little office his place was a
cushioned kneelingdesk at the right of the altar from which he
led his wing of boys through the responses. The falsehood of
his position did not pain him. If at moments he felt an impulse
to rise from his post of honour and, confessing before them all
his unworthiness, to leave the chapel, a glance at their faces
restrained him. The imagery of the psalms of prophecy
soothed his barren pride. The glories of Mary held his soul
captive: spikenard and myrrh and frankincense, symbolising
the preciousness of God's gifts to her soul, rich garments,
symbolising her royal lineage, her emblems, the lateflowering
plant and lateblossoming tree, symbolising the agelong gradual growth of her cultus among men. When it fell to him to

read the lesson towards the close of the office he read it in a veiled voice, lulling his conscience to its music.

Quasi cedrus exaltata sum in Libanon et quasi cupressus in monte Sion. Quasi palma exaltata sum in Gades et quasi plantatio rosae in Jericho. Quasi uliva speciosa in campis et quasi platanus exaltata sum juxta aquam in plateis. Sicut cinnamomum et balsamum aromatizans odorem dedi et quasi myrrha electa dedi suavitatem odoris.

His sin, which had covered him from the sight of God, had led him nearer to the refuge of sinners. Her eyes seemed to regard him with mild pity; her holiness, a strange light glowing faintly upon her frail flesh, did not humiliate the sinner who approached her. If ever he was impelled to cast sin from him and to repent the impulse that moved him was the wish to be her knight. If ever his soul, reentering her dwelling shyly after the frenzy of his body's lust had spent itself, was turned towards her whose emblem is the morning star, *bright and musical, telling of heaven and infusing peace,* it was when her names were murmured softly by lips whereon there still lingered foul and shameful words, the savour itself of a lewd kiss.

That was strange. He tried to think how it could be but the dusk, deepening in the schoolroom, covered over his thoughts. The bell rang. The master marked the sums and cuts to be done for the next lesson and went out. Heron, beside Stephen, began to hum tunelessly.

My excellent friend Bombados.

Ennis, who had gone to the yard, came back, saying:

—The boy from the house is coming up for the rector.

A tall boy behind Stephen rubbed his hands and said:

—That's game ball. We can scut the whole hour. He won't be in till after half two. Then you can ask him questions on the catechism, Dedalus.

Stephen, leaning back and drawing idly on his scribbler, listened to the talk about him which Heron checked from time to time by saying:

—Shut up, will you. Don't make such a bally racket!

It was strange too that he found an arid pleasure in follow-ing up to the end the rigid lines of the doctrines of the church and penetrating into obscure silences only to hear and feel the more deeply his own condemnation. The sentence of saint James which says that he who offends against one command-ment becomes guilty of all had seemed to him first a swollen phrase until he had begun to grope in the darkness of his own state. From the evil seed of lust all other deadly sins had sprung forth: pride in himself and contempt of others, cove-tousness in using money for the purchase of unlawful pleas-ure, envy of those whose vices he could not reach to and calumnious murmuring against the pious, gluttonous enjoy-ment of food, the dull glowering anger amid which he brooded upon his longing, the swamp of spiritual and bodily sloth in which his whole being had sunk.

As he sat in his bench gazing calmly at the rector's shrewd harsh face his mind wound itself in and out of the curious questions proposed to it. If a man had stolen a pound in his youth and had used that pound to amass a huge fortune how much was he obliged to give back, the pound he had stolen only or the pound together with the compound interest accruing upon it or all his huge fortune? If a layman in giving baptism pour the water before saying the words is the child baptised? Is baptism with a mineral water valid? How comes it that while the first beatitude promises the kingdom of heaven to the poor of heart the second beatitude promises also to the meek that they shall possess the land? Why was the sacrament of the eucharist instituted under the two species of bread and wine if Jesus Christ be present body and blood, soul and divinity, in the bread alone and in the wine alone? Does a tiny particle of the consecrated bread contain all the body and blood of Jesus Christ or a part only of the body and blood? If the wine change into vinegar and the host crumble into cor-ruption after they have been consecrated is Jesus Christ still present under their species as God and as man?

—Here he is! Here he is!

A boy from his post at the window had seen the rector come from the house. All the catechisms were opened and all heads bent upon them silently. The rector entered and took his seat on the dais. A gentle kick from the tall boy in the bench behind urged Stephen to ask a difficult question.

The rector did not ask for a catechism to hear the lesson from. He clasped his hands on the desk and said:

—The retreat will begin on Wednesday afternoon in honour of saint Francis Xavier whose feast day is Saturday. The retreat will go on from Wednesday to Friday. On Friday confession will be heard all the afternoon after beads. If any boys have special confessors perhaps it will be better for them not to change. Mass will be on Saturday morning at nine o'clock and general communion for the whole college. Saturday will be a free day. Sunday of course. But Saturday and Sunday being free days some boys might be inclined to think that Monday is a free day also. Beware of making that mistake. I think you, Lawless, are likely to make that mistake.

—I, sir? Why, sir?

A little wave of quiet mirth broke forth over the class of boys from the rector's grim smile. Stephen's heart began slowly to fold and fade with fear like a withering flower.

The rector went on gravely:

—You are all familiar with the story of the life of saint Francis Xavier, I suppose, the patron of your college. He came of an old and illustrious Spanish family and you remember that he was one of the first followers of saint Ignatius. They met in Paris where Francis Xavier was professor of philosophy at the university. This young and brilliant nobleman and man of letters entered heart and soul into the ideas of our glorious founder, and you know that he, at his own desire, was sent by saint Ignatius to preach to the Indians. He is called, as you know, the apostle of the Indies. He went from country to country in the east, from Africa to India, from India to Japan, baptising the people. He is said to have baptised as many as ten thousand idolaters in one month. It is said that his right arm had grown powerless from having been raised so often over the heads of those whom he baptised. He wished then to go to China to win still more souls for God but he died of fever on the island of Sancian. A great saint, saint Francis Xavier! A great soldier of God!

The rector paused and then, shaking his clasped hands before him, went on:

—He had the faith in him that moves mountains. Ten thousand souls won for God in a single month! That is a true conqueror, true to the motto of our order: *ad majorem Dei gloriam!* A saint who has great power in heaven, remember: power to intercede for us in our grief, power to obtain whatever we pray for if it be for the good of our souls, power above all to obtain for us the grace to repent if we be in sin. A great saint, saint Francis Xavier! A great fisher of souls!

He ceased to shake his clasped hands and, resting them against his forehead, looked right and left of them keenly at his listeners out of his dark stern eyes.

In the silence their dark fire kindled the dusk into a tawny glow. Stephen's heart had withered up like a flower of the desert that feels the simoom coming from afar.

*　　*　　*

—*Remember only thy last things and thou shalt not sin for ever*—words taken, my dear little brothers in Christ, from the book of Ecclesiastes, seventh chapter, fortieth verse. In the name of the Father and of the Son and of the Holy Ghost. Amen.

Stephen sat in the front bench of the chapel. Father Arnall sat at a table to the left of the altar. He wore about his shoulders a heavy cloak; his pale face was drawn and his voice broken with rheum. The figure of his old master, so strangely rearisen, brought back to Stephen's mind his life at Clongowes: the wide playgrounds, swarming with boys, the square ditch, the little cemetery off the main avenue of limes where he had dreamed of being buried, the firelight on the wall of the infirmary where he lay sick, the sorrowful face of Brother Michael. His soul, as these memories came back to him, became again a child's soul.

—We are assembled here today, my dear little brothers in Christ, for one brief moment far away from the busy bustle of the outer world to celebrate and to honour one of the greatest of saints, the apostle of the Indies, the patron saint also of your college, saint Francis Xavier. Year after year for much longer than any of you, my dear little boys, can remember or than I can remember the boys of this college have met in this very chapel to make their annual retreat before the feast day of their patron saint. Time has gone on and brought with it its changes. Even in the last few years what changes can most of you not remember? Many of the boys who sat in those front benches a few years ago are perhaps now in distant lands, in the burning tropics or immersed in professional duties or in seminaries or voyaging over the vast expanse of the deep or, it may be, already called by the great God to another life and to the rendering up of their stewardship. And still as the years roll by, bringing with them changes for good and bad, the memory of the great saint is honoured by the boys of his college who make every year their annual retreat on the days preceding the feast day set apart by our holy mother the church to transmit to all the ages the name and fame of one of the greatest sons of catholic Spain.

—Now what is the meaning of this word *retreat* and why is it allowed on all hands to be a most salutary practice for all who desire to lead before God and in the eyes of men a truly christian life? A retreat, my dear boys, signifies a withdrawal for a while from the cares of our life, the cares of this worka-day world, in order to examine the state of our conscience, to reflect on the mysteries of holy religion and to understand better why we are here in this world. During these few days I intend to put before you some thoughts concerning the four last things. They are, as you know from your catechism, death, judgment, hell and heaven. We shall try to understand them fully during these few days so that we may derive from the understanding of them a lasting benefit to our souls. And remember, my dear boys, that we have been sent into this world for one thing and for one thing alone: to do God's holy will and to save our immortal souls. All else is worthless. One thing alone is needful, the salvation of one's soul. What doth it profit a man to gain the whole world if he suffer the loss of his immortal soul? Ah, my dear boys, believe me there is nothing in this wretched world that can make up for such a loss.

—I will ask you therefore, my dear boys, to put away from your minds during these few days all worldly thoughts, whether of study or pleasure or ambition, and to give all your attention to the state of your souls. I need hardly remind you that during the days of the retreat all boys are expected to preserve a quiet and pious demeanour and to shun all loud unseemly pleasure. The elder boys, of course, will see that this custom is not infringed and I look especially to the prefects and officers of the sodality of Our Blessed Lady and of the sodality of the holy angels to set a good example to their fellowstudents.

—Let us try therefore to make this retreat in honour of saint Francis with our whole heart and our whole mind. God's blessing will then be upon all your year's studies. But, above and beyond all, let this retreat be one to which you can look back in after years when maybe you are far from this college and among very different surroundings, to which you can look back with joy and thankfulness and give thanks to God for having granted you this occasion of laying the first foundation of a pious honourable zealous christian life. And if, as may so happen, there be at this moment in these benches any poor soul who has had the unutterable misfortune to lose God's holy grace and to fall into grievous sin I fervently trust and pray that this retreat may be the turningpoint in the life of that soul. I pray to God through the merits of its zealous servant Francis Xavier that such a soul may be led to sincere repen-

tance and that the holy communion on saint Francis' day of
this year may be a lasting covenant between God and that
soul. For just and unjust, for saint and sinner alike, may this
retreat be a memorable one.

—Help me, my dear little brothers in Christ. Help me by
your pious attention, by your own devotion, by your outward
demeanour. Banish from your minds all worldly thoughts and
think only of the last things, death, judgment, hell and heaven.
He who remembers these things, says Ecclesiastes, shall not
sin for ever. He who remembers the last things will act and
think with them always before his eyes. He will live a good life
and die a good death, believing and knowing that, if he has
sacrificed much in this earthly life, it will be given to him a
hundredfold and a thousandfold more in the life to come, in
the kingdom without end—a blessing, my dear boys, which I
wish you from my heart, one and all, in the name of the Father and of the Son and of the Holy Ghost. Amen.

As he walked home with silent companions a thick fog
seemed to compass his mind. He waited in stupor of mind till
it should lift and reveal what it had hidden. He ate his dinner
with surly appetite and, when the meal was over and the
greasestrewn plates lay abandoned on the table, he rose and
went to the window, clearing the thick scum from his mouth
with his tongue and licking it from his lips. So he had sunk to
the state of a beast that licks his chaps after meat. This was
the end; and a faint glimmer of fear began to pierce the fog of
his mind. He pressed his face against the pane of the window
and gazed out into the darkening street. Forms passed this
way and that through the dull light. And that was life. The
letters of the name of Dublin lay heavily upon his mind, pushing one another surlily hither and thither with slow boorish
insistence. His soul was fattening and congealing into a gross
grease, plunging ever deeper in its dull fear into a sombre
threatening dusk, while the body that was his stood, listless
and dishonoured, gazing out of darkened eyes, helpless, per-
turbed and human for a bovine god to stare upon.

The next day brought death and judgment, stirring his soul slowly from its listless despair. The faint glimmer of fear became a terror of spirit as the hoarse voice of the preacher blew death into his soul. He suffered its agony. He felt the deathchill touch the extremities and creep onward towards the heart, the film of death veiling the eyes, the bright centres of the brain extinguished one by one like lamps, the last sweat oozing upon the skin, the powerlessness of the dying limbs, the speech thickening and wandering and failing, the heart throbbing faintly and more faintly, all but vanquished, the breath, the poor breath, the poor helpless human spirit, sobbing and sighing, gurgling and rattling in the throat. No help! No help! He, he himself, his body to which he had yielded was dying. Into the grave with it! Nail it down into a wooden box, the corpse. Carry it out of the house on the shoulders of hirelings. Thrust it out of men's sight into a long hole in the ground, into the grave, to rot, to feed the mass of its creeping worms and to be devoured by scuttling plumpbellied rats.

And while the friends were still standing in tears by the bedside the soul of the sinner was judged. At the last moment of consciousness the whole earthly life passed before the vision of the soul and, ere it had time to reflect, the body had died and the soul stood terrified before the judgmentseat. God, who had long been merciful, would then be just. He had long been patient, pleading with the sinful soul, giving it time to repent, sparing it yet awhile. But that time had gone. Time was to sin and to enjoy, time was to scoff at God and at the warnings of His holy church, time was to defy His majesty, to disobey His commands, to hoodwink one's fellow men, to commit sin after sin and sin after sin and to hide one's corruption from the sight of men. But that time was over. Now it was God's turn: and He was not to be hoodwinked or deceived. Every sin would then come forth from its lurkingplace, the most rebellious against the divine will and the most degrading to our poor corrupt nature, the tiniest imperfection and the most heinous atrocity. What did it avail then to have been a great emperor, a great general, a marvellous inventor, the most learned of the learned? All were as one before the judgmentseat of God. He would reward the good and punish the wicked. One single instant was enough for the trial of a man's soul. One single instant after the body's death, the soul had been weighed in the balance. The particular judgment was over and the soul had passed to the abode of bliss or to the prison of purgatory or had been hurled howling into hell.

Nor was that all. God's justice had still to be vindicated before men: after the particular there still remained the general judgment. The last day had come. Doomsday was at hand. The stars of heaven were falling upon the earth like the figs cast by the figtree which the wind has shaken. The sun, the great luminary of the universe, had become as sackcloth of hair. The moon was bloodred. The firmament was as a scroll rolled away. The archangel Michael, the prince of the heavenly host, appeared glorious and terrible against the sky. With one foot on the sea and one foot on the land he blew from the archangelical trumpet the brazen death of time. The three blasts of the angel filled all the universe. Time is, time was but time shall be no more. At the last blast the souls of universal humanity throng towards the valley of Jehoshaphat, rich and poor, gentle and simple, wise and foolish, good and wicked. The soul of every human being that has ever existed, the souls of all those who shall yet be born, all the sons and daughters of Adam, all are assembled on that supreme day. And lo the supreme judge is coming! No longer the lowly Lamb of God, no longer the meek Jesus of Nazareth, no longer the Man of Sorrows, no longer the Good Shepherd, He is seen now coming upon the clouds, in great power and majesty, attended by nine choirs of angels, angels and archangels, principalities, powers and virtues, thrones and dominations, cherubim and seraphim, God Omnipotent, God Everlasting. He speaks: and His voice is heard even at the farthest limits of space, even in the bottomless abyss. Supreme Judge, from His sentence there will be and can be no appeal. He calls the just to His side, bidding them enter into the kingdom, the eternity of bliss, prepared for them. The unjust He casts from Him, crying in His offended majesty: *Depart from me, ye cursed, into everlasting fire which was prepared for the devil and his angels.* O what agony then for the miserable sinners! Friend is torn apart from friend, children are torn from their parents, husbands from their wives. The poor sinner holds out his arms to those who were dear to him in this earthly world, to those whose simple piety perhaps he made a mock of, to those who counselled him and tried to lead him on the right path, to a kind brother, to a loving sister, to the mother and father who loved him so dearly. But it is too late: the just turn away from the wretched damned souls which now appear before the eyes of all in their hideous and evil character. O you hypocrites, O you whited sepulchres, O you who present a smooth smiling face to the world while your soul within is a foul swamp of sin, how will it fare with you in that terrible day?

And this day will come, shall come, must come; the day of death and the day of judgment. It is appointed unto man to die and after death the judgment. Death is certain. The time and manner are uncertain, whether from long disease or from some unexpected accident; the Son of God cometh at an hour when you little expect Him. Be therefore ready every moment, seeing that you may die at any moment. Death is the end of us all. Death and judgment, brought into the world by the sin of our first parents, are the dark portals that close our earthly existence, the portals that open into the unknown and the unseen, portals through which every soul must pass, alone, unaided save by its good works, without friend or brother or parent or master to help it, alone and trembling. Let that thought be ever before our minds and then we cannot sin. Death, a cause of terror to the sinner, is a blessed moment for him who has walked in the right path, fulfilling the duties of his station in life, attending to his morning and evening prayers, approaching the holy sacrament frequently and performing good and merciful works. For the pious and believing catholic, for the just man, death is no cause of terror. Was it not Addison, the great English writer, who, when on his deathbed, sent for the wicked young earl of Warwick to let him see how a christian can meet his end. He it is and he alone, the pious and believing christian, who can say in his heart:

> *O grave, where is thy victory?*
> *O death, where is thy sting?*

Every word of it was for him. Against his sin, foul and secret, the whole wrath of God was aimed. The preacher's knife had probed deeply into his diseased conscience and he felt now that his soul was festering in sin. Yes, the preacher was right. God's turn had come. Like a beast in its lair his soul had lain down in its own filth but the blasts of the angel's trumpet had driven him forth from the darkness of sin into the light. The words of doom cried by the angel shattered in an instant his presumptuous peace. The wind of the last day blew through his mind; his sins, the jeweleyed harlots of his imagination, fled before the hurricane, squeaking like mice in their terror and huddled under a mane of hair.

As he crossed the square, walking homeward, the light laughter of a girl reached his burning ear. The frail gay sound smote his heart more strongly than a trumpetblast, and, not daring to lift his eyes, he turned aside and gazed, as he walked, into the shadow of the tangled shrubs. Shame rose from his smitten heart and flooded his whole being. The image of Emma appeared before him and, under her eyes, the flood of shame rushed forth anew from his heart. If she knew to what his mind had subjected her or how his brutelike lust had torn and trampled upon her innocence! Was that boyish love? Was that chivalry? Was that poetry? The sordid details of his orgies stank under his very nostrils: the sootcoated packet of pictures which he had hidden in the flue of the fireplace and in the presence of whose shameless or bashful wantonness he lay for hours sinning in thought and deed; his monstrous dreams, peopled by apelike creatures and by harlots with gleaming jewel eyes; the foul long letters he had written in the joy of guilty confession and carried secretly for days and days only to throw them under cover of night among the grass in the corner of a field or beneath some hingeless door or in some niche in the hedges where a girl might come upon them as she walked by and read them secretly. Mad! Mad! Was it possible he had done these things? A cold sweat broke out upon his forehead as the foul memories condensed within his brain.

When the agony of shame had passed from him he tried to raise his soul from its abject powerlessness. God and the Blessed Virgin were too far from him: God was too great and stern and the Blessed Virgin too pure and holy. But he imagined that he stood near Emma in a wide land and, humbly and in tears, bent and kissed the elbow of her sleeve.

In the wide land under a tender lucid evening sky, a cloud drifting westward amid a pale green sea of heaven, they stood together, children that had erred. Their error had offended deeply God's majesty though it was the error of two children, but it had not offended her whose beauty *is not like earthly beauty, dangerous to look upon, but like the morning star which is its emblem, bright and musical*. The eyes were not offended which she turned upon them nor reproachful. She placed their hands together, hand in hand, and said, speaking to their hearts:

—Take hands, Stephen and Emma. It is a beautiful evening now in heaven. You have erred but you are always my children. It is one heart that loves another heart. Take hands together, my dear children, and you will be happy together and your hearts will love each other.

The chapel was flooded by the dull scarlet light that filtered through the lowered blinds; and through the fissure between the last blind and the sash a shaft of wan light entered like a spear and touched the embossed brasses of the candlesticks upon the altar that gleamed like the battleworn mail armour of angels.

Rain was falling on the chapel, on the garden, on the college. It would rain for ever, noiselessly. The water would rise inch by inch, covering the grass and shrubs, covering the trees and houses, covering the monuments and the mountain tops. All life would be choked off, noiselessly: birds, men, elephants, pigs, children: noiselessly floating corpses amid the litter of the wreckage of the world. Forty days and forty nights the rain would fall till the waters covered the face of the earth.

It might be. Why not?

—*Hell has enlarged its soul and opened its mouth without any limits*—words taken, my dear little brothers in Christ Jesus, from the book of Isaias, fifth chapter, fourteenth verse. In the name of the Father and of the Son and of the Holy Ghost. Amen.

The preacher took a chainless watch from a pocket within his soutane and, having considered its dial for a moment in silence, placed it silently before him on the table.

He began to speak in a quiet tone.

—Adam and Eve, my dear boys, were, as you know, our first parents and you will remember that they were created by God in order that the seats in heaven left vacant by the fall of Lucifer and his rebellious angels might be filled again. Lucifer, we are told, was a son of the morning, a radiant and mighty angel; yet he fell: he fell and there fell with him a third part of the host of heaven: he fell and was hurled with his rebellious angels into hell. What his sin was we cannot say. Theologians consider that it was the sin of pride, the sinful thought conceived in an instant: *non serviam: I will not serve.* That instant was his ruin. He offended the majesty of God by the sinful thought of one instant and God cast him out of heaven into hell for ever.

—Adam and Eve were then created by God and placed in Eden, in the plain of Damascus, that lovely garden resplendent with sunlight and colour, teeming with luxuriant vegetation. The fruitful earth gave them her bounty: beasts and birds were their willing servants: they knew not the ills our flesh is heir to, disease and poverty and death: all that a great and generous God could do for them was done. But there was one condition imposed on them by God: obedience to His word. They were not to eat of the fruit of the forbidden tree.

—Alas, my dear little boys, they too fell. The devil, once a shining angel, a son of the morning, now a foul fiend, came in the shape of a serpent, the subtlest of all the beasts of the field. He envied them. He, the fallen great one, could not bear to think that man, a being of clay, should possess the inheritance which he by his sin had forfeited for ever. He came to the woman, the weaker vessel, and poured the poison of his eloquence into her ear, promising her—O, the blasphemy of that promise!—that if she and Adam ate of the forbidden fruit they would become as gods, nay as God Himself. Eve yielded to the wiles of the archtempter. She ate the apple and gave it also to Adam who had not the moral courage to resist her. The poison tongue of Satan had done its work. They fell.

—And then the voice of God was heard in that garden, calling His creature man to account: and Michael, prince of the heavenly host, with a sword of flame in his hand appeared before the guilty pair and drove them forth from Eden into the world, the world of sickness and striving, of cruelty and disappointment, of labour and hardship, to earn their bread in the sweat of their brow. But even then how merciful was God! He took pity on our poor degraded parents and promised that in the fulness of time He would send down from heaven One who would redeem them, make them once more children of God and heirs to the kingdom of heaven: and that One, that Redeemer of fallen man, was to be God's onlybegotten Son, the Second Person of the Most Blessed Trinity, the Eternal Word.

—He came. He was born of a virgin pure, Mary the virgin mother. He was born in a poor cowhouse in Judea and lived as a humble carpenter for thirty years until the hour of His mission had come. And then, filled with love for men, He went forth and called to men to hear the new gospel.

—Did they listen? Yes, they listened but would not hear. He was seized and bound like a common criminal, mocked at as a fool, set aside to give place to a public robber, scourged with five thousand lashes, crowned with a crown of thorns, hustled through the streets by the jewish rabble and the Roman soldiery, stripped of His garments and hanged upon a gibbet and His side was pierced with a lance and from the wounded body of Our Lord water and blood issued continually.

—Yet even then, in that hour of supreme agony, Our Merciful Redeemer had pity for mankind. Yet even there, on the hill of Calvary, He founded the holy catholic church against which, it is promised, the gates of hell shall not prevail. He founded it upon the rock of ages and endowed it with His grace, with sacraments and sacrifice, and promised that if men would obey the word of His church they would still enter into eternal life but if, after all that had been done for them, they still persisted in their wickedness there remained for them an eternity of torment: hell.

The preacher's voice sank. He paused, joined his palms for an instant, parted them. Then he resumed:

—Now let us try for a moment to realise, as far as we can, the nature of that abode of the damned which the justice of an offended God has called into existence for the eternal punishment of sinners. Hell is a strait and dark and foulsmelling prison, an abode of demons and lost souls, filled with fire and smoke. The straitness of this prisonhouse is expressly designed by God to punish those who refused to be bound by His laws. In earthly prisons the poor captive has at least some liberty of movement, were it only within the four walls of his cell or in the gloomy yard of his prison. Not so in hell. There, by reason of the great number of the damned, the prisoners are heaped together in their awful prison, the walls of which are said to be four thousand miles thick: and the damned are so utterly bound and helpless that, as a blessed saint, saint Anselm, writes in his book on similitudes, they are not even able to remove from the eye a worm that gnaws it.

—They lie in exterior darkness. For, remember, the fire of hell gives forth no light. As, at the command of God, the fire of the Babylonian furnace lost its heat but not its light so, at the command of God, the fire of hell, while retaining the intensity of its heat, burns eternally in darkness. It is a never-ending storm of darkness, dark flames and dark smoke of burning brimstone, amid which the bodies are heaped one upon another without even a glimpse of air. Of all the plagues with which the land of the Pharaohs was smitten one plague alone, that of darkness, was called horrible. What name, then, shall we give to the darkness of hell which is to last not for three days alone but for all eternity?

—The horror of this strait and dark prison is increased by its awful stench. All the filth of the world, all the offal and scum of the world, we are told, shall run there as to a vast reeking sewer when the terrible conflagration of the last day has purged the world. The brimstone too which burns there in such prodigious quantity fills all hell with its intolerable stench; and the bodies of the damned themselves exhale such a pestilential odour that as saint Bonaventure says, one of them alone would suffice to infect the whole world. The very air of this world, that pure element, becomes foul and un-breathable when it has been long enclosed. Consider then what must be the foulness of the air of hell. Imagine some foul and putrid corpse that has lain rotting and decomposing in the grave, a jellylike mass of liquid corruption. Imagine such a corpse a prey to flames, devoured by the fire of burning brim-stone and giving off dense choking fumes of nauseous loath-some decomposition. And then imagine this sickening stench, multiplied a millionfold and a millionfold again from the millions upon millions of fetid carcasses massed together in the reeking darkness, a huge and rotting human fungus. Imag-ine all this and you will have some idea of the horror of the stench of hell.

—But this stench is not, horrible though it is, the greatest physical torment to which the damned are subjected. The torment of fire is the greatest torment to which the tyrant has ever subjected his fellowcreatures. Place your finger for a moment in the flame of a candle and you will feel the pain of fire. But our earthly fire was created by God for the benefit of man, to maintain in him the spark of life and to help him in the useful arts whereas the fire of hell is of another quality and was created by God to torture and punish the unrepentant sinner. Our earthly fire also consumes more or less rapidly according as the object which it attacks is more or less combustible so that human ingenuity has even succeeded in inventing chemical preparations to check or frustrate its action. But the sulphurous brimstone which burns in hell is a substance which is specially designed to burn for ever and for ever with unspeakable fury. Moreover our earthly fire destroys at the same time as it burns so that the more intense it is the shorter is its duration: but the fire of hell has this property that it preserves that which it burns and though it rages with incredible intensity it rages for ever.

—Our earthly fire again, no matter how fierce or widespread it may be, is always of a limited extent: but the lake of fire in hell is boundless, shoreless and bottomless. It is on record that the devil himself, when asked the question by a certain soldier, was obliged to confess that if a whole mountain were thrown into the burning ocean of hell it would be burned up in an instant like a piece of wax. And this terrible fire will not afflict the bodies of the damned only from without but each lost soul will be a hell unto itself, the boundless fire raging in its very vitals. O, how terrible is the lot of those wretched beings! The blood seethes and boils in the veins, the brains are boiling in the skull, the heart in the breast glowing and bursting, the bowels a redhot mass of burning pulp, the tender eyes flaming like molten balls.

—And yet what I have said as to the strength and quality and boundlessness of this fire is as nothing when compared to its intensity, an intensity which it has as being the instrument chosen by divine design for the punishment of soul and body alike. It is a fire which proceeds directly from the ire of God, working not of its own activity but as an instrument of divine vengeance. As the waters of baptism cleanse the soul with the body so do the fires of punishment torture the spirit with the flesh. Every sense of the flesh is tortured and every faculty of the soul therewith: the eyes with impenetrable utter darkness, the nose with noisome odours, the ears with yells and howls and execrations, the taste with foul matter, leprous corruption, nameless suffocating filth, the touch with redhot goads and spikes, with cruel tongues of flame. And through the several torments of the senses the immortal soul is tortured eternally in its very essence amid the leagues upon leagues of glowing fires kindled in the abyss by the offended majesty of the Omnipotent God and fanned into everlasting and ever increasing fury by the breath of the anger of the Godhead.

—Consider finally that the torment of this infernal prison is increased by the company of the damned themselves. Evil company on earth is so noxious that even the plants, as if by instinct, withdraw from the company of whatsoever is deadly or hurtful to them. In hell all laws are overturned: there is no thought of family or country, of ties, of relationships. The damned howl and scream at one another, their torture and rage intensified by the presence of beings tortured and raging like themselves. All sense of humanity is forgotten. The yells of the suffering sinners fill the remotest corners of the vast abyss. The mouths of the damned are full of blasphemies against God and of hatred for their fellowsufferers and of curses against those souls which were their accomplices in sin. In olden times it was the custom to punish the parricide, the man who had raised his murderous hand against his father, by casting him into the depths of the sea in a sack in which were placed a cock, a monkey and a serpent. The intention of those lawgivers who framed such a law, which seems cruel in our times, was to punish the criminal by the company of hateful and hurtful beasts. But what is the fury of those dumb beasts compared with the fury of execration which bursts from the parched lips and aching throats of the damned in hell when they behold in their companions in misery those who aided and abetted them in sin, those whose words sowed the first seeds of evil thinking and evil living in their minds, those whose immodest suggestions led them on to sin, those whose eyes tempted and allured them from the path of virtue. They turn upon those accomplices and upbraid them and curse them. But they are helpless and hopeless: it is too late now for repentance.

—Last of all consider the frightful torment to those damned souls, tempters and tempted alike, of the company of the devils. These devils will afflict the damned in two ways, by their presence and by their reproaches. We can have no idea of how horrible these devils are. Saint Catherine of Siena once saw a devil and she has written that, rather than look again for one single instant on such a frightful monster, she would prefer to walk until the end of her life along a track of red coals. These devils, who were once beautiful angels, have become as hideous and ugly as they once were beautiful. They mock and jeer at the lost souls whom they dragged down to ruin. It is they, the foul demons, who are made in hell the voices of conscience. Why did you sin? Why did you lend an ear to the temptings of fiends? Why did you turn aside from your pious practices and good works? Why did you not shun the occasions of sin? Why did you not leave that evil companion? Why did you not give up that lewd habit, that impure habit? Why did you not listen to the counsels of your confessor? Why did you not, even after you had fallen the first or the second or the third or the fourth or the hundredth time, repent of your evil ways and turn to God who only waited for your repentance to absolve you of your sins? Now the time for repentance has gone by. Time is, time was, but time shall be no more! Time was to sin in secrecy, to indulge in that sloth and pride, to covet the unlawful, to yield to the promptings of your lower nature, to live like the beasts of the field, nay worse

than the beasts of the field for they, at least, are but brutes
and have not reason to guide them: time was but time shall be
no more. God spoke to you by so many voices but you would
not hear. You would not crush out that pride and anger in
your heart, you would not restore those illgotten goods, you
would not obey the precepts of your holy church nor attend to
your religious duties, you would not abandon those wicked
companions, you would not avoid those dangerous temptations. Such is the language of those fiendish tormentors, words
of taunting and of reproach, of hatred and of disgust. Of
disgust, yes! For even they, the very devils, when they sinned
sinned by such a sin as alone was compatible with such angeli-
cal natures, a rebellion of the intellect: and they, even they,
the foul devils must turn away, revolted and disgusted, from
the contemplation of those unspeakable sins by which degraded man outrages and defiles the temple of the Holy Ghost,
defiles and pollutes himself.

—O, my dear little brothers in Christ, may it never be our
lot to hear that language! May it never be our lot, I say! In the
last day of terrible reckoning I pray fervently to God that not
a single soul of those who are in this chapel today may be
found among those miserable beings whom the Great Judge
shall command to depart for ever from His sight, that not one
of us may ever hear ringing in his ears the awful sentence of
rejection: *Depart from me, ye cursed, into everlasting fire
which was prepared for the devil and his angels!*

He came down the aisle of the chapel, his legs shaking and
the scalp of his head trembling as though it had been touched
by ghostly fingers. He passed up the staircase and into the
corridor along the walls of which the overcoats and water-
proofs hung like gibbeted malefactors, headless and dripping
and shapeless. And at every step he feared that he had already
died, that his soul had been wrenched forth of the sheath of
his body, that he was plunging headlong through space.

He could not grip the floor with his feet and sat heavily at
his desk, opening one of his books at random and poring over

it. Every word for him! It was true. God was almighty. God could call him now, call him as he sat at his desk, before he had time to be conscious of the summons. God had called him. Yes? What? Yes? His flesh shrank together as it felt the approach of the ravenous tongues of flames, dried up as it felt about it the swirl of stifling air. He had died. Yes. He was judged. A wave of fire swept through his body: the first. Again a wave. His brain began to glow. Another. His brain was simmering and bubbling within the cracking tenement of the skull. Flames burst forth from his skull like a corolla, shriek-ing like voices:

—Hell! Hell! Hell! Hell! Hell!

Voices spoke near him:

—On hell.

—I suppose he rubbed it into you well.

—You bet he did. He put us all into a blue funk.

—That's what you fellows want: and plenty of it to make you work.

He leaned back weakly in his desk. He had not died. God had spared him still. He was still in the familiar world of the school. Mr Tate and Vincent Heron stood at the window, talking, jesting, gazing out at the bleak rain, moving their heads.

—I wish it would clear up. I had arranged to go for a spin on the bike with some fellows out by Malahide. But the roads must be kneedeep.

—It might clear up, sir.

The voices that he knew so well, the common words, the quiet of the classroom when the voices paused and the silence was filled by the sound of softly browsing cattle as the other boys munched their lunches tranquilly, lulled his aching soul.

There was still time. O Mary, refuge of sinners, intercede for him! O Virgin Undefiled, save him from the gulf of death!

The English lesson began with the hearing of the history. Royal persons, favourites, intriguers, bishops, passed like mute phantoms behind their veil of names. All had died: all had been judged. What did it profit a man to gain the whole world if he lost his soul? At last he had understood: and human life lay around him, a plain of peace whereon antlike men laboured in brotherhood, their dead sleeping under quiet mounds. The elbow of his companion touched him and his heart was touched: and when he spoke to answer a question of his master he heard his own voice full of the quietude of humility and contrition.

His soul sank back deeper into depths of contrite peace, no longer able to suffer the pain of dread, and sending forth, as she sank, a faint prayer. Ah yes, he would still be spared; he would repent in his heart and be forgiven; and then those above, those in heaven, would see what he would do to make up for the past: a whole life, every hour of life. Only wait.

—All, God! All, all!

A messenger came to the door to say that confessions were being heard in the chapel. Four boys left the room; and he heard others passing down the corridor. A tremulous chill blew round his heart, no stronger than a little wind, and yet, listening and suffering silently, he seemed to have laid an ear against the muscle of his own heart, feeling it close and quail, listening to the flutter of its ventricles.

No escape. He had to confess, to speak out in words what he had done and thought, sin after sin. How? How?

—Father, I . . .

The thought slid like a cold shining rapier into his tender flesh: confession. But not there in the chapel of the college. He would confess all, every sin of deed and thought, sincerely: but not there among his school companions. Far away from there in some dark place he would murmur out his own shame: and he besought God humbly not to be offended with him if he did not dare to confess in the college chapel: and in utter abjection of spirit he craved forgiveness mutely of the boyish hearts about him.

Time passed.

He sat again in the front bench of the chapel. The daylight

without was already failing and, as it fell slowly through the
dull red blinds, it seemed that the sun of the last day was going
down and that all souls were being gathered for the judgment.

—*I am cast away from the sight of Thine eyes:* words
taken, my dear little brothers in Christ, from the Book of
Psalms, thirtieth chapter, twentythird verse. In the name of
the Father and of the Son and of the Holy Ghost. Amen.

The preacher began to speak in a quiet friendly tone. His
face was kind and he joined gently the fingers of each hand,
forming a frail cage by the union of their tips.

—This morning we endeavoured, in our reflection upon
hell, to make what our holy founder calls in his book of spiritual exercises, the composition of place. We endeavoured, that
is, to imagine with the senses of the mind, in our imagination,
the material character of that awful place and of the physical
torments which all who are in hell endure. This evening we
shall consider for a few moments the nature of the spiritual
torments of hell.

—Sin, remember, is a twofold enormity. It is a base consent
to the promptings of our corrupt nature to the lower instincts,
to that which is gross and beastlike; and it is also a turning
away from the counsel of our higher nature, from all that is
pure and holy, from the Holy God Himself. For this reason
mortal sin is punished in hell by two different forms of punishment, physical and spiritual.

—Now of all these spiritual pains by far the greatest is the
pain of loss, so great, in fact, that in itself it is a torment
greater than all the others. Saint Thomas, the greatest doctor
of the church, the angelic doctor, as he is called, says that the
worst damnation consists in this that the understanding of
man is totally deprived of divine light and his affection obsti-
nately turned away from the goodness of God. God, remember, is a being infinitely good and therefore the loss of such a
being must be a loss infinitely painful. In this life we have not
a very clear idea of what such a loss must be but the damned
in hell, for their greater torment, have a full understanding of

that which they have lost and understand that they have lost it through their own sins and have lost it for ever. At the very instant of death the bonds of the flesh are broken asunder and the soul at once flies towards God. The soul tends towards God as towards the centre of her existence. Remember, my dear little boys, our souls long to be with God. We come from God, we live by God, we belong to God: we are His, inalienably His. God loves with a divine love every human soul and every human soul lives in that love. How could it be otherwise? Every breath that we draw, every thought of our brain, every instant of life proceed from God's inexhaustible goodness. And if it be pain for a mother to be parted from her child, for a man to be exiled from hearth and home, for friend to be sundered from friend, O think what pain, what anguish, it must be for the poor soul to be spurned from the presence of the supremely good and loving Creator Who has called that soul into existence from nothingness and sustained it in life and loved it with an immeasurable love. This, then, to be separated for ever from its greatest good, from God, and to feel the anguish of that separation, knowing full well that it is unchangeable, this is the greatest torment which the created soul is capable of bearing, *pœna damni,* the pain of loss.

—The second pain which will afflict the souls of the damned in hell is the pain of conscience. Just as in dead bodies worms are engendered by putrefaction so in the souls of the lost there arises a perpetual remorse from the putrefaction of sin, the sting of conscience, the worm, as Pope Innocent the Third calls it, of the triple sting. The first sting inflicted by this cruel worm will be the memory of past pleasures. O what a dreadful memory will that be! In the lake of alldevouring flame the proud king will remember the pomps of his court, the wise but wicked man his libraries and instruments of research, the lover of artistic pleasures his marbles and pictures and other art treasures, he who delighted in the pleasures of the table his gorgeous feasts, his dishes prepared with such delicacy, his choice wines; the miser will remember his hoard of gold, the robber his illgotten wealth, the angry and revengeful and merciless murderers their deeds of blood and violence in which they revelled, the impure and adulterous the unspeakable and filthy pleasures in which they delighted. They will remember all this and loathe themselves and their sins. For how miserable will all those pleasures seem to the soul condemned to suffer in hellfire for ages and ages. How they will rage and fume to think that they have lost the bliss of heaven for the dross of earth, for a few pieces of metal, for vain honours, for bodily comforts, for a tingling of the nerves. They will repent indeed: and this is the second sting of the worm of conscience, a late and fruitless sorrow for sins committed. Divine justice insists that the understanding of those miserable wretches be fixed continually on the sins of which they were guilty and moreover, as saint Augustine points out, God will impart to them His own knowledge of sin so that sin will appear to them in all its hideous malice as it appears to the eyes of God Himself. They will behold their sins in all their foulness and repent but it will be too late and then they will bewail the good occasions which they neglected. This is the last and deepest and most cruel sting of the worm of conscience. The conscience will say: You had time and opportunity to repent and would not. You were brought up religiously by your parents. You had the sacraments and graces and indulgences of the church to aid you. You had the minister of God to preach to you, to call you back when you had strayed, to forgive you your sins, no matter how many, how abominable, if only you had confessed and repented. No. You would not. You flouted the ministers of holy religion, you turned your back on the confessional, you wallowed deeper and deeper in the mire of sin. God appealed to you, threatened you, entreated you to return to Him. O what shame, what misery! The Ruler of the universe entreated you, a creature of clay, to love Him Who made you and to keep His law. No. You would not. And now, though you were to flood all hell with your tears if you could still weep, all that sea of repentance would not gain for you what a single tear of true repentance shed during your mortal life would have gained for you. You implore now a moment of earthly life wherein to repent: in vain. That time is gone: gone for ever.

—Such is the threefold sting of conscience, the viper which gnaws the very heart's core of the wretches in hell so that filled with hellish fury they curse themselves for their folly and curse the evil companions who have brought them to such ruin and curse the devils who tempted them in life and now mock them and torture them in eternity and even revile and curse the Supreme Being Whose goodness and patience they scorned and slighted but Whose justice and power they cannot evade.

—The next spiritual pain to which the damned are subjected is the pain of extension. Man, in this earthly life, though he be capable of many evils, is not capable of them all at once inasmuch as one evil corrects and counteracts another just as one poison frequently corrects another. In hell on the contrary one torment, instead of counteracting another, lends it still greater force: and moreover as the internal faculties are more perfect than the external senses, so are they more capable of suffering. Just as every sense is afflicted with a fitting torment so is every spiritual faculty; the fancy with horrible images, the sensitive faculty with alternate longing and rage, the mind and understanding with an interior darkness more terrible even than the exterior darkness which reigns in that dreadful prison. The malice, impotent though it be, which possesses these demon souls is an evil of boundless extension, of limitless duration, a frightful state of wickedness which we can scarcely realise unless we bear in mind the enormity of sin and the hatred God bears to it.

—Opposed to this pain of extension and yet coexistent with it we have the pain of intensity. Hell is the centre of evils and, as you know, things are more intense at their centres than at their remotest points. There are no contraries or admixtures of any kind to temper or soften in the least the pains of hell. Nay, things which are good in themselves become evil in hell.

Company, elsewhere a source of comfort to the afflicted, will be there a continual torment: knowledge, so much longed for as the chief good of the intellect, will there be hated worse than ignorance: light, so much coveted by all creatures from the lord of creation down to the humblest plant in the forest, will be loathed intensely. In this life our sorrows are either not very long or not very great because nature either overcomes them by habits or puts an end to them by sinking under their weight. But in hell the torments cannot be overcome by habit. For while they are of terrible intensity they are at the same time of continual variety, each pain, so to speak, taking fire from another and reendowing that which has enkindled it with a still fiercer flame. Nor can nature escape from these intense and various tortures by succumbing to them for the soul is sustained and maintained in evil so that its suffering may be the greater. Boundless extension of torment, incredible intensity of suffering, unceasing variety of torture—this is what the divine majesty, so outraged by sinners, demands, this is what the holiness of heaven, slighted and set aside for the lustful and low pleasures of the corrupt flesh, requires, this is what the blood of the innocent Lamb of God, shed for the redemption of sinners, trampled upon by the vilest of the vile, insists upon.

—Last and crowning torture of all the tortures of that awful place is the eternity of hell. Eternity! O, dread and dire word. Eternity! What mind of man can understand it? And, remember, it is an eternity of pain. Even though the pains of hell were not so terrible as they are yet they would become infinite as they are destined to last for ever. But while they are everlasting they are at the same time, as you know, intolerably intense, unbearably extensive. To bear even the sting of an insect for all eternity would be a dreadful torment. What must it be, then, to bear the manifold tortures of hell for ever? For ever! For all eternity! Not for a year or for an age but for ever. Try to imagine the awful meaning of this. You have often seen the sand on the seashore. How fine are its tiny grains! And how many of those tiny little grains go to make up the small handful which a child grasps in its play. Now imagine a mountain of that sand, a million miles high, reaching from the earth to the farthest heavens, and a million miles broad, extending to remotest space, and a million miles in thickness: and imagine such an enormous mass of countless particles of sand multiplied as often as there are leaves in the forest, drops of water in the mighty ocean, feathers on birds, scales on fish, hairs on animals, atoms in the vast expanse of the air: and imagine that at the end of every million years a little bird came to that mountain and carried away in its beak a tiny grain of that sand. How many millions upon millions of centuries would pass before that bird had carried away even a square foot of that mountain, how many eons upon eons of ages before it had carried away all. Yet at the end of that immense stretch of time not even one instant of eternity could be said to have ended. At the end of all those billions and trillions of years eternity would have scarcely begun. And if that mountain rose again after it had been all carried away and if the bird came again and carried it all away again grain by grain: and if it so rose and sank as many times as there are stars in the sky, atoms in the air, drops of water in the sea, leaves on the trees, feathers upon birds, scales upon fish, hairs upon animals, at the end of all those innumerable risings and sinkings of that immeasurably vast mountain not one single instant of eternity could be said to have ended; even then, at the end of such a period, after that eon of time the mere thought of which makes our very brain reel dizzily, eternity would have scarcely begun.

—A holy saint (one of our own fathers I believe it was) was once vouchsafed a vision of hell. It seemed to him that he stood in the midst of a great hall, dark and silent save for the ticking of a great clock. The ticking went on unceasingly; and it seemed to this saint that the sound of the ticking was the ceaseless repetition of the words: ever, never; ever, never. Ever to be in hell, never to be in heaven; ever to be shut off from the presence of God, never to enjoy the beatific vision; ever to be eaten with flames, gnawed by vermin, goaded with burning spikes, never to be free from those pains; ever to have the conscience upbraid one, the memory enrage, the mind filled with darkness and despair, never to escape; ever to curse and revile the foul demons who gloat fiendishly over the misery of their dupes, never to behold the shining raiment of the blessed spirits; ever to cry out of the abyss of fire to God for an instant, a single instant, of respite from such awful agony, never to receive, even for an instant, God's pardon; ever to suffer, never to enjoy; ever to be damned, never to be saved; ever, never; ever, never. O what a dreadful punishment! An eternity of endless agony, of endless bodily and spiritual torment, without one ray of hope, without one moment of cessation, of agony limitless in extent, limitless in intensity, of torment infinitely lasting, infinitely varied, of torture that sustains eternally that which it eternally devours, of anguish that everlastingly preys upon the spirit while it racks the flesh, an eternity, every instant of which is itself an eternity, and that eternity an eternity of woe. Such is the terrible punishment decreed for those who die in mortal sin by an almighty and a just God.

—Yes, a just God! Men, reasoning always as men, are astonished that God should mete out an everlasting and infinite punishment in the fires of hell for a single grievous sin. They reason thus because, blinded by the gross illusion of the flesh and the darkness of human understanding, they are unable to comprehend the hideous malice of mortal sin. They reason thus because they are unable to comprehend that even venial sin is of such a foul and hideous nature that even if the omnipotent Creator could end all the evil and misery in the world, the wars, the diseases, the robberies, the crimes, the deaths, the murders, on condition that He allowed a single venial sin to pass unpunished, a single venial sin, a lie, an angry look, a moment of wilful sloth, He, the great omnipotent God, could not do so because sin, be it in thought or deed, is a transgression of His law and God would not be God if He did not punish the transgressor.

—A sin, an instant of rebellious pride of the intellect, made

Lucifer and a third part of the cohorts of angels fall from their glory. A sin, an instant of folly and weakness, drove Adam and Eve out of Eden and brought death and suffering into the world. To retrieve the consequences of that sin the Only Begotten Son of God came down to earth, lived and suffered and died a most painful death, hanging for three hours on the cross.

—O, my dear little brethren in Christ Jesus, will we then offend that good Redeemer and provoke His anger? Will we trample again upon that torn and mangled corpse? Will we spit upon that face so full of sorrow and love? Will we too, like the cruel jews and the brutal soldiers, mock that gentle and compassionate Saviour Who trod alone for our sake the awful winepress of sorrow? Every word of sin is a wound in His tender side. Every sinful act is a thorn piercing His head. Every impure thought, deliberately yielded to, is a keen lance transfixing that sacred and loving heart. No, no. It is impossible for any human being to do that which offends so deeply the divine majesty, that which is punished by an eternity of agony, that which crucifies again the Son of God and makes a mockery of Him.

—I pray to God that my poor words may have availed today to confirm in holiness those who are in a state of grace, to strengthen the wavering, to lead back to the state of grace the poor soul that has strayed if any such be among you. I pray to God, and do you pray with me, that we may repent of our sins. I will ask you now, all of you, to repeat after me the act of contrition, kneeling here in this humble chapel in the presence of God. He is there in the tabernacle burning with love for mankind, ready to comfort the afflicted. Be not afraid. No matter how many or how foul the sins if only you repent of them they will be forgiven you. Let no worldly shame hold you back. God is still the merciful Lord Who wishes not the eternal death of the sinner but rather that he be converted and live.

—He calls you to Him. You are His. He made you out of

nothing. He loved you as only a God can love. His arms are open to receive you even though you have sinned against Him. Come to Him, poor sinner, poor vain and erring sinner. Now is the acceptable time. Now is the hour.

The priest rose and, turning towards the altar, knelt upon the step before the tabernacle in the fallen gloom. He waited till all in the chapel had knelt and every least noise was still. Then, raising his head, he repeated the act of contrition, phrase by phrase, with fervour. The boys answered him phrase by phrase. Stephen, his tongue cleaving to his palate, bowed his head, praying with his heart.

> —*O my God!*—
> —*O my God!*—
> —*I am heartily sorry*—
> —*I am heartily sorry*—
> —*for having offended Thee*—
> —*for having offended Thee*—
> —*and I detest my sins*—
> —*and I detest my sins*—
> —*above every other evil*—
> —*above every other evil*—
> —*because they displease Thee, my God*—
> —*because they displease Thee, my God*—
> —*Who art so deserving*—
> —*Who art so deserving*—
> —*of all my love*—
> —*of all my love*—
> —*and I firmly purpose*—
> —*and I firmly purpose*—
> —*by Thy holy grace*—
> —*by Thy holy grace*—
> —*never more to offend Thee*—
> —*never more to offend Thee*—
> —*and to amend my life*—
> —*and to amend my life*—

*   *   *

He went up to his room after dinner in order to be alone with his soul: and at every step his soul seemed to sigh: at every step his soul mounted with his feet, sighing in the ascent, through a region of viscid gloom.

He halted on the landing before the door and then, grasping the porcelain knob, opened the door quickly. He waited in fear, his soul pining within him, praying silently that death might not touch his brow as he passed over the threshold, that the fiends that inhabit darkness might not be given power over him. He waited still at the threshold as at the entrance to some dark cave. Faces were there; eyes: they waited and watched.

—We knew perfectly well of course that although it was bound to come to the light he would find considerable difficulty in endeavouring to try to induce himself to try to endeavour to ascertain the spiritual plenipotentiary and so we knew of course perfectly well—

Murmuring faces waited and watched; murmurous voices filled the dark shell of the cave. He feared intensely in spirit and in flesh but, raising his head bravely, he strode into the room firmly. A doorway, a room, the same room, same window. He told himself calmly that those words had absolutely no sense which had seemed to rise murmurously from the dark. He told himself that it was simply his room with the door open.

He closed the door and, walking swiftly to the bed, knelt beside it and covered his face with his hands. His hands were cold and damp and his limbs ached with chill. Bodily unrest and chill and weariness beset him, routing his thoughts. Why was he kneeling there like a child saying his evening prayers? To be alone with his soul, to examine his conscience, to meet his sins face to face, to recall their times and manners and circumstances, to weep over them. He could not weep. He could not summon them to his memory. He felt only an ache of soul and body, his whole being, memory, will, understanding, flesh, benumbed and weary.

That was the work of devils, to scatter his thoughts and

overcloud his conscience, assailing him at the gates of the cowardly and sincorrupted flesh: and, praying God timidly to forgive him his weakness, he crawled up on to the bed and, wrapping the blankets closely about him, covered his face again with his hands. He had sinned. He had sinned so deeply against heaven and before God that he was not worthy to be called God's child.

Could it be that he, Stephen Dedalus, had done those things? His conscience sighed in answer. Yes, he had done them, secretly, filthily, time after time, and, hardened in sinful impenitence, he had dared to wear the mask of holiness before the tabernacle itself while his soul within was a living mass of corruption. How came it that God had not struck him dead? The leprous company of his sins closed about him, breathing upon him, bending over him from all sides. He strove to forget them in an act of prayer, huddling his limbs closer together and binding down his eyelids: but the senses of his soul would not be bound and, though his eyes were shut fast, he saw the places where he had sinned and, though his ears were tightly covered, he heard. He desired with all his will not to hear or see. He desired till his frame shook under the strain of his desire and until the senses of his soul closed. They closed for an instant and then opened. He saw.

A field of stiff weeds and thistles and tufted nettlebunches. Thick among the tufts of rank stiff growth lay battered canisters and clots and coils of solid excrement. A faint marshlight struggled upwards from all the ordure through the bristling greygreen weeds. An evil smell, faint and foul as the light, curled upwards sluggishly out of the canisters and from the stale crusted dung.

Creatures were in the field; one, three, six: creatures were moving in the field, hither and thither. Goatish creatures with human faces, hornybrowed, lightly bearded and grey as indiarubber. The malice of evil glittered in their hard eyes, as they moved hither and thither, trailing their long tails behind them. A rictus of cruel malignity lit up greyly their old bony faces.

One was clasping about his ribs a torn flannel waistcoat, another complained monotonously as his beard stuck in the tufted weeds. Soft language issued from their spittleless lips as they swished in slow circles round and round the field, winding hither and thither through the weeds, dragging their long tails amid the rattling canisters. They moved in slow circles, circling closer and closer to enclose, to enclose, soft language issuing from their lips, their long swishing tails besmeared with stale shite, thrusting upwards their terrific faces . . .

Help!

He flung the blankets from him madly to free his face and neck. That was his hell. God had allowed him to see the hell reserved for his sins: stinking, bestial, malignant, a hell of lecherous goatish fiends. For him! For him!

He sprang from the bed, the reeking odour pouring down his throat, clogging and revolting his entrails. Air! The air of heaven! He stumbled towards the window, groaning and almost fainting with sickness. At the washstand a convulsion seized him within; and, clasping his cold forehead wildly, he vomited profusely in agony.

When the fit had spent itself he walked weakly to the window and, lifting the sash, sat in a corner of the embrasure and leaned his elbow upon the sill. The rain had drawn off; and amid the moving vapours from point to point of light the city was spinning about herself a soft cocoon of yellowish haze. Heaven was still and faintly luminous and the air sweet to breathe, as in a thicket drenched with showers: and amid peace and shimmering lights and quiet fragrance he made a covenant with his heart.

He prayed:

—He once had meant to come on earth in heavenly glory but we sinned: and then He could not safely visit us but with a shrouded majesty and a bedimmed radiance for He was God. So He came Himself in weakness not in power and He sent thee, a creature in His stead, with a creature's comeliness and

lustre suited to our state. And now thy very face and form, dear mother, speak to us of the Eternal; not like earthly beauty, dangerous to look upon, but like the morning star which is thy emblem, bright and musical, breathing purity, telling of heaven and infusing peace. O harbinger of day! O light of the pilgrim! Lead us still as thou hast led. In the dark night, across the bleak wilderness guide us on to our Lord Jesus, guide us home.

His eyes were dimmed with tears and, looking humbly up to heaven, he wept for the innocence he had lost.

When evening had fallen he left the house and the first touch of the damp dark air and the noise of the door as it closed behind him made ache again his conscience, lulled by prayer and tears. Confess! Confess! It was not enough to lull the conscience with a tear and a prayer. He had to kneel before the minister of the Holy Ghost and tell over his hidden sins truly and repentantly. Before he heard again the foot-board of the housedoor trail over the threshold as it opened to let him in, before he saw again the table in the kitchen set for supper he would have knelt and confessed. It was quite simple.

The ache of conscience ceased and he walked onward swiftly through the dark streets. There were so many flag-stones on the footpath of that street and so many streets in that city and so many cities in the world. Yet eternity had no end. He was in mortal sin. Even once was a mortal sin. It could happen in an instant. But how so quickly? By seeing or by thinking of seeing. The eyes see the thing, without having wished first to see. Then in an instant it happens. But does that part of the body understand or what? The serpent, the most subtle beast of the field. It must understand when it desires in one instant and then prolongs its own desire instant after instant, sinfully. It feels and understands and desires. What a horrible thing! Who made it to be like that, a bestial part of the body able to understand bestially and desire bestially? Was that then he or an inhuman thing moved by a lower soul than his soul? His soul sickened at the thought of a torpid snaky life feeding itself out of the tender marrow of his life and fattening upon the slime of lust. O why was that so? O why?

He cowered in the shadow of the thought, abasing himself in the awe of God Who had made all things and all men. Madness. Who could think such a thought? And, cowering in darkness and abject, he prayed mutely to his angel guardian to drive away with his sword the demon that was whispering to his brain.

The whisper ceased and he knew then clearly that his own soul had sinned in thought and word and deed wilfully through his own body. Confess! He had to confess every sin. How could he utter in words to the priest what he had done? Must, must. Or how could he explain without dying of shame? Or how could he have done such things without shame? A madman, a loathsome madman! Confess! O he would indeed to be free and sinless again! Perhaps the priest would know. O dear God!

He walked on and on through illlit streets, fearing to stand still for a moment lest it might seem that he held back from what awaited him, fearing to arrive at that towards which he still turned with longing. How beautiful must be a soul in the state of grace when God looked upon it with love!

Frowsy girls sat along the curbstones before their baskets. Their dank hair hung trailed over their brows. They were not beautiful to see as they crouched in the mire. But their souls were seen by God; and if their souls were in a state of grace they were radiant to see: and God loved them, seeing them.

A wasting breath of humiliation blew bleakly over his soul to think of how he had fallen, to feel that those souls were dearer to God than his. The wind blew over him and passed on to the myriads and myriads of other souls on whom God's favour shone now more and now less, stars now brighter and now dimmer, sustained and failing. And the glimmering souls passed away, sustained and failing, merged in a moving breath. One soul was lost; a tiny soul: his. It flickered once and went out, forgotten, lost. The end: black cold void waste.

Consciousness of place came ebbing back to him slowly over a vast tract of time unlit, unfelt, unlived. The squalid scene composed itself around him; the common accents, the burning gasjets in the shops, odours of fish and spirits and wet sawdust, moving men and women. An old woman was about to cross the street, an oilcan in her hand. He bent down and asked her was there a chapel near.

—A chapel, sir? Yes, sir. Church Street chapel.

—Church?

She shifted the can to her other hand and directed him: and, as she held out her reeking withered right hand under its fringe of shawl, he bent lower towards her, saddened and soothed by her voice.

—Thank you.

—You are quite welcome, sir.

The candles on the high altar had been extinguished but the fragrance of incense still floated down the dim nave. Bearded workmen with pious faces were guiding a canopy out through a sidedoor, the sacristan aiding them with quiet gestures and words. A few of the faithful still lingered, praying before one of the sidealtars or kneeling in the benches near the confessionals. He approached timidly and knelt at the last bench in the body, thankful for the peace and silence and fragrant shadow of the church. The board on which he knelt was narrow and worn and those who knelt near him were humble followers of Jesus. Jesus too had been born in poverty and had worked in the shop of a carpenter, cutting boards and planing them, and had first spoken of the kingdom of God to poor fishermen, teaching all men to be meek and humble of heart.

He bowed his head upon his hands, bidding his heart be meek and humble that he might be like those who knelt beside him and his prayer as acceptable as theirs. He prayed beside them but it was hard. His soul was foul with sin and he dared not ask forgiveness with the simple trust of those whom Jesus, in the mysterious ways of God, had called first to His side, the carpenters, the fishermen, poor and simple people following a lowly trade, handling and shaping the wood of trees, mending their nets with patience.

A tall figure came down the aisle and the penitents stirred: and at the last moment, glancing up swiftly, he saw a long grey beard and the brown habit of a capuchin. The priest entered the box and was hidden. Two penitents rose and entered the confessional at either side. The wooden slide was drawn back and the faint murmur of a voice troubled the silence.

His blood began to murmur in his veins, murmuring like a sinful city summoned from its sleep to hear its doom. Little flakes of fire fell and powdery ashes fell softly, alighting on the houses of men. They stirred, waking from sleep, troubled by the heated air.

The slide was shot back. The penitent emerged from the side of the box. The farther slide was drawn. A woman entered quietly and deftly where the first penitent had knelt. The faint murmur began again.

He could still leave the chapel. He could stand up, put one foot before the other and walk out softly and then run, run, run swiftly through the dark streets. He could still escape from the shame. Had it been any terrible crime but that one sin! Had it been murder! Little fiery flakes fell and touched him at all points, shameful thoughts, shameful words, shameful acts. Shame covered him wholly like fine glowing ashes falling continually. To say it in words! His soul, stifling and helpless, would cease to be.

The slide was shot back. A penitent emerged from the farther side of the box. The near slide was drawn. A penitent entered where the other penitent had come out. A soft whispering noise floated in vaporous cloudlets out of the box. It was the woman: soft whispering cloudlets, soft whispering vapour, whispering and vanishing.

He beat his breast with his fist humbly, secretly under cover of the wooden armrest. He would be at one with others and with God. He would love his neighbour. He would love God Who had made and loved him. He would kneel and pray with others and be happy. God would look down on him and on them and would love them all.

It was easy to be good. God's yoke was sweet and light. It was better never to have sinned, to have remained always a child, for God loved little children and suffered them to come to Him. It was a terrible and a sad thing to sin. But God was merciful to poor sinners who were truly sorry. How true that was! That was indeed goodness.

The slide was shot to suddenly. The penitent came out. He was next. He stood up in terror and walked blindly into the box.

At last it had come. He knelt in the silent gloom and raised his eyes to the white crucifix suspended above him. God could see that he was sorry. He would tell all his sins. His confession would be long, long. Everybody in the chapel would know then what a sinner he had been. Let them know. It was true. But God had promised to forgive him if he was sorry. He was sorry. He clasped his hands and raised them towards the white form, praying with his darkened eyes, praying with all his trembling body, swaying his head to and fro like a lost creature, praying with whimpering lips.

—Sorry! Sorry! O sorry!

The slide clicked back and his heart bounded in his breast. The face of an old priest was at the grating, averted from him, leaning upon a hand. He made the sign of the cross and prayed of the priest to bless him for he had sinned. Then, bowing his head, he repeated the *Confiteor* in fright. At the words *my most grievous fault* he ceased, breathless.

—How long is it since your last confession, my child?

—A long time, father.

—A month, my child?

—Longer, father.

—Three months, my child?

—Longer, father.

—Six months?

—Eight months, father.

He had begun. The priest asked:

—And what do you remember since that time?

He began to confess his sins: masses missed, prayers not said, lies.

—Anything else, my child?

Sins of anger, envy of others, gluttony, vanity, disobedience.

—Anything else, my child?

—Sloth.

—Anything else, my child?

There was no help. He murmured:

—I . . . committed sins of impurity, father.

The priest did not turn his head.

—With yourself, my child?

—And . . . with others.

—With women, my child?

—Yes, father.

—Were they married women, my child?

He did not know. His sins trickled from his lips, one by one, trickled in shameful drops from his soul festering and oozing like a sore, a squalid stream of vice. The last sins oozed forth, sluggish, filthy. There was no more to tell. He bowed his head, overcome.

The priest was silent. Then he asked:

—How old are you, my child?

—Sixteen, father.

The priest passed his hand several times over his face. Then, resting his forehead against his hand, he leaned towards the grating and, with eyes still averted, spoke slowly. His voice was weary and old.

—You are very young, my child, he said, and let me implore of you to give up that sin. It is a terrible sin. It kills the body and it kills the soul. It is the cause of many crimes and misfortunes. Give it up, my child, for God's sake. It is dishonourable and unmanly. You cannot know where that wretched habit will lead you or where it will come against you. As long as you commit that sin, my poor child, you will never be worth one farthing to God. Pray to our mother Mary to help you. She will help you, my child. Pray to Our Blessed Lady when that sin comes into your mind. I am sure you will do that, will you not? You repent of all those sins. I am sure you do. And you will promise God now that by His holy grace you will never offend Him any more by that wicked sin. You will make that solemn promise to God, will you not?

—Yes, father.

The old and weary voice fell like sweet rain upon his quaking parching heart. How sweet and sad!

—Do so, my poor child. The devil has led you astray. Drive him back to hell when he tempts you to dishonour your body in that way—the foul spirit who hates Our Lord. Promise God now that you will give up that sin, that wretched wretched sin.

Blinded by his tears and by the light of God's mercifulness he bent his head and heard the grave words of absolution spoken and saw the priest's hand raised above him in token of forgiveness.

—God bless you, my child. Pray for me.

He knelt to say his penance, praying in a corner of the dark nave: and his prayers ascended to heaven from his purified heart like perfume streaming upwards from a heart of white rose.

The muddy streets were gay. He strode homeward, conscious of an invisible grace pervading and making light his limbs. In spite of all he had done it. He had confessed and God had pardoned him. His soul was made fair and holy once more, holy and happy.

It would be beautiful to die if God so willed. It was beautiful to live if God so willed, to live in grace a life of peace and virtue and forbearance with others.

He sat by the fire in the kitchen, not daring to speak for happiness. Till that moment he had not known how beautiful and peaceful life could be. The green square of paper pinned round the lamp cast down a tender shade. On the dresser was a plate of sausages and white pudding and on the shelf there were eggs. They would be for the breakfast in the morning after the communion in the college chapel. White pudding and eggs and sausages and cups of tea. How simple and beautiful was life after all! And life lay all before him.

In a dream he fell asleep. In a dream he rose and saw that it was morning. In a waking dream he went through the quiet morning towards the college.

The boys were all there, kneeling in their places. He knelt among them, happy and shy. The altar was heaped with fragrant masses of white flowers: and in the morning light the pale flames of the candles among the white flowers were clear and silent as his own soul.

He knelt before the altar with his classmates, holding the altar cloth with them over a living rail of hands. His hands were trembling, and his soul trembled as he heard the priest pass with the ciborium from communicant to communicant.

—*Corpus Domini nostri.*

Could it be? He knelt there sinless and timid: and he would hold upon his tongue the host and God would enter his purified body.

—*In vitam eternam. Amen.*

Another life! A life of grace and virtue and happiness! It was true. It was not a dream from which he would wake. The past was past.

—*Corpus Domini nostri.*

The ciborium had come to him.

IV

SUNDAY was dedicated to the mystery of the Holy Trinity, Monday to the Holy Ghost, Tuesday to the Guardian Angels, Wednesday to Saint Joseph, Thursday to the Most Blessed Sacrament of the Altar, Friday to the Suffering Jesus, Saturday to the Blessed Virgin Mary.

Every morning he hallowed himself anew in the presence of some holy image or mystery. His day began with an heroic offering of its every moment of thought or action for the intentions of the sovereign pontiff and with an early mass. The raw morning air whetted his resolute piety; and often as he knelt among the few worshippers at the sidealtar, following with his interleaved prayerbook the murmur of the priest, he glanced up for an instant towards the vested figure standing in the gloom between the two candles which were the old and the new testaments and imagined that he was kneeling at mass in the catacombs.

His daily life was laid out in devotional areas. By means of ejaculations and prayers he stored up ungrudgingly for the souls in purgatory centuries of days and quarantines and years; yet the spiritual triumph which he felt in achieving with ease so many fabulous ages of canonical penances did not wholly reward his zeal of prayer since he could never know how much temporal punishment he had remitted by way of suffrage for the agonising souls: and, fearful lest in the midst of the purgatorial fire, which differed from the infernal only in that it was not everlasting, his penance might avail no more than a drop of moisture, he drove his soul daily through an increasing circle of works of supererogation.

Every part of his day, divided by what he regarded now as the duties of his station in life, circled about its own centre of spiritual energy. His life seemed to have drawn near to eternity; every thought, word and deed, every instance of consciousness could be made to revibrate radiantly in heaven: and at times his sense of such immediate repercussion was so lively that he seemed to feel his soul in devotion pressing like fingers the keyboard of a great cash register and to see the amount of his purchase start forth immediately in heaven, not as a number but as a frail column of incense or as a slender flower.

The rosaries too which he said constantly—for he carried his beads loose in his trousers' pockets that he might tell them as he walked the streets—transformed themselves into coronals of flowers of such vague unearthly texture that they seemed to him as hueless and odourless as they were nameless. He offered up each of his three daily chaplets that his soul might grow strong in each of the three theological virtues, in faith in the Father, Who had created him, in hope in the Son Who had redeemed him, and in love of the Holy Ghost Who had sanctified him, and this thrice triple prayer he offered to the Three persons through Mary in the name of her joyful and sorrowful and glorious mysteries.

On each of the seven days of the week he further prayed that one of the seven gifts of the Holy Ghost might descend upon his soul and drive out of it day by day the seven deadly sins which had defiled it in the past; and he prayed for each gift on its appointed day, confident that it would descend upon him, though it seemed strange to him at times that wisdom and understanding and knowledge were so distinct in their nature that each should be prayed for apart from the others. Yet he believed that at some future stage of his spiritual progress this difficulty would be removed when his sinful soul had been raised up from its weakness and enlightened by the Third Person of the Most Blessed Trinity. He believed this all the more, and with trepidation, because of the divine gloom and silence wherein dwelt the unseen Paraclete, Whose symbols were a dove and a mighty wind, to sin against Whom was a sin beyond forgiveness, the eternal, mysterious secret Being to Whom, as God, the priests offered up mass once a year, robed in the scarlet of the tongues of fire.

The imagery through which the nature and kinship of the Three Persons of the Trinity were darkly shadowed forth in the books of devotion which he read—the Father contemplating from all eternity as in a mirror His Divine Perfections and thereby begetting eternally the Eternal Son and the Holy Spirit proceeding out of Father and Son from all eternity—were easier of acceptance by his mind by reason of their august incomprehensibility than was the simple fact that God had loved his soul from all eternity, for ages before he had been born into the world, for ages before the world itself had existed.

He had heard the names of the passions of love and hate pronounced solemnly on the stage and in the pulpit, had found them set forth solemnly in books, and had wondered why his soul was unable to harbour them for any time or to force his lips to utter their names with conviction. A brief anger had often invested him but he had never been able to make it an abiding passion and had always felt himself passing out of it as if his very body were being divested with ease of some outer skin or peel. He had felt a subtle, dark and murmurous presence penetrate his being and fire him with a brief iniquitous lust: it too had slipped beyond his grasp leaving his mind lucid and indifferent. This, it seemed, was the only love and that the only hate his soul would harbour.

But he could no longer disbelieve in the reality of love since God Himself had loved his individual soul with divine love from all eternity. Gradually, as his soul was enriched with spiritual knowledge, he saw the whole world forming one vast symmetrical expression of God's power and love. Life became a divine gift for every moment and sensation of which, were it even the sight of a single leaf hanging on the twig of a tree, his soul should praise and thank the Giver. The world for all its solid substance and complexity no longer existed for his soul save as a theorem of divine power and love and universality. So entire and unquestionable was this sense of the divine meaning in all nature granted to his soul that he could scarcely understand why it was in any way necessary that he should continue to live. Yet that was part of the divine purpose and he dared not question its use, he above all others who had sinned so deeply and so foully against the divine purpose. Meek and abased by this consciousness of the one eternal omnipresent perfect reality his soul took up again her burden of pieties, masses and prayers and sacraments and mortifications, and only then for the first time since he had brooded on the great mystery of love did he feel within him a warm movement like that of some newly born life or virtue of the soul itself. The attitude of rapture in sacred art, the raised and parted hands, the parted lips and eyes as of one about to swoon, became for him an image of the soul in prayer, humiliated and faint before her Creator.

But he had been forewarned of the dangers of spiritual exaltation and did not allow himself to desist from even the least or lowliest devotion, striving also by constant mortification to undo the sinful past rather than to achieve a saintliness fraught with peril. Each of his senses was brought under a rigorous discipline. In order to mortify the sense of sight he made it his rule to walk in the street with downcast eyes, glancing neither to right nor left and never behind him. His eyes shunned every encounter with the eyes of women. From time to time also he balked them by a sudden effort of the will, as by lifting them suddenly in the middle of an unfinished sentence and closing the book. To mortify his hearing he exerted no control over his voice which was then breaking, neither sang nor whistled and made no attempt to flee from noises which caused him painful nervous irritation such as the sharpening of knives on the knifeboard, the gathering of cinders on the fireshovel and the twigging of the carpet. To mortify his smell was more difficult as he found in himself no instinctive repugnance to bad odours, whether they were the odours of the outdoor world such as those of dung and tar or the odours of his own person among which he had made many curious comparisons and experiments. He found in the end that the only odour against which his sense of smell revolted was a certain stale fishy stink like that of longstanding urine: and whenever it was possible he subjected himself to this unpleasant odour. To mortify the taste he practised strict habits at table, observed to the letter all the fasts of the church and sought by distraction to divert his mind from the savours of different foods. But it was to the mortification of touch that he brought the most assiduous ingenuity of inventiveness. He never consciously changed his position in bed, sat in the most uncomfortable positions, suffered patiently every itch and pain, kept away from the fire, remained on his knees all through the mass except at the gospels, left parts of his neck and face undried so that air might sting them and, whenever he was not saying his beads, carried his arms stiffly at his sides like a runner and never in his pockets or clasped behind him.

He had no temptations to sin mortally. It surprised him however to find that at the end of his course of intricate piety and selfrestraint he was so easily at the mercy of childish and unworthy imperfections. His prayers and fasts availed him little for the suppression of anger at hearing his mother sneeze or at being disturbed in his devotions. It needed an immense effort of his will to master the impulse which urged him to give outlet to such irritation. Images of the outbursts of trivial anger which he had often noted among his masters, their twitching mouths, closeshut lips and flushed cheeks, recurred to his memory, discouraging him, for all his practice of humility, by the comparison. To merge his life in the common tide of other lives was harder for him than any fasting or prayer, and it was his constant failure to do this to his own satisfaction which caused in his soul at last a sensation of spiritual dryness together with a growth of doubts and scruples. His soul traversed a period of desolation in which the sacraments themselves seemed to have turned into dried up sources. His confession became a channel for the escape of scrupulous and unrepented imperfections. His actual reception of the eucharist did not bring him the same dissolving moments of virginal selfsurrender as did those spiritual communions made by him sometimes at the close of some visit to the Blessed Sacrament. The book which he used for these visits was an old neglected book written by saint Alphonsus Liguori, with fading characters and sere foxpapered leaves. A faded world of fervent love and virginal responses seemed to be evoked for his soul by the reading of its pages in which the imagery of the canticles was interwoven with the communicant's prayers. An inaudible voice seemed to caress the soul, telling her names and glories, bidding her arise as for espousal and come away, bidding her look forth, a spouse, from Amana and from the mountains of the leopards; and the soul seemed to answer with the same inaudible voice, surrendering herself: *Inter ubera mea commorabitur.*

This idea of surrender had a perilous attraction for his mind now that he felt his soul beset once again by the insistent voices of the flesh which began to murmur to him again during his prayers and meditations. It gave him an intense sense of power to know that he could by a single act of consent, in a moment of thought, undo all that he had done. He seemed to feel a flood slowly advancing towards his naked feet and to be waiting for the first faint timid noiseless wavelet to touch his fevered skin. Then, almost at the instant of that touch, almost at the verge of sinful consent, he found himself standing far away from the flood upon a dry shore, saved by a sudden act of the will or a sudden ejaculation: and, seeing the silver line of the flood far away and beginning again its slow advance towards his feet, a new thrill of power and satisfaction shook his soul to know that he had not yielded nor undone all.

When he had eluded the flood of temptation many times in

this way he grew troubled and wondered whether the grace which he had refused to lose was not being filched from him little by little. The clear certitude of his own immunity grew dim and to it succeeded a vague fear that his soul had really fallen unawares. It was with difficulty that he won back his old consciousness of his state of grace by telling himself that he had prayed to God at every temptation and that the grace which he had prayed for must have been given to him inasmuch as God was obliged to give it. The very frequency and violence of temptations showed him at last the truth of what he had heard about the trials of the saints. Frequent and violent temptations were a proof that the citadel of the soul had not fallen and that the devil raged to make it fall.

Often when he had confessed his doubts and scruples, some momentary inattention at prayer, a movement of trivial anger in his soul or a subtle wilfulness in speech or act, he was bidden by his confessor to name some sin of his past life before absolution was given him. He named it with humility and shame and repented of it once more. It humiliated and shamed him to think that he would never be freed from it wholly, however holily he might live or whatever virtues or perfections he might attain. A restless feeling of guilt would always be present with him: he would confess and repent and be absolved, confess and repent again and be absolved again, fruitlessly. Perhaps that first hasty confession wrung from him by the fear of hell had not been good? Perhaps, concerned only for his imminent doom, he had not had sincere sorrow for his sin? But the surest sign that his confession had been good and that he had had sincere sorrow for his sin was, he knew, the amendment of his life.

—I have amended my life, have I not? he asked himself.

*   *   *

The director stood in the embrasure of the window, his back to the light, leaning an elbow on the brown crossblind and, as he spoke and smiled, slowly dangling and looping the

cord of the other blind. Stephen stood before him, following
for a moment with his eyes the waning of the long summer
daylight above the roofs or the slow deft movements of the
priestly fingers. The priest's face was in total shadow but the
waning daylight from behind him touched the deeply grooved
temples and the curves of the skull. Stephen followed also
with his ears the accents and intervals of the priest's voice as
he spoke gravely and cordially of indifferent themes, the
vacation which had just ended, the colleges of the order
abroad, the transference of masters. The grave and cordial
voice went on easily with its tale, and in the pauses Stephen
felt bound to set it on again with respectful questions. He knew
that the tale was a prelude and his mind waited for the sequel.
Ever since the message of summons had come for him from
the director his mind had struggled to find the meaning of the
message; and during the long restless time he had sat in the
college parlour waiting for the director to come in his eyes had
wandered from one sober picture to another around the walls
and his mind wandered from one guess to another until the
meaning of the summons had almost become clear. Then, just
as he was wishing that some unforeseen cause might prevent
the director from coming, he had heard the handle of the door
turning and the swish of a soutane.

The director had begun to speak of the dominican and
franciscan orders and of the friendship between saint Thomas
and saint Bonaventure. The capuchin dress, he thought, was
rather too . . .

Stephen's face gave back the priest's indulgent smile and, not
being anxious to give an opinion, he made a slight dubitative
movement with his lips.

—I believe, continued the director, that there is some talk
now among the capuchins themselves of doing away with it
and following the example of the other franciscans.

—I suppose they would retain it in the cloister, said Stephen.

—O, certainly, said the director. For the cloister it is all right but for the street I really think it would be better to do away with, don't you?

—It must be troublesome, I imagine?

—Of course it is, of course. Just imagine when I was in Belgium I used to see them out cycling in all kinds of weather with this thing up about their knees! It was really ridiculous. *Les jupes,* they call them in Belgium.

The vowel was so modified as to be indistinct.

—What do they call them?

—*Les jupes.*

—O.

Stephen smiled again in answer to the smile which he could not see on the priest's shadowed face, its image or spectre only passing rapidly across his mind as the low discreet accent fell upon his ear. He gazed calmly before him at the waning sky, glad of the cool of the evening and the faint yellow glow which hid the tiny flame kindling upon his cheek.

The names of articles of dress worn by women or of certain soft and delicate stuffs used in their making brought always to his mind a delicate and sinful perfume. As a boy he had imagined the reins by which horses are driven as slender silken bands and it shocked him to feel at Stradbrook the greasy leather of harness. It had shocked him too when he had felt for the first time beneath his tremulous fingers the brittle texture of a woman's stocking for, retaining nothing of all he read save that which seemed to him an echo or a prophecy of his own state, it was only amid softworded phrases or within rosesoft stuffs that he dared to conceive of the soul or body of a woman moving with tender life.

But the phrase on the priest's lips was disingenuous for he knew that a priest should not speak lightly on that theme. The phrase had been spoken lightly with design and he felt that his face was being searched by the eyes in the shadow. Whatever he had heard or read of the craft of jesuits he had put aside frankly as not borne out by his own experience. His masters, even when they had not attracted him, had seemed to him always intelligent and serious priests, athletic and highspirited prefects. He thought of them as men who washed their bodies briskly with cold water and wore clean cold linen. During all the years he had lived among them in Clongowes and in Belvedere he had received only two pandies and, though these had been dealt him in the wrong, he knew that he had often escaped punishment. During all those years he had never heard from any of his masters a flippant word: it was they who had taught him christian doctrine and urged him to live a good life and, when he had fallen into grievous sin, it was they who had led him back to grace. Their presence had made him diffident of himself when he was a muff in Clongowes and it had made him diffident of himself also while he had held his equivocal position in Belvedere. A constant sense of this had remained with him up to the last year of his school life. He had never once disobeyed or allowed turbulent companions to seduce him from his habit of quiet obedience: and, even when he doubted some statement of a master, he had never presumed to doubt openly. Lately some of their judgments had sounded a little childish in his ears and had made him feel a regret and pity as though he were slowly passing out of an accustomed world and were hearing its language for the last time. One day when some boys had gathered round a priest under the shed near the chapel, he had heard the priest say:

—I believe that Lord Macaulay was a man who probably never committed a mortal sin in his life, that is to say, a deliberate mortal sin.

Some of the boys had then asked the priest if Victor Hugo were not the greatest French writer. The priest had answered that Victor Hugo had never written half so well when he had turned against the church as he had written when he was a catholic.

—But there are many eminent French critics, said the priest, who consider that even Victor Hugo, great as he certainly was, had not so pure a French style as Louis Veuillot.

The tiny flame which the priest's allusion had kindled upon

Stephen's cheek had sunk down again and his eyes were still fixed calmly on the colorless sky. But an unresting doubt flew hither and thither before his mind. Masked memories passed quickly before him: he recognised scenes and persons yet he was conscious that he had failed to perceive some vital circumstance in them. He saw himself walking about the grounds watching the sports in Clongowes and eating slim jim out of his cricketcap. Some jesuits were walking round the cycletrack in the company of ladies. The echoes of certain expressions used in Clongowes sounded in remote caves of his mind.

His ears were listening to these distant echoes amid the silence of the parlour when he became aware that the priest was addressing him in a different voice.

—I sent for you today, Stephen, because I wished to speak to you on a very important subject.

—Yes, sir.

—Have you ever felt that you had a vocation?

Stephen parted his lips to answer yes and then withheld the word suddenly. The priest waited for the answer and added:

—I mean have you ever felt within yourself, in your soul, a desire to join the order. Think.

—I have sometimes thought of it, said Stephen.

The priest let the blindcord fall to one side and, uniting his hands, leaned his chin gravely upon them, communing with himself.

—In a college like this, he said at length, there is one boy or perhaps two or three boys whom God calls to the religious life. Such a boy is marked off from his companions by his piety, by the good example he shows to others. He is looked up to by them; he is chosen perhaps as prefect by his fellow sodalists. And you, Stephen, have been such a boy in this college, prefect of Our Blessed Lady's sodality. Perhaps you are the boy in this college whom God designs to call to Himself.

A strong note of pride reinforcing the gravity of the priest's voice made Stephen's heart quicken in response.

—To receive that call, Stephen, said the priest, is the greatest honour that the Almighty God can bestow upon a man. No king or emperor on this earth has the power of the priest of God. No angel or archangel in heaven, no saint, not even the Blessed Virgin herself has the power of a priest of God: the power of the keys, the power to bind and to loose from sin, the power of exorcism, the power to cast out from the creatures of God the evil spirits that have power over them, the power, the authority, to make the great God of Heaven come down upon the altar and take the form of bread and wine. What an awful power, Stephen!

A flame began to flutter again on Stephen's cheek as he heard in this proud address an echo of his own proud musings. How often had he seen himself as a priest wielding calmly and humbly the awful power of which angels and saints stood in reverence! His soul had loved to muse in secret on this desire. He had seen himself, a young and silentmannered priest, entering a confessional swiftly, ascending the altarsteps, incensing, genuflecting, accomplishing the vague acts of the priesthood which pleased him by reason of their semblance of reality and of their distance from it. In that dim life which he had lived through in his musings he had assumed the voices and gestures which he had noted with various priests. He had bent his knee sideways like such a one, he had shaken the thurible only slightly like such a one, his chasuble had swung open like that of such another as he had turned to the altar again after having blessed the people. And above all it had pleased him to fill the second place in those dim scenes of his imagining. He shrank from the dignity of celebrant because it displeased him to imagine that all the vague pomp should end in his own person or that the ritual should assign to him so clear and final an office. He longed for the minor sacred offices, to be vested with the tunicle of subdeacon at high mass, to stand aloof from the altar, forgotten by the people, his shoulders covered with a humeral veil, holding the paten within its folds, or, when the sacrifice had been accomplished, to stand as deacon in a dalmatic of cloth of gold on the step below the celebrant, his hands joined and his face towards the people, and sing the chant *Ite, missa est*. If ever he had seen himself celebrant it was as in the pictures of the mass in his child's massbook, in a church without worshippers, save for the angel of the sacrifice, at a bare altar and served by an acolyte scarcely more boyish than himself. In vague sacrificial or sacramental acts alone his will seemed drawn to go forth to encounter reality: and it was partly the absence of an appointed rite which had always constrained him to inaction whether he had allowed silence to cover his anger or pride or had suffered only an embrace he longed to give.

He listened in reverent silence now to the priest's appeal and through the words he heard even more distinctly a voice bidding him approach, offering him secret knowledge and secret power. He would know then what was the sin of Simon Magus and what the sin against the Holy Ghost for which there was no forgiveness. He would know obscure things, hidden from others, from those who were conceived and born children of wrath. He would know the sins, the sinful longings and sinful thoughts and sinful acts, of others, hearing them murmured into his ears in the confessional under the shame of a darkened chapel by the lips of women and of girls: but rendered immune mysteriously at his ordination by the imposition of hands his soul would pass again uncontaminated to the white peace of the altar. No touch of sin would linger upon the hands with which he would elevate and break the host; no touch of sin would linger on his lips in prayer to make him eat and drink damnation to himself, not discerning the body of the Lord. He would hold his secret knowledge and secret power, being as sinless as the innocent: and he would be a priest for ever according to the order of Melchisedec.

—I will offer up my mass tomorrow morning, said the director, that Almighty God may reveal to you His holy will. And let you, Stephen, make a novena to your holy patron saint, the first martyr, who is very powerful with God, that

God may enlighten your mind. But you must be quite sure, Stephen, that you have a vocation because it would be terrible if you found afterwards that you had none. Once a priest always a priest, remember. Your catechism tells you that the sacrament of Holy Orders is one of those which can be received only once because it imprints on the soul an indelible spiritual mark which can never be effaced. It is before you must weigh well, not after. It is a solemn question, Stephen, because on it may depend the salvation of your eternal soul. But we will pray to God together.

He held open the heavy hall door and gave his hand as if already to a companion in the spiritual life. Stephen passed out on to the wide platform above the steps and was conscious of the caress of mild evening air. Towards Findlater's church a quartet of young men were striding along with linked arms, swaying their heads and stepping to the agile melody of their leader's concertina. The music passed in an instant, as the first bars of sudden music always did, over the fantastic fabrics of his mind, dissolving them painlessly and noiselessly as a sudden wave dissolves the sandbuilt turrets of children. Smiling at the trivial air he raised his eyes to the priest's face and, seeing in it a mirthless reflection of the sunken day, detached his hand slowly which had acquiesced faintly in that companionship.

As he descended the steps the impression which effaced his troubled selfcommunion was that of a mirthless mask reflecting a sunken day from the threshold of the college. The shadow, then, of the life of the college passed gravely over his consciousness. It was a grave and ordered and passionless life that awaited him, a life without material cares. He wondered how he would pass the first night in the novitiate and with what dismay he would wake the first morning in the dormitory. The troubling odour of the long corridors of Clongowes came back to him and he heard the discreet murmur of the burning gasflames. At once from every part of his being unrest began to irradiate. A feverish quickening of his pulses followed and a din of meaningless words drove his reasoned thoughts hither and thither confusedly. His lungs dilated and sank as if he were inhaling a warm moist unsustaining air and he smelt again the warm moist air which hung in the bath in Clongowes above the sluggish turfcoloured water.

Some instinct, waking at these memories, stronger than education or piety, quickened within him at every near approach to that life, an instinct subtle and hostile, and armed him against acquiescence. The chill and order of the life repelled him. He saw himself rising in the cold of the morning and filing down with the others to early mass and trying vainly to struggle with his prayers against the fainting sickness of his stomach. He saw himself sitting at dinner with the community of a college. What, then, had become of that deeprooted shyness of his which had made him loth to eat or drink under a strange roof? What had come of the pride of his spirit which had always made him conceive himself as a being apart in every order?

The Reverend Stephen Dedalus, S. J.

His name in that new life leaped into characters before his eyes and to it there followed a mental sensation of an undefined face or colour of a face. The colour faded and became strong like a changing glow of pallid brick red. Was it the raw reddish glow he had so often seen on wintry mornings on the shaven gills of the priests? The face was eyeless and sourfavoured and devout, shot with pink tinges of suffocated anger. Was it not a mental spectre of the face of one of the jesuits whom some of the boys called Lantern Jaws and others Foxy Campbell?

He was passing at that moment before the jesuit house in Gardiner Street, and wondered vaguely which window would be his if he ever joined the order. Then he wondered at the vagueness of his wonder, at the remoteness of his soul from what he had hitherto imagined her sanctuary, at the frail hold which so many years of order and obedience had of him when once a definite and irrevocable act of his threatened to end for

ever, in time and in eternity, his freedom. The voice of the
director urging upon him the proud claims of the church and
the mystery and power of the priestly office repeated itself
idly in his memory. His soul was not there to hear and greet it
and he knew now that the exhortation he had listened to had
already fallen into an idle formal tale. He would never swing
the thurible before the tabernacle as priest. His destiny was to
be elusive of social or religious orders. The wisdom of the
priest's appeal did not touch him to the quick. He was destined to learn his own wisdom apart from others or to learn
the wisdom of others himself wandering among the snares of
the world.

The snares of the world were its ways of sin. He would fall.
He had not yet fallen but he would fall silently, in an instant.
Not to fall was too hard, too hard: and he felt the silent lapse
of his soul, as it would be at some instant to come, falling,
falling but not yet fallen, still unfallen but about to fall.

He crossed the bridge over the stream of the Tolka and
turned his eyes coldly for an instant towards the faded blue
shrine of the Blessed Virgin which stood fowlwise on a pole in
the middle of a hamshaped encampment of poor cottages.
Then, bending to the left, he followed the lane which led up to
his house. The faint sour stink of rotted cabbages came towards him from the kitchengardens on the rising ground
above the river. He smiled to think that it was this disorder,
the misrule and confusion of his father's house and the stagna-
tion of vegetable life, which was to win the day in his soul.
Then a short laugh broke from his lips as he thought of that
solitary farmhand in the kitchengardens behind their house
whom they had nicknamed the man with the hat. A second
laugh, taking rise from the first after a pause, broke from him
involuntarily as he thought of how the man with the hat
worked, considering in turn the four points of the sky and then
regretfully plunging his spade in the earth.

He pushed open the latchless door of the porch and passed
through the naked hallway into the kitchen. A group of his

brothers and sisters was sitting round the table. Tea was nearly over and only the last of the second watered tea remained in the bottoms of the small glassjars and jampots which did service for teacups. Discarded crusts and lumps of sugared bread, turned brown by the tea which had been poured over them, lay scattered on the table. Little wells of tea lay here and there on the board and a knife with a broken ivory handle was stuck through the pith of a ravaged turnover.

The sad quiet greyblue glow of the dying day came through the window and the open door, covering over and allaying quietly a sudden instinct of remorse in Stephen's heart. All that had been denied them had been freely given to him, the eldest: but the quiet glow of evening showed him in their faces no sign of rancour.

He sat near them at the table and asked where his father and mother were. One answered:

—Goneboro toboro lookboro atboro aboro houseboro.

Still another removal! A boy named Fallon in Belvedere had often asked him with a silly laugh why they moved so often. A frown of scorn darkened quickly his forehead as he heard again the silly laugh of the questioner.

He asked:

—Why are we on the move again, if it's a fair question?

The same sister answered:

—Becauseboro theboro landboro lordboro willboro putboro usboro outboro.

The voice of his youngest brother from the farther side of the fireplace began to sing the air *Oft in the Stilly Night*. One by one the others took up the air until a full choir of voices was singing. They would sing so for hours, melody after melody, glee after glee, till the last pale light died down on the horizon, till the first dark nightclouds came forth and night fell.

He waited for some moments, listening, before he too took up the air with them. He was listening with pain of spirit to the overtone of weariness behind their frail fresh innocent voices.

Even before they set out on life's journey they seemed weary already of the way.

He heard the choir of voices in the kitchen echoed and multiplied through an endless reverberation of the choirs of endless generations of children: and heard in all the echoes an echo also of the recurring note of weariness and pain. All seemed weary of life even before entering upon it. And he remembered that Newman had heard this note also in the broken lines of Virgil *giving utterance, like the voice of Nature herself, to that pain and weariness yet hope of better things which has been the experience of her children in every time.*

*   *   *

He could wait no longer.

From the door of Byron's publichouse to the gate of Clontarf Chapel, from the gate of Clontarf Chapel to the door of Byron's publichouse and then back again to the chapel and then back again to the publichouse he had paced slowly at first, planting his steps scrupulously in the spaces of the patchwork of the footpath, then timing their fall to the fall of verses. A full hour had passed since his father had gone in with Dan Crosby, the tutor, to find out for him something about the university. For a full hour he had paced up and down, waiting: but he could wait no longer.

He set off abruptly for the Bull, walking rapidly lest his father's shrill whistle might call him back; and in a few moments he had rounded the curve at the police barrack and was safe.

Yes, his mother was hostile to the idea, as he had read from her listless silence. Yet her mistrust pricked him more keenly than his father's pride and he thought coldly how he had watched the faith which was fading down in his soul aging and strengthening in her eyes. A dim antagonism gathered force within him and darkened his mind as a cloud against her disloyalty: and when it passed, cloudlike, leaving his mind serene and dutiful towards her again, he was made aware

dimly and without regret of a first noiseless sundering of their
lives.

The university! So he had passed beyond the challenge of
the sentries who had stood as guardians of his boyhood and
had sought to keep him among them that he might be subject
to them and serve their ends. Pride after satisfaction uplifted
him like long slow waves. The end he had been born to serve
yet did not see had led him to escape by an unseen path: and
now it beckoned to him once more and a new adventure was
about to be opened to him. It seemed to him that he heard
notes of fitful music leaping upwards a tone and downwards a
diminished fourth, upwards a tone and downwards a major
third, like triplebranching flames leaping fitfully, flame after
flame, out of a midnight wood. It was an elfin prelude, endless
and formless; and, as it grew wilder and faster, the flames
leaping out of time, he seemed to hear from under the boughs
and grasses wild creatures racing, their feet pattering like rain
upon the leaves. Their feet passed in pattering tumult over his
mind, the feet of hares and rabbits, the feet of harts and hinds
and antelopes, until he heard them no more and remembered
only a proud cadence from Newman: *Whose feet are as the
feet of harts and underneath the everlasting arms.*

The pride of that dim image brought back to his mind the
dignity of the office he had refused. All through his boyhood
he had mused upon that which he had so often thought to be
his destiny and when the moment had come for him to obey
the call he had turned aside, obeying a wayward instinct. Now
time lay between: the oils of ordination would never anoint
his body. He had refused. Why?

He turned seaward from the road at Dollymount and as he
passed on to the thin wooden bridge he felt the planks shaking
with the tramp of heavily shod feet. A squad of christian
brothers was on its way back from the Bull and had begun to
pass, two by two, across the bridge. Soon the whole bridge
was trembling and resounding. The uncouth faces passed him
two by two, stained yellow or red or livid by the sea, and as

he strove to look at them with ease and indifference, a faint stain of personal shame and commiseration rose to his own face. Angry with himself he tried to hide his face from their eyes by gazing down sideways into the shallow swirling water under the bridge but he still saw a reflection therein of their topheavy silk hats, and humble tapelike collars and loosely hanging clerical clothes.

—Brother Hickey.

Brother Quaid.

Brother MacArdle.

Brother Keogh.

Their piety would be like their names, like their faces, like their clothes, and it was idle for him to tell himself that their humble and contrite hearts, it might be, paid a far richer tribute of devotion than his had ever been, a gift tenfold more acceptable than his elaborate adoration. It was idle for him to move himself to be generous towards them, to tell himself that if he ever came to their gates, stripped of his pride, beaten and in beggar's weeds, that they would be generous towards him, loving him as themselves. Idle and embittering, finally, to argue, against his own dispassionate certitude, that the commandment of love bade us not to love our neighbour as ourselves with the same amount and intensity of love but to love him as ourselves with the same kind of love.

He drew forth a phrase from his treasure and spoke it softly to himself:

—A day of dappled seaborne clouds.

The phrase and the day and the scene harmonised in a chord. Words. Was it their colours? He allowed them to glow and fade, hue after hue: sunrise gold, the russet and green of apple orchards, azure of waves, the greyfringed fleece of clouds. No, it was not their colours: it was the poise and balance of the period itself. Did he then love the rhythmic rise and fall of words better than their associations of legend and colour? Or was it that, being as weak of sight as he was shy of mind, he drew less pleasure from the reflection of the glowing sensible world through the prism of a language manycoloured and richly storied than from the contemplation of an inner world of individual emotions mirrored perfectly in a lucid supple periodic prose?

He passed from the trembling bridge on to firm land again. At that instant, as it seemed to him, the air was chilled and looking askance towards the water he saw a flying squall darkening and crisping suddenly the tide. A faint click at his heart, a faint throb in his throat told him once more of how his flesh dreaded the cold infrahuman odour of the sea: yet he did not strike across the downs on his left but held straight on along the spine of rocks that pointed against the river's mouth.

A veiled sunlight lit up faintly the grey sheet of water where the river was embayed. In the distance along the course of the slowflowing Liffey slender masts flecked the sky and, more distant still, the dim fabric of the city lay prone in haze. Like a scene on some vague arras, old as man's weariness, the image of the seventh city of christendom was visible to him across the timeless air, no older nor more weary nor less patient of subjection than in the days of the thingmote.

Disheartened, he raised his eyes towards the slowdrifting clouds, dappled and seaborne. They were voyaging across the deserts of the sky, a host of nomads on the march, voyaging high over Ireland, westward bound. The Europe they had come from lay out there beyond the Irish Sea, Europe of strange tongues and valleyed and woodbegirt and citadelled and of entrenched and marshalled races. He heard a confused music within him as of memories and names which he was almost conscious of but could not capture even for an instant; then the music seemed to recede, to recede, to recede: and from each receding trail of nebulous music there fell always one longdrawn calling note, piercing like a star the dusk of silence. Again! Again! Again! A voice from beyond the world was calling.

—Hello, Stephanos!

—Here comes The Dedalus!

—Ao! . . . Eh, give it over, Dwyer, I'm telling you or I'll give you a stuff in the kisser for yourself. . . . Ao!

—Good man, Towser! Duck him!

—Come along, Dedalus! Bous Stephanoumenos! Bous Stephaneforos!

—Duck him! Guzzle him now, Towser!

—Help! Help! . . . Ao!

He recognised their speech collectively before he distinguished their faces. The mere sight of that medley of wet nakedness chilled him to the bone. Their bodies, corpsewhite or suffused with a pallid golden light or rawly tanned by the suns, gleamed with the wet of the sea. Their divingstone, poised on its rude supports and rocking under their plunges, and the roughhewn stones of the sloping breakwater over which they scrambled in their horseplay, gleamed with cold wet lustre. The towels with which they smacked their bodies were heavy with cold seawater: and drenched with cold brine was their matted hair.

He stood still in deference to their calls and parried their banter with easy words. How characterless they looked: Shuley without his deep unbuttoned collar, Ennis without his scarlet belt with the snaky clasp, and Connolly without his Norfolk coat with the flapless sidepockets! It was a pain to see them and a swordlike pain to see the signs of adolescence that made repellent their pitiable nakedness. Perhaps they had taken refuge in number and noise from the secret dread in their souls. But he, apart from them and in silence, remembered in what dread he stood of the mystery of his own body.

—Stephanos Dedalos! Bous Stephanoumenos! Bous Stephaneforos!

Their banter was not new to him and now it flattered his mild proud sovereignty. Now, as never before, his strange name seemed to him a prophecy. So timeless seemed the grey warm air, so fluid and impersonal his own mood, that all ages were as one to him. A moment before the ghost of the ancient kingdom of the Danes had looked forth through the vesture of the hazewrapped city. Now, at the name of the fabulous artificer, he seemed to hear the noise of dim waves and to see a winged form flying above the waves and slowly climbing the air. What did it mean? Was it a quaint device opening a page of some medieval book of prophecies and symbols, a hawklike man flying sunward above the sea, a prophecy of the end he had been born to serve and had been following through the mists of childhood and boyhood, a symbol of the artist forging anew in his workshop out of the sluggish matter of the earth a new soaring impalpable imperishable being?

His heart trembled; his breath came faster and a wild spirit passed over his limbs as though he were soaring sunward. His heart trembled in an ecstasy of fear and his soul was in flight. His soul was soaring in an air beyond the world and the body he knew was purified in a breath and delivered of incertitude and made radiant and commingled with the element of the spirit. An ecstasy of flight made radiant his eyes and wild his breath and tremulous and wild and radiant his windswept limbs.

—One! Two! . . . Look out!

—O, cripes, I'm drownded!

—One! Two! Three and away!

—Me next! Me next!

—One! . . . Uk!

—Stephaneforos!

His throat ached with a desire to cry aloud, the cry of a hawk or eagle on high, to cry piercingly of his deliverance to the winds. This was the call of life to his soul not the dull gross voice of the world of duties and despair, not the inhuman voice that had called him to the pale service of the altar. An instant of wild flight had delivered him and the cry of triumph which his lips withheld cleft his brain.

—Stephaneforos!

What were they now but cerements shaken from the body of death—the fear he had walked in night and day, the incertitude that had ringed him round, the shame that had abased him within and without—cerements, the linens of the grave?

His soul had arisen from the grave of boyhood, spurning her graveclothes. Yes! Yes! Yes! He would create proudly out of the freedom and power of his soul, as the great artificer whose name he bore, a living thing, new and soaring and beautiful, impalpable, imperishable.

He started up nervously from the stoneblock for he could no longer quench the flame in his blood. He felt his cheeks aflame and his throat throbbing with song. There was a lust of wandering in his feet that burned to set out for the ends of the earth. On! On! his heart seemed to cry. Evening would deepen above the sea, night fall upon the plains, dawn glimmer before the wanderer and show him strange fields and hills and faces. Where?

He looked northward towards Howth. The sea had fallen below the line of seawrack on the shallow side of the breakwater and already the tide was running out fast along the foreshore. Already one long oval bank of sand lay warm and dry amid the wavelets. Here and there warm isles of sand gleamed above the shallow tide, and about the isles and around the long bank and amid the shallow currents of the beach were lightclad gayclad figures, wading and delving.

In a few moments he was barefoot, his stockings folded in his pockets and his canvas shoes dangling by their knotted laces over his shoulders: and, picking a pointed salteaten stick out of the jetsam among the rocks, he clambered down the slope of the breakwater.

There was a long rivulet in the strand: and, as he waded slowly up its course, he wondered at the endless drift of seaweed. Emerald and black and russet and olive, it moved beneath the current, swaying and turning. The water of the rivulet was dark with endless drift and mirrored the high-drifting clouds. The clouds were drifting above him silently and silently the seatangle was drifting below him; and the grey warm air was still: and a new wild life was singing in his veins.

Where was his boyhood now? Where was the soul that had hung back from her destiny, to brood alone upon the shame of her wounds and in her house of squalor and subterfuge to queen it in faded cerements and in wreaths that withered at the touch? Or where was he?

He was alone. He was unheeded, happy and near to the wild heart of life. He was alone and young and wilful and wildhearted, alone amid a waste of wild air and brackish waters and the seaharvest of shells and tangle and veiled grey sunlight and gayclad lightclad figures, of children and girls and voices childish and girlish in the air.

A girl stood before him in midstream, alone and still, gazing out to sea. She seemed like one whom magic had changed into the likeness of a strange and beautiful seabird. Her long slender bare legs were delicate as a crane's and pure save where an emerald trail of seaweed had fashioned itself as a sign upon the flesh. Her thighs, fuller and softhued as ivory, were bared almost to the hips where the white fringes of her drawers were like featherings of soft white down. Her slateblue skirts were kilted boldly about her waist and dovetailed behind her. Her bosom was as a bird's soft and slight, slight and soft as the breast of some darkplumaged dove. But her long fair hair was girlish: and girlish, and touched with the wonder of mortal beauty, her face.

She was alone and still, gazing out to sea; and when she felt his presence and the worship of his eyes her eyes turned to him in quiet sufferance of his gaze, without shame or wantonness. Long, long she suffered his gaze and then quietly withdrew her eyes from his and bent them towards the stream, gently stirring the water with her foot hither and thither. The first faint noise of gently moving water broke the silence, low and faint and whispering, faint as the bells of sleep; hither and thither, hither and thither: and a faint flame trembled on her cheek.

—Heavenly God! cried Stephen's soul, in an outburst of profane joy.

He turned away from her suddenly and set off across the strand. His cheeks were aflame; his body was aglow; his limbs were trembling. On and on and on and on he strode, far out over the sands, singing wildly to the sea, crying to greet the advent of the life that had cried to him.

Her image had passed into his soul for ever and no word had broken the holy silence of his ecstasy. Her eyes had called him and his soul had leaped at the call. To live, to err, to fall, to triumph, to recreate life out of life! A wild angel had appeared to him, the angel of mortal youth and beauty, an envoy from the fair courts of life, to throw open before him in an instant of ecstasy the gates of all the ways of error and glory. On and on and on and on!

He halted suddenly and heard his heart in the silence. How far had he walked? What hour was it?

There was no human figure near him nor any sound borne to him over the air. But the tide was near the turn and already the day was on the wane. He turned landward and ran towards the shore and, running up the sloping beach, reckless of the sharp shingle, found a sandy nook amid a ring of tufted sand-knolls and lay down there that the peace and silence of the evening might still the riot of his blood.

He felt above him the vast indifferent dome and the calm processes of the heavenly bodies; and the earth beneath him, the earth that had borne him, had taken him to her breast.

He closed his eyes in the languor of sleep. His eyelids trembled as if they felt the vast cyclic movement of the earth and her watchers, trembled as if they felt the strange light of some new world. His soul was swooning into some new world, fantastic, dim, uncertain as under sea, traversed by cloudy shapes and beings. A world, a glimmer, or a flower? Glimmering and trembling, trembling and unfolding, a breaking light, an opening flower, it spread in endless succession to itself, breaking in full crimson and unfolding and fading to palest rose, leaf by leaf and wave of light by wave of light, flooding all the heavens with its soft flushes, every flush deeper than other.

Evening had fallen when he woke and the sand and arid grasses of his bed glowed no longer. He rose slowly and, recalling the rapture of his sleep, sighed at its joy.

He climbed to the crest of the sandhill and gazed about him. Evening had fallen. A rim of the young moon cleft the pale waste of sky like the rim of a silver hoop embedded in grey sand; and the tide was flowing in fast to the land with a low whisper of her waves, islanding a few last figures in distant pools.

V

H E DRAINED his third cup of watery tea to the dregs and
  set to chewing the crusts of fried bread that were scattered near him, staring into the dark pool of the jar. The
yellow dripping had been scooped out like a boghole and the
pool under it brought back to his memory the dark turfcoloured water of the bath in Clongowes. The box of pawn-
tickets at his elbow had just been rifled and he took up idly
one after another in his greasy fingers the blue and white
dockets, scrawled and sanded and creased and bearing the
name of the pledger as Daly or MacEvoy.

1 Pair Buskins.
1 D. Coat.
3 Articles and White.
1 Man's Pants.

Then he put them aside and gazed thoughtfully at the lid of
the box, speckled with lousemarks, and asked vaguely:

—How much is the clock fast now?

His mother straightened the battered alarmclock that was
lying on its side in the middle of the kitchen mantelpiece until
its dial showed a quarter to twelve and then laid it once more
on its side.

—An hour and twentyfive minutes, she said. The right time
now is twenty past ten. The dear knows you might try to be in
time for your lectures.

—Fill out the place for me to wash, said Stephen.

—Katey, fill out the place for Stephen to wash.

—Boody, fill out the place for Stephen to wash.

—I can't, I'm going for blue. Fill it out, you, Maggie.

When the enamelled basin had been fitted into the well of

the sink and the old washingglove flung on the side of it he allowed his mother to scrub his neck and root into the folds of his ears and into the interstices at the wings of his nose.

—Well, it's a poor case, she said, when a university student is so dirty that his mother has to wash him.

—But it gives you pleasure, said Stephen calmly.

An earsplitting whistle was heard from upstairs and his mother thrust a damp overall into his hands, saying:

—Dry yourself and hurry out for the love of goodness.

A second shrill whistle, prolonged angrily, brought one of the girls to the foot of the staircase.

—Yes, father?

—Is your lazy bitch of a brother gone out yet?

—Yes, father.

—Sure?

—Yes, father.

—Hm!

The girl came back making signs to him to be quick and go out quietly by the back. Stephen laughed and said:

—He has a curious idea of genders if he thinks a bitch is masculine.

—Ah, it's a scandalous shame for you, Stephen, said his mother, and you'll live to rue the day you set your foot in that place. I know how it has changed you.

—Good morning, everybody, said Stephen, smiling and kissing the tips of his fingers in adieu.

The lane behind the terrace was waterlogged and as he went down it slowly, choosing his steps amid heaps of wet rubbish, he heard a mad nun screeching in the nuns' madhouse beyond the wall.

—Jesus! O Jesus! Jesus!

He shook the sound out of his ears by an angry toss of his head and hurried on, stumbling through the mouldering offal, his heart already bitten by an ache of loathing and bitterness. His father's whistle, his mother's mutterings, the screech of an unseen maniac were to him now so many voices offending and threatening to humble the pride of his youth. He drove their echoes even out of his heart with an execration: but, as he walked down the avenue and felt the grey morning light falling about him through the dripping trees and smelt the strange wild smell of the wet leaves and bark, his soul was loosed of her miseries.

The rainladen trees of the avenue evoked in him, as always, memories of the girls and women in the plays of Gerhart Hauptmann; and the memory of their pale sorrows and the fragrance falling from the wet branches mingled in a mood of quiet joy. His morning walk across the city had begun, and he foreknew that as he passed the sloblands of Fairview he would think of the cloistral silverveined prose of Newman, that as he walked along the North Strand Road, glancing idly at the windows of the provision shops, he would recall the dark humour of Guido Cavalcanti and smile, that as he went by Baird's stonecutting works in Talbot Place the spirit of Ibsen would blow through him like a keen wind, a spirit of wayward boyish beauty, and that passing a grimy marinedealer's shop beyond the Liffey he would repeat the song by Ben Jonson which begins:

> *I was not wearier where I lay.*

His mind, when wearied of its search for the essence of beauty amid the spectral words of Aristotle or Aquinas, turned often for its pleasure to the dainty songs of the Elizabethans. His mind, in the vesture of a doubting monk, stood often in shadow under the windows of that age, to hear the grave and mocking music of the lutenists or the frank laughter of waistcoateers until a laugh too low, a phrase, tarnished by time, of chambering and false honour, stung his monkish pride and drove him on from his lurkingplace.

The lore which he was believed to pass his days brooding upon so that it had rapt him from the companionships of youth was only a garner of slender sentences from Aristotle's poetics and psychology and a *Synopsis Philosophiæ Scho-*

lasticæ ad mentem divi Thomæ. His thinking was a dusk of doubt and selfmistrust lit up at moments by the lightnings of intuition, but lightnings of so clear a splendour that in those moments the world perished about his feet as if it had been fireconsumed: and thereafter his tongue grew heavy and he met the eyes of others with unanswering eyes for he felt that the spirit of beauty had folded him round like a mantle and that in revery at least he had been acquainted with nobility. But, when this brief pride of silence upheld him no longer, he was glad to find himself still in the midst of common lives, passing on his way amid the squalor and noise and sloth of the city fearlessly and with a light heart.

Near the hoardings on the canal he met the consumptive man with the doll's face and the brimless hat coming towards him down the slope of the bridge with little steps, tightly buttoned into his chocolate overcoat, and holding his furled umbrella a span or two from him like a diviningrod. It must be eleven, he thought, and peered into a dairy to see the time. The clock in the dairy told him that it was five minutes to five but, as he turned away, he heard a clock somewhere near him, but unseen, beating eleven strokes in swift precision. He laughed as he heard it for it made him think of MacCann and he saw him a squat figure in a shooting jacket and breeches and with a fair goatee, standing in the wind at Hopkins' corner, and heard him say:

—Dedalus, you're an antisocial being, wrapped up in yourself. I'm not. I'm a democrat: and I'll work and act for social liberty and equality among all classes and sexes in the United States of the Europe of the future.

Eleven! Then he was late for that lecture too. What day of the week was it? He stopped at a newsagent's to read the headline of a placard. Thursday. Ten to eleven, English; eleven to twelve, French; twelve to one, physics. He fancied to himself the English lecture and felt, even at that distance, restless and helpless. He saw the heads of his classmates meekly bent as they wrote in their notebooks the points they were bidden to note, nominal definitions, essential definitions and examples or dates of birth or death, chief works, a favourable and an unfavourable criticism side by side. His own head was unbent for his thoughts wandered abroad and whether he looked around the little class of students or out of the window across the desolate gardens of the green an odour assailed him of cheerless cellardamp and decay. Another head than his, right before him in the first benches, was poised squarely above its bending fellows like the head of a priest appealing without humility to the tabernacle for the humble worshippers about him. Why was it that when he thought of Cranly he could never raise before his mind the entire image of his body but only the image of the head and face? Even now against the grey curtain of the morning he saw it before him like the phantom of a dream, the face of a severed head or deathmask, crowned on the brows by its stiff black upright hair as by an iron crown. It was a priestlike face, priestlike in its pallor, in the widewinged nose, in the shadowings below the eyes and along the jaws, priestlike in the lips that were long and bloodless and faintly smiling: and Stephen, remembering swiftly how he had told Cranly of all the tumults and unrest and longings in his soul, day after day and night by night, only to be answered by his friend's listening silence, would have told himself that it was the face of a guilty priest who heard confessions of those whom he had not power to absolve but that he felt again in memory the gaze of its dark womanish eyes.

Through this image he had a glimpse of a strange dark cavern of speculation but at once turned away from it, feeling that it was not yet the hour to enter it. But the nightshade of his friend's listlessness seemed to be diffusing in the air around him a tenuous and deadly exhalation and he found himself glancing from one casual word to another on his right or left in stolid wonder that they had been so silently emptied of instantaneous sense until every mean shop legend bound his mind like the words of a spell and his soul shrivelled up, sighing with age as he walked on in a lane among heaps of dead language. His own consciousness of language was ebbing from his brain and trickling into the very words themselves which set to band and disband themselves in wayward rhythms:

> *The ivy whines upon the wall*
> *And whines and twines upon the wall*
> *The ivy whines upon the wall*
> *The yellow ivy on the wall*
> *Ivy, ivy up the wall.*

Did any one ever hear such drivel? Lord Almighty! Who ever heard of ivy whining on a wall? Yellow ivy: that was all right. Yellow ivory also. And what about ivory ivy?

The word now shone in his brain, clearer and brighter than any ivory sawn from the mottled tusks of elephants. *Ivory, ivoire, avorio, ebur.* One of the first examples that he had learnt in Latin had run: *India mittit ebur;* and he recalled the shrewd northern face of the rector who had taught him to construe the Metamorphoses of Ovid in a courtly English, made whimsical by the mention of porkers and potsherds and chines of bacon. He had learnt what little he knew of the laws of Latin verse from a ragged book written by a Portuguese priest.

> *Contrahit orator, variant in carmine vates.*

The crises and victories and secessions in Roman history were handed on to him in the trite words *in tanto discrimine* and he had tried to peer into the social life of the city of cities through the words *implere ollam denariorum* which the rector had rendered sonorously as the filling of a pot with denaries. The pages of his timeworn Horace never felt cold to the touch even when his own fingers were cold: they were human pages: and fifty years before they had been turned by the human fingers of John Duncan Inverarity and by his brother, William Malcolm Inverarity. Yes, those were noble names on the dusky flyleaf and, even for so poor a Latinist as he, the dusky verses

were as fragrant as though they had lain all those years in
myrtle and lavender and vervain; but yet it wounded him to
think that he would never be but a shy guest at the feast of the
world's culture and that the monkish learning, in terms of
which he was striving to forge out an esthetic philosophy, was
held no higher by the age he lived in than the subtle and
curious jargons of heraldry and falconry.

The grey block of Trinity on his left, set heavily in the city's
ignorance like a great dull stone set in a cumbrous ring, pulled
his mind downward; and while he was striving this way and
that to free his feet from the fetters of the reformed conscience
he came upon the droll statue of the national poet of Ireland.

He looked at it without anger: for, though sloth of the body
and of the soul crept over it like unseen vermin, over the
shuffling feet and up the folds of the cloak and around the
servile head, it seemed humbly conscious of its indignity. It
was a Firbolg in the borrowed cloak of a Milesian; and he
thought of his friend Davin, the peasant student. It was a
jesting name between them but the young peasant bore with it
lightly saying:

—Go on, Stevie, I have a hard head, you tell me. Call me
what you will.

The homely version of his christian name on the lips of his
friend had touched Stephen pleasantly when first heard for he
was as formal in speech with others as they were with him.
Often, as he sat in Davin's rooms in Grantham Street, wondering at his friend's wellmade boots that flanked the wall pair by
pair and repeating for his friend's simple ear the verses and
cadences of others which were the veils of his own longing and
dejection, the rude Firbolg mind of his listener had drawn his
mind towards it and flung it back again, drawing it by a quiet
inbred courtesy of attention or by a quaint turn of old English
speech or by the force of its delight in rude bodily skill—for
Davin had sat at the feet of Michael Cusack, the Gael—
repelling swiftly and suddenly by a grossness of intelligence or
by a bluntness of feeling or by a dull stare of terror in the eyes,

the terror of soul of a starving Irish village in which the curfew was still a nightly fear.

Side by side with his memory of the deeds of prowess of his uncle Mat Davin, the athlete, the young peasant worshipped the sorrowful legend of Ireland. The gossip of his fellowstudents which strove to render the flat life of the college significant at any cost loved to think of him as a young fenian. His nurse had taught him Irish and shaped his rude imagination by the broken lights of Irish myth. He stood towards this myth upon which no individual mind had ever drawn out a line of beauty and to its unwieldy tales that divided themselves as they moved down the cycles in the same attitude as towards the Roman catholic religion, the attitude of a dullwitted loyal serf. Whatsoever of thought or of feeling came to him from England or by way of English culture his mind stood armed against in obedience to a password: and of the world that lay beyond England he knew only the foreign legion of France in which he spoke of serving.

Coupling this ambition with the young man's humour Stephen had often called him one of the tame geese: and there was even a point of irritation in the name pointed against that very reluctance of speech and deed in his friend which seemed so often to stand between Stephen's mind, eager of speculation, and the hidden ways of Irish life.

One night the young peasant, his spirit stung by the violent or luxurious language in which Stephen escaped from the cold silence of intellectual revolt, had called up before Stephen's mind a strange vision. The two were walking slowly towards Davin's room through the dark narrow streets of the poorer jews.

—A thing happened to myself, Stevie, last autumn, coming on winter, and I never told it to a living soul and you are the first person now I ever told it to. I disremember if it was October or November. It was October because it was before I came up here to join the matriculation class.

Stephen had turned his smiling eyes towards his friend's

face, flattered by his confidence and won over to sympathy by the speaker's simple accent.

—I was away all that day from my own place over in Buttevant—I don't know if you know where that is—at a hurling match between the Croke's Own Boys and the Fearless Thurles and by God, Stevie, that was the hard fight. My first cousin, Fonsy Davin, was stripped to his buff that day minding cool for the Limericks but he was up with the forwards half the time and shouting like mad. I never will forget that day. One of the Crokes made a woeful wipe at him one time with his camaun and I declare to God he was within an aim's ace of getting it at the side of the temple. O, honest to God, if the crook of it caught him that time he was done for.

—I am glad he escaped, Stephen had said with a laugh, but surely that's not the strange thing that happened you?

—Well, I suppose that doesn't interest you but leastways there was such noise after the match that I missed the train home and I couldn't get any kind of a yoke to give me a lift for, as luck would have it, there was a mass meeting that same day over in Castletownroche and all the cars in the country were there. So there was nothing for it only to stay the night or to foot it out. Well, I started to walk and on I went and it was coming on night when I got into the Ballyhoura hills; that's better than ten miles from Kilmallock and there's a long lonely road after that. You wouldn't see the sign of a christian house along the road or hear a sound. It was pitch dark almost. Once or twice I stopped by the way under a bush to redden my pipe and only for the dew was thick I'd have stretched out there and slept. At last, after a bend of the road, I spied a little cottage with a light in the window. I went up and knocked at the door. A voice asked who was there and I answered I was over at the match in Buttevant and was walking back and that I'd be thankful for a glass of water. After a while a young woman opened the door and brought me out a big mug of milk. She was half undressed as if she was going to bed when I knocked and she had her hair hanging; and I thought by her figure and by something in the look of her eyes that she must be carrying a child. She kept me in talk a long while at the door and I thought it strange because her breast and her shoulders were bare. She asked me was I tired and would I like to stop the night there. She said she was all alone in the house and that her husband had gone that morning to Queenstown with his sister to see her off. And all the time she was talking, Stevie, she had her eyes fixed on my face and she stood so close to me I could hear her breathing. When I handed her back the mug at last she took my hand to draw me in over the threshold and said: *Come in and stay the night here. You've no call to be frightened. There's no one in it but ourselves. . . .* I didn't go in, Stevie. I thanked her and went on my way again, all in a fever. At the first bend of the road I looked back and she was standing at the door.

The last words of Davin's story sang in his memory and the figure of the woman in the story stood forth, reflected in other figures of the peasant women whom he had seen standing in the doorways at Clane as the college cars drove by, as a type of her race and his own, a batlike soul waking to the consciousness of itself in darkness and secrecy and loneliness and, through the eyes and voice and gesture of a woman without guile, calling the stranger to her bed.

A hand was laid on his arm and a young voice cried:

—Ah, gentleman, your own girl, sir! The first handsel today, gentleman. Buy that lovely bunch. Will you, gentleman?

The blue flowers which she lifted towards him and her young blue eyes seemed to him at that instant images of guilelessness; and he halted till the image had vanished and he saw only her ragged dress and damp coarse hair and hoydenish face.

—Do, gentleman! Don't forget your own girl, sir!

—I have no money, said Stephen.

—Buy them lovely ones, will you, sir? Only a penny.

—Did you hear what I said? asked Stephen, bending towards her. I told you I had no money. I tell you again now.

—Well, sure, you will some day, sir, please God, the girl answered after an instant.

—Possibly, said Stephen, but I don't think it likely.

He left her quickly, fearing that her intimacy might turn to gibing and wishing to be out of the way before she offered her ware to another, a tourist from England or a student of Trinity. Grafton Street, along which he walked, prolonged that moment of discouraged poverty. In the roadway at the head of the street a slab was set to the memory of Wolfe Tone and he remembered having been present with his father at its laying. He remembered with bitterness that scene of tawdry tribute. There were four French delegates in a brake and one, a plump smiling young man, held, wedged on a stick, a card on which were printed the words: *Vive l'Irlande!*

But the trees in Stephen's Green were fragrant of rain and the rainsodden earth gave forth its mortal odour, a faint incense rising upward through the mould from many hearts. The soul of the gallant venal city which his elders had told him of had shrunk with time to a faint mortal odour rising from the earth and he knew that in a moment when he entered the sombre college he would be conscious of a corruption other than that of Buck Egan and Burnchapel Whaley.

It was too late to go upstairs to the French class. He crossed the hall and took the corridor to the left which led to the physics theatre. The corridor was dark and silent but not unwatchful. Why did he feel that it was not unwatchful? Was it because he had heard that in Buck Whaley's time there was a secret staircase there? Or was the jesuit house extraterritorial and was he walking among aliens? The Ireland of Tone and of Parnell seemed to have receded in space.

He opened the door of the theatre and halted in the chilly grey light that struggled through the dusty windows. A figure was crouching before the large grate and by its leanness and greyness he knew that it was the dean of studies lighting the fire. Stephen closed the door quietly and approached the fireplace.

—Good morning, sir! Can I help you?

The priest looked up quickly and said:

—One moment now, Mr Dedalus, and you will see. There is an art in lighting a fire. We have the liberal arts and we have the useful arts. This is one of the useful arts.

—I will try to learn it, said Stephen.

—Not too much coal, said the dean, working briskly at his task, that is one of the secrets.

He produced four candlebutts from the sidepockets of his soutane and placed them deftly among the coals and twisted papers. Stephen watched him in silence. Kneeling thus on the flagstone to kindle the fire and busied with the disposition of his wisps of paper and candlebutts he seemed more than ever a humble server making ready the place of sacrifice in an empty temple, a levite of the Lord. Like a levite's robe of plain linen the faded worn soutane draped the kneeling figure of one whom the canonicals or the bellbordered ephod would irk and trouble. His very body had waxed old in lowly service of the Lord—in tending the fire upon the altar, in bearing tidings secretly, in waiting upon worldlings, in striking swiftly when bidden—and yet had remained ungraced by aught of saintly or of prelatic beauty. Nay, his very soul had waxed old in that service without growing towards light and beauty or spreading abroad a sweet odour of her sanctity—a mortified will no more responsive to the thrill of its obedience than was to the thrill of love or combat his aging body, spare and sinewy, greyed with a silverpointed down.

The dean rested back on his hunkers and watched the sticks catch. Stephen, to fill the silence, said:

—I am sure I could not light a fire.

—You are an artist, are you not, Mr Dedalus? said the dean, glancing up and blinking his pale eyes. The object of the artist is the creation of the beautiful. What the beautiful is is another question.

He rubbed his hands slowly and drily over the difficulty.

—Can you solve that question now? he asked.

—Aquinas, answered Stephen, says *Pulcra sunt quæ visa placent*.

—This fire before us, said the dean, will be pleasing to the eye. Will it therefore be beautiful?

—In so far as it is apprehended by the sight, which I suppose means here esthetic intellection, it will be beautiful. But Aquinas also says *Bonum est in quod tendit appetitus*. In so far as it satisfies the animal craving for warmth fire is a good. In hell however it is an evil.

—Quite so, said the dean, you have certainly hit the nail on the head.

He rose nimbly and went towards the door, set it ajar and said:

—A draught is said to be a help in these matters.

As he came back to the hearth, limping slightly but with a brisk step, Stephen saw the silent soul of a jesuit look out at him from the pale loveless eyes. Like Ignatius he was lame but in his eyes burned no spark of Ignatius' enthusiasm. Even the legendary craft of the company, a craft subtler and more secret than its fabled books of secret subtle wisdom, had not fired his soul with the energy of apostleship. It seemed as if he used the shifts and lore and cunning of the world, as bidden to do, for the greater glory of God, without joy in their handling or hatred of that in them which was evil but turning them, with a firm gesture of obedience, back upon themselves: and for all this silent service it seemed as if he loved not at all the master and little, if at all, the ends he served. *Similiter atque senis baculus,* he was, as the founder would have had him, like a staff in an old man's hand, to be left in a corner, to be leaned on in the road at nightfall or in stress of weather, to lie with a lady's nosegay on a garden seat, to be raised in menace.

The dean returned to the hearth and began to stroke his chin.

—When may we expect to have something from you on the esthetic question? he asked.

—From me! said Stephen in astonishment. I stumble on an idea once a fortnight if I am lucky.

—These questions are very profound, Mr Dedalus, said the dean. It is like looking down from the cliffs of Moher into the depths. Many go down into the depths and never come up. Only the trained diver can go down into those depths and explore them and come to the surface again.

—If you mean speculation, sir, said Stephen, I also am sure that there is no such thing as free thinking inasmuch as all thinking must be bound by its own laws.

—Ha!

—For my purpose I can work on at present by the light of one or two ideas of Aristotle and Aquinas.

—I see. I quite see your point.

—I need them only for my own use and guidance until I have done something for myself by their light. If the lamp smokes or smells I shall try to trim it. If it does not give light enough I shall sell it and buy another.

—Epictetus also had a lamp, said the dean, which was sold for a fancy price after his death. It was the lamp he wrote his philosophical dissertations by. You know Epictetus?

—An old gentleman, said Stephen coarsely, who said that the soul is very like a bucketful of water.

—He tells us in his homely way, the dean went on, that he put an iron lamp before a statue of one of the gods and that a thief stole the lamp. What did the philosopher do? He reflected that it was in the character of a thief to steal and determined to buy an earthen lamp next day instead of the iron lamp.

A smell of molten tallow came up from the dean's candle-butts and fused itself in Stephen's consciousness with the jingle of the words, bucket and lamp and lamp and bucket. The priest's voice too had a hard jingling tone. Stephen's mind halted by instinct, checked by the strange tone and the imagery and by the priest's face which seemed like an unlit lamp or a reflector hung in a false focus. What lay behind it or within it? A dull torpor of the soul or the dullness of the thundercloud, charged with intellection and capable of the gloom of God?

—I meant a different kind of lamp, sir, said Stephen.

—Undoubtedly, said the dean.

—One difficulty, said Stephen, in esthetic discussion is to know whether words are being used according to the literary tradition or according to the tradition of the marketplace. I remember a sentence of Newman's in which he says of the Blessed Virgin that she was detained in the full company of the saints. The use of the word in the marketplace is quite different. *I hope I am not detaining you.*

—Not in the least, said the dean politely.

—No, no, said Stephen, smiling, I mean . . .

—Yes, yes: I see, said the dean quickly, I quite catch the point: *detain.*

He thrust forward his under jaw and uttered a dry short cough.

—To return to the lamp, he said, the feeding of it is also a nice problem. You must choose the pure oil and you must be careful when you pour it in not to overflow it, not to pour in more than the funnel can hold.

—What funnel? asked Stephen.

—The funnel through which you pour the oil into your lamp.

—That? said Stephen. Is that called a funnel? Is it not a tundish?

—What is a tundish?

—That. The . . . the funnel.

—Is that called a tundish in Ireland? asked the dean. I never heard the word in my life.

—It is called a tundish in Lower Drumcondra, said Stephen laughing, where they speak the best English.

—A tundish, said the dean reflectively. That is a most interesting word. I must look that word up. Upon my word I must.

His courtesy of manner rang a little false, and Stephen

looked at the English convert with the same eyes as the elder brother in the parable may have turned on the prodigal. A humble follower in the wake of clamorous conversions, a poor Englishman in Ireland, he seemed to have entered on the stage of jesuit history when that strange play of intrigue and suffering and envy and struggle and indignity had been all but given through—a late comer, a tardy spirit. From what had he set out? Perhaps he had been born and bred among serious dissenters, seeing salvation in Jesus only and abhorring the vain pomps of the establishment. Had he felt the need of an implicit faith amid the welter of sectarianism and the jargon of its turbulent schisms, six principle men, peculiar people, seed and snake baptists, supralapsarian dogmatists? Had he found the true church all of a sudden in winding up to the end like a reel of cotton some finespun line of reasoning upon in-sufflation or the imposition of hands or the procession of the Holy Ghost? Or had Lord Christ touched him and bidden him follow, like that disciple who had sat at the receipt of custom, as he sat by the door of some zincroofed chapel, yawning and telling over his church pence?

The dean repeated the word yet again.

—Tundish! Well now, that is interesting!

—The question you asked me a moment ago seems to me more interesting. What is that beauty which the artist struggles to express from lumps of earth, said Stephen coldly.

The little word seemed to have turned a rapier point of his sensitiveness against this courteous and vigilant foe. He felt with a smart of dejection that the man to whom he was speaking was a countryman of Ben Jonson. He thought:

—The language in which we are speaking is his before it is mine. How different are the words *home, Christ, ale, master,* on his lips and on mine! I cannot speak or write these words without unrest of spirit. His language, so familiar and so foreign, will always be for me an acquired speech. I have not made or accepted its words. My voice holds them at bay. My soul frets in the shadow of his language.

—And to distinguish between the beautiful and the sublime, the dean added. To distinguish between moral beauty and material beauty. And to inquire what kind of beauty is proper to each of the various arts. These are some interesting points we might take up.

Stephen, disheartened suddenly by the dean's firm dry tone, was silent. The dean also was silent: and through the silence a distant noise of many boots and confused voices came up the staircase.

—In pursuing these speculations, said the dean conclusively, there is however the danger of perishing of inanition. First you must take your degree. Set that before you as your first aim. Then little by little, you will see your way. I mean in every sense, your way in life and in thinking. It may be uphill pedalling at first. Take Mr Moonan. He was a long time before he got to the top. But he got there.

—I may not have his talent, said Stephen quietly.

—You never know, said the dean brightly. We never can say what is in us. I most certainly should not be despondent. *Per aspera ad astra.*

He left the hearth quickly and went towards the landing to oversee the arrival of the first arts' class.

Leaning against the fireplace Stephen heard him greet briskly and impartially every student of the class and could almost see the frank smiles of the coarser students. A desolating pity began to fall like a dew upon his easily embittered heart for this faithful servingman of the knightly Loyola, for this halfbrother of the clergy, more venal than they in speech, more steadfast of soul than they, one whom he would never call his ghostly father: and he thought how this man and his companions had earned the name of worldlings at the hands not of the unworldly only but of the worldly also for having pleaded, during all their history, at the bar of God's justice for the souls of the lax and the lukewarm and the prudent.

The entry of the professor was signalled by a few rounds of Kentish fire from the heavy boots of those students who sat on the highest tier of the gloomy theatre under the grey cobwebbed windows. The calling of the roll began and the responses to the names were given out in all tones until the name of Peter Byrne was reached.

—Here!

A deep base note in response came from the upper tier, followed by coughs of protest along the other benches.

The professor paused in his reading and called the next name:

—Cranly!

No answer.

—Mr Cranly!

A smile flew across Stephen's face as he thought of his friend's studies.

—Try Leopardstown! said a voice from the bench behind.

Stephen glanced up quickly but Moynihan's snoutish face, outlined on the grey light, was impassive. A formula was given out. Amid the rustling of the notebooks Stephen turned back again and said:

—Give me some paper for God's sake.

—Are you as bad as that? asked Moynihan with a broad grin.

He tore a sheet from his scribbler and passed it down, whispering:

—In case of necessity any layman or woman can do it.

The formula which he wrote obediently on the sheet of paper, the coiling and uncoiling calculations of the professor, the spectrelike symbols of force and velocity fascinated and jaded Stephen's mind. He had heard some say that the old professor was an atheist freemason. O the grey dull day! It seemed a limbo of painless patient consciousness through which souls of mathematicians might wander, projecting long slender fabrics from plane to plane of ever rarer and paler twilight, radiating swift eddies to the last verges of a universe ever vaster, farther and more impalpable.

—So we must distinguish between elliptical and ellipsoidal. Perhaps some of you gentlemen may be familiar with the

works of Mr W. S. Gilbert. In one of his songs he speaks of
the billiard sharp who is condemned to play:

> *On a cloth untrue*
> *With a twisted cue*
> *And elliptical billiard balls.*

—He means a ball having the form of the ellipsoid of the
principal axes of which I spoke a moment ago.

Moynihan leaned down towards Stephen's ear and murmured:

—What price ellipsoidal balls! Chase me, ladies, I'm in the
cavalry!

His fellowstudent's rude humour ran like a gust through the
cloister of Stephen's mind, shaking into gay life limp priestly
vestments that hung upon the walls, setting them to sway and
caper in a sabbath of misrule. The forms of the community
emerged from the gustblown vestments, the dean of studies,
the portly florid bursar with his cap of grey hair, the president,
the little priest with feathery hair who wrote devout verses, the
squat peasant form of the professor of economics, the tall
form of the young professor of mental science discussing on
the landing a case of conscience with his class like a giraffe
cropping high leafage among a herd of antelopes, the grave
troubled prefect of the sodality, the plump roundheaded
professor of Italian with his rogue's eyes. They came ambling
and stumbling, tumbling and capering, kilting their gowns for
leap frog, holding one another back, shaken with deep fast
laughter, smacking one another behind and laughing at their
rude malice, calling to one another by familiar nicknames,
protesting with sudden dignity at some rough usage, whispering two and two behind their hands.

The professor had gone to the glass cases on the sidewall
from a shelf of which he took down a set of coils, blew away
the dust from many points and, bearing it carefully to the
table, held a finger on it while he proceeded with his lecture.
He explained that the wires in modern coils were of a compound called platinoid lately discovered by F. W. Martino.

He spoke clearly the initials and surname of the discoverer. Moynihan whispered from behind:

—Good old Fresh Water Martin!

—Ask him, Stephen whispered back with weary humour, if he wants a subject for electrocution. He can have me.

Moynihan, seeing the professor bend over the coils, rose in his bench and, clacking noiselessly the fingers of his right hand, began to call with the voice of a slobbering urchin:

—Please, teacher! Please, teacher! This boy is after saying a bad word, teacher.

—Platinoid, the professor said solemnly, is preferred to German silver because it has a lower coefficient of resistance variation by changes of temperature. The platinoid wire is insulated and the covering of silk that insulates it is wound on the ebonite bobbins just where my finger is. If it were wound single an extra current would be induced in the coils. The bobbins are saturated in hot paraffin wax . . .

A sharp Ulster voice said from the bench below Stephen:

—Are we likely to be asked questions on applied science?

The professor began to juggle gravely with the terms pure science and applied science. A heavybuilt student wearing gold spectacles stared with some wonder at the questioner. Moynihan murmured from behind in his natural voice:

—Isn't MacAlister a devil for his pound of flesh?

Stephen looked down coldly on the oblong skull beneath him overgrown with tangled twinecoloured hair. The voice, the accent, the mind of the questioner offended him and he allowed the offence to carry him towards wilful unkindness, bidding his mind think that the student's father would have done better had he sent his son to Belfast to study and have saved something on the train fare by so doing.

The oblong skull beneath did not turn to meet this shaft of thought and yet the shaft came back to its bowstring: for he saw in a moment the student's wheypale face.

—That thought is not mine, he said to himself quickly. It came from the comic Irishman in the bench behind. Patience. Can you say with certitude by whom the soul of your race was bartered and its elect betrayed—by the questioner or by the mocker? Patience. Remember Epictetus. It is probably in his character to ask such a question at such a moment in such a tone and to pronounce the word *science* as a monosyllable.

The droning voice of the professor continued to wind itself slowly round and round the coils it spoke of, doubling, trebling, quadrupling its somnolent energy as the coil multiplied its ohms of resistance.

Moynihan's voice called from behind in echo to a distant bell:

—Closing time, gents!

The entrance hall was crowded and loud with talk. On a table near the door were two photographs in frames and between them a long roll of paper bearing an irregular tail of signatures. MacCann went briskly to and fro among the students, talking rapidly, answering rebuffs and leading one after another to the table. In the inner hall the dean of studies stood talking to a young professor, stroking his chin gravely and nodding his head.

Stephen, checked by the crowd at the door, halted irresolutely. From under the wide falling leaf of a soft hat Cranly's dark eyes were watching him.

—Have you signed? Stephen asked.

Cranly closed his long thinlipped mouth, communed with himself an instant and answered:

—*Ego habeo.*

—What is it for?

—*Quod?*

—What is it for?

Cranly turned his pale face to Stephen and said blandly and bitterly:

—*Per pax universalis.*

Stephen pointed to the Csar's photograph and said:

—He has the face of a besotted Christ.

The scorn and anger in his voice brought Cranly's eyes back from a calm survey of the walls of the hall.

—Are you annoyed? he asked.

—No, answered Stephen.

—Are you in bad humour?

—No.

—*Credo ut vos sanguinarius mendax estis,* said Cranly, *quia facies vostra monstrat ut vos in damno malo humore estis.*

Moynihan, on his way to the table, said in Stephen's ear:

—MacCann is in tiptop form. Ready to shed the last drop. Brandnew world. No stimulants and votes for the bitches.

Stephen smiled at the manner of this confidence and, when Moynihan had passed, turned again to meet Cranly's eyes.

—Perhaps you can tell me, he said, why he pours his soul so freely into my ear. Can you?

A dull scowl appeared on Cranly's forehead. He stared at the table where Moynihan had bent to write his name on the roll, and then said flatly:

—A sugar!

—*Quis est in malo humore,* said Stephen, *ego aut vos?*

Cranly did not take up the taunt. He brooded sourly on his judgment and repeated with the same flat force:

—A flaming bloody sugar, that's what he is!

It was his epitaph for all dead friendships and Stephen wondered whether it would ever be spoken in the same tone over his memory. The heavy lumpish phrase sank slowly out of hearing like a stone through a quagmire. Stephen saw it sink as he had seen many another, feeling its heaviness depress his heart. Cranly's speech, unlike that of Davin, had neither rare phrases of Elizabethan English nor quaintly turned versions of Irish idioms. Its drawl was an echo of the quays of Dublin given back by a bleak decaying seaport, its energy an echo of the sacred eloquence of Dublin given back flatly by a Wicklow pulpit.

The heavy scowl faded from Cranly's face as MacCann marched briskly towards them from the other side of the hall.

—Here you are! said MacCann cheerily.

—Here I am! said Stephen.

—Late as usual. Can you not combine the progressive tendency with a respect for punctuality?

—That question is out of order, said Stephen. Next business.

His smiling eyes were fixed on a silverwrapped tablet of milk chocolate which peeped out of the propagandist's breastpocket. A little ring of listeners closed round to hear the war of wits. A lean student with olive skin and lank black hair thrust his face between the two, glancing from one to the other at each phrase and seeming to try to catch each flying phrase in his open moist mouth. Cranly took a small grey handball from his pocket and began to examine it closely, turning it over and over.

—Next business? said MacCann. Hom!

He gave a loud cough of laughter, smiled broadly and tugged twice at the strawcoloured goatee which hung from his blunt chin.

—The next business is to sign the testimonial.

—Will you pay me anything if I sign? asked Stephen.

—I thought you were an idealist, said MacCann.

The gipsylike student looked about him and addressed the onlookers in an indistinct bleating voice.

—By hell, that's a queer notion. I consider that notion to be a mercenary notion.

His voice faded into silence. No heed was paid to his words. He turned his olive face, equine in expression, towards Stephen, inviting him to speak again.

MacCann began to speak with fluent energy of the Csar's rescript, of Stead, of general disarmament, arbitration in cases of international disputes, of the signs of the times, of the new humanity and the new gospel of life which would make it the business of the community to secure as cheaply as possible the greatest possible happiness of the greatest possible number.

The gipsy student responded to the close of the period by crying:

—Three cheers for universal brotherhood!

—Go on, Temple, said a stout ruddy student near him. I'll stand you a pint after.

—I'm a believer in universal brotherhood, said Temple, glancing about him out of his dark, oval eyes. Marx is only a bloody cod.

Cranly gripped his arm tightly to check his tongue, smiling uneasily, and repeated:

—Easy, easy, easy!

Temple struggled to free his arm but continued, his mouth flecked by a thin foam:

—Socialism was founded by an Irishman and the first man in Europe who preached the freedom of thought was Collins. Two hundred years ago. He denounced priestcraft, the philosopher of Middlesex. Three cheers for John Anthony Collins!

A thin voice from the verge of the ring replied:

—Pip! pip!

Moynihan murmured beside Stephen's ear:

—And what about John Anthony's poor little sister:

> *Lottie Collins lost her drawers;*
> *Won't you kindly lend her yours?*

Stephen laughed and Moynihan, pleased with the result, murmured again:

—We'll have five bob each way on John Anthony Collins.

—I am waiting for your answer, said MacCann briefly.

—The affair doesn't interest me in the least, said Stephen wearily. You know that well. Why do you make a scene about it?

—Good! said MacCann, smacking his lips. You are a reactionary then?

—Do you think you impress me, Stephen asked, when you flourish your wooden sword?

—Metaphors! said MacCann bluntly. Come to facts.

Stephen blushed and turned aside. MacCann stood his ground and said with hostile humour:

—Minor poets, I suppose, are above such trivial questions as the question of universal peace.

Cranly raised his head and held the handball between the two students by way of a peaceoffering, saying:

—*Pax super totum sanguinarium globum.*

Stephen, moving away the bystanders, jerked his shoulder angrily in the direction of the Csar's image, saying:

—Keep your icon. If we must have a Jesus, let us have a legitimate Jesus.

—By hell, that's a good one! said the gipsy student to those about him. That's a fine expression. I like that expression immensely.

He gulped down the spittle in his throat as if he were gulping down the phrase and, fumbling at the peak of his tweed cap, turned to Stephen, saying:

—Excuse me, sir, what do you mean by that expression you uttered just now?

Feeling himself jostled by the students near him, he said to them:

—I am curious to know now what he meant by that expression.

He turned again to Stephen and said in a whisper:

—Do you believe in Jesus? I believe in man. Of course, I don't know if you believe in man. I admire you, sir. I admire the mind of man independent of all religions. Is that your opinion about the mind of Jesus?

—Go on, Temple, said the stout ruddy student, returning, as was his wont, to his first idea, that pint is waiting for you.

—He thinks I'm an imbecile, Temple explained to Stephen, because I'm a believer in the power of mind.

Cranly linked his arms into those of Stephen and his admirer and said:

—*Nos ad manum ballum jocabimus.*

Stephen, in the act of being led away, caught sight of Mac-Cann's flushed bluntfeatured face.

—My signature is of no account, he said politely. You are right to go your way. Leave me to go mine.

—Dedalus, said MacCann crisply, I believe you're a good

fellow but you have yet to learn the dignity of altruism and the responsibility of the human individual.

A voice said:

—Intellectual crankery is better out of this movement than in it.

Stephen, recognising the harsh tone of MacAlister's voice, did not turn in the direction of the voice. Cranly pushed solemnly through the throng of students, linking Stephen and Temple like a celebrant attended by his ministers on his way to the altar.

Temple bent eagerly across Cranly's breast and said:

—Did you hear MacAlister what he said? That youth is jealous of you. Did you see that? I bet Cranly didn't see that. By hell, I saw that at once.

As they crossed the inner hall the dean of studies was in the act of escaping from the student with whom he had been conversing. He stood at the foot of the staircase, a foot on the lowest step, his threadbare soutane gathered about him for the ascent with womanish care, nodding his head often and repeating:

—Not a doubt of it, Mr Hackett! Very fine! Not a doubt of it!

In the middle of the hall the prefect of the college sodality was speaking earnestly, in a soft querulous voice, with a boarder. As he spoke he wrinkled a little his freckled brow and bit, between his phrases, at a tiny bone pencil.

—I hope the matric men will all come. The first arts men are pretty sure. Second arts too. We must make sure of the newcomers.

Temple bent again across Cranly, as they were passing through the doorway, and said in a swift whisper:

—Do you know that he is a married man? He was a married man before they converted him. He has a wife and children somewhere. By hell, I think that's the queerest notion I ever heard! Eh?

His whisper trailed off into sly cackling laughter. The moment they were through the doorway Cranly seized him rudely by the neck and shook him, saying:

—You flaming floundering fool! I'll take my dying bible there isn't a bigger bloody ape, do you know, than you in the whole flaming bloody world!

Temple wriggled in his grip, laughing still with sly content, while Cranly repeated flatly at every rude shake:

—A flaming flaring bloody idiot!

They crossed the weedy garden together. The president, wrapped in a heavy loose cloak, was coming towards them along one of the walks, reading his office. At the end of the walk he halted before turning and raised his eyes. The students saluted, Temple fumbling as before at the peak of his cap. They walked forward in silence. As they neared the alley Stephen could hear the thuds of the players' hands and the wet smacks of the ball and Davin's voice crying out excitedly at each stroke.

The three students halted round the box on which Davin sat to follow the game. Temple, after a few moments, sidled across to Stephen and said:

—Excuse me, I wanted to ask you do you believe that Jean Jacques Rousseau was a sincere man?

Stephen laughed outright. Cranly, picking up the broken stave of a cask from the grass at his foot, turned swiftly and said sternly:

—Temple, I declare to the living God if you say another word, do you know, to anybody on any subject I'll kill you *super spottum*.

—He was like you, I fancy, said Stephen, an emotional man.

—Blast him, curse him! said Cranly broadly. Don't talk to him at all. Sure, you might as well be talking, do you know, to a flaming chamberpot as talking to Temple. Go home, Temple. For God's sake, go home.

—I don't care a damn about you, Cranly, answered Temple, moving out of reach of the uplifted stave and pointing at

Stephen. He's the only man I see in this institution that has an individual mind.

—Institution! Individual! cried Cranly. Go home, blast you, for you're a hopeless bloody man.

—I'm an emotional man, said Temple. That's quite rightly expressed. And I'm proud that I'm an emotionalist.

He sidled out of the alley, smiling slily. Cranly watched him with a blank expressionless face.

—Look at him! he said. Did you ever see such a go-by-the-wall?

His phrase was greeted by a strange laugh from a student who lounged against the wall, his peaked cap down on his eyes. The laugh, pitched in a high key and coming from a so muscular frame, seemed like the whinny of an elephant. The student's body shook all over and, to ease his mirth, he rubbed both his hands delightedly, over his groins.

—Lynch is awake, said Cranly.

Lynch, for answer, straightened himself and thrust forward his chest.

—Lynch puts out his chest, said Stephen, as a criticism of life.

Lynch smote himself sonorously on the chest and said:

—Who has anything to say about my girth?

Cranly took him at the word and the two began to tussle. When their faces had flushed with the struggle they drew apart, panting. Stephen bent down towards Davin who, intent on the game, had paid no heed to the talk of the others.

—And how is my little tame goose? he asked. Did he sign too?

Davin nodded and said:

—And you, Stevie?

Stephen shook his head.

—You're a terrible man, Stevie, said Davin, taking the short pipe from his mouth. Always alone.

—Now that you have signed the petition for universal peace, said Stephen, I suppose you will burn that little copybook I saw in your room.

As Davin did not answer Stephen began to quote:

—Long pace, fianna! Right incline, fianna! Fianna, by numbers, salute, one, two!

—That's a different question, said Davin. I'm an Irish nationalist, first and foremost. But that's you all out. You're a born sneerer, Stevie.

—When you make the next rebellion with hurleysticks, said Stephen, and want the indispensable informer, tell me. I can find you a few in this college.

—I can't understand you, said Davin. One time I hear you talk against English literature. Now you talk against the Irish informers. What with your name and your ideas . . . Are you Irish at all?

—Come with me now to the office of arms and I will show you the tree of my family, said Stephen.

—Then be one of us, said Davin. Why don't you learn Irish? Why did you drop out of the league class after the first lesson?

—You know one reason why, answered Stephen.

Davin tossed his head and laughed.

—O, come now, he said. Is it on account of that certain young lady and Father Moran? But that's all in your own mind, Stevie. They were only talking and laughing.

Stephen paused and laid a friendly hand upon Davin's shoulder.

—Do you remember, he said, when we knew each other first? The first morning we met you asked me to show you the way to the matriculation class, putting a very strong stress on the first syllable. You remember? Then you used to address the jesuits as father, you remember? I ask myself about you: *Is he as innocent as his speech?*

—I'm a simple person, said Davin. You know that. When you told me that night in Harcourt Street those things about your private life, honest to God, Stevie, I was not able to eat my dinner. I was quite bad. I was awake a long time that night. Why did you tell me those things?

—Thanks, said Stephen. You mean I am a monster.

—No, said Davin, but I wish you had not told me.

A tide began to surge beneath the calm surface of Stephen's friendliness.

—This race and this country and this life produced me, he said. I shall express myself as I am.

—Try to be one of us, repeated Davin. In your heart you are an Irishman but your pride is too powerful.

—My ancestors threw off their language and took another, Stephen said. They allowed a handful of foreigners to subject them. Do you fancy I am going to pay in my own life and person debts they made? What for?

—For our freedom, said Davin.

—No honourable and sincere man, said Stephen, has given up to you his life and his youth and his affections from the days of Tone to those of Parnell but you sold him to the enemy or failed him in need or reviled him and left him for another. And you invite me to be one of you. I'd see you damned first.

—They died for their ideals, Stevie, said Davin. Our day will come yet, believe me.

Stephen, following his own thought, was silent for an instant.

—The soul is born, he said vaguely, first in those moments I told you of. It has a slow and dark birth, more mysterious than the birth of the body. When the soul of a man is born in this country there are nets flung at it to hold it back from flight. You talk to me of nationality, language, religion. I shall try to fly by those nets.

Davin knocked the ashes from his pipe.

—Too deep for me, Stevie, he said. But a man's country comes first. Ireland first, Stevie. You can be a poet or mystic after.

—Do you know what Ireland is? asked Stephen with cold violence. Ireland is the old sow that eats her farrow.

Davin rose from his box and went towards the players,

shaking his head sadly. But in a moment his sadness left him and he was hotly disputing with Cranly and the two players who had finished their game. A match of four was arranged, Cranly insisting, however, that his ball should be used. He let it rebound twice or thrice to his hand and struck it strongly and swiftly towards the base of the alley, exclaiming in answer to its thud:

—Your soul!

Stephen stood with Lynch till the score began to rise. Then he plucked him by the sleeve to come away. Lynch obeyed, saying:

—Let us eke go, as Cranly has it.

Stephen smiled at this sidethrust. They passed back through the garden and out through the hall where the doddering porter was pinning up a notice in the frame. At the foot of the steps they halted and Stephen took a packet of cigarettes from his pocket and offered it to his companion.

—I know you are poor, he said.

—Damn your yellow insolence, answered Lynch.

This second proof of Lynch's culture made Stephen smile again.

—It was a great day for European culture, he said, when you made up your mind to swear in yellow.

They lit their cigarettes and turned to the right. After a pause Stephen began:

—Aristotle has not defined pity and terror. I have. I say . . .

Lynch halted and said bluntly:

—Stop! I won't listen! I am sick. I was out last night on a yellow drunk with Horan and Goggins.

Stephen went on:

—Pity is the feeling which arrests the mind in the presence of whatsoever is grave and constant in human sufferings and unites it with the human sufferer. Terror is the feeling which arrests the mind in the presence of whatsoever is grave and constant in human sufferings and unites it with the secret cause.

—Repeat, said Lynch.

Stephen repeated the definitions slowly.

—A girl got into a hansom a few days ago, he went on, in London. She was on her way to meet her mother whom she had not seen for many years. At the corner of a street the shaft of a lorry shivered the window of the hansom in the shape of a star. A long fine needle of the shivered glass pierced her heart. She died on the instant. The reporter called it a tragic death. It is not. It is remote from terror and pity according to the terms of my definitions.

—The tragic emotion, in fact, is a face looking two ways, towards terror and towards pity, both of which are phases of it. You see I use the word *arrest*. I mean that the tragic emotion is static. Or rather the dramatic emotion is. The feelings excited by improper art are kinetic, desire or loathing. Desire urges us to possess, to go to something; loathing urges us to abandon, to go from something. These are kinetic emotions. The arts which excite them, pornographical or didactic, are therefore improper arts. The esthetic emotion (I use the general term) is therefore static. The mind is arrested and raised above desire and loathing.

—You say that art must not excite desire, said Lynch. I told you that one day I wrote my name in pencil on the backside of the Venus of Praxiteles in the Museum. Was that not desire?

—I speak of normal natures, said Stephen. You also told me that when you were a boy in that charming carmelite school you ate pieces of dried cowdung.

Lynch broke again into a whinny of laughter and again rubbed both his hands over his groins but without taking them from his pockets.

—O I did! I did! he cried.

Stephen turned towards his companion and looked at him for a moment boldly in the eyes. Lynch, recovering from his laughter, answered his look from his humbled eyes. The long slender flattened skull beneath the long pointed cap brought before Stephen's mind the image of a hooded reptile. The eyes, too, were reptilelike in glint and gaze. Yet at that instant, humbled and alert in their look, they were lit by one tiny human point, the window of a shrivelled soul, poignant and selfembittered.

—As for that, Stephen said in polite parenthesis, we are all animals. I also am an animal.

—You are, said Lynch.

—But we are just now in a mental world, Stephen continued. The desire and loathing excited by improper esthetic means are really unesthetic emotions not only because they are kinetic in character but also because they are not more than physical. Our flesh shrinks from what it dreads and responds to the stimulus of what it desires by a purely reflex action of the nervous system. Our eyelid closes before we are aware that the fly is about to enter our eye.

—Not always, said Lynch critically.

—In the same way, said Stephen, your flesh responded to the stimulus of a naked statue but it was, I say, simply a reflex action of the nerves. Beauty expressed by the artist cannot awaken in us an emotion which is kinetic or a sensation which is purely physical. It awakens, or ought to awaken, or induces, or ought to induce, an esthetic stasis, an ideal pity or an ideal terror, a stasis called forth, prolonged and at last dissolved by what I call the rhythm of beauty.

—What is that exactly? asked Lynch.

—Rhythm, said Stephen, is the first formal esthetic relation of part to part in any esthetic whole or of an esthetic whole to its part or parts or of any part to the esthetic whole of which it is a part.

—If that is rhythm, said Lynch, let me hear what you call beauty: and, please remember, though I did eat a cake of cowdung once, that I admire only beauty.

Stephen raised his cap as if in greeting. Then, blushing slightly, he laid his hand on Lynch's thick tweed sleeve.

—We are right, he said, and the others are wrong. To speak of these things and to try to understand their nature and, having understood it, to try slowly and humbly and constantly to express, to press out again, from the gross earth or what it brings forth, from sound and shape and colour which are the prison gates of our soul, an image of the beauty we have come to understand—that is art.

They had reached the canal bridge and, turning from their course, went on by the trees. A crude grey light, mirrored in the sluggish water, and a smell of wet branches over their heads seemed to war against the course of Stephen's thought.

—But you have not answered my question, said Lynch. What is art? What is the beauty it expresses?

—That was the first definition I gave you, you sleepy-headed wretch, said Stephen, when I began to try to think out the matter for myself. Do you remember the night? Cranly lost his temper and began to talk about Wicklow bacon.

—I remember, said Lynch. He told us about them flaming fat devils of pigs.

—Art, said Stephen, is the human disposition of sensible or intelligible matter for an esthetic end. You remember the pigs and forget that. You are a distressing pair, you and Cranly.

Lynch made a grimace at the raw grey sky and said:

—If I am to listen to your esthetic philosophy give me at least another cigarette. I don't care about it. I don't even care about women. Damn you and damn everything. I want a job of five hundred a year. You can't get me one.

Stephen handed him the packet of cigarettes. Lynch took the last one that remained, saying simply:

—Proceed!

—Aquinas, said Stephen, says that is beautiful the apprehension of which pleases.

Lynch nodded.

—I remember that, he said. *Pulcra sunt quæ visa placent.*

—He uses the word *visa,* said Stephen, to cover esthetic apprehensions of all kinds, whether through sight or hearing or through any other avenue of apprehension. This word, though it is vague, is clear enough to keep away good and evil which excite desire and loathing. It means certainly a stasis and not a kinesis. How about the true? It produces also a stasis of the mind. You would not write your name in pencil across the hypothenuse of a rightangled triangle.

—No, said Lynch, give me the hypothenuse of the Venus of Praxiteles.

—Static therefore, said Stephen. Plato, I believe, said that beauty is the splendour of truth. I don't think that it has a meaning but the true and the beautiful are akin. Truth is beheld by the intellect which is appeased by the most satisfying relations of the intelligible: beauty is beheld by the imagination which is appeased by the most satisfying relations of the sensible. The first step in the direction of truth is to understand the frame and scope of the intellect itself, to comprehend the act itself of intellection. Aristotle's entire system of philosophy rests upon his book of psychology and that, I think, rests on his statement that the same attribute cannot at the same time and in the same connection belong to and not belong to the same subject. The first step in the direction of beauty is to understand the frame and scope of the imagination, to comprehend the act itself of esthetic apprehension. Is that clear?

—But what is beauty? asked Lynch impatiently. Out with another definition. Something we see and like! Is that the best you and Aquinas can do?

—Let us take woman, said Stephen.

—Let us take her! said Lynch fervently.

—The Greek, the Turk, the Chinese, the Copt, the Hottentot, said Stephen, all admire a different type of female beauty. That seems to be a maze out of which we cannot escape. I see however two ways out. One is this hypothesis: that every physical quality admired by men in women is in direct connection with the manifold functions of women for the propagation of the species. It may be so. The world, it seems, is drearier than even you, Lynch, imagined. For my part I dislike that way out. It leads to eugenics rather than to esthetic. It leads you out of the maze into a new gaudy lectureroom where Mac-

Cann, with one hand on *The Origin of Species* and the other hand on the new testament, tells you that you admired the great flanks of Venus because you felt that she would bear you burly offspring and admired her great breasts because you felt that she would give good milk to her children and yours.

—Then MacCann is a sulphuryellow liar, said Lynch energetically.

—There remains another way out, said Stephen, laughing.

—To wit? said Lynch.

—This hypothesis, Stephen began.

A long dray laden with old iron came round the corner of sir Patrick Dun's hospital covering the end of Stephen's speech with the harsh roar of jangled and rattling metal. Lynch closed his ears and gave out oath after oath till the dray had passed. Then he turned on his heel rudely. Stephen turned also and waited for a few moments till his companion's illhumour had had its vent.

—This hypothesis, Stephen repeated, is the other way out: that, though the same object may not seem beautiful to all people, all people who admire a beautiful object find in it certain relations which satisfy and coincide with the stages themselves of all esthetic apprehension. These relations of the sensible, visible to you through one form and to me through another, must be therefore the necessary qualities of beauty. Now, we can return to our old friend saint Thomas for another pennyworth of wisdom.

Lynch laughed.

—It amuses me vastly, he said, to hear you quoting him time after time like a jolly round friar. Are you laughing in your sleeve?

—MacAlister, answered Stephen, would call my esthetic theory applied Aquinas. So far as this side of esthetic philosophy extends Aquinas will carry me all along the line. When we come to the phenomena of artistic conception, artistic gestation and artistic reproduction I require a new terminology and a new personal experience.

—Of course, said Lynch. After all Aquinas, in spite of his

intellect, was exactly a good round friar. But you will tell me about the new personal experience and new terminology some other day. Hurry up and finish the first part.

—Who knows? said Stephen, smiling. Perhaps Aquinas would understand me better than you. He was a poet himself. He wrote a hymn for Maundy Thursday. It begins with the words *Pange lingua gloriosi.* They say it is the highest glory of the hymnal. It is an intricate and soothing hymn. I like it: but there is no hymn that can be put beside that mournful and majestic processional song, the *Vexilla Regis* of Venantius Fortunatus.

Lynch began to sing softly and solemnly in a deep bass voice:

> *Impleta sunt quæ concinit*
> *David fideli carmine*
> *Dicendo nationibus*
> *Regnavit a ligno Deus.*

—That's great! he said, well pleased. Great music!

They turned into Lower Mount Street. A few steps from the corner a fat young man, wearing a silk neckcloth, saluted them and stopped.

—Did you hear the results of the exams? he asked. Griffin was plucked. Halpin and O'Flynn are through the home civil. Moonan got fifth place in the Indian. O'Shaughnessy got fourteenth. The Irish fellows in Clarke's gave them a feed last night. They all ate curry.

His pallid bloated face expressed benevolent malice and, as he had advanced through his tidings of success, his small fatencircled eyes vanished out of sight and his weak wheezing voice out of hearing.

In reply to a question of Stephen's his eyes and his voice came forth again from their lurkingplaces.

—Yes, MacCullagh and I, he said. He's taking pure mathematics and I'm taking constitutional history. There are twenty subjects. I'm taking botany too. You know I'm a member of the field club.

He drew back from the other two in a stately fashion and placed a plump woollengloved hand on his breast, from which muttered wheezing laughter at once broke forth.

—Bring us a few turnips and onions the next time you go out, said Stephen drily, to make a stew.

The fat student laughed indulgently and said:

—We are all highly respectable people in the field club. Last Saturday we went out to Glenmalure, seven of us.

—With women, Donovan? said Lynch.

Donovan again laid his hand on his chest and said:

—Our end is the acquisition of knowledge.

Then he said quickly:

—I hear you are writing some essay about esthetics.

Stephen made a vague gesture of denial.

—Goethe and Lessing, said Donovan, have written a lot on that subject, the classical school and the romantic school and all that. The *Laocoon* interested me very much when I read it. Of course it is idealistic, German, ultraprofound.

Neither of the others spoke. Donovan took leave of them urbanely.

—I must go, he said softly and benevolently. I have a strong suspicion, amounting almost to a conviction, that my sister intended to make pancakes today for the dinner of the Donovan family.

—Goodbye, Stephen said in his wake. Don't forget the turnips for me and my mate.

Lynch gazed after him, his lip curling in slow scorn till his face resembled a devil's mask:

—To think that that yellow pancakeeating excrement can get a good job, he said at length, and I have to smoke cheap cigarettes!

They turned their faces towards Merrion Square and went on for a little in silence.

—To finish what I was saying about beauty, said Stephen, the most satisfying relations of the sensible must therefore correspond to the necessary phases of artistic apprehension. Find these and you find the qualities of universal beauty.

Aquinas says: *ad pulcritudinem tria requiruntur, integritas,
consonantia, claritas*. I translate it so: *Three things are needed
for beauty, wholeness, harmony and radiance*. Do these correspond to the phases of apprehension? Are you following?

—Of course, I am, said Lynch. If you think I have an
excrementitious intelligence run after Donovan and ask him to
listen to you.

Stephen pointed to a basket which a butcher's boy had
slung inverted on his head.

—Look at that basket, he said.

—I see it, said Lynch.

—In order to see that basket, said Stephen, your mind first
of all separates the basket from the rest of the visible universe
which is not the basket. The first phase of apprehension is a
bounding line drawn about the object to be apprehended. An
esthetic image is presented to us either in space or in time.
What is audible is presented in time, what is visible is presented in space. But, temporal or spatial, the esthetic image is
first luminously apprehended as selfbounded and selfcon-
tained upon the immeasurable background of space or time
which is not it. You apprehend it as *one* thing. You see it as
one whole. You apprehend its wholeness. That is *integritas*.

—Bull's eye! said Lynch, laughing. Go on.

—Then, said Stephen, you pass from point to point, led by
its formal lines; you apprehend it as balanced part against part
within its limits; you feel the rhythm of its structure. In other
words the synthesis of immediate perception is followed by
the analysis of apprehension. Having first felt that it is *one*
thing you feel now that it is a *thing*. You apprehend it as
complex, multiple, divisible, separable, made up of its parts,
the result of its parts and their sum, harmonious. That is
consonantia.

—Bull's eye again! said Lynch wittily. Tell me now what is
claritas and you win the cigar.

—The connotation of the word, Stephen said, is rather
vague. Aquinas uses a term which seems to be inexact. It

baffled me for a long time. It would lead you to believe that he had in mind symbolism or idealism, the supreme quality of beauty being a light from some other world, the idea of which the matter is but the shadow, the reality of which it is but the symbol. I thought he might mean that *claritas* is the artistic discovery and representation of the divine purpose in anything or a force of generalisation which would make the esthetic image a universal one, make it outshine its proper conditions. But that is literary talk. I understand it so. When you have apprehended that basket as one thing and have then analysed it according to its form and apprehended it as a thing you make the only synthesis which is logically and esthetically permissible. You see that it is that thing which it is and no other thing. The radiance of which he speaks is the scholastic *quidditas,* the *whatness* of a thing. This supreme quality is felt by the artist when the esthetic image is first conceived in his imagination. The mind in that mysterious instant Shelley likened beautifully to a fading coal. The instant wherein that supreme quality of beauty, the clear radiance of the esthetic image, is apprehended luminously by the mind which has been arrested by its wholeness and fascinated by its harmony is the luminous silent stasis of esthetic pleasure, a spiritual state very like to that cardiac condition which the Italian physiologist Luigi Galvani, using a phrase almost as beautiful as Shelley's, called the enchantment of the heart.

Stephen paused and, though his companion did not speak, felt that his words had called up around them a thoughtenchanted silence.

—What I have said, he began again, refers to beauty in the wider sense of the word, in the sense which the word has in the literary tradition. In the marketplace it has another sense. When we speak of beauty in the second sense of the term our judgment is influenced in the first place by the art itself and by the form of that art. The image, it is clear, must be set between the mind or senses of the artist himself and the mind or senses of others. If you bear this in memory you will see that art necessarily divides itself into three forms progressing from one to the next. These forms are: the lyrical form, the form wherein the artist presents his image in immediate relation to himself; the epical form, the form wherein he presents his image in mediate relation to himself and to others; the dramatic form, the form wherein he presents his image in immediate relation to others.

—That you told me a few nights ago, said Lynch, and we began the famous discussion.

—I have a book at home, said Stephen, in which I have written down questions which are more amusing than yours were. In finding the answers to them I found the theory of esthetic which I am trying to explain. Here are some questions I set myself: *Is a chair finely made tragic or comic? Is the portrait of Mona Lisa good if I desire to see it? Is the bust of Sir Philip Crampton lyrical, epical or dramatic? Can excrement or a child or a louse be a work of art? If not, why not?*

—Why not, indeed? said Lynch, laughing.

—*If a man hacking in fury at a block of wood,* Stephen continued, *make there an image of a cow, is that image a work of art? If not, why not?*

—That's a lovely one, said Lynch, laughing again. That has the true scholastic stink.

—Lessing, said Stephen, should not have taken a group of statues to write of. The art, being inferior, does not present the forms I spoke of distinguished clearly one from another. Even in literature, the highest and most spiritual art, the forms are often confused. The lyrical form is in fact the simplest verbal vesture of an instant of emotion, a rhythmical cry such as ages ago cheered on the man who pulled at the oar or dragged stones up a slope. He who utters it is more conscious of the instant of emotion than of himself as feeling emotion. The simplest epical form is seen emerging out of lyrical literature when the artist prolongs and broods upon himself as the centre of an epical event and this form progresses till the centre of emotional gravity is equidistant from the artist himself and from others. The narrative is no longer purely personal. The personality of the artist passes into the narration itself, flowing round and round the persons and the action like a vital sea. This progress you will see easily in that old English ballad *Turpin Hero* which begins in the first person and ends in the third person. The dramatic form is reached when the vitality which has flowed and eddied round each person fills every person with such vital force that he or she assumes a proper and intangible esthetic life. The personality of the artist, at first a cry or a cadence or a mood and then a fluid and lambent narrative, finally refines itself out of existence, impersonalises itself, so to speak. The esthetic image in the dramatic form is life purified in and reprojected from the human imagination. The mystery of esthetic like that of material creation is accomplished. The artist, like the God of the creation, remains within or behind or beyond or above his handiwork, invisible, refined out of existence, indifferent, paring his fingernails.

—Trying to refine them also out of existence, said Lynch.

A fine rain began to fall from the high veiled sky and they turned into the duke's lawn, to reach the national library before the shower came.

—What do you mean, Lynch asked surlily, by prating about beauty and the imagination in this miserable Godforsaken island? No wonder the artist retired within or behind his handiwork after having perpetrated this country.

The rain fell faster. When they passed through the passage beside the royal Irish academy they found many students sheltering under the arcade of the library. Cranly, leaning against a pillar, was picking his teeth with a sharpened match, listening to some companions. Some girls stood near the entrance door. Lynch whispered to Stephen:

—Your beloved is here.

Stephen took his place silently on the step below the group of students, heedless of the rain which fell fast, turning his eyes towards her from time to time. She too stood silently among her companions. She has no priest to flirt with, he thought with conscious bitterness, remembering how he had seen her last. Lynch was right. His mind, emptied of theory and courage, lapsed back into a listless peace.

He heard the students talking among themselves. They spoke of two friends who had passed the final medical examination, of the chances of getting places on ocean liners, of poor and rich practices.

—That's all a bubble. An Irish country practice is better.

—Hynes was two years in Liverpool and he says the same. A frightful hole he said it was. Nothing but midwifery cases. Half a crown cases.

—Do you mean to say it is better to have a job here in the country than in a rich city like that? I know a fellow . . .

—Hynes has no brains. He got through by stewing, pure stewing.

—Don't mind him. There's plenty of money to be made in a big commercial city.

—Depends on the practice.

—*Ego credo ut vita pauperum est simpliciter atrox, simpliciter sanguinarius atrox, in Liverpoolio.*

Their voices reached his ears as if from a distance in interrupted pulsation. She was preparing to go away with her companions.

The quick light shower had drawn off, tarrying in clusters of diamonds among the shrubs of the quadrangle where an exhalation was breathed forth by the blackened earth. Their trim boots prattled as they stood on the steps of the colonnade, talking quietly and gaily, glancing at the clouds, holding their umbrellas at cunning angles against the few last raindrops, closing them again, holding their skirts demurely.

And if he had judged her harshly? If her life were a simple rosary of hours, her life simple and strange as a bird's life, gay in the morning, restless all day, tired at sundown? Her heart simple and wilful as a bird's heart?

* * *

Towards dawn he awoke. O what sweet music! His soul was all dewy wet. Over his limbs in sleep pale cool waves of light had passed. He lay still, as if his soul lay amid cool waters, conscious of faint sweet music. His mind was waking slowly to a tremulous morning knowledge, a morning inspiration. A spirit filled him, pure as the purest water, sweet as dew, moving as music. But how faintly it was inbreathed, how passionlessly, as if the seraphim themselves were breathing upon him! His soul was waking slowly, fearing to awake wholly. It was that windless hour of dawn when madness wakes and strange plants open to the light and the moth flies forth silently.

An enchantment of the heart! The night had been enchanted. In a dream or vision he had known the ecstasy of seraphic life. Was it an instant of enchantment only or long hours and days and years and ages?

The instant of inspiration seemed now to be reflected from all sides at once from a multitude of cloudy circumstance of what had happened or of what might have happened. The instant flashed forth like a point of light and now from cloud on cloud of vague circumstance confused form was veiling softly its afterglow. O! In the virgin womb of the imagination the word was made flesh. Gabriel the seraph had come to the virgin's chamber. An afterglow deepened within his spirit, whence the white flame had passed, deepening to a rose and ardent light. That rose and ardent light was her strange wilful heart, strange that no man had known or would know, wilful from before the beginning of the world: and lured by that ardent roselike glow the choirs of the seraphim were falling from heaven.

> *Are you not weary of ardent ways,*
> *Lure of the fallen seraphim?*
> *Tell no more of enchanted days.*

The verses passed from his mind to his lips and, murmuring them over, he felt the rhythmic movement of a villanelle pass through them. The roselike glow sent forth its rays of rhyme; ways, days, blaze, praise, raise. Its rays burned up the world, consumed the hearts of men and angels: the rays from the rose that was her wilful heart.

> *Your eyes have set man's heart ablaze*
> *And you have had your will of him.*
> *Are you not weary of ardent ways?*

And then? The rhythm died away, ceased, began again to move and beat. And then? Smoke, incense ascending from the altar of the world.

> *Above the flame the smoke of praise*
> *Goes up from ocean rim to rim.*
> *Tell no more of enchanted days.*

Smoke went up from the whole earth, from the vapoury oceans, smoke of her praise. The earth was like a swinging smoking swaying censer, a ball of incense, an ellipsoidal ball. The rhythm died out at once; the cry of his heart was broken. His lips began to murmur the first verses over and over; then went on stumbling through half verses, stammering and baffled; then stopped. The heart's cry was broken.

The veiled windless hour had passed and behind the panes of the naked window the morning light was gathering. A bell beat faintly very far away. A bird twittered; two birds, three. The bell and the bird ceased: and the dull white light spread itself east and west, covering the world, covering the roselight in his heart.

Fearing to lose all, he raised himself suddenly on his elbow to look for paper and pencil. There was neither on the table; only the soupplate he had eaten the rice from for supper and the candlestick with its tendrils of tallow and its paper socket, singed by the last flame. He stretched his arm wearily towards the foot of the bed, groping with his hand in the pockets of the coat that hung there. His fingers found a pencil and then a cigarette packet. He lay back and, tearing open the packet, placed the last cigarette on the windowledge and began to

write out the stanzas of the villanelle in small neat letters on
the rough cardboard surface.

Having written them out he lay back on the lumpy pillow,
murmuring them again. The lumps of knotted flock under his
head reminded him of the lumps of knotted horsehair in the
sofa of her parlour on which he used to sit, smiling or serious,
asking himself why he had come, displeased with her and with
himself, confounded by the print of the Sacred Heart above
the untenanted sideboard. He saw her approach him in a lull
of the talk and beg him to sing one of his curious songs. Then
he saw himself sitting at the old piano, striking chords softly
from its speckled keys and singing, amid the talk which had
risen again in the room, to her who leaned beside the mantel-
piece a dainty song of the Elizabethans, a sad and sweet loth
to depart, the victory chant of Agincourt, the happy air of
Greensleeves. While he sang and she listened, or feigned to
listen, his heart was at rest but when the quaint old songs had
ended and he heard again the voices in the room he remembered his own sarcasm: the house where young men are called
by their christian names a little too soon.

At certain instants her eyes seemed about to trust him but
he had waited in vain. She passed now dancing lightly across
his memory as she had been that night at the carnival ball, her
white dress a little lifted, a white spray nodding in her hair.
She danced lightly in the round. She was dancing towards him
and, as she came, her eyes were a little averted and a faint
glow was on her cheek. At the pause in the chain of hands her
hand had lain in his an instant, a soft merchandise.

—You are a great stranger now.

—Yes. I was born to be a monk.

—I am afraid you are a heretic.

—Are you much afraid?

For answer she had danced away from him along the chain
of hands, dancing lightly and discreetly, giving herself to none.
The white spray nodded to her dancing and when she was in
shadow the glow was deeper on her cheek.

A monk! His own image started forth a profaner of the

cloister, a heretic franciscan, willing and willing not to serve, spinning like Gherardino da Borgo San Donnino, a lithe web of sophistry and whispering in her ear.

No, it was not his image. It was like the image of the young priest in whose company he had seen her last, looking at him out of dove's eyes, toying with the pages of her Irish phrasebook.

—Yes, yes, the ladies are coming round to us. I can see it every day. The ladies are with us. The best helpers the language has.

—And the church, Father Moran?

—The church too. Coming round too. The work is going ahead there too. Don't fret about the church.

Bah! he had done well to leave the room in disdain. He had done well not to salute her on the steps of the library. He had done well to leave her to flirt with her priest, to toy with a church which was the scullerymaid of christendom.

Rude brutal anger routed the last lingering instant of ecstasy from his soul. It broke up violently her fair image and flung the fragments on all sides. On all sides distorted reflections of her image started from his memory: the flowergirl in the ragged dress with damp coarse hair and a hoyden's face who had called herself his own girl and begged his handsel, the kitchengirl in the next house who sang over the clatter of her plates with the drawl of a country singer the first bars of *By Killarney's Lakes and Fells,* a girl who had laughed gaily to see him stumble when the iron grating in the footpath near Cork Hill had caught the broken sole of his shoe, a girl he had glanced at, attracted by her small ripe mouth as she passed out of Jacob's biscuit factory, who had cried to him over her shoulder:

—Do you like what you seen of me, straight hair and curly eyebrows?

And yet he felt that, however he might revile and mock her image, his anger was also a form of homage. He had left the classroom in disdain that was not wholly sincere, feeling that perhaps the secret of her race lay behind those dark eyes upon which her long lashes flung a quick shadow. He had told himself bitterly as he walked through the streets that she was a figure of the womanhood of her country, a batlike soul waking to the consciousness of itself in darkness and secrecy and loneliness, tarrying awhile, loveless and sinless, with her mild lover and leaving him to whisper of innocent transgressions in the latticed ear of a priest. His anger against her found vent in coarse railing at her paramour, whose name and voice and features offended his baffled pride: a priested peasant, with a brother a policeman in Dublin and a brother a potboy in Moycullen. To him she would unveil her soul's shy nakedness, to one who was but schooled in the discharging of a formal rite rather than to him, a priest of eternal imagination, transmuting the daily bread of experience into the radiant body of everliving life.

The radiant image of the eucharist united again in an instant his bitter and despairing thoughts, their cries arising unbroken in a hymn of thanksgiving.

> *Our broken cries and mournful lays*
> *Rise in one eucharistic hymn.*
> *Are you not weary of ardent ways?*
>
> *While sacrificing hands upraise*
> *The chalice flowing to the brim,*
> *Tell no more of enchanted days.*

He spoke the verses aloud from the first lines till the music and rhythm suffused his mind, turning it to quiet indulgence; then copied them painfully to feel them the better by seeing them; then lay back on his bolster.

The full morning light had come. No sound was to be heard: but he knew that all around him life was about to awaken in common noises, hoarse voices, sleepy prayers. Shrinking from that life he turned towards the wall, making a cowl of the blanket and staring at the great overblown scarlet flowers of the tattered wallpaper. He tried to warm his perish-ing joy in their scarlet glow, imagining a roseway from where he lay upwards to heaven all strewn with scarlet flowers. Weary! Weary! He too was weary of ardent ways.

A gradual warmth, a languorous weariness passed over him, descending along his spine from his closely cowled head. He felt it descend and, seeing himself as he lay, smiled. Soon he would sleep.

He had written verses for her again after ten years. Ten years before she had worn her shawl cowlwise about her head, sending sprays of her warm breath into the night air, tapping her foot upon the glassy road. It was the last tram; the lank brown horses knew it and shook their bells to the clear night in admonition. The conductor talked with the driver, both nodding often in the green light of the lamp. They stood on the steps of the tram, he on the upper, she on the lower. She came up to his step many times between their phrases and went down again and once or twice remained beside him forgetting to go down and then went down. Let be! Let be!

Ten years from that wisdom of children to his folly. If he sent her the verses? They would be read out at breakfast amid the tapping of eggshells. Folly indeed! The brothers would laugh and try to wrest the page from each other with their strong hard fingers. The suave priest, her uncle, seated in his armchair, would hold the page at arm's length, read it smiling and approve of the literary form.

No, no: that was folly. Even if he sent her the verses she would not show them to others. No, no: she could not.

He began to feel that he had wronged her. A sense of her innocence moved him almost to pity her, an innocence he had never understood till he had come to the knowledge of it through sin, an innocence which she too had not understood while she was innocent or before the strange humiliation of her nature had first come upon her. Then first her soul had begun to live as his soul had when he had first sinned: and a tender compassion filled his heart as he remembered her frail pallor and her eyes, humbled and saddened by the dark shame of womanhood.

While his soul had passed from ecstasy to languor where had she been? Might it be, in the mysterious ways of spiritual life, that her soul at those same moments had been conscious of his homage? It might be.

A glow of desire kindled again his soul and fired and fulfilled all his body. Conscious of his desire she was waking from odorous sleep, the temptress of his villanelle. Her eyes, dark and with a look of languor, were opening to his eyes. Her nakedness yielded to him, radiant, warm, odorous and lavish-limbed, enfolded him like a shining cloud, enfolded him like water with a liquid life: and like a cloud of vapour or like waters circumfluent in space the liquid letters of speech, symbols of the element of mystery, flowed forth over his brain.

Are you not weary of ardent ways,
Lure of the fallen seraphim?
Tell no more of enchanted days.

Your eyes have set man's heart ablaze
And you have had your will of him.
Are you not weary of ardent ways?

Above the flame the smoke of praise
Goes up from ocean rim to rim.
Tell no more of enchanted days.

Our broken cries and mournful lays
Rise in one eucharistic hymn.
Are you not weary of ardent ways?

While sacrificing hands upraise
The chalice flowing to the brim,
Tell no more of enchanted days.

And still you hold our longing gaze
With languorous look and lavish limb!

Are you not weary of ardent ways?
Tell no more of enchanted days.

*   *   *

What birds were they? He stood on the steps of the library to look at them, leaning wearily on his ashplant. They flew round and round the jutting shoulder of a house in Molesworth Street. The air of the late March evening made clear their flight, their dark darting quivering bodies flying clearly against the sky as against a limphung cloth of smoky tenuous blue.

He watched their flight; bird after bird: a dark flash, a swerve, a flash again, a dart aside, a curve, a flutter of wings. He tried to count them before all their darting quivering bodies passed: six, ten, eleven: and wondered were they odd or even in number. Twelve, thirteen: for two came wheeling down from the upper sky. They were flying high and low but ever round and round in straight and curving lines and ever flying from left to right, circling about a temple of air.

He listened to the cries: like the squeak of mice behind the wainscot: a shrill twofold note. But the notes were long and shrill and whirring, unlike the cry of vermin, falling a third or a fourth and trilled as the flying beaks clove the air. Their cry was shrill and clear and fine and falling like threads of silken light unwound from whirring spools.

The inhuman clamour soothed his ears in which his mother's sobs and reproaches murmured insistently and the dark frail quivering bodies wheeling and fluttering and swerving round an airy temple of the tenuous sky soothed his eyes which still saw the image of his mother's face.

Why was he gazing upwards from the steps of the porch, hearing their shrill twofold cry, watching their flight? For an augury of good or evil? A phrase of Cornelius Agrippa flew through his mind and then there flew hither and thither shapeless thoughts from Swedenborg on the correspondence of birds to things of the intellect and of how the creatures of the air have their knowledge and know their times and seasons because they, unlike man, are in the order of their life and have not perverted that order by reason.

And for ages men had gazed upward as he was gazing at birds in flight. The colonnade above him made him think vaguely of an ancient temple and the ashplant on which he leaned wearily of the curved stick of an augur. A sense of fear of the unknown moved in the heart of his weariness, a fear of symbols and portents, of the hawklike man whose name he bore soaring out of his captivity on osierwoven wings, of Thoth, the god of writers, writing with a reed upon a tablet and bearing on his narrow ibis head the cusped moon.

He smiled as he thought of the god's image for it made him think of a bottlenosed judge in a wig, putting commas into a document which he held at arm's length and he knew that he would not have remembered the god's name but that it was like an Irish oath. It was folly. But was it for this folly that he was about to leave for ever the house of prayer and prudence into which he had been born and the order of life out of which he had come?

They came back with shrill cries over the jutting shoulder of the house, flying darkly against the fading air. What birds were they? He thought that they must be swallows who had come back from the south. Then he was to go away for they were birds ever going and coming, building ever an unlasting home under the eaves of men's houses and ever leaving the homes they had built to wander.

> *Bend down your faces, Oona and Aleel,*
> *I gaze upon them as the swallow gazes*
> *Upon the nest under the eave before*
> *He wander the loud waters.*

A soft liquid joy like the noise of many waters flowed over his memory and he felt in his heart the soft peace of silent spaces of fading tenuous sky above the waters, of oceanic silence, of swallows flying through the seadusk over the flowing waters.

A soft liquid joy flowed through the words where the soft long vowels hurtled noiselessly and fell away, lapping and flowing back and ever shaking the white bells of their waves in mute chime and mute peal and soft low swooning cry; and he felt that the augury he had sought in the wheeling darting birds and in the pale space of sky above him had come forth from his heart like a bird from a turret quietly and swiftly.

Symbol of departure or of loneliness? The verses crooned in the ear of his memory composed slowly before his remembering eyes the scene of the hall on the night of the opening of the national theatre. He was alone at the side of the balcony, looking out of jaded eyes at the culture of Dublin in the stalls and at the tawdry scenecloths and human dolls framed by the garish lamps of the stage. A burly policeman sweated behind him and seemed at every moment about to act. The catcalls and hisses and mocking cries ran in rude gusts round the hall from his scattered fellowstudents.

—A libel on Ireland!
—Made in Germany!
—Blasphemy!
—We never sold our faith!
—No Irish woman ever did it!
—We want no amateur atheists.
—We want no budding buddhists.

A sudden swift hiss fell from the windows above him and he knew that the electric lamps had been switched on in the reader's room. He turned into the pillared hall, now calmly lit, went up the staircase and passed in through the clicking turnstile.

Cranly was sitting over near the dictionaries. A thick book, opened at the frontispiece, lay before him on the wooden rest. He leaned back in his chair, inclining his ear like that of a confessor to the face of the medical student who was reading to him a problem from the chess page of a journal. Stephen sat down at his right and the priest at the other side of the table closed his copy of *The Tablet* with an angry snap and stood up.

Cranly gazed after him blandly and vaguely. The medical student went on in a softer voice:

—Pawn to king's fourth.

—We had better go, Dixon, said Stephen in warning. He has gone to complain.

Dixon folded the journal and rose with dignity, saying:

—Our men retired in good order.

—With guns and cattle, added Stephen, pointing to the titlepage of Cranly's book on which was printed *Diseases of the Ox*.

As they passed through a lane of the tables Stephen said:

—Cranly, I want to speak to you.

Cranly did not answer or turn. He laid his book on the counter and passed out, his wellshod feet sounding flatly on the floor. On the staircase he paused and gazing absently at Dixon repeated:

—Pawn to king's bloody fourth.

—Put it that way if you like, Dixon said.

He had a quiet toneless voice and urbane manners and on a finger of his plump clean hand he displayed at moments a signet ring.

As they crossed the hall a man of dwarfish stature came towards them. Under the dome of his tiny hat his unshaven face began to smile with pleasure and he was heard to murmur. The eyes were melancholy as those of a monkey.

—Good evening, captain, said Cranly, halting.

—Good evening, gentlemen, said the stubblegrown monkeyish face.

—Warm weather for March, said Cranly. They have the windows open upstairs.

Dixon smiled and turned his ring. The blackish monkeypuckered face pursed its human mouth with gentle pleasure: and its voice purred:

—Delightful weather for March. Simply delightful.

—There are two nice young ladies upstairs, captain, tired of waiting, Dixon said.

Cranly smiled and said kindly:

—The captain has only one love: sir Walter Scott. Isn't that so, captain?

—What are you reading now, captain? Dixon asked. *The Bride of Lammermoor?*

—I love old Scott, the flexible lips said. I think he writes something lovely. There is no writer can touch sir Walter Scott.

He moved a thin shrunken brown hand gently in the air in time to his praise and his thin quick eyelids beat often over his sad eyes.

Sadder to Stephen's ear was his speech: a genteel accent, low and moist, marred by errors: and listening to it he wondered was the story true and was the thin blood that flowed in his shrunken frame noble and come of an incestuous love?

The park trees were heavy with rain and rain fell still and ever in the lake, lying grey like a shield. A game of swans flew there and the water and the shore beneath were fouled with their greenwhite slime. They embraced softly, impelled by the grey rainy light, the wet silent trees, the shieldlike witnessing lake, the swans. They embraced without joy or passion, his arm about his sister's neck. A grey woollen cloak was wrapped athwart her from her shoulder to her waist: and her fair head was bent in willing shame. He had loose redbrown hair and tender shapely strong freckled hands. Face. There was no face seen. The brother's face was bent upon her fair rainfragrant hair. The hand freckled and strong and shapely and caressing was Davin's hand.

He frowned angrily upon his thought and on the shrivelled mannikin who had called it forth. His father's gibes at the Bantry gang leaped out of his memory. He held them at a distance and brooded uneasily on his own thought again. Why were they not Cranly's hands? Had Davin's simplicity and innocence stung him more secretly?

He walked on across the hall with Dixon, leaving Cranly to take leave elaborately of the dwarf.

Under the colonnade Temple was standing in the midst of a little group of students. One of them cried:

—Dixon, come over till you hear. Temple is in grand form.

Temple turned on him his dark gipsy eyes.

—You're a hypocrite, O'Keeffe, he said, and Dixon's a smiler. By hell, I think that's a good literary expression.

He laughed slily, looking in Stephen's face, repeating:

—By hell, I'm delighted with that name. A smiler.

A stout student who stood below them on the steps said:

—Come back to the mistress, Temple. We want to hear about that.

—He had, faith, Temple said. And he was a married man too. And all the priests used to be dining there. By hell, I think they all had a touch.

—We shall call it riding a hack to spare the hunter, said Dixon.

—Tell us, Temple, O'Keeffe said, how many quarts of porter have you in you?

—All your intellectual soul is in that phrase, O'Keeffe, said Temple with open scorn.

He moved with a shambling gait round the group and spoke to Stephen.

—Did you know that the Forsters are the kings of Belgium? he asked.

Cranly came out through the door of the entrance hall, his hat thrust back on the nape of his neck and picking his teeth with care.

—And here's the wiseacre, said Temple. Do you know that about the Forsters?

He paused for an answer. Cranly dislodged a figseed from his teeth on the point of his rude toothpick and gazed at it intently.

—The Forster family, Temple said, is descended from Baldwin the First, king of Flanders. He was called the Forester. Forester and Forster are the same name. A descendant of

Baldwin the First, captain Francis Forster, settled in Ireland and married the daughter of the last chieftain of Clanbrassil. Then there are the Blake Forsters. That's a different branch.

—From Baldhead, king of Flanders, Cranly repeated, rooting again deliberately at his gleaming uncovered teeth.

—Where did you pick up all that history? O'Keeffe asked.

—I know all the history of your family too, Temple said, turning to Stephen. Do you know what Giraldus Cambrensis says about your family?

—Is he descended from Baldwin too? asked a tall consumptive student with dark eyes.

—Baldhead, Cranly repeated, sucking at a crevice in his teeth.

—*Pernobilis et pervetusta familia,* Temple said to Stephen.

The stout student who stood below them on the steps farted briefly. Dixon turned towards him saying in a soft voice:

—Did an angel speak?

Cranly turned also and said vehemently but without anger:

—Goggins, you're the flamingest dirty devil I ever met, do you know.

—I had it on my mind to say that, Goggins answered firmly. It did no one any harm, did it?

—We hope, Dixon said suavely, that it was not of the kind known to science as a *paulo post futurum.*

—Didn't I tell you he was a smiler? said Temple, turning right and left. Didn't I give him that name?

—You did. We're not deaf, said the tall consumptive.

Cranly still frowned at the stout student below him. Then, with a snort of disgust, he shoved him violently down the steps.

—Go away from here, he said rudely. Go away, you stinkpot. And you are a stinkpot.

Goggins skipped down on to the gravel and at once returned to his place with good humour. Temple turned back to Stephen and asked:

—Do you believe in the law of heredity?

—Are you drunk or what are you or what are you trying to say? asked Cranly, facing round on him with an expression of wonder.

—The most profound sentence ever written, Temple said with enthusiasm, is the sentence at the end of the zoology. Reproduction is the beginning of death.

He touched Stephen timidly at the elbow and said eagerly:

—Do you feel how profound that is because you are a poet?

Cranly pointed his long forefinger.

—Look at him! he said with scorn to the others. Look at Ireland's hope!

They laughed at his words and gesture. Temple turned on him bravely, saying:

—Cranly, you're always sneering at me. I can see that. But I am as good as you any day. Do you know what I think about you now as compared with myself?

—My dear man, said Cranly urbanely, you are incapable, do you know, absolutely incapable of thinking.

—But do you know, Temple went on, what I think of you and of myself compared together?

—Out with it, Temple! the stout student cried from the steps. Get it out in bits!

Temple turned right and left, making sudden feeble gestures as he spoke.

—I'm a ballocks, he said, shaking his head in despair. I am. And I know I am. And I admit it that I am.

Dixon patted him lightly on the shoulder and said mildly:

—And it does you every credit, Temple.

—But he, Temple said, pointing to Cranly. He is a ballocks too like me. Only he doesn't know it. And that's the only difference I see.

A burst of laughter covered his words. But he turned again to Stephen and said with a sudden eagerness:

—That word is a most interesting word. That's the only English dual number. Did you know?

—Is it? Stephen said vaguely.

He was watching Cranly's firmfeatured suffering face, lit up now by a smile of false patience. The gross name had passed over it like foul water poured over an old stone image, patient of injuries: and, as he watched him, he saw him raise his hat in salute and uncover the black hair that stood up stiffly from his forehead like an iron crown.

She passed out from the porch of the library and bowed across Stephen in reply to Cranly's greeting. He also? Was there not a slight flush on Cranly's cheek? Or had it come forth at Temple's words? The light had waned. He could not see.

Did that explain his friend's listless silence, his harsh comments, the sudden intrusions of rude speech with which he had shattered so often Stephen's ardent wayward confessions? Stephen had forgiven freely for he had found this rudeness also in himself towards himself. And he remembered an evening when he had dismounted from a borrowed creaking bicycle to pray to God in a wood near Malahide. He had lifted up his arms and spoken in ecstasy to the sombre nave of the trees, knowing that he stood on holy ground and in a holy hour. And when two constabularymen had come into sight round a bend in the gloomy road he had broken off his prayer to whistle loudly an air from the last pantomime.

He began to beat the frayed end of his ashplant against the base of a pillar. Had Cranly not heard him? Yet he could wait. The talk about him ceased for a moment: and a soft hiss fell again from a window above. But no other sound was in the air and the swallows whose flight he had followed with idle eyes were sleeping.

She had passed through the dusk. And therefore the air was silent save for one soft hiss that fell. And therefore the tongues about him had ceased their babble. Darkness was falling.

Darkness falls from the air.

A trembling joy, lambent as a faint light, played like a fairy host around him. But why? Her passage through the darken-

ing air or the verse with its black vowels and its opening
sound, rich and lutelike?

He walked away slowly towards the deeper shadows at the
end of the colonnade, beating the stone softly with his stick to
hide his revery from the students whom he had left: and
allowed his mind to summon back to itself the age of Dowland
and Byrd and Nash.

Eyes, opening from the darkness of desire, eyes that
dimmed the breaking east. What was their languid grace but
the softness of chambering? And what was their shimmer but
the shimmer of the scum that mantled the cesspool of the
court of a slobbering Stuart. And he tasted in the language of
memory ambered wines, dying fallings of sweet airs, the proud
pavan: and saw with the eyes of memory kind gentlewomen in
Covent Garden wooing from their balconies with sucking
mouths and the poxfouled wenches of the taverns and young
wives that, gaily yielding to their ravishers, clipped and
clipped again.

The images he had summoned gave him no pleasure. They
were secret and enflaming but her image was not entangled by
them. That was not the way to think of her. It was not even
the way in which he thought of her. Could his mind then not
trust itself? Old phrases, sweet only with a disinterred sweet-
ness like the figseeds Cranly rooted out of his gleaming teeth.

It was not thought nor vision though he knew vaguely that
her figure was passing homeward through the city. Vaguely
first and then more sharply he smelt her body. A conscious
unrest seethed in his blood. Yes, it was her body he smelt: a
wild and languid smell: the tepid limbs over which his music
had flowed desirously and the secret soft linen upon which her
flesh distilled odour and a dew.

A louse crawled over the nape of his neck and, putting his
thumb and forefinger deftly beneath his loose collar, he caught
it. He rolled its body, tender yet brittle as a grain of rice,
between thumb and finger for an instant before he let it fall
from him and wondered would it live or die. There came to his
mind a curious phrase from Cornelius a Lapide which said

that the lice born of human sweat were not created by God with the other animals on the sixth day. But the tickling of the skin of his neck made his mind raw and red. The life of his body, illclad, illfed, louseeaten, made him close his eyelids in a sudden spasm of despair: and in the darkness he saw the brittle bright bodies of lice falling from the air and turning often as they fell. Yes; and it was not darkness that fell from the air. It was brightness.

Brightness falls from the air.

He had not even remembered rightly Nash's line. All the images it had awakened were false. His mind bred vermin. His thoughts were lice born of the sweat of sloth.

He came back quickly along the colonnade towards the group of students. Well then, let her go and be damned to her. She could love some clean athlete who washed himself every morning to the waist and had black hair on his chest. Let her.

Cranly had taken another dried fig from the supply in his pocket and was eating it slowly and noisily. Temple sat on the pediment of a pillar, leaning back, his cap pulled down on his sleepy eyes. A squat young man came out of the porch, a leather portfolio tucked under his armpit. He marched towards the group, striking the flags with the heels of his boots and with the ferule of his heavy umbrella. Then, raising the umbrella in salute, he said to all:

—Good evening, sirs.

He struck the flags again and tittered while his head trembled with a slight nervous movement. The tall consumptive student and Dixon and O'Keeffe were speaking in Irish and did not answer him. Then, turning to Cranly, he said:

—Good evening, particularly to you.

He moved the umbrella in indication and tittered again. Cranly, who was still chewing the fig, answered with loud movements of his jaws.

—Good? Yes. It is a good evening.

The squat student looked at him seriously and shook his umbrella gently and reprovingly.

—I can see, he said, that you are about to make obvious remarks.

—Um, Cranly answered, holding out what remained of the halfchewed fig and jerking it towards the squat student's mouth in sign that he should eat.

The squat student did not eat it but, indulging his special humour, said gravely, still tittering and prodding his phrase with his umbrella:

—Do you intend that . . .

He broke off, pointed bluntly to the munched pulp of the fig and said loudly:

—I allude to that.

—Um, Cranly said as before.

—Do you intend that now, the squat student said, as *ipso facto* or, let us say, as so to speak?

Dixon turned aside from his group, saying:

—Goggins was waiting for you, Glynn. He has gone round to the Adelphi to look for you and Moynihan. What have you there? he asked, tapping the portfolio under Glynn's arm.

—Examination papers, Glynn answered. I give them monthly examinations to see that they are profiting by my tuition.

He also tapped the portfolio and coughed gently and smiled.

—Tuition! said Cranly rudely. I suppose you mean the barefooted children that are taught by a bloody ape like you. God help them!

He bit off the rest of the fig and flung away the butt.

—I suffer little children to come unto me, Glynn said amiably.

—A bloody ape, Cranly repeated with emphasis, and a blasphemous bloody ape!

Temple stood up and, pushing past Cranly, addressed Glynn:

—That phrase you said now, he said, is from the new testament about suffer the children to come to me.

—Go to sleep again, Temple, said O'Keeffe.

—Very well, then, Temple continued, still addressing

Glynn, and if Jesus suffered the children to come why does the church send them all to hell if they die unbaptised? Why is that?

—Were you baptised yourself, Temple? the consumptive student asked.

—But why are they sent to hell if Jesus said they were all to come? Temple said, his eyes searching in Glynn's eyes.

Glynn coughed and said gently, holding back with difficulty the nervous titter in his voice and moving his umbrella at every word:

—And, as you remark, if it is thus I ask emphatically whence comes this thusness.

—Because the church is cruel like all old sinners, Temple said.

—Are you quite orthodox on that point, Temple? Dixon said suavely.

—Saint Augustine says that about unbaptised children going to hell, Temple answered, because he was a cruel old sinner too.

—I bow to you, Dixon said, but I had the impression that limbo existed for such cases.

—Don't argue with him, Dixon, Cranly said brutally. Don't talk to him or look at him. Lead him home with a sugan the way you'd lead a bleating goat.

—Limbo! Temple cried. That's a fine invention too. Like hell.

—But with the unpleasantness left out, Dixon said.

He turned smiling to the others and said:

—I think I am voicing the opinions of all present in saying so much.

—You are, Glynn said in a firm tone. On that point Ireland is united.

He struck the ferule of his umbrella on the stone floor of the colonnade.

—Hell, Temple said. I can respect that invention of the grey spouse of Satan. Hell is Roman, like the walls of the Romans, strong and ugly. But what is limbo?

—Put him back into the perambulator, Cranly, O'Keeffe called out.

Cranly made a swift step towards Temple, halted, stamping his foot, crying as if to a fowl:

—Hoosh!

Temple moved away nimbly.

—Do you know what limbo is? he cried. Do you know what we call a notion like that in Roscommon?

—Hoosh! Blast you! Cranly cried, clapping his hands.

—Neither my arse nor my elbow! Temple cried out scornfully. And that's what I call limbo.

—Give us that stick here, Cranly said.

He snatched the ashplant roughly from Stephen's hand and sprang down the steps: but Temple, hearing him move in pursuit, fled through the dusk like a wild creature, nimble and fleetfooted. Cranly's heavy boots were heard loudly charging across the quadrangle and then returning heavily, foiled and spurning the gravel at each step.

His step was angry and with an angry abrupt gesture he thrust the stick back into Stephen's hand. Stephen felt that his anger had another cause but, feigning patience, touched his arm slightly and said quietly:

—Cranly, I told you I wanted to speak to you. Come away.

Cranly looked at him for a few moments and asked:

—Now?

—Yes, now, Stephen said. We can't speak here. Come away.

They crossed the quadrangle together without speaking. The birdcall from *Siegfried* whistled softly followed them from the steps of the porch. Cranly turned: and Dixon, who had whistled, called out:

—Where are you fellows off to? What about that game, Cranly?

They parleyed in shouts across the still air about a game of billiards to be played in the Adelphi hotel. Stephen walked on alone and out into the quiet of Kildare Street. Opposite Maple's hotel he stood to wait, patient again. The name of the hotel, a colourless polished wood, and its colourless quiet front stung him like a glance of polite disdain. He stared angrily back at the softly lit drawingroom of the hotel in which he imagined the sleek lives of the patricians of Ireland housed in calm. They thought of army commissions and land agents: peasants greeted them along the roads in the country: they knew the names of certain French dishes and gave orders to jarvies in highpitched provincial voices which pierced through their skintight accents.

How could he hit their conscience or how cast his shadow over the imaginations of their daughters, before their squires begat upon them, that they might breed a race less ignoble than their own? And under the deepened dusk he felt the thoughts and desires of the race to which he belonged flitting like bats, across the dark country lanes, under trees by the edges of streams and near the poolmottled bogs. A woman had waited in the doorway as Davin had passed by at night and, offering him a cup of milk, had all but wooed him to her bed; for Davin had the mild eyes of one who could be secret. But him no woman's eyes had wooed.

His arm was taken in a strong grip and Cranly's voice said:

—Let us eke go.

They walked southward in silence. Then Cranly said:

—That blithering idiot Temple! I swear to Moses, do you know, that I'll be the death of that fellow one time.

But his voice was no longer angry and Stephen wondered was he thinking of her greeting to him under the porch.

They turned to the left and walked on as before. When they had gone on so for some time Stephen said:

—Cranly, I had an unpleasant quarrel this evening.

—With your people? Cranly asked.

—With my mother.

—About religion?

—Yes, Stephen answered.

After a pause Cranly asked:

—What age is your mother?

—Not old, Stephen said. She wishes me to make my easter duty.

—And will you?

—I will not, Stephen said.

—Why not? Cranly said.

—I will not serve, answered Stephen.

—That remark was made before, Cranly said calmly.

—It is made behind now, said Stephen hotly.

Cranly pressed Stephen's arm, saying:

—Go easy, my dear man. You're an excitable bloody man, do you know.

He laughed nervously as he spoke and, looking up into Stephen's face with moved and friendly eyes, said:

—Do you know that you are an excitable man?

—I daresay I am, said Stephen, laughing also.

Their minds, lately estranged, seemed suddenly to have been drawn closer, one to the other.

—Do you believe in the eucharist? Cranly asked.

—I do not, Stephen said.

—Do you disbelieve then?

—I neither believe in it nor disbelieve in it, Stephen answered.

—Many persons have doubts, even religious persons, yet they overcome them or put them aside, Cranly said. Are your doubts on that point too strong?

—I do not wish to overcome them, Stephen answered.

Cranly, embarrassed for a moment, took another fig from his pocket and was about to eat it when Stephen said:

—Don't, please. You cannot discuss this question with your mouth full of chewed fig.

Cranly examined the fig by the light of a lamp under which he halted. Then he smelt it with both nostrils, bit a tiny piece, spat it out and threw the fig rudely into the gutter. Addressing it as it lay, he said:

—Depart from me, ye cursed, into everlasting fire!

Taking Stephen's arm, he went on again and said:

—Do you not fear that those words may be spoken to you on the day of judgment?

—What is offered me on the other hand? Stephen asked. An eternity of bliss in the company of the dean of studies?

—Remember, Cranly said, that he would be glorified.

—Ay, Stephen said somewhat bitterly, bright, agile, impassible and, above all, subtle.

—It is a curious thing, do you know, Cranly said dispassionately, how your mind is supersaturated with the religion in which you say you disbelieve. Did you believe in it when you were at school? I bet you did.

—I did, Stephen answered.

—And were you happier then? Cranly asked softly. Happier than you are now, for instance?

—Often happy, Stephen said, and often unhappy. I was someone else then.

—How someone else? What do you mean by that statement?

—I mean, said Stephen, that I was not myself as I am now, as I had to become.

—Not as you are now, not as you had to become, Cranly repeated. Let me ask you a question. Do you love your mother?

Stephen shook his head slowly.

—I don't know what your words mean, he said simply.

—Have you never loved anyone? Cranly asked.

—Do you mean women?

—I am not speaking of that, Cranly said in a colder tone. I ask you if you ever felt love towards anyone or anything.

Stephen walked on beside his friend, staring gloomily at the footpath.

—I tried to love God, he said at length. It seems now I failed. It is very difficult. I tried to unite my will with the will of God instant by instant. In that I did not always fail. I could perhaps do that still . . .

Cranly cut him short by asking:

—Has your mother had a happy life?

—How do I know? Stephen said.

—How many children had she?

—Nine or ten, Stephen answered. Some died.

—Was your father. . . . Cranly interrupted himself for an instant: and then said: I don't want to pry into your family affairs. But was your father what is called well-to-do? I mean when you were growing up?

—Yes, Stephen said.

—What was he? Cranly asked after a pause.

Stephen began to enumerate glibly his father's attributes.

—A medical student, an oarsman, a tenor, an amateur actor, a shouting politician, a small landlord, a small investor, a drinker, a good fellow, a storyteller, somebody's secretary, something in a distillery, a taxgatherer, a bankrupt and at present a praiser of his own past.

Cranly laughed, tightening his grip on Stephen's arm, and said:

—The distillery is damn good.

—Is there anything else you want to know? Stephen asked.

—Are you in good circumstances at present?

—Do I look it? Stephen asked bluntly.

—So then, Cranly went on musingly, you were born in the lap of luxury.

He used the phrase broadly and loudly as he often used technical expressions as if he wished his hearer to understand that they were used by him without conviction.

—Your mother must have gone through a good deal of suffering, he said then. Would you not try to save her from suffering more even if . . . or would you?

—If I could, Stephen said. That would cost me very little.

—Then do so, Cranly said. Do as she wishes you to do. What is it for you? You disbelieve in it. It is a form: nothing else. And you will set her mind at rest.

He ceased and, as Stephen did not reply, remained silent. Then, as if giving utterance to the process of his own thought, he said:

-—Whatever else is unsure in this stinking dunghill of a

world a mother's love is not. Your mother brings you into the world, carries you first in her body. What do we know about what she feels? But whatever she feels, it, at least, must be real. It must be. What are our ideas or ambitions? Play. Ideas! Why, that bloody bleating goat Temple has ideas. MacCann has ideas too. Every jackass going the roads thinks he has ideas.

Stephen, who had been listening to the unspoken speech behind the words, said with assumed carelessness:

—Pascal, if I remember rightly, would not suffer his mother to kiss him as he feared the contact of her sex.

—Pascal was a pig, said Cranly.

—Aloysius Gonzaga, I think, was of the same mind, Stephen said.

—And he was another pig then, said Cranly.

—The church calls him a saint, Stephen objected.

—I don't care a flaming damn what anyone calls him, Cranly said rudely and flatly. I call him a pig.

Stephen, preparing the words neatly in his mind, continued:

—Jesus, too, seems to have treated his mother with scant courtesy in public but Suarez, a jesuit theologian and Spanish gentleman, has apologised for him.

—Did the idea ever occur to you, Cranly asked, that Jesus was not what he pretended to be?

—The first person to whom that idea occurred, Stephen answered, was Jesus himself.

—I mean, Cranly said, hardening in his speech, did the idea ever occur to you that he was himself a conscious hypocrite, what he called the jews of his time, a whited sepulchre? Or, to put it more plainly, that he was a blackguard?

—That idea never occurred to me, Stephen answered. But I am curious to know are you trying to make a convert of me or a pervert of yourself?

He turned towards his friend's face and saw there a raw smile which some force of will strove to make finely significant.

Cranly asked suddenly in a plain sensible tone:

—Tell me the truth. Were you at all shocked by what I said?

—Somewhat, Stephen said.

—And why were you shocked, Cranly pressed on in the same tone, if you feel sure that our religion is false and that Jesus was not the son of God?

—I am not at all sure of it, Stephen said. He is more like a son of God than a son of Mary.

—And is that why you will not communicate, Cranly asked, because you are not sure of that too, because you feel that the host too may be the body and blood of the son of God and not a wafer of bread? And because you fear that it may be?

—Yes, Stephen said quietly. I feel that and I also fear it.

—I see, Cranly said.

Stephen, struck by his tone of closure, reopened the discussion at once by saying:

—I fear many things: dogs, horses, firearms, the sea, thunderstorms, machinery, the country roads at night.

—But why do you fear a bit of bread?

—I imagine, Stephen said, that there is a malevolent reality behind those things I say I fear.

—Do you fear then, Cranly asked, that the God of the Roman catholics would strike you dead and damn you if you made a sacrilegious communion?

—The God of the Roman catholics could do that now, Stephen said. I fear more than that the chemical action which would be set up in my soul by a false homage to a symbol behind which are massed twenty centuries of authority and veneration.

—Would you, Cranly asked, in extreme danger commit that particular sacrilege? For instance, if you lived in the penal days?

—I cannot answer for the past, Stephen replied. Possibly not.

—Then, said Cranly, you do not intend to become a protestant?

—I said that I had lost the faith, Stephen answered, but not that I had lost selfrespect. What kind of liberation would that be to forsake an absurdity which is logical and coherent and to embrace one which is illogical and incoherent?

They had walked on towards the township of Pembroke and now, as they went on slowly along the avenues, the trees and the scattered lights in the villas soothed their minds. The air of wealth and repose diffused about them seemed to comfort their neediness. Behind a hedge of laurel a light glimmered in the window of a kitchen and the voice of a servant was heard singing as she sharpened knives. She sang, in short broken bars, *Rosie O'Grady*.

Cranly stopped to listen, saying:

—*Mulier cantat.*

The soft beauty of the Latin word touched with an enchanting touch the dark of the evening, with a touch fainter and more persuading than the touch of music or of a woman's hand. The strife of their minds was quelled. The figure of woman as she appears in the liturgy of the church passed silently through the darkness: a whiterobed figure, small and slender as a boy and with a falling girdle. Her voice, frail and high as a boy's, was heard intoning from a distant choir the first words of a woman which pierce the gloom and clamour of the first chanting of the passion:

—*Et tu cum Jesu Galilæo eras.*

And all hearts were touched and turned to her voice, shining like a young star, shining clearer as the voice intoned the proparoxyton and more faintly as the cadence died.

The singing ceased. They went on together, Cranly repeating in strongly stressed rhythm the end of the refrain:

> *And when we are married,*
> *O, how happy we'll be*
> *For I love sweet Rosie O'Grady*
> *And Rosie O'Grady loves me.*

—There's real poetry for you, he said. There's real love.

He glanced sideways at Stephen with a strange smile and said:

—Do you consider that poetry? Or do you know what the words mean?

—I want to see Rosie first, said Stephen.

—She's easy to find, Cranly said.

His hat had come down on his forehead. He shoved it back: and in the shadow of the trees Stephen saw his pale face, framed by the dark, and his large dark eyes. Yes. His face was handsome: and his body was strong and hard. He had spoken of a mother's love. He felt then the sufferings of women, the weaknesses of their bodies and souls: and would shield them with a strong and resolute arm and bow his mind to them.

Away then: it is time to go. A voice spoke softly to Stephen's lonely heart, bidding him go and telling him that his friendship was coming to an end. Yes; he would go. He could not strive against another. He knew his part.

—Probably I shall go away, he said.

—Where? Cranly asked.

—Where I can, Stephen said.

—Yes, Cranly said. It might be difficult for you to live here now. But is it that that makes you go?

—I have to go, Stephen answered.

—Because, Cranly continued, you need not look upon yourself as driven away if you do not wish to go or as a heretic or an outlaw. There are many good believers who think as you do. Would that surprise you? The church is not the stone building nor even the clergy and their dogmas. It is the whole mass of those born into it. I don't know what you wish to do in life. Is it what you told me the night we were standing outside Harcourt Street station?

—Yes, Stephen said, smiling in spite of himself at Cranly's way of remembering thoughts in connection with places. The night you spent half an hour wrangling with Doherty about the shortest way from Sallygap to Larras.

—Pothead! Cranly said with calm contempt. What does he know about the way from Sallygap to Larras? Or what does he know about anything for that matter? And the big slobbering washingpot head of him!

He broke out into a loud long laugh.

—Well? Stephen said. Do you remember the rest?

—What you said, is it? Cranly asked. Yes, I remember it. To discover the mode of life or of art whereby your spirit could express itself in unfettered freedom.

Stephen raised his hat in acknowledgment.

—Freedom! Cranly repeated. But you are not free enough yet to commit a sacrilege. Tell me, would you rob?

—I would beg first, Stephen said.

—And if you got nothing, would you rob?

—You wish me to say, Stephen answered, that the rights of property are provisional and that in certain circumstances it is not unlawful to rob. Everyone would act in that belief. So I will not make you that answer. Apply to the jesuit theologian Juan Mariana de Talavera who will also explain to you in what circumstances you may lawfully kill your king and whether you had better hand him his poison in a goblet or smear it for him upon his robe or his saddlebow. Ask me rather would I suffer others to rob me or, if they did, would I call down upon them what I believe is called the chastisement of the secular arm?

—And would you?

—I think, Stephen said, it would pain me as much to do so as to be robbed.

—I see, Cranly said.

He produced his match and began to clean the crevice between two teeth. Then he said carelessly:

—Tell me, for example, would you deflower a virgin?

—Excuse me, Stephen said politely, is that not the ambition of most young gentlemen?

—What then is your point of view? Cranly asked.

His last phrase, soursmelling as the smoke of charcoal and disheartening, excited Stephen's brain, over which its fumes seemed to brood.

—Look here, Cranly, he said. You have asked me what I would do and what I would not do. I will tell you what I will do and what I will not do. I will not serve that in which I no longer believe whether it call itself my home, my fatherland or my church: and I will try to express myself in some mode of life or art as freely as I can and as wholly as I can, using for my defence the only arms I allow myself to use—silence, exile, and cunning.

Cranly seized his arm and steered him round so as to head back towards Leeson Park. He laughed almost slily and pressed Stephen's arm with an elder's affection.

—Cunning indeed! he said. Is it you? You poor poet, you!

—And you made me confess to you, Stephen said, thrilled by his touch, as I have confessed to you so many other things, have I not?

—Yes, my child, Cranly said, still gaily.

—You made me confess the fears that I have. But I will tell you also what I do not fear. I do not fear to be alone or to be spurned for another or to leave whatever I have to leave. And I am not afraid to make a mistake, even a great mistake, a lifelong mistake and perhaps as long as eternity too.

Cranly, now grave again, slowed his pace and said:

—Alone, quite alone. You have no fear of that. And you know what that word means? Not only to be separate from all others but to have not even one friend.

—I will take the risk, said Stephen.

—And not to have any one person, Cranly said, who would be more than a friend, more even than the noblest and truest friend a man ever had.

His words seemed to have struck some deep chord in his own nature. Had he spoken of himself, of himself as he was or wished to be? Stephen watched his face for some moments in silence. A cold sadness was there. He had spoken of himself, of his own loneliness which he feared.

—Of whom are you speaking? Stephen asked at length.

Cranly did not answer.

*　　*　　*

20 *March:* Long talk with Cranly on the subject of my revolt. He had his grand manner on. I supple and suave. Attacked me on the score of love for one's mother. Tried to

imagine his mother: cannot. Told me once, in a moment of thoughtlessness, his father was sixtyone when he was born. Can see him. Strong farmer type. Pepper and salt suit. Square feet. Unkempt grizzled beard. Probably attends coursing matches. Pays his dues regularly but not plentifully to Father Dwyer of Larras. Sometimes talks to girls after nightfall. But his mother? Very young or very old? Hardly the first. If so, Cranly would not have spoken as he did. Old then. Probably, and neglected. Hence Cranly's despair of soul: the child of exhausted loins.

21 *March, morning:* Thought this in bed last night but was too lazy and free to add it. Free, yes. The exhausted loins are those of Elisabeth and Zachary. Then he is the precursor. Item: he eats chiefly belly bacon and dried figs. Read locusts and wild honey. Also, when thinking of him, saw always a stern severed head or deathmask as if outlined on a grey curtain or veronica. Decollation they call it in the fold. Puzzled for the moment by saint John at the Latin gate. What do I see? A decollated precursor trying to pick the lock.

21 *March, night:* Free. Soulfree and fancyfree. Let the dead bury the dead. Ay. And let the dead marry the dead.

22 *March:* In company with Lynch followed a sizable hospital nurse. Lynch's idea. Dislike it. Two lean hungry greyhounds walking after a heifer.

23 *March:* Have not seen her since that night. Unwell? Sits at the fire perhaps with mamma's shawl on her shoulders. But not peevish. A nice bowl of gruel? Won't you now?

24 *March:* Began with a discussion with my mother. Subject: B.V.M. Handicapped by my sex and youth. To escape held up relations between Jesus and Papa against those between Mary and her son. Said religion was not a lying-in hospital. Mother indulgent. Said I have a queer mind and have read too much. Not true. Have read little and understood less. Then she said I would come back to faith because I had a restless mind. This means to leave church by backdoor of sin and reenter through the skylight of repentance. Cannot repent. Told her so and asked for sixpence. Got threepence.

Then went to college. Other wrangle with little roundhead rogue'seye Ghezzi. This time about Bruno the Nolan. Began in Italian and ended in pidgin English. He said Bruno was a terrible heretic. I said he was terribly burned. He agreed to this with some sorrow. Then gave me recipe for what he calls *risotto alla bergamasca*. When he pronounces a soft *o* he protrudes his full carnal lips as if he kissed the vowel. Has he? And could he repent? Yes, he could: and cry two round rogue's tears, one from each eye.

Crossing Stephen's, that is, my green, remembered that his countrymen and not mine had invented what Cranly the other night called our religion. A quartet of them, soldiers of the ninetyseventh infantry regiment, sat at the foot of the cross and tossed up dice for the overcoat of the crucified.

Went to library. Tried to read three reviews. Useless. She is not out yet. Am I alarmed? About what? That she will never be out again.

Blake wrote:

> *I wonder if William Bond will die*
> *For assuredly he is very ill.*

Alas, poor William!

I was once at a diorama in Rotunda. At the end were pictures of big nobs. Among them William Ewart Gladstone, just then dead. Orchestra played *O, Willie, we have missed you*.

A race of clodhoppers!

25 *March, morning:* A troubled night of dreams. Want to get them off my chest.

A long curving gallery. From the floor ascend pillars of dark vapours. It is peopled by the images of fabulous kings, set in stone. Their hands are folded upon their knees in token of weariness and their eyes are darkened for the errors of men go up before them for ever as dark vapours.

Strange figures advance from a cave. They are not as tall as men. One does not seem to stand quite apart from another. Their faces are phosphorescent, with darker streaks. They peer at me and their eyes seem to ask me something. They do not speak.

30 *March:* This evening Cranly was in the porch of the library, proposing a problem to Dixon and her brother. A mother let her child fall into the Nile. Still harping on the mother. A crocodile seized the child. Mother asked it back. Crocodile said all right if she told him what he was going to do with the child, eat it or not eat it.

This mentality, Lepidus would say, is indeed bred out of your mud by the operation of your sun.

And mine? Is it not too? Then into Nilemud with it!

1 *April:* Disapprove of this last phrase.

2 *April:* Saw her drinking tea and eating cakes in Johnston, Mooney and O'Brien's. Rather, lynxeyed Lynch saw her as we passed. He tells me Cranly was invited there by brother. Did he bring his crocodile? Is he the shining light now? Well, I discovered him. I protest I did. Shining quietly behind a bushel of Wicklow bran.

3 *April:* Met Davin at the cigar shop opposite Findlater's church. He was in a black sweater and had a hurleystick. Asked me was it true I was going away and why. Told him the shortest way to Tara was *via* Holyhead. Just then my father came up. Introduction. Father, polite and observant. Asked Davin if he might offer him some refreshment. Davin could not, was going to a meeting. When we came away father told me he had a good honest eye. Asked me why I did not join a rowingclub. I pretended to think it over. Told me then how he broke Pennyfeather's heart. Wants me to read law. Says I was cut out for that. More mud, more crocodiles.

5 *April:* Wild spring. Scudding clouds. O life! Dark stream of swirling bogwater on which appletrees have cast down their delicate flowers. Eyes of girls among the leaves. Girls demure and romping. All fair or auburn: no dark ones. They blush better. Houp-la!

6 *April:* Certainly she remembers the past. Lynch says all women do. Then she remembers the time of her childhood—

and mine if I was ever a child. The past is consumed in the present and the present is living only because it brings forth the future. Statues of women, if Lynch be right, should always be fully draped, one hand of the woman feeling regretfully her own hinder parts.

6 *April, later:* Michael Robartes remembers forgotten beauty and, when his arms wrap her round, he presses in his arms the loveliness which has long faded from the world. Not this. Not at all. I desire to press in my arms the loveliness which has not yet come into the world.

10 *April:* Faintly, under the heavy night, through the silence of the city which has turned from dreams to dreamless sleep as a weary lover whom no caresses move, the sound of hoofs upon the road. Not so faintly now as they come near the bridge: and in a moment as they pass the darkened windows the silence is cloven by alarm as by an arrow. They are heard now far away, hoofs that shine amid the heavy night as gems, hurrying beyond the sleeping fields to what journey's end— what heart?—bearing what tidings?

11 *April:* Read what I wrote last night. Vague words for a vague emotion. Would she like it? I think so. Then I should have to like it also.

13 *April:* That tundish has been on my mind for a long time. I looked it up and find it English and good old blunt English too. Damn the dean of studies and his funnel! What did he come here for to teach us his own language or to learn it from us? Damn him one way or the other!

14 *April:* John Alphonsus Mulrennan has just returned from the west of Ireland. (European and Asiatic papers please copy.) He told us he met an old man there in a mountain cabin. Old man had red eyes and short pipe. Old man spoke Irish. Mulrennan spoke Irish. Then old man and Mulrennan spoke English. Mulrennan spoke to him about universe and stars. Old man sat, listened, smoked, spat. Then said:

—Ah, there must be terrible queer creatures at the latter end of the world.

I fear him. I fear his redrimmed horny eyes. It is with him I must struggle all through this night till day come, till he or I lie dead, gripping him by the sinewy throat till . . . Till what? Till he yield to me? No. I mean him no harm.

15 *April:* Met her today pointblank in Grafton Street. The crowd brought us together. We both stopped. She asked me why I never came, said she had heard all sorts of stories about me. This was only to gain time. Asked me, was I writing poems? About whom? I asked her. This confused her more and I felt sorry and mean. Turned off that valve at once and opened the spiritual-heroic refrigerating apparatus, invented and patented in all countries by Dante Alighieri. Talked rapidly of myself and my plans. In the midst of it unluckily I made a sudden gesture of a revolutionary nature. I must have looked like a fellow throwing a handful of peas into the air. People began to look at us. She shook hands a moment after and, in going away, said she hoped I would do what I said.

Now I call that friendly, don't you?

Yes, I liked her today. A little or much? Don't know. I liked her and it seems a new feeling to me. Then, in that case, all the rest, all that I thought I thought and all that I felt I felt, all the rest before now, in fact . . . O, give it up, old chap! Sleep it off!

16 *April:* Away! Away!

The spell of arms and voices: the white arms of roads, their promise of close embraces and the black arms of tall ships that stand against the moon, their tale of distant nations. They are held out to say: We are alone. Come. And the voices say with them: We are your kinsmen. And the air is thick with their company as they call to me, their kinsman, making ready to go, shaking the wings of their exultant and terrible youth.

26 *April:* Mother is putting my new secondhand clothes in order. She prays now, she says, that I may learn in my own life and away from home and friends what the heart is and what it feels. Amen. So be it. Welcome, O life! I go to encoun-

ter for the millionth time the reality of experience and to forge in the smithy of my soul the uncreated conscience of my race.

27 *April:* Old father, old artificer, stand me now and ever in good stead. *needs guidance*

Dublin 1904
Trieste 1914

A Note on the Text

For this definitive edition, Chester G. Anderson compared Joyce's final fair-copy manuscript, in his own handwriting, now in the National Library of Ireland, with all the texts published in England and America, and with lists of corrections and changes noted by Joyce, some of which were never made in any of the published versions. Mr. Anderson then prepared an extensive list of possible corrections in the current Viking-Compass edition. Richard Ellmann, the editor of Joyce's letters, was asked to act as arbiter, and reviewed the final selection.

Mr. Anderson's complete study, with a critical text of the novel noting all the variants, appears in a monograph accepted as his doctoral thesis at Columbia University in 1962.

This new edition has been set as nearly as possible page-for-page with the old, so that references based on the old text will not differ by more than one page.

The People
Next Door

The People
Next Door

Bettye Griffin

KENSINGTON PUBLISHING CORP.

DAFINA BOOKS are published by

Kensington Publishing Corp.
850 Third Avenue
New York, NY 10022

Special book excerpts or customized printings can also be created to fit specific needs. For details, write or phone the office of the Kensington Special Sales Manager: Kensington Publishing Corp., 850 Third Avenue, New York, NY 10022. Attn. Special Sales Department. Phone: 1-800-221-2647.

Dafina Books and the Dafina logo Reg. U.S. Pat. & TM Off.

ISBN 0-7394-5131-6

First Kensington Trade Paperback Printing: April 2005

Printed in the United States of America

In memory of Peter A. Griffin
(1952–1992)
Missing you now and always

Acknowledgments

Many people have supported and encouraged me since I've been writing, and at this time I'd like to thank every one of them. Since I can't possibly name you all, let's just say that you know who you are.

Special thanks to my husband, Bernard Underwood, who after all these years continues to awe and inspire me and who, among other things, provided the saying that kicks off Chapter 27.

To my mom, Mrs. Eva M. Griffin, for being the absolute best.

To my agent, Elaine English, who believed in this project from day one.

To Kimberly Rowe-Van Allen, whose input was invaluable, as always.

To Karen Bell, formerly of the B. Dalton Jacksonville Landing, the most professional bookstore manager I've known. I'll miss signing at your store. Happy retirement.

Finally, since this story is about an extended family, I want to acknowledge Bonnie Golden Underwood, Dawn Henderson Stewart, Yolanda Flynn Stewart, and Stephen Stewart, all of whom have proven that Will and Jada don't have the patent on getting along with the ex; and to the offspring who benefitted from all the good feelings: Timothy and Katrina Underwood; Cheri and Jamila Stewart.

And a special shout-out to the Williams family of Gary, Indiana.

Your basic extended family today includes your ex-husband or wife, your ex's new mate, your new mate, possibly your new mate's ex, and any new mate that your new mate's ex has acquired.

—Delia Ephron

CHAPTER 1

To deprive misfortune of its power.
—Anonymous, on perseverance

Excitement bounced off the walls of Lisa and Darrell Canfield's SUV like a rubber ball as they approached the highway exit ramp. After weeks of looking at land and more land, Lisa had an instinctive feeling they were about to find the perfect spot to build their dream house.

She soon learned she was wrong.

Darrell scowled. "I don't get it. What the hell is this?"

She glanced at her husband, then back at the road, unable to hide her dismay. The salesperson had described Northeast Jacksonville as an undiscovered paradise, an oasis of lush green lawns and graceful homes, but all she saw was forest. No gas stations, convenience stores, or fast food restaurants that usually marked highway exits. Nothing at all but an uninhabited jungle that from the air probably looked like giant bunches of broccoli.

She tried to mask her disappointment. "Maybe the agent was envisioning how the area will look five years from now."

"Then maybe we ought to come back in five years," he fired back.

"Oh, you." She playfully poked his arm. "Hey, I see something up ahead."

Signs of life appeared, but not good signs. Trailers sat on both sides of the street, front yards littered with rusted bicycles and old tires.

Darrell's scowl deepened. "Look at this mess."

Lisa frowned at the mobile homes perched on cement blocks. Most of them had peeled, exposing the steel underneath. But they weren't crowded together, like they were in those tacky trailer parks. The large lots they sat on gave her pause. She wondered if the residents owned the land as well. Maybe they were land rich and cash poor, hoping someone would make an offer for their property. Now that the area was being developed, their dreams of a big payday were probably about to come true.

"I agree it looks awful," she said, "but since we're here, we might as well go ahead and look at the land. There's the sign for the subdivision up ahead on the right—"her voice broke off as a large building came into view on the left.

"Oh, no. A school? Forget it, Lisa, it's not gonna work." Darrell's eyes narrowed to angry slits. "I don't want to live this close to a school." He thumped the steering wheel. "What the hell is wrong with these developers? They need to think before they start clearing land by schools and raggedy trailers and expect people to come in and build upscale homes. This isn't Monopoly money we're spending."

She sighed. He was right. This property had too many strikes against it. "Let's just turn around."

Darrell steered into a U-turn, his mouth set in a hard line. "This is getting to be a real pain in the butt," he said. "Finding the right plans was hard enough, but I thought once we had them, finding a place to build would be a snap. Maybe we should just stay in St. Marys and see about adding on a bedroom and bath for Mom."

Lisa fought the panic rising from her belly and tried to sound calm and reasonable. "I know it's discouraging, Darrell, but we can't give up. The new house plan is perfect for us. And moving to Jacksonville means we won't have that long commute to work." She let that sink in for a few seconds. "Remember when Cary sprained his ankle in gym class? I must have sat in traffic on the Fuller Warren Bridge for a half hour trying to get to his school to pick him up."

"Yeah, I know."

She could tell he was weakening and rushed on. "You promised we'd build a new place in Jacksonville if I took the job at Costco."

"Yeah, I know. You're right, but I'm tired of looking at these crummy lots. When was the last time we just relaxed all weekend?"

She understood how he felt. She was beat, too. Every Sunday for weeks they'd toured Jacksonville, looking at model homes. Their need for a larger home was more pressing now that Darrell's recently widowed mother wanted to move in with them. They thought that finding a blueprint that met their defined needs as well as their wish list would be their biggest challenge, and while it wasn't easy, they'd done it. Their twin boys, Cary and Courtney, would share a bedroom much larger than the one they had now. Paige, Lisa's daughter from her first marriage, and Devon, Darrell's daughter from his, would still have their own rooms, but they would no longer have to share a bathroom with the boys—a huge convenience for appearance-conscious fifteen-year-old females. And they'd gotten Darrell's mother the first floor quarters she wanted.

Darrell was excited about the quiet nook off the master bath where he could work. As manager of the Jacksonville branch of a nationwide brokerage house, he liked to check on the European markets every morning before work. Lisa's favorite feature was the pool bath accessible from the patio. No more tracking chlorinated water through the house.

Finding the place to build was proving to be even harder. Darrell liked the idea of building in a subdivision with homes of similar value. He said living with all those ridiculous community regulations was worth it because no one could put a tiny cottage or patio home next door and make their place look silly and grandiose. But he refused to look at any subdivision that included the word "Plantation" in its title, saying generations of his ancestors had prayed to get off the plantations and he wasn't bringing his family to live on one, regardless of it being strictly symbolic.

Unfortunately, many of the nicest subdivisons were called This or That Plantation, with attractive homes surrounded by sprawling, shade-supplying oak trees, usually close to the picturesque St. Johns River that weaved through Jacksonville. Lisa looked longingly beyond the brick walls at the stately homes and lush green trees and wished she could get Darrell to change his mind. All the sites they'd seen were unacceptable, and she feared they would never find a place to build.

One by one, each prospective homesite was ruled out as being too isolated, too congested, or in unsuitable environments, near schools, trailers, steel electric towers, or outdated strung-up telephone wires. In this region, city government tended to do things backward when it came to construction. First they green-lighted the building of new communities for hundreds of residents, and not until everyone moved in did they realize the roads needed to be widened to handle increased traffic, or that those ugly phone, electric, and cable wires needed to be run underground, or that the drainage wasn't sufficient. Whatever the reason, the result was always the same, snarls of both traffic and tempers as drivers took curvy, narrow detours around huge hills of dirt while construction was underway.

By now Lisa and Darrell had spent almost as much time scouting locations as they had looking at model homes.

"Which way are we going now?" Darrell asked.

"Get back on the highway. We have to cross the bridge to look at the next place. After that we can stop by Michael's and Kim's."

"I didn't hear lunch on that list. I'm hungry."

"Kim said they'd have something for us." Lisa's voice sounded weary even to her own ears. Darrell reached across the center console and patted her hand.

"Don't worry," he said. "I promise we'll soon be enjoying our Sunday afternoons at home like we used to."

She sighed loudly. "I hope so."

Lisa saw the hopeful glint in Kim's eye when her friend opened her front door and knew what would follow. She shook her head before Kim could ask.

"Oh, no. And you had such a good feeling about today. What happened?"

"A big bust. The first place was so bad we ended up turning around without going in," Lisa said as she and Darrell walked with Kim to the patio. They took a moment to greet Kim's husband Michael, who was grilling hamburgers.

Darrell took over the job of sautéing onion slices on the side burner as he recounted the unacceptable scenery in the first neighborhood. "The second place was better," he said. "It's all new, and everything we need is right there, supermarket, dry cleaner, pharmacy, movies, restaurants, even new schools for the kids. Plus it's close to work."

"So what's wrong with it?" Michael asked with a confused shrug.

"They put the homes too close together," Lisa said, "just twelve feet on both sides."

Kim nodded. "Yeah . . . most people don't like having a lot of grounds to care for. Too much work."

"That's why they make riding lawn mowers. I like my privacy," Darrell said in the that's-the-last-word tone Lisa knew so well.

"The man in the sales office tells us the only way we can get around that would be if we bought two lots," she explained to Kim and Michael. "But we don't think we should have to spend all that money for something we should be getting already. That's the trouble with a lot of these subdivisions."

"We're sick of the whole thing," Darrell said. He held out a platter for Michael to transfer the meat to, then brought it over to the table where Lisa and Kim sat. The air was scented with the flavorful aroma of onion, beef, and barbecue sauce.

They were joined by the Gillespie's seven-year-old daughter Alicyn. For a few minutes no one spoke as they dressed their burgers, unless it was to ask for the rolls or condiments to be passed their way.

"I'm sorry you guys are having so much trouble," Kim said as she tore open a large bag of ridged potato chips. "When we went looking, we found this place almost right away."

"Of course," Michael said with a smile, "our requirements weren't quite as stringent as yours."

"I do love your house," Lisa said. "I can't believe you guys moved in just before Christmas. It's barely been six weeks, and it looks like you've lived here for years." The Gillespies lived in a new subdivision bordering the St. John's River. Although they hadn't been able to secure one of the prime riverfront lots, which had sold quickly in spite of premium prices, the quiet wooded area where their house sat was almost as pleasant.

"Too bad they're all sold out. We'd love to have our best friends for neighbors," Kim said. "But your house would be too big for the lots here anyway." She drew in her breath. "Michael! Around the corner, at the tip of the boulevard . . ."

He snapped his fingers. "Of course! That'd be perfect!"

"You two want to tell us what you're talking about, or is it a secret?" Darrell asked crankily, prompting Lisa to place a reassuring palm on his shoulder. Their frustrating search had turned her usually affable husband into a real grouch.

"We went bike riding one day after we moved in," Kim explained. "We turned north on the boulevard to see how far it went. It ends right around the corner in a peninsula on the river. People have put up some gorgeous homes, I'm talking candidates for magazine covers, and last I saw there were still a few lots for sale. You have to see the street. It's breathtaking, with the river right behind their backyards and a view of downtown."

"We can ride over there after lunch," Michael said.

"Sure, we'd love to."

"Hi there!"

Lisa's hips did a slight jump from her chair, startled by the strange male voice just a few feet away. A man had come around the back of the house. She decided he had to be a neighbor, or else he would have used the front door.

"Hey, Ernie," Michael said. "What's up?"

"Not a thing. Just finishing up some yard work." The man approached, nodded at Lisa and Darrell and waited expectantly, his hand reaching to pull out an empty chair.

Michael performed introductions before Ernie could sit, identifying him as the owner of the house next door and adding, "I'll have to catch up with you later, Ernie. We're going to finish lunch and then go out for a minute."

Ernie hastily lowered his hand from the chair back. "Oh, sure. See you later. Nice meeting you folks," he said with a nod.

"Likewise." Darrell waited until Ernie disappeared around the corner and then spoke in a low voice. "Is it me or is he kind of pushy? He was about to sit down, even though he could see we were eating, and nobody invited him to join us. What kind of neighbors do you have, anyway?"

Kim shot a concerned glance at her daughter, but Alicyn seemed more engrossed in the old sitcom on the patio TV than in what the adults were saying. "When we first moved in, he and his wife were very helpful," Kim said softly, "but it wasn't long before we noticed they seemed a little too interested in what we have and what we do. And, of course, who we know," she added with a grin. Then she rolled her eyes. "I'll bet Ernie wasn't anywhere near his yard. He just cut his grass yesterday."

"Oh, come on, Kim. Lighten up a bit," Michael said. "So what, he's a little curious. You make him sound like an old washerwoman. It's the New Yorker in you. You're suspicious of everybody." He laughed. "Did I ever tell you guys that when we got a toddler seat for Alicyn attached to Kim's bike, that she rode around with a ten-pound sack of potatoes in it for a week because she wanted to make sure it was strong enough?"

"All right, so maybe I don't like to take people's word for anything," Kim admitted as Darrell and Lisa laughed. "But I still say Ernie wasn't working in his yard. He probably saw that Durango outside and wanted to see who it belonged to."

"Now Kim, you don't want to forget the good neighbor policy," Lisa teased.

"Yeah, well, somebody should remind Ernie that the best good neighbor policy is the one that goes, 'Keep your distance.' "

Lisa helped Kim clean up after they ate. As they worked in the kitchen, Kim said, "I know you said it was okay for Darrell's mother to live with you, but isn't she causing a lot of problems already? You wouldn't be going crazy with a new house if it wasn't for her. I hope this isn't an omen of things to come."

"No, I can't put this on her. The main reason we're getting a new house is so we'll be closer to the kids when we're at work. When Ma Canfield found out we planned to leave Georgia, she said she didn't want to be left behind. I can understand her wanting to be near us now that Pa Canfield's gone."

Kim chuckled. "Whenever I hear you refer to your in-laws it makes me think of Ma and Pa Kettle. You'd think your mother-in-law was ninety years old instead of in her sixties. But since Missus Canfield's coming to live with you, I'm glad you're at least getting a new house out of it. I know I'd be a wild woman if *my* mother-in-law said she wanted to move in with us."

Lisa chuckled. "No one believes me when I tell them I get along well with my mother-in-law. Her birthday's the day before mine, and we're a lot alike. My mother's the one who'd drive me crazy, getting up at six A.M. to dust and mop, or not being able to sleep if there's as much as a dirty fork in the kitchen sink. But I'm worried about Darrell. He's serious about staying in Georgia and adding on a bedroom and bath for his mother, and I don't want to do that. I hope this property is as nice as you say, because it's make or break time."

"I don't think you'll be disappointed." Kim wiped her hands on a dish towel. "I'm done. I'll get Alicyn, and we'll go."

They got into the Gillespie's Impala, Kim and Lisa flanking Alicyn in the backseat. Michael turned left onto the main road, which curved to the right before ending in a large cul-de-sac partially surrounded by water. Several impressive homes stood on the riverfront and others were in the process of being built. Only two empty lots remained.

Lisa gasped. Kim was right; the block was breathtaking. The view of the St. John's River, with the skyline of downtown Jacksonville on the other side, was stunning. The houses were spaced at least twenty feet apart, maybe even twenty-five, and the side view of existing homes revealed the proportions of lawn in the back were as generous as those in front. She leaned forward and gripped Darrell's arm in excitement. "It's perfect."

"Our house would fit in fine with these. And it's not even a subdivision, so there won't be any community regulations."

They drove back and forth, eventually deciding the first of the available lots was best because it had a better view of downtown. Michael parked, and they got out for a closer look.

"It looks like we'll be able to crack open that bottle of champagne we've been saving after all," Kim said happily.

"I think this is it," Lisa said. She glanced at Darrell for confirmation and was surprised to see an apprehensive expression on his face.

"It's going to be expensive, you know, a waterfront lot like this," he said slowly.

"Darrell, we've been sitting on the profits from that dot-com stock you sold for a couple of years now."

"I know, and this is probably going to take all of it. You realize this lot will cost half as much as the house, maybe more. We might have to hold off on getting new furniture. Remember, I'm not a radiologist like Brad."

Lisa made a face at the mention of her first husband. In the dozen years since their divorce, she and Brad Betancourt managed to put all the bad feelings behind them and move on with their respective personal lives while still being good parents to Paige. Brad was co-owner of a busy diagnostic center and made big bucks, but she didn't like to hear Darrell compare himself negatively to Brad. Darrell had done well for them. Besides, the earnings from her own career added nicely to their income, which was more than she could say for that lazy woman Brad married, whose lifestyle could be a soap opera. "The Rich and the Restless," starring Suzanne Betancourt. *She'd* want to rush out and redecorate a new house, even if there wasn't anything wrong with the old furnishings, just for the heck of it. Yeah, silly Suzanne. Her definition of disposable income was something to be disposed of.

Lisa linked her arm through Darrell's, thoughts of Brad's wife fading fast. "We'll do fine. We don't need new furniture. I'm not like Lucy Ricardo or some other scatterbrained fifties housewife who only wants to spend, spend, spend. The important thing is that we hung in there and didn't give up. This is our reward." She squeezed his arm affectionately. "Just think, Darrell. After everything we've been through, now we have both the plans of our house and a location for it. In six months or so our beautiful new house will be standing on this very land."

CHAPTER 2

The we of me.
—Carson McCullers, on family

The very next day, Lisa and Darrell met with the real estate agent who was handling the sale of the property. The man's attitude irritated Lisa. After inviting them to sit, he reminded them of the price, as if he expected them to suddenly get up and say with embarrassment that they'd made a mistake. When Darrell said he was aware of the cost, the agent, a middle-aged man with thinning sandy brown hair and a pink plaid shirt that practically screamed Kmart, took his time opening their floor plan. "Wow. Quite a large house," he said as he looked it over. "Over four thousand square feet."

"The other homes on the cul-de-sac appear to be in that same range," Darrell said. He spoke casually, but Lisa could tell by the coldness in his eyes that he was just as annoyed by the man's patronizing attitude as she was.

"Yes, that's true. Got a big family, do you?"

"Two girls, two boys, and my mother will be moving in with us," Darrell replied.

"Nice. Well, this lot can easily accommodate the dimensions of your house."

"We'll be putting in a pool as well," Lisa said.

The agent nodded. "There's plenty of room for that, as long as it's not Olympic size." He chuckled.

She wondered why he had turned amiable, and then he asked a

question. "Uh . . . may I inquire what line of work you're in, Mister Canfield?"

She nodded knowingly. So that was it. He wanted to know how they could afford the expensive property. She suppressed a smile as Darrell named their employers but not their professions—answering without really answering. "We're in the process of arranging our financing," he added without pause. "I'd like to give you a binder in the meantime." He named a figure. "Is that sufficient?"

"Yes, that'll do fine." The agent quietly waited as Lisa took the checkbook from her purse and wrote out a check. Darrell had effectively halted his curiosity. To ask again about their careers after Darrell's evasive reply would make him look desperately curious, and he knew it.

She handed the check to Darrell, who glanced at it before handing it to the agent. She took the receipt he wrote, and they all shook hands and said good-bye.

"That wasn't too bad, eh?" Darrell said when they were in the car.

"It wasn't exactly pleasant, either. Do you suppose he asks white buyers what *they* do for a living?"

"Maybe he does, but I'm sure he doesn't look at them with that 'How can they possibly afford this?' look."

"He can be as surprised as he wants to be, but he can't stop us from buying the land."

"That's right. We won't have to see him again anyway. The financing for the lot will be included in our mortgage."

On Saturday, they brought their children and Darrell's mother down to Jacksonville to look at the site.

Darrell's mother, Esther, drew in her breath when they turned into the cul-de-sac. "Oh, this is lovely!" The river, visible through the large spaces between houses and from the empty lots, glistened in the sunlight.

"Wow! Is our house gonna look like that?" Cary asked, pointing to the first residence on the street, an impressive two-story tan stucco mansion with a reddish-brown Spanish tile roof.

"Actually, no," Lisa replied. "Our house is going to be very nice, and probably just as large, but it's a different style altogether."

"And it's going to be right here," Darrell said, stopping the Durango in front of their lot.

The twins, sitting in the third-row seat, were the last ones out, but quickly ran in front of everyone, not stopping until they got to the center of the property. Cary, his sprained ankle healed, did cartwheels, while Courtney held his arms outstretched and shouted, "This is where my room's gonna be!"

"When will it be finished?" Devon asked.

Lisa placed an arm around the child who technically was her stepdaughter but in her heart was as much hers as Paige and the twins. It pleased her to see Devon show interest. She had grown rather pensive lately, and Lisa suspected it came from a lack of contact with her mother. Darrell's first wife, Paula, lived outside of Houston and had recently remarried a much younger man. The ceremony had taken place last fall, and Devon hadn't been invited to spend her Christmas vacation in Texas like she'd done for years. Paula claimed it was only because she needed more time to adjust to her new marriage. Darrell said she probably didn't want her new husband's family and friends to know she had a teenage daughter, and Lisa wondered if there could be something to his theory. Paula had always seemed to be a little on the vain side, but surely that was carrying vanity too far.

She squeezed Devon's shoulder. "We should be able to move in right after school lets out. That'll be nice, won't it? You and Paige will be able to start your junior year in a new school rather than transfer midsession."

"What school, Mom?" Paige asked.

"Daddy and I haven't decided yet. Kim said the public schools in this area aren't so hot, so we'll have to check the private ones."

"I want to go back by the river," Esther said.

"Come on, Ma, I'll walk with you," Darrell said, offering her his arm.

Devon walked with them, with Lisa and Paige trailing behind. "Do you like our new neighborhood?" Lisa asked her daughter.

"Sure, Mom, it's fine. I see the people next door have a boat out back. Are we getting one?"

"Well, I really don't know. Darrell hasn't mentioned wanting a boat, but if he wants one I guess we'll get one. It doesn't have anything to do with what the neighbors have." She glanced at her daughter. "You know, it's been longer than usual since you've been down to see your father. I hope you're planning to go next weekend."

"I am. Can I tell him we're moving?"

"Of course. He'll probably be thrilled to know you'll be living closer to St. Augustine." She knew Suzanne would be as curious as Brad would be happy, but it wasn't like Lisa could prevent her from knowing about their plans. Telling Brad was as good as telling Suzanne.

Lisa really couldn't complain. Her encounters with Brad and Suzanne were limited to dropping Paige off or picking her up, and that was plenty. She didn't want to get in their business, and she didn't want them in hers. She doubted Paige would say anything about the new house in front of Suzanne anyway, and Brad might not feel it important enough to mention to her later. Paige had never warmed up to her stepmother, whom she said treated her politely but not really like part of the family.

"Okay." Paige raced across the ground, which sloped downward as it neared the river, to join the others. The patches of crabgrass growing here and there in the sand looked nothing like the lush green blades surrounding the occupied homes, but sod wouldn't be laid until construction was complete.

Lisa remained where she stood, hands stuffed in the pockets of her jeans, deep in thought. Even after all these years, the thought of Suzanne Hall—and that's how she thought of her, not as Suzanne Betancourt, but as Suzanne Hall—filled her with annoyance.

From the very first day Lisa walked into the diagnostic center Brad co-owned and asked for him, she felt wary of the pretty new receptionist. She would never forget Suzanne's look of surprise mixed with envy when she identified herself as Brad's wife. She could practically feel Suzanne thinking how much she'd like to reverse their roles.

While Lisa never witnessed inappropriate dress or behavior on Suzanne's part—once Suzanne started working for Brad she made it a point to stop by often—she always felt there was a connection between Suzanne's hiring and the unraveling of her marriage to Brad. Brad always promised they would enjoy a life of comfort once he became established, and after he purchased a partnership in the radiology center it looked like they were on their way. Lisa had looked forward to the future after a long struggle—the lean period during Brad's last years of medical school, his internship, residency, and the early years of his career, when she hardly saw him and had to raise Paige and handle everything on the home front by herself. But his promise had crumbled like feta cheese, and instead of a life of luxury and privilege, she became a single parent. It was Suzanne who got to enjoy the benefits of being a doctor's wife without having made a single sacrifice.

Suzanne didn't even work, not that she'd ever had much of a career anyway. Answering the phones, checking in patients, and making appointments at the diagnostic center had been the extent of her vocation, and when she married Brad she promptly retired. If it wasn't for Brad, she'd still be answering phones . . . or selling girdles at J.C. Penney.

In the period during Lisa's separation and ultimate divorce from Brad, she had spent a lot of time feeling old, unattractive, and dazed. She'd been thirty-one, looked as good as ever, and remained sharp-witted enough not to make any errors when filling prescriptions. Still, she couldn't understand what had gone wrong between them. She didn't believe Brad's claim that it had nothing to do with Suzanne, especially after it got back to her that he was dating his receptionist. In Lisa's mind, that woman had forced herself between them as sure as if she chopped her way in with an ax.

Even after the divorce, Lisa devoted more time than she should have to wondering how her life had gotten so off track. That day her car broke down in the rain on the way to work she felt like breaking down herself, setting free all her pent-up rage and frustration by screaming uncontrollably until she had no voice left. A male motorist stopped and offered assistance, plus the security of a large golf umbrella. She used his cell phone to call the auto club, and he stayed with her until the tow truck came. That motorist's name was Darrell Canfield. He was divorced and the custodial parent of a daughter just three months younger than Paige. He took her phone number when they parted, and two years later they were married. The happily-ever-after that Lisa had dreamed of when she was married to Brad became a reality with Darrell.

She was about to join the others when they began walking back toward her. As she waited for them, she turned her attention to the partially constructed house next door.

"Are you thinking what I *think* you're thinking?" Darrell asked when he stood opposite her.

She gave him a devilish smile. "It'll only take a minute. Maybe we'll get some decorating ideas for our place."

He turned to his mother. "Ma, will you keep an eye on the twins? We're going to walk through the house next door."

Esther cast a baleful glance at the unfinished building. "Doesn't look like there's much to see."

"There probably isn't, but it gets to be a habit when you've done this as much as we have. Be back in a minute."

Unpainted drywall helped define the various rooms of the house, but the floors were unfinished and sawdust was everywhere, racing up her nostrils like ants scurrying into a dark hole. "I like the way you have to step down when you come in," Lisa said as they walked into the wide foyer. Darrell nodded, then quickly took off to explore.

"There's a lot of rooms in here," he called out as he rushed from room to room. It irked her to no end how he could cover an entire house, no matter how large, in three minutes or less, then yell at her to hurry up. She liked to take her time.

"It doesn't look this big from the outside," he continued. "You can get lost in here."

"Look at this kitchen, Darrell. Granite countertops." She stroked the smooth surface, which retained the cool temperature of the North Florida winter in the unheated house. "I'll bet they just put these in. This must have cost a fortune, but it's beautiful. No seams, and the corners are rounded. And look how nice the design matches the wood of the cabinets."

He shrugged, as she knew he would. He wasn't a kitchen type of guy. "There's an upstairs, too. I'm going up."

"Wait for me."

The others were waiting in the car when they returned. "How was it?" Esther asked.

"A lot bigger than it looks," Darrell replied. "It had so many bedrooms I lost count. They probably have a lot of kids."

"I guess you'll find out soon enough." Esther glanced at the unfinished house, then at the rest of the block. So how come neither of you asked what *I* think about where we'll be living?"

Darrell and Lisa exchanged guilty looks. She gestured for him to answer, mouthing, "She's *your* mother."

"We weren't trying to ignore you, Ma. I guess we figured you'd just tell us without our asking." He cleared his throat. "So what *do* you think?"

"I wasn't expecting such a fancy neighborhood. I think you guys might be getting a little uppity, buying property on the river next to

these . . . mansions. Next thing I know you'll leave the Baptist church
to become Presbyterians."

"Well, Ma, you saw how big our new house is when we took you
through the model. We have to put it up in a neighborhood with similar houses, or else it'll lose value. We thought you'd like living on the
river."

"Umph. At least the water doesn't stink. And it's good to know your
friends live nearby, 'cause I sure don't think you'll find any black folks
on this street."

Lisa knew her mother-in-law's trepidation came from her having
lived all her sixty-plus years in southern Georgia. Her own parents, up
in Columbus, were just as cynical. "There are plenty of other black
families in the Gillespies' subdivision, Ma Canfield, so don't worry
about us being the only ones for miles around."

"That's good. Nothing against the white folks, but I get uncomfortable if I don't see any brown faces."

Lisa turned around to face the rear seats. "We're going to stop by
Michael's and Kim's for just a minute."

"We don't have to stay too long, do we, Mom?" Paige asked. "Devon
and I were planning on going to the movies at four."

"We're just going to stop by and say hello. We'll be there a half
hour at the most."

Lisa kept her word to Paige. They stayed at the Gillespies' only long
enough to exchange thoughts on the new neighborhood and have a
cold drink. Cary and Courtney, happily playing with Alicyn, were re-
luctant to leave, but finally broke away when Lisa pointed out they
would soon be able to spend time together all the time.

Michael and Kim walked them outside, and Lisa and Darrell delayed getting in the truck, instead standing by it to talk.

"C'mon, Daddy," Devon said impatiently from her seat in the center row, jabbing her watch.

"Yeah, yeah, we're coming."

Kim nudged Lisa's side. "Here comes Ernie and his wife," she said,
nodding toward a late-model white Altima pulling into the driveway
next door. "Watch them walk over and say hello."

She met Kim's eyes with a raised eyebrow. "I think a wave would be
sufficient, don't you? After all, we only saw him that one time, and
we've never met his wife."

"Are you kidding? This is Ernie's chance to find out all about you since Michael cut him short last week. I told you they're nosy."

Sure enough, Ernie approached them, along with a plump brown-skinned woman. "Hey there."

Greetings were exchanged all around, and Ernie presented his wife, Flo. "It's nice to see you two again. Do you live around here?"

"Not yet, but four or five months from now we will," Darrell said.

"We're going to be neighbors? How nice!" Flo said. "You'll like living in Villa Saint John. I've noticed a few 'for sale' signs. Personally, I think it's silly for people to go to all the expense of building a house, live in it for a year or two, and then sell." She sighed theatrically. "I guess that's what happens when people live beyond their means." A lock of her center-parted chin-length hair fell toward her left eye, and in a smooth motion she pushed it back.

"I think most of those who sell quickly are naval officers who've been transferred," Michael said.

Ernie nodded. "That's true." He looked at Darrell. "If the sellers are desperate enough, you can get their price down. That can be an advantage to buying a house that's practically new rather than having one custom built, like Flo and I did. But why will it be so long before you move in?"

Darrell glanced at Lisa before answering, the corners of his mouth turned up ever so slightly. "They haven't even broken ground yet."

Both Flo and Ernie looked confused. "Broken ground?" Flo repeated. "I don't get it. There aren't any empty lots left, and the neighboring subdivisions are all built up, too."

"We're not building in a subdivision," Lisa said. "We bought a lot around the corner, on the river."

She wished she had a camera so she could have made a permanent record of Ernie's and Flo's wide-eyed, dropped mouth expressions for posterity. This was clearly the last thing they expected to hear.

Ernie recovered first, but his voice had risen about half an octave. "You're building a place on the river?"

Darrell nodded. "Michael and Kim showed us the land last week. We'd been looking all over Jacksonville for a suitable property and couldn't find anyplace 'til then."

"You live outside of Jacksonville now?" Flo asked.

"Yes, we're up in Georgia."

"Darrell, we've really got to go," Lisa said quickly, deciding they'd answered enough questions. "Remember the girls want to make the four o'clock show."

They said their good-byes and got in the truck, waving as they drove off. The Hickmans still stood with Michael and Kim, but Lisa noticed Kim's hand on Michael's arm, as if she were trying to rush him into the house.

"Who was that?" Esther wanted to know.

"They live next door to the Gillespies." Darrell chuckled. "Did you notice how shocked they seemed when I told them where we're building?"

"I think they were embarrassed, too," Lisa said. "As they should have been. To listen to them talk you'd think we couldn't afford to buy when they were putting up Villa Saint John, while their place was"— she raised two curved index fingers to signify quotation marks— " 'custom built.' "

"Who are they to make assumptions about what you can and can't afford?" Esther sounded miffed.

"They're nobody, Ma Canfield," Lisa said. "We don't even know them. Kim said they're the type who want to know everybody's business. We got away before they could ask us too many questions, but you'll notice they stayed right there with Michael and Kim."

Darrell chuckled. "Kim looked like she was ready to make a quick escape herself. You know, I feel a little sorry for them. Pain-in-the-neck neighbors are no joke. I hope we fare better."

CHAPTER 3

Your prisoner; if you let it go you are a prisoner to it.
—John Ray, on secrets

Lisa frowned when Paige raised the volume on the car radio. "For heaven's sake, turn that down."

Paige did, and then Lisa asked, "Do you have any special plans for this weekend with your father?"

"No, not really, Mom. It's just that I haven't been down there in a while, and I figured this would be a good time 'cuz Kenya's coming over later."

"Any special occasion?"

Paige shrugged. "Suzanne mentioned they're having some people over to watch some boxing match on pay-per-view. Her mother and brothers will be there, too."

"Well, you be sure to offer to help Suzanne. If she's entertaining for the evening, she'll need it." Her pleasant tone disguised her distaste for the idea of Paige getting friendly with Suzanne's sixteen-year-old sister. From photographs Lisa had seen of the girl, she was a future home wrecker in the making, an opinion she felt was best kept to herself.

"It won't just be for the evening. Kenya and the rest of her family are spending the night."

"Just from Palatka? It's not like they have a long drive to get home."

"No, but they stay over a lot."

Lisa wondered how Brad felt about the Halls en masse descending on his home for weekend visits so often. She flipped on her turn signal and steered into the strip mall. "Is that Daddy over there?" she said, pointing with a raised chin.

"Yeah, that's him."

She pulled up driver-to-driver, even if Brad sat considerably higher in his new Escalade. He was obviously pleased with the vehicle, but to her it looked hideously huge. She loved her Mercedes wagon. It was already eight years old when she and Darrell bought it five years ago, and it was big enough for the entire family, even Ma Canfield, without being a three-ton behemoth. She felt uncomfortable driving anything too large and left the Durango for Darrell's use.

"Hi," she said. "Hope you weren't waiting long."

"Hi. No, just two or three minutes. It was really nice of you to drive all the way down here to meet me." The strip mall was at the southern tip of Duval County, near the stables where he and the kids went horseback riding every week.

"Not a problem." She didn't tell him she liked shopping at the mall's anchor, a supermarket chain that had no stores up her way.

"Why don't we make it easy on you tomorrow and meet up north. There's a strip mall with a Wal-Mart right after the bridge."

"I know it. That'll work." She smiled at her ex-husband, who, as she'd expected, was alone. She couldn't remember the last time she'd seen Suzanne. It was almost an unwritten rule that she not come along when Brad picked up Paige unless it absolutely couldn't be avoided.

Brad looked good. He had a fair sprinkling of gray in his hair, but that was about right. He was three years older than she, so he'd be turning forty-six this year. He had always gone for the clean-shaven look, managing to avoid the razor bumps that prompted so many black men to grow beards.

She waited until Paige tossed her nylon gym bag in the backseat of the Escalade and climbed in front beside Brad before waving goodbye. "You guys have fun. I'll see you tomorrow."

Suzanne tossed her cigarette butt on the ground, looking up from the romance novel she was reading as Bradley Junior and Lauren galloped past on horseback. "Hold on," she yelled through cupped hands. They looked so sweet in their jodhpurs and boots. She loved seeing them ride. Her kids' experience with horses wasn't limited to those ancient, slow-moving ponies at children's parties. They knew how to control the animal, how to stop, start, speed up, and slow down. A couple years ago, she'd read a celebrity magazine interview in which the woman said her kids went horseback riding regularly. At that moment, she decided to enroll Bradley and Lauren for lessons. She would never go near a horse—they frightened her, and they smelled bad— but she was determined her kids would do everything other privileged kids did . . . because *they* were privileged.

She turned her head just in time to see Brad approaching with Paige. Her chest constricted the way it always did when she saw the living proof of her husband's marriage to another woman. But Paige was an all right kid, even if she did look more and more like her mother as she matured. Paige adored Bradley and Lauren, and often baby-sat if she and Brad wanted to go out for a quiet dinner alone or run an errand. The truth was Paige could be awfully convenient to have around.

Still, Suzanne couldn't control the resentment that flared each time she saw Brad's daughter. If she had her way, her children would be the *only* children. How nice it would be to forget Lisa ever existed.

The thought of Brad's ex always made her feel lacking. Lisa came from one of the leading black families of Columbus, Georgia, and she was a college graduate who worked as a pharmacist. Most of the wives of Brad's friends had professional careers, and being around them made Suzanne feel insignificant and stupid, like the poor girl from Palatka she'd been before she married.

Suzanne answered her last phone call right after she accepted Brad's proposal, citing potential awkwardness in taking instructions from senior clerical staff at the diagnostic center. Brad agreed his office manager and others would feel like they had to treat her with kid gloves now that she was his fiancée. The plan had been for her to find work elsewhere, but then she lamented how difficult it would be to work every day while planning their wedding. By then she had moved in with him, and he told her not to worry about getting another job— a response she'd counted on.

She hadn't worked a day since. When they returned from their honeymoon, she immediately became immersed in redecorating the house, changing it from a bachelor pad to something more befitting Brad's new status as a family man. Then she got pregnant with Bradley Junior, cementing her future as a stay-at-home wife and mother.

She enjoyed her life as mistress of the house. Let the wives of Brad's colleagues have their careers and their full-time household help. She was content to spend her days instructing her three-times-a-week cleaning woman, sending Bradley and Lauren off to school, working out, shopping, reading her romance novels, and puttering around in the kitchen.

In contrast, Lisa had gone back to work after she had her twins, and Suzanne liked to think it was because her family needed the money. Lisa's second husband was a stockbroker, and while he probably made a decent living, no way could he make as much as Brad. Besides, with their twins and Lisa's husband's daughter plus Paige they had twice as many kids, although of course Brad contributed to Paige's support. It pleased her that she, a girl from an undistinguished single-parent family in Palatka, had ended up with a wealthier lifestyle than the girl from the black elite.

Buoyed by her thoughts of economic superiority, Suzanne greeted Paige with more affection than usual. "I was just telling your father that we don't see enough of you these days, and Bradley and Lauren have missed you," she said, squeezing her stepdaughter's hand.

"I've missed you guys, too. It's been so long since I've ridden, I hope the horse doesn't throw me."

"Well, you two enjoy your ride. Brad, now that you're back I'm going to drive to the supermarket. I'll be back soon." That bench was starting to get uncomfortable and with the numerous horses passing by the air smelled like a school gymnasium after a basketball game. She kissed Brad good-bye and tucked her book inside her large purse. It was entertaining, but not any great shakes. She'd never read anything as wonderful as her own real-life fairy tale romance, and she probably never would.

Suzanne usually went to the supermarket after spending a few minutes watching Brad and the kids ride on Saturday mornings. From the time she moved into Brad's house, she had learned to write down what she needed the moment she thought about it, and to always carry her list with her. They lived in St. John's County, under a St. Augustine post office jurisdiction, but their home's physical location was about halfway between Jacksonville and St. Augustine, which translated to the middle of nowhere. If she ran out of something not stocked by the convenience store, her only option was a ten-mile drive to the nearest supermarket in Ponte Vedra Beach. She wished someone would build a market closer, but that was doubtful. There simply wasn't a heavy residential concentration where they lived.

She awkwardly guided the SUV into a parking space. She liked driving the Escalade, but still had difficulty parking it; it was so big. At least the spaces at this newer shopping center had been painted wider than the previous standard to accommodate today's monster SUVs.

She lingered a few minutes outside the store while she finished her cigarette, then stubbed out the butt in the standing ashtray and went inside. She took a cart and immediately steered it toward the display of Hamburger Helper. The kids loved the stuff, even if Brad hated it, and it was on sale this week. Not that she had to worry about what was on sale, but youthful habits tended to stay with a person. Besides, everybody loved a bargain. Didn't plenty of well-heeled folks shop at Wal-Mart?

She was turning the cart around to head to the produce department at the far end of the store when she noticed a woman on the checkout line who looked a lot like Lisa. Suzanne hastily held up a box of cereal, pretending to look at the label while she watched the woman transfer her purchases from the shopping cart to the belt. When the woman turned sideways, Suzanne saw she was right.

She grudgingly conceded that Lisa looked good. She had to be in her forties by now, but could easily pass for thirty-five. The simple pageboy with bangs hid any lines she might have on her forehead, and Suzanne liked to think there were lines aplenty underneath. She wore jeans, and the elastic border of her leather bomber jacket showed off her still-trim waistline.

She turned her attention to Lisa's purchases. Lots of packages of meat wrapped in white paper, plus other dietary staples. She recognized various sale items, but no Hamburger Helper. What was up with that? It might not be gourmet dining, but it made a quick, filling meal. Did Lisa have the same I-don't-want-to-eat-that-shit attitude as Brad did?

Her eyes narrowed as she glanced at Lisa's purchases again. Anything wrapped in white paper came from the butcher block, where they kept steaks, chops, seafood, and boneless chicken on ice. The good stuff. It was just like Lisa to turn up her nose at anything ordinary. She always acted like she'd been the one to think of putting adhesive on maxi pads.

Suzanne's shoulders slumped, and she quickly backed into the aisle. Lisa had no reason to turn around, but if she did happen to take her eyes off her purchases, Suzanne wasn't about to be seen with a cart full of Hamburger Helper.

Brad beamed at his oldest daughter. "It's been too long since I've seen you, Paige." After fifteen minutes riding at a nice clip, they'd slowed down to let the horses rest. "I hope you've been staying out of trouble."

"Just waiting for my birthday so I can get my driver's license."

"Is that why you haven't been down, because you're preparing for your test?"

"Oh, no. I'm sure I'll pass on my first try," Paige said with the unwavering confidence of a fifteen-year-old. "It's just that when I'm at your house I miss out on things like going to the movies or to the mall. You live so far from everything, and there aren't any kids my age where you live."

He nodded thoughtfully. "You know, when I first bought that house, I loved being out in the country, but lately I've been thinking more and more about selling, getting someplace closer to town."

"That would be great, Daddy."

"Even Bradley and Lauren are getting more social since they've started school, and Suzanne's always driving them to this one's house and that one's house. We're spending so much time in Jacksonville, I can't help feeling maybe we ought to live there."

"Well, that's where you work."

"Yeah, I know, even though I can't say I mind commuting. I find the drive relaxing. But there are plenty of advantages to moving to Jacksonville, believe me."

"I know. Mom and Darrell are building a new house there."

"They are?"

"Yep. They showed us where last week. It's somewhere on the river. It took them forever to make up their minds, first about the house and then where to put it."

Her impatience made him smile. "Buying a house is a little more involved than buying a pair of shoes, Paige."

"Yeah, I know, but still. Mom says we'll move in around June. It's gonna be bigger than where we live now. Devon and I still have our own rooms, plus Ma Canfield is going to live with us."

"That was nice of your mother to agree to that."

"Oh, Ma Canfield's okay. You just have to get used to her being so blunt. She embarrassed one of my friends the other week. My friend is kinda chubby, and we were eating, and Ma Canfield said, 'You're a pretty girl, but you might want to stay away from that macaroni and cheese.' I wished I could disappear."

"If she's prone to making that type of remark, you might want to keep her away from your friends before you lose them all," he said with a chuckle.

"I know. C'mon Daddy, let's ride some more." Paige dug her heels into her horse's sides, and he did the same.

The rhythmic sound of hooves hitting the ground ruled out conversation, so Darrell considered the feasibility of moving to Jacksonville. Most appealing was its considerable distance from Palatka and his in-laws. More and more, he found himself thinking he simply couldn't tolerate Suzanne's family. Her brothers had no ambition beyond their present two-bit jobs, and her sister dressed way too provocatively for a sixteen-year-old. The entire family, including their mother, seemed to subscribe to the what's-yours-is-mine school of thought. Arlene, his mother-in-law, was already talking about moving in with them after she retired, an idea he found unappealing, for wherever Arlene went, her sons and daughter were sure to follow.

This afternoon would mark the second time in three weeks that his in-laws came for an overnight visit. He was ready to have a serious talk with Suzanne about her family's constant intrusions, but since that problem might be eliminated if they moved to Jacksonville, he'd raise that topic first. He expected her to balk. He still remembered how excited she'd been when he first showed her the house they lived in now, which he'd purchased while they were still dating. He was sure she found its proximity to her family in Palatka just as appealing as its distance from Paige in Georgia. Suzanne had always been kind of funny where his daughter was concerned.

Brad watched as his brother-in-law Derrick rummaged around the refrigerator, Matthew close enough to look over his shoulder. Both were large men, six feet plus and well over two hundred pounds. "We ordered some platters and some chicken for the fight," Brad said pointedly. Didn't they ever eat at home?

"Yeah, I heard Suzanne say she was driving to Ponte Vedra to pick them up, but I'm hungry. I know y'all got somethin' good to eat in here. Ah, here we go." Derrick straightened up, a large plastic container of leftover red beans, rice, and sausage in his hand.

"Heat up the whole thing," Matthew said. "I'll eat half."

"Listen, fellas, I'm sure Suzanne told you we're having some friends over to watch the fight," Brad began. "I need you two to watch what you say, ay? Keep it appropriate, if you know what I mean."

"White dudes, huh?" Matthew asked.

"Actually, yes." He felt a little embarrassed. He shouldn't have to point out to grown men that they shouldn't make remarks like, "That niggah's out cold," in mixed company, but his brothers-in-law weren't particularly classy guys. He'd already told Suzanne not to get a vegetable platter for fear they would double dip. He'd been to plenty of social functions and seen people who should know better indulge in that unsanitary practice, but like his parents always said, ignorant or crass behavior always looked much worse when the offender was black. Same thing with crime. He always held his breath when TV news reporters described the arrest of an alleged criminal, hoping those arms poking out from the jacket perpetrators usually put over their heads wouldn't be brown. If they weren't, he silently thanked God. If they were, he shook his head sadly at the loss of yet another black man to the prison system.

"Don't you know any black doctors?" Derrick asked.

"Of course. One of them is coming tonight. But I don't limit my associations to other black people." He knew his explanation was pointless. Living a life free of social limitations was something neither Derrick nor Matthew would know anything about.

He watched as the two of them bickered over who had more food on their plate and resolved to check tomorrow's real estate ads on the sly. He'd deal with any objections Suzanne had later.

After more than ten years, he'd had it with his freeloading in-laws.

CHAPTER 4

One woman's poison is another woman's meat.
—variation of a proverb

Lisa reclined on the bed, her head resting on a pile of pillows, while Darrell sat in an armless chair on the other side of his nightstand. The PBS documentary on the history of segregation was heartbreaking as well as infuriating. She'd have to think of what her ancestors went through the next time she found herself frustrated over some minor inconvenience, like the washing machine going on the fritz or her car not starting.

"Wow," she said when it was over. "I give those people a lot of credit. I don't know if I could have handled what they did."

"You'd be surprised at what you can do when you have no choice. Our own parents went through hell right here in Georgia when they were young." He held up a glass containing ice and watery-looking purple liquid. "Get me a refill, will you?" he said as the phone began to ring.

"Let me get this first. It better not be for the girls. They know better than to tell anybody to call here after nine o'clock on a school night." She reached for the receiver, ignoring the reflexive urge to wait until the second ring before picking it up. She had more important things to do than worry about the caller wondering if she'd been sitting by the phone. "Hello. Oh, hi Paula. How are you? . . . Good . . . Oh, I'm well, thanks . . . Sure, he's sitting right here. Hold on." She handed the receiver to Darrell before taking his glass, as well as the bowl that had held popcorn, and leaving the room.

He was still talking when she returned a few minutes later. "I don't think it'll be a problem, but of course that's up to Lisa," he was saying. "I'll talk to her about it and get back to you tomorrow, huh?"

She put the glass down on a coaster and sat on the edge of the bed, staring at him with open curiosity. What was up to her?

"All right, talk to you then. 'Bye." He hung up and turned to her. "Paula wants to bring Devon up to her timeshare in Hilton Head for spring break. She says she'll fly into Jacksonville and rent a car to drive there from here. It's only about three-and-a-half hours."

"And she wants to stay here a night or two? You know I don't have a problem with that, Darrell. She's stayed with us before." Funny how the animosity she felt toward Brad's wife Suzanne didn't extend to her husband's ex, but the situation was entirely different. Paula had been the one to leave Darrell years ago. She'd given him custody of Devon, who was a mere toddler at the time, and never tried to get either of them back. Lisa saw no point in harboring any bad feelings. If anything, Paula's loss had been her gain.

"There's something else. She wants to bring Paige to Hilton Head with them to keep Devon company."

"That's sweet of her. But what about her husband? We really don't have anyplace for him to sleep, Darrell. Paula always stays with Devon in her room. I don't feel Devon should have to leave her room to bunk with Paige to accommodate someone we don't even know, do you?"

"Don't worry, he's not coming here. He's flying directly to Hilton Head. Apparently he's a golf fanatic and doesn't want to lose any time coming to pick up Devon."

She made a face. "In other words, he treats her like a stepchild. Has Devon even met this dude?"

"Of course. She's the one who told us how young he is, remember?"

"Oh, that's right. I guess Paula wouldn't have volunteered anything so juicy as her marrying a thirty-year-old if she didn't have to." Lisa giggled.

"Devon met him a couple of times last year. She said he was all right, but I get the feeling he's the type who'll simply tolerate her existence rather than make any effort to get to know her."

She nodded knowingly. Shades of Suzanne's attitude toward Paige.

"It's up to Paige if she wants to go, but my hunch is she won't want to pass on tennis and the beach. Now, if we could only find someone to pawn the boys off on, we could get a nice spring break ourselves." She wiggled her eyebrows suggestively, but her attempt at humor went ignored.

Darrell twisted his lower lip, the way he always did when he was thinking. "You know what Paula's doing, don't you? This is her way of spending time with Devon without being at home, where she'd have to tell everyone she has a daughter who's almost sixteen."

"I still find it hard to believe that Paula would go through all that just to hide the fact that she's a little older than her husband. After all, I'm older than you."

"By one year, Lisa. And our kids are the same age. But Paula's got to be close to forty by now, and her husband's only about thirty. That's a big difference." He shook his head. "She's always been pretty absorbed with her looks. If I know her, she's telling her new social set she's thirty. If she acknowledges Devon's her daughter, that'll mean she was having sex at thirteen."

"Oh, my."

"She's caught between the proverbial rock and hard place," Darrell continued. "If she gives her true age, she'll be scrutinized for crow's feet and other signs of aging by the other wives and girlfriends in her husband's circle. If she doesn't tell her age and introduces Devon as her daughter, the fellows will liken her to the Energizer bunny because she's been fucking since adolescence."

"If she wants to pretend to be younger, fine, but it's not right for her to compromise Devon to do it. Devon used to see Paula three or four times a year, but she hasn't seen her at all since last summer." Lisa wrinkled her nose. "And that excuse about needing time to adjust to a new marriage is a load of crap. I think Devon feels abandoned, poor thing."

"I think so, too," Darrell said, taking a gulp of his soda. "But when Paula gets here, she and I are going to straighten this out. Of course, she'll deny her motives, so it won't be pretty."

At Darrell's suggestion, they drove down to Jacksonville to see their lot on Sunday. The last six weeks had been spent getting their financing in order, putting their present home up for sale, and meeting with the builder to discuss locations of phone jacks and upgrades, like a raised toilet and shower bars in Ma Canfield's bathroom. Darrell's mother enjoyed excellent health at sixty-eight, had no difficulty moving about, but they felt in another ten years they'd be glad they had these extras installed now.

The preliminary work had been as tedious as it was necessary, and they were both excited to see that construction was finally beginning. The land was cleared and smoothed, and their future home outlined with elevated wood strips. Then the pipes for the plumbing were put in. Now the previously staked-out outline was a large block of flat concrete. Lisa walked on it, her hand touching the cool metal pipes in wonder. Their new house was undergoing a metamorphosis from a blueprint to a reality before their eyes. She found it terribly exciting, but the children didn't share her enthusiasm. The twins took one look at the foundation and the pipes protruding from it and asked in unison, "Is that all?" in voices ringing with disappointment. The girls' reactions weren't much either, just quick nods followed by asking when they were going home.

"I think maybe we should have left the kids at home," she said to Darrell.

"It could have been worse. Ma might have come," he replied. He tried to imitate his mother's voice. " 'I didn't ride all the way down there just to look at some hole in the ground.' "

"Your mother's all right with me. There's no BS in her, just blunt honesty. I've learned not to ask her anything unless I'm sure I want to hear her answer."

They turned at the sound of an approaching car on the quiet street. A white Lexus pulled up in front of the house under construction next door. A dark-haired mustached man got out on one side, and a blond woman on the other. Three children got out from the backseat, one through one door and two through the other.

The children ran straight into the house, and the man approached them, the woman trailing a few feet behind him. "Hi, I'm Joe Ianotti. This is my wife, Jenny. Looks like we're going to be neighbors."

Darrell grinned and shook his hand. "Darrell Canfield. My wife, Lisa."

Lisa nodded, her shoulders suddenly stiff. Jenny Ianotti's smile seemed forced. Lisa wished she could see her eyes, but they were hidden behind large dark-tinted sunglasses. Joe Ianotti might have no objections to their being neighbors, but his wife was clearly unhappy.

Lisa faced her future neighbors, part defiant and part cautious. "You have children, I see," she said, feeling she had to say something.

"Yes. Thirteen, nine, and seven. I understand most of the families on this block have kids," Joe said.

"Our twin boys are about the same age as your younger ones; they're eight," Darrell said.

Jenny glanced over at the children. "Are they identical?"

Lisa hadn't expected Jenny to make any small talk and was pleasantly surprised. Maybe her first instinct was wrong, and Jenny had some other matter on her mind. "No, they're fraternal," she said. "I've never dressed them alike. Personally, I feel that's damaging to kids' personalities, making them think they're part of a set rather than two individuals."

"You're probably right," Jenny said. "What about your daughters? Are they twins, too? They look like they're the same size."

"No, only the boys are twins. The girls just happen to be the same size." Paige and Devon were often mistaken for fraternal twins, but Lisa didn't elaborate. She saw no need for complete strangers to know their family history. If they were going to be neighbors, there was plenty of time to get to know each other.

They chatted for a few minutes about the irony of building such an upscale residential area in a below-average school district. After a few minutes, the Ianottis excused themselves and went inside their home.

"They seem like all right people," Darrell remarked.

She shrugged. "He was nice, but she seemed a little standoffish, at least at first."

"I think they just had a fight. She looked like she's been crying."

She looked at him incredulously, her chin lowered and her shoulder raised. "Crying? How could you tell?"

"She was dabbing at her eyes when she thought no one was looking. And her nose was running."

She shrugged. "Another good reason to have plenty of space between houses. That way we won't have to hear it when she screams that she hates him, or when he screams back that he should have listened to his mother and married an Italian girl." She giggled and reached for Darrell's hand. "Come on, let's make sure our foundation doesn't have any cracks."

CHAPTER 5

Lying and boasting are the same.
—Welsh Proverb

Flo was out of breath by the time she got to the cul-de-sac. She'd started speed walking in what was probably a futile attempt to get in shape for the summertime, and she liked walking by the river. This had to be one of the prettiest blocks in Jacksonville.

She stopped to let her heart rate slow in front of the concrete foundation that hadn't been there a few days ago. This was probably the beginning of the house those friends of Kim and Michael Gillespie were building. The timing was right for construction to begin. She'd met them in mid-January, and now it was March.

She could tell from the size of the foundation that it was going to be a large house, but of course people didn't buy property of this caliber just to put up two-room cottages. Besides, the Canfields' Durango had been full of people that day, four or five kids, from what she could tell.

Flo felt her throat constrict with wanting as she walked along the sand surrounding the outline of the foundation. She paused at the rear, admiring the view of the river and the lone sailboat floating by on this Wednesday afternoon. The brown water looked almost blue, an illusion from the bright sunlight.

She felt an overpowering urgency to know all about Darrell and Lisa Canfield. What did they do for a living? How could they afford such an expensive house, especially with all those kids?

Michael and Kim weren't any help when it came to getting information. Even that day after the Canfields drove off and Ernie had hinted, "Your friends must be pretty well off to be able to afford to build a house on the river," they just shrugged and agreed, but they didn't elaborate. Maybe they didn't like to talk about it because they were jealous that their friends obviously had more money than they did. Some people were like that.

Flo certainly wasn't jealous of them. Hell, she didn't even know them. But she would love to have a house right on the river. She didn't like these newcomers coming along and seizing the position she and Ernie worked so hard to achieve—that of the most affluent black couple in the neighborhood. They had a nicer house, nicer furniture, and nicer cars than those of everyone they knew in Villa St. John . . . and they had the bills to prove it.

She walked back around to the front of the foundation, swinging her arms with renewed energy after her brief rest. She circled the block, admiring the completed homes. The house next door to the Canfields looked like it was complete. The owners should be moving in soon. Two cars were parked in front of it now. Maybe the buyers were taking the final walk through the finished product before the closing.

Flo slowed down her approach as a blond woman with oversized sunglasses like the kind Jackie Onassis used to wear came out, accompanied by an older woman in a suit. They talked briefly, and the older woman gave the blonde a hug. Then the blonde got into the white Lexus and started the engine, lifting her sunglasses momentarily to dab at her eyes before driving away. What was that about? Had someone died or something?

The other woman, holding some kind of poster in her right hand, waved as the woman drove off, then bent to insert the poster in the ground by its wire legs. Flo realized it was a For Sale sign. How odd. Hadn't someone contracted to have the house built? Builders rarely put up luxury houses in mere hopes that someone would come along and buy them; they waited for the buyers to come to them.

Maybe the purchaser's financing fell through or something. That would explain why the blond woman was crying. *I'd cry, too, if I'd built a house that pretty and had to give it up.* Flo had been all through the house, both before the drywall was up and after. It looked rather unpretentious from the outside, almost like a New England seaside cottage with its dormer windows, but she knew it was huge, with a kitchen to make even the most untalented of cooks feel like they were Martha Stewart or B. Smith. The builders had put a lagoon-style pool in the back, with a terra cotta-colored tiled deck that probably cost as much as it had to carpet Flo's whole house. But on this block of wealthy residents things like waterfalls, whirlpools, and decorative decks were common.

She was heading for home when she saw Kim bike riding with her daughter. She waved, and Kim stopped. "I thought you might want to know. I talked to Carol about the hearse."

The neighbors who lived on the other side of the Gillespies had taken to parking a white hearse in their driveway, much to the dismay of everyone on the block. "Oh, yeah? What'd she say?"

"She said that she doesn't see a problem with it being there, that it's just a vehicle like any other. You should see the thing, Flo. She uses it like it's a station wagon or a minivan, driving it to the market or the bank. I know her family are funeral directors, but this is ridiculous."

Flo was glad that Carol and her husband lived next to Kim and Michael and not her and Ernie. Bad enough to have a hearse parked two doors down, but worse to have it right next door. "So what can we do about it?"

I'm asking everyone on our street to file a formal complaint with the homeowner's association."

"But are they really breaking any regulations?"

"It's not on the list of definite no-no's, like the clause against above-ground pools, but a hearse falls under the category of 'undesirable appearance.' I mean, who's going to think to put it in writing that residents aren't to park hearses in front of their homes?" Kim shook her head. "It's like living next door to Herman and Lily Munster."

"Mommy, can we go now?" an impatient Alicyn asked.

"In a minute." Kim smiled at Flo.

"Hold up, Alicyn," she called to her daughter. Then, turning to Flo, she said, "Nice day for some exercise. Gotta get it in now before it gets too hot."

"I heard that. Hey, it looks like they're starting work on your friends' house."

"Yes, Lisa told me the foundation is down. We're headed over that way now."

"It looks like it's a pretty large house."

Kim shrugged. "Well, they've got a large family."

Flo was torn between asking precisely how large the Canfield family was or how large the house was. She quickly decided which was the more valuable piece of information. "Do you know how many square feet it is?"

"Are you kidding? I barely know the size of my own house. Why would I know that about someone else's?"

Flo realized she'd gone too far. Kim's incredulous expression showed how taken aback she was by the question. It was time to turn on the charm. "Anyway, I'll bet it'll be really lovely," she said sweetly. "Ernie and I would have built over here if we were putting up a larger place. Even with the guest bedroom and the bonus room, our house is really too small to be on this block."

"These lots are very expensive, Flo."

A knot formed in her gut. Did Kim think she and Ernie couldn't afford a riverfront lot? They couldn't, of course, but no one was supposed to know that but them. They had worked hard to give the impression of being without financial limitations. "I'm sure they are, but that's not a hindrance for us," she said, keeping her tone light and breezy. "Knowing our house wouldn't fit in with the others was what made us go to Villa Saint John instead. By then all the prime lots there had already been sold."

Flo didn't like Kim's "Yeah, right" smile, but decided it was best not to comment on it. After all, people who really had money wouldn't care if a neighbor thought they were full of shit. She merely smiled with what she hoped was the proper amount of haughtiness, bid Kim and Alicyn good-bye, and speed-walked home.

She was out of breath by the time she reached her front door. She breathed heavily as she leaned against the inside front door. After a few seconds, she opened her eyes. What she saw as she moved forward made her smile, as it always did. The Bombay chest in the foyer, the exotic fish in the floor-tank nestled so perfectly in a niche in the wall, the Thomasville dining room set and accent tables, and the glass-sided staircase leading from the family room to the loft and bonus room upstairs, flanked by her beloved painted plaster dog statues. They'd collected just about every breed, Dalmatians, boxers, German shepherds, Dobermans, even a huge Saint Bernard they kept just inside the front door.

She went to the kitchen and checked the timer. The meat loaf had another twenty-five minutes to go. Gregory went straight from school to work at the supermarket and would eat when he came home at seven-thirty, but Ernie would probably be home shortly after it came out. He'd called her at work to say he needed to stay at the office and finish something.

She washed her hands and went about setting the table. She and Ernie had been married for nineteen years. He could be a flirt with other women sometimes, but she didn't think he'd ever cheated on her. Ernie wasn't ugly by any means, but he was far from the best-looking man she'd ever seen, and in recent years he'd gotten a little pudgy. She was no beauty herself, but she got by. Once she lost this excess weight that had sneaked up on her over the years, she'd turn heads again.

Still, sometimes she wondered if Ernie was up to something other than work. Whenever she called his office he was there, but someone else could be there with him as well. Ernie was the manager of human resources, and she knew there were plenty of women willing to overlook a man's lack of movie-star looks if he held a good job.

That job was what allowed them to live the way they did, and Flo was grateful. Ernie may have been promoted purely by being in the right place at the right time, but he'd done well in his work, and that was no accident.

Life was good, she thought as she went to take a shower. Now, if they could just get a few of the bills for all this high living paid off. . . .

CHAPTER 6

Where you live with your loved ones.
—Anonymous, on home

"That was good," Brad said breathlessly as he climbed off Suzanne and lay on his back in the king-size bed. He watched Suzanne stretch and her mouth form an O-shaped yawn. "Tired?"

"Actually, yes. I'm gonna sleep real good tonight. Bringing Bradley to that party in Jacksonville today wore me out. And tomorrow I'll have to drive back up there to pick Lauren up from her sleepover."

He reached for the remote control and flipped on the TV. He felt all revved up, the way he often did after sex. Besides, she'd just handed him the perfect opportunity to discuss moving. "Maybe it's time for us to get another house," he said casually.

She frowned as she lit a cigarette. "Another house? Why?"

"A couple of reasons I can think of. We've really outgrown the neighborhood. You've mentioned that maybe we should live somewhere more upscale."

"Yes, but—"

"And this house is so far from everything. You said it yourself. Two trips to Jacksonville in two days. Maybe we ought to just live up there."

"I don't know about living in Jacksonville, Brad. I like it down here. Sure, I'd like to upgrade to a nicer place, but there are plenty of other upscale communities in St. John's County."

"A lot of which are like this, in the middle of nowhere. Wouldn't it be nice not to fear forgetting something from the grocery store?"

"Well, yes, but there are plenty of other places that aren't as far removed as this is, Brad."

"Let's at least see what's out there, both in northern Saint John's and in Jacksonville. It can't hurt."

She exhaled, smoke pouring from her like a chimney. "All right, if you want to," she said wearily.

Suzanne tried to relax, but her stomach muscles felt constricted and her jaw ached. She'd had a bad feeling about the whole thing, ever since Brad first broached the idea of getting another house. A sixth sense told her he wanted to focus on Jacksonville, even though he said they would also check out St. Johns County. And now they were doing the last thing she wanted, driving up to Jacksonville to see a house. *It was all GI Joe's fault,* she thought with annoyance. He should stick to treating indigestion and stomach ulcers and stay out of people's business.

She wasn't sure of the best way to handle the situation. Just last weekend, Brad gently told her he felt her family should cut back on their visits, perhaps come for a few hours in the afternoon and forget about the overnighters. "I want to be able to spend time with just you and the kids when I'm off, and I'm starting to feel like our immediate family has doubled," he'd said.

Then that night he brought up the idea of moving to Jacksonville. It was like he was waiting for just the right moment to pounce on her like a cat jumping at catnip, and he did . . . right after she complained about how tired she was after bringing Bradley into town for a birthday party and Lauren to a sleepover, from which she'd have to pick her up the next day. She wished she could take the words back, but how could she have known what Brad had up his sleeve? And now he was telling her about a brand new house his colleague needed to unload. Everything was happening too fast. She couldn't help suspecting that Brad had it all planned.

Once he explained that GI Joe—Brad had dubbed him that because he specialized in gastrointestinal disorders—and his wife were breaking up, there was nothing she could do but agree to look at it. Part of her was curious to see what type of house Joe and his soon to be ex-wife were putting up. Suzanne had always liked Joe's wife. She, too, hadn't gone any further than high school, nor did she work outside the home. Like Suzanne, when Joe's wife entertained, she stuck to casual dining, not those stuffy cocktail parties or sit-down dinners Brad's other friends invited them to. Suzanne hated going to functions where they served hors d'oeuvres she didn't recognize and entrees so unusual she had to pause and see which utensil the others used. The conversation always centered on medical matters, politics, or the economy. You had to be a big brain to participate. What did she care about what Alan Greenspan did? She wasn't even sure who he was, just that he had something to do with finance.

Suzanne liked her life just the way it was. She didn't like the idea of having more distance between her and her family. They needed to be close to her, and she needed to be close to them. They were the only ones besides Brad who made her feel like she could be herself; she didn't have to have a Ph.D. in order to be somebody. Sure, she'd love a new house, just not in Jacksonville.

They'd still been dating when Brad bought the house they lived in now. He was in the early years of his practice and was paying back student loans, plus the business loan for the diagnostic center, and he'd splurged on a used late model Jaguar sports car, the very car they rode in now. It was a nice enough house, in a gated community with a wide front porch and sitting on an acre lot. Eventually he'd had a pool put in, but Suzanne felt they lived too simply for their income, almost beneath their position. Their neighbors were ordinary working people, teachers, bankers, department store managers. She wouldn't mind living in a more exclusive community, like other lawyers and doctors, now that Brad was well established and they could afford it.

Just not in Jacksonville. Her shoulders squared. Brad could show her a hundred houses there, and she wouldn't like any of them. She'd find a perfect place for them in St. John's County, where they wouldn't be so far from her mother and siblings, and their open admiration of her that her ego had come to depend on.

It annoyed her that they hadn't even gotten there to see it yet and he was talking like they'd bought the damn place. "See, there's a Publix," he said with a wave of his hand as they passed an attractive strip mall on a corner. "Joe said the house is only a few minutes away. It'll be nice to live close to a supermarket again, won't it?"

She sighed. "We're just going to *look* at the house, Brad. Or is there something you've forgotten to tell me?"

"No, of course not. You know I'd never buy a house without discussing it with you. This'll be my first time seeing it, too. Joe wouldn't even tell me a lot about it, just that we'd love it. But I really like the idea of living in Jacksonville, Suzanne. I'll be closer to work, the kids will be closer to school, and we'll probably get to see more of Paige. This place isn't isolated like we are now, and I'm sure there'll be other kids her age in the neighborhood."

Suzanne practically snapped her neck in her haste to stare at him. "So you think we see too much of *my* family, but you want your daughter to visit more often. Does that sound fair to you? Because it doesn't to me." Damn it. It was all part of a plan he'd devised to shut her family out of their lives.

"That's different, Suzanne. Paige is my daughter. Just because she doesn't live with us doesn't make her any less a part of our family. I have responsibilities to her, and I want to be a part of her life. On the other hand, I have no obligations to your mother and siblings, but I feel like I'm supporting them two days out of every week."

She exhaled loudly, then stared straight ahead. Like it was her fault her family wasn't well off and had to struggle. Why shouldn't they enjoy the lifestyle Brad could afford whenever they could? Brad, who'd come from a middle-class household in Macon, was always sending his parents money, and there was plenty to go around. Business was booming, both at the diagnostic center and with the interventional procedures he performed at the hospital, thanks to a shortage of radiologists in North Florida. The three Subway franchises he owned in Jacksonville were raking in a fortune, and their vacation property in Maine was frequently rented when they weren't in residence. She stuck out her lower lip and crossed her arms over her chest, more determined not to like the house.

She caught her breath when they followed the curve of the road and it suddenly ended, revealing impressive-looking homes surrounded on three sides by the St. Johns River. She could see the attractive architecture of downtown Jacksonville on the opposite shore. "This is a pretty block," she said with more enthusiasm than she meant to show. She was careful to sound casual with her next words. "I suppose the house is nearby?"

"It's right here." Brad stopped in front of a tan stucco house with attractive brick accents. A For Sale sign sat out front.

"Here! Where anybody can just drive up to it unannounced? Where's the gate?"

"This isn't a gated community, Suzanne. Most places on the Saint

Johns aren't, just like the majority of houses out at the beach aren't in gated communities."

She didn't have to pretend not to like what she saw. It took only a glance to see this was the plainest house on the block, though the slope of the roof suggested it was large and a three-brick pattern placed at intervals at each corner gave it an elegant touch, as did the brick-paved driveway. She glanced around at the other homes. One looked like a Spanish mansion, another had an elegant wide front window that revealed a curving staircase. Even the house under construction next door was going to be large. She could tell from the wood skeleton. The houses on the other side of the street that weren't on the water were also impressive, but there was nothing stately about this house. If anything, those protruding windows upstairs made it look like an ordinary sea cottage.

"I like living in a gated community, Brad. I feel protected. Here anybody can show up at our front door."

"So you get an occasional Girl Scout selling cookies and trick-or-treaters once a year, probably kids from the neighborhood. I don't think you'll be hounded by encyclopedia salesmen or Fuller Brush men, Suzanne, and the Jehovah's Witnesses probably don't even know this block exists." He took the keys and got out. "Come on, let's go in. The agent's waiting."

"Just what we need, a real estate agent following our every move," she grumbled as she gracefully stepped out of the Jaguar.

She was pleased when the agent greeted them and then said, "I'll wait out here while you look around." "It's an Arthur Rutenberg house, so prepare to be impressed."

Suzanne wrinkled her nose. She doubted it. The name Arthur Rutenberg meant nothing to her. She'd never heard of him.

She kept her expression impassive as she walked into the house. The foyer, living room, and dining room had attractive cherry hardwood floors, while the kitchen floor was inlaid with a rustic tile. The other floors were covered by a beige carpet with multicolored specks.

The master suite took up an entire wing. But it was the family room that took her breath away. Sliding glass doors lined the long wall facing the back of the house and a shorter one on the side, allowing for an unobstructed view of the lanai and beyond, the St. Johns River and downtown.

"I've never seen doors so long," Suzanne remarked.

"No, they're standard size," Brad said. "Three on that side and four over there. See how each one is set back a little from the next? They're each on their own track."

She shrugged, unimpressed.

"That means they open all the way. The effect would be—Wait, I'll show you." One by one he slid open all seven doors, and suddenly the family room and the lanai became one huge area, part indoors, part out, separated by a single shallow step down.

The spacious, screened-in lanai was floored with cement the color of terra cotta. The high ceiling added to the open feel. A lagoon-style pool, complete with foliage at its border, was positioned on the left, with an L-shaped stone fireplace centered at the rear. Nestled in the right-hand corner was a compact U-shaped kitchen with white Formica cabinets on the top and bottom, a tiny sink, an under-counter refrigerator, and a large built-in metal grill.

"Hey, check this out," Brad said as he inspected the grill. "It's not only a grill, but a smoker and a rotisserie as well. It's a fabulous setup for entertaining."

Suzanne was thinking the same thing. The simplest of menus would be elegant served in this setting. How impressed everyone would be, even if she served beans and franks. GI Joe sure had good taste. God, it must have killed Joe's wife to give all this up to go live in an apartment somewhere, even if she'd never gotten to move in.

"Just picture how nice it'll look out here with plenty of patio furniture and a TV," Brad said. "It's just like Joe to choose the plainest façade he could find and turn it into a showplace. He's never been the type to put on airs. That's one reason I like him so much."

"He certainly did seem to go all out. But why is the water in the pool so dark? It looks like a pond."

They walked closer to the pool. "The cement inside must be a darker color. That would make the water look dark, too," Brad guessed. "It's supposed to look like a pond, more like a swimming hole rather than a pool. That's why it's surrounded by plants, and why there's no ladder. You can jump in from anywhere, but the only way to get out is by the steps in the shallow end."

Suzanne stared at the deep blue water. She'd been nervous when Brad had their pool put in after Bradley and Lauren became reasonably good swimmers, courtesy of lessons from the Y. Suzanne had never learned to swim herself. Brad had offered to teach her, and she'd actually taken a lesson or two, but after that their schedules just hadn't meshed. He'd offer to give her a lesson right after she'd been to the hairdresser, and she hadn't wanted to get her hair wet. Eventually they abandoned the idea altogether, but she'd always felt a little uncomfortable, knowing she could do little if one of the kids were to get in trouble in the water. Suzanne generally doted on her children, but out of her own fear and sense of inadequacy she'd yelled at Bradley on more than one occasion when she caught him in the pool unsupervised. To ease her fears she had a new lock installed on the back door, one that she could also lock from the inside. She kept the fence door locked as well, so Bradley couldn't access the pool from the yard.

"But it's chlorinated, and if they'd used lighter colored cement it would look just as bright as our pool at home," Brad continued. "C'mon, let's look at the rest of the inside."

Suzanne noted with interest that the first floor had four other bedrooms in addition to the master suite, with a sixth bedroom plus a bonus room upstairs. She lost count of all the bathrooms. Too bad it was so far from Palatka, or else she'd be all for buying it. It was fabulous, and so big. Hell, there was enough room in here for her entire family to move in. . . .

Her mind began spinning like spokes on a speeding bicycle. Maybe that was the answer. She wouldn't mind moving to Jacksonville if her family came, too!

CHAPTER 7

God's gift of a do-it-yourself kit.
—Lawrence Eisenberg, on free will

Suzanne's mouth opened in a reflex action as the idea formed. Not that she'd want her mother and siblings to live with them on a permanent basis. Her brothers could be awfully loud and uncultured sometimes, and her mother enjoyed the contents of their liquor cabinet more than Suzanne felt comfortable with. Besides, Brad would never stand for her family staying for any extended period of time, not after he'd complained about them being around just on Saturdays and Sundays. Maybe they could contact the builder and arrange for this same house to be built somewhere in St. Johns County.

No, Brad wouldn't go for that. Why start from scratch and wait six or nine months when this house was available now? Building a replica would probably cost more money, and Brad was always looking for a bargain. And they'd never find such a pretty riverfront setting. There had to be a way for her to get this house *and* have her family nearby.

What if her family moved in with them for a transition period of six months or so? That would give her mother enough time to have desperately needed repairs made to her house, sell it at a profit, and save up for a nice place nearby while she lived with them rent-free. Once they had relocated, they could come over all the time.

Work wouldn't present a problem. Suzanne's mother was a post office clerk. All she had to do was transfer to a Jacksonville branch. She wouldn't lose a thing.

Suzanne began working out the logistics in her head. The large bedroom in the right rear wing, on the other end from the master suite, with a full bath right outside its door, would be perfect for her mother. Of the three bedrooms on the other side of the first floor, one would be Bradley's and one Lauren's, her sister Kenya could use the third one. Matthew and Derrick could share the smaller bonus room upstairs. As grown men in their twenties, they were a little old to be sharing a bedroom, but she wanted the larger upstairs room to be a playroom for Bradley and Lauren. Half the time the boys were out somewhere anyway. They might even decide to stay in the house in Palatka and pay their mother rent.

The challenge would be getting her plan to work without Brad putting his foot down. Suzanne knew him well enough to know that his good nature didn't lend itself to being pushed. It had to be presented as a short-term situation, with a certain amount of desperation attached. If her mother transferred to a Jacksonville post office and had no place lined up to live, surely Brad would agree to let them stay until they found an apartment, but of course it would be a slow process finding one both affordable and decent. Brad might fuss at first, but he'd get used to their being around. Six months would go by in no time.

Her stomach churned, as if protesting her plan. She'd never plotted behind Brad's back before, and it didn't feel right. But hadn't he done it first, orchestrating this whole thing with the house? It had all been too convenient to be anything else. First he proceeded to eliminate her family coming for the weekend, then he dropped the hint about looking for a new house in Jacksonville, and presto! Within a week, one had suddenly become available. The fact that it was a luxurious showplace and she could easily picture herself presiding over it was beside the point. If anything, she should feel guilty about having so much while her family had so little.

Suzanne absolutely hated the idea of her family living in that awful house in Palatka. Her mother couldn't afford to pay the mortgage and make repairs, too, not with her other living expenses. Her brothers weren't much help, spending most of Friday's paycheck before Monday rolled around. The kitchen drawers were falling out, the bathtub was cracked, and the faucet handles came off unless they were turned ever so gingerly. So what if they wanted to spend their weekends in nicer surroundings? She had done well by marrying Brad, and she saw no reason why her mother and siblings couldn't benefit as well, particularly Kenya, her little sister who had just turned seventeen.

Suzanne had remarked to Brad that her mother's house was practically falling down, but instead of offering to help as she hoped he would, he'd merely commented that it wouldn't be that way if the boys would pitch in and help with maintenance costs. Knowing how he felt, Suzanne didn't dare pay for the repairs herself. Brad paid all the household bills and scrutinized them thoroughly. Instead, she helped where she could, in small ways Brad wouldn't object to. She often took Kenya shopping and to get her nails done. She wanted her sister to attract the right husband, at a younger age than she had been when she met Brad, where she'd get to be the first and only wife and not have to cope with exes and other children, like she did with Lisa and Paige. Eligible men were being snapped up earlier and earlier these days, often as early as high school. If a girl looked shabby, she didn't stand a chance.

And Kenya had another strike against her. Most people in Palatka knew she had been the result of a brief affair their divorced mother had with a man who disappeared soon after. If Kenya came to Jacksonville, no one would know.

Suzanne occasionally wondered what might have transpired between her and the boy she had a crush on in high school had she had a better family pedigree. In hindsight, she knew that Eric Davidson, the son of the local funeral director, had never taken her seriously, but she didn't realize it at the time. His family had probably ingrained in him not to get attached to any of those poor little girls around Palatka. She'd given him her virginity when she was sixteen, and she'd been thrilled to be his prom date. Her mother went into debt on a knockout ensemble that far outshone those bargain basement dresses the other girls had worn.

Their affair continued even after Eric went off to Morehouse, with letters, phone calls, and passionate lovemaking during his visits home. She even got up to Atlanta a few times to visit him at school. Eric's parents always treated her with kindness. There was none of that being ushered into the study and being heartlessly told that she wasn't good enough for their son, like she'd seen in countless movies and read in countless romance novels.

Eric's plan was to settle in Atlanta after college and begin a career in marketing. She'd been expecting him to at least ask her to move to Atlanta to be near him, and at best ask her to marry him, but shortly before earning his M.B.A., Eric became engaged to a Spelman girl, someone from a distinguished family background similar to Lisa Canfield's. When Suzanne expressed shock at the news, he calmly stated that they'd had a great time over the past six years, but that he'd always known a marriage between them wouldn't work. He held two college degrees, while she'd squeaked through high school with a C- average. He needed a wife who could hold her own with anyone about anything, and she always felt so uncomfortable meeting new people and showed little interest in current events. Eric seemed genuinely surprised at her hurt reaction. Hadn't those potential problems occurred to her?

It hadn't. All Suzanne wanted was to marry him and have his children. She believed everything else would fall into place.

Heartbroken, Suzanne had relocated to Jacksonville not long afterward, just for a change of pace. She rented a tiny apartment and barely managed to keep the rent paid. Eventually, she was hired as a receptionist at a diagnostic center and met Brad. When they got married, she had announcements printed up and sent one to Eric's parents, who still lived in Palatka, so they'd be sure to let Eric know she'd ended up just fine. She rarely thought about him anymore. All she wanted was to be surrounded by the people she loved.

Not only did Suzanne look out for her family, she truly felt comfortable around them. She couldn't say the same for Brad's doctor friends. Their wives were all teachers or bank officers or business owners, and she was always afraid she'd make a slip that would make her look silly. Her family, on the other hand, were just regular folks. Not only did they love her for who she was, but they practically worshiped her because she'd gotten out of the ghetto by snagging a rich husband, and they looked up to her. She needed that. In the outside world, she was a minor being at best. As the recipient of her family's reverence, she became someone special, someone important.

"This is great!" Brad exclaimed as he came from upstairs. "It's got more room than we have now. I figure we can fix up a playroom for the kids in the bonus room and put a computer in there for them as well, or maybe put a desk in that large corner in the hall. The second room up there can be a fitness room. We can set up the treadmill, the exercise bike, and the Bowflex in there, plus a TV and a watercooler. And that large bedroom opposite our room will be perfect for Paige."

She clenched her fists for a few seconds and quickly relaxed them. She'd had the same idea about a playroom for Bradley and Lauren, but an exercise room? What was wrong with getting the garage wired for climate control—if it wasn't already—and working out in there, like they did now? This was Florida. Nobody used garages to park their cars in. It wasn't like they had to worry about snow or hail. Basements were rare in this region because the swampy land made digging too deep impractical, so people used their garages like basements, for storage or for recreation.

And that remark about reserving a room for Paige! Brad made it sound like his daughter would be moving in with them. She didn't need to have her own bedroom in their house. She already had one at Lisa's. Let her stretch out on a couch in the playroom when she visited.

"Or we could make a room for Paige on the other side, close to Bradley and Lauren's rooms," he continued.

Suzanne realized she had to say something. If she didn't speak up soon, he'd know something was wrong, and she certainly couldn't tell him what she was planning. "We've got plenty of time to work it out," she said weakly.

"What do you think of the kitchen?"

"I think it's beautiful. I like the tile on the countertops. It's really pretty."

"It's granite. Joe must have forked out four or five grand for that."

She was annoyed at herself for choosing the wrong word. "I also like the way they covered the fridge with the same wood as the cabinets."

"I like the whole thing."

That wasn't surprising. He'd made it perfectly clear that he hadn't seen anything he didn't like. She liked it, too, but she didn't want to make it too easy for him. "It looks awfully plain from the outside."

"That's all right. We don't have to prove anything to anybody."

Maybe not, but she wanted everyone on the block to know their place was as nice as theirs, probably nicer.

He pinched her cheek. "So what do you think, Suzie Q? It sounds like you might have changed your mind and can picture our family living here."

She knew he was feeling victorious that she'd been won over. But she saw no point in pretending she didn't like it. "Yes, I can," she admitted. "It's so much nicer than what we have now. But what about the kids' school?"

"There's no reason why they'd have to switch, at least not right away."

"But isn't this North Jacksonville? Their school is in Mandarin."

"This is Arlington. Mandarin's on the other side of town, and I'm sure the school will still send a bus to pick them up. It's still a little far, but not as far as going all the way to Saint Augustine. Joe said there's another Country Day School near here, so next semester we can transfer them." He smiled at her. "Think we should make an offer?"

She shrugged. "All they can say is no." She could hardly believe it. This house was lovelier than any she'd ever seen. Wait 'til her so-called friend Liloutie Braxton saw it. Suzanne related to Liloutie a little better than she did to most of the other wives—them both being African-American—but Liloutie could be hard to stomach sometimes. She was always asking them in that condescending way of hers if they were ever going to get a new house. This might not be as grand as that mansion Liloutie and her cardiologist husband Calvin had over in San Jose, but it was nicer without being as . . . what was the word? Showy.

"It's in move-in condition, although I'd like to have some work done before we move in. It needs paint for one thing. These white walls are too bland. We'll have to pick up some paint samples and decide what colors we want with which rooms, unless you'd rather wallpaper. What do you think about getting a wall mural painted on the playroom wall?"

"That's a great idea," she said eagerly. He had such good taste.

"Looks like we're going to be doing some shopping," Brad continued. "I definitely want some drapes to cover those sliding glass doors. In the winter it'll get drafty with all that glass. Besides, anyone passing by on a boat will be able to look dead in here at us. That's a must." Seeing the disappointment in her eyes, he added, "Don't worry, we can pull them back when we're entertaining. But the rods will have to be custom-made for the length we'll need."

"We'll need some new furniture for the extra bedrooms, too," Suzanne said, perking up. She loved to shop. Maybe she could talk Brad into letting her redo the whole house. No, he probably wouldn't go for that. Their present furniture was only a few years old and still in great condition; there was no need to replace it. Besides, they still had to sell the house in St. Augustine. If it didn't sell right away, Brad would have to put out a huge sum each month for both mortgages.

Her rapid change of heart startled her. Talk about an unexpected occurrence. She'd been determined not to like the house, but it was so gorgeous, so impressive, that it had won her over, and now she couldn't wait to live in it.

With her *entire* family.

CHAPTER 8

Your length in years.
—Anonymous, on age

Lisa parked in the driveway and grabbed her purse and keys, anxious to get inside. Paula had arrived today. She'd rented a car at the airport and driven to the house, and Darrell left work early to meet her there. Lisa hadn't spoken to him since just before he left his office and was eager to know how their talk about Devon went.

"Hi," she called out as she entered the front door.

She found Paige in the kitchen. "That meat smells good." Because she worked until six, Lisa frequently seasoned roasts or hams or chickens in the morning, instructing the girls on when to put them in the oven so the family could sit down to dinner by seven.

She pressed the button for the oven light and bent so she could see the thermometer through the window. "I think it'll be done in another ten minutes at the most." She straightened up, scowling as her hand reached to soothe her lower back. "I can't bend over like I used to. I'm glad we're getting a wall oven put in the new house."

Paige moved close to her and whispered, "Aren't you going to ask about Miss Paula?"

"Yes. Is she here?"

Paige nodded. "She's in Devon's room. Mom, she's pregnant."

Lisa sucked in her breath. "She is? I'm surprised Devon didn't say anything to us."

"She didn't know until she saw her. Miss Paula said she wanted to surprise her. She's due the beginning of August."

"That's a surprise, all right." Lisa wondered if it was wise of Paula to keep her pregnancy a secret. Devon would probably interpret it as just another way of keeping her shut out, and Lisa couldn't blame her. "Where's Darrell?"

"He went to the store. The boys went with him. You know how they are, always trying to get him to buy them some sunflower seeds or candy."

Lisa hated to question Paige, but she couldn't bear to wait for Darrell to return. He could easily be gone for another half hour. "How did Devon take Paula's big news?"

"She was shocked. You should have seen her face."

"Do you know if Darrell spent any time talking with Paula this afternoon?"

"They were out back when Devon and I got home from school. Miss Paula came in and said hi to Devon and me, and then she went back outside to Darrell." Paige glanced to see if anyone was approaching before continuing in a low voice. "I couldn't hear what they were saying, but I could see them when I was putting the meat in the oven, and they looked like they were mad at each other. I don't think I've ever seen Darrell mad, but his face was all twisted up, and so was hers. Then when they finally came in the house, Miss Paula went to see Devon in her room, and they've been in there ever since. Usually Devon and I do our homework together upstairs, but after she saw Miss Paula was pregnant she went straight to her room. What's going on, Mom?"

Lisa hesitated only a moment. Paige was almost sixteen, old enough to know the truth, or at least what she and Darrell suspected. Devon might even have said something to her about it. "Darrell and I are concerned because Paula seems to be completely wrapped up in her new husband, and now I guess with the new baby."

"And she doesn't have time for Devon anymore," Paige concluded. "I'm not blind, Mom."

"Has Devon said anything to you about it?"

"Only that she didn't know when she'd get back to Texas to see her mother again. I asked her why, and she just shrugged. She's not blind, either. But it's always been weird between those two. Devon went to live with Darrell when he and Miss Paula broke up, even though she was only two or three years old. Devon says it was Miss Paula's idea for her to stay with him, and then she ran off to Texas."

A question begged to be asked, and Lisa felt compelled to ask it. She didn't know why, for she was pretty sure she already knew the answer. Maybe her ego needed to be stroked for some reason. "You mean you wouldn't have wanted to live with your daddy after he and I broke up?"

"Nah. I was still a mommy's girl when I was three. I don't even remember seeing a whole lot of Daddy back then. He was always working. He would've ended up leaving me with a baby-sitter, probably Suzanne." The way she wrinkled her nose told Lisa how little Paige thought of that idea. "Anyway, this whole thing makes me wonder how important Devon is to Miss Paula."

"I'm afraid Devon's wondering the same thing. Darrell plans to discuss the situation with her. That's probably why you saw him and Paula being hostile with each other. I'll find out how things went when he gets back." She glanced at her watch. "I wish he'd hurry." Lisa gestured to two cans on the counter. "Put the green beans on for me, will you? I'm going to change clothes."

"Sure, Mom."

Paula faced her daughter. Devon's resemblance to Darrell was immediately recognizable. She was fortunate to also be pretty, for every man's face didn't work on girl children. The lack of resemblance between her and her daughter actually worked in her favor for what she had planned, but she had to choose her words carefully. She'd already made a slip with Darrell about the circumstances of her marriage, and he'd been furious.

"Devon, I just had a long talk with your father. He seems to think I'm pushing you in the background in favor of Andre. You don't think that, do you?"

She shrugged. "I haven't seen you since last summer, Mom. What am I supposed to think?"

Paula squirmed uncomfortably. Devon was so matter-of-fact. Not only did she look like Darrell, she had his personality. That shouldn't come as a surprise, since he'd raised her. "I know, dear, but it isn't because I didn't want to be with you. Marriage is very difficult, and I've already failed once when it didn't work out between your daddy and me. Andre and I needed time to get comfortable with each other, to get to know each other's daily routines."

"What would have happened if I lived with you, Mom? Would you have sent me away to live with Daddy so you could have time to get to know Andre's routine?"

Paula sucked her teeth. "That's a pointless question, Devon, and you know it. You've always lived with your father. When our marriage broke up, I didn't have a penny to my name and had to get established. I wanted a new start, so I moved to Houston and stayed with my friend Rhonda until I had a job and could afford to get my own place. It simply wasn't the right setting for a two-year-old."

"You only stayed with Rhonda for a few months."

"Yes, but by the time I got settled in my own place, you were so happy living with Daddy we decided it would be best if you stayed there. Then he met Lisa, and you and Paige became such good friends, and eventually sisters. You would've resented having to leave all that behind to come live with me in a strange city." She studied Devon's expression, which didn't look like she disagreed. Encouraged, she reached out and took one of Devon's hands in both of hers. "I want to thank you for being so patient with me. I'm hoping you'll come to stay with us for a while when the baby's born."

"Really, Mom?"

Paula's heart swelled at the hopeful note in Devon's voice. "Of course, sweetheart. The baby's due August first. You can come the end of July and stay three weeks. I know you'll be starting school around the twentieth of August, so you'll want to get back in time to get ready."

Devon hugged her. "I'm so glad, Mom. I hope I didn't hurt your feelings. Maybe I just expected the worst. You never said anything about having me come this summer, and then when I saw you're having another baby . . . I felt I was being replaced."

"No one can replace my little girl." Paula stroked Devon's hair, savoring the moment and dreading what she had to say next. "But there's just one thing," she began. She felt Devon's back go rigid just before abruptly pulling away.

"What's that?" Devon asked, her voice low with suspicion.

If Paula didn't know it was impossible, she would have thought Devon knew what was coming. Devon's actions told her she wasn't trusted, and that hurt. It was almost too much, but she had to do this;

she'd promised Andre. She took a deep breath. "Devon . . . You know Andre's younger than me. He's only thirty-one. We do a lot of socializing with his friends. One night I was talking with some of the girls, and when the subject of age came up, I was, well . . . I took off ten years."

"Ten years! They think you're twenty-eight?"

"I expected them to tell me they knew I was lying, but they accepted it. I didn't really know how to tell them the truth, so I've gone along with it ever since."

"But Andre knows how old you are."

"Yes, he's always known. But he thinks it's a good idea to let the others go on thinking I'm younger. You know how people like to tease. It might get uncomfortable for us."

"So what're you going to tell them when I show up? That you had me when you were in middle school?"

"No. I want to say you're . . . my stepdaughter from my first marriage."

"*What!* Your *step*daughter! I already have a stepmother, Mom. Lisa. I can't believe this. You actually want to tell all these lies just so Andre's friends won't gossip about you?"

"Do this for me, Devon, please. It's really very simple. Everybody knows I was married before. All we have to do is say you're my first husband's daughter that I'm still close to. We'll still see each other as often as we used to, and none of my new friends will think it's odd. It'll be our little secret." She rested her palm on Devon's shoulder. "I know it's asking a lot of you, Devon, but this is very important to me. Can't you understand that?"

Devon's voice shook, but her expression remained stoic. "You don't want me to tell anybody I'm your daughter."

"None of the new people you'll be meeting, no. With people you've already met, it's fine. You won't get confused. We never see his friends and my friends at the same time."

"Hmph. I guess with all the lies you tell, you *can't.*"

Paula winced.

The zest seemed to have ebbed out of Devon's slim frame. She shrugged listlessly. "All right, Mom. I don't like it, but I'll go along."

"Oh, sweetheart, thank you!" Paula held out her arms again, but Devon ignored her and stood up.

"I'd better help Paige with dinner," she said tonelessly. "It's going on seven. Lisa should be home by now."

"I'll be out in just a minute to say hello." Paula rose, her expanded belly causing only minimal delay. She pulled Devon into her arms and rocked her from side to side, trying to ignore her daughter's unresponsiveness, the way her arms hung stiffly at her sides. "My beautiful little girl. You've made your Mommy so happy."

"Good."

Devon's tone sounded flat and spiritless, like she couldn't care less. Instinct told Paula to merely let go, so she kissed Devon's cheek and stepped back. Without a word, Devon slipped out of the room.

Paula turned to the mirror over the double-wide dresser. At almost five-and-a-half months, she still looked graceful. Her baby was a neat round bundle under her blouse. It had been a long time since she'd had a baby, and she'd been worried about how she would look as her pregnancy advanced. Thank God she hadn't blown up all over. She didn't even want to think about how hard it would be to get the added pounds off after she gave birth, now that she was older. It had been a snap after Devon's birth, but she wasn't twenty-two anymore.

She inspected herself carefully in the mirror. It was hard work trying to be ten years younger than she was, but she carried it off well. She'd had her hair lightened to a rich sable brown with auburn highlights. She wore it straight and long, down to her shoulder blades, layered shorter in the front, parted in the middle. Not only was it youthful, but complimentary, since her hair had always been on the thin side. She hoped they'd have that Rogaine perfected for women in another ten or fifteen years; she suspected she'd need it by then.

She brushed a little more color on her cheeks and closed her eyes until she felt her facial muscles relax. Then she headed toward the kitchen.

"I think I'll have another biscuit," Paula said after the twins were given permission to be excused from the table.

"No need to be shy. You're eating for two," Lisa said with a smile.

"I've always hated it when women use pregnancy as an excuse to eat everything in sight. But this bread is really good." She halved it with her knife. "Everything was good."

"The girls are a big help to Lisa," Darrell said proudly.

"It's either that or eat dinner at nine o'clock every night if we wait for me to get home and cook," Lisa said.

"Daughters are wonderful, aren't they?" Paula smiled at Devon. "Pass me the butter, will you, sweetheart?"

"Sure, Paula."

She gasped. Her eyes went from Devon's impassive demeanor to the shocked expressions of Darrell, Lisa, and Paige, then back to Devon, who calmly placed the tub of butter in front of her. She struggled to get words to form in her throat.

But nothing was wrong with Darrell's vocal cords. "Since when do you call your mother by her first name, Devon?" he demanded.

"She didn't tell you?"

"Tell me what?"

"Well, we agreed that when I go to Texas—"

The scraping of Paula's chair interrupted Devon's words. "Excuse me," Paula said. She dropped the uneaten biscuit on her plate and left the room as quickly as her bulk would allow. She closed the bedroom door behind her and leaned on the dresser, fighting back tears.

How could Devon do that to her? Hadn't they agreed it would be their little secret? Okay, so she'd merely put out the suggestion. Devon hadn't exactly agreed, but Paula certainly hadn't expected her to announce the plan in front of Darrell, Lisa, and Paige. It wasn't any of their business, and Devon knew it. Darrell would have a fit, especially after this afternoon, when she'd accidentally mentioned that she and Andre had a formal wedding, not the simple civil ceremony at City Hall that she told him and Devon they'd had. Devon was her father's daughter, all right. Darrell didn't rant or rave, but he believed in payback.

Damn! She should have known Devon had something up her sleeve when she agreed so quickly to hide her identity. She had this all planned, to strike back where it hurt the most.

Paula straightened, breathing hard, one hand resting on her swollen abdomen. She could just imagine what was being said at the dining room table. Darrell would be in any minute to chew her out.

She lost the battle to hold back tears, and they spilled onto her carefully made-up cheeks in large wet drops. She was walking a tightrope, trying to make everyone happy, but her husband had gone on to Hilton Head without her, and her daughter had disowned her. She wanted so badly to please both of them, but her efforts had done nothing but make her the recipient of their anger and annoyance.

Her shoulders slumped in defeat at the knock she'd known would come. She recognized Darrell's voice. "Paula, it's me."

Here it comes. "Come in, Darrell."

But the lecture she expected didn't come. Instead he looked at her with pity in his eyes and said, "It looks like you've just lost your daughter, Paula. I hope he's worth it," and then left her alone with her misery.

CHAPTER 9

The price of progress.
—Anonymous, on problems

"It doesn't look like Joe and Jenny have moved in yet," Lisa said, glancing at the completed house next door. "That's odd. The house certainly looks like it's ready. Joe especially seemed anxious to get in."

"I haven't seen them in weeks," Darrell said. "Not since that time I told you about, when she went storming out the front door and he followed, and then he drove off burning rubber." He shook his head. "Those two are going to be trouble. I can feel it."

They entered the shell that would eventually be their home. A concrete floor had been laid, but the construction was in the early process of wood frame, and the lack of drywall made it difficult to determine which room was which.

"I don't think I'll be able to find my room without getting lost," Esther lamented.

"Don't worry, Ma," Darrell said. "It'll be a lot easier to identify the rooms once the walls are up."

"I can pick out the closets because they're so small," Devon said.

"And the bathrooms because of the pipes," Paige added. "And the stairs."

They walked single file through the maze of wood, identifying the various rooms for Esther's benefit. Darrell had brought the camcorder along to make a permanent record of the construction for their family library, and the kids provided amusing moments for him to capture on film: Devon primping before an imaginary mirror in the bathroom, Paige pretending to wash dishes in the hole that would eventually be a kitchen sink, and the boys looking out the oblong openings of their bedroom windows.

Even Esther said the construction was progressing nicely as they left.

"That's because we stay on top of the builders," Darrell explained. "Either Lisa or I are here almost every day. Last Thursday we got a couple of sandwiches from the Publix deli and had a picnic at lunchtime. They know we're watching them."

"Look, Mom, there's a car like Daddy's," Paige said, pointing at a cream-colored Escalade parked in front of the house next door. "Same color and everything."

"I guess Joe bought a new car."

"I like our Durango better," Cary said.

"They're both too big, if you ask me," Lisa said with a grunt. Darrell unlocked her door, and she popped it open. She had one leg in when Paige suddenly shouted.

"Look! It *is* Daddy!"

Lisa looked toward the Escalade, but her gaze soon shifted to the front door of the house; Brad emerged alongside Suzanne, followed by their son and daughter. She gasped. What were they doing in the Ianottis' house?

Paige had run to greet Brad, her arms outstretched. Lisa could tell Brad and Suzanne were both surprised—no, *shocked*—to see her. *Their shock is about to be compounded,* she thought as she headed in their direction.

Darrell quickly came around the side of the Durango to join her. "What the hell are they doing here?" he hissed.

"Visiting, I hope."

"There's no one living here to visit, Lisa."

"I'm grasping here, but I can't come up with any logical explanation."

"Well, we're about to find out what's going on," Darrell muttered.

They didn't have to inquire. Paige's excited voice carried in their direction. "You *bought* this house? Are you serious?"

God, I hope not. Lisa shot a frantic glance at Darrell.

"Mom, Darrell, you'll never guess!" Paige said. "Daddy's going to be moving in here, right next door to us!"

Lisa watched as Brad looked taken aback and Suzanne's hand flew to her mouth.

"Next door to *you*? Wait. You guys are moving *there*?" Brad pointed to the skeletal beginnings of their house.

"I told you Mom and Darrell were building a new house on the river," Paige said happily, oblivious to the tension in the air.

"Paige, please," Lisa interrupted. "We haven't even had a chance to say hello."

"Hello, neighbor," Darrell said to Brad, extending his hand.

Brad grasped and shook it. "Is this for real?" he asked. "I mean, are you really building next door to us?"

"To be frank, Brad," Darrell said good-naturedly, "when we signed the contract, we didn't know our dream house included having you as a next-door neighbor. If we had, I don't mind telling you we probably would've done something different."

"I think I'm in shock," Suzanne said. She shook her head as if trying to clear it. "Are we actually going to be living next door to each other?"

Lisa, too, was numb. "I don't get it. What happened to Joe and Jenny?" she asked.

"They're getting a divorce," Brad said.

"Why doesn't that surprise me," Darrell said. "I was just telling Lisa, every time I saw those two they had either just finished an argument or were just getting started on a new one."

"Joe's one of my colleagues. He has a GI practice locally and sends me referrals all the time," Brad explained. "He knew I was thinking about moving closer to work, so he called me about the house after he and Jenny broke up. Suzanne and I took one look at it and fell in love. We arranged to take it over."

"Of course, it's not too late for us to find another place we like just as well," Suzanne added quickly.

"Of course it's too late, Suzanne," Brad said with annoyance. "We closed last week. That means we've taken possession, even if we haven't moved in. We've already had the painters in. We just drove up to see the work they did. Next week, we've got men coming to do the wainscoting, the window treatments, the wallpaper, and to hook up the cable. The moving van's scheduled for Friday."

"Well, Lisa and I might not have taken possession of our place yet, but as you can see it's half built, and it's not like we can just abandon it," Darrell said. "We went through all kinds of changes, first with finding the perfect blueprint and then the right setting. I guess there's nothing to do now but learn to live with it." He looked at Lisa meaningfully.

Lisa had been secretly pleased by Brad's reaction to Suzanne's ridiculous suggestion that they find another house, but now she bristled at the look Darrell gave her, like he was warning her to be on her best behavior. He knew damn well that wasn't necessary, and she resented being treated like a child. "Excuse me," she said frostily as she moved away.

Suzanne glared at Brad. How dare he chastise her in front of Lisa and her husband!

But Brad was too busy agreeing with Darrell to even notice her fury. "At least we won't be living on top of each other," he was saying. "It might be far from ideal, but it should work out all right." Then he glanced at Suzanne's murderous expression. "What?"

Darrell sensed they were about to get into it and quickly excused himself. He didn't want to witness them argue. He had problems of his own. Lisa's poisonous stare and abrupt departure told him she was upset with him. He'd better catch up with her and calm her down.

Lisa was talking to Paige a few yards away, but it was Devon who caught his eye as she walked toward the truck, her head down and her shoulders slumped. Lisa's hurt feelings would have to wait. Something was troubling his daughter. "Dev, wait up."

"I was gonna wait for you guys in the car," she said when they faced each other.

"Something wrong?"

She stuffed her hands in her jeans pockets. "I'm already sick of hearing Paige go on and on about how glad she is that we'll be living next door to her daddy and her little brother and sister."

"Surely you don't begrudge her that. After all, your daddy and little brothers are right in the same house as you. Paige just wants what you've got."

"*She's* the one who has everything. It's not fair."

"Come on, Dev. What's Paige got that you haven't got?"

"She's got her driver's license, for one."

"That's only because she's three months older than you. Come June you'll have yours, too."

"Her daddy's going to buy her a car."

He stiffened. Why hadn't Lisa told him about Brad's plans? Surely she knew about it. "I hadn't heard about that."

"Paige told me he's getting her a PT Cruiser."

"Devon, I know how appealing that is to a kid your age, but I can't afford to buy you a car like that. I hadn't planned on getting you kids a car at all, because you'd have to share it and I can picture you two arguing about whose turn it is. You'll have to drive your mother's car when it's convenient for her to let you use it."

"A station wagon! You're kidding, aren't you, Daddy?"

"I'm dead serious."

"Well, if Paige has her own and I have my own, there won't be any arguing about who gets to drive. We can each go about our own business," Devon said brightly.

He hesitated, hating to disappoint her. "We'll see what we can do about getting you a car down the road. But I'm not making any promises, Devon, and it definitely won't be anytime soon. We've got some big expenses coming up with the new house, new furniture, getting our family plus Ma moved in . . . the list goes on and on."

"That's what I mean, Daddy. Paige has everything. And she'll soon have both her parents close by."

He sighed. This was harder to address than the car issue. "You know I feel it was terribly wrong of your mother—of Paula—to ask you to deny who you are because of her own vanity. I wish things were different. But it's not like you have no mother figure in your life. Grandma's always been there for you, and Lisa loves you as much as she loves Paige and the boys. She's been a part of your life almost as long as Grandma has."

"I know, Daddy. But Paige's little sister and brother were so happy to see her today. I can't help thinking that Mom's—I mean Paula's—baby won't even get to know who I am. Paula will be too afraid it'll let out her big secret in front of her stupid friends once it learns how to talk."

Darrell sighed. "Devon, I know this is extremely difficult for you, and frankly, I'm at a loss for how to handle it. You can always talk it over with a professional counselor, like I suggested when you came back from Hilton Head."

"I know, but I still don't want to. Right now I'm going to go sit with Grandma, if that's all right with you."

"Go ahead. Tell her we'll be along soon."

The back door of the truck opened, and Esther poked her head out. "Nobody said anything about being here all day," she said pointedly.

"All right, Ma," Darrell said wearily. "Give me a minute to round everybody up."

He rounded up Lisa, Paige, and the twins, who were standing off to the side having their own conversation with Brad and Suzanne's youngsters while they played with their pet beagle. "Time to go," he said.

Paige gave Brad and her half siblings good-bye hugs before racing after the twins and climbing in the truck.

"If there's any good to come out of this little mishap, it's the benefit to my little girl," Brad remarked, smiling after her.

"She's definitely thrilled that you'll be right next door," Lisa said, beaming. She glanced at Suzanne just in time to see her rolling her eyes and asked icily, "Something wrong, Suzanne?"

"No, Lisa, nothing's wrong," Suzanne replied with an equal degree of frostiness.

"I think it's time to go," Brad said quickly.

"Come on, Lisa, Ma's been waiting a long time," Darrell said just as quickly, tugging at her arm.

"What's the matter with you?" Darrell hissed as he and Lisa walked toward the truck.

"I can't stand that bitch. She clearly hates the idea of Paige living next door. She actually rolled her eyes when we were saying how happy this coincidence has made Paige. I know how she is, Darrell. She thinks her kids are the only ones who count. Well, Paige is Brad's child, too, just as much as those two she had."

"Brad loves Paige. I'm sure he'll never let Suzanne forget about her."

"Maybe so, but I'm so mad I could spit. Suzanne has always resented Paige because she's mine. Paige said she never feels like she's part of their family because of the way Suzanne treats her."

"How does she treat her?"

"Overly polite."

"So Paige would prefer Suzanne fuss at her like she does with her own kids?"

"She'd better not fuss at Paige."

"Then I don't know what you're talking about, Lisa. You don't want her to be too polite, you don't want her to fuss. This sounds like a no-win situation."

"It's hard to explain. Suzanne is sweet to Paige, but it's an insincere sweet. There's no warmth. Paige has always felt the phoniness. Suzanne just wants to stay on Brad's good side, and she knows he'd give her hell if she tries any stuff with Paige."

They split up temporarily to climb in on opposite sides of the Durango. When Darrell started the engine and steered into a U-turn, Lisa adjusted the speaker so the music played louder in the back. "Of all people to move next door. I'd take Joe and Jenny Ianotti and their arguments over Brad and Suzanne anytime."

He shrugged. "So would I, but the bottom line is we can't start over. We're not doctors, like Joe, where we can make a few phone calls and get someone to take over the financing while we look for something else. We'll have to work it out because there's virtually no other choice. I want you to promise me something, Lisa."

She looked at him suspiciously. "What?"

"I want you to make an honest effort to get along with Suzanne."

"I can promise you, Darrell, that I'll be pleasant and polite, but if she makes any more faces or derogatory comments regarding my child, the gloves come off."

He merely looked at her and said nothing. She met his gaze and held it until he had to look away to focus on the road in front of them. On that point, she wasn't backing down.

"So we're going to be living next to your ex, Lisa, huh?" Esther said from the second row.

"Yes, Ma Canfield. Unfortunately, it's too late for us to get out of it."

"His wife looked like a pretty little thing. The kids looked cute, too."

Lisa exhaled loudly. The last thing she wanted to hear was how pretty Suzanne was.

"Bradley's a jerk," Cary said. "He said me and Courtney have girls' names."

"He did?" Lisa said angrily, jerking her head to look at her sons.

"Yeah, but we set him straight," Courtney said. "Cary told him he's named after a famous movie star who's on a stamp, and I told him my name is for both boys and girls."

"Good for you," Darrell said. "We can't have anybody saying you boys are a couple of sissies."

"But they've got a nice puppy, Daddy," Cary said. "Can Courtney and I get a dog?"

"We'll see."

They fell silent, suddenly aware of rising voices in the third row, where the girls sat. Darrell lowered the radio volume so they could listen.

"What's wrong with you, Devon?" Paige was saying, her voice higher pitched than usual in agitation.

"Why does something have to be wrong with me just because I said I don't want to go to the mall?"

"You're just mad because I can drive by myself and you can only drive if Mom or Darrell are chaperoning you."

"Shut up, Paige."

"Hey!" Darrell said sharply. "What's up with you two?"

"All I did was ask Devon if she wanted to go to the mall when we got home," Paige said.

"I believe I heard you putting on some airs about having your driver's license," Lisa said. "It easily could have been you with a later birthday, you know."

"Then you also must have heard her tell me to shut up," Paige said. "Why haven't you gotten on her for that? Why am *I* the bad guy?"

"That's enough, Paige," Darrell said. "Your mother and I are going to be getting on both of you when we get home, so I don't want to hear anymore about it for now. As far as I'm concerned *everybody* can shut up."

Lisa sighed. "What a fine afternoon this turned out to be. We left our house a happy family, and now we're all bickering worse than Jenny and Joe Ianotti. You and I, Devon and Paige, even the twins with Bradley Junior. And I'm sure that down in Saint Augustine everything is just dandy with Brad and Suzanne." *Just like always,* she thought bitterly. *Suzanne ends up smelling like the proverbial rose while my life goes to ruin.*

Suzanne braced herself for a lecture. She knew something was coming the minute Brad suggested the kids sit in the third row of the Escalade.

He didn't disappoint her. "All right, what just happened with you and Lisa back there?" he demanded.

Damn it, she hadn't meant to roll her eyes, but all that talk about Paige was getting on her nerves. The last thing she wanted was for

Paige to be in and out of their house every five minutes, reporting everything she saw to Lisa. Suzanne had reacted honestly, but she knew it had been a mistake to let Lisa see her. But if Brad noticed, it would have been a lot worse.

She decided innocence would work best. "What do you mean?"

"What did you do to set Lisa off?"

"What did *I* do? Not what did *she* do, but what *I* did. Well, I didn't do anything, Brad. Lisa's always hated me. You know that. She's just trying to create problems between you and me, maybe even break us up. And she'll have plenty of opportunity once they move in." She sighed theatrically. "It's going to be a real challenge, being neighbors with them. Just think, I'm leaving my family behind in Palatka to live in Jacksonville next door to your ex-wife." *And your daughter,* she added silently, not daring to say it aloud. She could get away with criticizing Lisa, but she knew Paige was off limits.

"Listen, Suzanne. I know you're not happy about this. I don't think any of us are except for Paige. But we've spent a lot of money on this house, and who knows how long it'll take for the old house to sell. In the meantime, that's two mortgages I'm responsible for. You want to get new furniture, and I already told you I'm buying Paige a car . . ."

She bit her lower lip to keep from making a face.

". . . so we're stuck. You and Lisa will simply have to learn to get along. And you've got to get used to the idea of seeing a lot more of Paige, now that she'll be living so close. I guess there's no point in setting up a bedroom for her, since she won't be coming to spend entire weekends anymore. She'll probably never even spend the night, unless she baby-sits Bradley and Lauren late and is asleep herself."

Suzanne brightened. Not having to have a room designated for Paige in their new house made her feel a lot better. That was the one crimp in her plan to have her family move in with them; she'd allotted that room for her mother. "But what I don't understand is how Lisa and her husband can afford to build on a riverfront lot in the first place. They must have paid as much as we did for the land. Of course, we easily could have afforded to buy in Epping Forest or Queen's Harbor if we had wanted to, and they never could do that." She tapped her fingernails against the truck door. "Her husband's father died recently. I wonder if he had a lot of life insurance."

"I was wondering how they could afford it, too," he confessed. "But I don't think it was life insurance." That smug look on Suzanne's face bothered him. He knew she'd like nothing else than to believe Lisa's new house had materialized out of a man's death rather than out of her and Darrell's own efforts or success. "Darrell's a stockbroker. He might have made a good investment. Of course, Lisa makes good money, too."

Suzanne frowned at the mention of Lisa and her high-paying job. "Maybe we should have gotten a house in a gated community after all," she said. She hated Brad's financial conservatism, the way he preferred to live below their means. "I've got a bad feeling about this, Brad. Look at what just happened, you talking to me like I'm a child. I might not have a college education and a pharmacy degree like Lisa does, but I'm no dummy."

"I already apologized to you once for that, Suzanne. I was just upset to learn that the house being constructed next to ours was theirs, like we all were. That's the only reason I was a little short with you. It had nothing to do with Lisa and her education and her job." He sighed. Suzanne had always been suspicious of Lisa, and Lisa was equally suspicious of Suzanne.

In all these years, he'd never been able to convince Lisa that nothing had gone on between him and Suzanne while he and Lisa were still married. The change in Lisa's personality had dealt the death knell to their marriage, not any interest in other women. Lisa had become accustomed to running the household during the frantic period of his residency, but she continued to run things once he got settled, not even bothering to consult him with decisions she'd made half the time. Her whole manner changed, and eventually it became unbearable, with her telling him about decisions she'd made after the fact, not discussing it with him, and making judgments. He wanted his wife to be a partner, not a commanding officer.

He'd never mentioned to Lisa that he'd taken Suzanne to lunch a few times in those early days. He took a special interest in her because she was a sister, and she was bright, too bright to be sitting in that receptionist's chair asking clients to sign in and making follow-up appointments. Brad was a firm believer in helping uplift their people. He hadn't gotten to be a doctor without encouragement and assistance from others, and he wanted to give back to the community. But he hadn't thought of Suzanne as anything other than a bright young girl—well, a *fine* bright young girl—until after he and Lisa had separated. When he was free to date again, he looked at Suzanne through the eyes of a single man, not a married one interested in helping her improve herself, and she was the one he asked out. Within a week he was hooked.

He'd never regretted marrying Suzanne. She continued to look great, even after two babies. She was a fair if unimaginative cook, as long as she didn't try to serve him that nasty Hamburger Helper. Their sex life was still dynamite. She enjoyed the life he'd made possible for her, and unlike Lisa, she never forgot that he had the last word.

Funny how that career he visualized for her in the beginning had never panned out. But it was for the best. A career was fine for a bright young receptionist in his office, but not for his wife. Careers meant financial independence, and while he would always be grateful that Lisa was able to support the two of them and Paige in those early days, he liked the fact that if it wasn't for him Suzanne wouldn't have a dime to her name. Maybe if Lisa hadn't earned as much as she did, they never would have gotten divorced.

But it wasn't like he was still in love with Lisa. What happened between them was old news. They'd both made new lives, happy ones, as far as he knew. Suzanne had his heart now, and he found it reassuring to know they would never have the same problem that destroyed his marriage to Lisa.

He just hoped Suzanne knew he meant it when he said he expected her to be cordial to the Canfields, because his plans for life in his fabulous new home didn't include listening to his present wife complain day after day about his former wife.

CHAPTER 10

The fruit of evil as often as the root of it.
—Henry Fielding, on money

"The girls are in their rooms," Lisa reported to Darrell after she finished preparing the ham, and macaroni and cheese. "We still have about an hour before dinner is ready. Did you want to talk to them now?"

"First I need to ask you something."

"Sure, what?"

"Why didn't you tell me Brad is getting Paige a car?"

She didn't expect him to ask her that, and she realized belatedly that her surprise showed on her face. "I'm sorry, Darrell. I knew that would make things difficult for Devon, so I've been trying to talk him into putting it off until next year, when we'll be able to get a car for Devon, too. That way each girl will have their own vehicle, and they'll stay friends."

"I understand your trying to protect Devon's feelings, but that doesn't explain why you didn't fill me in."

"I just . . . I just figured if I could talk Brad into waiting, there wasn't much point in telling you about it. It's not like I was trying to hide it from you or anything." But she did feel like she had to protect him, an emotion she knew would insult his male pride. Over the years, Darrell had made occasional comments about not having as much money as Brad, usually in an apologetic manner, and it always pained her to hear him admit it. She suspected Brad was wondering how they could even afford the location of their new house. Unlike Brad and Suzanne, they had to be careful about their spending and spent considerable time budgeting and prioritizing.

New cars every couple of years weren't important, but private school tuition for the kids was, both for quality of education and their own peace of mind. Most of the school shootings they'd heard about took place in public school districts in wealthier communities. They'd yet to hear of any kids going berserk with guns in private schools.

While they sometimes hired professionals to complete special jobs around the house, they did this only if they absolutely had to. They would do the painting, ceiling fan installation, and other decorating themselves, and not until after they moved in. They couldn't afford to have their house prepared beforehand by painters and wainscots, like Brad could.

Money really did make the world go round, but she wished it didn't. How was Darrell supposed to feel, knowing Brad was all set to buy Paige a car when they couldn't afford to buy one for Devon right now? Since the beginning, they'd made it a point to treat the two girls equally. When one received something special just for the heck of it, the other did, too, with the exception of their birthdays. They continued the practice when the twins were born, but it had originated to prevent Paige and Devon from feeling like the proverbial stepchild.

"You thought I'd feel lacking somehow because Brad can afford to do things I can't," he guessed.

She moved to face him. "Does it make me such a bad person to want to protect your feelings, the same as I want to protect the way we've always treated the girls?"

"I'm a big boy, Lisa. I don't need you to protect me. I'm a grown man, not a little boy. And you're my wife, not my mother."

Damn it, she should have known he'd react that way. "Darrell, that's not fair—"

"Maybe it isn't, but it's how I feel. I don't want you feeling you have to shield me from the fact that Brad has more money than we do. I've always known that."

"But I hate to hear you say it."

"It's a fact. You can't tiptoe around it to spare my feelings. And we can't tiptoe around it to spare Devon's feelings, either."

"But she's having such a hard time," Lisa said, sounding sympathetic but a tad whiny. She quickly changed her tone back to normal.

"Her own mother has rejected her. You mark my words, Paula will raise this new baby as hers for all the world to see while Devon is explained away as a stepchild from a marriage that no longer exists. I can't imagine how awful that makes Devon feel."

"I know we're not equipped to handle the way she feels, Lisa, but she's refused to see a counselor. I love Devon and I know you love her too, and I hate to see her unhappy, but we can't walk on eggshells around her for fear she'll get depressed. You shouldn't have to try to convince Brad to hold off on doing something nice for his daughter because you're worried about Devon's reaction. What'd you tell him, anyway?"

"Just that this wasn't a good time. I did say there was a problem with Devon, but naturally I didn't say what it was."

"He doesn't even need to know that much. It's none of his damn business. But since you told him, what'd he say?"

She hesitated, then plunged ahead. If she hadn't been evasive in the first place, they wouldn't be having this conversation now. "He said he's sorry Devon's having a rough time and he doesn't mean to sound cold, but Devon isn't his daughter, and he doesn't feel Paige should go without in order to spare Devon's feelings."

"He's absolutely right. I'd feel the same way if I were in his shoes. We all have to live in this world, Lisa."

"I know, but I didn't like seeing the girls argue. They've been best friends since they were preschoolers. I'd hate to see it fall apart because of jealousy."

"So would I, but if Devon is old enough to operate a motor vehicle, she's old enough to understand that some people have more than others. I already told her that this isn't a good time for us to buy her a car, and that in the meantime when she gets her license, she can drive your car at your convenience. And I made sure she understands from the jump that when she does get a car it's not going to be an expensive PT Cruiser like Paige has, but a five-thousand-dollar Honda or Saturn like all the other kids drive. And if she gives us a hard time or starts moping around all the time, I'm sending her to a counselor whether she wants to go or not. She's not going to make our lives miserable." He tapped her elbow. "Come on, let's go talk to them now."

He held the bedroom door open, and Lisa walked through it silently. Her home life was slowly unraveling like a knit sweater. Was it a mere coincidence for all these problems to surface the same day she saw Brad and Suzanne? She hoped this wasn't a sign of what lay ahead, because after they moved to Jacksonville she'd be seeing a lot more of Mr. and Mrs. Betancourt, which was way too often for each encounter to bring her bad luck.

CHAPTER 11

A favorite weapon of the assassins of character.
—Ambrose Bierce, on rumors

Suzanne surveyed their newly moved belongings. She had directed the movers where to place the furniture, but boxes had merely been stacked in the designated rooms. It looked like she'd have to forego afternoons at the mall until she got this mess cleaned up.

She glanced at her watch. It was after three. Before she started unpacking, she should go outside and wait for the kids' school bus. They were picked up this morning at the old house, but she'd notified the school of their move and instructed them to bring them to the new place this afternoon.

She leashed Buster, the kids' beagle, walked past Brad, who was settling the bill with the movers, and went out the front door, Buster's leash in one hand, pack of Newports in the other. Brad hated her smoking, and while she couldn't help thinking that he acted more like a pulmonologist than a radiologist, she did try not to do it around him or the children. She walked to the curb and lit up, her eyes pealed toward the entry to the cul-de-sac.

Restless, she began to walk in that direction, hoping to see the first glimpse of the yellow school bus as it rounded the corner.

"Hi there!"

Suzanne smiled at the chubby brown-haired woman who greeted her with such friendliness. "Hi!"

"You must be waiting for the school bus."

"Yes, I am. We just moved this morning, and this'll be the first time the kids come home to the new house."

"Well, welcome to the neighborhood. I'm Ann Sorensen."

"Suzanne Betancourt. Thank you. And this is Buster," she said, nodding at the dog.

"Hiya, fella!" Ann bent to rub the top of Buster's head. "Are you from Jacksonville, Suzanne?" she asked as she straightened up.

Suzanne never told people she was from Palatka. Like any other small town, it had its share of well-off folks, but it had a reputation of being a hick town, probably because of its hick-sounding name. Better to say where she had moved from. "No, Saint Augustine, but this is much closer to my husband's office." Not job, office. She liked the important way that sounded. She waited for Ann to ask what her husband did.

Ann merely nodded. "Well, you're sure to like it here. The neighbors are friendly, and all the kids get along. How old are yours?"

"Seven and nine. My son is the oldest."

"We have two girls and a boy. Our son is ten, and our girls are seven and twelve. What school do your kids go to?"

"The Country Day."

Ann's face lit up. "So do ours! Maybe our daughters will be in the same class."

"Oh, I don't think so, at least not this year. Our kids went to the Country Day in Mandarin before we moved, and we decided to keep them there, at least for the time being. We'll switch them to Arlington when the new school year begins."

"They'll have a much shorter ride every day, that's for sure. But the kids will get acquainted, I'm sure, just from seeing each other outside."

"And I know my kids'll feel a lot better about changing schools if they know some of their schoolmates in advance." Suzanne smiled warmly.

"Oh, here they are now," Ann said, as a small school bus pulled into the street. Five children got off, and two Asian girls waved at Ann before crossing the street. Ann proudly presented her brood of rather ordinary-looking youngsters to Suzanne before saying, "I'm going to go in now. I hope you don't have to wait too much longer."

"Oh, I'm sure the bus will be here any minute." Suzanne slipped her hand through the loop in the leash so she could take out another cigarette.

"Well, feel free to knock on my door anytime if there's anything I can do."

"Thanks, Ann. I'll talk to you later."

Suzanne smiled as she lit another cigarette. Ann Sorensen seemed like a nice enough person. Suzanne felt a little disappointed that she hadn't gotten the opportunity to share Brad's occupation with Ann, but at least Ann hadn't seemed shocked to see she had black neighbors, definitely a point in her favor. Ann was obviously a stay-at-home mom, so they had something in common. Suzanne felt relieved to hear the neighbors were friendly people. She'd have to do her best to meet all of them and form an alliance, and quickly. She imagined herself hosting a coffee klatch for her new friends and sharing her distress over her husband's first wife moving right next door to her. She could paint Lisa as a bitterly jealous woman. Maybe the other women would avoid her, too, after she moved in.

Suzanne knew her thoughts were more suitable for a scheming ten-year-old than a mature thirty-seven-year-old woman, but she couldn't deny how good the thought of shutting Lisa out socially made her feel.

CHAPTER 12

A residential area changing for the worse.
—John Ciardi, defining neighborhood

Lisa brought her station wagon to a gentle stop in front of her future house. Her eyes focused on Brad's house next door. She
knew they'd moved in last week. A pale green Jaguar sat in the driveway.

She sucked her teeth in annoyance. Surely their house was equipped
with an automatic garage door opener. It was just like Suzanne not to
use her garage so everyone could see she drove a Jag.

As Lisa walked toward the front door of her home-in-progress, she
began to feel excited. This would be the first time she'd seen it in over
a week, since that awful day they'd run into Brad and Suzanne. She
would swear the gray in her hair—still not enough to be noticeable to
anyone other than her hairdresser, thank God—had doubled since
then.

She chose to go straight home from work when Brad went to see it
Thursday, having the crampy, generally icky feeling her period brought.
She'd never had much in the way of difficulty with menstruation until
she reached forty, when it began to really wipe her out. These last ten
years or so were going to be a bitch. She'd felt lousy all weekend, and
while yesterday she felt better, when the pharmacy closed at six she
preferred to go straight home without stopping. Darrell had planned
to meet her here tonight, but he'd gotten tied up at the office.

She moved quickly, eager to see the kitchen cabinets Darrell told her had been installed. She opened the door and wiped her feet out of ingrained habit. It was hardly necessary since the rough floors hadn't yet been carpeted. The first of what she knew would be many coats of white paint covered the walls, making the rooms look a lot more pleasant than dull gray drywall. Just looking at the unfinished structure made her feel good, and she couldn't hold back her smile. This was the house of her dreams, and damn it, she was going to enjoy living here with Darrell and the kids, no matter who lived next door.

Flo ran a hand over the kitchen cabinetry in the Canfield's new house. They were done in white with round porcelain knobs, and two of the doors were glass with white wood trim. She imagined the kitchen appliances would be white as well. She thought Darrell and Lisa would have gone with that stainless steel that was all the rage now, but white had its advantages. One, it never went out of style, and two, it always looked so crisp and bright. Flo's kitchen appliances were stainless steel, but she was getting tired of constantly wiping down the refrigerator. It streaked every time anyone touched it, and Ernie and Gregory tended to push it shut with the palms of their hands rather than use the handle.

She heard a noise toward the front of the house and realized that someone had closed the front door and was walking toward the kitchen. Oh, heavens, what if it was the Canfields? It probably was, for the construction workers had already left for the day. She had to get out without being discovered.

She tiptoed toward the back door and hurried out, crouching so she couldn't be seen through the windows, her heart pounding an allegro rhythm. She breathed heavily when she finally reached the street. A dark green Mercedes wagon was parked in front of the Canfield house. When she met them at Kim and Michael Gillespie's they were riding in a navy Durango, but of course they would have two cars. Still, this wasn't the type of vehicle she imagined either Darrell or Lisa would drive. It was a Mercedes, and it had no dents in it, but it looked at least ten years old. Hell, even she and Ernie had two fairly new cars. Unfortunately, they also had eight hundred dollars in car payments every month. But people who lived in neighborhoods like this were *supposed* to trade in their cars every two or three years. It was all part of the image—new cars sitting in the driveways of new houses. Look at that beautiful Jaguar sedan parked in the driveway of the house next

door. The For Sale sign she'd seen the real estate agent put up was
gone, and now someone had obviously moved in.

Flo resumed walking, swinging her arms vigorously. She went to the
edge of the cul-de-sac and circled around, crossing the street again so
she'd be in front of the Canfield's house instead of across from it.
Maybe she'd be lucky enough to bump into whoever was viewing the
house as they left. Since Michael and Kim weren't forthcoming with
any information about their friends, she'd have to get it herself. After
all these months, she still didn't know if Darrell and Lisa actually were
well-off or just show-offs who drove an SUV they couldn't really afford
and were building a house they couldn't really afford, like Ernie said.

She made a mental note to cook something for them when they
moved in. That would certainly be a nice way to kick off a friendship
and subsequently find out all about them.

Flo slowed down as she crossed the street, wishing there was some
way she could delay walking until she saw someone come out of the
house, but she couldn't since it would be perceived as loitering. That
could be dangerous for a black woman hanging around a white neighborhood. Someone might call the cops. No, all she could do was stop and
pretend to be catching her breath or massaging sore leg muscles before continuing.

She was almost in front of the newest house in the neighborhood,
just one house away from the Canfield home, when the garage door
opened and a young black woman clad in a white sweatshirt, navy
sweat pants, and white gym shoes came out, wheeling a trash bin. *She
must be the housekeeper.* Too bad. She'd always imagined most house-
keepers in private households to be middle-aged, heavy-set women in
their fifties, like in the movies. This woman seemed awfully young to
spend the rest of her life picking up after rich white folks, but hey, she
supposed it was better than cleaning toilets and changing sheets for
tips at the Holiday Inn.

Flo wondered if the lady of the house was a stay-at-home mom who
needed a hand keeping all those rooms clean, or if she worked at
some responsible high-paying job and didn't handle the domestic angle
at all. Then again, the owners might have hired temporary household
help just to assist with getting settled. Moving could be a real pain in
the butt.

The woman took a drag on her cigarette and smiled at Flo. "Hello.
Nice day for a walk, huh?"

Flo considered merely nodding pleasantly and moving on, then decided it wouldn't hurt to stop and chat. She'd just have to make sure this woman knew *she* was nobody's household help or a resident of those semi-swank apartments a mile or so down the road, but a homeowner in the neighborhood. "It's starting to get a little warm now," she said, breathing deeply as she stuffed her hands inside her jeans pockets. "Soon I'll have to go back to using my treadmill with the AC on, but I try to walk outdoors ever since we moved here. The scenery is so lovely to look at."

"You're right, it's real pretty around here." The woman glanced around with a pleased smile. "We just moved in last week, and I've only met a few people. Do you live on this block?"

Flo hoped she hadn't gasped audibly. This woman dressed so casually and enjoying a cigarette break while she took out the trash, *lived* here? Could there actually be *two* black families moving onto this block of half-million-dollar-plus homes? This was incredible! Wait till she told Ernie. "I live in Villa Saint John. It's the subdivision right around the corner."

"Oh, yes, I've seen it. It's very attractive, especially that building with the fountain at the entrance."

"That's the clubhouse. There's tennis courts behind it, and a swimming pool for people who don't have their own." Flo hoped her voice sounded haughty enough to suggest she wouldn't be caught dead using a community pool. "I usually circle a few streets in Villa Saint John, then come over here, walk to the end of the street, turn around and go back home and circle it again. That gives me about a mile-and-a-half."

"Wow. You do that every day?"

"I try to, unless it's raining. I'm seeing benefits from it, too. I've gotten firmed up and I've lost a few pounds." Flo took in the other woman's skin and facial features. The ponytail extending from her crown was a classic favorite of young girls, but this was no girl. Flo put her age at somewhere in her middle thirties. She'd probably caught her long hair in a band to keep it out of her face while she worked around the house. Hell, she'd do the same herself for her walks if her hair was long enough, and she was forty-one, but since it only came to her chin she pushed it back with a headband.

She decided it was time for introductions. "I'm Flo Hickman, by the way."

"Suzanne Betancourt."

"You have a lovely home." Flo didn't mention how intimately she knew the layout of the six bedrooms, bonus room, and five baths, even though she hadn't been inside in a while. The builders started locking it right after they put in the carpeting.

"Oh, thank you. We love it. We actually lucked into it. A business associate of my husband's had it built, but then his marriage broke up. He told my husband about it, and we fell in love the minute we saw it."

Flo wondered if Suzanne's business-associated husband could be white. The average black man certainly couldn't afford a house like this, unless he was doing something illegal or played defensive end for the Jacksonville Jaguars. She wished their offspring would show up so she'd know for sure. Whatever he was, he made damn good money, especially if Suzanne didn't work. Of course, Flo didn't know if Suzanne was just taking some time off for the move or if she stayed home all the time. "I thought I'd seen a For Sale sign out front for a couple of days."

Suzanne laughed. "Yes, it didn't take us long to decide to buy it." Her eyes narrowed suddenly as she focused on something over Flo's shoulder.

Flo followed her glance and saw Lisa Canfield coming out of her house. Why would Suzanne be unhappy to see Lisa, a woman she probably hadn't even had a chance to meet? Was she the queen bee type who resented a second affluent black family moving onto the block? She glanced back at Suzanne, who seemed to have forgotten she was standing there and was still glaring. The situation had fabulous potential, and Flo knew just how to bring it to a boil.

"Hi, Lisa!" she called, waving enthusiastically. To her surprise, Lisa walked over to them.

"Hi. Flo, isn't it?"

She tried not to look hurt at Lisa's uncertainty about her name. After all, they'd only met that one time. "Yes. I'm just out taking my daily constitutional. How's the house coming along?"

Lisa shrugged. "It's coming, I guess. I don't see a whole lot of changes other than the ones Darrell told me about when he was here last week."

Flo was all ready to introduce Lisa to Suzanne when Lisa chattily asked, "So Suzanne, how's the settling in process going?"

"Pretty slowly, but I'm definitely much better organized than we were right after we moved in," Suzanne replied.

Flo's sharp senses picked up on the caution in Suzanne's voice. She was growing more curious by the second. How did these two know each other?

"I've still got quite a lot to do," Suzanne continued, sounding more sure of herself. "Another week should do it."

"How wonderful!"

Flo followed the conversation incredulously. "You two know each other?" She was further captivated when it appeared that neither woman wanted to answer the question.

Finally, Lisa said, "Yes, we know each other. But we didn't know we'd be neighbors until last week."

"Wow," Flo said. "I'll bet there's an interesting story behind that."

Ernie leaned forward eagerly. "So what'd they say?"

"Nothing, not really," Flo said. "Lisa said she had to go, and Suzanne reminded me how they happened to buy the house, through her husband's business associate."

"Yeah, yeah. But that doesn't tell you how they know each other."

"I don't think Suzanne wanted to say. They might know each other, but I don't think they're friends. I definitely sensed some hostility between them from the way Suzanne looked at Lisa. And Lisa seemed almost too nice, like she really didn't mean it." Ernie wasn't a fan of the old *I Love Lucy* show, so it wouldn't make sense to give him the analogy she was thinking of, but watching Suzanne and Lisa interact reminded her of the way Lucy and her nemesis Carolyn Appleby interacted, with phony friendliness that barely covered the animosity beneath.

"Damn! I'd love to know what the deal is behind that. Suzanne didn't mention what kind of business her husband's in, did she?"

"No, but don't worry," she said confidently. "I'm sure to find out. I'm going to bake a pound cake tonight and bring it over there tomorrow. I'm sure she'll invite me in, and one thing will lead to another."

"Just make sure you find out what she and her husband do."

"Don't worry, honey. You can count on me."

CHAPTER 13

You reap what you sow.
—The New Testament

"Pause that, will you, Darrell?" Lisa asked as she grabbed the ringing phone. "Hello . . . Oh, hi Paula. How are—Yes, she's here. I don't know why she didn't grab the phone herself. Hold on a minute." She covered the receiver and yelled, "Devon!"

Her second daughter appeared in the doorway. "Yes?"

"It's your—It's Paula." Lisa was still struggling to adjust to the shifting roles she and Paula played in Devon's life.

"Okay. I'll take it in my room."

Lisa, sitting sideways on the sofa with her feet in Darrell's lap, playfully massaged his penis with her heel while she waited for Devon to get her bedroom extension. She gently replaced it in its cradle when Devon's voice came through the wire. "Brr," she said with a mock shiver.

He'd closed his eyes, and she knew from the way he had grown rigid against her foot that he was enjoying the massage. "You cold?" he finally said, not opening his eyes.

"No. I'm just reacting to Paula. She's been real chilly lately, ever since she came to pick up Devon for vacation. I was asking how she was, and she cut me off and asked for Devon."

He opened his eyes. "That's just like her," he said so angrily that Lisa's foot immediately froze in position. "It's inconvenient for her to be Devon's mother, but she doesn't want *you* to be her mother, either."

"I never tried to take Paula's place," she said hastily, withdrawing her foot. She wanted it understood that while she would always be there for Devon, she'd done nothing to manipulate the situation in any way. "Devon made her own decision to call me 'Mom,' and she never would have done that if Paula hadn't told her she didn't want anyone to know she's her real daughter."

"Paula knows she brought this on herself. That's why she's taking it out on you. But I won't have her calling our house and being rude to you."

She put a hand on his shoulder. "No, Darrell, don't say anything to her. That'll only make it worse. If it gets really bad, I'll say something to her myself, in a nice way."

"All right. But she'd better not try any of that shit with me." He shook his head. "She's really got a hell of a nerve." He lowered his voice. "I just hope Devon never finds out Paula had a wedding and didn't invite her."

"But don't you think Paula had a point when she said she thought it best not to say anything about it because it was during the school year, and she didn't want to pull Devon out of school to fly to Texas?" she asked. "I have to agree that with all a bride has to do in those few days before her wedding, she probably wouldn't have had much time to spend with Devon anyway, and of course she'd leave for her honeymoon right after. But if it was me, I'd plan my wedding for a time when my daughter was out of school, because I wouldn't want to remarry without her being there."

"Exactly. And since Paula scheduled her wedding for October, that tells me she never planned on telling anyone she has a child."

"I'll bet she wanted to kick herself for letting that slip out."

"You should have seen her face," Darrell said. "I accused her of neglecting Devon and she got all defensive. She was trying to make the point that she needed time to adjust to a new marriage, but it came out as 'ever since my wedding' instead of 'ever since I got married.' I didn't even have to ask her what she meant by 'wedding.' As soon as the words were out, she got all flustered, drawing her breath in and covering her mouth with her hand."

"What did you say?"

"I asked her what happened to City Hall. She gave some bullshit story about how her husband had never been married before, and how she and I got married with only our parents present because she was pregnant with Devon, so they felt they should have a little something. She claims they only had fifty people."

"But Devon wasn't one of them."

"And I don't believe it was some small affair with just their closest friends, either," Darrell said grimly. "They probably had two hundred people there. If she lied about city hall, it's no stretch to lie about how many guests she had. You know, I'm starting to think this whole thing with shutting Devon out was Paula's husband's idea. I never met the guy, of course, but he sounds like the type who'd try something like that. After all, he let his pregnant wife make that drive from South Georgia to Hilton Head with just two kids in the car while he flew straight there, didn't he?"

Lisa frowned as she shook her head. "I don't get it. How could any woman let some man talk her into denying her own daughter?"

"Like I said to her, I hope he's worth it." He playfully wiggled her big toe and held out the remote. "You ready to get back to the movie?"

She sighed. Before Paula called she'd been planning on getting an early afternoon quickie. Lord knew she had Darrell all ready for it. He'd probably gone down by now, so they might as well just watch the rest of the movie. "Yeah, go ahead."

Lisa stretched when the credits on the DVD began to roll, then checked her watch. "The ham needs about another twenty minutes. When it comes out, we probably should take that ride down to Jacksonville."

"I'll pick up Ma now to save time. By the time I get back, you can take out the ham and we'll go."

"Can I drive, Daddy?" Devon asked from the kitchen, where she was pouring herself a glass of juice.

"Sure."

"How's Paula, Devon?" Lisa asked.

"She's okay. Let's go, Daddy."

Lisa got up and ejected the DVD, placing it back in its case. The best thing about these things was that they didn't have to be rewound, like VHS tapes. "Here. Why don't you drop this off, since you're passing the store."

Paula reached inside the refrigerator for the container of skim milk. Maybe some time in the recliner with the Sunday paper would relax her nerves. She hated it when Lisa answered the phone when she called Devon. But if she didn't take the action of calling Devon, she feared they would never talk at all. Lord knows Devon hadn't called *her* in weeks.

Her hand shook a little as she poured the milk. Everything had changed since she went to Georgia to pick up Devon and Paige for spring vacation. The girls had a fabulous time together in Hilton Head, but it hadn't been the same. Paula winced every time her daughter called her by her first name. Devon still treated her with respect, but showed no affection. Paula suspected Lisa was getting that, and it infuriated her.

It wasn't fair. *She* was Devon's mother, not Lisa. *She* was always buying Devon gifts for no special reason and shipping them to Georgia. *She* paid part of Devon's school tuition. Maybe she hadn't seen Devon as much as she should have since she married Andre, but couldn't anyone understand how difficult her situation was? It was difficult enough to be a bride and then a new wife while simultaneously being a good mother, but it was impossible when married to Andre. He needed a lot of attention, and a person could only pull themselves in so many directions.

Surely it hadn't been such a bad thing for her to ask one little favor of Devon. She'd never denied Devon a thing in her life, but when the tables were turned and she needed something from Devon it was suddenly so awful. No, it wasn't fair.

"Paula, get me a beer, will ya?"

"Sure." Her tone sounded pleasant but inside she was annoyed. Sometimes she thought the only time Andre ever ate or drank was if she brought his food and liquid to him. What was he going to do when she went to the hospital to have the baby, keep an Igloo and microwave next to the family room couch? She liked being needed, but not to this degree. Andre was just plain lazy.

She brought him a bottle of Michelob and then settled in the chair with her milk. She pushed herself into a reclining position, feeling bloated, fat, and every one of her nearly thirty-nine years. She wondered how long she would be able to keep up this charade before time caught up with her. Ten years was a whole lot of years to subtract from her age. Now she wished she'd just told the truth that night with Andre's friends when they started talking about how old they were. She'd still be able to claim her daughter as her own. She and Andre would just have to get used to being ribbed every now and then. As long as she looked good, she had nothing to be ashamed of. Those Hollywood actresses often bragged about being older than their husbands or boyfriends, and a lot of them looked closer to their real ages than she did to hers.

She picked up the paper. Her eyes focused on the headline, but she didn't really see it. Twinges of truth fought their way through her wall of defense. Maybe she should have insisted they put off the wedding until Christmas, or even the spring so Devon could have been a part of it. She wondered if Andre's rush stemmed less out of eagerness to marry her and more out of the desire to conceal the fact that she had a teenage daughter from his parents and friends.

Paula shut her eyes tightly. No, that was too painful to consider. Andre loved her. He'd said he wouldn't be able to take vacation at Christmastime, and that he didn't want to wait until spring to get married. Sure, she'd had no problem getting pregnant with Devon—the pregnancy was the only reason she and Darrell had gotten married in the first place—but she was older now, he'd said. Delaying their wedding by six months might negatively impact her fertility, and didn't they want children? Lord knew his parents wanted a grandchild. They already had a collection of business cards from some of the best preschools in Houston, and Paula had no doubt they'd pick up the entire tab. Andre's father, Leonard Haines, was a top criminal attorney.

She gave in once he promised to never mention the wedding to Devon. It was best for her daughter to think they'd merely gone off to City Hall and said their vows and not had one hundred sixty guests in a flower-decorated church and then celebrated at a lavish reception hall. But because of her carelessness, Darrell knew the circumstances of their marriage. She didn't know if he had told Devon, but she guessed he hadn't. Devon would be hurt if she knew the truth, and Darrell wouldn't want to do that.

Shutting her eyes didn't lock out her guilt and shame. She knew she shouldn't have permitted Andre to convince her to go along with this deception. He'd go on about his merry way, his life completely unchanged, while her relationship with her daughter would never be the same. Andre was sure to insist they not tell their child who Devon really was, and that would surely wield the death knell to the relationship between mother and daughter. Paula remembered Darrell's words, "I hope he's worth it," and suddenly found herself catching a sob in her throat.

The sound was muffled by Andre's belch. "Hey Paula, what's for lunch?"

CHAPTER 14

A penny for your thoughts.
—Sir Thomas More

Lisa's stomach fluttered with each step she took as they approached the front door of Brad's house. In spite of her promise to herself not to let it bother her, it was still hard to believe that her first husband and his second family would be living right next door to her. What was that Kim had said when she told her? "I don't blame you, Lisa. What woman wants to live next to somebody she used to fuck every night?"

Paige answered the door after Darrell pushed the chime. She hugged Lisa like they'd been separated for weeks.

"Well, you certainly must have had a nice weekend," Lisa said with pleased surprise.

Brad came up behind Paige. "Hey, guys. Why don't you come and sit down while Paige gets her things?"

Darrell glanced at Lisa. When she nodded he said, "Maybe for just a minute."

They all paused to wipe their feet. Brad shook Darrell's hand and gave Lisa his standard quick, impersonal hug. She wondered if he was aware that he only hugged her when Suzanne wasn't around, or if it was an unconscious distinction on his part. He said hello to the twins and took both of Esther's hands in his. He'd met her only once or twice over the years. Lisa couldn't hear what Brad was saying, but she guessed he was acknowledging the loss of Esther's husband last year.

"Where's Devon, Mom?" Paige asked.

"She wanted to stay home, and Darrell said it was all right since we wouldn't be gone that long."

They followed Paige to a side hallway that led to a family room and adjacent breakfast area and gourmet kitchen. "Nice setup," Darrell said, looking out to the open patio beyond. "But does it close up? In the summer your AC will choke, and in the winter you'll freeze."

"They're sliding glass doors," Paige said. "They tuck into panels outside. Because there's a nice breeze today Suzanne opened them. Go on out."

They all stepped down onto the patio. Behind them, Lisa heard Esther praising the loveliness of the home to Brad.

Suzanne was sitting in a lounge chair, her mother and sister nearby. Lisa wasn't surprised to see Arlene and Kenya Hall. If they visited frequently when Brad lived in St. Augustine, she doubted the visits would stop just because they now lived in Jacksonville. If anything, the longer distance gave them a more credible reason to hang around all weekend. Again she wondered how Brad felt about his in-laws' constant presence.

"Oh, hello," Suzanne said, her offhand tone suggesting she had no idea they were coming.

Lisa knew better. She breathed in noisily but forced herself to smile. Not only was Suzanne expecting them, but she'd have had those glass doors open even if it'd been ninety degrees outside, just to make sure they saw the stunning effect of the open lanai.

Suzanne greeted them one by one, and Brad introduced her and her mother to Esther. At Suzanne's insistence they sit down, Esther took a chair next to Arlene and the two women began chatting.

"Can I get you guys something to drink?" Suzanne offered. "I've got some sweet iced tea and some pop in the fridge."

"That'd be great. I think we're all thirsty," Darrell said.

"I'll fix them, Suzanne," Paige said. "C'mon Kenya, help me out."

Watching the two girls giggling together in the outdoor kitchen made Lisa glad Devon had asked Darrell if she could stay home after they returned from picking up Esther. At least Kenya's cleavage was covered up today, but the crop top she wore showed off her tight abs, and her jeans hugged her generous behind the way paper casing fit sausage. Lisa suspected the girl didn't feel complete unless she was showing some skin. She wished someone would tell her she didn't have to dress that way to get attention; her pretty face and Beyoncé-like figure warranted a second look.

"Where're the kids?" Darrell asked.

"They're watching a movie over at one of the neighbors," Brad said.

"You have a lovely home, Suzanne," Lisa said. She was proud of how genuine she sounded, but she wasn't lying. The house was a damn magazine layout. An outdoor kitchen and stone fireplace? Glass walls that rolled back to make one huge screened-in area? This was the life. And it could have been hers. It *should* have been hers.

She bit her lip. My God, what was she thinking, *should have been hers?* She had no feelings for Brad anymore, at least not that way. She loved Darrell with all her heart. With him she had the relationship of mutual love and respect she craved, and he'd given her Cary and Courtney. It wasn't her working alone most of the time, the way it had been when she was married to Brad—him telling her to handle their business as best she saw fit and then complaining that she made decisions without consulting him. By the end she'd wanted to strangle him. It had been a damned-if-she-did and damned-if-she-didn't type situation, and just before the end she felt he baited her deliberately just to start arguments. No, the love between them had gone a long time ago. If you asked her, he'd allowed his M.D. degree to go to his head. She just wished he hadn't married Suzanne. The type of lifestyle Brad provided was too damn good for somebody like her, someone who'd come from nowhere.

"Oh, thank you," Suzanne said. "We love it."

"She's done a marvelous job with decorating," Brad said proudly.

"And Lisa, I wanted to tell you how wonderful our new house-keeper is," Suzanne said. "Her name's Teresita, and we use her three days a week. I'd recommend her highly if Tuesday and Thursday would work for you. I'm sure you'll have to get someone new like we did because your old housekeeper won't commute." She smiled sweetly.

Lisa knew Suzanne wanted to hear her say she didn't use a cleaning woman regularly, but she wasn't about to admit they only got some-one to help out when they were about to have house guests or to en-tertain. "Thanks. I'll keep that in mind," was all she said.

"How's your place coming along?" Brad asked.

"Actually, pretty good," Darrell said. "It's right on schedule, and we've got a buyer for our house in Brunswick."

"Is your new place an Arthur Rutenberg model, too?" Suzanne asked.

"Rutenberg? Oh, you mean *Rute*nberg," Lisa said, pronouncing the name correctly with a short "U," whereas Suzanne had elongated it, like in "root." She smiled sweetly in response to Suzanne's glare. "No, our place was designed by ICI."

"It's good that you've got a buyer all lined up," Brad said. "Now that we're settled in here we'll be putting our old place on the market."

Lisa felt her jaws go rigid. Brad spoke as casually about paying two mortgages as if he'd asked Paige for a glass of iced tea. And who knew how long it would take for his old place to sell? Meanwhile, they had been forced to live in a museum the last few months, keeping the house showroom-spotless and removing all signs of personalization, like family photos and shopping lists on the refrigerator, so prospective buyers could picture the house furnished with their own personal mementos. That was no longer an issue now that they'd accepted an offer and the buyers had secured financing, but another challenge lay ahead. She had to coordinate the move into their new house while simultaneously leaving the old one in good condition for the buyers. She'd probably have to drive all the way up to Georgia to sweep, vacuum, mop, and scrub after they moved their things out, time she'd much rather devote to getting settled in the new house. It irritated her that Suzanne would be spared that headache because Brad's income allowed her the luxury of doing one thing at a time.

She sipped the iced tea Paige brought her, hoping it would stop the angry pounding in her head.

"We're really enjoying living here," Brad was saying. "I think you guys will love it, too. The neighbors are friendly, but they don't get into your business." He chuckled. "You know, I still have to laugh whenever I think of our situation. Paige told me you guys were building a new house on the river, but the Saint Johns is such a long-ass river. What are the odds of us buying next door to each other?" True to his word, he laughed, and Darrell joined him. Suzanne managed a halting smile that didn't quite reach her eyes. Lisa didn't even try. She didn't think it was funny.

Deciding she'd had enough of their situation, she turned to Cary and Courtney, who were sitting near the pool. "Drink up, boys. We need to get going."

* * *

"Well, that was nauseating," she said softly when they were in the truck so only Darrell could hear. Paige was sitting directly behind Darrell, and Lisa didn't want her voice to carry. She'd never said anything against Brad to their daughter, and she never would.

Darrell looked at her thoughtfully but didn't reply.

"What a beautiful house," Esther said. "I've only seen places that pretty in the movies or in magazines. That patio was stunning. I wish I could have seen the rest of it."

"It's real nice, Ma Canfield," Paige said. She launched into a complete description.

Lisa busied herself by looking out the window and humming loudly to herself, drowning out Paige's voice. She had no interest in hearing about Suzanne's fancy new house. Like Darrell said, some people simply had more than others, and they had to accept it. This type of thing probably wasn't all that unusual even within the same family. Now she knew exactly how Devon must feel when she looked at Paige's PT Cruiser while she had no car of her own.

Right now Lisa felt like a poor relation herself, seeing that gorgeous house and hearing about Suzanne's wonderful cleaning woman. What the hell did Suzanne need a cleaning woman for? It wasn't like she worked. What else did she have to do all day?

Lisa had heard just about all she could stand of Suzanne and her lifestyle of the rich and useless. The next time they had to pick up Paige from Brad's, she'd send the boys next door to get her while she and Darrell checked out the progress the construction workers had made. This chummy socializing needed to stop right now. She and Darrell weren't friends with Brad and Suzanne and never would be. She wanted their relationship to be as Brad described the rest of the neighbors, pleasant but distant. No coming over to have coffee or to borrow eggs.

She glanced over at Darrell. He stared straight ahead at the road in front of him, but she'd known him long enough to be able to pick up on when something was troubling him. He hadn't said a word since they'd been in the truck. What was on his mind? And why had he looked at her so funny when she said the visit had nauseated her?

CHAPTER 15

One who has the same enemies you have.
—Abraham Lincoln, defining friend

Suzanne scrubbed four baking potatoes with a toothbrush she kept especially for that purpose. She had to admit it certainly was convenient to have a supermarket just a few miles away. Gone forever were the days of living in virtual fear that she would forget something she absolutely couldn't do without and have to drive a total of twenty miles to get it.

She opened the upper door of the double wall oven and placed the potatoes alongside the eye round roast, which sent out a delicious beefy aroma to the kitchen and beyond. She inhaled with a satisfied sigh, then took the plastic bag of fresh green beans from the vegetable crisper in the fridge and stood over the sink as she rinsed them and snapped off the ends. When the doorbell rang she dried her hands with a paper towel and went to answer it. She should probably check on Bradley and Lauren anyway. They were out riding their bicycles with Ann Sorensen's kids.

Ann and her husband Bill had invited their whole family over for an informal dinner the first week they moved in. Their kids had become fast friends. Suzanne had expected to be grilled like the steaks and burgers Bill Sorensen cooked, but they didn't ask a lot of questions, and they didn't seem particularly impressed when they learned what Brad did. If anything, Brad was the one to show interest when Bill said his law specialty was personal injury and medical malpractice. They spent a good part of the evening debating the effect the sizable damage awards were having on doctors in the state.

It had been a fun evening, and they would include the Sorensens when they did their first entertaining in the new house next weekend, which would also be a small, informal dinner of grilled meats and vegetables.

Suzanne found herself hoping Ann was at the door now. She'd welcome a social visitor after a day of solitude.

A quick peek out of one of the narrow windows flanking the door revealed Flo, the walker from Villa St. John. Suzanne opened the door eagerly.

"Hi, Flo. I'm so glad you stopped by. I'm so sorry I was on my way out last week when you brought that wonderful cake over."

"Oh, I understand. How'd the kids make out at the dentist?"

"No cavities."

"Good."

"The cake is delicious. All of us are enjoying it. There's maybe four slices left."

"Glad to hear it. I hope it's all right, my coming by like this, but I figured you'd probably be done with the cake plate."

"Of course. I would have brought it to you sooner, but I don't know exactly where you live in Villa Saint John. I transferred the cake to my glass plate the same day you brought it over, so the container's all ready for you. Why don't you come in for a bit? I'm making dinner and I'd love some company."

"Sure."

"I just want to take a quick look and see if I see the kids. They're out here somewhere, riding their bikes."

"Two of them?"

"Yes, a boy and a girl, nine and seven."

"That must have been them I saw just a minute ago. They went down that side street." Flo cocked her head toward the street. When she straightened a lock of hair fell toward her eye and she casually pushed it back. "They were riding their bikes right next to the curb, along with a couple of white kids."

"Good. We told them not to ride in the street."

"They'll be fine. There's very little traffic on these streets, and the people who drive go very slowly because they know neighborhood kids are out."

Suzanne smiled and opened the door wider. "Come on in."

"Your home is lovely," Flo said as they walked through the foyer.

"Thank you." She couldn't resist putting on just a little bit. "It's really much larger than it looks from the outside. My husband goes for the unobtrusive look." She'd heard Brad use that word to describe their house and decided she liked it. She'd resolved to improve her vocabulary and make more of an effort to fit in with Brad's educated friends.

"Oh, it's just beautiful," Flo said. "It reminds me of the homes up north. I'm from Boston, you know."

Suzanne noticed Flo's head moving from side to side as she took in the living room and dining room furnishings. She regretted having not drawn back the drapes in the family room and opening the sliding doors. To do it now would seem showy. She'd have to wait until another time to let Flo see it. But she looked forward to Flo's reaction when she saw the kitchen with its sumptuous granite countertops and smooth oak cabinets with braided dark metal inlay, and the butler's pantry with wet bar and built-in wine cooler. Or maybe she should say wine *cellar*. She'd have to make sure she was using the correct term. Wine cooler sounded so ordinary. People might think she was talking about a simple stainless steel bucket, or worse, a four-pack of Bartles and James. But wouldn't a wine cellar be an actual cellar? She'd have to ask Brad. He knew she wasn't the smartest or most sophisticated woman in the world, but he never made fun of her. No wonder she loved him so much.

To her disappointment, Flo said nothing when they entered the kitchen. Perhaps she felt she'd already paid enough compliments. She might even be jealous. Villa St. John was a nice subdivision, but the homes there were just a little above average, selling for maybe between one-fifty and the low two hundreds. Yes, that was it. Flo was probably envious and wished she could live in such a fine house. What other explanation could there be? It wasn't as though she'd ever been in this kitchen before.

"I'll bet you could stand a cold drink," Suzanne offered graciously.

"I sure could. Walking always makes me thirsty. Ice water will do fine. No calories." Flo chuckled.

"Have a seat." Suzanne gestured toward the bar stools on the opposite side of the island, across from the sink.

Flo sniffed. "Something smells delicious."

"Thanks. I've got a roast beef in the oven." Suzanne had finally gotten out of the habit of saying "roast beast," an expression she'd used since childhood that hadn't matured with the rest of her. It wasn't until Brad told her it sounded rather silly coming from an adult that she made a conscious effort to quit. She held a tall glass to the ice dispenser, then filled it with water from the dispenser next to it. "We generally eat as soon as my husband gets home from work. He'll be here in about forty-five minutes."

Over the course of drinking a single glass of water, Flo managed to find out Suzanne's husband was a radiologist who owned his own diagnostic center, get a close enough look at the furnishings of the living, dining, and family rooms to determine they were expensive, and see the spectacular patio. She also saw a photograph of the entire family and confirmed Suzanne hadn't married white to get all this. Of course seeing the tall, good-looking black man smiling for the camera had only been a formality, for their kids certainly hadn't looked like they were biracial. But the real scoop came as she was leaving.

Flo drained the last of her water and stood up, picking up the plastic cake plate and cover Suzanne had taken from one of the cabinets. The remainder of the pound cake sat in a domed glass pedestal plate on the kitchen counter. "I enjoyed visiting with you, Suzanne, but I've got to get home and check on my own dinner. I'm roasting a pork loin, and I put it in before I set out on my walk. Besides, your husband will be home soon."

"I'm so glad you stopped by. And thanks again for the cake."

"You and your husband will have to come over one night and have dinner with us," Flo suggested. "How about Saturday? You can bring the children, but I'm afraid they might be bored. Our son is seventeen. I'm afraid I couldn't even help you with recommending a babysitter, although I'm sure there's plenty of them in the neighborhood."

"Oh, that's all right. I'll have a baby-sitter right next door when Paige moves in, and she'll be visiting again before that."

Lines of confusion formed between Flo's eyebrows. "Paige? Who's that, Lisa's daughter?"

Suzanne had spoken naturally, forgetting that Flo didn't know about her relationship to Lisa. She hadn't meant to reveal their history so soon. No point in trying to cover now, she might as well tell the truth. "Yes. She's also my stepdaughter. My husband and Lisa used to be married to each other."

Flo drew in her breath sharply and looked horrified, like she'd just stumbled across a dead body. "And she's moving next door? Your husband's ex? Oh, Suzanne. That's . . . that's got to be terribly awkward for you . . . and for her, too. How did it happen?"

"A terrible coincidence. We didn't know they were building next door until after we'd closed on this house." Maybe her blunder wouldn't be such a bad thing after all. Flo was the first black person she'd met in the neighborhood, even if she lived in Villa St. John and not on this block. She would be the link to meeting the other African-American neighbors. Suzanne could put her original plan into effect, the one that hadn't materialized with her own neighbors.

She had met the other families who lived on the cul-de-sac, but the coffee klatches she envisioned with the other wives hadn't materialized. Except for Ann, the rest of the women worked and didn't have much time for socializing. During the day the street looked like a convention of Molly Maids was being held, with hatchback vehicles from various cleaning services in front of every house. She might not have been able to shut Lisa out of the social circle of the block, but she might be successful at making Lisa persona non grata among their own people.

"I'm not happy about it," she confided. "Lisa's about my least favorite person in the world. She's always resented me and blamed me for breaking up her marriage. But Brad and I never even had a date until after he and Lisa had broken up. I'm really apprehensive about how this is all going to work out, but I love our new house and I'm sure Lisa loves hers."

"Oh, you'll work it out, I'm sure," Flo said sympathetically. "And in the meantime, as you said, you'll have a baby-sitter living right next door."

"I appreciate your support, Flo. We'd love to have dinner at your place on Saturday night. I'm sure my husband doesn't have anything planned. Don't worry about the kids. I'll get my mother to drive up and watch them." She wrote her name and phone number on a memo pad, and Flo did the same for her.

Suzanne walked Flo to the front door. It was time for the kids to come in, which Bradley well knew. She planned to go out and flag them down, but was delighted to see them heading toward the garage on their bicycles, along with Ann's son and younger daughter. Could it be that Bradley had actually checked his watch? Or maybe it was Ann's kids who'd done the checking, for Bradley could be awfully obstinate sometimes. He had a tendency to do as he wanted, not as he was told. At nine years old he was still young enough for corporal punishment, but she'd only spanked him one time, when she caught him in the pool after she'd told him to get out. Her preferred method was to threaten him with punishment, like no TV or no bicycle or that old standby, wait-till-your-father-comes-home, but she suspected that he knew she really didn't mean it. She figured he'd be a real handful by the time he became a teenager.

She headed toward the open garage so she could close the door and lock the garage entry to the house. The kids were home and it would soon be getting dark. She waved good-bye to Flo. "I'm glad you came by. See you Saturday."

Suzanne had a warm feeling at her core. It was nice to have a friend.

CHAPTER 16

Nothing more than mouth-to-mouth recitation.
—Anonymous, on gossip

Flo placed a bowl of mixed munchies on the coffee table. The NBA game had just started, and Ernie was busy telling the fellows all the information she had provided for him about the people around the corner. He was clearly enjoying his moment in the spotlight.

"Yeah, the husband's some big shot doctor," he was saying. "Owns his own clinic over by Southpoint someplace."

"You met him yet?" Larry Barnes asked.

"No, not yet. But Flo's friends with the wife, and she invited them over for dinner tomorrow."

She smiled. She and Suzanne weren't exactly friends. She couldn't even remember Suzanne's last name, only that it started with a "B." But at least Ernie was giving her some credit. It was the least he could do.

"So we got some rich black folks livin' in the neighborhood, huh?" George Morton remarked.

"And not just one family. The house going up next to them is owned by Michael's friends, remember?"

"Oh, that's right. You told us about that."

"Well, here's something I didn't tell you. This doctor who's already moved in used to be married to the wife who's about to move in. They've even got a kid together."

"Aw, c'mon, man," George Morton said. "Who buys a house next to their ex? Unless he's still messin' with her. One wife ain't enough for him?"

"Is one enough for you, George?" Larry teased.

"No, nothing like that," Ernie said. "Remember, his first wife's married again, too. When the doc and his wife bought their house after the original builders changed their mind, they didn't know his ex and her husband were putting up the house next door."

Flo fiddled around in the kitchen, listening to Ernie recount how Suzanne and her husband had happened to buy the house. She'd cursed her timing the day she brought Suzanne the pound cake just as Suzanne was leaving to bring her kids to the dentist, but she'd hit pay dirt when she went to retrieve her container. It was too soon to hope for a tour of the house, but she was thrilled to have seen and learned as much as she had.

She'd met Ernie at the door as soon as she heard his car pull up, just bursting to tell him about it.

"So the husband's a doc, huh? And he's not a white boy."

"That was just a theory I had, but their kids didn't look like they're mixed, and when I saw a family portrait in their family room I knew for sure. He's black. But they're rich, Ernie, really rich. You should see their house."

"She took you through it?"

"No, but I saw a lot of the downstairs. I knew they had expensive kitchen cabinets and marble countertops, but their refrigerator is one of those new three-door models, and it's finished in the same oak as the cabinets, right down to the metal braid by the borders. The dining room has floor-to-ceiling windows overlooking the pool. And two of the walls in their family room are long connecting sliding glass doors that really open up the view of the river. What a great setting for a party. There's a stone fireplace out on the patio, and a kitchen, too."

"You've been all through that house, Flo," Ernie said, sounding annoyed. "Why didn't you tell me all this before?"

"Because I couldn't get in after the builders started locking it at night. I remember noticing a lot of sliding doors when I walked around the back, but I didn't realize they could all be open at the same time. I've never seen anything like that."

"Sounds like it's real nice."

"Ernie, we have to get real. It's more than 'real nice.' These people have more money than we can ever hope to have. They've got a plasma TV over the fireplace in their family room that's easily five feet wide."

"That's no big deal. The prices of those have gone down a lot in the last couple of years. Do they have a home theater set up in their bonus room with a big screen TV?"

"I don't know. I told you I didn't get upstairs. But to think we can compete with them is just foolish, I tell you. If we try, people are just going to laugh at us." She suspected their neighbors might be laughing already. She and Ernie hadn't taken a vacation since they'd taken occupancy, and people were starting to notice. She was sure she saw George and Larry's gazes meet in amusement when, after talking about their respective travel plans, Larry had asked Ernie where they were going and Ernie said he didn't know. It wouldn't do for anyone to figure out they couldn't afford to go away.

"So they've got a plasma TV. It's still not as big as the big screen we have upstairs."

"But you know it cost more, Ernie. And for all we know they've got a home theater, too. Remember the layout? That house has two bonus rooms upstairs. I'm sure they're not sitting empty, and I'm sure they're not bedrooms. They only have two kids. Or two and a half."

He jumped on her cryptic remark with his usual zeal. "Why do you say two and a half? Is she pregnant?"

That was when she told him about the connection between Suzanne's husband and Lisa Canfield. That blew him away.

Now it was Larry and George's turn to be stunned as Ernie told them about the marital connection between the two families. Flo could tell he was enjoying himself. Ernie loved being the one always in the know, the one who knew anything worth knowing about anyone in the neighborhood. If someone was selling their house, he knew about the job transfer or promotion that prompted the sale, and he also managed to find out the asking price. If they were going on vacation, he knew where. If they had to suddenly leave town, he knew who was ill or who had died. Whenever someone new moved in, Ernie found out where they worked and what they did almost immediately. And he had no problem with passing on what he knew to anyone who would listen.

Flo raised her eyebrows thoughtfully. If a woman talked the way Ernie did, she'd be labeled a gossip. But he had a way of extracting information that seemed so casual, people probably didn't even realize they were being interrogated. Sometimes she did feel he overdid his need to know everything, like the time he stopped at George's house simply because he saw Larry's car in the driveway. He told her George acted like he didn't want to let him in, and he seemed downright annoyed when Ernie asked if Larry was there, saying Larry had just stopped by for a minute and was getting ready to leave. Ernie rode past an hour later just to see, and Larry's car was still there. He came home fuming. She tried to tell him they couldn't expect to be included every time their neighbors got together. It wasn't like George was giving a party, she'd said. If Larry's car was the only one in the driveway, maybe they had something to discuss that was only between the two of them.

But Ernie carried on like a little kid, insisting he'd been snubbed. He even kept to himself for a little while after that, but it didn't last very long. Soon he was right back into the swing of it.

She didn't share Ernie's desire to be the first one to know all, the latest news, but she did share his wish that none of the black people in the neighborhood surpass them material-wise. That hadn't been a problem until Suzanne and her family moved in. No way could she and Ernie live as well as a doctor's family, no matter what Ernie said. The jury was still out about the Canfields—for all she knew Lisa and her second husband might be doctors, too—but at least they felt comfortably ensconced ahead of everyone else here in Villa Saint John.

Larry and his wife, Sondra, were lucky to be living here at all, since they had four children. All their kids were boys, and all of them had unfortunately inherited Larry's round head and wide-spaced eyes. Their house was no great shakes, and their furniture nothing to write home about, but how they were able to afford a house in Villa St. John in the first place mystified Flo. Larry delivered packages for UPS, and Sondra only worked part-time as a bank teller while the kids were in school. Then again, maybe they *couldn't* really afford the house and so many kids. Sometimes their boys looked downright shabby, and whenever they were over and she served refreshments, they ate like they were starving.

Gail and George Morton's house was the smallest model in the development, just three bedrooms and a living room that had to double as a family room, and while it was comfortable and certainly furnished nicer than that cheap Rooms to Go stuff Larry and Sondra had, there was nothing spectacular about it.

Then, of course, there were the Gillespies right next door, the newest residents of the neighborhood. Unlike the Mortons and the Barnes, who were in their early and mid thirties, the Gillespies were about the same age as she and Ernie. They were nice enough people—Michael was supposed to come over and watch the game with the fellows tonight—but closemouthed, whether it was about themselves or their friends, the Canfields. Flo hadn't even seen their entire house, even though she'd been over there several times. That didn't seem fair. She and Ernie had taken them through theirs the first time they had them over, like they did with everybody. She wondered if Kim and Michael had a reason for not wanting anyone to see the rest. Maybe the private areas were a raggedy contrast to their beautifully decorated living, dining, and family rooms.

Most of the other black couples in Villa St. John were older, in their fifties, and didn't really socialize other than a friendly hello when they passed on the street or met at homeowner's association meetings. There was one other couple in their forties, the Princes, whom they had tried to befriend at a homeowner's association meeting, only to have their efforts met with a chilly reception. Some people preferred to keep to themselves, and that was all right . . . as long as the couple weren't friendly with the Barneses or the Mortons, and they weren't. Both Sondra and Gail had observed that the Princes struck them as being standoffish.

She called out, "I've got it, Ernie," when the doorbell chimed through the house. She stopped to admonish George's two young daughters not to play with the expensive life-sized statue of a German shepherd at the foot of the stairs. She didn't understand why George had to bring them with him in the first place. Two- and three-year-old girls had no interest in basketball. She wondered if Gail had wanted to get them out of the house so she'd have some time to herself. That wasn't very considerate. Surely Gail had known George wouldn't watch them, that it would fall on *her* shoulders.

Flo shook her head. The little Morton girls were cute with their chubby cheeks and long braids, but sometimes she felt George and Gail thought their daughters' cuteness excused them from behaving. Right now she really didn't feel like being bothered.

After sending George's daughters back to the family room, she opened the front door and saw Michael Gillespie holding a six-pack of Icehouse, with two of Larry's kids pressing close behind him.

Damn. If these two had shown up now, the other two would soon follow. They usually came in pairs. She was half tempted to ask the kids to wait at the door and send Larry out to them.

"Hi, Michael. The guys are in the family room. Go on back."

"Thanks, Flo." He headed toward the hall.

She glanced at the Barnes kids again and made a quick decision. "And can you tell Larry that someone's here to see him?" she called after Michael.

"Sure."

"We came to watch the game with Daddy," the oldest boy, Larry Junior, said.

She didn't know how to respond. Damn, if Larry's kids wanted to watch the game why didn't Larry just stay home with them? They had a damn TV set. She'd been so happy when Larry showed up alone today. Those boys of his might be all right in their own home environment, with its dark-colored furniture and rugs, but her house was hardly childproof. One of them had spilled bright red fruit punch on her tan Berber carpet the last time he was here. She'd told him to drink it in the breakfast nook, but he'd ignored her and ventured into the family room, where he promptly knocked the glass over. That same day, the youngest had fallen into the pool while running outside—even though he'd been told not to—and had to go home to change into dry clothes.

Larry's stocky build soon filled the archway just beyond the foyer. "Hey, squirts! You come to watch the game with your old man?"

"Yeah."

"Well, come on! We're missing it." He waved them forward, and they would have rushed in if Flo didn't block them with her arm across the door. "Wait a minute, fellas. Wipe your feet first."

"Yeah, guys," Larry said with a touch of impatience. "You know better than that."

After the boys were inside, Flo went to the laundry room. The dryer had stopped, so she began folding clothes and linens. She didn't feel like refereeing the Barnes kids tonight, nor supervising the Morton girls. Let Ernie do it. Lord knows Larry and George wouldn't. Did her neighbors think she was running a day care center or something?

She was anxious to finish up the laundry. She usually did it on Saturday, but there'd been so much work at the office that her supervisor asked her to come in tomorrow morning. She agreed, welcoming the idea of extra money to help pay the bills. If she was lucky, they'd stay this busy and she could get in fifteen or twenty overtime hours a month. She might make enough to pay off the equipment and furniture in the home theater upstairs. Getting into medical billing had been a wise choice—health care was one of the few fields that continued to grow while so many others were dragging. The loss of either of their jobs would be catastrophic.

Flo shook her head as her hands deftly rolled Ernie's T-shirts. Sometimes she thought he believed his own publicity, that he was a high-powered director of Human Resources and she was a supervisor instead of a mere data entry operator. He'd been a mere clerk when the manager resigned. It was a relatively small company, so the executive staff agreed to give him a trial at the job. He'd grown along with the company, but Flo was realistic enough to know he'd never get another job at that level. Although Ernie had attended numerous seminars for human resource professionals over the years, he didn't have a four-year degree, or even a two-year degree. One year of college meant absolutely nothing in today's job market.

She hoped he wouldn't feel he had to go out and make another big-ticket purchase in a futile attempt to prove to everyone that they had just as much disposable income as Suzanne and her doctor husband. They had more important things to do with their money. Gregory would be ready for college next year, and as it was, he'd have to do his first two years at FCCJ, the local community college. They couldn't afford to send him anywhere more expensive. If they didn't get their finances under control, they wouldn't be able to afford even that.

Her mouth set in a hard line as she rolled Ernie's undershirts. Between the two of them, they brought in a nice income. They shouldn't have a care in the world, but Ernie's extravagant spending habits were pushing them toward the poor house. Every time one of the neighbors bought something new for their homes Ernie tried to best them, like the extravagant Christmas lighting he'd charged because Larry Barnes bought a set of reindeer with moving heads. Their yard looked like the Las Vegas Strip, and their electric bill had more than doubled. Then there was the outdoor bar George Morton had so proudly shown them the last time they were over there. The very next weekend Ernie came home with an entire new set of lawn furniture—a round table with umbrella, chaises, end tables, side chairs—all because he didn't want George to show them up.

They'd had a huge argument when he spent twelve thousand dollars on a used late model VW Bug for Gregory. All the other kids in
the neighborhood drove models from the early nineties. She felt that
was good enough for Gregory as well, but Ernie insisted their son
should have something better than the rest of the kids. Gregory had
eagerly agreed to help with the payments—she and Ernie paid half of
the monthly note—but he could have helped out just the same, and
not have to work as hard as he did, if he drove a less expensive car.
Twenty-five hours a week was a lot for a seventeen-year-old high school
junior who had to keep his grades up. He should be home now, watching the play-off game with Ernie, instead of scanning groceries at Winn-
Dixie for minimum wage.

She stiffened at the sound of the doorbell. It had to be Larry's other
two boys. Then she relaxed and continued with her folding. If Ernie
called out to her to get the door she probably wouldn't hear him up
here anyway.

She scooped up a stack of folded sheets and towels and headed for
the linen closet, pausing in the wide hall leading to the front door.
Larry and Ernie were both counting out change. She recognized the
Domino's Pizza logo on the shirt of the man who stood waiting, and
then she noticed two large white boxes resting on top of the Bombay
chest, no doubt dripping grease all over it. No one told her they'd ordered pizza. She'd better go make sure all the kids ate at the table, or
else she'd have to cope with hard-to-remove tomato and grease stains
over every surface, including the wall.

She had all four kids sitting at the table and was pouring them
some Sprite—specifically chosen because it wouldn't leave a stain if it
spilled—when Larry's other two boys showed up around the back.
The screen door by the pool was locked, and they called out to their
father to let them in. Larry jumped up and unlocked the door.

"Gee, they musta seen the deliveryman coming," Larry Junior said.

Flo had to agree.

CHAPTER 17

Home is where you go when other places close.
—Joseph Laurie

Brad smiled naturally for the first time that evening as he shook hands with Flo and Ernie and said good night. Now he understood how Suzanne felt when she was around his business associates, people she had nothing in common with. The evening had dragged on forever.

"Well, that's over," he remarked as he and Suzanne walked to the Jaguar.

"Was it so bad?"

"It was awful. But you certainly made it easy for them." He opened the passenger door for her.

"I did? How?"

He gestured for her to wait while he walked around to the driver's side. "In case you didn't notice, they were pumping you for information all night," he said as he fastened his seat belt. "And you were only too happy to tell them what they wanted to know."

"I was?"

He mimicked the questions and her replies. " 'Nice people, Darrell and Lisa. We met them a couple of times. Are they doctors, too?' 'Oh, no. Lisa's a pharmacist. Darrell manages an investment house.' 'It looked like they had a lot of kids with them the day we met them.' 'They have twin boys a little younger than our Bradley. Paige lives with them, and so does Darrell's daughter from his first marriage. And

Darrell's mother will be living with them, too.' " He returned to his normal speaking voice. "Damn, girl, you practically provided their whole life stories. Didn't you feel me nudging your leg under the table?"

"Oh, I don't care. It's not like I was talking about *our* business."

"That's another thing. Be very careful of these people, Suzanne. They're the type who'll try to find out everything, including our bank balance and the size of my draw."

"Don't be silly, Brad. Nobody cares what size drawers you wear."

"I'm not talking about my underwear. I'm talking about my salary, what I draw from the business every month. I know their type, Suzanne. They've managed to make a little money, so they fill their house with a lot of things they feel are everyone's ideal, like that gold-plated silverware and that colossal chandelier. They're obsessed with what everybody else has."

"That chandelier did seem too big and fussy, but I did think the silverware was pretty."

"I think it's gaudy, just like that overly ornate chandelier. Maybe it'd be pretty if it was real gold, but you know it isn't. Their whole house is overdone. It's like they want to fit in as much as they can to try to impress people with their belongings, but it looks like a junkyard with all those ceramic dogs all over the place."

"I guess it was a little crowded."

"Listen, Suzanne, I don't want to sound like a snob. You know my family is lower middle class, so I know how it feels to achieve a higher standard of living than your parents had. I may have done all right for myself, but I don't go around talking about how my house is custom built and my pool is custom built and my lawn is custom maintained, like the two of them were saying. Did you hear Ernie spout that crap about how the local high school is one of the best in the city?"

Suzanne smiled. "Yes, in response to your telling them Bradley and Lauren go to the Country Day."

"That's why they tried to say how good the public school is, because that's where their son goes. Anyway, I'm telling you right now that I have no intention of becoming friends with these people. If you want to be buddies with the wife, that's fine, but don't expect us to engage in any more of these cozy just-the-four-of-us evenings. And when you're around them, just remember what I said about not talking so much." He turned into their driveway. "You want me to park in the garage?"

"Sure, go ahead."

He pressed the remote control to open the garage door. He noticed his mother-in-law's battered Buick in the driveway. That was another source of annoyance. Not only had Suzanne accepted Flo's invitation without even consulting him—just because he had nothing else planned didn't mean he wanted to spend an evening with Flo and Ernie—she'd also arranged for her mother to come up and stay with Bradley and Lauren, and she'd brought all three of her kids along. It was too late for them to drive back to Palatka now, so they'd be hanging around all day tomorrow. Last Sunday only Arlene and Kenya had come for the day, but this was something else. He'd better not see them again next weekend, or else he and Suzanne were going to have it out.

He shook his head. If Suzanne thought she was going to get her family up here to Jacksonville every week, she was about to be disappointed. It didn't matter if they came for the weekend or just an afternoon. He worked hard, and he didn't want outsiders underfoot all the time in his home when he was off.

A box of Popeye's chicken sat on the kitchen counter. Empty containers of side dishes littered the nearby space.

Arlene was watching TV in the family room, but got up hastily at the sound of their greeting. "We didn't expect you back so soon," she said as she disposed of the trash and wiped down the counter, restoring the kitchen to order. "Did you have a nice time?"

"Oh, it was lovely," Suzanne said.

"Did you meet their son?"

"No, he was out for the evening."

Brad listened to the exchange curiously. Obviously Arlene and Suzanne had discussed Flo and Ernie before. If he knew Arlene, and after all this time he felt he did, she wanted to snare their son for Kenya. Arlene knew nothing about the Hickmans other than they had a house in Villa St. John, but as far as she was concerned that gave them class. Not that he cared. If anything, he was all for Kenya marrying somebody who could support her in style. Then his mother-in-law could go live with *them* when she retired.

Derrick, then Matthew, emerged from the stairs, both wearing sharply creased chinos and short-sleeved shirts. Brad could smell their cologne from eight feet away. "We're going to check out a club," Derrick said. "See you later."

"Do you have the key I gave you?" Suzanne asked.

Brad looked at her sharply. He could understand if she removed her own key and gave it to Derrick to use just for tonight, but it sounded like she'd given him one of the extras, just like she'd given her mother a card that opened the entry gate at their old community in St. Augustine. He didn't want them letting themselves into his house any time they wanted, damn it. If anyone who didn't physically live here should have a key, it would be Paige, and he felt reasonably certain Suzanne hadn't offered *her* one.

"He has your key?" he asked Suzanne as his brothers-in-law left.

She looked embarrassed. "No. I gave him one of the spares. Remember, at the closing we got four."

"Well, you make sure you get it back before they leave tomorrow," he said, not caring if Arlene heard him. It was probably best for her to know right off the bat how he felt. He sighed. He'd taken a drink at the Hickmans', but he could use another one to cap off what had been a trying evening. A drink and sex would be even better, but Suzanne had a tendency to sit up and talk to her mother after she baby-sat, probably telling her all about the evening, and he was too tired to wait for her. He was doing more and more surgical procedures these days, spending almost as much time at the hospital as he did at the diagnostic center.

He removed a highball glass from an upper cabinet, filled it with ice, then took out the Captain Morgan spiced rum. Oh, yeah. This would go down his throat a lot smoother than that rotgut-tasting stuff Ernie had served. Ernie had mixed it in the kitchen, out of his line of vision, probably because it was a cheap brand.

"What've we got to mix this with?" he asked Suzanne.

She promptly opened the refrigerator. "We've got some Coke left." She handed him the plastic liter.

Brad stirred the drink with his finger. "Ladies, I'm going to say good night." He pinched Suzanne's ass on the way out, hoping she'd get the message and would hurry in.

Suzanne sprawled in a club chair in the family room and sighed heavily after he left.

"Anything wrong, dear?" her mother asked.

"No, not really. Brad's just a little cranky tonight. He doesn't like my new friend. He said she and her husband just want to get into our business."

"And you don't think that's the case?"

"No, not really. I know if I was her and saw someone moving in this big house with two Jaguars and an Escalade I'd be a little curious, too. But I think she and her husband were trying to give us the impression they have as much as we do."

"That's ridiculous," Arlene said confidently. "How could they?"

"I think it was just talk. They were saying things like they'd considered building on this street before deciding their house was too small, and they went on and on about how they had everything built to their personal specifications, stuff like that."

"Complete foolishness. No wonder Brad's so grumpy. He's worked too hard all week to have to be subjected to the company of a couple of wannabees. But I'm afraid us being here doesn't help the situation. He seemed annoyed that Derrick has a key to the house."

"He was. I'm sorry, Mom."

"Don't you worry. But I think it'll be best if we wait two or three weeks before we come back. You can always drive down with Bradley and Lauren to see us in the meantime."

"Are the kids in bed yet?"

"Upstairs watching TV with Kenya. They're fine." Arlene took a sip of her drink. "Derrick and Matthew will be disappointed that they can't come back for a bit. They were excited about going to the night-club tonight."

"I'm sorry, Mom, but I do think you're doing the right thing. We'll have to move slowly"—she lowered her voice to a whisper—"or else the plan won't work."

Arlene followed her example and spoke softly. "I already put in for a transfer."

Suzanne blinked in surprise. Her mother hadn't wasted any time. "Let's hope it doesn't come through before you can use it."

"Don't worry, honey. You've got it worked out just fine. You don't think Brad wouldn't invite us to stay with you once I start working up here, do you? Like you said, I've got a real need to stay here with you. I still have to pay the mortgage until the house sells, and my car's likely to give out if I try making that long commute every day." She squeezed Suzanne's arm. "Don't worry, honey. It'll probably take months for the house to sell, maybe even a year or two. Kenya can transfer to the high school up here, and the boys can stay in the house until it sells. Of course, they might want to come up here for the weekends."

For the first time Suzanne began to feel uneasy. A year or two? It sounded like her mother planned to stay with them a lot longer than the original plan of six months. In hindsight she realized she hadn't specified a time frame, she'd just said "for a while." How could she tell her mother a year or two was too long a stay? "I'm afraid Brad might suggest Derrick and Matthew just stay there and pay the mortgage for you, Mom. After all, they both work."

"Oh, but they don't make that much money. Matthew's saving up for a car, and after Derrick pays his car note and child support for that girl's baby he barely has anything left."

Suzanne noticed her mother said "that girl's baby" like Derrick's ex had gotten pregnant by herself. "But there's two of them, Mom, and your house note isn't that much."

"That's the beauty of it, dear. There's a big difference between the mortgage I've had for fourteen years and today's rents. Once I see how much the rents are up here, that'll give me the perfect excuse to stay with you longer. So don't you worry." Arlene drained the remainder of her glass. "I'm going to refresh this."

Suzanne eyed the clear gin bottle, wondering how many shots her mother had poured herself tonight. In recent years it seemed like her mother had developed an increasing dependency on alcohol. Sometimes Suzanne thought that marrying Brad had done little more than allow her mother to change her tastes from beer to Beefeater. But once she got out of that awful house with its torn linoleum and threadbare carpet and moved in with them, her life would change. Maybe she'd meet people who liked to do something besides sit around and drink. Kenya, too, would benefit, meeting nice boys from nice families, like Flo and Ernie's son.

As for Derrick and Matthew, Suzanne doubted the move would affect them other than to give them new and different places to hang out on the weekends. They didn't seem to be interested in anything else. No wonder Brad was so down on them. When he was Derrick's age, he was already starting his residency at Emory Medical Center in Atlanta. Derrick and Matthew both worked at the Putnam Medical Center, but Derrick was an orderly and Matthew did maintenance.

She said good night to her mother and eagerly headed toward the bedroom where Brad waited. She still didn't like scheming behind his back, but she had to get her family out of that miserable house in Palatka. Leaving them behind while she lived the good life in Jacksonville simply wasn't an option.

She just hoped she wasn't making a serious mistake.

CHAPTER 18

When the stream of life flows according to our wishes.
—Cicero, on prosperity

Lisa had taken a week's vacation when they moved the second week in June. Now that she'd changed jobs, she was back to only two weeks off per year, but she didn't want to spend all of it unpacking.

Her entire life revolved around the move weeks before it had actually occurred. All her free time was spent packing. They spent the last few days before the move eating out for lunch and dinner. When the movers came for the furniture and boxes, she stayed behind, armed with a vacuum, bucket, broom, mop, and an all-purpose cleaning agent. She didn't want the new owners to think they were a bunch of pigs.

She thought of Suzanne as she wiped down cabinets, appliances, baseboards, and window sills, picturing her leaving behind a huge mess in her old house without so much as a backward glance. Only when she saw the paint on her rag and realized she'd scrubbed too hard did she force herself to forget about Suzanne and concentrate solely on her work. The sooner she finished, the sooner she could drive down to Jacksonville and be with her family . . . and begin the process of organizing, unpacking, and decorating her new home. . . .

Once in the new house, Lisa threw herself into her chores and was satisfied with her progress at week's end. After the first few days, the house had been made reasonably functional, with the kitchen completely unpacked and the furniture in place. Darrell hammered curtain rods into place, and Lisa learned how to use his power drill and helped him hang the blinds. She didn't want the windows covered with sheets and blankets for more than two days, hating the ghetto way it looked.

Devon's sixteenth birthday fell on their first Friday in the house, and Darrell announced he was taking everyone to dinner that night to celebrate. Lisa ordered Devon's favorite red velvet cake from Publix and carefully placed it in the back of the Durango, with the plan to get the waitstaff to serve it after they finished eating.

"All right, everybody, ten minutes," Lisa yelled, feeling like a director on a movie set. "I hope everyone heard me," she said to Darrell.

"Use the intercom."

"Oh, I forgot." She walked to the intercom by the light switch, held a button down, and calmly requested that everyone be ready to leave in ten minutes. "I guess that's that." She groaned at the sound of the doorbell. "Who's that, I wonder?"

"Maybe it's Michael and Kim."

"Nah, they're coming over tomorrow for dinner, remember? I'll go see who it is." She buttoned the top back button of her dress and plodded barefoot to the front door. "Who is it?" she called.

"Flo and Ernie Hickman from Villa Saint John," a woman's voice replied.

Lisa frowned for a moment before she placed their identity. She couldn't imagine why Kim and Michael's nosy neighbors had come calling, but nonetheless she wanted to make a good impression. She whirled around, anxious to determine how much the Hickmans would be able to see through an open front door. Only the living room was straight ahead, and fortunately it looked fine. The black baby grand that dominated the room shone like new leather shoes, as did the black accent tables. She opened the door and smiled. "Hello there!"

"Hi," Flo said. "Kim mentioned you guys had just moved in."

"We thought we'd bring you something to snack on, so you won't have to take time out from unpacking to cook," Ernie added, holding out a large brown paper bag.

"I baked you an apple pie, too," Flo said. "It's our way of saying welcome to the neighborhood."

"How nice of you," Lisa said, genuinely touched by the gesture. She reached to accept the bag from Ernie. "I'd love to invite you in, but we're all about to go out to dinner. It's my daughter's birthday."

"How nice. How old is she?" Flo asked.

"Sixteen."

"No party?" Ernie asked.

"Nobody really has sweet sixteen parties anymore," Lisa said with a smile. "I'm afraid you're dating yourself, Ernie."

"Well, we're sorry we caught you at a bad time," Flo said. "I hope you guys enjoy your dinner. Where're you going, Red Lobster?"

Lisa didn't want to say she never ate at Red Lobster or anyplace else with that annoying bright overhead lighting. "The birthday girl wants to go to TGI Friday's, so that's where we're going."

"We'll have to catch you guys another time," Ernie said. "But I don't think you can carry all this, Lisa. Can I give you a hand?"

He was right. She didn't even know what was in the bag she held, but whatever it was, it was still warm. The last thing she wanted to do was drop the pie while trying to protect her palms from the heat of the bag. And no one else was around to help. Darrell was still getting dressed. "That's a good idea. Come in," she said, stepping back and pulling the door open wider.

"Your place looks all settled," Flo said chattily as they followed her to the kitchen.

"Oh, we've got plenty to do yet, but it's coming along."

"Nice place," Ernie said.

"Thanks."

"All right, who's in my house?" a harsh voice demanded.

It had become a household tradition for Darrell to demand to know who was visiting whenever he heard strange voices, but poor Ernie looked so startled that suddenly Lisa felt embarrassed. "It's Kim and Michael's neighbors, Darrell," she called. "Come on out."

Darrell emerged and greeted the Hickmans jovially, not using their names.

Lisa knew he sidestepped the issue because he didn't remember. "Look what Flo and Ernie brought us," she said pointedly as she unwrapped a golden brown chicken that must have weighed at least six pounds.

"Hey, that was real nice of you folks."

"We were glad to do it. We know how hectic moving time is," Flo said.

The twins came running from around the corner. "We're ready, Daddy."

"Right on time. These are our boys, Cary and Courtney. Boys, say hello to Mister and Missus, uh . . ."

"Hickman," Ernie supplied.

The boys mumbled hello and shook Ernie's hand.

"They look a lot alike, but they're not quite identical, are they?" Flo asked.

"That's right, they're fraternal," Lisa said.

"I'm taller," Courtney said proudly, standing straight to accent the inch difference in their heights.

"So what. I can still beat you," Cary said.

"Hey boys, take it easy, will you?" Darrell said easily as the twins took pokes at each other. Then he turned to the Hickmans. "Flo, Ernie, I'm sorry we can't invite you to stay a while, but I'm sure Lisa explained we're celebrating our daughter's birthday this evening."

"Oh, we understand," Flo said.

"Another time, maybe," Ernie added.

"Are you two doing anything tomorrow night?"

Lisa looked at Darrell curiously. Nice as it had been of the Hickmans to roast a chicken and bake a pie for them, she didn't feel they owed them anymore than a thank you, which they'd already conveyed. She hardly felt it necessary to invite them over for an evening. Had he forgotten what Kim and Michael said about how nosy they were?

"Actually, no," Ernie said after exchanging a glance of confirmation with Flo.

"Why don't you come over tomorrow evening, say about eight?" Darrell suggested. "We'll rent a movie or something."

"We'd love to," Flo said.

The girls and Esther showed up. "My stomach's crying out for some of those ribs basted in Jack Daniels," Esther said in a tone that suggested she was ready to leave right this minute.

Lisa smiled; when her mother-in-law was ready to go, she was ready to go. But she had a point. Who knew how long they'd have to wait for a table?

"Okay, Ma, we're going," Darrell said.

The Hickmans walked outside with them. They waved good-bye before getting into their Altima and driving off.

Darrell turned to Lisa when they were all seated in the car. "Did you bring the cake?" he mouthed.

She nodded. "Darrell, why did you invite Flo and Ernie over tomorrow night? If they're as bad as Kim says, I don't want to get involved with them. It's not like we owe them anything, other than the return of their Pyrex dish."

"I was just trying to be nice. Since Kim and Michael are coming tomorrow, we can all get together this one time and see what happens. We don't have to be best buddies, but I think it'd be nice if we were a little friendly with the other families in the neighborhood. We never got beyond impersonal hi-how-are-you's with our neighbors in St. Marys."

"Most of them were retired. We had nothing in common," she pointed out, adding, "the twins used to play with their visiting grandchildren, for crying out loud."

"All right, but a lot of the people here are in our age group. I think we should give them a chance. Don't forget, that's how we met Michael and Kim, and they're the best friends we've ever had."

Michael Gillespie had an apartment a few doors down in the complex where Darrell moved with Devon after he and Paula broke up. The two men became friendly and started playing tennis together. After Lisa came into the picture, she was introduced to Michael's girlfriend Kim. The couples hit it off so well that Lisa and Darrell served as matron of honor and best man when Michael married Kim two years later. Those were happy days. Paige and Devon were little girls together, and Lisa felt a lot less harried than she did now, probably because she was younger and didn't have the added stress of teenage daughters who drove. And, of course, she didn't have Brad and Suzanne living next door.

"Yes, they are our best friends, and I trust what they say about their neighbors," she said. At Darrell's determined stare, she added with a sigh, "But I suppose we ought to make up our own minds about them. It was awfully nice of them to welcome us the way they did." It was more than Brad and Suzanne had done. While their neighbors on the other side, Ann and Bill Sorensen, had come over and introduced themselves and brought homemade fudge brownies, the Betancourts hadn't been heard from.

"It'll be fine, Lisa. You'll be able to return Flo's pie plate to her. We know there's no way a pie will last more than twenty-four hours with our brood. We don't have to see them anymore after tomorrow if we don't want to. But they can't be that bad. Even Michael gets together with Ernie occasionally."

* * *

"Happy sixteenth birthday to me!" Devon squealed after they had sung to her and she blew out the candles. "I hope I can get to the license bureau next week."

"Just enjoy the day, Devon," Darrell suggested easily. "The DMV isn't going anywhere."

"I'll bring you on Wednesday," Lisa said. "I need to get there myself and get a Florida license. Darrell, Ma Canfield, Paige—you guys will have to do the same."

"Did your mother call you back, Devon?" Esther asked. She'd answered the phone when Paula called earlier. Devon and Paige were out, having gone to the local supermarkets to fill out job applications.

"If she did I wasn't home again. She put a note in my birthday card saying she'd be sending me something special soon. I can't wait to see what it is."

Lisa was curious herself. She hoped Paula would follow through with the surprise she'd promised and not forget about it. Devon appeared truly happy these days, like her old self, which delighted Lisa. That emotion had been missing from Devon's young life lately. She didn't want Paula to mess things up.

The next morning, Lisa and Darrell drove to the consumer warehouse where she worked to do some stock-up shopping. Lisa had deliberately let the freezer in their garage in St. Mary's become empty so she wouldn't have to worry about the food defrosting during the move, and now it was time to fill it up. She selected several chickens, hams, and roasts.

"Here's some ground beef," Darrell said, placing a ten-pound package in their cart. "How are we on steaks? I saw some real nice ones."

"We're low on everything so get them."

They were browsing the aisles when Darrell stopped in front of a paddleboat on display. "Hey, this is cute. We can take the twins out in this and do some fishing."

"Correction. *You* can take the twins out fishing. I'll go when you just want to take a ride. It's great cardiovascular exercise, like riding a bike."

"It's got grooves for drinks and even a cooler or a portable TV set. And it seats six." His eyes scanned the surrounding area, looking for the price. "Not bad. You want to get it?"

"Can we afford to right now? We'll have to get life jackets for everyone, too."

"We'll stop at the sporting good store on the way home for those. But let's get it. You know how this place is. You've got to buy the stuff when you see it. Two weeks from now they might be sold out. We'll put it on the American Express. By the time the bill comes in I'll have the cash."

They had a stockman put the large box on the cargo rack on top of the truck. The kids were excited about the boat when they arrived back home. After Darrell enlisted help from Bill Sorensen next door getting the unwieldy box down—there'd been no answer at Brad's— all of them helped Darrell put it together, handing him the tools he needed like obedient OR nurses.

Lisa divided the large packages of meat into smaller portions and wrapped them in white freezer paper. When she finished, she went to see how the boat was coming along. "Anything I can do to help?"

"Nah, we're just about done."

"In that case I'm going to make some tuna fish for lunch."

"Great. We'll take it out and eat on the boat."

An hour later, they all piled into the boat, armed with tuna fish sandwiches, bottled soda, and a portable CD player. Lisa felt the pull in her calves as she pushed the pedals in a circular motion.

"We're hardly moving," Courtney complained.

"That's because we're carrying a full load," Darrell replied. "We'll just float once we get further out."

"I thought we were going downtown," Devon said.

"We could, but we're not. That's a lot farther than it looks," Darrell said. "Remember, this boat is foot controlled. You always want to save enough strength for the return trip or else you'll be stuck in the middle of the river. You could find yourselves in real trouble, especially if it starts storming."

"I don't want you girls trying to go all the way downtown," Lisa added. "It's not like you can dock this and leave it unattended. Anyone can get in and paddle away with it. Not very quickly, of course, but what're you gonna do, jump in the Saint Johns and swim after them?"

"Ahoy there!"

Everyone's head turned in the direction of the voice, not knowing if the greeting was meant for them or another boater.

"It's Daddy!" Paige said. "He's out on his boat." She began waving frantically.

"Stop, Paige, he sees us," Lisa snapped. She didn't mean to sound so short, but it just slipped out.

Brad steered his boat to within a few yards of where they floated.

Darrell whistled. "Nice boat, Captain. What is it, twenty, twenty-two feet?"

"Twenty-five."

"Bet you could do some serious fishing in that."

"Not today I can't. I've been out for hours and haven't caught a thing," Brad said with a laugh. "You guys look nice and relaxed."

"We are," Lisa said quickly.

Bradley appeared, an orange life jacket covering his neck and chest. Lisa wondered what it was like below deck. "Hey, Paige," he said, waving. Then he made a face. "You guys have a funny boat."

Lisa wanted to slap him.

"We do not," Cary yelled.

"Be quiet, Bradley," Brad said. To Darrell he said, "I used to dock her at the marina. Now I'm going to keep her in the boathouse out back."

"Where's Lauren, Daddy?" Paige asked.

"She's out with Suzanne. They dropped us off at the marina this morning so we could pick up the boat. I don't know if they're back home yet or not. But we're about ready to head in. Darrell, maybe we can try our luck fishing next week. Bring the boys along."

"Count me in."

Brad waved, then started the engine and drove off, his unbuttoned shirt flying out behind him. Lisa caught the name painted in red on the bow—*The Suzie Q.* She sighed and turned away.

Darrell turned to the twins. "Well, fellas, looks like we'll be going out with—" he paused, trying to come up with an appropriate term for the twins to use to address Brad, "Doctor Brad on the big boat next weekend. Do you think you can manage to spend a few hours around Bradley without throwing him overboard?"

Everyone laughed, but Lisa could only manage a smile. A few minutes ago, she thought their new paddle boat was just adorable, but it would look like a joke docked next to Brad's fully equipped vessel, which looked sturdy enough for a trip to the Bahamas. She'd known from Paige that Brad had a boat, but it never occurred to her that Brad would start docking it at their private pier.

She took a moment to be grateful that Suzanne hadn't been on deck to see them powering their new boat with their feet like the Flintstones. Lisa knew Suzanne would enjoy nothing better than to wave triumphantly as Brad powered up their motor and left them behind in a trail of foamy water.

CHAPTER 19

Why don't you come up some time and see me?
—Mae West in *She Done Him Wrong*, 1933

Ernie hastily unlocked his kitchen window so he could open it. He'd just caught a glimpse of Michael and Kim Gillespie leaving their house with their daughter, and he wanted to catch them before they got into their car. "Hey!" he called to them. "Y'all change your mind about going over to Darrell's?"

"No. We're going over now," Michael said.

"I thought we could ride over together." Ernie watched as Michael and Kim exchanged glances. He didn't get it. It was only seven o'clock. He could have sworn Darrell said to come over about eight.

"Actually, Ernie, we were invited for dinner, so we're going a little earlier," Kim said. "We didn't get to see Devon yesterday for her birthday. We've known her all her life, you know."

He noticed the brightly wrapped package little Alicyn Gillespie held. A birthday present for the Canfield girl. He felt disappointed. When he'd seen Michael that morning while they were both working in their yards he'd casually said, "Flo and I were invited over to Darrell's place tonight." The last thing he'd expected to hear was that Michael and Kim would be there, too. Now his confidence deflated even further to learn that the Gillespies were going over for dinner, while he and Flo had only been invited for afterward. Embarrassed, he said, "In that case we'll see you in about an hour," then closed the window.

"What's going on?" Flo said as she entered the kitchen. "Did I just hear you calling out to somebody?"

"Yeah. I just saw Michael and Kim leaving. I thought maybe something had come up for them and they wouldn't be able to make it over to Darrell's. It turns out they were invited over there to *dinner*."

"Well, Ernie, they've known each other a long time. Didn't Michael say they were neighbors ten, twelve years ago?"

"Yeah, but I don't see why Darrell couldn't invite us for dinner as well. It's not like they can't afford to feed two more people. I'll bet they're serving something real nice, too."

"To listen to you talk you'd think our refrigerator is empty," Flo said, sounding rankled. "They hardly know us. We're lucky they invited us over at all. Don't worry about it, huh?" She placed a reassuring hand on his shoulder. "It's after seven. I'm going to take a shower and get dressed."

"Okay."

Flo hadn't come out of the bedroom yet when the doorbell rang at 7:40. Ernie answered the door to see George Morton standing on the other side. He noticed George didn't have the ladder he'd borrowed three weeks ago. He hoped George wasn't coming to ask for another favor. He and Gail were the neediest damn people he'd ever seen. Either their cars were breaking down and they needed rides, or they needed someone to baby-sit their daughters—with them it was always something.

"I just came to see what you were doing tonight," George said.

Ernie stood a little straighter. "Flo and I are going over to the new neighbors for dinner. You know, around by the river," he added at George's confused expression. "Those friends of Michael's I told you about."

"Oh. Well, if they're friends of his, how'd *you* rate getting invited over there?"

"Flo fixed some food for them after they moved in and they invited us over. They're always entertaining. You should see their house." He whistled, completely comfortable with the fibs he told. He had no idea how often Darrell and Lisa Canfield entertained; he hadn't seen but one room of their house, and he and Flo hadn't been invited for dinner, but he figured George didn't have to know any of that. After the disappointment with Michael, Ernie at least wanted George to think he and Darrell were buddies, that he had access to a connection that was closed to George and Larry.

"What do they do, anyway?" George asked.

Ernie recalled what Suzanne had said the other week at dinner. "He's a stockbroker, and she's a pharmacist."

George whistled appreciatively. "They must be raking in the big bucks. I wish I could see their place," he said enviously. "I'll bet they got some nice shit."

"Why don't you come by? You can always say you're looking for me. Maybe you'll get lucky and they'll invite you to stay."

"Where is their house exactly?"

"On the cul-de-sac around the corner, the fourth house on the left, I think. My car will be in the driveway, and so will Michael's." Ernie glanced at his watch. "We'll be leaving in about twenty minutes. Stop by around nine-thirty. We ought to be through with dinner by then."

"All right. See ya later, man."

Lisa laughed at Kim's recounting of her and Michael's encounter with Ernie. "You should have seen his face," Kim was saying. "He looked so hurt that he hadn't been asked to dinner, too."

"I told Kim I'm beginning to feel like he's monitoring all our comings and goings," Michael said. "He's got this knack of showing up whenever we leave the house or come home."

"And when we have company," Kim added. "Like the way he came over when you guys were over the day we showed you the lot."

"We'd better get this table cleared off," Esther said, gesturing for everyone to pass their plates down to her. "It's nearly eight o'clock, and from what I'm hearing I don't think these people are the type to show up late. We probably don't need to have any food lying around. You don't want to rub it in."

"I'll help, Grandma," Devon said. She got up and squeezed Kim affectionately. "Thanks again for the straw bag, Aunt Kim." She paused to give Michael a quick hug as well.

"We're glad you liked it."

The twins disappeared to their room upstairs, Alicyn Gillespie close behind, and Paige began removing condiment jars from the table.

"I love eating outside," Kim remarked.

"Hopefully a month from now we'll be having dinner by our pool," Michael said.

"It's too bad you guys didn't decide to put one in earlier. You've already missed almost two months of the season," Darrell said.

"I know. We just couldn't make up our minds if this was the best time to do it," Michael said. "But if we're in business by the third week in July, we'll still get plenty of use of it this year."

"That's right," Lisa agreed. "If you lived up north you'd be silly to wait until now to have a pool put in, but the summer here is much longer. You can still swim into October. Anyone for dessert?"

"No, I'm still full. Those salmon steaks were fabulous," Kim said. Darrell and Michael also declined.

Lisa checked her watch as the doorbell chimed. "Two minutes after eight. I should have known. Darrell, why don't you go let in your new best friend?"

Everyone chuckled. "Yeah, right," Darrell said as he pushed back his chair and got up. "Be right back."

He returned minutes later with Flo and Ernie. Enthusiastic hellos went all around, and the Hickmans joined them at the oblong table.

"This is a beautiful table," Flo said, running her hand over the cedar. "You don't often see patio furniture that can accommodate so many people."

"We've got a large family, and we believe in eating together, so we had to have a table for eight," Darrell said. "As it was our boys had to grab chairs from the other table and squeeze in, since tonight we were ten."

"Did you have a nice party?" Ernie asked. Lisa noticed his sharp eyes sweep the table, looking for any vestiges of their dinner. She was suddenly grateful to Esther for her foresight. She half expected him to ask if they'd put the food away yet.

She smiled. "Oh, yes. Devon had a wonderful birthday. Quiet, spent with family and friends, but nice all the same."

"When they get to be teenagers it's nice if you can keep them at home," Flo said chattily.

"I was admiring your piano last night," Ernie said, looking at the baby grand through the large paned living room window. "Does anyone play?"

"Everybody but me," Darrell answered with a laugh.

"I believe everyone should learn how to play a musical instrument," Lisa said. "Paige and Devon don't take lessons anymore, but Cary and Courtney still do. I took lessons for five or six years when I was a kid." She paused. "I *don't* believe in forking out big bucks for a piano or anything else we don't use, just for show."

"What'd it run ya, about fifteen grand?" Ernie asked.

Lisa merely stared at him incredulously.

Flo hastily jumped into the breach. "Oh, I wouldn't want to buy a piano if no one played either."

"Every Christmas Eve the whole family gives a concert, with everyone taking a turn playing a solo," Kim said. "It's really very sweet."

"It's a good way to keep the girls from getting too rusty," Lisa said with a smile.

"Can I get you guys anything to drink?" Darrell asked.

"Sure," Michael said, prompting laughter because the query had been directed toward Flo and Ernie.

"You got any cognac, Darrell?" Ernie wanted to know.

"You name it, I've got it. Follow me. Michael, bring your glass with you."

"And mine too, dear," Kim prompted.

Flo leaned forward, pausing to brush back a falling lock of hair with her fingers. "Is that wine you're drinking, Kim?"

"Yes, Chardonnay."

"I'll have some of that," Flo said to Ernie.

At nine-thirty they were still on the patio, having dessert—a choice between Flo's apple pie and leftovers from Devon's birthday cake— and watching the first of three bouts of unknown heavyweight boxers on HBO when the door chimed again. "Let the girls get it," Darrell said to Lisa.

"But it's dark out," she objected.

"They know better than to open the door for someone they don't know."

"Lisa, have your daughters met many kids in the neighborhood yet?" Flo asked.

"Not yet, but I'm sure they will before long."

"Our son is about their age. He's seventeen. He'll be happy to introduce them to kids at the high school."

"Does he go to Episcopal?" Lisa asked. "That's where we're planning on sending the girls."

Flo glanced at Ernie. "Uh . . . actually, he goes to the public school."

"Oh, I see," Lisa said. She looked up expectantly as Paige opened the patio door.

"Mister Hickman, someone's here to see you," Paige said.

Lisa's eyes widened, and Darrell's forehead wrinkled with his frown.

"Oh, that must be George," Ernie said matter-of-factly. "Where is he?"

"Outside. There are two of them."

"You left them outside?" he said in obvious surprise.

"Of course. They're strangers." Paige looked at Darrell uncertainly.

"I think you'd better go out and talk to your friends, Ernie," Darrell said firmly.

"Um . . . yeah. Excuse me." Ernie went inside the house.

"That's odd," Lisa remarked. "How would anyone know where to find Ernie?"

"Our son must have told them we were here," Flo murmured.

"I didn't think your son knew where we lived," Darrell said, his tone suggesting he *shouldn't* have known.

Flo's words tumbled out nervously. "He doesn't, not exactly. He just knows you live on this street. Whoever it is must have looked for our car in your driveway."

"It must be some kind of emergency," Kim said. She sounded concerned, but her sparkling eyes and slight smile suggested she didn't believe it for a minute. "Why else would anyone go to a stranger's house to ask to speak with a guest?"

Flo shifted uncomfortably. "Yes, I'm sure it's something urgent."

A knockdown in the fight stopped conversation temporarily, but when the boxer got up and the match resumed Darrell said, "Excuse me. I want to make sure everything's all right with Ernie."

Darrell returned almost immediately with Ernie. "Who was looking for you?" Flo asked anxiously.

"Nobody but George and Larry."

"Was anything wrong?"

"No, they just wanted to know what I was doing tonight." Ernie leaned back in his chair and focused on the boxers, oblivious to the incredulous looks that passed between Lisa, Darrell, Kim, and Michael.

But Flo wasn't. The moment the final fight ended in a first-round knockout she said, "It's time to go, Ernie."

"It's early yet."

"Actually," Lisa said as she stifled a yawn, "it's later than you think. After eleven. We've got a full day of unpacking tomorrow. It's my last chance before going back to work."

"I'll go up and get Alicyn," Kim said.

"You guys got an upstairs?" Ernie asked.

"Yes. We put the boys up there because they've got more energy than the rest of us to run up and down," Darrell said.

"This house is pretty big, huh? I'd love to see the rest of it," Ernie hinted.

"Sorry," Lisa said breezily, "but it's too messy to show to anyone. Besides, it's late. My mother-in-law is probably in bed, and the girls might be, too."

"Can I help you clean up, Lisa?" Flo offered.

"Thanks, Flo, but I've got everything under control. I'm just gonna toss these glasses in the dishwasher with the dinner dishes and go to bed myself."

"It was a lovely evening," Flo said. "Thanks so much for inviting us."

"Yeah, we had fun," Ernie said. He shook hands with both Darrell and Michael. They all walked toward the front door. "Hey, where's Kim?" Ernie asked.

"If I know her she's probably cleaning up the mess the kids made," Lisa said. "I told her not to worry about it."

"Oh."

Silence followed. "C'mon, Ernie, let's go," Flo said.

He hesitated. "You guys sure Kim's all right?"

"Of *course* she's all right," Michael said with amusement. "Don't worry, Ernie. I won't leave without her."

"I know that. It's just that she's been gone a long time—"

"And there's really no need for us to wait," Flo interrupted meaningfully. "Good night, all."

The moment they were in the car Flo let him have it. "What was that all about, having George and Larry coming over here to look for you?"

"George said he wanted to come over and check out Darrell's place."

"Check it out? What for, a future robbery?"

"Don't be silly, Flo. I mentioned how nice it was when he stopped by earlier, and he said he wished he could see it, too."

"You barely saw it yourself. And after that stunt you just pulled we probably never will."

"George doesn't know what I saw. Anyway, I figured Darrell would answer the door and would invite George in once he said he was a friend of mine. I didn't expect him to send his kid to see who it was. And I didn't tell George to bring Larry along."

"You shouldn't have told George to come at all. You should have seen Lisa and Darrell look at each other like they thought you were nuts or something. You don't have your friends knock on people's doors looking for you, especially if they don't even know each other. Did you catch how annoyed Darrell sounded when he suggested you go see what your friends wanted? I was so embarrassed."

"You're overreacting, Flo."

"The hell I am. Like I said, they'll probably never invite us over to their place again."

"Sure they will. We'll invite them to dinner, the way we did with Brad and Suzanne. They'll want to reciprocate. Remember how Suzanne said they'd be inviting us to their housewarming party in a few weeks?"

"I told you, it's not a housewarming. Suzanne said they're just having a party to celebrate being in their new house. You only call it a housewarming if you want your guests to bring gifts. It makes sense for them to not want gifts. What could we or anyone else possibly get Brad and Suzanne that they can't get for themselves?"

He licked his lips. "Whatever. I just know I want to be invited to every party both Darrell and Brad give, large or small. I'll bet between the two of them they're always having something. Did you notice how good it smelled on Darrell's patio? They must have grilled some kind of fish, maybe tuna. I thought I smelled corn on the cob, too."

Flo sighed. She, too, wanted to be included on the guest lists of both the Canfields and the Betancourts, and she didn't want to do anything that would get their names crossed off. From the very beginning, she'd felt there was something different about them, just like she'd sensed something different about Kim and Michael Gillespie, and now she knew what it was. They had class. They didn't grow up poor like she and Ernie had, living in an ugly housing project with the smell of urine in the elevators and drug addicts curled up in the hallways and stairwells. Building a large, fancy house wasn't an achievement for them, like it had been for Ernie and her, but what was expected.

These were the type of people she wanted to associate with, people who were clearly a cut above the Mortons and the Barneses. She wanted her son to eventually find a wife in that circle of privileged black folks. But if any of this was to materialize, she and Ernie would have to be very careful of how they acted. "Well, when the Betancourts give their party, just don't go telling George and Larry that it's okay for them to come a-knocking."

CHAPTER 20

*Does it really matter what these affectionate people do, so long as they
don't do it in the streets and frighten the horses?*
—Mrs. Patrick Campbell, British actress, on an alleged
homosexual affair between two actors

"Is it safe?" Kim said in an exaggerated whisper as she peeked around the corner of the family room where the others sat.

"Where've you been?" Lisa said. "We were about to send a cavalry for you."

"I was trying to wait for Flo and Ernie to leave."

"They didn't want to go, or at least he didn't," Michael said. "Flo had to practically drag him by the ears."

"What'd I tell you?" Kim said triumphantly.

"Tell him what?" Lisa asked.

Kim sat down next to Michael on the love seat. "I told Michael that Ernie wouldn't want to leave without us because he was afraid he'd miss something. He even suggested we drive over together."

"Well, he was definitely hanging back," Darrell said. "But I'm glad he's gone. I'm done with him. I don't like his friends coming to my house to look for him."

"He surprised me with that," Michael said. "I figured even *he* wouldn't have the nerve to have George and Larry show up at your place when he barely knows you himself and when you don't know his friends at all." He shook his head. "You'd think the two of them would know better, even if Ernie doesn't."

"None of them know jack," Kim said disdainfully. "Those are the nosiest bunch of guys I've ever seen. No class whatsoever. They're like old washerwomen. All they want to do is get in your house so they can see what you've got."

"Well, I don't know his friends," Darrell declared, "don't want to know them, and what Lisa and I have or don't have isn't any of their damn business. If somebody wants to contact him while he's at someone's house, let them call on his cell phone. That should include their son. If he's old enough to stay home by himself, he's old enough to make a phone call if he needs help."

"Did you say anything to him about those guys coming over?" Lisa asked.

"I just said the whole thing struck me as very odd. If they knew he was over here they already knew he had plans for the evening, so why show up to ask what he was doing? Ernie just shrugged and said they kind of look up to him and always want to be in on everything he does because he's a little older than they are."

"I feel sorry for Flo," Lisa remarked. "She seemed embarrassed by the whole thing. But I guess we can cross them off our list."

"We sure can," Darrell said.

"Don't sweat it," Michael said. "I won't be seeing that much of him anymore myself, now that you guys are right around the corner. Hey Kim, where's Alicyn? I thought you were bringing her down."

"I wanted to give us a few minutes to talk about what happened. And I wanted to see the new paddle boat," Kim said.

"At this time of night?" Michael said.

"There's a dim light down at the dock. I just want to see it real quick. Don't give me a hard time just because you've seen it already," Kim countered.

"It'll only take a minute," Lisa said, taking her friend's arm. "We'll be right back," she said over her shoulder as they left the room.

"Oh, how cute!" Kim exclaimed when they were at the dock. "And it's got a roof on it to keep the sun out. You and I will have to take this out for a spin one day soon."

"Sure. As long as we don't run into Suzanne." Lisa had told Kim about running into Brad and Bradley the very first time they took the boat out, and how embarrassed she'd felt.

"If we do I'll just wave at her. Don't let her get to you, Lisa. You've got nothing to be ashamed of. If you and Darrell wanted to get a fancy boat like they've got I'm sure you could afford one."

Kim's remark made Lisa remember what she had said to Paige so many months ago when Paige asked if they were getting a boat like their neighbors. "If we want a boat we'll get one," she had said. "It doesn't have anything to do with what the neighbors have." At the time she hadn't known the neighbors in question would be her former husband and his wife. She didn't understand why that made such a difference—it shouldn't—but it did.

"Listen, I'm not ashamed to see that you and Darrell have more money than Michael and me," Kim continued. "We could never afford a house like this, not a cop and a secretary. But it doesn't bother us. We're happy for you guys."

"That's because you're our friends. Maybe that's the key. I just hate the idea of Darrell and Brad going fishing together."

Kim shrugged. "I think it's nice that the two of them are making the best of what could be a really unpleasant situation."

"They've always gotten along," Lisa admitted. "Maybe in the very beginning there was a little tension and distrust, but they've had a lot of time to get used to each other. But maintaining civility doesn't mean they have to become best buddies, does it?"

Kim placed a reassuring palm on Lisa's shoulder. "Just be glad that Darrell isn't as angry as you are about them living next door, or else you'd have real problems. He knows that Brad doesn't have to be his enemy, and after all this time it would be silly. You've been married to Darrell a lot longer than you were married to Brad. Let them go fishing together. It won't hurt anything, and it might help." She giggled. "You and Suzanne have had plenty of time to get used to each other, too, but we all know the two of you won't be going out shopping together anytime soon."

"Got that right," Lisa agreed heartily.

"I've said my piece. Come on, let's go back in." Kim turned and walked a few steps, then stopped and drew in her breath.

"What?"

"Shh. Look over there, at Brad's pool."

Lisa saw two figures in the water. At first she thought Suzanne and Brad were merely skinny dipping, but she gasped as it registered that they had carried it to the next level and were making love. Courtesy of the pool lights, Lisa saw Suzanne's feet resting on Brad's shoulders and her arms wrapped around his neck. The water level prevented her from seeing Brad's movements, but from the way Suzanne had her head thrown back Lisa presumed his hips were moving back and forth. "Oh, my," she said, her hand resting on her heart like a schoolgirl pledging allegiance to the flag.

"It's a little early to assume no one is up to see them, don't you think?" Kim hissed. "It's not even eleven-thirty."

"I guess they thought they were safe because no one takes their boats out this late."

"They should have turned off the lights in the pool."

They stood, transfixed, until Suzanne slumped forward onto Brad and he leaned back against the pool's edge.

"Well, she looks satisfied," Kim whispered. "Tell me, was he that good?"

"I don't remember," Lisa whispered back. She really didn't. Over ten years of satisfying sex with only Darrell had dulled her memory of anyone she had known previously, including her first husband. But she wished she and Darrell had the freedom to make love outdoors. The twins went to bed early, but Esther and the girls didn't. Just another pleasure Suzanne had that she didn't. Her mouth set in a hard line. "Let's make a run for it before they see us."

Darrell and Michael looked up expectantly when they returned, but before anyone could say anything the phone began to ring. "Who could be calling this late?" Lisa asked.

"Maybe somebody for one of the girls," Darrell said. "I know it's the weekend, but it's eleven-thirty. They shouldn't be getting any calls after eleven." He picked up the extension. "Hello?"

Lisa could tell right away something was wrong from the way Darrell's features froze. Instinctively she went to stand next to him.

"When did it happen?" he was asking. "Oh, no. That was Devon's birthday, you know. A helluva reminder every year . . . How's she doing? . . . Yes, I'm sure she's devastated, but is she at least all right physically? . . . Oh, I see. I'm so sorry about this, for both her and her husband as well. Yes, I can take it down."

Lisa quickly pulled a pad and paper out of an end table drawer and gave them to him.

"Yes, I'm ready." Darrell repeated a phone number. "All right, Rhonda. Thanks a lot. We'll call her tomorrow. Uh-huh. Good night." He hung up. "That was Paula's friend Rhonda. Paula tripped over their dog yesterday and fell onto the sharp edge of a table. Her husband brought her to the hospital, but they couldn't keep her from going into premature labor. The baby was seriously hurt in the fall, and he didn't make it."

"Oh, no," Lisa lamented, a sentiment echoed by Kim and Michael. "Is she all right?"

"She'll heal, but because of complications the doctors have told her they're not sure if she'll be able to carry another baby to term."

CHAPTER 21

O what a tangled web we weave, when first we practise to deceive.
—Sir Walter Scott

Paula knew she looked awful, for she'd cried inconsolably through much of the night. But she made no moves to improve her appearance. Her world had fallen apart. Her little boy had only lived three hours, and she might never have another. Even if she could, children weren't interchangeable. No one would ever replace the infant she'd named Drew.

The door of her private room swung open, and she braced herself for another check of her vital signs. Nothing like starting the day with someone jabbing a thermometer in your mouth. A nurse had woken her up during the night to do the same, in spite of her pleas to be left alone, that she was still breathing.

Andre appeared, not a nurse. "Good morning," he said.

She grunted. "What's good about it?"

"You're alive, Paula."

"So what? Drew's dead." She added softly, "And I wish I was, too."

He grabbed her hand and squeezed it. "Don't talk like that, Paula. I'm hurting, too. But we have to go on."

She stared at him dubiously. "I think you're starting to believe your own publicity machine, Andre. May I remind you that I'm what the doctors call, 'advanced maternal age.' That line about, 'There will be other babies,' probably doesn't apply to me."

"They weren't sure, remember? I'll bet you're pregnant again in a couple months."

"The doctor wants me to wait at least six months before trying. I'll be forty by then. It's not going to be easy. And there's the increased risk of miscarriage."

His smile vanished. "You didn't tell me you can't start trying again right away."

"Two days ago we were about to become parents. Now we have to face the fact that we might not have kids at all." She stared at him defiantly. "Kinda changes the way you feel about things, doesn't it?"

"No, of course not," he said, too hastily to be convincing. "Listen, why don't you let me help you spruce up? I know my parents will be by to see you, and possibly some other folks as well."

She blew out her breath in annoyance. "I hope there won't be a steady stream of people coming to see me, Andre. Your parents are different, of course, since they're family, but I just lost my baby and I don't feel like putting up a brave front."

"Everyone's sensitive to our situation, Paula. They said they'd follow my recommendation. Actually, I told them it'd be best to wait until after you're home. I was just hoping that if you thought people were coming you'd want to fix up a little."

"Well, I don't."

"Our friends might not be coming, but don't forget my parents."

"They'll have to see me looking less than sparkling, not to mention my actual age. What's wrong, Andre? Do they think I'm twenty-nine, too?"

"No. They think you're thirty-five." He looked at her sheepishly. "But you already know that."

She had agreed to subtract four years from her age at his suggestion that his parents, anxious for a grandchild, might be concerned that she might be too old to conceive. It seemed like such a little thing at the time, but suddenly she felt angry for allowing his weakness to extend to her. She was eight-and-a-half years older than him. So the fuck what? She had nothing to be ashamed of. Why was she putting on this elaborate charade to cover it up, like she'd done something shameful, like served time in prison or made a porn movie? Just so Andre's friends wouldn't tease him about their age difference? They were grown men, for crying out loud, too old to be carrying on like little children at the playground. So his wealthy parents would be more accepting of her if she was only a few years older than him and didn't already have children? It wasn't like Devon had been born out of wedlock. She knew the elder Haineses would never accept that. They'd probably resent the fact that she and Darrell had a hasty marriage ceremony after she became pregnant, but they'd never know. She could come clean without revealing every little detail. Surely her in-laws didn't expect her to be a virgin.

He opened his mouth to say something else, but at that moment her doctor came in and asked Andre to give them some privacy for a few minutes.

He was all smiles when he returned. The doctor had left several minutes before, so she presumed Andre had spoken with him in the hall. "The doctor just told me you'll be able to go home tomorrow," he said.

"Yes, thank God. One of my wishes came true. The only other one is to hear from Devon."

"Did Rhonda talk to her?"

She wanted to ask if he really cared. He'd hedged when she asked him to call Jacksonville and tell Darrell what happened, finally saying he didn't feel comfortable calling her ex, so she asked her friend Rhonda to do it instead. She knew now that he wanted nothing at all to do with that part of her life and that he wished it didn't exist. "Rhonda talked to Darrell last night."

"I guess Devon will be disappointed about not coming this year."

She looked at him through narrowed eyes. "What do you mean, 'not coming this year'? Why would she change her plans now?"

"She was coming to see the new baby. Now that we've lost him . . ."

"She was coming to see *me*, her mother. She'll be disappointed to hear about Drew, but that doesn't mean she doesn't need to see me. And I need to see her."

"Won't that look a little strange? She was supposed to help out with the baby."

"I don't give a shit *how* it looks," she said angrily. "She's my daughter, Andre, not some baby-sitter. It was wrong of me to deny her because you're so damn concerned with what everyone will think. I'm ready to tell everybody the truth."

"You can't do that, Paula. Maybe we should have handled it differently, but it's too late to do anything about it now. Confessing that we lied will look worse than lying."

"I don't care. I came this close"—she snapped her fingers—"to losing Devon. After I told her about your little proposal to hide her identity she put Lisa in the role *I* should be in. It's probably too late to do anything about that, but she's still my daughter. I'm tired of pretending to be somebody I'm not, Andre. I never should have gone along with any of it."

She recalled what else he said to her the night he brought her to meet his parents. She'd just accepted his marriage proposal and was eager for them to approve of her, which was why she went along with being four years younger. "By the way, they know you're divorced, but I didn't tell them you have a daughter," he'd said as they were getting out of the car. "My parents are funny about those things." She'd been puzzled and hurt, and she asked how she was supposed to explain who Devon was when she came to their wedding. "We'll figure out something," he'd vaguely replied.

Her jaw set in resentment at the memory. "Figure out something" turned out to mean not inviting Devon to the wedding or to visit after they were married, and planning to pass her off as a former stepdaughter when she did.

"*You're* the one who told everybody you were twenty-eight," he said evenly. "That wasn't my idea."

"I was kidding when I said that. I was sure someone would call me on it, but no one did. It was *your* suggestion not to tell them I was only joking."

"Listen, Paula, I didn't come down here to fight with you." He sounded weary.

"I know you didn't. And I'm not trying to give you a hard time. But I'm not happy, Andre. I don't want to live a lie anymore."

He sighed. "Why don't I let you get some rest? We can talk about it later."

"All right." She felt sure he wanted to call his parents and tell them she was still too upset to see anyone. That was fine by her, she really didn't feel like seeing them anyway. She hugged him back when he bent and wrapped his arms around her. Maybe he really did understand. . . .

Paula thought about her in-laws as she lay in the quiet, sterile room. They were so desperate to be grandparents. In hindsight, she should be grateful they hadn't insisted she take a fertility test, like the prospective wives of royalty. Had her baby lived, and if she was blessed with a successful pregnancy, the first and most likely only Haines grandchild would receive the world on a platter.

Devon, on the other hand, had no wealthy grandparents to dote on her. Paula didn't want her to ever go without anything she truly wanted. Her heart had broken for her daughter when Darrell told her that Paige's father had given her a real cute car for her sixteenth birthday and that Devon wanted one too, but he couldn't afford the expense right now. Paula had known what was coming even before Darrell asked if there was anything she could do to help.

She sympathized with Devon, who through no fault of her own had been doled the part of poor relation to her stepsister. But she had held back from making a commitment, saying it wasn't a good time for her to cough up any extra cash. She knew Darrell and Lisa thought she was trying to wiggle out of helping; she only hedged because she wanted to make absolutely sure she could do it. She'd since assessed her financial situation and planned to get the check in the mail yesterday, right after she called Florida to wish Devon a happy birthday. Devon hadn't been home, and Paula had taken that devastating fall before she had a chance to call back or get to the mailbox. She'd send it off as soon as she got back home.

Maybe it was the ticket to getting her daughter back.

CHAPTER 22

*Lord help the mister who comes between me and my sister . . . Lord help
the sister who comes between me and my man.*
—"Sisters, Sisters," lyrics by Irving Berlin

Devon opened the front door. "Hello," she said eagerly to the
handsome young man who stood on the other side.

"Hi. I'm Gregory Hickman. I came to pick up my mom's pie plate."

"Yes, my mother said you were coming." She opened the door
wider. "Come in, and I'll get it for you." Suddenly she felt nervous. He
was so fine . . . why couldn't she think of anything to say to him?

"Do you like living in Jacksonville?" he asked as they walked toward
the kitchen.

"It's nice so far. But I don't know many people. I guess we—my sister and me—won't get to meet a lot of kids until school starts."

"How old is your sister?"

"Sixteen, same age as me."

"Are you twins?"

"No. Technically, we're stepsisters. My father and her mother got
married when we were five." With embarrassment she realized she
hadn't even told him her name. "I'm Devon, by the way."

"Nice to meet you, Devon." Gregory looked around the kitchen.
"Nice place."

"Thank you."

Lisa entered the kitchen, wearing a matching sarong over her one-
piece print swimsuit. "You must be Flo's son. Gregory, isn't it?"

"Yes, Mrs. Canfield."

"Your mother bakes a wonderful apple pie. We all enjoyed it."

"I think so, too, thank you."

"I see you've met my daughter Devon," Lisa said as she refilled her drinking glass with iced tea.

"Yes, I have. I was just telling her that a couple of kids are coming over to my house Friday night if she and her sister would like to come and meet some of them."

"Oh, how sweet of you. I'm sure Devon and Paige would be happy to join you and your friends." Lisa glanced at Devon and immediately understood what the teen was silently trying to tell her. "Well, don't feel like you have to rush off, Gregory. Stay and have something to drink. Devon, where are your manners?"

"I was just going to offer him some iced tea," Devon said happily.

"Sure, I'd love some." Gregory turned to Lisa. "My mother doesn't need her pie plate right away."

Lisa merely smiled at the explanation. "Well, if you two will excuse me. I just came in to get some more to drink." Glass in hand, she returned to her deck chair. Darrell and the twins were playing ball in the water and doing a great deal of splashing, so she was content to read her book where it would stay dry. After they finished, she'd get in the floating pool chair. Working with two non-consecutive days off had taken some getting used to. She often spent her Wednesdays working around the house, but Sundays were all hers. She planned to lounge around all day like a true lady of leisure. Darrell had promised to do the cooking, and Paige had offered to go to the store for her.

The sound of laughter drifted out of the house. Apparently Devon and Gregory were having a good time.

Lisa had been surprised to see how good-looking Gregory Hickman was. Like the late John F. Kennedy, Jr., he had gotten the best from both parents, so much that he didn't really resemble either of them. The teenager personified the expression "tall, dark, and handsome." She and Darrell definitely found Ernie's overbearing personality intolerable, but she certainly had no objection if Devon wanted to be friends with his son.

The striped beach ball bounced out of the pool and rolled to the corner of the screened patio. Courtney hopped out of the water to retrieve it.

Darrell swam to the edge closest to Lisa's chair. "Lisa, is Ma home yet?"

"No, but she'll probably walk in any minute now. I know it's after one."

"I told her I'd take her out in the boat after she got back from church. Did she go to her old church in St. Marys?"

"As far as I know. I think she'd prefer it if all of us went with her to a new church."

Courtney tossed the ball to Cary, and their game resumed. Lisa resettled with her book. After a few minutes Paige came out. "I'm back, Mom. I left your change on the table."

"Thanks for going for me." Lisa glanced inside. "Did you meet Gregory?"

"Yes, outside. He was just leaving." She whistled. "I hope the rest of his friends are as cute as he is."

The back door swung open one more time. Devon came out, her hand over her heart, feigning light-headedness. "Is he hot or what?"

"How long was he here before I got back?" Paige asked.

"I hope long enough for him to decide he likes me."

"Sometimes it only takes a second, like when he saw *me.*"

"He barely knew you were there, he was so busy looking at *me,*" Devon said in an I'm-cute-and-I-know-it voice.

"Oh, puh-leese."

Lisa began to feel uncomfortable as the girls volleyed back and forth. Their tone was light and bantering, but she didn't like the idea of Paige and Devon competing for the attention of the same young man. "I wouldn't worry about it if I were you," she said. "You're going to be meeting other fellows on Friday, and both of you might see someone you like better. As long as it's not the same guy."

"Well, I've got to go see what I'm gonna wear," Devon said. Paige rushed in the house behind her, apparently with the same idea.

Lisa closed her eyes and said a silent prayer. After all Devon's resentment about Brad moving next door and Paige getting a car, the girls had made up and were getting along pretty well these days. All she could do was hope for the best with this latest challenge.

She looked up curiously at the sound of voices coming from the side of the house. She swung her legs around to one side of the lounge and got up. Might as well investigate.

"Hi, Ma Canfield. We were beginning to worry about you." Then she glanced at her mother-in-law's companion. Arlene Hall, of all people. She was dressed in a knit tank top and denim capri pants. A set of knee pads rested on the ground a few feet away from a gardening fork and spade. "Hello, Missus Hall. You look busy."

"Just doing a little landscaping. I'm afraid my daughter doesn't care much for gardening."

No profit in it, Lisa thought, smiling brightly.

"Suzanne was all ready to hire a professional, but I said it was ridiculous for her to spend all that money to hire a professional to put down flowers when I love to do it," Arlene continued. "That girl always wants to pay someone to do something. She doesn't know how it is to have no other choice but to do it yourself if you want it done at all." She smiled happily. "Your mother and I were just discussing a few ideas for arrangements."

"Well, please be careful. It's awfully hot to be working outside," Lisa said.

"Oh, I've got my drink right next to me, so I'm keeping cool."

Lisa glanced at the tall plastic cup of what appeared to be grapefruit juice that rested on a third, worn knee pad. From the faint smell of alcohol on Arlene's breath, she presumed it was spiked. The corners of her mouth did a slight upturn. The way she felt right now she wouldn't care if Arlene keeled over, not after that remark about how Suzanne preferred to hire people to do the chores. Arlene clearly enjoyed flaunting Suzanne's lack of financial restrictions as much as Suzanne herself did. The way Arlene talked Suzanne had never known any other kind of life, but Lisa knew better.

"Ma Canfield, I think Darrell and the boys are waiting for you," she said calmly.

"Oh, that's right. Arlene, I've got to go, but I'm sure I'll see you again soon."

"All right, Esther. Enjoy your afternoon."

Lisa waved good-bye, then held the screen door open for her mother-in-law. The pool was empty. Darrell and the twins had probably gone in to change into dry clothes. "I see you and Missus Hall are on a first-name basis," she commented.

"Why not? She's here just about every weekend, and she's pleasant enough, if you're willing to overlook her always mentioning how well-off Suzanne is into every conversation."

"I hate people who brag," Lisa said flatly.

"It does gets tiresome. But she's proud that her daughter married so well. I guess I can't blame her for that." Esther opened the door to the house, and they went inside.

"Why? Because her daughter married a doctor?" Lisa asked, incredulous. "I'm proud of Cary and Courtney because they made the A and B honor roll, and I'm proud of Paige and Devon for passing their road tests on the first try. Those are accomplishments they studied and worked toward. Marrying a man who's got some bucks is hardly an accomplishment."

"Arlene might do her fair share of bragging, but I think she envies me a little because I live here with you. I get the feeling she'd like nothing better than to live with Suzanne."

"I guess so, since she seems to spend all her weekends here. Her own place mustn't be too comfortable, or maybe Brad just has a better stocked liquor cabinet."

"She's just up for the day. Her other kids are at home in Palatka. But I do think she drinks, poor thing. I smelled it on her."

"So did I."

"Hi, Ma," Darrell said as he emerged from the master bedroom clad in a T-shirt emblazoned with the name of his employer and a pair of cutoffs.

"Hi, dear. I'm just going to put on some shorts, and then I'll be right with you." Esther went off toward her room.

"Are the girls going with you?" Lisa asked Darrell.

"No, they're going to the mall so Devon can spend her birthday money."

"Together?"

"I think Devon's still a little jealous of Paige's car, but I think she's learning to accept it, even enjoy it a little," Darrell said. "There's plenty of room for you in the boat if you want to come out with us."

"No thanks. I'm going to get in the pool chair with my book and a nice cool glass of iced tea." She'd decided not to go out in the boat unless it was in the last hour or so before dark. She wasn't about to give Suzanne the chance to bring out her twenty-five-footer and snicker at them.

Life in the house of her dreams had become one big competition, and she didn't like it at all.

CHAPTER 23

The most voluble of the emotions.
—Frank M. Colby, on self-esteem

"Ernie, we just *have* to go somewhere this summer," Flo said firmly.

"We can't take a vacation. Your family is coming down, remember? We're gonna give our annual barbecue."

"That doesn't mean anything. All we have to do is set aside a week and tell them not to plan on coming then because we'll be out of town."

He looked up from the newspaper he was reading. "What's going on with you? Why are you so hell bent on us taking a vacation all of a sudden?"

"Because we haven't been anywhere since we moved into this house," Flo said wistfully. They hadn't done a whole lot of traveling even *before* they'd moved into the house, just an annual trip up to see their families in Boston with stops to see the sights in the historical cities they drove through, like Savannah, Charleston, Richmond, D.C., Philadelphia, and New York. But there was a lot more to travel than the Eastern Seaboard. "George and Gail are going to Las Vegas to celebrate their anniversary. Even Larry and Sondra are taking a four-day cruise to the Bahamas."

"What about all those round-headed boys? Surely they aren't going, too?"

"Larry's mother is coming to take care of them." Flo momentarily entertained the facetious idea of Sondra Barnes cutting her kids' food and clothing budgets in order to pay for her and Larry's trip. Flo quickly decided that was absurd, but hell, if the parents of four raggedy, skinny boys could take a nice vacation, then she and Ernie should be able to go away, too.

"Well, I don't know, Flo. You're the one who's always saying we can't afford to take a trip."

"We can't, but the overtime I'm working has helped a lot with the bills. We still owe way too much money," she added, not wanting him to think they were out of danger and start spending again, "but a little trip won't cost that much. We don't have to go far. I'd settle for spending four or five days in Saint Augustine Beach or Daytona. Just as long as we're out of Jacksonville. We just can't stay home another summer and entertain our families. People are going to start noticing we never go anywhere, if they haven't already."

"And how'd that look, us driving twenty-five miles to Saint Augustine for a so-called vacation when George is going across the country and Larry is going out of the country?"

"We don't have to tell them that's where we're going, Ernie. We can tell them we're going to Aruba or Barbados or someplace like that."

"It'd be different if we really could go to one of those places, but I don't know if I want to spend all that time in Saint Augustine."

"Why not? You afraid you'll miss something here?"

"Of course not," he said, so quickly she knew he was lying. "But what about Gregory? He won't want to travel with us, and we can't leave him home alone for five days. It would be different if we were just going away overnight."

"We can always send him up to Boston."

"He'll hate it."

Flo knew he was right. When Gregory was small, he enjoyed going to Boston to play with his many cousins. Even when he was a little older, he found the history of Boston intriguing and wanted to see all the sights, the Paul Revere house, the Bunker Hill monument, and the rest. But while at first Gregory had found the inner-city atmosphere that was home to his relatives a refreshing change, by now he'd outgrown them, and their environment simply looked shabby to him. None of his cousins on either her side or Ernie's had any ambitions in life other than to graduate high school and get a car and an apartment . . . naturally, in the same neighborhood where they'd lived all their lives.

She and Ernie, too, had outgrown their families, who all gushed about how lovely their home was and marveled that so many black families lived in the subdivision. She remembered how they'd all watched *Waiting to Exhale* on HBO on one of her visits, just before she and Ernie contracted to have their house built. They kept saying, "Come on, black folks don't live like that," at the sight of the adobe palace belonging to Angela Bassett's character. Well, maybe black folks didn't enjoy such comforts in Roxbury, but they certainly did all over the South and the Midwest. Flo had heard there were sections of Atlanta and Houston that looked just as impressive as Beverly Hills and were full of black people. She had kept quiet, finding it a little sad to realize these people, her family and Ernie's, knew so little about anything outside of their own limited world.

She wished she knew someone who could take Gregory in for a few days while she and Ernie were gone. Sondra's household was too crowded and disorganized, and Gail's was too small. Flo sighed. Even though she lived right next door to Kim Gillespie, their relationship was one of cordiality rather than real friendship. Kim had always been pleasant but kept her at a distance. Flo felt it was out of envy, that Kim was jealous of all the nice things she and Ernie had. Why else would they suddenly decide to put in a pool and act so nonchalant about it? They hadn't said a word. Ernie got it out of Michael after they noticed the huge pile of dirt being dug up in the Gillespies' backyard.

Actually, Flo's friendships with Gail and Sondra couldn't really be called genuine. They got together only because their husbands were buddies. They always had a good time, but their contact was tied in to that of the fellows. Nobody went off shopping together or to see one of those chick flicks at the movies. Sondra was too busy with her large family, and Gail's world revolved around those girls of hers. The only woman in the neighborhood Flo could actually call a friend was Suzanne Betancourt, but even they hadn't gotten to the point where she felt comfortable asking if Gregory could stay there. Flo was still hoping Suzanne would issue a return invitation for dinner, but she hadn't, at least not yet. But she and Suzanne talked and saw each other regularly, and she and Ernie had been invited to the party the Betancourts were giving in a couple of weeks. It was sure to be a major event, one to which Kim Gillespie wouldn't be invited, and neither would anyone else from Villa St. John. Even Lisa and Darrell wouldn't be there, in spite of their living right next door, not the way Suzanne felt about Lisa.

Flo began to feel better. This little problem with Gregory wouldn't stop them from taking a vacation. All they had to do was get her parents down here a week early so he wouldn't be home alone. They'd have free reign of the house and her Altima to drive. As fascinated as they were with the house and the pool, surely they'd want to venture out, maybe go over to the Regency shopping area and see a movie. It wasn't like either of her parents could swim. For that matter neither could she, and Ernie had barely managed to pass the requirements to get into the Navy. Summers in Boston were so short, and they weren't among the highfalutin folks with summer homes on the Vineyard.

Flo could count the number of times she'd been in her pool on one hand. She'd gotten in a float once and drifted off into the deep end, and no one was around to help her. She had to use her hands to paddle back to where she could stand up. The experience had terrified her.

Besides the risk of getting into water over her head, the chlorine was murder on her hair. The pool's main purpose was to complement their house, which in their eyes would have looked incomplete without it. Gregory got more use out of it than her or Ernie. Even now there must be fifteen kids out there, splashing and having a good time. She and Ernie encouraged Gregory to bring his friends over. It was the best way to see what kind of crowd he was running with. Most of them were from Villa St. John or the surrounding, equally nice subdivisions, but a few came from those cement block ranch houses that dotted Old Arlington or even those run-down drug-ridden apartment complexes, so naturally she and Ernie were concerned. Kids from the low-income sector were most likely to get into trouble with things like theft, drugs, and alcohol. Some of them had atrocious manners, greeting her with hand signals or with expressions like, "Hey," that might be appropriate directed at their contemporaries—or, as her parents used to say, toward a horse—but not the parent of a friend. Whatever happened to "Hello, Missus Hickman," like she had been taught to do? When Flo was growing up even the child from the poorest family had been trained to speak to adults with courtesy and respect.

That wasn't a problem with Lisa's kids, Paige and Devon. They'd had excellent home training, and they were both cute as buttons. Flo had no trouble identifying which one was Lisa's natural daughter and which one was her stepdaughter. Paige looked like a younger version of Lisa, while Devon closely resembled Darrell. They were the type of girls she'd like Gregory to hook up with, girls from a good family background. Either one of them would do nicely, although Paige, as the daughter of a doctor, probably had a slight edge. After all, Paige drove a PT Cruiser, which had probably cost more than Gregory's Bug, and Devon had no car.

Flo didn't want Gregory to marry as young as she and Ernie had—in this day and age marriage at twenty-one and twenty-three wasn't practical—but at seventeen she felt him old enough to at least make the acquaintance of his future wife.

Her thoughts were interrupted by the sound of Ernie's voice. "Hey, Flo, it looks like Lisa and Darrell are next door at the Gillespie's."

"Well, it's only natural for them to visit. They can't expect Kim and Michael to go to their house all the time."

"I wonder why didn't they invite us, too? We had a good time together last Saturday." At the faint sound of an approaching car, Ernie discreetly glimpsed through the blinds. "I don't believe it," he said in a loud whisper. "It's that couple from the other block pulling into the Gillespies' driveway. What's their name . . . the ones who seemed so stuck up."

"Ben and Stacy Prince?" Flo said, rising. This she had to see, for she never expected to see those two socializing with anyone in the subdivision. They'd been so reserved when she and Ernie approached them. But there they were, getting out of their car and heading for the Gillespies' front door.

For the first time she was grateful for the curve in the road that allowed them a view of the Gillespies' driveway from their kitchen window. Her feelings had been hurt when the Princes rebuffed their attempts at friendship, but she'd been mollified when everybody else wrote them off as a bunch of snobs. Now that she'd seen them going over to Kim's, she felt like she'd been socked in the stomach. What did Michael and Kim have that she and Ernie didn't? Wasn't *their* house more elegant than the Gillespies'? Didn't *they* have newer cars?

"Why don't we go over and say hello," Ernie suggested.

"I thought you were playing cards with George and Larry tonight?"

"I can play with them anytime. I'd rather see what's going on next door. We can say we just wanted to get away from the noise Gregory and his friends are making, but not go too far in case he needs us for something."

Flo took a moment to consider that. "Let me check on the kids first. They were coming out of the pool the last I looked and changing into dry clothes. They'll probably move into the loft and do some dancing. I want to make sure no one drapes wet swimsuits or towels on our furniture. Some of these kids don't know any better," she said contemptuously. "Besides, I don't want to leave the house while anyone's still in the pool."

"You're right, we're liable for their safety," Ernie agreed. "It's best to wait a half hour or so anyway. It'd be too obvious if we rushed over there right away."

Lisa, Kim, and Stacy Prince settled at the table in the breakfast nook with their plates while their husbands gathered in the family room.

"Lisa, when's the last time you played golf?" Stacy asked.

"Oh, it's been ages. But I'll probably get back into it now that I'm getting a little old for tennis. All that running leaves me winded nowadays."

"I like it," Kim said. "It keeps me thin."

"I try to hit the links once or twice a month," Stacy said. "Ben indulges me, but I'm afraid that once he starts playing with Michael and Darrell I'll seem inadequate to him."

Lisa smiled. "In that case we'll have to get together for nine holes one Sunday. It'll have to be a Sunday; I work Saturdays."

"I'd love to." Stacy turned to Kim. "You know, I'm ashamed of myself for not meeting you sooner, Kim. It's just that I'd met some of the people who live here in Villa Saint John and they turned me right off."

"Would that be Ernie and Flo Hickman, our next-door neighbors?" Kim said with a smile.

"Yes, how did you know?"

"Lucky guess," Kim said, her eyes shining.

"Ben and I saw them at a homeowner's association meeting," Stacy said. "They acted like we were best friends or something, just because we were the only other black ones there."

"I hate when people assume that because you're both black you're supposed to pair off," Lisa said.

"Well, between the two of them, they must have asked us a dozen questions with all the subtlety of a machine gun," Stacy continued. " 'Where are you from?' 'What do you do?' 'Where do you work?' 'How many kids do you have?' 'How old are they?' 'How large is your house?' 'Who was your builder?' " She dissolved into laughter. "We wanted to run for our lives. Anyway, that unpleasant experience gave us the impression that all the black families here were trying to outdo each other, and we didn't want any part of it."

Lisa liked Stacy Prince more each minute. She and Ben were a little older than the rest of them, but not by much. She put Stacy in her mid forties and Ben close to fifty. Their two boys were both in college. "I know what you mean," Lisa said. "We invited them over last weekend. They'd done something nice for us, and Darrell felt we should reciprocate. When Darrell said he manages the Jacksonville branch of an investment firm, Ernie actually asked him if he made more than six figures. Can you imagine the nerve?"

"What did Darrell say?" Stacy asked.

"He looked as shocked as I felt, and then he just said, 'Look closely, Ernie, and you'll see the amount of my salary lightly tattooed on my forehead for all the world to see.' "

"And Ernie looked, too!" Kim shrieked. "It was a riot!"

They were still laughing when the doorbell chimed. Kim's laughter changed to wide-eyed panic. "Oh, no. I hope this isn't Ernie now. It seems like every time there's a car he doesn't recognize in our driveway he makes up some excuse to come by just so he can see who's here." She pushed her chair back. "I'm going to get it before Michael does, so I can nip it in the bud." To Michael she called, "I'll get it!"

Flo shrank back as the closing door came closer and closer to her face. She'd never been so humiliated in her life.

"Well, I'll be . . ." Ernie scratched his head. "What's wrong with people nowadays?"

"Let's not stand here. We'll go home and talk about it in private." Hot tears stung Flo's eyes. She could hardly believe it. Kim Gillespie had come to the door, stepped outside and closed it behind her, like she didn't want them to be able to see in, and listened to Ernie explain how they wanted to get away from the noise the kids were making. But instead of inviting them in, she'd apologetically stated that this wasn't a good time because they had company. Before either of them knew what was happening she was wishing them a pleasant evening and had slipped back inside, closing the door in their unbelieving faces.

They hurried back, so anxious to get inside that they treaded on their beautifully manicured front lawn rather than going up the front walk.

"It's just like that time when George wouldn't let me in when Larry was over there," Ernie complained. "Company! What's so special about the Canfields and the Princes?"

"Maybe they're having dinner," Flo said, her voice tinged with sarcasm.

He grunted. "I'll bet if we told Kim something happened to one of the Canfield girls she would have let us in in a hurry."

Flo looked at him sharply. "But they're fine. We couldn't make something like that up. If they don't want us, they don't want us." She squared her shoulders. "Let's just forget it, Ernie."

Devon pretended to be glancing around the room, but she was focused on Paige, who was dancing with Gregory. Panic rose in her like the evening tide. Gregory hadn't danced with *her*. Did that mean he liked Paige better?

She was sick of coming in second to her sister. Every time she looked at that maroon PT Cruiser she wanted to kick in one of its fenders. Paige had been real nice about it, even let her drive sometimes when they went out together, but that didn't change the fact that Paige had a car and she didn't. Even Lisa—even though she called Lisa "Mom" and referred to her as her mother, in Devon's thoughts she was still Lisa—rarely turned her down when she requested to use the station wagon. It might be kind of old timey, but at least it was a Mercedes. Lisa had even had a CD changer installed. But she longed to have a car of her own. And she wanted the attentions of Gregory Hickman all to herself. Let Paige envy *her* for once and see how it felt.

She forced herself to smile as she sneaked another glance their way. The last thing she wanted to do was get caught looking evil, like the way the other girls present looked at her and Paige.

Devon spent a few minutes talking to one of the guys—he seemed to like her and he was nice enough, but he wasn't as fine as Gregory—

and then suddenly Paige came to stand on her other side and Gregory was asking *her* to dance.

She was still smiling when the gathering ended at ten—they'd gone over at five, swam for two hours, eaten hot dogs and burgers Gregory's father grilled, and then changed into dry clothes and gone up to the loft above the family room to listen to music and dance.

Devon was glad she had driven the Mercedes tonight. She wanted Gregory to know she wasn't always a passenger in Paige's car but that she had a license, too. Their parents were still next door at the Gillespies'; she could see their Durango in the driveway.

They stood on the outside of the car, Devon by the driver's side with keys in hand and Paige on the passenger side, and said good-bye to the other guests. Gregory stood by the car's hood.

One of the girls, a tall, slim type who'd been careful not to get her ponytail wet while in the pool—Devon suspected it was fake—looked at the station wagon and tittered as she walked past. Devon found it amusing that the girl then climbed in the backseat of a red Grand Prix driven by one of the boys. *She's laughing at what I'm driving, but she has to get a ride with somebody.*

Gregory glanced after her. "Don't mind Shanequa. She's got a way about her sometimes."

He was too polite to say she was jealous. She liked that. Nice boys didn't talk about girls behind their backs, even if the girl was a real ho.

"Do all the kids go to your school?" she asked.

"Yeah. I've known them for two years, ever since we moved here. They're a nice group. We're all set to graduate next May." His eyes went from Devon to Paige. "I hope you guys had fun."

They assured him they had.

The driver of the Grand Prix honked as he drove off, and Devon realized they had to leave, too. "Call anytime, Gregory," she said. She couldn't say call *me* and she didn't want to say call *us,* so she settled for something less direct and hoped he knew what she meant. "Your mom should have our number."

"Okay. Are you guys working?"

"We're starting Monday at the Publix on Fort Caroline Road."

"Oh, I work at the Winn-Dixie just down from there."

Instantly, Devon regretted her choice of employer.

"Y'all gonna be on registers?" he asked.

"Right after we finish training," Paige answered.

Gregory nodded. "That's when they teach you how the register works and about all the fruits and vegetables. Make sure you learn real good. I'm gonna come in and buy a rutabaga or something, and you'll have to know what it is." They laughed. "Are y'all gonna be on days or nights?"

"It'll vary," Devon said.

"Okay. I'll give you guys a call next week."

Devon hoped that meant he'd give *her* a call.

CHAPTER 24

Just another day in paradise.
—Phil Colins

Suzanne relaxed in a padded chaise longue on the patio, flipping through the pages of a book on weddings by Martha Stewart. Usually Martha's ideas were too highbrow for her, and of course no one was getting married, but she figured first-class entertaining followed the same basic guidelines. She wanted their first big party in the new house to be a smashing success, and nothing else but the best would do. Every idea in this book would work for them except wedding cakes.

She was determined to stop being so nervous at social functions. After all this time it was ridiculous. She'd been married to Brad for over ten years. Besides, as hostess she'd have plenty to do and thus a valid reason to excuse herself from conversations that were over her head.

This would be the largest party they'd ever given. Practically everyone they knew had been invited . . . even, to her dismay, Lisa and her husband. When she'd looked at Brad with surprise, he said it would be different if they were giving something small and intimate, but it wouldn't be right to have a party this large and not invite Lisa and Darrell. Ann Sorensen from down the street was coming with her husband, and so were the people who lived on the other side of them, the white guy with the pretty Chinese wife. No, that wasn't right. Suzanne didn't know if Vicky Frasier's origins were Chinese, Japanese, Korean, or Filipino. She had to stop referring to all Asians as Chinese, another bad habit from childhood that would embarrass her if she ever said it in public.

Suzanne tapped her index finger on a page featuring a sprawling cloth-covered table with all types of hors d'oeuvres, hot and cold. That would be perfect. Everything on one Y-shaped table—actually three cloth-covered tables. She wanted it just like the picture, with the cold foods like fruit, raw vegetables, and salads in bowls within larger bowls full of ice, and the hot foods like wings and those flaky stuffed phyllo dough triangles served straight from the chafing dishes. She'd order a presliced pound cake, some napoleons and other pastries, and chocolate-dipped strawberries. Her mouth watered just thinking about it.

She wanted to have an exact idea of what she wanted before the caterer—no, Brad said she was called an event planner and would oversee everything, not just the menu—arrived, and she was due any moment.

This party was going to be fabulous.

Bradley bounded out from the kitchen. "Mom, can we go swimming?"

"No, not now. I'm expecting someone. You and Lauren can swim later."

"Can we go over Paige's and go in her pool?"

"No," she said curtly. "You don't have to use anyone else's pool. You have your own. It's not going to kill you to wait a few hours to go in. You've got plenty of other things to keep you occupied." She didn't want her kids in Lisa's pool, even if Lisa wasn't there to see it. That big-mouth Paige was sure to mention it to her when she got home from work. Suzanne didn't like the idea of Bradley and Lauren playing with Lisa's twins. She sensed Bradley envied that the Canfield boys always had each other to play with, while he only had a little sister. And Lauren had met another seven-year-old through the twins, a little girl named Alicyn, who lived in the same subdivision as Suzanne's friend Flo. Apparently Alicyn's parents were friends of Lisa and Darrell. Lauren talked about her all the time, calling Alicyn and Ann Sorensen's daughter her two best friends. As happy as it made Suzanne to see her introverted daughter make friends, she wished there wasn't any connection to Lisa. And she hated the idea of Bradley being envious of anything Lisa's kids had.

Bradley retreated, returning five minutes later. "Mom, I called Paige, and she says she'll take us bowling if it's okay with you."

That was different. She wouldn't turn down the opportunity to get the kids out of her hair for a few hours, as long as they weren't in Lisa's pool. She'd always said Paige could come in handy sometimes. "All right. Get my purse, will you, and I'll give you some money." The doorbell rang. It had to be the party planner. Damn, she wouldn't even have a chance to tell Paige to drive carefully. "And hurry up."

Paige took care to keep her arm straight as she rolled the ball. She held her breath as it swiftly made its way down the center of the lane, gaining momentum as it rolled. When it knocked down every single pin, she jumped for joy.

Bradley and Lauren slapped her palm, and Gregory gave her a quick hug. Impersonal as it was, it sent a shiver through her entire body.

What a marvelous stroke of luck that Devon had awakened with cramps, and Bradley had called and asked her to take him and Lauren someplace while their mother had company. It had given her the perfect opportunity to call Gregory and ask if he'd like to come along while she took her little brother and sister bowling.

She really liked Gregory, but he was so . . . well, *nice*. Sometimes she thought he regarded her and Devon as nothing but pals. Paige wished she could change that, wished she could get him to choose which one of them he liked best.

Her thoughts were interrupted by joyful shouts as Bradley's second ball knocked down the remaining pins. Gregory picked him up and lifted him high in the air. "I'm the champ," Bradley yelled, pounding his chest. When Gregory put him down Lauren, who wanted everything Bradley got, insisted he pick her up as well. He obliged.

Paige felt Gregory must be the most personable boy she'd ever met. He knew how to behave around little kids like Lauren and Bradley, around kids their own age, and around grown-ups, like her mother and Darrell. This seemed all the more incredible when she considered his parents. His father was a complete doofus. She still couldn't believe how amazed he acted when she hadn't invited his friends into their house that night they came looking for him. And his mother seemed nice enough, but she was too nosy. The few times Paige had been over there, she must have asked at least five questions about her family. She'd politely wiggled out of answering.

"Hey Paige, it's your turn," Gregory said.

She removed her ball from the automated rack and stepped up to the line.

"Hey, you're up!" Paige exclaimed when she saw Devon in the kitchen fixing a sandwich. "You feeling better?" She stiffened when Devon stared at her coldly without speaking. "What's up with you?"

"Did you have a nice time out with Gregory?"

"As a matter of fact, yes. We bowled two games. Bradley and Lauren came with us."

"So that's supposed to make it all right?"

"If Cary and Courtney weren't at day camp this week I'd have brought them, too. You act like Gregory and I were on a date or something."

"You didn't waste any time calling him, did you? You must have gone to the phone the minute you heard I wasn't feeling good."

Paige crossed her arms defiantly. "So tell me something, Dev. How'd you know I was with Gregory in the first place?"

Devon first looked embarrassed, then raised her chin defiantly. "Because I called him. When he wasn't home, I tried his cell. He said he was bowling with you."

"Why'd you call him?"

"Because I wanted to ask him something," Devon said, her tone suggesting it was none of Paige's business.

"Like would he come and see you, maybe, since you knew I was out and you'd get to be alone with him?"

"That wasn't it."

"Yeah, right. Don't accuse me of being sneaky when *you're* the one who's doing all the scheming." Paige stalked off toward her bedroom.

Lisa felt the tension in the air when she came home from work, right along with the distinctive scent of frying chicken. Darrell and Esther were doing the cooking, talking in low voices, with Esther constantly looking toward the hallway leading to the girls' rooms. Through the window she could see the boys—Darrell had picked them up after work—swimming under Paige's watchful eye. Devon wasn't around. That alone hinted something was wrong. Usually the girls were both in the pool with their brothers, and sometimes Esther was in the water as well. Lisa knew Devon was having cramps when she left the house in the morning, but her cramps generally weren't so bad they kept her in bed all day.

"Hi," Lisa said. "Is Devon still not feeling well?"

"They had a fight," Esther said.

"Who, Devon and Paige?"

"Yes. Over that boy."

Lisa's shoulders slumped. "Oh, no. They weren't hitting each other, were they?"

"No," Esther replied. "It was strictly verbal. Devon feels Paige went behind her back by calling to ask him to go bowling with her, knowing Devon wouldn't go because she didn't feel well."

Lisa's forehead wrinkled. "I thought Paige took Bradley and Lauren to the bowling alley."

"Apparently she left out a little detail about the Hickman boy going, too," Darrell said. "But there's two sides to this. Paige talked to Ma, too."

"Paige told me she pointed out that the only way Devon knew that boy went along was because she called him herself to invite him over while Paige was out, but Devon denied it," Esther said.

Lisa slumped against the counter. "Lord, what a mess."

"They yelled at each other back and forth. By the time I came out to see what all the fuss was about Paige had gone to her room. They haven't spoken to each other all afternoon," Esther continued. "I didn't leave the house today, other than to make a quick trip to CVS to pick up my medication. They've pretty much kept to their rooms."

Lisa looked at Darrell for help. "I was afraid something like this might happen. What are we going to do, Darrell?"

"Tell them we're not going to put up with any of this game-playing crap."

She sighed. "I saw this coming the moment they both said they liked him. It was a friendly rivalry when it started, but now it's turned ugly."

"The ironic part is, if he liked either one of them in that special way I think they'd know it by now," Darrell said. "But they're all just friends. He hasn't shown any particular interest in either one of them. For all we know he's gay. That would really be a hoot for the girls to stop speaking over some boy who likes boys."

"Devon was sleeping when I checked on her a little while ago," Esther said.

"I won't wake her," Darrell said, "but when she gets up the four of us are going to sit down and talk."

Dinner was more subdued than usual. Lisa was glad Devon woke up in time to join them.

"Can I be excused, Daddy?" Courtney asked, a question quickly echoed by Cary.

"Look at all that meat you guys left on those chicken bones," Darrell said after a quick inspection of their plates. "Y'all have to learn to clean your bones. Look at mine."

"Daddy, you can suck a chicken bone so dry no one would believe it had ever had any meat on it to begin with," Cary said. They all laughed, even Devon.

"All right, all right, go on," Darrell said good-naturedly.

"Scrape your plates good before you put them in the dishwasher," Lisa warned.

Esther quickly pushed back her chair. "I'm done myself. I'll make sure they do it right."

Lisa knew her mother-in-law wanted to give her and Darrell a chance to talk to Paige and Devon alone.

"Darrell, you and Ma Canfield can really fry some good chicken," Paige said in admiration. She licked her fingers, then dried them off with a well-used napkin, which she tossed atop her plate with a flourish. "I guess I'll see you guys later." Plate in hand, she proceeded to get up.

"Sit down, Paige," Darrell ordered.

Lisa noted Paige's startled look. Darrell rarely spoke to her with such vehemence. But she lowered herself back into her chair. "What's up?"

"Your mother and I understand you two had an argument today," Darrell said. "Even a deaf man could tell you two didn't have two words to say to each other at dinner."

"We'd like to know what's going on," Lisa added.

The two girls looked at each other, then began talking simultaneously, and Darrell silently held up a hand. The talking promptly stopped.

"One at a time," Lisa said. "Go, Paige."

They listened as each girl recounted her story.

"I think it would be a terrible mistake for you two to let a boy come between you," Lisa said after Devon had finished, but even as she spoke she knew it was much more than that. Devon was still jealous of Paige for having a car and for having her father and half siblings right next door. She didn't want to feel that she'd lost out to Paige again.

"Look at yourselves," Darrell added. "You've known this boy for several weeks now, and nothing's happened. Don't you realize he just wants to be friends with the both of you? You've known each other since you were three years old. You're family. Do you really think it makes sense to be mad at each other over the attentions of some boy?"

Both girls hedged, then confessed that it didn't.

"I think we'll excuse ourselves," Darrell said, reaching for his plate. "We'll be back in five minutes, and we're expecting you to be friends again."

"I think it'll be all right," Lisa said as she rinsed the plates and silverware and put them in the dishwasher.

"It's going to have to be. I'm telling you, Lisa, I'm not having the two of them going around mad at each other," Darrell said. "As far as I'm concerned they both tried to pull a fast one, and they both got caught being sneaky." He thumbed through the mail she had left on the counter and held up an envelope. "Here's something from Paula."

"What's she want?" Lisa asked absently. She was still thinking about what he'd just said. *They both got caught being sneaky.* The remark bothered her. Did he feel a need for Paige to share the blame with Devon? If so, she certainly didn't agree. She saw nothing wrong with Paige asking Gregory if he wanted to go along with her to the bowling alley, since Devon was sick. It struck her as perfectly natural for sixteen-year-olds to want someone their own age to go along when going someplace with much-younger siblings.

"Tell you in a minute." He tore the envelope open. A check fell out. "Whoa!"

"Isn't it a little soon for her to be sending money for Devon's tuition?"

"It's not for tuition. She sent five thousand dollars for Devon's car."

She raised an eyebrow. Now he had her full attention. "No, she didn't."

"She says this is the surprise she told Devon she was sending." Darrell read the handwritten note. "She says she can't bear to think of

Devon being unhappy, watching Paige drive around in her car while she doesn't have one. She says she hopes this will be enough to get her behind the wheel of something cute until we have some free cash, and that she sent it to us instead of Devon because we know how much we want to spend."

"It sounds like she expects us to cough up five grand ourselves."

"We were going to do it anyway, weren't we?"

His reasoning caught Lisa off guard. "Well . . . yes."

"I didn't expect Paula to come through with anything, much less five thousand dollars. I didn't think she could afford to write a check that large on top of Devon's tuition and all the other stuff she sends her."

"Her husband can. Devon said his family is rich."

"Yeah, right. Like he gives a shit about Devon and her misery. But as long as this check doesn't bounce, I don't care where it came from. We should be able to get her something real nice for ten thou, and we won't be spending any more than we planned to." Lisa's eyes grew wide. Paula's check sure had Darrell singing a different tune. Before he'd insisted that Devon would get basic transportation for a few thousand dollars, and now he wanted to get her "something real nice." She knew the change came as a direct result of the PT Cruiser Brad had bought for Paige. Darrell might say he wasn't in competition with Brad, but his actions said otherwise.

She decided not to point out his reversal. It really didn't matter. Like Darrell said, they were going to spend at least five grand anyway. Paula's contribution was gravy. And at least Devon wouldn't feel like Paige got the inside of the egg while she got the shell.

"We can use Paula's money as a down payment and finance the rest," Darrell was saying. "When I get my bonus we'll pay it off. I really don't want to dip into our savings unless it's a true emergency."

"I agree." *At least he doesn't feel that getting Devon a car isn't an emergency*, Lisa thought.

Darrell glanced at his watch. "Time to check on the girls. I'm sure they've kissed and made up by now. But let's not say anything to Devon about the check just yet. You and I can go car shopping and pick something out in the right price range, maybe a couple of choices, before we tell her about it and let her pick her favorite. But we'll have to do it soon, or else she'll think Paula forgot about her and she'll start getting the blues again. I'll call Paula later and let her know how we're handling it, so she won't wonder why she hasn't heard from Dev." He jovially pinched Lisa's rear as he passed her on his way to the dining room.

Lisa remained in place, her back to the counter, her palms resting on the countertop. Instinct told her Paula was up to something. Lisa sympathized with her for the accident that harmed her unborn baby, but she wondered if the baby's death had been the factor to make Paula suddenly decide to concentrate on the child she had. Her motive was strictly one of convenience, not of what was right.

Surely nothing good would come from that.

CHAPTER 25

*Keeping up with the Joneses was a full-time job with my mother and
father. It was not until many years later that I realized how much
cheaper it was to drag the Joneses down to my level.*
—Quentin Crisp

Suzanne glanced at the vehicle she passed in her brand new Lexus
SC-430 as she and Flo rode down Arlington Expressway. The convertible hardtop was down, courtesy of a push-button control, and as
she expected, the driver of the car she passed did a double take.

"Oh Suzanne, this is fabulous!" Flo exclaimed. She brushed her
hair out of her eyes.

"I thought Brad would never get rid of that old Jag," Suzanne said.
Lord knew she'd tried to get him to trade it in. The car, which he'd
bought while he was still married to Lisa and represented his first
splurge, still looked and ran great, but after all these years the novelty
had long since worn off. Suzanne felt someone of Brad's stature
shouldn't be driving a fourteen-year-old car, even if it was a Jaguar.
People might think he couldn't afford anything better.

As glad as she'd been to see Brad turn in the old Jaguar, she did
have fond memories of it. The first time she'd gotten in it was when
Brad invited her to lunch. She'd been so excited about the prospect
of sitting beside him in the passenger seat, where Lisa always sat. He'd
explained he felt she had potential to be more than a receptionist
and asked her what she wanted to do with her life. It had all been very
innocent, with Brad's attitude bordering on the paternal. Brad had
explained that long ago someone had taken an interest in him, encouraged him to be whatever he wanted, and that was why he was a

doctor today. It was important, he said, for the black people of America to try to lift themselves up. Suzanne had been so impressed with his sincerity that she had made up her mind then and there that what she wanted was to be his wife, a goal that had a major challenge whose name was Lisa.

She hadn't liked Lisa from the first day she flounced into the office. Lisa hadn't been rude or anything, it was her mannerisms that raised Suzanne's hackles, the easy way she'd asked for "Doctor Betancourt," the way she arched a well-shaped eyebrow when Suzanne asked her name, the slight amusement in her tone and expression when she replied, "His wife." Suzanne imagined how wonderful Lisa's life must be as the wife of a doctor. From office scuttlebutt she learned Lisa had her own career as a pharmacist, and her jealousy increased tenfold.

Suzanne was careful not to drop any hints that would reveal her interest in Brad on the subsequent occasions when he took her to lunch, afraid that if he knew how she felt the occasional invitations would stop. She took to dressing up on Fridays, and when he complimented her she would casually remark she had a date. She'd hoped he would be jealous and had been frustrated when he showed no reaction.

The sight of the photo of Lisa holding their little girl on Brad's desk filled Suzanne with despair, and the day she saw them coming back from lunch together, Lisa sitting beside Brad in the sleek Jaguar, she felt physically ill. How foolish of her to think she could come between Brad and Lisa. Lisa looked right at home in the passenger seat of the Jag, whereas she'd probably looked like an excited kid receiving a rare treat. Women like Lisa from those high-class backgrounds always ended up with the cream of the crop. It wasn't fair.

In the weeks that followed, Suzanne privately rejoiced when the technician's gossip about Dr. Betancourt arguing with his wife over the telephone reached her ears, but even though the photo of Lisa and their daughter was eventually replaced by one of the daughter alone, Brad's behavior toward her remained perfectly appropriate. It wasn't until one Friday after his divorce that he looked at her and said, "Hot date tonight?" She'd smiled at him and said doubtfully, "I don't know how hot it's going to be," as a joke, but the way he looked at her told her the lightbulb had finally lit up. The following week he discreetly asked her out.

He'd courted her in the Jaguar. Finally, *she* was the one always sitting beside him in the two-seater. They'd had some great make-out sessions in that car.

She could still remember that first night they'd made love. She'd gone to the restroom of the restaurant, removed her underwear and stuffed it in her purse, and once they were in the car lifted her short skirt so he could see she wore nothing beneath. He immediately reached for her, bringing her to orgasm with his finger on the way back to his bachelor pad. It was a miracle he hadn't lost control of the car on I-95, with one hand on the wheel and the other firmly attached to her crotch. Truck drivers looked into the low-sitting vehicle as it passed and smiled down at them knowingly, but she hadn't cared. Those guys probably saw all kinds of stuff going on in cars as they drove from Maine to Florida.

Since they'd been married, Brad usually commuted to work in the Jaguar, leaving her with the choice between the newer Jag sedan and the Escalade for her use. Every couple of years one of the auto manufacturers would come out with a new sleek sports model that caught his eye, but he never actually went to test drive a vehicle until he saw the Lexus. He'd been attached to it like Crazy Glue since he'd driven it home from the dealer, but today was Saturday and he'd gone fishing with Bradley and Lauren, so she finally had a chance to take it out.

She'd looked forward to taking the new car for a ride as a driver, rather than a passenger with Brad at the wheel. Flo had been all too happy to accept when Suzanne asked if she wanted to come along.

The breeze hit them from the top and the sides. Suzanne had tied her long hair back in a ponytail. A few short wisps blew in the wind, tickling her forehead and the sides of her scalp. As she watched Flo push her hair back for what had to be the tenth time since they'd been riding, she wished she could hand her a barrette to hold it back. Suzanne was beginning to suspect that Flo deliberately combed her hair so that one lock would continually fall into her eye and she could casually brush it back. Maybe that repetitive action made Flo feel like her chin-length locks were a lot longer than they were, but after a while it just looked silly.

"Ernie would love this," Flo said.

"I would have asked him to come along if there'd been room," Suzanne lied. The car did have a backseat, but its sole purpose was to eliminate the "no backseat" criteria insurance companies used to define sports cars and thus cut the premium. For the sake of symmetry, the designer had put headrests on both the front and backseats, but any attempt to sit in the back would be futile. Even an infant in a car seat would feel cramped back there; leg room virtually did not exist. It was convenient to hold packages only.

Suzanne was glad to have a valid excuse for not including Ernie. She knew Ernie wanted nothing better than to get tight with Brad. Whenever she went over to see Flo, Ernie always asked about Brad and usually dropped a loaded comment, like how much he liked to fish. Suzanne knew he wanted her to pass on the remark to Brad so that he would in turn invite Ernie out on the boat, but she didn't bother. She knew her husband well enough to know he meant it when he said he didn't want to be bothered with Ernie.

Sometimes even she was turned off by Ernie's pushy ways. Just a little while ago, when she picked Flo up, he had said, "Nice ride, Suzanne. What'd you guys pay for this, about sixty K?" She didn't have to pretend to be appalled.

As Flo sang along with the Randy Crawford disc in the CD player, Suzanne considered the irony that Brad had taken Darrell Canfield and his twin boys on the boat today, and this wasn't the first time. They'd all gotten rather chummy, both Brad and Darrell as well as Bradley and the twins. If Suzanne had her way, she would have preferred Ernie fill the role of neighborhood pal. Yeah, he could be obnoxious at times, but she still felt he was a better choice for a friend than Lisa's husband. On the other hand, in a crazy kind of way she supposed it was good. If Brad had any feelings left for Lisa, he certainly wouldn't want to hang out with the man she was now married to.

Suzanne didn't feel there was much chance of Brad retaining feelings for Lisa. *She* was the one he loved. And why not? She made sure she stayed in shape and took care of him sexually, not that she had to pretend because he knew how to drive her wild. They had great times making love in the pool after the kids were asleep and the neighbors safely in their homes. But just knowing that Brad had once hit the sheets with Lisa with the same fervor he showed with her and produced Paige with her made Suzanne a little crazy. And that damn Lisa made her feel so insignificant, with her pharmacy degree and her fancy family background.

Lisa's maternal grandfather had been a local civil rights leader, and their family name was revered among the residents of Columbus, Georgia. Being around Lisa made Suzanne feel like a poor little nobody. Things would be so much better if someone else lived next door, even an annoying type who mowed his lawn every Sunday morning at seven A.M.

Suzanne didn't understand how Darrell and Lisa had been able to afford to buy that prime lot and put up such a large house in the first place. From the outside, it looked larger than theirs. She'd never been inside it, but Flo had, and she'd assured Suzanne it wasn't nearly as nice as theirs.

Flo broke into Suzanne's thoughts. "Are you all ready for the party?"

"Everything's all arranged. It's going to be all buffet."

"Even for the kids?"

"I'm not having any kids attend," Suzanne said. "Even Bradley and Lauren won't be there. They'll be in the house, but not at the party."

"Don't most of your friends have kids?"

"Sure, but I'm not inviting them. Let them get baby-sitters. Kids don't belong at adult parties, at least as far as I'm concerned. They run around and make noise and splash water all over everybody."

Flo seemed surprised by the observation. "Oh. Well, you've been working so hard on this. I'm sure you'll be glad when it's all over."

"I'm going to be relaxing. Next weekend we're going up to Maine."

"What's up there?"

"Our summer house," Suzanne said casually.

"You've got a summer house?"

Suzanne loved the impressed tone in Flo's voice. Flo might act like she believed she and Ernie were financial equals to her and Brad—which was just plain ridiculous—but every now and then she let it slip that she was in awe of them, and that was precisely how Suzanne wanted her to feel. "Oh, yes. A three-bedroom cabin on a lake. It's rustic-looking on the outside, but it's got all the conveniences. It's really lovely."

"That's a lot of room. Does your mother go with you?"

Suzanne made a face at the idea. "She went up there with me and the kids once or twice in the spring when Brad couldn't get away, but when Brad and I go we only bring our kids." As much as she wanted her family out of their present living conditions, she didn't feel she had to bring them along on vacation. Even if her plan worked and

Brad said they could stay with them, they definitely wouldn't be accompanying them when they went to Maine for Christmas. She wanted vacation time reserved for the family—her, Brad, and the children. *Their* children, which didn't include Paige. Fortunately, after going with them the first few years, Paige decided there wasn't enough to do up there and didn't want to go anymore.

"Have you and Ernie taken your vacation yet?" Suzanne asked.

"No. We're planning to go down to Aruba next month, but my parents will be coming down from Boston for a visit in a few weeks, and possibly a few other family members. That way Gregory won't be alone in the house. Gregory's very trustworthy," she added hastily, "but I'm not so sure about some of his friends."

"I heard about some kids in suburban Chicago who tore up their friend's parents' house while they were away," Suzanne remarked. "It's good you and Ernie won't have to worry."

"Yes, it works out perfectly. My family gets to spend a week in Florida, and Ernie and I can go away. Ernie's family doesn't like to travel, so we have to go up there to see them. We go every year for Thanksgiving. Somehow the holidays feel more authentic when it's a little chilly outside."

"We love having Christmas in Maine," Suzanne said. "Will this be your first trip to Aruba?"

"Uh, yes."

"You'll love it. Are you staying at the Occidental?"

Flo hesitated. "I really don't remember, but no, that doesn't sound like it."

"Well, let's stop at the mall. We can both get some new clothes for our respective trips."

Flo needed both hands to carry the heavy shopping bags, one from Dillard's and one from Belk. She'd had no choice but to join in once Suzanne started picking up stuff. Like Suzanne, she hadn't looked at any price tags.

"What the hell is all that?" Ernie demanded, scowling at the bags.

"Don't worry, it's all going back. I got hoodwinked into buying all this stuff. When I told Suzanne we're going to Aruba, she insisted we go to the mall and shop. She and Brad are going up to Maine next week. They own a cabin up there."

"Own, or rent?"

Flo sighed. Not again. If Ernie didn't realize the Betancourts were wealthy by now he never would. "It's not like I asked to see the deed, but I'm sure they own it. Three bedrooms, she said."

"Wow. I wish we could go with them. We could drive up, and all we'd have to pay for would be gas for the car, instead of spending four nights in a hotel in Daytona, plus eating out three meals a day."

"I'm sure they're flying, Ernie."

"That doesn't mean we'd have to. It's cheaper to drive."

Flo merely shrugged. The only time Ernie wanted to open his wallet was when he was trying to impress someone. Other than that he was as tight as the skin on a drum.

"Damn, I wonder why they haven't invited us over," Ernie said. "I know you see a lot of Suzanne, but I haven't seen Brad since the day they came over here to dinner."

"I know he's terribly busy with his radiology practice."

"Not busy enough to go fishing with Darrell, or golfing with his doctor buddies."

"Ernie, you don't golf."

"He doesn't know that. He's never asked me."

It pained Flo to say what she was thinking, but she wanted his opinion on it. "Maybe he feels you can't afford it."

"Can't afford it? He's been here, Flo." Ernie waved his hand around like a TV spokesmodel. "Does this look like the house of someone who can't afford golf, or anything else?"

"No, of course not, but it's more than just the house. He might be thinking about other things, like how we send our only son to public school. Brad and Suzanne have two in Country Day, plus Brad's daughter will go to Episcopal. Even with her living with Lisa, I'm sure Brad's picking up at least part of the tab for her schooling. He might think we can't afford to send Gregory to a better school, and if he thinks that, he might think you can't afford other things as well."

"So what. Everybody else's kids go to public school."

Flo knew that wasn't true and suspected Ernie did, too, but she didn't want to burst his bubble by pointing that out. But something was definitely wrong. For July Fourth they planned a cookout and invited all the neighbors: George and Gail Morton, Larry and Sondra Barnes, Michael and Kim Gillespie, Brad and Suzanne Betancourt, and even Darrell and Lisa Canfield, who had never been to their home. Flo was especially anxious to erase the bad impression Ernie left on the

Canfields the night they were there. In the end, only the Mortons and the Barneses had come, complete with their children. In hindsight Flo felt Suzanne had a valid point about not inviting kids to an adult function. Youngsters could hardly be excluded from a holiday cookout, which were traditional times for families to spend together, but by the end of the day Flo wished they could have been. Larry's youngest boy slipped on the deck while running—which he'd been told a hundred times not to do—and busted his lip. George's younger daughter had the runs, but George apparently didn't feel that meant she couldn't be brought into the pool. She had to stop him, saying that her condition would put them all at risk for *E. coli.* Didn't he know that? Or was it he simply didn't care because it wouldn't be his problem if they had to drain and sanitize the pool at considerable expense because his daughter had taken a dump in it?

Sometimes Flo felt that George and Larry were both jealous of their pool. Larry was always asking if he could bring the kids to go swimming. Thank heaven she had Gregory to fall back on. "Gregory's having friends over, and I'm afraid he wouldn't want to have younger kids around," she would say. And George always made sure to pack swimsuits on the frequent occasions he and Gail asked her to baby-sit the girls. Lord knew neither couple ever turned down an invitation to come over, but nevertheless she'd managed to keep the Barnes boys out of her pool except maybe three or four times this season.

Flo wouldn't have minded the presence of George's sick girls and Larry's unruly boys as much if the other three invited couples had come, but none of them had. Suzanne apologetically said she didn't want to be around Lisa, which Flo could understand. She certainly wouldn't relish spending time with any of Ernie's exes, either. But then Lisa called to say she and Darrell wouldn't be able to make it. Lisa hadn't offered any explanation, and while Flo was curious, she hadn't wanted to ask. Kim Gillespie next door had been ambivalent, saying she and Michael and their daughter had other plans but would try to stop by if it wasn't too late when they got home. Flo wasn't surprised when they didn't. When she saw Kim a few days later she asked how they spent their holiday, and Kim had replied with a cryptic, "With some friends."

When Flo told Suzanne that Lisa wasn't coming, she hoped Suzanne would change her mind and come after all. Instead, Suzanne said she and Brad had already made plans to spend the day at home with their kids and her mother and siblings. This had disappointed Flo most of all. Lisa and Suzanne would be two fresh, new faces among the group, and she'd looked forward to flaunting her friendship with them in front of Gail and Sondra. She'd already dropped a few casual remarks alluding to Gregory's association with Lisa's teenage daughters, hinting that he couldn't decide which one he wanted to start dating because he liked them both. It had thrilled her when Gail wistfully said she wished Lisa's twin boys were young enough to play with her girls. Flo knew what she meant. It was never too early to get your kids in with the right people.

Flo had also made sure to mention Suzanne's upcoming party several times in front of Gail and Sondra, enjoying their envious expressions as they asked question after question about it. She couldn't wait to describe it to them in luscious detail after it was over. She wanted to see more of those "I-wish-we'd-been-invited" looks on their faces.

But that was only part of Flo's goal. She hadn't been successful in infiltrating the social circle of either the Betancourts or the Canfields the way she'd hoped. Having Suzanne Betancourt alone in her corner wasn't enough. She had to get the rest of them, Brad, Lisa, and Darrell, to see that she and Ernie deserved to be their friends.

She sighed. She had time. The party was still a week away. Right now she had to plan how to get back to the mall and return all these clothes she couldn't afford to keep.

CHAPTER 26

All right, Mr. De Mille. I'm ready for my close-up.
—Gloria Swanson in *Sunset Boulevard,* 1950

Suzanne leisurely ran the curling iron down the length of her long auburn-tinted hair. The caterers were busy preparing the hors d'oeuvres for the party. Her family had come up this morning, and Brad greeted them so warmly Suzanne was glad they'd cut back on their visits. In the past weeks, she and the kids drove down to Palatka on Saturdays after the kids' equestrian lessons, and her mother sometimes came up for the day on Sundays, sometimes with Kenya and other times alone, but there had been no overnight stays and no sign of Derrick and Matthew since that first time, the night she and Brad had had dinner at the Hickman's. Her mother had told her she'd been offered a position at a Jacksonville post office to replace someone who was retiring at the end of the month, which worried Suzanne because she hadn't expect it to happen so quickly. But Brad's pleasant attitude gave her hope that he would at least allow her mother and Kenya to stay with them.

All of them discussed the party menu at lunch this afternoon, and Brad had tactfully gotten the point across that no one was to lower a bitten end of a vegetable back into the dip. He accomplished this under the guise of instructing Bradley and Lauren on proper etiquette, as they would make a brief appearance at the party to eat before retreating into the house. The surprised expressions Suzanne had seen on her sibling's faces told her that they hadn't realized how unsanitary double dipping was, but at least now they knew.

She'd never felt so relaxed just before entertaining, but there truly wasn't anything to worry about. Teresita, their housekeeper, had cleaned the house thoroughly yesterday. While the guests would be limited to using the pool bath, which had no access to the main house, she knew people would wander inside, and those who'd never been here before would ask to see the rest of the house. Suzanne planned to honor all requests and wanted it to look showroom perfect. Her main concerns had been possible glitches in the food preparation and potential friction between Brad and her family members. Both were under perfect control. Of course, she'd have to watch her mother and make sure she didn't consume too many orange blossoms. . . .

Brad had asked Suzanne to see to it that Kenya didn't wear anything too revealing, so she had taken her sister shopping and bought her a jungle print dress that hugged her generous hips rather snugly but bared only her back. For herself, Suzanne had chosen a white cotton dress with a V neck in both the front and back, printed with oversize poppies in yellow, pink, and orange. The wide waist fit her snugly, and the full skirt fell nearly to her ankles. She'd had her hair newly relaxed and wrapped, and she knew she looked good. Every man present was bound to keep an admiring eye on her tonight, even, she thought wickedly, Darrell Canfield. Maybe her walls weren't decorated with college degrees and professional certificates like Lisa and the other women, but she looked as good as any of them.

Brad's voice suddenly filled the large bathroom, amplified by the tiled walls. "Suzanne, it's just past seven-thirty. I doubt anyone will show up before eight, but you probably need to come ou—" He broke off when she turned to face him. "Wow!" he said. "You look great."

She broke into a smile, then held out the sides of her full skirt and did a curtsey. "I'm happy you approve."

They stood admiring each other for a moment. Brad was casually dressed in a windowpane pattern tan and yellow shirt, tan slacks, and a pale yellow sports coat. Even after ten years of marriage, Suzanne still found herself marveling that this handsome, successful man belonged to her.

"I'll be right there," she said, taking a moment to coax and finger comb her hair into that just-a-bit-tousled look. To her surprise, Brad remained where he stood, simply watching her as she turned off the

curling iron and returned it to the shelf inside the island in the center of the large bathroom. She faced the mirror one more time and
tossed her hair over one shoulder, loving the way it fell into place. She
felt qualified to do a shampoo commercial, the kind where the models lift and fan their hair with their fingers and let it fall, looking all
shiny and bouncy. The bottom strands had just enough curl to look
like a natural bend.

She and Brad entered the living room together, their hands entwined.
The house looked photo-shoot perfect. The wood floors gleamed, the
living room with its tan, brown, and orange color scheme looked bright
and cheerful, the dining room regal, and the family room cozy. The
sounds of Spyro Gyra drifted throughout the house and onto the lanai,
courtesy of the CD in the built-in intercom system.

The sliding glass doors were all in the open position, and her mother,
wearing a green-and-white belted print dress, sat poolside, like she
wanted to stake out a good seat for the evening early. Suzanne shot a
disapproving glance at the glass in her hand. *She's starting early, I see.*

"Oh, don't you look lovely," Arlene gushed when Suzanne stepped
onto the lanai.

"Thanks, Mom."

"Isn't she beautiful, Brad?" Arlene pressed.

Suzanne expected him to blow her mother off with a "Yeah, yeah,"
but instead he quietly stated, "She takes my breath away." The serious
way he looked at her told her he meant it. Her heart swelled, and a
tiny part of her wished the evening was over so she and Brad could retreat to the privacy of their bedroom. There would be some serious
lovemaking going on in there tonight, and just thinking about it
made her toes elevate in her high-heeled sandals.

Paige and Devon were the first guests to arrive, along with Darrell's
mother, who took a choice seat next to Suzanne's mom. "Guests," was
precisely how Suzanne thought of them. She knew Brad would be furious at her for not considering his daughter a part of the family, but
she couldn't help it. Paige would watch their home for them while
they were up in Maine, and Suzanne was already trying to come up
with a way she could delicately tell her that she didn't want Lisa
snooping around in the house while they were away. Lisa hadn't been
able to conceal how impressed she'd been that day they'd come to
pick up Paige while they were still living in Georgia, and Suzanne sus-

pected Lisa had been chomping at the bit for them to go away so she could have Paige show her the rest of it. But she also knew a wrong choice of words would make Paige run straight to Brad and complain. Paige was good for doing that. The girl was a whiner.

Suzanne gave grudging credit to Paige's appearance. She looked quite nice in a navy blue polka dot culotte with halter neckline. Devon, too, looked great in a pink-and-green floral minisheath against a white background. But she felt that Kenya with her form-fitting dress and goddess braids would blow them out of the water. Just because Kenya had grown up without the advantages Brad's and Darrell's daughters enjoyed didn't mean she had to come in third. If Suzanne had her way, Kenya would get the prize and leave the other two in the dust.

Suzanne was inspecting the buffet table when Brad came up behind her. "Look who's coming," he said softly. "Didn't I tell you they'd be the first ones here? And mark my words—they'll be the last ones to leave, I'll bet."

Suzanne looked up to see Flo and Ernie at the side entrance to the screened lanai. One of the waiters was also doing door duty. Suzanne had asked that all invitees' names be checked off, just to make sure no one got in that didn't belong. She'd never forget that scene in the movie *Working Girl* when Harrison Ford and Melanie Griffith crashed a wedding, eating, drinking, and dancing like they'd been invited, with the bride and groom each assuming they'd been on the other's guest list.

The first thing Suzanne noticed as Flo and Ernie approached was how their outfits clashed. Flo's strapless royal blue dress with full skirt looked awful next to Ernie's kelly green crew shirt and gray suit. She wondered if they were even aware of how terrible the colors looked together. "Hello!" she said enthusiastically.

Flo began gushing immediately. "Oh, Suzanne, how beautiful everything looks! You didn't tell me it was going to be like this! What a classy touch, having to make sure our names are on the guest list before we're admitted. It makes it so exclusive! And I just *loooove* those tree lights on the lawn and those thick candles outlining the path to the door. It'll look beautiful once it gets dark. Look at those buffet tables, just groaning with food. . . ." She finally stopped, perhaps having run out of things to praise.

"Thank you, Flo," Suzanne said graciously, proud of how it came out just a tad smug.

"Long time no see, Brad," Ernie said, extending his hand.

"What can I say? The work never stops," Brad said as they shook.

"Flo tells me you two are heading up to New England next week. Got a summer house up there."

Brad glanced at Suzanne, an unreadable expression in his eyes. "Yes, we've got a little place up in Maine we try to get up to two or three times a year. I'm looking forward to it."

"I'll bet it's real pretty up there. Flo and I are from New England, you know, Boston, but we've never been to Maine."

"Yes, I recall hearing you're from Boston."

"We generally don't get up that way in the summer anymore; we go around Thanksgiving. Tell me, is your place on the water?"

"It's not on the Atlantic, but it's on a lake."

"Not a lot of 'us' up that way, are there?" Ernie asked.

Suzanne saw Brad's gaze shift to the entrance, where his friend Calvin Braxton and his wife were giving their names to the waiter. "Not a lot, but we do have a limited presence."

"Remember *The Shawshank Redemption*, Ernie?" Flo said. "That prison was set in Maine from the forties through the sixties, and there were plenty of other black men incarcerated there besides poor Morgan Freeman."

"Yeah, probably got sent up for rubbing out the peckerwoods," Ernie said with a laugh. "That'll get a black man a life sentence faster'n anything."

Suzanne forced a smile through stiff lips. Her eyes darted around to see if anyone else was at the door. Ernie had made no attempt to lower his voice, and while she wasn't concerned about the feelings of the mostly white waitstaff—they were only help—she didn't want him making any inappropriate remarks that might offend their friends. Fortunately, all she saw were Calvin and Liloutie Braxton, who as African-Americans wouldn't feel insulted. None of the other guests had yet arrived.

Ernie was still talking. "Anyway, Flo and I would just love to visit Maine in the summer."

"We hope you'll think about it," Brad said. As Ernie beamed he added, "I'll give you my rental agent's number. We rent the property when we're not using it, and it's always nice when we know the renters personally. And it has heat, in case you're interested in spending some time there while you're visiting Boston in the fall." He grinned. "Please excuse us, we have to greet our new arrivals." He guided Suzanne by the elbow and led her to the Braxtons, but not before Suzanne noted the crestfallen look on Ernie's face. Clearly his expectations had risen when Brad said he hoped they would consider going to Maine, but he hadn't expected to be offered the phone number of a rental agent. He hadn't been able to conceal his disappointment at being told they were welcome as paying renters, not as guests.

"That was mean, Brad," she whispered.

"He had it coming. Who the hell does he think he is? I barely know the man. He's not here five minutes before he lays it out for us to invite him to vacation with us. He's nothing but a fucking freeloader. And I'm disappointed you even told them we have a summer place. Like I told you, I don't want them in our business."

"It was only in passing, Brad. Flo and I were talking about vacation plans, that's all."

"You should know by now that any time you tell her anything, she's going to run right to Ernie and tell him all about it. But we'll talk later." Brad had been whispering, but he returned to a normal voice as he greeted Calvin.

Suzanne embraced Liloutie. Privately, she called the woman who hailed from St. Croix "Liloutie the highfaloutie." A top recruiter for Robert Half, she and Calvin, a cardiologist, lived in one of Jacksonville's most exclusive gated communities, also on the St. Johns River. Suzanne still remembered Liloutie's raised eyebrow when she learned Suzanne and Brad were moving into a non-gated community. But Suzanne had the last laugh the first time she and Brad played host to the Braxtons, when Liloutie had obviously been wowed by the new house.

She appeared equally impressed by the setup tonight. The bartender had set up shop behind the counter of the outdoor kitchen, while the attractive cloth-covered buffet tables were set up near the pool. "Who was your caterer, Suzanne?" she asked.

Suzanne named the event planner she and Brad had contracted.

"Well, they did a fabulous job. I never thought it would be this nice. Just look at that beautiful buffet table."

"Yes, I just told them what I wanted, and they made it," Suzanne said sweetly. She wanted to smack Liloutie for saying outright that she didn't think their party would be as nice as the ones she and Calvin gave. She'd always had a bit of a patronizing attitude, both because of her job and, Suzanne felt, because her salary combined with Calvin's put them well above Brad's lone income. The way Liloutie acted, she and Brad were a charity case or something.

By eight-thirty the party was in full swing. Lisa and Darrell had arrived; Lisa looking crisp in a polka-dotted red dress and red strappy sandals. She'd had her thick locks cut in a very short, straight style, which Suzanne reluctantly conceded was stunning on her. She went with Brad to greet them, and while she stood a full three inches taller than Lisa, standing opposite Brad's ex never failed to make Suzanne feel like a little kid.

"Nice party," Darrell remarked. "Lisa and I should be able to select our future caregivers from among your guests, since we're living down here now. Brad, why don't you point out an internist for us, an OB–GYN for Lisa, a pediatrician for the kids, and a geriatric specialist for Ma?"

They all laughed, and as Darrell and Brad began chatting about the many physicians in attendance, Suzanne decided she really should make an effort to be nice to Lisa. It might be unpleasant, but it wouldn't kill her. And Brad would be pleased. "I'm glad your mother-in-law could come, Lisa, but who's taking care of the boys?"

"The Frasiers' son. He's watching half the kids on the block, I think. I know Ann Sorensen's kids are over there."

"Is he old enough to be baby-sitting?"

"A little young for so many kids, but he's fifteen and in high school. And because they live right on the other side of you, he won't have far to go if he needs help. Are Bradley and Lauren here?"

"Yes, in the house. They came out a little while ago to fix their plates. We check on them every so often." Suzanne was relieved when Brad excused them and grabbed her hand to greet GI Joe Ianotti and his date. She'd done her duty and wouldn't have to say anything to Lisa the rest of the night.

Brad frequently changed the CDs, keeping a steady stream of mingle music playing. The bartender kept busy making mixed drinks, including strawberry daiquiris and piña coladas courtesy of two blenders on the counter. The waiters passed trays of specialty hors d'oeuvres. On more than one occasion, Suzanne glimpsed Ernie Hickman scrutinizing the contents suspiciously and talking to the waitstaff, probably to ask what they were. *Strictly NC,* she thought.

Suzanne found it less amusing when she noticed Derrick and Matthew, who had come down when the party had really gotten started, doing the same thing. She walked over to them and quietly described the contents of every hors d'oeuvre on the buffet. "This way you won't have to ask the waiters. And for God's sake, try not to make faces at something you don't recognize," she said. "It looks so childish, and there are sophisticated people here tonight."

"Yeah, sure," Matthew said. "I think I'll just stick to the shrimp."

"I'm gonna get me a drink," Derrick said.

Suzanne's expression remained impassive, but she couldn't help thinking that Derrick put away nearly as much alcohol as their mother did.

When her brothers went on their way, she did a quick survey of the lanai, making sure everyone looked happy. She practically dashed over to meet Gregory Hickman when she saw him at the door. She took his arm. "I'm so glad you could join us tonight, Gregory."

"I would have gotten here earlier, except I had to work until six."

"That's quite all right. We're going to be here for hours yet. I'll bring you to the girls. I know they'll be happy to see you. Oh, and my sister is here tonight also. I don't believe you've met her. She's about your age." They stopped in front of the corner where all three girls sat. "Look who's here, girls. And Gregory, may I present my sister, Kenya Hall."

She smiled at Gregory's rapt expression as he and Kenya traded hellos. He barely glanced at Paige and Devon, and they both looked a little dejected. The look they exchanged suggested they knew they had both lost.

Suzanne had hoped for this reaction. Paige would never confide in her—Lisa had probably warned her not to—but Flo, unable to hide the pride in her voice, had mentioned that both girls were interested in her son. *Score another one for the underdog,* she thought as she watched Gregory offer to get Kenya a glass of pop.

As far as she was concerned, the party was a success.

CHAPTER 27

"Oh," said the blind man, "can't you see?"
—Bernard Underwood

Darrell bit off half of a miniature quiche. "I really like these," he said.

"So I see," Lisa said with a smile. "Did you ever figure out what's in it?"

"Mmm . . . I recognize mozzarella cheese and tomato. Maybe a little pesto thrown in for extra flavor," he mused. "Whatever it is, it's great. Between this and those stuffed phyllo dough triangles I can make a meal. Keep 'em coming," he said to the waiter, who promptly raised the tray. Darrell helped himself to two more. "Nice party, isn't it?" he remarked to Lisa while he ate.

"Yeah, I didn't know Suzanne had it in her. I'm sure Brad was looking over her shoulder telling her what to order, or else we'd be feasting on pigs in a blanket and deviled eggs, like we're at a picnic or something. That's more her speed."

"Why don't you cut the girl some slack, Lisa?"

"Because she's a little nobody who sashayed out of the swamp and is trying to pass herself off as having some background," she said flatly. "And I know she doesn't, even if she's got the rest of you fooled. I'll never understand what Brad saw in her."

"I'm going to get another drink."

She looked at his retreating back curiously, startled by his abrupt departure. And why didn't he offer to get her a drink as well? He could see her glass was down to diluted liquid.

"Hi, Mom."

She hadn't seen Paige approaching. Her daughter's sad expression made her look like she'd lost the proverbial best friend. "As the bartender said to the horse, 'Why the long face?' "

Paige laughed in spite of herself. "Oh, Mom, that's so corny."

"It made you laugh, didn't it? Now tell me what's wrong."

"Oh, it's Kenya."

That figures. "What'd she do?"

"I've been trying to get Gregory to like me for weeks, and all she does is say hello and his mouth falls open like he's never seen a girl before."

Lisa had noticed the eyes of grown men who should know better following the teenager around the lanai. The girl was a sex magnet, even reasonably covered up, and the dress she wore accented her prominent behind. She wasn't the type any female with a lick of sense would trust around her man. Lisa had gotten the same discomforting feeling about Suzanne the first time she laid eyes on her so many years ago, and of course before it was over she was out of a husband.

But secretly Lisa felt relieved that Gregory Hickman had chosen Kenya over her daughters. "I guess this means you and Devon don't have anything to argue about anymore, do you?"

Paige looked embarrassed. "I guess not."

Devon joined them, popping the last of a broccoli stalk into her mouth and then rubbing her palms together. "Did Paige tell you about Gregory and Kenya?"

Lisa put a comforting arm around her shoulder. "She did, and I was telling her there's no reason for the two of you to be at odds with each other anymore."

"There's not much reason to hang around here anymore, either," Devon said gloomily.

"You got that right," Paige agreed. "Nothing here but old folks."

Lisa rolled her eyes. "All right now, let's not be unkind." She placed her near-empty glass on the tray of a passing waiter and draped her other arm around Paige. "But since I'm so old I'm probably wise as well, so let me share a little bit of what I've learned about life. You two are going to find that every boy you find attractive isn't necessarily going to fall at your feet. Some, like Gregory, will just want to be friends. Others won't respond to you at all. It doesn't mean you're not attractive, because both of you are beautiful. That's just the way it goes sometimes." She paused, knowing this wasn't the appropriate setting to add what she wanted to say. After glancing around and being certain no one was listening, she said, "But I hope the two of you never let another boy come between you again, ever. We're family, and that's a sacred relationship that should come first for you until the day you get married and create your own families." She patted both girls' shoulders, then let her hands drop to her sides. "And that's all I've got to say on the subject. Now enjoy the party."

"Are these your daughters?" one of the women asked.

Lisa proudly introduced the girls. After everyone had moved on, she wandered to the buffet table and helped herself to two more of those giant shrimp, then backed away. She looked around furtively. Where was Darrell? He'd been gone a long time, and when he left he'd seemed annoyed for some reason.

She had the feeling that something was off-kilter somehow when he did return to her, in spite of her asking him repeatedly if he was all right. He responded with a terse, "I'm fine," that did nothing to ease the tension. But she knew him well enough to know he wouldn't speak about anything that troubled him in public. Whatever it was, he'd tell her when they got home. Maybe he'd witnessed Ernie Hickman doing something obnoxious.

Surely he wasn't upset with *her.*

Flo shifted her weight to her other foot. She didn't belong in this group, or at least she didn't once they started talking about the rising costs of school tuition. Someone asked her what school her children went to, and she smiled and said, "We have one son who's in college prep. It's a public school, but you have to apply and be accepted, and they have an excellent reputation." No one seemed shocked by the admission, but she wanted to get away before anyone asked her a question she couldn't answer. It also wouldn't hurt to fill Ernie in on the lie she told in case someone asked him where Gregory attended school.

She spotted him dancing in an open space with that woman with the funny name, Lil-something. She might have a weird name, but she looked smashing in a simple white strapless minidress with a black floral appliqué embroidered on the bottom right. The color really set off her dark skin, and her slim build only reminded Flo of the extra weight she still carried despite a regular routine of brisk walking. She could only stare at the woman with envy. Some women just never put on pounds, no matter how many kids they had or how old they got. And the woman's black hair grazed her shoulders, with a gardenia pinned on one side. Damn, why could everybody except her grow hair? Even Gail Morton's two little girls had more hair than she had.

When the song ended, she fully expected Ernie to join her, but instead he followed Lil, or whatever her name was, to the buffet table. He stood closer to her than what was necessary, or even proper, Flo noted with sinking spirits. She hastily turned away. That woman was married and here with her husband; surely Ernie knew that. How could he embarrass her like this in front of Suzanne and Lisa?

Lisa was the first familiar face she recognized. Suzanne had shared how upset she'd been when Brad insisted they invite the Canfields, but at this moment Flo couldn't have been happier to see her. "Hi, Lisa," she said, forcing herself to sound cheerful. "It's so nice to see you again. I love your hair."

"Thanks, Flo."

"Are you all settled now?"

"Pretty much so, yes."

"Have you been on vacation yet?" This seemed as good a time as any to find out what the Canfields' plans were, if they had any. Secretly she hoped Lisa would say they weren't going anywhere. She'd love to know that she and Ernie weren't the only ones who couldn't afford a trip. But she was in for a disappointment.

"Not yet," was all Lisa said.

Flo tried again. "I'm sorry you and Darrell weren't able to join us on the Fourth, but you'll have to come over to see us one night. It's been too long since we've gotten together." Was it just her imagination, or did her remark make Lisa look acutely uncomfortable?

"Yes, we'll be sure to do that," Lisa replied, so pleasantly that Flo decided she'd imagined the pained look on her face. "Actually, we spent the Fourth over in your subdivision. Do you know Ben and Stacy Prince? They live two streets over from you, I believe."

"Yes. I, uh, didn't know you knew them."

"Kim and Michael introduced us."

Flo's jaw felt like it had been lined with lead, but she managed a tight little smile. "We haven't seen too much of Kim and Michael lately, either."

"I guess we're all busy. You know how it is. They're having a pool put in, you know."

Flo was tempted to retort that she doubted they were doing the work themselves. But she couldn't let Lisa see how much it bothered her that Lisa and Kim preferred the company of the Princes to that of her and Ernie. "Yes, I know," she said. Then she allowed herself a covert glance over at the buffet table. Ernie was still standing next to that woman, and they both held plates. Flo didn't like the cozy way they smiled at each other. She didn't know the whereabouts of the woman's husband, but as far as she was concerned it was time to break up this little flirtation. She excused herself and walked over to Ernie. "Hello."

"Hey, Flo!" Ernie greeted. "Liloutie and I were just talking about you."

"Were you, now?" she asked dryly, brushing her hair away from her face to conceal her self-consciousness. Next to the petite Liloutie she felt bigger than a pregnant elephant.

"Your husband is charming, Flo," Liloutie said. "And speaking of husbands, I'm sure mine is wondering where I am. I think he's in the house. Excuse me."

"So you were talking about me?" Flo asked after Liloutie left. "What did you say?"

"All about how you walk all over the neighborhood for exercise."

"Oh, great. What'd you do, ask her how she stays so slim and then tell her how your wife walks and walks and she's still overweight?"

"Come on, Flo. I'm just trying to be sociable."

"Well, if you got any closer to her, you would have been on top of her, Ernie," she hissed. "How could you act like that? How would it make you feel if some man was all up in my face?"

"Oh, stop overreacting. I told you it was harmless."

"You've done this before, Ernie. Every time we go anywhere and there's a new female face, you're all over her like a cheap plaid suit. I'm sick of it, and I'm sick of *you*."

She turned and walked into the house.

Lisa and Darrell wandered off in different directions. She could see Darrell, who had gotten into a discussion in the family room. She enjoyed herself regardless, mingling with the other guests, both the ones she knew, like Ann and Bill Sorensen and other neighbors; and ones she didn't, all the while doing her best to avoid Flo Hickman. She was afraid Flo might try to pin her down to a specific evening for her and Darrell to go over there, and neither of them wanted to go. She hadn't expected to see Flo and Ernie here; they didn't strike her as being Brad's type of people. They must have done the same thing for Brad and Suzanne as they had for her and Darrell, showed up on their doorstep with prepared food in a neighborly act to disguise their curiosity, but she still found it puzzling. Surely Brad recognized them for being the nosy types they were and felt the same way about them as she and Darrell did. Then a lightbulb lit up inside her brain. The Hickmans wouldn't fool Brad, but they'd probably fooled Suzanne. God, she was dumb.

The latest group she was chatting with disbanded when someone came along and said, "Suzanne's about to give another tour." She knew from the raves of the guests who'd already gone that Suzanne was taking people through the house in small groups and wished she could go, too, but of course that wouldn't do.

Lisa moved on to another group, introducing herself as the Betancourts' next-door neighbor. She had no intention of providing any further details, but soon realized it was no secret, at least among the women present. Lisa found it amusing that the expression of every woman she had talked to, whether black, white, Middle Eastern, Asian, or Indian, changed to one of knowing the moment she said she lived next door. Suzanne had certainly been keeping herself busy telling everyone about her husband's ex building a house next to them, no doubt leaving out the fact that construction on their house had already been started before Suzanne and Brad even knew this street existed.

From the quick looks up and down, expressions that so plainly read, "No *wonder* Suzanne's so upset," Lisa decided that Suzanne had also forgotten to mention that she had remarried years ago, instead painting her as a vengeful ex-spouse determined to get her former husband back. It was nice to know that at almost forty-three she could still elicit that kind of reaction, but she wished these women knew she was happily married.

"Who's the jerk in the gray suit?"

Brad followed Calvin Braxton's gaze. "Oh, him," he said, settling on Ernie. "He lives down the street. Suzanne's friends with his wife, so we had to invite them, but he's a real nitwit."

"I'll say. Liloutie said she thought she'd never be able to shake him, but even driving home the point that she's married didn't stop him. I was inside talking, or else I would have gotten her away from him."

"He's obviously insecure," Liloutie added. "Here I am, a total stranger, and he's telling me all about his custom built house in the subdivision down the street. 'You and your husband will have to come and see us,' he said. Can you believe saying that to someone you've just met, like we're old friends?"

"He's the type who wants everybody to see his house," Brad explained. "He and his wife have got so much bric-a-brac in that place you can hardly walk through without breaking something, but they're just as proud as they can be."

"Tell him what else he said, Lil," Calvin urged.

"Oh, yes," she said. "He told me I looked nice, and before I know it he's going on about how he wishes his wife would lose thirty pounds. Then the wife shows up and gives me a dirty look like I'm trying to take away her man. I felt sorry for her." She made a mock shiver. "Whatever does Suzanne see in people like that?"

"I wish I knew," Brad admitted.

CHAPTER 28

The party's over; it's time to call it a day.
—"The Party's Over," lyrics by Betty Comden and Adolph Green

Paige and Devon left the party at about eleven, first stopping next door to retrieve the twins. When Esther announced she was ready to go home a half hour later, Lisa and Darrell went with her.

"Did you have a nice time, Ma Canfield?" Lisa asked.

"Wonderful. That food was great. I must have eaten a dozen of those shrimp. I would've eaten more, but they filled me up. I've never seen shrimp so large. I hope it doesn't give me nightmares."

"I'm sure you'll be fine."

"The boy I saw with Arlene's younger daughter, is that the one Devon and Paige are always talking about?"

"Yes. Apparently, he's decided he likes her better than either of our girls."

"Just as well," Esther said lightly.

Lisa glanced at Darrell, expecting him to say something at this news, but he remained silent. "But I think they've both learned a lesson about letting anyone come between them, and that makes it worthwhile."

The moment they got into the house Darrell said good night. "Tell the boys I'll see them in the morning," he said to Lisa.

"Okay." She looked after him anxiously, unable to shake the feeling that something was wrong. "I'll be in shortly," she added, but he didn't look back, nor did he acknowledge her statement.

She checked on the boys, who were so worn out after an evening of play that they were already in their beds and nearly asleep. Then she bade her mother-in-law good night and entered the master suite. "All right," she said to Darrell. "Now that we're alone, don't you think you'd better tell me what has you wound so tight? Did Ernie say something thoughtless to you?"

"Ernie has nothing to do with it. And all I have to say, Lisa, is that if you want Brad back maybe you should let him know."

"If I want Brad . . ." she repeated incredulously. "What are you talking about, Darrell? I haven't had any feelings for Brad in years, since before I met you."

"It doesn't sound that way to me. You sound like a bitter woman whose husband just left her for someone glamorous and younger. You don't sound like someone who's long since found happiness with someone else and moved on, and that's what makes me wonder." He unbuttoned his shirt so forcefully she expected to see buttons flying. "What the hell difference does it make to you what Brad sees in Suzanne, or where she came from? I don't care if she's the daughter of Swamp Thang. It's none of your damn business."

Glamorous and younger? Glamorous and younger? Lisa hated herself for thinking it, but the first thing that stuck in her mind wasn't Darrell's hurt feelings, but that he'd referred to Suzanne that way. She forced the matter out of her mind. Her husband's feelings were hurt; she had to reassure him. "It's not that I have any feelings for Brad. It's just that I dislike Suzanne so much."

"I'm not crazy about her myself, especially after you told me how she rolled her eyes that first day outside the house when you mentioned Paige. And I've seen her try to bait you, trying to make sure you never forget that she and Brad have more money than you and I." His eyes narrowed suddenly. "Or is that the problem, that you envy her lifestyle?"

"Of course not, Darrell—"

"Listen, Lisa, I may not have the initials 'M.D.' after my name, but I make a good living. Our house isn't as fancy as Brad's place, but it's hardly a shack. Nor would we starve if you didn't work. In case you forgot, before we started looking for a house in Jacksonville, I gave you that choice. If you wanted to stay home we'd look for an ordinary house in a good public school district, but you said you wanted to keep working. Since we can't maintain this house plus the kids' tuition without a dual income, it's too damn late now for you to change your mind and want to be a stay-at-home mom like Suzanne."

She wanted to scream at him to stop it; she couldn't stand hearing him talk this way. "Darrell, stop! I never said I envied Suzanne's lifestyle. I just . . . I feel it's too good for someone like her. I know it's wrong of me, that I'm not the one who gets to make those decisions, but I can't help it."

"You'd better help it, Lisa. I'm sick of hearing all your snide little comments." Darrell pulled off his slacks and, in a move unusual for him, dropped them on the floor. "Good night." He climbed into bed in his underwear, his back to her.

Lisa felt shaken. She and Darrell seldom had such strong disagreements. She couldn't remember the last time she'd seen him so upset. Had she actually complained so much that he felt she still wanted Brad, or was he merely being oversensitive?

"You want to turn out the light?" he grumbled, so harshly that her shoulders inadvertently twitched. She hastily complied with his request, slipping out of her dress in the lit walk-in closet. She slipped into their king-size bed, knowing he would keep his distance and it would be like sleeping alone.

And as she lay in the dark, she kept thinking it was all Suzanne's fault.

Suzanne moaned in pleasure. She knew it excited Brad when she did that, but he was inside her so deep she couldn't help the sounds escaping from her throat. She bucked against him wildly, feeling her breasts bounce each time she raised her hips. When he reached down and fingered her clit, she squealed as her climax began. He soon joined her. When it ended, he rolled off her and lay next to her on his back, panting.

"That was so good it makes me want a cigarette," he said.

"But you don't smoke, Brad."

"I know. That's how good it was. I might have one of yours."

She laughed. "The evening was perfect, wasn't it?"

"Everybody had a good time. I just hope Ernie didn't offend all our guests."

"I'm sure he didn't."

"He sure put off Liloutie and GI Joe. Liloutie said he was coming on to her, telling her she had a nice figure and then complaining about his wife being overweight."

"No, he didn't!"

Brad shrugged. "The guy's got less class than summer vacation. Hey, he's *your* friend."

"No, not really. Flo's my friend, he just comes with her. What'd he say to GI Joe?"

"Apparently he found out that Joe was the original owner of the house, and he came right out and asked if it cost more than a half mil. Joe said he couldn't believe it." Brad chuckled deep in his throat. "The first ones to arrive and the last ones to leave. They're really something else, those two."

"Well, Flo really is nice, even if Ernie's on the uncouth side."

"Yeah, well, just remember what I said about not telling them our business." He reached over and tweaked her breast. "That was great sex, Suzie Q. But I'm not up to a round two tonight. I'm gonna roll over and go to sleep, if that's okay with you."

"Sure, go ahead. I'm going to sleep, too. You wore me out."

Suzanne had a smile on her face as she closed her eyes ten minutes later. Brad was already asleep. He placed a possessive hand on the curve of her hip and sighed contentedly.

She loved it when everything went the way it was supposed to with no glitches. Their first party would be talked about for months to come. Kenya had succeeded with Gregory where both Paige and Darrell's daughter had failed. And Brad hadn't raised a single objection about her family's presence. Only one thing bothered her, something that threatened to keep her awake well into the night.

She and Brad had been chatting with GI Joe and his date—it hadn't taken him long to find someone after the breakup with Jenny—and Joe asked her how she liked the house. When Suzanne said they loved it, Joe turned to Brad and said, "Aren't you glad you mentioned to me that you were thinking about moving to Jacksonville? I never would have thought to ask you if you'd be interested in my little palace, and if you hadn't said what you did, Prakash from Pulmonary might be living here today."

She felt her face freeze. Had it all been a coincidence and not a carefully orchestrated scheme, like she'd thought? Joe's words suggested it had been nothing more than an innocent series of events, and suddenly she was filled with shame for plotting with her mother behind Brad's back. The voice of her conscience told her she had done wrong.

She feared it would come back to haunt her.

"Not a bad way to spend an evening," Ernie remarked as he unlocked their front door. The Bug in the driveway and the lone light in the foyer told them Gregory had gone to bed. "At least I got to see their whole house."

Flo didn't reply right away. When they reached the bedroom and closed the door behind them, she finally said, "I guess if that woman agreed to go out with you it would have been perfect."

"Come on, Flo. I told you it wasn't anything but me trying to be friendly. But that wasn't a very friendly crowd. It was nice to see some brothers there. I figured it'd only be white guys. They just seemed a little on the snooty side to me, all of them. I'd say something to get into the conversation and they'd get these funny looks on their faces."

Flo felt her anger toward him weakening. Ernie could act immature at times, even downright thoughtless, but she'd loved him since she was fifteen years old and she knew she always would. She didn't like to hear that anyone had been rude to him. "What'd you think of their house?" she asked, wanting to change the subject.

He sat in the corner chair, resting his hands on the arms. "It's fabulous. You're right, Flo. There's no way we can compete with that, even if they don't have a home theater."

She smiled, knowing how difficult it was for Ernie to admit someone had them beat.

"I'm satisfied to know them well enough to get invited to their parties," Ernie continued. "That buffet alone must have cost Brad a fortune. I could have done without all that fancy stuff, but the shrimp and crab cakes were great."

"Suzanne told me some of them were lobster."

"Well, they were all good." He patted his slightly protruding belly. "Maybe you should offer to take some of the leftovers off their hands. I checked, and there were plenty."

"Suzanne's coming over tomorrow with her mother and sister. If she brings some food with her I won't refuse, but I don't think it would be right for me to ask, Ernie. I doubt she'll give away crab cakes and jumbo shrimp, anyway. Those two items probably cost more than anything on those tables. There was plenty of other, cheaper food left, chicken wings, stuffed clams, raw vegetables."

"All right, if you say so. Hey, what was with Darrell and Lisa being there? I sure as hell didn't expect to see *them*."

"Didn't I tell you? Brad insisted they invite them. Suzanne didn't want to."

"I'll bet she didn't. That Lisa's a fox."

Once again Flo's annoyance grew. She wished Ernie would be more considerate of her feelings and compliment her once in a while. To listen to him, everybody looked great except her.

"Darrell didn't have too much to say, either," Ernie added. "What about Lisa? She talk to you?"

Flo shrugged. "She was all right, I guess." But Lisa's appearance at the party had been a disappointment. She'd thought Lisa would've been a lot more receptive than she'd been, since most of the other women there seemed to know each other. But Lisa did know the other couples from the block, and she moved easily from group to group, seeming to fit right in. Flo was too shy to do much mingling, but the guests she'd spoken with had been outgoing, introducing themselves and bringing her into the conversation.

She hung up her dress and slipped into a nightgown. "All of the women were nice, actually. But don't judge the fellas too harshly, Ernie. It's not like they could let their inner homeboy out and be down with it. They probably felt they had to act dignified. You have to consider the company. Most of the guests were white."

"Yeah, that's what they think. A lot of them damn East Indians are darker than me. I wonder if they consider themselves white."

Flo couldn't care less about how East Indians classified themselves. "Did Gregory tell you he has a tentative date with Suzanne's sister Kenya next Saturday?"

"What's this tentative shit? She holding out for a better offer?"

"No, it's just that she's not sure if she'll be up this way next weekend. She'll have to check with her mother. I'm real happy about it."

"Yeah, well, I'd hold off on ordering a china pattern if I were you. Personally, I'd rather see him with Brad's daughter. After seeing that new Lexus and that house, we *know* they've got big bucks. What's Suzanne's mother got?"

"Probably not a whole lot. She works for the post office."

"And you're excited about Gregory taking her daughter out? Why, for God's sake?"

"Don't take the Lord's name in vain, Ernie."

"Sorry. It slipped out. But why?"

"Because if everything goes the way it's supposed to, Kenya and her mother will be moving in with Suzanne and Brad, so after a while there won't be much difference between Kenya and Paige. Even Paige doesn't *live* there."

Ernie immediately leaned in closer. "Oh, yeah? They're movin' in?"

"But don't say anything to Brad if you see him, Ernie. He doesn't know yet."

"He probably won't like it much."

"Oh, I'm sure Suzanne knows Brad won't like it. I think that's why she told me in the first place. She was looking for my approval. She was saying how much she misses her family, especially her mother. Of course I told her I understood, although I really don't."

He grunted. "Well, I'm glad you don't miss *your* mother so much where you want her and your father to move in with *us.*"

The next morning, Flo straightened up in anticipation of Suzanne's visit. She'd offered to help Suzanne tidy up her house after the party, but Suzanne had said she'd leave it for the maid to do on Monday with a flippancy Flo found intriguing. She couldn't imagine being so casual about household help. How wonderful it would be if she could afford a maid to pick up after Ernie and Gregory, both of whom were slobs of Oscar Madison magnitude. Sometimes she felt she hardly had time to sit down and enjoy her surroundings, between all the vacuuming, dusting, wiping, and mopping, especially in the bathrooms. Anyone would think a grown man and one who was nearly grown would be able to aim into the toilet and not spill onto the floor. She couldn't let Suzanne and her mother see those suspicious little puddles.

Suzanne had accepted right away when Flo suggested she bring her mother and Kenya by her house today. Brad, she'd said, had plans to play golf and would be gone all afternoon. Flo had a hunch that

Suzanne wanted her mother to see she'd made friends in the neighborhood.

Flo sensed something odd about Suzanne's relationship with her mother. She understood Suzanne's wanting to impress her with how well she was doing—hell, she wanted to impress Mrs. Hall herself—but no one as old as Suzanne should feel they needed approval from a parent anymore. But Flo welcomed the opportunity to get to know Suzanne's mother and sister, especially since Gregory had taken a liking to young Kenya.

She had just finished with her housework when Gail Morton called at noon. Could Flo keep her girls for an hour while she and George ran to Home Depot? "I hate to bring them around all those high shelves packed with heavy building supplies," she said.

Flo turned her down. Even over the phone she could hear the surprise in Gail's voice, but the truth was Flo had gotten fed up with Gail and George and their kids. Yes, they were cute little girls, but the way their parents fussed over them they would soon know it. You just didn't tell children repeatedly how cute they were. Gail and George both seemed to think that everyone found their daughters as irresistible as they did. Besides, Flo knew there was no way the Mortons would be back in an hour. Villa St. John must have a dozen teenage girls who baby-sat for short or long periods. Of course, they had to be *paid* for their services. Gail's strategy was to call Flo or Sondra Barnes, say she and George would only be gone for an hour, and then get "delayed" and show up three hours later full of apologies, having received free baby-sitting services. Flo was beginning to think that getting people to do things for them for nothing was how they'd come up with the money to build their house. But that's what she'd expect from people like that, people who were young and uncultured.

Flo would love to do "couple" things with Suzanne and Brad, like go out to dinner or spend evenings at each other's homes, but she rarely saw Brad. Suzanne's suggestions to get together usually occurred when he was out on his boat or on the golf course or somewhere. From that first night they'd had dinner together, she sensed Brad had no interest in befriending Ernie, and after last night she knew for sure. She wished Ernie hadn't dropped those hints that he wanted to go to Maine with the Betancourts. She felt Brad had enjoyed leading Ernie on for a big letdown, behavior she perceived as

unnecessary and even a bit cruel. So what if Ernie had gone overboard in his enthusiasm. He hadn't been mean, but Brad had. If he
hadn't been their host, she would have told him so.

Flo knew she should forget about forging a husbands-and-wives
friendship with the Betancourts. She was grateful to at least have established an alliance with Suzanne. Lisa Canfield was another matter
entirely. All Flo's overtures led nowhere. She'd have to focus on Kim
and Michael Gillespie next door. They were the key to getting in with
Lisa and Darrell. She had to get Kim and Michael to include her and
Ernie when they had people over, like the Princes, so they could make
a second, better impression. Ernie reported having seen both the
Canfield and Gillespie vehicles in the Princes' driveway last Sunday.
He couldn't see the back of the house, but they were probably swimming and cooking out. What else was there to do on a Sunday afternoon? Flo desperately wanted to dump George and Gail with their
aren't-they-adorable girls and Larry and Sondra with their unruly
boys and get in with this more cultured, better behaved group. She'd
made a special effort last night to be gracious to Lisa. She feared
Ernie may have permanently put off the Canfields early on, too, by
having George and Larry go to their house looking for him.

Flo knew Ernie didn't mean to sound boorish, even if he came off
sounding that way sometimes. They both came from the ghetto and
were proud of what they'd accomplished, justifiably so, she felt. What
they had trouble accepting was that some folks had done even better,
had more. Plenty of folks, she was learning. They'd grown so accustomed to being the leaders that relinquishing their position wasn't
easy. She'd initially been shocked to see that two black couples were
building on the exclusive riverfront, but she'd gotten used to the
idea. Ernie was just getting there, but he had to learn to control his
curiosity. She'd asked him to stop asking about people's salaries or
how much they had paid for their belongings. She hoped he hadn't
asked anyone last night.

"Ernie," she said, "are you going over to Michael's this afternoon?"

"Nah, I told Larry I'd be by. I figure Darrell might be at Michael's
and steal my thunder."

Flo knew what he meant. *He* wanted to be the one to inform the
others about the Betancourts' party, not have Darrell do it. He
wanted to impress George and Larry, something that could be done

without changing a single fact. But Flo knew he'd embellish the details nevertheless.

"Maybe I'll stop by there later," he said, glancing at the Gillespie home through the kitchen window. "Like if I see Ben Prince's car there."

She smiled. Maybe Ernie felt that they needed to upgrade their friends, too.

CHAPTER 29

My toughest fight was with my first wife.
—Muhammad Ali

Lisa stared at Darrell, confused. "You and Devon are going out? I thought you and I were going over to Kim and Michael's."

"It really isn't that important that we go today, is it? Can't we go over there anytime?"

"Of course," she said quickly. "Are you bringing the boys with you?"

"No, this time it's just me and Devon."

"In that case I guess I'll see you guys when you come back," she said stiffly. No point in pretending she didn't find his behavior upsetting. She wondered where he planned to take Devon, but knew his secrecy was deliberate. If he'd wanted her to know, he would have told her. His anger of last night had carried over to this new day.

For the first time in a long time Lisa felt a boundary between herself and Devon as if Devon were one of those little glass-covered figurines in a shadowbox. Devon had been a part of their household since the beginning, and Lisa considered her as much her child as Paige and the twins, but Darrell's hush-hush attitude made it painfully clear that she didn't have the right to insist upon knowing where Darrell was taking her, the way she could if he was taking the twins out. Devon was Darrell's daughter, and he could justifiably, if rather insensitively, tell her it was none of her business. It would be different if she'd legally adopted Devon, but of course she hadn't because

Paula had always taken an active interest in Devon's upbringing, or at least she had until she remarried.

She called Kim to tell her they had a change in plans and would see her and Michael another time. She'd hoped to make it a quick conversation, but Kim wanted to know all about the party. "Maybe I can get some ideas for when Michael and I celebrate our pool being completed," she explained.

Lisa dutifully recited the menu items and told Kim about the decorative lighting.

"That's a fresh idea, palm tree lights. I guess I can rent them, huh?"

"Probably, from a party planner. They did look pretty, but don't be surprised if Flo comments about how Suzanne had the same ones at her party."

"Flo? *She* was there?"

"She sure was." Lisa nodded her head, even though Kim couldn't see her. "She and Ernie both. I was surprised, too. From what I observed, Flo's latched onto Suzanne."

"I didn't know. We haven't seen much of them since you guys moved in. Michael's more likely to hang out with Darrell than with Ernie, and I'm glad. I wish there was a way I could get around not inviting them to our pool party, but I guess I can't. I'll have to invite all the neighbors."

"You don't sound too thrilled at the prospect."

"You wouldn't either, if you knew these people," Kim replied. "I've had it with Ernie. The last time he was here he pulled out his cell phone and started calling his friends and telling them to come over."

Lisa drew in her breath. "Did they come?"

"Larry and George came over right away. Some other guy we didn't even know showed up on our doorstep, too."

"Good Lord, what'd you do?"

"Michael didn't want to be mean, so he just let them in. When he told me about it, I told him that was the final straw, and none of them have set foot in our house since. That's why I wasn't surprised when Larry and George showed up at your house that night." Kim sighed. "Now that I think about it, I'm tempted not to invite them after all."

Lisa laughed. "It sounds like they'll just crash it anyway. Formal invitations don't mean anything to those people. Unless you do what Suzanne did and have someone at the door checking off names."

Talking to Kim cheered her up a bit. Lisa turned on the TV and channel surfed. A movie on the Lifetime network caught her attention briefly. A teenage girl was shouting at her mother the way those white kids always seemed to get away with doing, at least on TV. Lisa doubted anyone she knew would tolerate that behavior. Still, the conflict between mother and daughter reminded her of that between Devon and Paula.

Lisa realized that in order for Devon to receive a birthday card from Paula with the promise of a forthcoming surprise in time for her birthday, Paula had decided to send the check days before she fell and injured her baby, not after. Still, Lisa wondered if she'd increased the amount out of guilt, or if she had merely hoped that a check would make Devon reclaim her as her mother. Lisa felt no child should be given love based on the whims of his or her parents, but that's exactly what was happening to poor Devon.

She blinked. Could Darrell be taking Devon car shopping? He'd said he wanted to pick out something for her beforehand so she wouldn't run to the most expensive car on the lot, but maybe he'd changed his mind. Paula's check had probably cleared by now.

Wouldn't he discuss such a big step with her first? They always consulted each other before making any major purchases. But Darrell had been so upset with her last night. She wanted to put the episode behind them and get on with their lives. She was prepared not to make any remarks that could be interpreted as a longing for Brad or jealousy of Suzanne's lifestyle.

She turned off the television and busied herself by removing all the food from the refrigerator, cleaning the glass shelves, the shelves on the inside of the door, and even the crispers, and then putting the food back, throwing out things like expired sour cream and uneaten leftovers. She found the chore invigorating and then proceeded to wipe down the kitchen cabinets with water mixed with wood soap.

She heard the front door open, and Cary came bounding into the kitchen. "I'm thirsty," he announced.

"I hope you remembered to wipe your feet."

"Yeah, I did." He took a plastic cup from the first shelf in the cupboard and filled it with water from the dispenser, then moved it to the adjacent dispenser and added ice.

"Cary, I wish you wouldn't do that," Lisa said wearily. "When you use water it's not a problem, but when you pour juice first and then add ice, the juice splashes up and makes a sticky mess. It's very hard to clean, and a big buildup can disable the dispensers altogether and make me have to call for service. I've told you this before," she reminded him.

"I'm sorry, Mom. I guess I forgot." Head leaning back, he gulped down the water like an empty gas tank. "Where's Daddy?" he asked as he placed the cup in the sink.

"He went out with Devon."

"Where'd they go?"

"I don't know. I guess they'll tell us when they get back. Where's Courtney?"

"He's outside with Bradley." Cary wiped his mouth on his sleeve. "We're riding our bikes. I gotta go so I can catch up with them."

"You be careful, Cary."

"I will. 'Bye."

Lisa gave him a head start, then went to the front door and opened it. There wasn't much traffic on their street or the side street that branched off it, but Cary was only eight years old. A child in a hurry would probably be more likely to make a careless move. She just wanted to make sure he was following the safety rules.

She relaxed when Cary looked both ways before crossing to the opposite side of the street. She wasn't too keen on the idea of Cary and Courtney playing with Bradley. From what she'd seen of the boy, he had a real discipline problem. She couldn't count how many times she'd arrived home from work and seen Suzanne in front of her house screaming at him to come in. His response was usually to wave at her and say he'd be right there, and then pedal in the other direction. An exasperated-looking Suzanne would merely go back inside.

Lisa mentioned the boy's disrespectful behavior to Darrell, who had gone fishing with them on Brad's boat twice. Darrell reported Bradley was a model child around his father, news that didn't come as a surprise to Lisa. It figured that Suzanne couldn't control the boy. Bradley was more likely to obey Paige, his big sister, than he would his mother.

As far as Brad and Suzanne's daughter Lauren, Lisa wondered if she was all there. Lisa didn't think she'd ever heard the girl say more than ten words; she just stared at everyone with those enormous eyes of hers. But Paige hadn't mentioned anything about her little sister having any type of defect or delay, and Lisa felt it would be improper to bring up the matter. Maybe the little girl was just shy.

Lisa had just returned to the kitchen when Paige ambled out of the hall where her bedroom was. "Where's Devon, Mom?"

"Out somewhere with Darrell."

"Oh. I wish they'd brought me with them. I'm bored, Mom."

"You can always clean your room," Lisa suggested with a smile.

"Come on, Mom, it's my day off."

She looked at her daughter squarely, suddenly annoyed. "You know what, Paige, it's my day off, too, and that means I don't want to listen to you whine about how bored you are." Without another word, she walked past Paige onto the lanai.

Esther had taken advantage of the twins' being outside by getting in the pool, swimming gracefully, her arms making little semicircular ripples in the water but no splashes, for her head with its perfectly styled gray hair remained dry and above the water. She usually swam ten laps a day. Lisa admired her mother-in-law's skill at swimming without getting her hair wet. Now that she'd cut her own hair she'd have to learn to do the same thing. Her other two choices were to avoid the pool altogether or to do a wash, blow-dry, and curl every time she went in. She'd just have to tell the boys not to splash while she was swimming.

Lisa sat in a chaise longue and picked up the newspaper beside it, scanning the sale circulars. She didn't even notice Esther coming up the pool steps.

"Where's Darrell?" Esther asked as she toweled off.

Lisa began to feel a little irritated at constantly being questioned, but at the same time she knew she wasn't being fair. Of course the other members of their family would inquire about Darrell and Devon's whereabouts. "He took Devon out somewhere." She watched Esther's gaze turn curious as she sat in a matching chaise, and at that moment decided her mother-in-law was the best person for her to confide in.

"I'm afraid Darrell's a little upset with me, Ma Canfield," she admitted.

"You two looked fine last night. But of course," she added, "I've lived long enough to know how your whole life can change in a matter of a few seconds."

"Well, this isn't exactly a life-changing event. It's just that Darrell feels . . . Let me ask you, Ma Canfield. Have I given you the impression that I want Brad back or that I'm jealous of Suzanne?" As Lisa asked the question, she fully expected Esther to assure her she'd never thought no such thing, but the way Esther immediately averted her eyes suggested that wasn't what she thought at all. "Ma Canfield?" Lisa prompted.

"I wouldn't say you act like you want Brad back," Esther began, "but I do get the feeling you're jealous of Suzanne. Now, don't be upset with me," she cautioned. "I noticed it that day we drove down to check on the house and pick Paige up after Suzanne and Brad moved in. When you saw those marble countertops in the kitchen, that gorgeous patio, the outdoor fireplace and kitchen, the lagoon pool . . . Lisa, dear, it was all over your face. You wanted all that for yourself."

"Oh," she said softly. "I didn't realize." But even as she said the words, she knew in her heart that as much as she loved Darrell, she wished he made the money Brad made. Yes, she did feel that what Suzanne had should be hers, only with Darrell, not Brad, as a husband. In a deep pocket of her heart, she still resented Brad for wanting to have it both ways. He'd never complained when she was the primary breadwinner, working, raising Paige, and running their household by herself while he came home and collapsed into bed. She tried to talk to him about the decisions they had to make, but he always told her to handle it the way she felt was best. Then all of a sudden his residency was over, he had more time on his hands, and he expected her to consult him on every little thing. Those last months with him had been pure hell. Funny. It seemed like centuries ago. Darrell had been the one to put her broken heart back together, make her forget how hurt she'd been when Brad left her. She wouldn't trade him for anything.

She felt so guilty. She and Darrell had a good life together, surrounded by comforts and conveniences. She had no right to want more. And she'd never felt this way until Brad and Suzanne became their neighbors. She'd allowed herself to be caught up in a crazy cycle of the Jones syndrome. It didn't bother her that Ann and Bill Sorensen had a boat, but she hated seeing Brad's. How had this happened?

If Esther noticed her distress, she didn't comment on it. Instead she said, "I'm not saying I can't imagine how you must feel, Lisa. Your husband hires an attractive young girl to answer his phones at his office, and eventually that girl replaces you in his life. This type of thing happens all the time. I saw a movie on TV—actually it was *two* movies—based on a true story that happened out in California. A woman married to a very successful attorney became so incensed when he left her for his secretary that she stole their house key from one of their children, let herself in their house in the middle of the night, and shot both of them dead. I think her name was Betty Broderick. Of course, the way the movie depicted her, she had some kind of mental problem that coincided with the collapse of the marriage." She reached out and closed her hand around Lisa's upper arm. "I know I'd be terribly hurt if that happened to me. And I'm sure it's very selfish of me to say this, but I can't be too sorry Suzanne came along. If she hadn't, you wouldn't be my daughter-in-law. Darrell might have chosen a second wife I couldn't stomach any more than the first."

"You never cared much for Paula, did you, Ma Canfield?"

"No. I thought she was too young from the very beginning, and youth often means stupidity. I wasn't surprised when she got pregnant with Devon, but I had a bad feeling about them getting married."

"You were against it?"

"Not entirely, but I couldn't shake the feeling that Paula really wasn't ready to be a mother or a wife. But I didn't want my grandchild to be born out of wedlock, so I went along and just hoped I was wrong." Esther sighed. "It's very painful to see your child enter a marriage that you're sure will fail. And, of course, it did. By the time Devon turned two, Paula had grown bored and wanted out. By the time Devon turned three, Paula had run off to her friend's in Texas and left Devon for Darrell to raise. And he did a fabulous job."

Lisa smiled at the memory. "I remember he used to say the only things he *couldn't* do for a child was give birth and breast-feed, but that he had everything else covered."

"My son is a wonderful father," Esther said. "But that Paula, she's worthless. She's only there for Devon when it's convenient, like sending a check to buy Devon a car right after she loses her baby. Hmph. If she does have another baby, Devon will probably never hear from her again. But I don't think it'll happen. God don't like ugly, you know."

Lisa pointed out that Paula had indicated she would be sending a check before her miscarriage. "I guess the biggest worry is what kind of effect this will all have on Devon," Lisa said. "I hate to think of her growing up thinking it's right to show affection when it's beneficial for her and withhold it when it isn't."

"It wouldn't be a bad idea for you and Darrell to sit her down and talk to her about it."

Lisa's smile dissolved as she gazed at the clear aqua water of the pool. "Right now I can't picture Darrell and me sitting down to do anything, Ma Canfield. In all the years we've been together, I've never seen him so upset as he was last night. You know he never really gets mad, but I feel like there's something raging inside him, anger he didn't show to me but that I can *feel*"—she clenched her fists and held them in front of her chest—"and it terrifies me, Ma Canfield, because I've never seen it before. He didn't even tell me where he went with Devon. He's never done that before." She dropped her hands to her sides, letting them rest palms down on the edges of the chaise. "I feel so helpless, like my marriage is in danger of falling apart any minute and there's nothing I can do about it but stand and watch."

"I think you might be exaggerating just a little bit, Lisa," Esther said soothingly. "I hardly think your marriage is in jeopardy over this. Darrell's a man. You hurt his pride. I know that's a man's most vulnerable spot, but I'm sure he'll get over it. Especially if you watch what you say from now on," she added meaningfully.

Lisa felt better. Esther was probably right. In thirteen years together—nearly ten of them as husband and wife—most of the disagreements she and Darrell had were limited to minor disagreements here and there. She simply wasn't used to being on the outs with him. But even when they'd had arguments, he'd never looked so cold and unyielding as he had last night. This morning hadn't been much better.

It suddenly occurred to Lisa that Darrell must have told his mother about the check Paula sent, since *she* hadn't. Lisa wondered if Esther also knew where Darrell and Devon had gone, but pride wouldn't allow her to ask.

She'd just have to wait and see.

CHAPTER 30

If there is strife and contention in the home, very little else can
compensate for it.
—Lawanna Blackwell

Suzanne watched nervously as her mother and Brad walked back from the pier behind their house. They seemed to be companionable, but Brad seldom wore his emotions openly. She supposed it was part of being a doctor. You had to put on a good face to keep your patients' spirits up, even if they were dying.

She forced herself to concentrate on the latest romance she was reading. Surely she could do that for the sixty seconds it would take for them to get to where she sat on the lanai.

"I'm going to pull those weeds I saw growing this morning," Arlene said.

Suzanne noticed she was smiling. Did that mean Brad had agreed?

He took a seat opposite her, his knees far apart and body leaning slightly forward. "Your mother tells me she put in for a transfer to a Jacksonville post office," he said.

She kept her voice light. "She mentioned she wanted to do that because she misses me so much. You know we've always been close, but in the time since we moved up here she's had the opportunity to get used to my being in Jacksonville. She won't really go through with it."

"Well, guess again. She's been offered a position here at the Merrill Road Post Office."

"You're kidding!" It came out remarkably well, considering the news came as no surprise. Suzanne hated pretending, but she saw no other way to handle it.

"People at the post office retire all the time. Anyway, she's trying to work out the logistics. If she takes the job, she'll need to be at work the second week in August."

"That's just a few weeks away, Brad."

"I know, right around the start of school for Kenya. It presents a logistical nightmare."

"She's thinking about taking the job?"

"Yes, she is. Uh . . . she asked if she and Kenya could stay with us while she looks for an apartment. She's not going to sell the house. Derrick and Matthew will stay there." He chuckled. "They're actually going to pay the mortgage every month, if you can believe it."

At the moment she didn't care about her brothers. She just wanted to know what Brad had told her mother. "What'd you tell her, Brad?"

He looked out at the skyline for a few moments. "I told her I wouldn't object if you didn't, but that I feel we should put some kind of time limit on it."

Suzanne's mouth suddenly went dry. "Time limit?"

"Yeah, one month, two at the most. If we make that understood from the outset we won't have to worry about them still living with us six months from now. Things like that do happen, Suzanne."

She didn't get it. Why the hell had her mother been smiling like she was so happy if Brad said she could only stay with them until the middle of October? "Well, it's all right with me," she said. "I appreciate you allowing my mother and sister to stay with us. I know my family can be hard to deal with at times."

"It's all right. I'm glad we can help," he said. "I think it'll be good for Arlene and Kenya to get out of that house. It's time for your brothers to be on their own. Maybe now they'll take some responsibility, since there won't be anyone there to do for them." He shook his head. "To tell you the truth, it'll be a lot easier to live with your mother and sister than with your brothers. *They're* the ones who're hard to take. They're too damn old to be so irresponsible."

Suzanne swallowed hard. Things had gone from bad to worse. First Brad put a cap on the time her mother and Kenya could stay with them, and now he'd made it clear that the same door open to them was closed to Derrick and Matthew. So much for her mother's plan of having the boys join them later.

"Where'd they go, anyway?" Brad asked.

"They offered to go to the store for me."

"That's a first. I can't imagine them offering to go to the store unless you let them take the Lexus," he said with a laugh.

"I did."

Brad slapped his palms against his thighs. "You did *what?*"

"Nothing's going to happen to the car, Brad."

"That is a fifty-five-thousand-dollar car, Suzanne. You know how careless your brothers are. How could you just hand over the keys like that?" He glanced at his watch. "How long have they been gone?"

"Maybe a little longer than they should be, but—"

"See? Store, my ass. They're probably halfway to the beach by now if I know the two of them. You might not see them for hours. You're so gullible sometimes, Suzanne." He rose and disappeared into the house.

Suzanne blinked furiously, trying to hold back tears. Just last night she'd been on top of the world. How could everything fall apart so quickly? Her mother and sister would only be able to stay with them for a short time, and she had to face the possibility her brothers might damage their expensive new car. Brad was right. It didn't take this long to drive the few miles to Publix and back. All types of awful things might have happened. Whoever was driving—and she was sure they'd argued over who got to drive or who had driven longer—might be so busy profiling that they ran into a stopped car in front of them. They might even have gotten on the highway and be speeding dangerously.

She swung her eyes to one side of the chaise and got up. Derrick had a cell phone. She'd better get the number and call and find out where the hell they were.

Derrick claimed he and Matthew were on their way back. "There were a couple of things they didn't have at Publix," he said, "so we had to go to the Wal-Mart Supercenter."

"All the way out there?" She should have known. They had to take the Arlington Expressway to get to Wal-Mart, no doubt moving at a speed higher than the posted limit. "Well, just get back as soon as you can," she said. "Brad's a little anxious about the car."

It was another twenty minutes before they returned, toting blue plastic bags with "Wal-Mart" printed across one side in black letters. "I thought you went to Publix first," Suzanne said.

Matthew shrugged. "When we saw they were out of turkey breasts we just decided to get everything from one store. It seemed easier that way."

"Hey. I see you're back," Brad called from the adjoining family room. "Everything okay?"

"The car's fine, man," Derrick said.

"It rides great," Matthew said. "I know you just got it, but talk to me when you're ready to trade it in."

Suzanne shot a worried look Brad's way, afraid he might say something insulting, but he just glanced at Matthew with amusement and turned his attention back to the Sunday paper. The idea of Matthew, who had never owned a vehicle, coughing up enough money to buy a sports car, even a used one, was just plain silly, but she hoped Brad wouldn't say so. She knew how little patience he had for people who made ridiculous statements. That was why he'd deliberately misled Ernie Hickman last night when Ernie hinted so obviously about going along with them to Maine. Poor Ernie had looked downright comical in his shock when Brad said their vacation house could be rented. Even Flo had been obviously taken aback. Suzanne had been glad when Brad led her away, for she'd been tempted to burst out laughing. The more she saw of Ernie the more uncouth and raw he seemed, but Flo was her friend. Suzanne didn't want to hurt her feelings.

Suzanne had started dinner when Brad called out to her from the family room. "Hey, Suzie Q, put some of those shrimp on a plate for me, will you?"

"Sure." She turned to the refrigerator and began lifting the foil from the platters of leftovers. "That's funny," she said aloud.

"What's funny?"

"I don't see the shrimp. I'm sure I've gone through everything. Come to think of it, I don't see the crab and lobster cakes, either."

"Well, look again," Brad said. "They've got to be in there somewhere. There was a ton of it left last night."

"Maybe I missed them," she agreed. She began to repeat the task with no luck.

Brad joined her. "Find them?" he asked.

"No. Brad, I'm wondering . . . well, when the boys left they asked if they could take some food so they wouldn't have to fix dinner. I told them it was all right—"

"Oh, shit. Don't tell me they walked off with all that shrimp."

"The lobster and crab too, I'm afraid."

He slammed his palm on the counter. "Damn it! I'm sick of your brothers, Suzanne. Who the fuck do they think they are, coming to my house and walking off with the best food? What'd they leave for us, raw vegetable sticks?"

"I'm sorry, Brad."

"I know it's not your fault, but the next time I see those two I'm going to tell them about themselves."

"I can still fix you a plate, but it'll be wings, mini-quiches, and stuffed phyllo dough, things like that."

"Go ahead." He headed back for the family room.

After Suzanne had fixed Brad's snack and gotten dinner started, she went to talk to her mother, who was busy tending to the numerous flowering plants that lined the front of the house. "Mom, what's going on? Brad told me the longest you and Kenya can stay here is two months, and he doesn't want the boys to come at all. Why'd you look so happy?"

"Because he said we can stay," Arlene replied matter-of-factly. "Once we get here, I can come up with a way to extend it, no matter what Brad says."

"I don't know about that, Mom. Brad generally sticks to his guns."

"Not when his mother-in-law is concerned. Don't worry, dear. You just leave it to me. When it comes to these things I know what'll happen. Didn't I tell you your friend's son would invite Kenya to stay there when you and I left?"

Suzanne felt her mother's prediction regarding Gregory Hickman and Kenya was just a lucky guess anyone could have made. Gregory was clearly enchanted with Kenya. Of course he wouldn't want her to leave. She wasn't convinced that Brad would relent, and she only saw disappointment in store for her mother. She sighed heavily and prepared to go back into the house. When she got to her front door, she glanced next door at Lisa's. Lisa's mother-in-law already lived with them, so she obviously didn't have any problems in that area. Hell, Lisa probably didn't have any problems at all.

* * *

Lisa decided to calm her nerves by mixing and shaping salmon cakes for dinner. Ordinarily she hated putting her hands in the sticky mixture, but this afternoon she wanted to be busy.

Where *was* Darrell? Three-thirty and not a peep from him. She wondered if he'd be home for dinner.

Paige wandered into the kitchen for about the tenth time, carrying a balled-up load of laundry. "Mom, when's Devon and Darrell coming back?"

"I don't know, Paige," Lisa said in a carefully measured tone.

"Well, where'd they go?"

"I don't know, Paige."

"Why are you talking so funny?"

"I don't know, Paige," she repeated a second time in the exact same modulation. She sighed in relief when Paige continued on to the laundry room and left her in peace.

"We're home!"

Lisa looked up expectantly as Devon and Darrell entered the kitchen. "Hi! I was wondering if you'd gotten lost. You two have been gone a long time."

"Guess what?" Devon said excitedly. "Daddy bought me a car!"

Lisa raised an eyebrow. *Daddy* bought her a car? "He did?"

"Well, Mom helped," Devon admitted.

Mom? *Mom?* "Yes, I know about the check she sent," Lisa said tightly. She glanced at Darrell, who had reached for a bag of potato chips on top of the refrigerator and was nonchalantly munching on them, his expression impassive.

"And guess what, Lisa?" Devon continued, oblivious to Lisa's tenseness. "It's a Mustang!"

Lisa? She merely stared at her daughter.

"Oh, I'm sorry," Devon said. "It's just that I get confused when I get excited. I didn't mean to call you Lisa. I meant to call you Mom." She beamed. "I guess I've got *two* moms."

Lisa smacked the salmon cake she was forming with so much force the fragile mixture fell apart on the plate. *Before Paula sent that check, you had only one mother,* she thought bitterly.

"Wait 'til you see it." Devon was still unaware of Lisa's distress. "It's royal blue, and it has a moonroof, just like Paige's Cruiser. It's *gorgeous.*"

"Sounds lovely." Lisa's voice cracked a bit. She quickly cleared her throat to cover.

"We couldn't finalize the deal today because it's Sunday," Devon said, "but they'll do everything tomorrow, and I should be able to get it on Tuesday." She hopped up and down like she'd just won the lottery. "I've got to go tell Paige." She ran off in the direction of their respective bedrooms, calling her sister's name.

Lisa was happy to see her go. She wanted a chance to talk to Darrell privately.

"So you got Devon a car," she said to him.

"Yeah, we got a good deal."

"Exactly how good a deal did 'we' get, if you don't mind my asking?" She shrugged. "But I guess it really isn't any of my business, since you and *Paula* got it for her."

"Don't be so touchy, Lisa. Devon didn't mean anything by that, and you know it."

"Well, pardon me for finding it ironic that 'Paula' "—she held up her fingers like quote marks—"suddenly becomes 'Mom' again after she springs for the down payment."

"It's a little more than just the down payment, Lisa. She paid for almost half the car."

Her eyes narrowed into slits. "Oh, so that makes it all right?"

"I didn't mean it that way. Listen, I don't see what the big deal is. We already talked about doing this for Devon."

"Yes, *we* did, but I had no idea *you* were doing it today. If you recall, you were very careful not to fill me in on your plans when you left this morning."

Darrell replaced the plastic clip that held the bag of chips closed, tossed it back on the fridge, and silently went out the way he'd come in, leaving her to glare after him.

CHAPTER 31

"What you take when you can no longer take what you've been taking."
—Earl Wilson, on vacation

Brad liked watching Suzanne brush her hair. She did it the exact same way every night as part of her before-bed ritual, kneeling on the bed in her nightgown and first vigorously brushing the left, then the right, and then lowering her head and brushing from the nape. He could say this much for his wife—she really took good care of herself. She looked great. And she didn't slather a lot of oily stuff all over her face at night or come to bed wearing rollers or a rag tied around her hair like some slave. She insisted on covering their pillows with slippery satin pillowcases to protect her hair, but he'd gotten used to them.

He smiled when his favorite part came—she tossed her head back and her hair flew up, then into place. It was just like the scene from that old movie with Rita Hayworth, the one they showed in the scene from *The Shawshank Redemption* that had driven all the prisoners wild. "Is your scalp tingling?" he asked.

"Mmm."

"This thing I'm watching will be over in about twenty minutes."

"All right." She slid under the sheets and picked up her latest romance novel.

"I'll probably be a little late getting home tomorrow. I've got a few things to finish up before we go," he said.

"Mom wanted to know if she could move some things in while we're away," Suzanne remarked matter-of-factly.

"Absolutely not. I don't want your mother snooping around my house when I'm not here. I can just see her driving the Jag, and I'm sure Derrick and Matthew would love to get their hands on the keys to the Lexus. Forget it, Suzanne. We'll only be gone ten days. Let her move in when we get back. All she and Kenya have to bring are their clothes, not furniture or anything heavy. They can do that in one trip."

"My mother wouldn't snoop around, Brad," Suzanne said indignantly. "If anything, I thought you'd like the idea of having someone here all the time to keep an eye on the house."

"That's why we have an alarm system, Suzanne. Besides, we have three vehicles. We can easily park two of them in the driveway. And Paige will be in and out."

"Yes, and so will Lisa, I'm sure."

He cast her a sidelong glance. "What's that supposed to mean?"

She shrugged. "Just a hunch. I've got a feeling that Lisa's the one who'll be doing all the, as you put it, 'snooping around,' courtesy of Paige."

"That's ridiculous, Suzanne. Lisa's not the snoopy type, for one thing; and Paige knows better than to let anyone who's not a member of the immediate family go wandering through our home. Your mother, on the other hand, will be driving the Jaguar and handing the keys to the Lexus to Kenya or your brothers if they show up. Pardon me for saying this, but I happen to have more faith in my daughter than in your mother."

Suzanne exhaled loudly before returning her attention back to her book.

Lisa's curiosity soon overpowered the guilt she felt. She knew she had no business in Brad and Suzanne's master bathroom, but it was breathtaking, and almost as large as the bedroom itself. It had to be, or else they'd trip over the large hexagon-shaped island in its center whenever they moved. She and Darrell had his-and-her sinks, but they were on the same side and separated only by maybe two feet of countertop. Brad and Suzanne each had an entire mirrored wall to themselves. Suzanne's portion included a built-in vanity, and like the kitchen the countertops were granite, as was the top of the island.

Their walk-in closets—two of them, unlike the single large closet she and Darrell shared—were actually inside of the bathroom. Lisa allowed herself to peek only because the sliding doors had been left open. The built-in shelving, drawers, and shoe racks had probably come with the house as an optional upgrade. She and Darrell had theirs installed after they moved in.

It seemed like a natural thing to do, offering to go along with Paige when she noted she hadn't checked her father's house yet today. The sun was setting, and it was such a large house. If it had been earlier in the day, Lisa wouldn't have thought anything of it, but she hadn't liked the idea of Paige going over there alone just before dark. When she said as much, Paige suggested she come along.

The house seemed so quiet and still when they walked in. Buster, Brad's beagle, had flown to Maine with the rest of the family, so there was no barking to greet them. They both gasped aloud when the lights suddenly snapped on in the kitchen, living room, and family room. Then Paige laughed. "It's the timer," she said between chuckles. "But you know what, Mom? I'm glad you came with me."

"Me, too. But tomorrow you make sure you get here earlier. And bring Devon with you. I'd feel better. I don't like the idea of you checking all these rooms by yourself, even if it's two in the afternoon." She rubbed the back of Paige's neck affectionately. "Are you sure you wouldn't rather be up in Maine with your father than here at home? You don't feel left out or anything, do you?"

"Definitely. Maine is pretty and everything, and I liked going up there when I was younger, but now there's not much for me to do, and nobody to do anything with. It's worse than Daddy's old house in Saint Augustine."

"I'm surprised Suzanne didn't bring her sister along to keep you company."

"I asked Daddy if she could come, but he said that would create a problem because Missus Hall would want to come, too, and so would Derrick and Matthew. I even asked if Devon could come, but he said Suzanne would complain about that, too."

"That sounds like Suzanne, all right," Lisa said with a smile.

She would have been content to sit in the living room while Paige checked the various rooms, but Paige insisted she come along, saying she was afraid to do it alone. So Lisa got to see the private areas of Brad and Suzanne's house: the laundry room with its tomato-red walls and front-loading washer and dryer on a back-saving platform, Bradley's primary color-decorated bedroom and Lauren's frilly pink one, the guest rooms, the huge playroom upstairs with its colorful circus scene wall mural and comfortable oversized U-shaped sectional in the middle of the room, air-pop popcorn maker, and built-in handsome mahogany shelving for the twin computers and the large flat screen TV. It even had a miniature Simmons Beautyrest mattress in one corner for Buster. Buying a mattress for a dog struck Lisa as sloppy spending, but she'd never been particularly fond of dogs. The twins, accustomed to playing with Buster as well as the pets of other kids on the block, had been asking for a puppy of their own. She and Darrell had already agreed to surprise them with one for their birthday in December, but he'd sleep on the floor someplace.

She was equally impressed by the exercise room. *No wonder Brad is in such great shape,* she thought as she eyed the Bowflex, treadmill, stationary bicycle, and stepper. He had the equivalent of a private gym right here in his home. A wall-mounted TV and watercooler provided maximum comfort while exercising. She and Darrell had a treadmill in the small nook off their private bath, but she was the only one who used it. He went in there strictly to check the stock market on the computer.

I'm not being disloyal, she assured herself. *I'm just pointing out the truth.* So what if Suzanne had granite-topped counters in a bathroom large enough to play ball in. So what if Bradley and Lauren had a playroom all to themselves equipped with two computers, rather than a much smaller bonus room that all four of her own kids shared and constantly argued about who got to use the lone computer. So what if Darrell was starting to get a little thick through the middle and Brad was buff. None of that meant she wanted Brad back. Still, she'd better not be too enthusiastic if Darrell asked her what she thought of Brad's place. He'd apologized to her for being so secretive and said it was only because he'd been upset. On the surface, everything seemed all right between them, but she still felt an underlying tension whenever Brad's name came up, and she didn't want to aggravate it. Darrell had even stopped going out on Brad's boat, instead taking the twins out in the paddleboat. The situation was definitely awkward, but she felt confident that in time the bad feelings would fade.

"Are you ready?" she said to Paige.

"Yes, let's go. This place feels really creepy when it's empty and quiet." After reactivating the security alarm, Paige held the key poised to latch the front door behind them.

Lisa turned to watch as Paige locked the door, then instinctively tried to turn the knob. "Okay, it's done," Paige said. They turned around to face the street, ready to cross the grass to their own house.

And found themselves being watched from across the street by Flo Hickman.

"This is nice, isn't it?" Flo said, reaching for Ernie's hand as they strolled the beach at Destin.

"It's all right. It's costing a damn arm and a leg. What was wrong with Daytona?"

"Because Destin is one of the nicest beaches in Florida, a lot cleaner than Daytona. More like Aruba, where we're supposed to be. Besides, summer is the best time to come here. In January the rates will triple."

"I wish Brad had invited us to go to Maine."

"Listen, we couldn't have gone anyway. I already told Suzanne we had reservations for Aruba this week. What would it look like if we'd canceled to go to Maine? I'll tell you," she continued, not waiting for him to reply, "it would've looked like we had no reservations in the first place. People don't up and do things like that. So you should just forget it." Sometimes her husband behaved like a little kid. She couldn't believe he was still hung up on going to Maine after what Brad had said at the party.

"Yeah, I guess so. It's just that we're spending so much money."

"We aren't spending all that much, no more than you do on all that stuff you buy to impress the neighbors."

"We've got a reputation to protect, Flo."

"Not if it's going to put us in the poorhouse," she hissed.

"All right, all right. I haven't bought anything lately."

"You just spent three hundred dollars on a stereo from Costco last week, just because George bought a Bose Wave CD player. There wasn't anything wrong with our old stereo. Ernie, we're in serious debt. We maxed out ten grand on one card, and we're getting close to the five grand limit on another. Even with the money we make, we can't keep up with debt reduction the way we should. We still owe fifteen hundred on the home theater."

"Ah, that ain't nothing. We'll have that paid off in no time."

"It's taking a long time. After we finish paying the mortgage, our car notes, plus Gregory's car, the credit cards, and the rest of our monthly expenses, there's not a lot left, even with the overtime I've been working. This time next year we'll have college tuition for Gregory." She sighed. "I wish you had better health insurance. They take an awful lot out of your check. And my job charges even more."

"That might get better soon."

"How? Are they getting a different plan?"

"Sort of. The rumor mill says we're going to merge with our competitor here in Jacksonville. A bigger company should be able to offer a better benefits package."

Flo caught her breath in her throat. "Merge? What does that mean for your job?"

"Right now the whole thing's just a rumor, but if it happens I'll be fine. The company will be double, so they'll need enough people to handle all the staff. Even if they don't, I've got more seniority than the HR manager at the other company." He rubbed his stomach when it made a growling noise. "Come on, this salt water is making me hungry. Let's see if we can grab a cheap lunch."

CHAPTER 32

What some invent and the rest enlarge.
—Jonathan Swift, on gossip

"Thanks so much for stopping by, Ann, Bill," Lisa said to her neighbors. "I'm sorry you couldn't stay longer."

"We are, too," Bill Sorensen said, "but I've got an early meeting in the morning with a new client."

"And we really need to check on our brood," Ann added.

"I understand. My birthday would have to fall on a Sunday this year. I guess everybody else will be leaving in the next hour or so. Good night, y'all." Lisa waved to her neighbors. She liked the Sorensens. They'd been friendly from the day they moved in, coming over to introduce themselves and bringing brownies Ann had made. Ann and Bill came over whenever she and Darrell had a get-together and in turn invited them whenever they entertained. Lisa gave them credit, for it wasn't every white person who felt comfortable in a house full of black folks. Darrell had joked privately that it was like living next door to Hillary and that other Bill, the Clintons.

Darrell had also teased her about turning forty-three. He wouldn't be forty-two until September second, so for the next couple of weeks the one-year difference in their ages seemed like two. But Lisa welcomed his joviality. Relations between them had been strained since the night of Brad's party two weeks ago, and his giving this birthday celebration for her suggested they were on the mend. Ma Canfield's birthday was the day before hers, and they'd all celebrated by going to dinner at a seafood restaurant in Mandarin that Darrell and the twins knew from having gone there with Brad one day while they were out on the boat. The restaurant turned out to be every bit as nice as they said it was, and they all enjoyed it.

Except Devon, who wasn't there. To everyone's surprise, Paula had gone ahead and made reservations for Devon to visit her in Texas the latter half of July, which had been the original plan. Lisa and Darrell both felt a little sad to see Devon get on the airplane and take off, but they were undeniably happy for her. Lisa expected Paula to come up with some feeble excuse for canceling the visit after she lost her baby, that the check she'd sent for Devon's car was meant solely as a consolation prize.

The dual events of Devon getting a car of her own and Gregory Hickman dating Suzanne's sister Kenya had served to restore the girls' friendship. Once more they were in and out of each other's rooms and could be heard giggling through closed doors. Lisa hoped they'd learned their lesson as far as letting any boy come between them.

Kim, Michael, and Alicyn Gillespie were the last to leave, along with Ben and Stacy Prince. Lisa and Darrell walked them outside, and her eyes wandered to Brad's house next door. Paige said they were due back today. From this angle, she couldn't tell if their Escalade was in the driveway, and if they were home they probably parked it in the garage anyway to make bringing in their bags easier. The lights, set with timers, had been on every night from dusk until eleven or so, so that gave no clues. They'd been gone a week and a half, and although Lisa didn't see them every day, just knowing they were far away gave her a wonderful carefree feeling.

Just like knowing they were back made her feel heavy-hearted.

Suzanne stretched lazily on the sectional in the kids' playroom upstairs. "It's good to be home."

"Yes, it is," Flo agreed. They'd just finished working out in the exercise room next door and were now enjoying a snack of lemonade and popcorn.

"That's right, you were away, too. Did you enjoy Aruba?"

"Oh, it was wonderful. Very quiet. We didn't do a whole lot of anything, just walked on the beach, went for drinks at night. Naturally, we dropped a bundle in the casino."

"It doesn't really matter if you don't do anything special," Suzanne said. "What's most important is that you do it someplace other than home."

"I agree. I just wish I hadn't left my camera in that restaurant. Such a beautiful place, and no pictures to remember it by." The lie rolled off Flo's lips with surprising ease. This would be her safety mechanism. She and Ernie couldn't show photographs of a trip they hadn't taken if their camera had been lost. "So did Paige stay here while you were away?"

"No, but Brad asked her to keep an eye on things. Even with the alarm and the timers automatically turning the lights on and off, he says it's still good to have someone do a physical check. Did you see her going in or out and think she was staying here?"

"Yes, I saw her and Lisa coming out."

"Lisa? You saw Lisa coming out of *my* house?"

"Yes. I was out walking the night before we left, and I saw them coming out as I was passing by. Lisa looked . . . well, she had this look on her face like she was dazzled."

Suzanne's jaws immediately began to ache. "What dazzled her was probably my bedroom, my bathroom, my exercise room, and everything else there is to see in my house. That bitch! She probably couldn't wait for me to leave town so she could get all into my business. Doggone it, I *told* Brad that would happen."

Flo leaned forward eagerly. She'd hoped she'd be able to casually work into the conversation her sighting of Lisa leaving Suzanne's house. Suzanne's reaction was more volatile than she expected. "What do you think Brad'll say?" she prodded.

"He'll probably say she was just looking out for Paige. He's always sticking up for her."

"I guess that drives you nuts," Flo said.

"You're damn right it does." Suzanne grasped her hands tightly together. "Look at me, I'm getting all upset. I guess there's no point. There's nothing I can do about it now, and I already know Brad won't say anything." She relaxed, loosening her grip on her hands, and sighed. "I've got a lot to do this week. My mother and sister are moving to Jacksonville; they're going to be staying with us for a while."

"Yes, I know. Gregory mentioned it. He's been talking to Kenya on the phone pretty often since they met. He's really looking forward to her moving up here."

"I'm looking forward to it myself," Suzanne said, smiling.

CHAPTER 33

The road to hell is paved with good intentions.
—George Bernard Shaw

Paula couldn't remember the last time she'd felt so happy. She'd taken a week off from her position as manager of a reservations call center to spend with her daughter. They did something together every day: the mall, the bowling alley, even a trip to Six Flags Astroworld.

Andre made his displeasure about the matter known in his subtle manner. He treated Devon politely, but whenever Paula asked him if he wanted to join them in the evening or on the weekend he always had an excuse ready. Once they were alone, he projected a decidedly chilly demeanor.

She knelt beside him on the floor as he laid on his bare back, clasped hands supporting the back of his head, and repeatedly raised to touch his elbow to the opposite raised knee. "Your body's in prime shape, Andre," she said admiringly, reaching out to lightly stroke his well-developed chest and his flat stomach. He was such a handsome man. She shifted into a reclining position next to him and used her most alluring tone. "I hope you plan on sharing it with me tonight."

"No, I don't want it to interfere with your time with Devon."

Taken aback, she straightened her spine. "You're being silly. Our making love has nothing to do with my spending time with Devon, and you know it."

He continued his exercise with annoying precision, performing four crunches before bothering to even answer her. "I'm just trying to be considerate, Paula. I don't want you to be too tired to spend time with your child."

So that was it. He hated the fact that her daughter lived and breathed while their baby had died. "I'm not going to apologize for having a child, Andre, if that's what you're waiting for. I know you blame me for losing the baby, but that's not right. It was an accident."

"I didn't say it was your fault, you just *said* I did."

She let out an exasperated sigh and got up. "One thing I don't understand," she said as she settled into bed, "how am I supposed to get pregnant again if we don't have sex?"

He stopped mid-rise, then quickly resumed the exercise. At least she'd gotten a reaction from him, but Paula felt no victory, only sadness. He had changed from the man who had once professed adoration and love for her to one consumed by bitterness, jealousy, and an obsession with having a baby. She suspected his parents and their almost fanatical wish for grandchildren were the root of the problem. They were probably nagging him to death. She wished they would butt out.

When he climbed into bed and positioned himself on his side facing the other direction, she considered for the first time the possibility that their marriage might not survive.

On the way back from Six Flags, Devon started complaining of belly pain. At first Paula wasn't worried. "We did eat a lot of junk food," she reminded her daughter.

"Yeah, I guess so."

"When we get home you take an Alka-Seltzer and go to bed. You'll feel better in the morning."

But Devon didn't feel better. She emerged from the guest room while Paula and Andre were having breakfast. "Mom, the pain's gotten sharper," she said weakly, her palm resting on her right abdomen and her body bent forward at the waist.

"It's probably just indigestion," Andre said in a dismissive manner. "Why don't you sit down and have some breakfast? It'll probably take the pain away."

"No!" The forcefulness of Paula's tone came as a surprise to her own ears. "It's more than that. She's practically doubling over." She wiped her mouth with a napkin and got up from the table, plate in hand. "Devon, I'm going to take you to the emergency room."

"Come on, Paula, you're overreacting," Andre said with a scowl. "You'll end up spending the whole day in the ER while they do a bunch of expensive, unnecessary tests. We were supposed to go to the show later, remember?"

She spun around so quickly she nearly dropped her plate. "Devon isn't feeling well, Andre. That takes precedence over everything for me, even your plans to see a movie." She placed her plate in the sink and put a palm to her daughter's forehead. "You feel warm, Devon. But we won't stop to confirm you've got a fever. We'll let them take your temperature at the hospital. Come on, let's go."

In the car, Devon continued to clutch her left lower abdomen. Paula saw tears of pain in her eyes, which only made her own anger flare. How dare Andre suggest it was merely a case of indigestion?

"Andre doesn't like my being here, does he, Mom?"

Paula had dreaded this question, but she'd been expecting it. Devon was no dummy. She'd have to be missing a few brain cells not to pick up on his cavalier attitude toward her discomfort. "I'm afraid my husband is going through a me-me-me phase," she said. "It all seems to have started when I lost the baby."

"Believe me, Mom, it started before that."

Paula simply couldn't bring herself to agree aloud, although she did feel Devon's assessment was dead on. "I think it's painful for him to see anyone with their children right now, even me."

"I'm really sorry about what happened to you, Mom. And I wish it hadn't happened on my birthday."

"I know you do, sweetheart. It doesn't seem fair to be that far along and then have something happen to your baby so suddenly." She sighed. "I guess that was God's way of telling me I'd done wrong to the child I already had. I'll never forgive myself, Devon, for shunting you off to the background like I did."

"Mom—"

"No, don't say anything to try to make me feel better. I know what I did hurt you, and when you started calling me Paula I realized just how much. You give as good as you get, Devon. Sometimes that's what it takes to open someone's eyes. Thank goodness it wasn't too late for me to reclaim my status as your mother."

"No, but I still call Lisa 'Mom,' too," Devon said, sounding meek because of her pain. "This whole thing really made me think, and it occurred to me that Lisa's the one who raised me. People think of me as Lisa Canfield's daughter." She smiled, suddenly realizing that she and her stepmother shared a surname. Paige was the outsider in their household, the only one named Betancourt. Not that it really mattered because they were all family, from her grandmother right down to her twin brothers. Paige would always be her best friend. "I hope you don't mind my doing that."

"Well, maybe just a little," Paula admitted. "But I can't deny the major role Lisa played in raising you, along with your grandmother, and of course your father. We can't forget him." She tried to chuckle, but it didn't come out right. She gazed at the road in front of her. Her parents and Darrell's parents had been right sixteen years ago. They'd married too young, or at least *she* had. She'd allowed Devon to stay in Darrell's care simply because she didn't want to cope with the challenges of being a single parent, of arranging for baby-sitters every time she wanted to go somewhere. She'd been young and selfish, and because of that she now had to share her daughter with Lisa.

Two-and-a-half hours later, Paula called Andre from the hospital. "They sent Devon for a scan of her abdomen and pelvis. They just got the results back," she said. "That little tummy-ache you said she had is actually appendicitis."

"Oh! Paula, I had no idea."

"Yes, I'm sure you didn't. Fortunately, I followed my own instincts."

The air was heavy with silence until Andre finally asked, "So they're going to remove her appendix?"

"I'm sure they will in the end, but right now they're waiting for a surgeon to consult. So I'm going to be here for a while." She waited expectantly, praying he would say he'd be right over to wait with her.

"Well, it doesn't take long to do an appendectomy, only about forty minutes."

"And your point is?" she asked in a voice that could freeze Prestone.

"Ah . . . tell you what," he said. "It'll probably be a little while before the consult shows up. Let me finish washing the car and change clothes, and I'll come by with some lunch for you and we'll wait together. I can be there in about an hour."

Her breath came out in a relieved torrent. "That'll work."

"In the meantime, you need to call Darrell and let him know."

"I've already called him."

"Oh? You called him before you called me?"

"Devon is his child, Andre. Of course I called him right away."

"I realize that, but I'm your husband now, not Darrell. A few minutes' delay wouldn't have made any difference. He's too far away to do anything about it."

"Puh-leese. Ever since Devon's been here you've been distancing yourself from me. When she said she was sick you tried to downplay it. And now you have the nerve to get insulted because I called her father first when I found out she needs surgery? Like you said, it was only a matter of a few minutes between calling him and calling you. So what if Darrell's in Florida and can't hop in the car and come right over? It's not like *you're* dropping what you're doing to rush down here. I'm in the emergency room. If you come I'll be happy to see you. Good-bye, Andre."

She hung up, seething. She'd never seen a more insecure person in her life, male or female. Andre simply couldn't accept he couldn't come first for her in all matters. She was trying to be patient only because she knew her own role in his attitude. By agreeing not to invite Devon to visit during the past year, she had condoned his actions. Nothing, even putting her foot down about being separated from her daughter again, would ever change that. She'd never forgive herself for what she'd done, regardless of her good intentions. Instead of placating him, she should have tried to convince him that Devon was an enhancement to their family, not a threat.

She had an odd feeling that Devon's hospitalization and surgery would be the catalyst for the lies to end and the truth to come out.

CHAPTER 34

"God gives us our relatives—thank God we can choose our friends."
—Ethel Watts Mumford

Suzanne gasped. Kenya's bedroom was in complete disarray. She'd been up for hours, but her double bed remained unmade. The carpet could barely be seen through the clothing-littered floor. Suzanne hadn't realized her little sister was so sloppy. Well, while she was staying here she'd have to stop spending so much time in front of the mirror in favor of a little more time with a dust cloth and vacuum.

Suzanne thought Bradley had been exaggerating when he complained that the bathroom was a mess in the week since Kenya and their mother had moved in, but if Kenya treated the bathroom like she did her room, Bradley certainly had a legitimate protest. Suzanne rarely checked the bathroom in the kids' wing, leaving it to the housekeeper to take care of. Now that she thought of it, Teresita had been around working later than usual last week, probably because of the mess.

Suzanne returned the door to the partially closed position she'd found it in, then out of curiosity checked the bathroom. No big mess there, but Teresita had just been in yesterday, so Kenya had had little time to create one.

Suzanne sighed. It looked like she'd have to sit Kenya down for a little chat. Looking good would go a long way toward catching a man, but being a slob wouldn't help her keep him.

Suzanne recalled that as a child her own inclination leaned toward untidiness. By the time she was an adolescent, she decided she liked things neat. Not that her personal preference had nothing to do with it. Her mother demanded she keep her room clean, and that was that. But Suzanne knew older mothers tended to be more lenient with their children, and her mother probably hadn't had the stamina to repeat orders over and over again to a strong-willed child, especially since she was raising that child by herself.

Suzanne's parents had separated when she was six. They reconciled a few years later, had Derrick and Matthew, then split for good. Kenya hadn't been born until years later, after a brief affair of Arlene's. Anyone who lived in Palatka knew that even though Kenya used the surname Hall she had a different father. Here in Jacksonville, Suzanne saw no reason for anyone to know about their mother's indiscretion. Some people might see Kenya's out-of-wedlock birth as a detriment, especially the type of family she hoped Kenya would eventually marry into.

Flo seemed to be pushing Gregory toward Kenya pretty strongly, but the Hickmans weren't the type of family Suzanne wanted for Kenya's in-laws. Suzanne regarded Flo and Ernie as ordinary people who'd made a little money and constructed a halfway decent house, but who obviously lacked true taste. Ernie's sometimes boorish behavior and the way their house was stuffed with furniture and knickknacks attested to that. Not that Suzanne minded Kenya going out with Gregory. He was a nice enough young man, with none of his father's crudeness. He'd probably end up being her prom date next spring. But if Kenya didn't develop better habits, she'd end up marrying someone like him and living in an overcrowded trophy house of her own, when she could do so much better.

It had only been a week, but Suzanne feared it had been a mistake to allow her mother and sister to move in. Her mother was drinking to excess, and Brad had threatened to start locking the cabinet where they kept the alcohol. Kenya's sloppiness was disruptive. Even the normally complacent Lauren had complained about all the cosmetics crowding the counters and the clothes on the bathroom floor. Worst of all, Derrick and Matthew, instead of enjoying free reign of the house in Palatka the way she thought they would, were coming up to visit today and would spend the night. Brad's features had hardened when Suzanne gave him the news. She knew he was thinking the same thing she was—that they would be up every weekend for the next two months. She sensed a blowup coming.

When she mentioned the visit to her mother, Arlene had merely shrugged. "They have to bring me my mail."

"You could have arranged to have it forwarded, Mom. Or the boys could mail it to you, at least the important stuff."

"Oh. I didn't think of that. But I don't want to tell Derrick and Matthew they can't come, Suzanne. They like it here in Jacksonville."

Suzanne knew what her mother was thinking. What harm could there be in the boys coming up for the weekend when they had so much room? The situation had quickly gotten out of hand.

She found that the laundry she'd been doing when she peeked into Kenya's room helped her think. Funny, but while she allowed Teresita to wash just about everything else, she didn't like anyone else handling her lingerie or Brad's underwear.

She'd been plagued with fear that something would go terribly wrong ever since the night of their party, when she learned that finding this house had been a mere coincidence and not a plot on Brad's part. She felt ashamed of herself for her secret plan to get her family here. She didn't want to open the proverbial can of worms by confessing what she'd done to Brad. She'd apologize to him for her family's intrusion the first chance she got. She loved her mother, her sister, and her brothers, and she wanted the best for them . . . but not if it meant them coming between her and her husband.

She was putting the newly dried and folded undergarments away when Brad entered their bedroom, the front of his T-shirt wet with sweat and a towel around his neck. Despite his post-workout state, she hastily put the stack of clothing down and wrapped her arms around his waist. "I'm so sorry, Brad," she said. "I honestly didn't think my family being here would cause . . . so much stress for us."

"I did. That's why I told your mother she'd have to find her own place within sixty days. But don't worry, Suzie Q. I think we can survive another seven weeks. Then we'll get our home back to ourselves." He gently removed her arms. "Come on, you don't want to get all sweaty." He went to his highboy, removing fresh underwear. "That was a good workout. Why don't I take you out to lunch after I get changed, just the two of us? Your mother can watch the kids."

"Sure." In spite of his assurance, she nonetheless looked after him with a worried expression as he went to take a shower. She'd have to break it to her mother that she'd have to forget about trying to extend the time she spent here with them, that she'd have to find an apartment and move into it on time. And she had to talk to her sister about her being such a pig.

"Kenya," Suzanne said as she joined her sister in the family room, "you've got to stop being so messy. A family of four could be living under all those clothes on your floor."

Kenya looked up from the *Sister to Sister* magazine she held. "Oh, that. I'm going to clean it up. As soon as I get back from Saint Augustine."

"What's in Saint Augustine?"

"Gregory has to go down there for something, and he asked me to go along with him. I just love riding in that VW Bug of his."

"Didn't you say you're going to the show tonight?"

"Yes, but that's not 'til later."

Suzanne sighed. "Kenya, I'm afraid you'll either have to skip the movie or Saint Augustine."

"Why? I said I'd clean my room."

"I know you, Kenya. When you get back you'll say you have to go get your nails done. Then when you get back after that you'll say your nails need more time to really get dry all the way through. Then you'll be showered, changed, and out of here to the movies with Gregory. And your room will look just the way it does now."

"Suzanne, I promise I'll clean it up."

Suzanne felt herself weakening. "Tell you what. Go ahead and go this afternoon. But if you don't have that mess cleaned up by the time Gregory comes to pick you up tonight, you don't go to the movies. Deal?"

Kenya broke into a grin. "Deal!"

"Mom, can you keep an eye on Bradley and Lauren?" Suzanne asked. "Brad and I are gonna go out for a bit."

"Sure, no problem. I'm going to be tending to my perennials anyway, so I'll watch them," Arlene replied. "The kids are outside somewhere. So where're you and Brad off to?"

Suzanne had her answer ready. "We have a lunch date. Last week was pretty frantic. We didn't get to spend a lot of time together." She felt her answer was forthright as a dental drill, but her mother's next words proved she'd missed the point.

"Derrick and Matthew will be here soon," Arlene said. "I'm sure they'd have wanted to go with you."

"I'm sure they'd like to," Suzanne noted wryly, "but they couldn't have, even if they were here already. The whole point is for Brad and me to have some time alone. That's why our children aren't going." Sometimes her mother could really be dense. How could she possibly think they would take Derrick and Matthew out to lunch and leave Bradley and Lauren, their own children, behind at home?

"Oh, I see," Arlene said briskly. "Well, stop and pick up a bottle of Beefeater on your way back, will you?"

"Uh . . . I'm sure we're not out of it, Mom. We had a full bottle just last weekend."

"I don't think so. It's empty, and no way did I drink an entire fifth just since last weekend."

"I don't want to argue with you, Mom," she said softly.

"Oh, never mind. I'll just drink the Grey Goose."

Suzanne enjoyed lunch. Brad had wanted to go to that Middle Eastern place in the Publix shopping center, but didn't object when she protested, saying she really didn't care for the cuisine. Brad had developed a taste for it from his colleagues at the hospital who hailed from that part of the world, and she saw no reason why he couldn't enjoy it over lunch with them. She suggested Thai, but the restaurants specializing in that cuisine didn't open until later in the day to serve dinner. They ended up going to Applebee's for all the rib tips they could eat. They held hands as they left the restaurant. Suzanne felt young and carefree, and very much in love. She took time out to say a prayer of thanks that her marriage hadn't been damaged by her deception . . . and of gratefulness for her second chance. She wouldn't let her family get to her over the next seven weeks, and she wouldn't give in if her mother tried to convince her to let them stay on.

Upon returning home, she refused to be rattled when Derrick and Matthew both grilled her about where she and Brad had eaten. She gave them the same explanation she had her mother. "My husband and I had a date. If you're hungry there's plenty of food in the refrigerator," she said breezily.

"Y'all didn't bring nothin' back for us?" Matthew asked.

She hoped Brad in the adjacent family room couldn't hear them. "Why would we? There's plenty to eat here."

"Yeah, leftovers. It's not the same as restaurant food," Derrick complained.

Suzanne lowered her chin to her chest and cast an incredulous look their way. "Am I doing something to keep you two from going out to eat?"

Derrick answered without hesitation. "No, but since you just came back it would've been easier, that's all."

It amazed her that neither of them seemed the least bit embarrassed.

"That reminds me, fellas," Brad began, walking toward them. "Speaking of leftovers, we had a lot of jumbo shrimp and crab and lobster cakes left over after our party, but when I went to fix a plate Sunday afternoon I couldn't find any of it. Do you two have any idea what happened?"

"Derrick and I took some," Matthew said. "Suzanne said it was okay."

"You did more than take *some*, Matthew," Suzanne interjected. "You took it *all*. I didn't say it was okay to do that."

"But y'all had so much other stuff left," Derrick reasoned, "stuff we didn't like that much."

"That doesn't give you the right to walk off with the entire supply. There are other people who enjoy shrimp, crab, and lobster, too," Brad said. "I'm telling you here and now not to ever do that again."

Both Derrick and Matthew glanced at Suzanne, waiting to see if she would say anything in their defense. Only on seeing her rigid stance, arms crossed in front of her chest, did they mumble and nod agreement.

"Suzanne, I need a favor."

Stretched out on the sofa with her head resting on a pillow on Brad's lap as they watched TV with her mother, Suzanne smiled up at her sister. "You need to borrow a piece of jewelry, hon?"

"No. It's just that I didn't get to clean my room."

She stiffened. "And?"

"Can I go to the movie if I promise to do it tomorrow?"

"No, Kenya. We had a deal, remember?"

"Oh, come on, Suzanne. I had a busy afternoon. We were longer in Saint Augustine than we planned, and then we stopped at Winn-Dixie so Gregory could introduce me to the store manager—you know I'm trying to get a job there—and there just wasn't time to clean up."

"We had a deal, Kenya, and I'm sticking to it, even if you're not."

Kenya turned to Arlene, who sat in a nearby swivel chair. "Mom!"

Arlene spoke up immediately. "Suzanne, why don't you let her go?"

"Mom, she and I made a deal. Kenya was all for it until she couldn't keep up her end."

"But just this once wouldn't hurt, would it?"

"Mom, please. Stay out of it."

"If Mom says I can go, I should be able to go," Kenya said stubbornly. "*She's* my mother, not you."

"That's true, but the room you're keeping like a pigpen is in *my* house, Kenya," Suzanne said sternly, sitting up.

"Why do I have to clean it? Isn't that why you have a maid?"

Brad spoke up. "Yes, we have a housekeeper, and she works very hard. But all she does in Bradley's and Lauren's rooms is change the sheets, because Suzanne and I want them to learn how to pick up after themselves. I haven't seen your room, Kenya, but from what I hear it would be enough to make Teresita quit if she had to clean it." When she lowered her head, he spoke more gently. "I think you need to admit you blew it and cut your losses. Clean up your mess and keep it clean, and you won't have to worry anymore about not being able to go out."

Kenya put her hand on her hip. "Well, I think this sucks," she said. "I'll be glad when we're out of here." She stalked out.

Brad turned his attention back to the television.

"Suzanne, don't you think you were too hard on her?" Arlene asked. "What's she supposed to tell Gregory?"

"I'm disappointed in you, Mom. You'd never let *me* get away with being so sloppy when I was her age." Suzanne's gaze went to the ever-present highball glass at her mother's side and wondered if this new lenience had anything to do with her increased alcohol consumption. "Kenya's spoiled. She's accustomed to everyone doing for her, but she needs to learn discipline and stop trying to weasel out of her responsibility." Suzanne held her chin high in defiance. "I painted a picture for her earlier, telling her exactly what I saw happening if she tried to go to Saint Augustine this afternoon and on a date tonight, that she wouldn't have time to clean her room. She insisted that wouldn't happen, but it has. I don't care what she tells Gregory. I'm not going to allow her to keep such a nasty room in my home, and that's that."

CHAPTER 35

After a storm comes a calm.
—Matthew Henry

Lisa glimpsed the dashboard clock. Funny how it took her the same amount of time to get home every night. Working until six made for less traffic and therefore more regularity. She should be home within ten minutes, and she couldn't get there fast enough. The slice of pizza she'd had for lunch had faded hours ago. God bless Ma Canfield, who had offered to make dinner those afternoons when both Paige and Devon were scheduled to work. They had left the supermarket in favor of a Subway Brad owned near the mall when Brad told Paige he was having trouble keeping reliable help.

Lisa hadn't liked the idea of the girls working once school had started, especially since the mall was farther away from home than Publix, but Darrell felt it would help them develop a good work ethic early on. They compromised, telling the girls they would be able to work only if they maintained an average no lower than B-minus. It seemed to be working out. The girls only worked about ten hours a week. Besides, once school activities began they would quit, or go in only if the restaurant was understaffed. Devon planned to go out for the girl's basketball team, while Paige had gotten on the dance team as a late replacement.

As Lisa drove through an intersection, she saw a flash of movement through her right peripheral vision. She turned her head to identify it—something crashed into her car, slamming her body into the driver door as glass shattered on the other side.

Lisa recognized the Durango as it screeched to a halt some yards away. Darrell jumped out and ran to her. "Are you all right?"

She willingly stepped into his embrace. "I'm a lot better now that you're here." There was no sound more sickening than that of a traffic accident, the screeching brakes, the shattering glass, the crashing sound of steel on steel. For a frightening moment, she feared she'd been injured, but she was able to simply place her hand on the door and open it and get out. "But I'm afraid the car has had it." She felt his hand increase the pressure on her back.

"As long as *you're* all right. We can always get another car. You're irreplaceable." He cupped her cheek, then lowered his hand to capture hers. "Come on, let's go look."

The damage extended down most of the right side of the Mercedes. Lisa knew little about auto bodies, but even she could tell the impact of the crash had bent the frame. The passenger windows had been shattered, and the windshield had sustained several cracks. "My God," Darrell said softly. "Good thing he hit you on the passenger side, or else they'd be loading you into an ambulance right now."

"She," Lisa corrected. "It was a woman. She's over there, with the police officer. Getting a citation for running a red light."

He squeezed her hand. "I'm really glad you're okay, Lisa."

"I'll be fine. My neck snapped at the impact, that's all. I got hit just as I was turning to see what was coming toward me." She rubbed the right side of her neck. "I've already got a funny feeling there. I think I may have strained it or something."

"I'm taking you to the emergency room right now."

"Darrell, I'm so hungry. Can we go home for a minute first? Besides, I'd like to see the kids."

"I guess that's best. They'll feel better after they see you're okay, too."

"Missus Canfield? I just wanted to say again how sorry I am," the other driver, a plump woman of about thirty, said, sounding sincere. "My son developed a fever at school today, and my mother had to pick him up. I was rushing over there to see him, and I . . . I guess I wasn't paying attention."

"Do you have a ride home?" Lisa asked.

"My mother is getting a neighbor to stay with my son so she can come get me. My husband's in the Navy, stationed in the Persian Gulf," the woman explained. She noticed Lisa rubbing her neck. "I hope your neck isn't too bad."

"I'm going to bring her to the emergency room so they can check it out," Darrell said.

"We'll be in touch with your insurance company," Lisa added.

"She seemed sincerely sorry," Darrell said after they were in the truck.

"Part regret and part guilt. I think she was on the phone when she ran that light. Naturally, she didn't tell the policeman that." Lisa sighed. "She was probably talking to her son. I feel kind of sorry for these Navy wives. It's hard trying to do it all by yourself when your husband's away for months at a time."

"Those long separations are why Navy families have a sky-high divorce rate." Darrell glanced at the smashed front end of the other motorist's Chevy, which was being loaded onto a tow truck. "Looks like we're not the only ones who'll be going car shopping."

"Look at the bright side. At least we won't have to find a good body shop," Lisa said.

Lisa reached to turn off the alarm, but a shooting pain through her shoulder made her abruptly lower her arm. A surprised gasp escaped from her lips, but because Darrell had already left for work no one heard it. Their bedroom was isolated in the right front corner of the house. She decided to lay quietly for a few moments, let the pain subside and then try to get up slowly. Fortunately for her, she had set her alarm to the soothing sounds of birds chirping in the forest, so she didn't mind the sound continuing. If it was one of those buzzing noises, she'd yank the cord out of the wall, no matter how much pain the motion gave her.

The pain had caught her by surprise, even though the emergency room physician had warned her she might feel worse in the morning. She'd have to call her Wednesday relief pharmacist and see if he could fill in for her for the next few days. The first thing she'd do after making sure the twins got off to school okay—the girls' high school classes began earlier, and they were gone by now—would be to take a hot shower. Maybe if she felt up to it this afternoon, she'd get Ma Canfield to take her to pick up the rental vehicle their insurance provided as interim transportation.

She laid her head against the pillow and blew out her breath in frustration. Bad enough to have her family's finances disrupted by the expense of having to purchase a new car because a worried mother wasn't concentrating on the traffic signals, but to have to cope with this pain on top of it made for a double insult.

"How does it feel?" the car rental agent inquired eagerly.

Lisa decided all the employees had been specifically trained to show such enthusiasm, but she wasn't in the mood for a lot of BS. "Well, if you really want to know, it feels very small and very cheap."

"Oh, I'm so sorry. What kind of vehicle do you usually drive?"

"A Mercedes wagon. It was old, but those types of cars are built to last forever. Unfortunately, I think the insurance company will write it off."

"Well, I suppose a Ford Escort is something of a comedown when you're accustomed to driving a Mercedes," the agent said. "Do you plan on purchasing another?"

"Another car, yes. Another Mercedes, I don't think so. We got lucky to find that one."

"You might want to visit our used vehicle lot on Atlantic Boulevard. We sell all types of models, SUVs, two-seaters, sedans, convertibles, luxury."

She decided their training must also include strict instructions to always refer to cars as "vehicles." Why couldn't they just call a spade a spade? It was ridiculous, like a HoJo employee avoiding the word "motel." "Thanks. I'll give it a look." But not now. Her neck was already beginning to stiffen. All she wanted to do was go home and take one of those muscle relaxants the ER physician had prescribed for her.

She had just turned onto her street when she saw the Lexus roll out of the Betancourts' driveway. It had to be Suzanne going out at this time of day; surely Brad was at work. Damn. Of all times for Suzanne to choose to leave her home in a sixty-thousand-dollar Lexus sports car while she was behind the wheel of a cheesy Escort. Damn that insurance company.

Lisa was tempted to speed up and cut Suzanne off to get into her driveway, but the last thing she wanted to do was be involved in another accident, especially one she caused. She had no choice but to sit and wait for Suzanne, who was going straight and had the right of way.

As the seconds passed, she grew impatient. What was taking Suzanne so long? Hell, not only could she have turned into her driveway by now, she could have been in her damn garage.

Suzanne, already driving slowly, peered into the Escort, presumably out of curiosity to see who was showing up at their house in the early afternoon. She stopped alongside it, effectively blocking Lisa from turning, and depressed her driver side window. "Hi, Lisa," she said cheerfully. "New car?"

Exasperated, Lisa pulled around the Lexus and made an awkward semi-U-turn to her driveway just as Suzanne began pulling forward, not caring about being rude. Suzanne had it coming for being such a bitch. That crack she made hadn't deserved a response.

It came as no surprise to Lisa and Darrell when the insurance company declared the Mercedes a total loss. "Any idea what type of car you'd like to get?" Darrell asked.

"I really hadn't given it much thought," she confessed. "I've been so annoyed about the whole thing. They're giving us practically nothing for the Mercedes because it's so old. On top of that we'll have two car payments, something we've always avoided. Not to mention the money we'll have to take from savings to make the down payment." She sighed. "I sure hope you get a big bonus in December. We still have Devon's car to pay off yet."

"Well, I'm not saying to go out and get another Mercedes, but you're going to be driving whatever you get for a long time, so at least get something you like. As long as it's within reason, we'll handle the expense."

Lisa took a deep breath. He had a point, and all things considered, a new car was a small price to pay. It could almost be considered a bonus, for she'd known from the moment he ran to her at the crash site that their marital strain had ended. She'd assured him when she called that she was all right, but he'd clearly been terrified at the mere thought of something happening to her. Sometimes that's what it took to realize what was really important.

She would never allow Brad and Suzanne to come between them again.

CHAPTER 36

I'm afraid the masquerade is over.
—"(I'm Afraid) The Masquerade is Over," lyrics by
Herb Magidson and Allie Wrubel

Flo rushed to meet Ernie when she heard his key in the lock. "You were right," she said when he was inside. "It probably wasn't such a good idea for Gregory to get involved with Kenya. She may be living in Brad and Suzanne's house, but just as a poor relation. She's gonna go to the same school as Gregory, and she'll take the bus to get there. I stopped in at Publix and left at the same time Paige and Devon were getting off work. It was their last day. They told me they're going to be working at a Subway on Monument Road. Brad owns it."

"He owns a Subway?"

"More than one, apparently. Paige mentioned that's the one closest to where they live. They're going to be working just a few hours a week so they can concentrate on their studies and school activities. But Kenya is working at Winn-Dixie with Gregory." She frowned. Gregory should be playing basketball, a sport he loved, but he couldn't because the practice and game schedule would interfere with his work. He had to work to help pay for his Bug. Another difference between them and the Canfields.

"Anyway," she continued, "she's definitely a poor relation. While Paige and Devon are at cheerleading practice or whatever they're going to be doing, Kenya will be ringing up people's groceries."

Flo chirped away, finally stopping when she noticed the gloomy expression Ernie wore. "What is it, hon?" When he didn't reply she began to feel a sense of urgency. "Ernie, tell me what's wrong."

He stuffed his hands in his pockets and spoke in a monotone. "They just laid me off."

She drew in her breath. "Laid you off! I don't understand. You said they would need all of you in Human Resources to handle the larger number of employees."

"They decided they didn't need two managers at two manager salaries."

"I still don't get it. You said if it came to that, that the person from the other company didn't have the seniority you have!"

"She doesn't. It was close, actually, but I still had more time. It came down to the fact that she's got a degree and I don't. At least that's what they said. I think it was just their way of getting rid of the brother and keeping the white woman."

"They laid you off," Flo repeated, gasping. It had suddenly become difficult to breathe in the well-ventilated room, and her knees felt like they'd buckle at any moment. The enormity of the hole they were in began to sink in. What would they do about their mortgage? Their bills? There was no way she could handle it all on her salary. Ernie made significantly more than she did.

"My salary will continue for the next ten weeks," Ernie said. "I won't be able to apply for unemployment before that."

"What's that, two hundred dollars a week?" she said sardonically. Damn it, she *told* him time and time again that his spending habits would ruin them. But he just *had* to have a home theater furnished with two extra-long curved leather sofas and a special platform to elevate the one in the rear, just to impress people. Heaven knew they hardly ever used the damn thing. And he just had to have a twenty-five-hundred-dollar Bombay chest in the foyer, for the same reason. And whenever one of their neighbors got something new for their house, he immediately rushed out to get the same thing, usually trying to outdo them, just so no one would say they couldn't afford it. As soon as they got back from Destin, George Morton proudly stated he and Gail were making over their bedroom closet with supplies they'd purchased from Home Depot. Ernie responded by promptly calling in a representative from The Space Place for an in-home consultation, then told everyone *their* closet was being remodeled by professionals. She could tell from George's tight-lipped expression that he found the copycat action annoying.

But Flo knew she couldn't put all the blame on Ernie. She enjoyed their surroundings as much as he did, enjoyed being thought of as the couple who had everything. Nothing compared to the oohs and aahs she heard when taking visitors through the house. And then there was that trip to Destin, which had been her idea. The bill for that hadn't even come in yet. What were they going to do? Whatever would they tell the neighbors?

"Well, I'd like to avoid collecting unemployment if possible," Ernie said. "I'm going to start looking for a job right away. If I get one I won't have to worry about trying to make it on two hundred a week."

"And just what type of job do you think you can get with no college degree?" Flo wailed. If only he had followed his superior's advice and gone to weekend college to finish his bachelor's. He was dreaming if he thought he'd be able to land another Human Resource Manager position again. The best he'd be able to do was a clerical job. That wouldn't pay much, and who knew how long it would take to materialize? "Do you realize the effect this is going to have on our finances?" she said, her voice high-pitched in panic. "We can't afford this house. We can't afford our cars." And they couldn't afford to have fifteen thousand dollars in credit card debt on top of all their already high living expenses. They'd be disgraced, humiliated. She covered her face with her palms and began to sob.

He quickly embraced her. "Listen, Flo, the first thing we have to remember is not to panic. Right now we have my same check coming in for the next ten weeks. That's more than two months' full salary. If I can find something right away it'll be like a bonus check. We also have our savings, plus retirement funds we can raid if we have to. We still have time to plot a strategy to raise money. And as for George, Larry, and Michael, none of them have to know I've lost my job. I'm sure it'll all work out."

Flo wished she could feel as confident as he did.

"Did you see Lisa's new convertible?" Arlene said to Suzanne as they got in the Escalade for a trip to the supermarket. Brad had taken the Lexus to work today, and the SUV was more practical to pack groceries in than the sedan.

Suzanne sucked her teeth. "Yeah, I've seen it. Cloth seats, canvas top. I'm not impressed. She just wanted something sporty after she saw our new Lexus and got that car because it was the best she could afford. She's always copying Brad and me. I heard her boys saying they wished they had a puppy while they played with Buster, so I guess that'll be next. Not a purebred, like a beagle or a Dalmatian, but some mutt."

"There it is in the driveway," Arlene said as they passed the Canfields' house, nodding toward the cranberry-colored Sebring. "I wonder whose Cadillac that is next to it."

"Didn't I tell you? Lisa's parents are visiting from Georgia. Brad insisted on going over there the other night and saying hello. He wanted me to go with him, but I have no interest in meeting his former in-laws." Suzanne shrugged. "Bad enough he wanted me to go over there with him after Lisa's accident." She could still see the concern in his eyes when Paige called and told him that Lisa had been in an accident and her car totaled. The next day, he had come home from work with two buckets of fried chicken and two identical sets of side dishes from KFC, saying he wanted them to bring one set next door and wish Lisa a speedy recovery in person. She had gone along only because she sensed he felt strongly about it, the way he had about inviting Lisa and Darrell to their party, and she hadn't wanted to start an argument by refusing to accompany him.

Lisa had come to the door wearing a padded collar around her neck. Suzanne had taken perverse pleasure in the look of discomfort on Lisa's face. She supposed it was mean of her, but it wasn't like Lisa had suffered any type of permanent injury. In time her neck would heal and she'd be good as new.

The only good thing that came out of her well wishes was getting a glimpse of the Canfield home. Suzanne still smarted over the thought of Lisa traipsing freely throughout her house while they were in Maine, but she knew complaining to Brad would be futile. He'd defended Lisa when she brought up the mere possibility of her snooping around in their absence, so surely if she told him what Flo had seen he'd have an excuse for Lisa's being there. Just thinking about it made Suzanne furious.

She'd gone next door planning to pick the place apart mentally, but to her surprise Lisa's house was tastefully decorated, even elegant. All right, she hadn't expected it to be jammed with stuff like Flo's— she knew Lisa had better taste than that—but she hoped it would contain furnishings of less than premium quality. That hadn't been the case. Instead, she saw parquet hallways and muted neutral carpeting, light-upholstered furniture, marble-topped accent tables, and walls painted dramatic colors like sea green and royal blue. The layout wasn't bad either. Lisa, Darrell, and their kids might not have as large an income as Brad, but they nevertheless lived pretty damned good from what she could see.

Suzanne had also noticed how quick Darrell was to see to Lisa's needs. Her accident had obviously shaken him up. He repeatedly said how different things might have been if the car had hit Lisa on the other side, that God must have been looking out for her. Suzanne found herself a little jealous of Darrell's devotion to Lisa, for her own home life had become tense since the arrival of her family. Derrick and Matthew showed up to spend a second consecutive weekend, and since that time Brad's presence at home had become scant. Each weekend day he went either fishing or golfing and managed to be gone most of the day. Just before Lisa's accident, he'd announced that the following week he would be attending a medical convention in Pittsburgh, an event he'd originally passed on.

Suzanne felt helpless and frustrated by Brad's reluctance to spend time at home. She knew her family's extended presence was the reason for his absence, even if he didn't come right out and say so. He assured her everything was fine, but she felt increasingly unhappy. Even their sex life had been compromised, for having extra people in the house meant they couldn't skinny dip like they used to. Her mother went to bed early, but her sister and brothers stayed up late and might see them.

As she watched Darrell fuss over Lisa, for the first time Suzanne considered that money wasn't everything. Lisa might not have an Arthur Rutenberg house with a Jaguar, an Escalade, and a Lexus in the garage, but she and Darrell seemed so happy together. Could it be Lisa's marriage was more secure than hers?

"You're awfully quiet today," Arlene commented.

Her mind raced to concoct an excuse. She certainly couldn't tell her mother she was wishing that her mother and Kenya would hurry and move out so she and Brad could have their lives back. It had been difficult enough telling her she had to forget about any schemes she had to stay on. "Oh, I'm just trying to think if there's anything we need that I might have forgotten to write down. I've gotten a little lazy when it comes to keeping a list since we moved."

Arlene chuckled. "That's understandable. If I were you I probably wouldn't write anything down at all, now that you can drive to the store in just a few minutes."

Suzanne felt relieved to arrive at the supermarket. She'd rather concentrate on her grocery list than on how happy Lisa and Darrell were.

"Looks like Gregory's here," Suzanne said as she pulled into her driveway after completing her shopping. Gregory's bright blue Bug was neatly parked behind her mother's Buick.

"He's a nice boy," Arlene said. "And crazy about Kenya."

Suzanne activated the garage door and drove in.

"I'll help you bring in the bags," Arlene said. "No point in bothering Kenya if she has company."

"You and I can handle it," Suzanne agreed. She opened the hatchback, and she and her mother each grabbed a handful of bags. Suzanne unlocked the door to the house and led the way to the kitchen. The bags she held by looped handles were just inches from the floor, so she gently lowered them to the floor and peeked in the family room. The house seemed so quiet, no TV or music playing. Maybe Kenya and Gregory were studying.

No one was there. She crossed back into the kitchen and into the dining room. She gasped at the sight of Kenya and Gregory locked in a feverish embrace on the living room sofa, his hands roaming all over Kenya's body.

Arlene came up behind Suzanne. "What is it?" she asked anxiously. The sound of her voice alerted Kenya and Gregory to the fact that they were no longer alone in the house. "Kenya!" Arlene exclaimed in shock.

"Mom! Suzanne!" Breaking away from Gregory, Kenya hastily pulled down her blouse, which had been up around her chest. "What are you doing here?"

"I live here, Kenya," Suzanne said coldly.

"I . . . I meant Mom."

"They gave me a day off because they need me to work Saturday," Arlene explained sternly. "Now, what's going on here?"

"Do you really have to ask?" Suzanne said caustically. "Kenya, what the hell is wrong with you? Bradley and Lauren will be home any minute. It could have been them walking in on you like this!"

Gregory rose. "Mrs. Hall, Mrs. Betancourt. I'm so sorry. I guess I got carried away."

"I think you should leave, Gregory," Suzanne stated quietly.

He looked uncertainly at Kenya.

"It's all right. Go. We'll talk later," she said. He left with one last pleading look at Suzanne and Arlene.

"Where's Teresita?" Suzanne demanded.

"She left right after I got home. Her work was finished, and I told her I'd let the kids in. I'm sorry. Like Gregory said, we got carried away. We didn't hear you come in. If you'd come in the front door we would have."

Suzanne shook her head. "I think you'd better handle this," she said to her mother. "And for God's sake, this is no time to go easy on her." She returned to the kitchen, where she proceeded to put away her purchases, making two more trips to the truck to unload.

Her mother returned as she was finishing up. "Well, I grounded her," Arlene said. "She's to come straight home from school and work, and she won't be able to see Gregory this weekend."

"How long will it last?"

"Through next weekend. I hope I can count on you to help me enforce it, Suzanne, since I'll be at work most days."

"Of course, Mom."

Brad shook his head. "It won't be as easy as you make it sound."

"I don't see why not, Brad. If I'm not home, Teresita will be here. That's the only time I go out in the afternoon, when I know she'll be here when the kids get home from school."

"But there's more to it than that, Suzie Q. Gregory drives Kenya to school, drives her home, drives her to work and then home again. I see lots of loopholes. She can always call in sick to work and go over his house to hang out. Maybe you should say something to alert his mother."

"I don't want Flo to know I caught my little sister making out with her son! It's embarrassing."

"In that case you run the chance of Flo catching them over there."

"I'd be mortified if that happened, Brad." Suzanne frowned, unhappy with either option. Then she raised her chin triumphantly. "No, it won't happen. Flo told me Ernie is doing this huge project for work, and they're letting him work at home. So they can't go there." She exhaled in relief.

"All right, so you're probably covered. Of course, you wouldn't have this problem at all if your sister wasn't so fast. I'm just glad Bradley and Lauren didn't walk in on them. You know how impressionable Lauren is."

"Kenya's seventeen, Brad. That's certainly old enough to have hormones."

"And I'm sure she's acted on them. I doubt she's a virgin."

She shrugged. *Neither was I at her age.* It wouldn't do to say that. She kept her hurt over her first love, Eric Davidson, dumping her so many years ago in the deepest recesses of her heart. Best to change the subject. "Only three more weeks to go before they move out."

"I wish your mother hadn't rented an apartment so close. I realize she wants to stay in the same school district so Kenya won't have to switch, but that complex a half mile down the road means they'll still be around all the time."

"Not all the time." Suzanne spoke a bit hesitantly. "Brad . . . I hope you're planning on staying close to home this weekend. You've been gone so much."

"Yeah, I guess I have. It's easier to forget that we're under siege when I'm not around to see it. But I'll stick close by this weekend. Maybe you and I can go to the show or something."

Derrick and Matthew drove up Friday night instead of Saturday because they wanted to attend a special event at one of the clubs. Suzanne was thrilled when they prepared to return to Palatka Saturday afternoon. It meant two less people in the house the rest of the weekend.

"I had a letter from a real estate agent asking me to call her," Arlene remarked. "Someone has made an offer on the house."

"It's not even up for sale, is it?" Brad said.

"No, but he's an investor, and he wants to buy it. I guess he'll fix it up and rent it out, or maybe sell it."

"Are you considering selling, Mom?" Suzanne asked.

"I'm thinking about it, yes. It was a good offer, considering the work the house needs."

"Wait a minute, Mom," Derrick said. "What's gonna happen to Matthew and me if you sell the house out from under us?"

"Come on, Derrick," Brad said easily. "You knew your mother was going to sell the house eventually. Does it make that big a difference if it's now or three months from now?"

"He's right, Derrick," Matthew agreed. "I don't know about you, but I wanna come up to Jacksonville, too."

"And what, commute to Palatka?" Derrick said sarcastically. "That's where your job is. It'd be kinda hard to get there without a car."

"For your information, I just talked to the bank last week about getting a car loan. They told me how much I'll be able to borrow. If I come up here, I should be able to get a job at one of the local hospitals, and I can get a second job at Brad's Subway, like Paige."

"Whoa," Brad said. "What's this about working at my restaurant?"

"Paige said she's only gonna be there until football season starts and she gets busy with the dance team, and even now she only works a few hours a week because she has practice. I figure I can take her place. I'm gonna put in for the night shift on my applications at the hospitals, so I can have my afternoons free to bring in some extra cash. Maybe I'll be able to take some college classes eventually, or get in trade school. That's another reason for me to work nights. Besides, the night shift gets paid more."

"It sounds like you've given this a lot of thought," Brad remarked.

"I have. I don't want to just get by, Brad. I want something like this for myself." Matthew waved his hand at the room.

"My manager has had to fire a lot of people who aren't reliable," Brad said. "You understand you won't be given any special consideration because you're my brother-in-law. But if you're really serious about this, we'll talk."

"Bet."

CHAPTER 37

It's simple: Either you have discipline or you haven't.
—Edmund H. North

Paige felt her forehead. She didn't *feel* warm. That was a good sign. But she was all congested, and it hurt every time she swallowed. She'd first noticed the symptoms yesterday at work. She'd hoped she would feel better today, but if anything she felt worse.

She plodded barefoot to the kitchen, a robe carelessly thrown over her shorty pajamas, where she found Darrell having his morning coffee. "Darrell, I don't feel good."

He looked at her sympathetically. "I've got to tell you, you don't look so good either. Where does it hurt?"

"I'm all stuffed up, and my throat is sore. I just feel run down."

"Yeah, back in the day we used to call it iron poor blood. Why don't you go back to bed? I'll let Lisa know. She'll be in to check on you as soon as she gets up."

"Thanks, Darrell."

"Hey, you just take it easy so you'll feel better."

Paige slept most of the day away. At dinnertime, Lisa brought her a bowl of chicken chowder. "I'm going to call your father," she said. "There's no way you'll be able to baby-sit for Bradley and Lauren tomorrow."

Paige slapped her palm to her forehead. "Oh, Mom, I forgot all about that."

"Of course you did. You're sick." Lisa reached for the receiver on Paige's bedside table. The voice of Goofy, whose likeness stood on top of a platform, greeted her with a cheery "Hello!" The telephone had been a Christmas gift to Paige the year she was thirteen. Devon's room was equipped with a Winnie the Pooh phone. "How do you speed dial Daddy?" Lisa asked.

"Three pound."

Lisa punched the two keys. The call went through right away. "Hello Suzanne, it's Lisa. May I speak with Brad?" She shook her head. Even through the phone, she could feel Suzanne's resentment at her calling. "Hi Brad," she said when he finally picked up. She sensed Suzanne had deliberately delayed telling him she was on the phone just to extend her wait.

But she had more important things on her mind than Suzanne's games. "I'm sitting here with Paige in her room. She's not feeling well . . . Oh, she's all stuffed up and her throat is painful . . . No, no fever. All right. We're right here. 'Bye."

"He's coming over," Lisa announced as she replaced the receiver. Goofy promptly announced, "Good-bye." She glared at it. "I don't know how you can stand that thing talking all the time. Anyway, Daddy wants to take a look at your throat."

"Well, I don't see any inflammation," Brad said as Lisa looked on anxiously. "That's a good sign. No patchy white spots, either. And your ears looked fine." He reached for a miniature spray can. "All right, open wide again. I'm going to spray your throat. It'll help ease the pain you feel when you swallow."

"Do you think she needs an antibiotic?" Lisa asked.

"Nah. I don't see any sign of infection, and she doesn't have a fever. It's probably just viral. But if her symptoms aren't gone completely in a few days a throat culture wouldn't be a bad idea."

He and Lisa turned at the sound of a tapping on the open door. Devon stood in the doorway. "Wow, a house call," she said as she joined them. "Is Paige going to be all right, Doctor Brad?"

"Well, if you two had any plans for this weekend, I'm afraid she won't be able to participate. But by next week she should be fine."

"Daddy, I'm so sorry I won't be able to baby-sit for you and Suzanne tomorrow," Paige said.

"Don't you worry about that, or anything else," Brad assured her.

"If I didn't work Saturdays I'd watch Bradley and Lauren myself, Brad," Lisa said.

"Maybe I can help," Devon offered. "I'm off tomorrow. What time are you supposed to be there?"

"From about eight in the morning until about one or two," Paige said. "Daddy and Suzanne are going to help Miss Arlene and Kenya move to their new apartment."

"Devon, it'd be great if you could help us out," Brad said. "I'd pay you the same as what I give Paige, six dollars an hour."

"Sure, I'd be glad to."

Lisa beamed. "I think that's wonderful!"

"Hey, so do I," Brad said. "Thanks a lot, Devon. We'll see you at eight-thirty tomorrow morning, all right?"

"I'll be there."

Devon looked at her watch for the third time in ten minutes. She knew it wouldn't help Doctor Brad and Miss Suzanne get home any earlier, but Bradley was really being difficult. What was it about substitute teachers and baby-sitters that made kids want to see how much they could get away with?

This might be one of the last opportunities for swimming this season, unless you were a polar bear. Although it was October and the seemingly endless summer heat was finally tapering off, today the temperature was going up to high eighties. The water temperature had also dipped, but the Betancourts had some kind of gizmo that heated the water as it went through the pump. Bradley and Lauren took advantage of the heat by spending the morning in the pool. Devon joined them, floating in a pool chair with a glass of iced tea and a magazine. She must have told Bradley five times already not to splash water, but he continued to do it. If Cary or Courtney ignored her like that she'd smack them upside the head, but they wouldn't do that. Her little brothers were good kids; they listened. Bradley Betancourt, on the other hand, seemed to think the world was his kingdom.

He certainly had his younger sister under his thumb. At noon, Devon had asked if they were ready to have lunch. Lauren simply looked at Bradley, who shook his head and said no. She asked again at twelve-thirty with the same response. At one o'clock, she didn't bother to ask. "All right guys, I'm fixing lunch, and y'all are gonna eat. I don't care what you say, I know you're hungry by now."

Bradley reacted the way she figured he would, by whining, "Oh, maaaaan."

"I mean it. Now, out of the pool."

"We have to get out?" Lauren asked, disappointed.

"Lauren, I can't see you that well from the kitchen, and you can't be in the water unsupervised."

"But we're only in three feet," Bradley protested. He had finally settled down into a game of Tic Tac Toe on a floating board.

"It doesn't matter," Devon said. "Anything can happen. And you might as well get used to the idea of being out of the water for a while. You'll have to wait an hour after you eat for your food to digest before you can go back in again."

"Our daddy doesn't make us wait that long," Bradley said.

"Well, Bradley, your daddy's a doctor. If you were to start drowning he'd know exactly what to do," Devon said good-naturedly. "And maybe you'll get your wish. Your mommy and daddy should be here any minute." She hoped. She didn't know how much more of Bradley she could take. How could Paige stand being around him?

Devon waited until both children had stepped out of the pool and sat in lounge chairs. Bradley removed the remote control for the TV from the drawer in the outdoor kitchen. The TV, perched high on a built-in shelf, lit up, showing Robin Williams in drag as *Mrs. Doubtfire.* He and Lauren pulled up chairs to watch.

"Okay, guys," Devon said. "Grilled cheese sandwiches coming right up." She went into the house.

As she worked in the spacious kitchen, she periodically glanced out the window to make sure Bradley and Lauren were behaving themselves. As she buttered six slices of bread, she found her thoughts going to her mother in Texas. She'd noticed a lot of tension between her mother and Andre when she came home from the hospital after her appendectomy. Andre barely spoke to either of them, and even his mother, who'd always been affectionate, seemed a little cold when she called for him and Devon answered the phone. She'd asked her mother about it, but Paula just told her not to worry about anything other than getting well.

Devon had been glad to leave that stress-filled house and fly home. Her mother called her regularly, and she'd instructed Devon to use her cell phone number to contact her. She sidestepped Devon's questions about Andre, and Devon wondered if he and her mother were no longer living together.

As she put away the bread and butter, she glanced at the wall clock. The Betancourts were running later than she expected. When the phone began to ring, she guessed they were calling to say they were on their way home.

She glanced outside again at the children as she reached for the receiver. But the male voice didn't belong to Doctor Brad.

"Hello, Missus Betancourt, this is Gregory."

"Hi, Gregory. This is Devon."

After a moment of silence, he said, "Did I dial the wrong number? I was looking for Kenya."

"No, no. I'm just here baby-sitting for Doctor Brad and Miss Suzanne." She figured he'd wonder why she was baby-sitting for Paige's brother and sister. "Paige was going to do it, but she got sick yesterday."

"Oh, sorry to hear that. I was just calling to see if Kenya was in, or to get her new phone number if she's not there."

"I don't think they've finished moving yet. I was hoping this would be Doctor Brad calling to let me know how much longer they'll need me. I've been here since early this morning." She held her hand palm down over the large skillet and determined the preheating period was done. She placed three of the bread slices in the pan butter side down and placed three slices of cheese on each.

"Oh, all right. I guess I'll call back later. Hey, are you going to the big game Friday night?" Their respective high schools were scheduled to play each other.

"I wouldn't miss seeing the chance to see you guys get clobbered," she said as she turned to the window for another quick check of her charges.

"Clobbered, huh? Well, let me tell you . . ."

"It's hot out here," Bradley said, his arms crossed and his lower lip poked out. "I want to get back in the water."

"Bradley, no," Lauren objected. "Devon said not to."

"So what? I'm not scared of Devon." Bradley promptly went to the steps of the pool. Seconds later he was on his back in the center of the deep end, happily floating. "This is a whole lot cooler than sitting outside. I can even see the TV from here. You ought to come in."

"No. Devon'll be mad."

"Ah, let her get mad. She can't do anything to us. She's not part of our family."

Lauren turned her attention back to the movie. Soon she was laughing at Robin Williams' antics at housecleaning while wearing old-lady garb.

Bradley, able to see the screen from the center of the pool, laughed, too, but he suddenly got a sharp pain in his calf. He clutched his right foot, an action that caused him to flip over facedown. He quickly rolled over. "My leg!" he called to Lauren. "I got a pain. I can't stay up!" He flapped his arms wildly, struggling to reach the edge of the pool that was out of his reach.

Lauren merely laughed at him.

Brad glanced at the rear of the Escalade. The third row of seats had been removed, and the second row lay flat to allow it to be packed. "The truck doesn't look too bad, considering we used it as a moving van," he remarked to Suzanne. "I'm going to come in and get something to eat, and then I'll drive over to the car wash and have it vacuumed out. The kids'll probably want to come along. They get a kick out of driving through the car wash."

"That's one of the few things that'll get them out of the pool," Suzanne said. "I'm sure they're swimming, hot as it is out here today. Poor Devon probably thinks we got lost." She pushed the passenger door open.

When Brad proceeded to do an inspection of the truck she said, "I'll see you inside. I'm going to go around back. I'm sure the kids are in the pool."

Bradley's arms were tired. He wouldn't be able to stay above the water much longer. Why was Lauren laughing? Did she think he was just playing around? "Lauren, I'm not kidding," he managed to gasp before he slipped beneath the surface.

Devon laughed as she checked the bottom of the bread with a spatula. "Well, I'll guess we'll just see who beats who Friday night." She'd missed talking with Gregory. Now that she'd had time to accept his preference for Kenya as a girlfriend, she found she still liked the idea of being friends with him. Friendship lasted longer than boyfriends anyway. He and Kenya could break up at any time, but *she'd* still be able to have a nice conversation with him.

She turned sharply at the sound of the door opening. Lauren's words came out half spoken and half crying. "Devon, come quick! It's Bradley!"

She told Gregory she had to go, simultaneously removing the skillet from the heat and then ran outside, just in time to witness Suzanne drop her purse as she screamed. Devon watched, transfixed to the spot, as Suzanne ran to the deep end of the pool and jumped in. Her heart thumping in panic, Devon finally realized those eddies in the deep end of the water came from Bradley's small form. She rushed to action, retrieving the long metal pole from its holder on the side of the house. "Lauren, find your father," she ordered as she held the pole out for Suzanne, who appeared to be struggling to stay afloat, to grab onto.

Suzanne had managed to pull Bradley's head above the water, and he was sputtering. Her heavy gym shoes weighted her down. With one hand tightly wrapped around her son's chest, she used her other hand to grasp the bar. Devon slowly pulled it toward the pool's shallow end.

Brad came running around the corner as Suzanne was leading Bradley up the pool stairs. "What happened?!" he shouted.

"Check him," Suzanne said, panting.

"My God. Bradley!" Brad turned his son around and, leaning behind him, pushed his fist into the boy's chest. Water poured from Bradley's mouth, a smaller amount from his nostrils. "Daddy," he said weakly, crying.

"It's all right," Brad said, dropping to one knee to embrace him. "You're all right, thank God."

Suzanne choked back a sob, then turned to Devon. "What the hell happened?" she asked accusingly. "I come home and find my son drowning, and you're inside the house instead of out here watching him."

"I was making lunch. I told Bradley and Lauren to get out of the pool, and they did. They were watching TV. I was watching them while I was cooking."

"Not very well, obviously, since you didn't see him go back in."

"I checked them just before the phone rang."

Suzanne's mouth dropped open. "The *phone?* You were on the *phone* while my son nearly drowned? I don't believe this! Talking with some boy, I'll bet. If I hadn't walked through that door when I did—" she pressed her fingertips against her eyebrows, then lowered her hands into tightly clenched fists. "Get out!" she screamed. "Get out of my house this minute!"

Devon looked wildly at Brad, but he was busy comforting Bradley. When he did look at her, his eyes were damp. "Go home, Devon," he said quietly.

"I'm sorry," she whispered. Sobbing, she ran into the house to collect her things.

CHAPTER 38

Can't we all just get along?
—Rodney King, after the 1992 Los Angeles riots

Lisa, playing the theme from *Titanic* on the piano, looked up when she heard the front door open. "Hi, Devon. How'd it go?" She hastily got up at the sound of a whimper. Devon ran into her arms. She rubbed her daughter's back. "What's wrong, Devon? Tell me what's happened."

"Doctor Brad and Miss Suzanne . . . they're mad at me, but it wasn't my fault, Mom. It wasn't." She began to sob again.

"Shh. Daddy is cleaning the pool. Let's go out so the three of us can talk about this together. But I'm sure it can't be that bad." She put her arm around Devon, and together they went out to the patio.

Darrell immediately sensed something was wrong and took over comforting his daughter. The three of them sat down at a round table, Darrell pulling his chair close to Devon's so he could hold her hand in both of his. She haltingly recounted how she had ordered the children out of the pool, checked on them every few minutes while she was cooking, and how Lauren had come running for help at the precise moment Suzanne had come home to find Bradley foundering in the water. "Miss Suzanne screamed at me to get out. Even Doctor Brad told me to leave," she concluded with a sob.

Lisa and Darrell looked at each other. "Do you think we should go over?" she asked.

"Yes, but not until later. Give them a chance to calm down. They've just had a frightening experience, and that's all they're thinking about right now. I don't blame them. Thank God Bradley's all right."

"I'm so glad you were able to get Suzanne and Bradley to safety with the pole, Devon," Lisa said.

"Yes, that was a good thing," Darrell agreed. "But I wish you hadn't been on the phone. It makes it look a little worse than it would have if you'd merely been making lunch." When Devon's face wrinkled with the threat of fresh tears, he added quickly, "but of course Bradley had no business getting back in the water after you told him to get out."

"I always said he was a brat," Lisa muttered. "Half the time he ignores Suzanne."

"That's another reason to wait until later to go see them," Darrell said. "They might realize the role Bradley played in what happened to him instead of putting all the blame on my girl."

"It's seven-thirty," Lisa said to Darrell. "Why don't we go see how things are next door? I don't want to leave the boys alone too long."

"What do you mean, leave them alone? Mom's here. Paige is here."

"I'd like to come along, if you don't mind," Esther said. "I know you two will make sure Brad and Suzanne treat Devon right, but I have a stake in this, too. She's my grandchild, and she's having a very difficult year. Besides, you might need me to referee. With this being such a sensitive situation it might get out of control, and who's better suited to calm flaring tempers than the senior member of the group?"

"I'm going, too," Paige said.

"I don't know, Paige," Lisa said. "You're still not feeling that well. I know I said it was all right for you to come, but now I'm thinking maybe you should stay home and rest."

"But, Mom! *I* was the one who was supposed to baby-sit for Bradley and Lauren. And if it had been me, Daddy and Suzanne wouldn't have thrown me out the way they did Devon." Paige threw a pleading look at Darrell.

"Amen to that," Esther muttered.

"She's right," Darrell said to Lisa. "They wouldn't have thrown Paige out. They would have hugged her and told her everything was gonna be okay . . . or at least Brad would have."

"I want to be there for Devon," Paige insisted.

Lisa broke into a smile. "I think that's very sweet. All right. Why don't you go get Devon and tell her we're ready to go." Suddenly, she felt very glad Esther was coming along. She was right—the sensitive circumstances could easily turn ugly before it was all over.

When they stood in front of the double doors of Brad's home, Lisa hoped Brad would answer the door and not Suzanne, who would probably take one look at them and slam it in their faces.

Lisa and Darrell stood in front, Devon between them, with Esther and Paige behind. Darrell put a protective arm around Devon just before the door opened, and then they were face to face with Brad. "Hi," Lisa said. "Devon told us what happened, and we just wanted to make sure Bradley was okay."

Brad stepped back and held the door open. They filed inside, one at a time. Lisa briefly curled her hand around Brad's upper arm as she passed him. He and Darrell shook hands, then he held his arms open for Devon, who came next. "I was going to come see you tonight. I've been thinking about you all afternoon. I'm afraid Suzanne and I may have been a little hard on you because we were shook up about Bradley. I apologize."

Lisa's heart wrenched when Devon's face wrinkled, as if she were going to cry, but she composed herself and merely nodded.

"Besides," Brad continued, "I owe you some money."

At that Devon actually smiled. Brad counted out some bills and handed them to her, then embraced Paige. "Are you feeling better, honey?"

"A little bit."

Esther reached out and took both of Brad's hands. "I'm so glad your little boy is all right," she said sincerely.

"Thank you, Missus Canfield. He's in his room, taking it easy after all the excitement." He waved his hand toward the living room. "Please, everybody sit down. I'll get Suzanne." He went off in the direction of what Lisa knew was the master bedroom.

After a few minutes had gone by, she glanced at her watch. "It seems like it's taking them an awfully long time to come out," she whispered. "I wonder if it's because Suzanne doesn't want to see us and he's trying to coax her out."

"Shh!" Darrell said. "I think they're coming."

Suzanne appeared, wearing a tank top, shorts, white leather flip flops, and a stony expression. A towel was wrapped around her hair. Lisa decided her hair must be a mess after its encounter with the chlorine of the pool.

"Hello, everyone," Suzanne said quietly, bordering on monotone as she took a seat in one of the twin Provincial chairs. "Brad tells me you were all concerned about Bradley. He's going to be fine."

"Did you have to bring him to the emergency room?" Esther asked.

"No, I managed to get all the water out of him," Brad replied. "He really didn't need further treatment."

"We also had another reason for coming," Darrell began. "We'd have to be really dense if we didn't recognize the potential for some lingering bad feelings from what happened this afternoon."

"Well, I don't know about Brad," Suzanne said with just a touch of hostility, "but *I'm* certainly not going to forget anytime soon that my son almost drowned today."

"I think the important thing here, Suzanne, is to realize that both Devon and Bradley learned valuable lessons today," Darrell said calmly.

Suzanne's voice, on the other hand, came out shrill and accusing. "*Bradley!*" she said, practically shrieking. She leaned forward in her chair. "Bradley did nothing wrong. We entrusted the care of our children to *your* daughter"—she accented her words with a pointed finger, which she quickly withdrew—"but instead of watching them, she's talking on the phone with some boy. So what, she told them to get out of the water. You don't leave children unattended near a pool. If your daughter is old enough to be baby-sitting, Darrell, she's certainly old enough to know that."

Darrell's eyes had narrowed at Suzanne's pointing finger. "Wait a minute, Suzanne," Lisa said before he could reply. "I agree that children shouldn't be left unattended while they're in the water, but kids Bradley and Lauren's age are old enough to know that 'stay out of the pool' means just that, *stay out of the pool.* Bradley is nine years old, not three."

Suzanne rose and approached Lisa. "You've got a helluva nerve, coming in *my* house and telling me my son has a comprehension problem."

"That's not what I said," Lisa fired back. "If anything, he has a *behavior* problem."

"Uh, Lisa," Darrell cautioned.

She knew if he had been sitting next to her he would have nudged her, but Devon sat between them on the sofa. But she didn't care. If Suzanne believed the blame for this near-tragic incident lay expressly on Devon's shoulders, she was dreaming. "Well, he does."

"Wait a minute," Brad said, holding out his hand palm out, like a policeman directing traffic. "In all honesty, I do feel Bradley has some responsibility in what happened."

"Brad!" Suzanne sounded shocked.

He helped her back into her chair. "I talked to Lauren privately after I put Bradley to bed," he said. "She said Devon told them they had to stay out of the water while she was making their lunch because she couldn't see the pool from the kitchen. According to Lauren, Devon also said that after they ate they'd have to wait at least an hour before they went back in."

"And I told him I'm not a doctor like you are," Devon said softly, speaking for the first time.

"Lauren said Bradley complained about everything Devon said, that he didn't want to get out of the water," Brad continued. "According to Lauren, Devon didn't go into the house until she and Bradley were sitting in lounge chairs watching television. They were only sitting about five minutes before Bradley said he was going back in the pool. When Lauren reminded him of what Devon had said, she quoted him as saying, 'I'm not afraid of Devon.' And of course he went in and got a Charley horse." He paused a moment to glance around at everyone in the room. "Now, there's no way I can vouch for Devon when she says she looked out of the window every few minutes, but I believe her."

"Thank you, Doctor Brad," Devon said softly. "And it's the truth. I did check on them."

Suzanne, now holding her arms crossed over her chest, exhaled loudly. "Well, I guess we should give Devon a gold star for doing such a fine job."

"Suzanne, it could have happened to anybody," Darrell said. The patience and calmness in his voice just moments before was gone. Now he just sounded exasperated. "You can't put this all on Devon's shoulders."

"My son was left in your daughter's care," Suzanne repeated. "I came home just in time to see him thrashing around in eight feet of water, going down for the third time, with no one to help him. If I had come in through the front door instead of right around the back . . .

taken two minutes to go to the bathroom . . ." her voice cracked. She closed her eyes and shielded them with her hands, sobbing quietly.

Brad moved behind her and put strong hands on her shoulders. "Suzanne, don't torture yourself like this. This all happened very quickly; these things always do. You happened to walk in at the same moment Lauren was getting Devon. Devon would have gotten Bradley out of the water. She's a good swimmer, and she was clear-headed enough to give you that pole to grab onto, or else both you and Bradley . . . might not be here right now."

She raised her head. "I talked to Bradley," she said in a choked voice. "I sat with him until he went to sleep. You must have been talking to Lauren at the same time. But Bradley said Devon *didn't* tell them they had to stay out of the pool, and he asked her if he could go back in and she said yes."

"He's a liar, Suzanne," Lisa said flatly as Devon drew in her breath in shock.

Suzanne leaned forward again, her eyes flashing angrily. "I've had it up to *here* with you, Lisa"—she ran a hand across the front of her throat in a swift motion—"and your attacks on my son's character."

"Bradley is not the little angel you think he is, Suzanne, and I think it's high time you realized that. I've seen you calling out to him to come in when he's riding his bike, and I've seen him turn around and head in the opposite direction." Lisa wanted to throttle Suzanne, but she tried her best to sound gentle. "If he disobeys you, his mother, what makes you think he's going to obey Devon?"

"My son is a good boy," Suzanne said stubbornly.

"Yeah, well, Al Capone's mother said the exact same thing about him." Lisa almost laughed at Suzanne's openmouthed expression of indignation.

But Suzanne quickly recovered from her shock. "If you ask me, you need to get a life of your own and stay out of my business. What do you do, sit by the window and wait for me and my kids to go outside so you can watch us? I already know that you wait for us to go out of town so you can go all through my house."

At that everyone looked puzzled. Lisa silently cursed Flo Hickman for blabbing about seeing her and Paige leaving the Betancourt home. She didn't dare meet Paige's eyes, she knew that would only bring out the guilt Paige felt. Instead she said, "What the hell are you talking about, Suzanne?"

"You know damn well what I'm talking about. Don't play ignorant with me."

"Well, *I* don't know what you're talking about," Brad said, "but I've got a feeling it's got nothing to do with what we're discussing now."

"That's right, stick up for her," Suzanne snarled. "Bradley's wrong, and now I'm wrong, but Lisa's always right."

"Stop it!"

All heads turned to look at Paige, from whom the outburst had come.

"I hate seeing all of you at each other's throats like this," Paige said, her voice shaking. "This is all my fault. If I hadn't been sick I would have been able to stay with Bradley and Lauren. The same thing easily could have happened to me, but Daddy, you guys wouldn't have jumped on me the way you jumped on Devon because I'm your daughter and she's not. But she's my sister, and it's not right."

Lisa stole a glance at Suzanne, knowing she wouldn't want to be reminded of Paige being a member of her family. *So help me, if she as much as blinks I'm gonna slap her.*

"May I say something?" Esther asked humbly as Brad went to soothe Paige.

"Please," he said over his shoulder.

"Well, I wanted to point out to Suzanne that since the children gave such differing accounts of what happened, one of them is not telling the truth. Now Darrell's my only child, so I never had to worry about he-said, she-said, but my natural instinct would be to doubt the one who'd find him or herself in trouble if the truth came out."

Suzanne merely sat with an unreadable expression. Lisa knew she wouldn't dare tell Esther to butt out, no matter how much she might have wanted to.

"That said," Esther continued, "I have to say that I agree with my son. It's not about assigning blame, it's about being grateful that everything turned out okay, and about taking steps to avoid this ever happening again."

Everyone except Suzanne nodded.

"Why don't we get all the kids together tomorrow," Darrell suggested. "We'll have a safety drill, teach them what to do if someone should get into trouble in the water."

"That's not a bad idea," Brad said. "Lauren also told me that at first she thought Bradley was playing a joke on her, and that when she realized he wasn't she just stood there not knowing what to do before she ran to get Devon. When someone's going down for the third time a few seconds is all it takes to make the difference between life and death. The first instinct is often to jump in after the person, but that can be a fatal mistake. Even if you're a strong swimmer, a person who fears drowning can fight you in panic instead of allowing themselves to be pulled to safety. A lot of would-be heroes have drowned that way. Suzanne, wait. I didn't mean—" he said quickly as she stormed out of the room. He went after her a few steps, then halted. "Damn!" he said under his breath.

The way Brad went back and forth between his wife and daughter made Lisa think of a tennis ball.

"I guess she thinks you meant that she didn't use good judgment by jumping in after Bradley when she can't swim herself," Devon said.

"Yeah, I think you're right," Brad agreed.

"This is probably a good time for us to leave," Darrell said, rising. "You'll want to calm Suzanne down, and we've been here long enough anyway. Our boys are alone next door."

"Yeah, all right. See you tomorrow."

CHAPTER 39

Affluenza.
—A new psychological term to describe an excessive
desire to consume material goods

"Hi, Flo!" Suzanne said into the receiver. "What a coincidence. I was just about to call you. I haven't seen too much of you lately. Where've you been?"

"Oh, we've been so busy at work. I just got a promotion, you know."

"No, you didn't mention it." *That seemed odd.* Flo wasn't one to keep quiet about how well she and Ernie were doing. "Congratulations."

"Thank you. I was just calling to see if you were busy this afternoon."

"No. I was going to call you. I'd like to get out of the house for a few hours."

"You can always come over here. What's up?"

"Our next-door neighbors are coming over, and I don't want to be here."

"Is everything okay over there? Gregory mentioned he was talking with Devon while she was baby-sitting your kids yesterday, and she had to hang up because of some emergency. I called you last night to see if everything was okay, but Brad said you were sleeping."

"I was. We had quite a bit of excitement around here yesterday, and a near tragedy." Suzanne filled Flo in on the details of the incident.

"Oh, no. Suzanne, I feel terrible. I mean, it was my son Devon was on the phone with."

"There's no reason for you to feel bad, Flo. Gregory didn't do anything wrong. He didn't know the kids were by the pool. That was Devon's responsibility, and that's why I'm so upset. They're all coming over here for a lesson in pool safety, and I don't feel like seeing any of them."

"Why don't you just come over here?"

"I'll do that. Thanks a lot, Flo." She hung up the phone, feeling grateful to have such a good friend.

Flo sat in her kitchen nook, one elbow on the table and her hand raised. She resisted the urge to rest her chin on her hand, for then she'd look as bored as she felt. Suzanne had been carrying on about Lisa for twenty minutes, and it had gotten old. It would be different if she'd say something Flo hadn't heard before, spilled an interesting tidbit she could casually pass on to Gail or Sondra, but it was just the same stuff over and over.

"Suzanne," she said patiently, "I think you might be exaggerating just a little bit. It really isn't that bad. I know the situation is difficult for you, but come on. It's got to be hard for Lisa, too. Wouldn't you feel a little odd if someone you used to sleep with, the father of your child, bought the house next door to you, especially if you have it in for the new wife?"

"I'm hardly new, Flo. I've been married to Brad for almost eleven years. But the way Brad always sticks up for her makes me wonder if he wants to sleep with her again."

"Brad's never given me any indication that he wants anyone else but you." Over Suzanne's shoulder Flo noticed Ernie gesturing to get her attention. "Excuse me a minute."

"What is it?" she asked when they had moved into the hall, safely out of Suzanne's earshot.

"Just wanted to give you a heads up," he said. "When I was talking to George, Gail wanted to know if you were doing anything today. I told her no, so that means she'll probably come over with him."

"Oh, great," she said with an annoyed sigh. "I guess that means Sondra will show up, too. And of course all the kids will show up. Gail never goes anywhere without those girls, and Sondra's boys will show up two at a time."

"I hope you don't mind too much," he said apologetically. "I figured you'd get a kick out of letting Gail see you kicking back with Suzanne."

She hadn't thought of that. It wouldn't be a bad idea for Gail and Sondra to see her being girlfriends with Suzanne. Flo had been a little embarrassed at the party Kim and Michael gave when their pool was completed. She'd bragged to Gail and Sondra about her friendship with Lisa, but Lisa had little to say to her other than basic pleasantries, preferring to spend her time with mutual friends of hers and Kim's and with those snooty Princes. Flo was certain her sharp-eyed neighbors had noticed the snub and were laughing at her behind her back.

"Oh, it's all right," she said to Ernie. "I just hope nobody's expecting lunch." That was the problem with George and Larry. Many a time she and Ernie had been guests in their homes they'd been offered only beer or pop, but the two of them would frequently ask if they had anything to eat. Likewise, when Ernie offered them a beer, they'd come right out and ask if he had any Hennessy because they knew the cognac was a favorite of Ernie's. Ernie, always eager to impress, never refused them, especially when Michael Gillespie was around. But they'd seen little of Michael lately, who appeared to have shifted his attentions to Darrell and Lisa and Ben and Stacy Prince.

As far as George and Larry, Flo couldn't help feeling she and Ernie were being used. Or perhaps they'd become victims of their own publicity. George and Larry probably felt no shame in asking for food or expensive liquor because they felt she and Ernie could afford to share it with them. Maybe if she and Ernie hadn't bragged so much things would be different. . . .

"I'm going to put out some of those crackers from Wal-Mart, and that spinach dip."

"Forget the spinach dip. There's some onion soup mix in the pantry. Let's mix up some onion dip. It'll be cheaper." They had to be careful with every dime they spent. Ernie had accepted a position in Human Resources at one of the insurance companies before his severance pay ran out. The salary was less than half of what he had been previously earning. Flo stretched each dollar until George Washington screamed for mercy. The second job she'd taken doing additional medical billing helped, and of course she continued to volunteer for weekend overtime when her full-time position warranted it. She'd managed to renegotiate new payment terms with their creditors, so they were getting by, but just barely. They'd been reduced to renting a room in their house to a college student for the extra money it brought in, and she wasn't about to spend anything extra on the likes of those freeloading neighbors of theirs.

Flo rejoined Suzanne at the table, where Suzanne promptly resumed her verbal criticism of Lisa. "Honestly, Flo, I'm at the point now where I'd like nothing better than to put our house on the market, much as I love it, and find another one. I feel like my life isn't my own anymore. Lisa's always copied me, from the very beginning. Right after Brad and I got married she announced she was marrying Darrell. After I got pregnant with Bradley, she got pregnant with her twins. We buy a sports car, she buys a convertible, not that what she drives can compare in any way to our Lexus. I'm so sick of her I can scream."

Flo hastily rose when the doorbell rang. Gregory was at work, and she hadn't heard the doorbell. Only one other person had a key, their renter, Sharif. She hoped to catch him before Suzanne saw him. But he was too quick, having unlocked the door—he rang it only as a courtesy—and bounded toward the kitchen before she reached the hall. "Hi, Miss Flo; it's me." The young man nodded at Suzanne before putting his six-pack of bottled water in the fridge and disappearing toward the bedrooms. Flo smiled after him weakly, wishing Suzanne hadn't seen him and knowing what would follow.

"Who was that?" Suzanne asked.

"Oh, that's Sharif," she replied lightly. "He's the son of friends of ours from Fernandina. He's enrolled at UNF and was looking for someplace to stay off campus. Since we've got two extra bedrooms we don't use we told him he could stay with us. He's really no trouble."

"Oh, that was nice."

Flo shrugged. "Anything for a friend."

Suzanne felt better by the time she returned home several hours later. Some of Flo and Ernie's neighbors had come over to watch the game, and the way they fussed over her made her temporarily forget Brad's making nice with the Canfields at home. One of the women— she didn't remember either of their names—said she'd heard from Flo how wonderful her housewarming party had been. Suzanne recognized it as a hint to be invited to the next party she and Brad gave. *Not likely,* she thought smugly. But the sucking up was just what her ego needed to make her feel important. Funny. If she was still

Suzanne Hall from Palatka, living in a shabby efficiency apartment in Mandarin and struggling to get by from check to check, nobody would pay her any attention, but as the wife of Bradley Betancourt, Sr., M.D., everybody she met wanted to be her friend. The power of money could never be ignored.

CHAPTER 40

Children are now tyrants, not the servants, of their households.
—Socrates

Paige didn't see any of her father's cars in the driveway, but she rang the bell anyway. Her science paper was due on Monday, and she wanted him to look it over so she could turn it in and forget about it. She hated science. Besides, he'd said he'd be around all afternoon, so maybe he'd be back soon.

Or maybe he was home and had parked in the garage. The driveway was occupied only by Miss Arlene's blue Regal, so Paige presumed Suzanne was out with her mother. Miss Arlene and Kenya had moved out last month, but they lived just down the street and were still a constant presence on the weekends.

Kenya answered the door. "Hi!" she said.

"Hi, Kenya. Is my father here?"

"No, he's playing golf. He should be back soon. Mom and Suzanne are out shopping. I'm watching the kids."

Paige stiffened. It had been weeks since Suzanne had asked *her* to watch Bradley and Lauren. Suzanne was probably still holding a grudge about that incident with Devon and Bradley that she'd tried so hard to blame on Devon.

"Why don't you come in and wait?" Kenya suggested. "Everybody should be getting in soon."

"Okay." Paige followed Kenya inside. "Where're the kids?"

"Out back playing. They'll probably get back on their bikes in a few. I think Bradley's trying to stick around so he can peek at what Suzanne brings home. She's already started Christmas shopping."

"That's Bradley for you," Paige said with a smile.

"No move without a reason," Kenya agreed. "Hey, have you seen that new Chris Rock movie?"

They were talking about the movie, Paige trying not to be jealous when Kenya let it be known that she'd seen it with Gregory, when they were startled by the appearance of a bloody, crying Bradley.

"Bradley, what happened?" Paige said, secretly pleased that her brother had come to her for comfort rather than his aunt.

"I fell and hit my head on the bench," he said between sobs. "It hurts."

Paige gingerly fingered the skin around the gaping forehead wound. "I can't tell for sure, but I think you literally busted your head open."

"Here's a dish towel," Kenya said, handing Paige a plain white towel trimmed in red stitching.

Paige took it and pressed it against Bradley's head, all the while trying to comfort him. At least he'd stopped crying. A subdued Lauren sought solace from Kenya.

"I'm going to call Suzanne and tell her to come home," Kenya said.

"I think you should call Daddy, too. This looks like a big cut. I think it'll have to be stitched."

Suzanne and Arlene arrived home first. Bradley lay on one of the twin sofas in the family room, his cloth-covered head resting on Paige's lap, alternating between soft whimpers and a repeated sizzling sound of pain as Paige did her best to comfort him.

"My poor baby!" Suzanne exclaimed. She lifted the blood-soaked towel and inspected the cut. "Oh, my. That's going to need stitches."

"Here, give that towel to me," Arlene said. "It's soaked. He needs a fresh one. I'll get it."

"Will it hurt?" Bradley asked in a small voice as Suzanne gingerly removed the folded dish towel from his forehead and handed it to her mother.

"Stitches never hurt," Suzanne replied. "They'll give you something to numb you, so you won't even feel the needle. It's like going to the dentist and getting that shot of Novocain. You remember how you can't even feel your own tongue?"

"Will you come with me, Mommy?"

"I promise you that either myself or Daddy will be right there with you, and maybe both of us if the doctor says it's okay. So don't you worry." She bent forward and kissed his cheek.

"I'm sorry, Suzanne," Kenya said. "He and Lauren were running around with Buster out back. I told them to be careful around that concrete bench. Bradley must have tripped."

Suzanne stood with her arm around Lauren, who stared at her brother with the fear only a child can experience. "Oh, that's all right, hon," Suzanne said. "These things happen, no matter how careful we are. No one can watch a child every minute."

Paige stared at her stepmother in stunned disbelief. She'd expected Suzanne to express annoyance at Kenya for not keeping a closer eye on the kids, but her casual dismissal of any blame demonstrated a stark contrast to the way she'd treated Devon under similar circumstances.

She decided to point it out. "Suzanne, I think it's sweet of you to be so understanding of Kenya, but do you realize how differently you acted when Devon was watching the kids and the same type of thing happened?"

"It was an accident, Suzanne," Kenya repeated quickly, as if afraid her sister would have a sudden change of heart.

"I know that," Suzanne said coldly. She turned to Paige. "Paige, you're out of line. These two situations are completely different. And I don't want to hear anything else about it."

"Bradley, raise up," Paige said abruptly. "I'm going to go now, but I'll fix the pillows so you can put your head on them, all right?"

"Aren't you coming with me, Paige, when I get stitched up?" Bradley asked.

"No, but I'll see you when you get back home. Okay?"

"Okay."

"I'm leaving," Paige announced after settling Bradley's head at a comfortable angle. "See you later, Kenya." She cast a frosty stare on her stepmother and spoke with equal chill. "Good-bye, Suzanne."

"She's mad, Suzanne," Kenya remarked with wide-eyed concern after Paige left.

"So what. She's got a hell of a nerve, telling me about the way I behave. With any luck, she's angry enough to stay out of my house for a while." The wheels of Suzanne's mind were already turning. All she had to do was make sure she spoke to Brad before Paige did. She didn't want Paige trying to win sympathy, like she had that night their two families talked after Bradley almost drowned. Those crocodile tears might have softened everybody up, but they hadn't done anything for *her.*

Arlene appeared with a fresh towel. "I've got the other one soaking in cold water in the laundry room."

"Thanks, Mom." Suzanne knelt in front of Bradley and replaced the towel, dabbing at the fresh blood. "Now Bradley, I'm sorry you got hurt, but next time you'll have to listen to what Auntie Kenya tells you."

"I feel so bad," Kenya said. "I know how Bradley pretty much does what he wants to do. Paige and I should have gone out back where I could have kept a better eye on him."

"So the only reason you went inside was because Paige came over?" Suzanne asked, already thinking, *This is all Paige's fault.*

Kenya hesitated before answering. "No, I was in the house even before she rang the bell. I wanted to watch TV, and there was too much glare on the TV outside."

Paige went out the front door just as her father pulled up. "Hey," Brad said breathlessly as he hopped out of the Lexus. "Where're you off to? And how's Bradley?"

"He says his cut stings, and it's pretty ugly, but I'm sure he'll be okay. I'm leaving, Daddy. I'll be back later."

He frowned. Paige appeared upset. "Is something wrong?"

"Ask your wife," she said before breaking into a run.

Brad rushed inside. He found Suzanne hovering over a reclining Bradley, Arlene, Kenya, and Lauren sitting nearby. Lauren jumped up and ran to him, crying. "Daddy!"

He bent and picked her up. "I'm sure Bradley's all right, sweetheart. Don't worry, okay?" he said. When she nodded, he walked to the sofa where Bradley lay. "Here, let me have a look," he said to his son. He placed Lauren back on her feet and bent to lift the dishcloth from Bradley's forehead. "What are we going to do with you, man?" he said playfully. You're just getting all marked up."

"I fell."

"I know. We're going to have to bring you to the hospital and get you stitched up."

"Will it hurt, Daddy?"

"I already told him it won't," Suzanne said. "But do you think there'll be a scar?"

"You won't feel a thing, pal," Brad said to his son. "I think the worst of it is over. You just sit tight for a few minutes with Grandma and Aunt Kenya. I need to talk to Mommy for a minute." He gently recovered Bradley's wound, then gestured with his head for Suzanne to come with him.

"Lauren, are you coming with me to the hospital?" Bradley was asking as they retreated.

When they stood in the living room, on the other side of the kitchen, Brad turned to Suzanne. "What happened with Paige? I ran into her as she was leaving, and she seemed upset."

She sighed. "Oh, she got her nose out of joint because I pointed out to her that *I'm* Bradley's mother and that I'll determine who gets reprimanded, not her."

"Reprimanded for what?"

"Oh, she expected me to start hollering at Kenya because she was supposed to be watching Bradley when he fell."

"Well, why wasn't she? Where was she?"

"She was in the house with Paige." Suzanne wished she could suggest the incident had been Paige's fault. "There's nothing wrong with that. Bradley and Lauren were playing on our own property. It wasn't like they were by the pool."

"No, they were just by the river."

Her head jerked back at the sarcasm in his voice. Where had that come from? Surely he wasn't annoyed with her. *She* hadn't done anything wrong.

"I want to know exactly what was said," Brad said sternly.

"Well, naturally Kenya was upset that Bradley had hurt himself while she was baby-sitting. I told her that no one could watch a child every minute. Right away Paige jumps in and says I wasn't nearly as understanding when Bradley almost drowned, insinuating that I was showing favoritism because my sister was the one doing the baby-sitting. Like it was really the same thing," she said with a sneer. "I already told you what I said to that." She turned an indignant gaze on Brad. "Imagine her saying that to me! So she got annoyed, and then she left."

Brad's expression remained unyielding. "You were wrong, Suzanne."

"I was wrong! Oh, I get it," she said with a knowing nod. "You stick up for Paige just like you stick up for Lisa, take their side against me."

"I'm not against you, Suzanne. I don't think you realize the irony here. The two situations are a lot more similar than you realize. I shouldn't have to draw you a picture. You think about it for a while. Maybe after you spend a few minutes on it you'll realize you owe Paige an apology. And Devon as well."

Suzanne stood watching as he went toward their bedroom. His support for Paige and Lisa had gone too far. No way did she owe Paige an apology, and it stunned her to think he could believe that. This time she'd been so sure he would side with her, provided she gave him the true version of what transpired before Paige could make up things to make her look bad. Hot tears stung her eyes.

She walked slowly through the kitchen back to the family room.

"Oh Suzanne, I'm so sorry," Kenya gushed. "Was Brad very upset?"

"He was, but I ought to be used to it by now," she said bitterly. "If I'm on one side and his ex and his daughter are on the other, I know who he'll stand with."

"Well, you really can't blame him," Kenya said. "It's hard to argue when something bad happens to Bradley while Devon's watching him and she gets in trouble, and then something bad happens to him when I'm watching him and everything's okay."

Suzanne merely stared at her sister.

At the hospital, Suzanne chose to wait outside while Brad accompanied Bradley in the treatment area of the emergency room. They had left Lauren at home in the care of her grandmother and aunt.

Suzanne relished the time alone to think. Maybe her judgment *had* been a little slanted with regard to Bradley. Even Kenya had said it wasn't fair to treat her differently from the way she had Devon. Kenya also acknowledged that Bradley often did just as he pleased, regardless of what he had been told. Suzanne couldn't deny her son had a headstrong streak. She'd been embarrassed when Lisa witnessed events of Bradley disobeying her.

Then there was that other pool incident, the one at the old house. Back then Bradley again ignored her orders and had gone in the water even though she told him not to. Suzanne had been grateful that she saw him and ordered him out before anything bad happened, just as he was heading toward the deep end. Since then she'd tucked the unpleasant memory away in the recesses of her mind, but now it fought its way out and demanded she remember. One thing for certain. She'd have to start being a lot tougher on Bradley.

But Bradley's discipline could wait. She would have to swallow her pride and apologize to Paige, and she supposed to Devon, too. The thought made her feel a little ill. She wished she could substitute almost any other unpleasant deed for it, but of course she couldn't. Now that she'd forced herself to look upon her behavior honestly, she understood what Brad had meant. Paige was right. If only she'd kept her big mouth shut, or even called Kenya into another room under the pretense of reprimanding her, she wouldn't have to go to the Canfield house now with her tail between her legs.

They stopped to pick up pizza and wings on the way home. Suzanne felt too nervous to eat; her tummy was doing somersaults. Brad probably thought she was sulking, but she wanted to go next door and say what she had to say and get it over with. She'd tell him about the apology after the fact. "I'm going out for a minute," she announced.

"Suzanne, can you let Mom know we're eating?" Kenya asked.

"Where is she?"

"Outside somewhere messing with dirt and stuff, like she's always doing."

Suzanne found her mother on the side of the Canfield house, talking with Darrell's mother. "Hi, Mom. Hello, Missus Canfield."

After both women acknowledged her and her mother confirmed Bradley was all right, Suzanne said, "Mom, I just wanted you to know we brought home some take-out food, in case you were ready to eat."

"Thanks, dear," Arlene said. "I'll be in shortly. I'm just sharing some of my gardening tips with Esther."

"Your mother missed her calling, Suzanne," Esther said. "She should be running a greenhouse."

"She's very talented," Suzanne agreed. "We get more compliments about our landscaping, including requests for the business card of the person who does it." She smiled. "If you'll excuse me a moment, I need to go see Paige."

As she walked around to the front of the Canfield house, a spray of cold water suddenly saturated her shoulder. She quickly stepped out of the way, looking up just in time to see Lisa cover her mouth with her hand as her eyes widened.

"Suzanne, I'm so sorry," Lisa said. "I was trying to get *him*." Laughing, she aimed the hose at Darrell, who stood on the other side of the soapsud-covered Durango.

Darrell mopped his face with his T-shirt. "Great," he said. "I won't have to take a shower tonight." To Suzanne he said, "I hope we didn't get you too bad."

"Oh, that's all right. I'll change as soon as I get home. I was wondering if Paige was in."

If Lisa was surprised by her request to see Paige, she didn't show it. "Yes, she's inside. Go on in, the door's open," she said.

"Tell Brad I'll see him tomorrow at nine," Darrell said. At Suzanne's quizzical look he added, "We're playing golf with Michael Gillespie and Ben Prince from Villa Saint John. The losers buy the Bloody Marys."

"I'll do that." As Suzanne approached the front door, she marveled at Darrell's easy friendship with Brad. Didn't it bother him, as the second spouse, to be living so close to his wife's former husband, the father of her firstborn child?

She turned at the sound of Lisa squealing. Apparently Darrell had gotten control of the hose and turned it on her, for her entire side was soaked, both her T-shirt and her shorts. Suzanne chuckled as Lisa wrung the excess water out of her shirt.

The front door was ajar, as Lisa had said, but Suzanne felt uncomfortable merely walking in, so she rang the bell. Paige answered the door. Her smile of greeting soon transformed into a straight line, hostility pouring from her like water from the hose her mother had outside.

Suzanne took a deep breath, reminding herself this was a mere child. "Paige, I wanted to know if I could speak to you and Devon for a minute."

Curiosity now flared in Paige's dark eyes. "Sure. Come in."

Suzanne followed Paige to the family room, where Devon sat watching something on television. "Paige, you're missing it." Her eyes widened, obviously surprised to see Suzanne.

"Suzanne wanted to know if she could talk to us for a minute," Paige explained.

"Of course, if it's a bad time . . . if you're watching a movie, I can always come back later," Suzanne said.

"Oh no, that's all right," Devon said hastily, simultaneously reaching for the remote control and lowering the volume.

"Your timing is perfect. The boys are outside, so they won't bother us," Paige said brightly as she plopped onto a chair.

Suzanne preferred to stand. She clasped her hands in front of her and began to speak. "I came to apologize . . . to both of you," she began. The words stuck a little in her throat. "Paige, you were right about what you said earlier. I didn't want to accuse my sister of being inattentive to my children only because she's my sister. I had no problem accusing Devon because she's not a member of my family."

"I'm glad you understand how I felt, Suzanne," Paige said. "Thanks a lot."

Suzanne tried to smile. "When I stop to think about it, both situations really have to do with Bradley not doing as he was told. I'm going to have to do something about that."

"Is Bradley okay?" Devon asked.

It didn't surprise Suzanne that Devon knew about Bradley's fall. Paige had probably filled everyone in on what happened when she got home. Suzanne knew she'd never have any secrets as long as Paige lived next door. She resisted the urge to frown and forced herself to sound pleasant. Theirs would never be an ideal situation, but that wasn't why she was here. "He's going to be fine. The doctor stitched him up good as new. Right now he's enjoying being on the injured list and having everyone fuss over him."

"That's good news," Paige said. "I feel a lot better, both about Bradley and about what you just said."

"I feel a lot better too, Miss Suzanne," Devon added.

The tenseness in Suzanne's shoulders dissolved. The girls had accepted her apology so easily. For that she was grateful. They could have made it difficult for her, and she would have ended up leaving in a huff before she allowed herself to grovel. "I hope we can get past this," she said sincerely. "Devon, I'd be happy to have you sit with Bradley and Lauren anytime. And Paige, you know the door's always open. I promise you both I'll do my best to be fair in the future." She unfolded her hands. "Anyway, that's what I came to say. I'll go home now and see after Bradley."

Both Paige and Devon got up and walked with her to the door. "Thanks for coming, Miss Suzanne," Devon said.

"Devon, you don't have to call me 'Miss Suzanne.' Your sister has always called me just plain Suzanne, and I think you should, too. We'll just let your brothers use the 'Miss,' since they're so much younger than you."

"Okay, Suzanne," Devon said, giggling at the unfamiliar casualness.

They paused at the front door. "I'm really glad we cleared the air," Suzanne said. "I'll see you girls soon, okay?"

"Okay. Thanks for coming, Suzanne," Paige said.

Lisa and Darrell were nowhere to be seen. Since the Durango had been thoroughly rinsed, Suzanne assumed they had gone in to clean up. Just as well they weren't there. She really didn't feel like seeing them again anyway, the happy couple making a game out of washing their truck, while at her own house her husband had made it clear he was displeased with her behavior.

Her mother and Mrs. Canfield were gone as well, but she wasn't through with encountering members of the Canfield family. Cary and Courtney, bike riding in single file with some other neighborhood kids, stopped when they reached her. "Miss Suzanne, is Bradley coming outside?" one of them asked. They didn't look as much alike as they used to, or maybe she was just getting used to them, but she still didn't know which one was which.

"Not tonight, boys," she said. "Bradley had a little accident and hurt his head this afternoon, so he's taking it easy. But I'm sure he'll be outside tomorrow."

"Okay. See you later." They pedaled off to catch up with their friends.

Suzanne smiled after them, and it suddenly occurred to her that everyone in their two households had formed an alliance. Her mother and Darrell's mother, Brad and Darrell, Bradley and the Canfield twins . . . everyone but her and Lisa.

There were probably too many deep-rooted feelings for her and Lisa to ever be friends, but that didn't mean they had to hate each other. Just being cordial would make their status as neighbors so much more pleasant.

And best of all, it would strengthen her *own* marriage.

CHAPTER 41

All my skinfolk ain't my kinfolk.
—Zora Neale Hurston

"Let me open the door, Mom, please?"
Suzanne handed Bradley her keys. She must be getting old. These days when she turned off the car engine the kids were out before she had even unsnapped her seat belt. "Go ahead, unlock it. And don't spill that ice cream on the floor."

"I won't."

"I won't," Lauren echoed.

Suzanne picked up the large bag with the kids' new shoes and hit the button to automatically lock all the doors before slamming the driver's side door shut. Realizing she hadn't checked the day's mail, she walked toward the curb.

At that moment, Lisa steered her new Chrysler into her driveway. She got out and headed for her own mailbox. A queasy feeling instantly formed in Suzanne's gut. She hadn't seen much of Lisa since she went over there to apologize to Paige and Devon, and when she had, it'd been in passing. She felt good about those quick waves of hello she made when driving past, but a face-to-face encounter was something else. She fought the urge to turn around and run to the safety of her house. Hadn't she vowed to be cordial to Lisa? Hadn't Lisa been nice to her?

"Hi," Lisa said as she approached her mailbox, which was just a few feet from Suzanne's on the edge of their respective property lines. "I see we've got the same idea."

"The mailman was late today," Suzanne said shyly.

"I've been running errands all afternoon." Lisa chuckled. "Some way to spend my day off. If I'd gone to work I'd be getting ready to go home by now. There's always so much to do when the holidays get close."

They each fell silent as they perused the contents of their mail. "By the way," Lisa said, "will you and Brad still be in town on the twentieth of next month? I know your family spends Christmas in Vermont, but that's the date of our Christmas party and we'd love for you to come."

"Actually, we go to Maine. But we don't leave until the twenty-third. We'd love to come."

"Wonderful." Lisa turned, perhaps sensing movement near. Flo Hickman approached, swinging her arms vigorously at her sides. "Hello, Flo."

"Hi, Lisa, Suzanne."

Suzanne smiled. "Out for your walk?"

"Yes. We're getting into the best time of year to do this, the coolest months." Flo brushed her hair away from her eye in the gesture Suzanne knew so well. "You guys doing all right?"

"Fine. How's the new job going?"

"Busy, but I love it."

"Are you all ready for Thanksgiving?" Lisa asked.

"That's right, you're going to Boston, aren't you, Flo?" Suzanne said.

"Um . . . actually, this year we're staying home. I'll probably have to go in on Friday. My promotion has changed a lot of things. So much more responsibility. We did invite our families to come down and spend it with us, but they decided not to." Flo rubbed her palms together. "Well, if you'll excuse me, I'd better finish my walk so I can get home before my dinner catches fire."

"Oh, sure," Suzanne said as Lisa murmured agreement. "See you later."

"I'm so glad you and Brad can make the party," Lisa said to Suzanne as Flo moved on.

"We wouldn't miss it." Suzanne looked after Flo curiously.

"Something wrong?" Lisa asked.

"Uh . . . no, not really. I was just wondering about Flo. She seems so different lately."

"I like it. For once she didn't ask a million questions." Lisa drew in her breath. "Sorry. I shouldn't have said that. I know she's your friend."

"I'm not so sure. I never hear from her anymore, and whenever I call her she's too busy to talk." Suzanne took one last glance at Flo swinging her arms as she walked to the end of the cul-de-sac and then turned to Lisa. "She should consider herself lucky that their families turned them down. Brad's parents are coming to spend Thanksgiving weekend with us."

"I'm sure you'll enjoy them. Nothing should spoil your first holiday season in the new house. Besides, Mister and Missus Betancourt are nice people."

"I guess I can't complain, not after my family stayed with us for weeks." But Brad's parents had always given Suzanne the impression they preferred Lisa to her as a daughter-in-law. She felt the familiar resentment toward Lisa build, then bit her lower lip to stop it. It wasn't Lisa's fault Brad parents liked her so much. She owed it to both their families to keep the peace. Brad would be so proud of her. . . . If she kept a fair outlook, she'd never have to worry about him siding with Lisa ever again. "You and Darrell will have to come over and say hello to them," she said graciously as they began walking toward their homes.

"Thanks. We'll do that."

Suzanne looked up as her garage door rumbled in opening. Bradley came out, wheeling his bicycle. "Mom, can I go riding?"

"No, Bradley. It'll be dark soon."

Safely away from the Jaguar in the driveway, Bradley straddled his bike and pedaled toward the curb. "C'mon, Mom. Just once around the block. It's not gonna get dark *that* quick."

"Bradley Betancourt, you get back inside right now. I said no and I *mean* no," she said sternly.

Bradley stared at her, unaccustomed to this side of his mother.

Suzanne stared right back at him. "Don't make me tell you again," she said, her voice low and threatening.

Bradley promptly got off his bike, turned around, and walked it back inside.

"And make sure you close the garage door!" she called after him. Then she turned to Lisa, who had stopped where she stood to witness the scene. She wore a slight smile, Suzanne noted. She sighed. "Kids. What're you going to do with them?"

"Let them know who's boss, like you just did," Lisa said with a smile.

"I'd better get in. See you later, Lisa."

" 'Bye, Suzanne."

Flo, now on the return leg of her walk, watched with a mixture of envy and sadness as Suzanne and Lisa disappeared behind their respective front doors, into a world she now knew she'd never get to be part of. She'd heard what Lisa said to Suzanne as she continued her walk. She gleaned that Suzanne would be attending a party Lisa was hosting. It didn't surprise her that Lisa hadn't invited her and Ernie. The friendly, neighborly relationship between them had stumbled that first night at the Canfields' and never recovered.

What Flo *did* find surprising was the way Suzanne's intense dislike of Lisa had dissolved like an Alka-Seltzer tablet in water. Flo wondered what had happened to make the two of them so buddy-buddy.

She also knew Suzanne was probably wondering what had happened to their own girlfriend status. Flo saw no point in trying to continue with their friendship. Their lives were too different. Her financial situation wasn't a temporary setback, but one that would last for the rest of her working life. At an age where she should be enjoying the fruits of her labor, she found herself working more hours than ever and still struggling to pay the bills, and as she got older it would become more difficult to keep the pace. She knew sooner or later Suzanne would give up and stop calling, if she hadn't already. Flo didn't care. Now that her own life had gone down the tubes, she simply couldn't stomach Suzanne anymore. They had nothing in common now, not that they ever had.

Life truly wasn't fair. Why should she have to bust her ass every day while Suzanne had such an easy life? Suzanne served no useful purpose at all. She contributed absolutely nothing to society. She didn't even clean her own house. All she did was lounge around reading those silly romance novels, work out, and spend her husband's money when she wasn't complaining about Lisa living next door, or at least she had before she and Lisa became pals.

Flo massaged her wrists. All the keying she did was starting to affect her. The last thing she needed was a case of carpal tunnel syndrome. It surprised her that she had the energy to take a walk, but she'd al-

ready gained seven pounds from constantly sitting. She vowed to start
walking again at least three times a week.

Sometimes Flo wondered if her efforts were worth the results. Even
with two jobs, her net pay had pretty much stayed the same as it had
been because of the large sum deducted for health insurance benefits. It didn't make sense for Ernie to enroll in his new job's plan; the
premiums were higher, and the benefits not as good.

Their lives had changed so much from just a few short months ago.
In addition to the extra medical billing she did two nights a week,
Ernie had gotten a second job as a line cook at a restaurant. Between
their two schedules, they spent more time out than at home, and Gregory
had free reign of the house. God only knew what he and Kenya were
doing while she and Ernie were at their night jobs.

Flo spent weekends trying to get caught up on her housework and
handling their household bills, which took considerable time because
of the juggling required to match up payments with paydays. The
three-fifty a month they got from Sharif helped a lot. She just prayed
no one would find out that story about knowing his parents was pure
fabrication, that they hadn't known each other before he rented the
room from them.

She feared the whole house of cards she and Ernie had so carefully
constructed was about to fall down. The promotion she made up had
occurred months ago. How long could anyone believe she was so busy
because of new responsibilities that weren't new anymore? No, she had
too many problems to want to be bothered with Suzanne. She probably shouldn't even be walking here on Easy Street anymore. She didn't
belong here, and she didn't want to know the people who did.

Before she passed the two neighboring houses, she felt the puddles
form in her eyes, and as she finished walking past them, she had to
wipe her eyes to keep them from spilling over.

CHAPTER 42

All's well that ends well.
—William Shakespeare

Lisa looked on proudly as Courtney played the closing chords of "Christmastime Is Here," while Paige sang the tune popularized on a Peanuts holiday cartoon. She raised her hands in front of her face and applauded with gusto. Their other guests clapped as well.

Their holiday party and mini-concert had become a tradition in their family, with her and the children choosing a different carol every year to perform for their guests.

Everyone had pitched in to help decorate the eight-foot-tall Christmas tree, which stood tall and proud in a corner of the formal living room, just a few feet from the piano. Its green lights provided the only light other than the light above the keyboard and the crystal chandelier overhead, which had been set to dim.

Because of the limited seating in the area, most of the observers stood. Esther, Arlene Hall, and one of Esther's friends from St. Marys filled the sofa, while a woman who was due to deliver a baby in February sat in the chair. Darrell and the boys had provided folding chairs for Esther's other friends, all of whom were over sixty-five, who were present. The group had moved to this area specifically for the concert, the actual festivities taking place in the family room, where a burning log crackled in the fireplace and music from prerecorded tapes and CDs played, Christmas carols mixed in with everyday music.

Lisa closed the concert with a jazzy rendition of *What Child Is This?*

She rose from the piano bench and gestured for the kids to join her. They clasped hands and bowed to their appreciative audience. Darrell kissed them all, waved a hand their way and announced, "My family, y'all." Lisa felt she would burst with happiness. She could actually feel the love in the room. The air was thick with it.

For this intimate annual event, she and Darrell invited their closest friends, many of whom came from Georgia. They had also included their neighbors, who had invited them to their own earlier holiday celebrations. Because Kenya Hall asked if she could bring Gregory Hickman as her date, Lisa had even extended an invitation to his parents, Flo and Ernie.

The air buzzed with voices as Lisa and Darrell led the way back to the family room, passing the kitchen, where Suzanne and Brad's housekeeper Teresita busily arranged another batch of hors d'oeuvres. Lisa always encouraged their friends to bring their children along, saying it was a family affair. Most of the young people present went upstairs to the bonus room, where they would remain until the buffet was served.

Flo and Ernie brought up the rear in the move to the other room. "Look at all those gifts under the tree," Ernie said wistfully. "They're gonna have a great Christmas."

"They have a large family, Ernie." Flo tried to sound matter-of-fact, but all through the concert she couldn't stop staring at the beautifully wrapped packages of varying sizes, stacked six or seven deep under the tree in a horseshoe design around three sides. She thought about their own tree, which also had packages around it, but the bulk of them were empty. Ernie said he wanted anyone who came to the house to think they were exchanging a lot of gifts, even if the boxes contained nothing.

"I wish we could come back here after Christmas, after the gifts have been opened, so we could see what's in them," he said.

Flo wished the same thing, but she didn't dare hope for another invitation, not even to what she had learned was an annual function, unless Gregory happened to still be seeing Kenya a year from now. She had learned, if Ernie hadn't, that when it came to the Canfields and the Betancourts they'd always be on the outside looking in. "Yeah, well, I wouldn't plan on it if I were you."

"I don't believe it," Kim said to Lisa in the privacy of the kitchen, with only Teresita present. "I've been here nearly two hours, and not a single question out of Flo. I was sure she'd at least ask me if Teresita works here full time."

"Is this okay, Miss Lisa?" Teresita asked, holding up a tray of assorted hors d'oeuvres.

"Yes, that's fine," Lisa said.

After Teresita left, Kim mimicked her Spanish accent. "Mees Leesa, Mees Leesa." She giggled. "But the uniform's a nice touch."

"Oh, she wears it when she's cleaning for Suzanne, just maybe not a pink one. Gray, I think."

Kim raised an eyebrow. "Don't tell me Suzanne's invited you over for coffee."

"No, of course not. The only reason I know about Teresita's uniform is because I've seen her bringing out the trash. Suzanne and I won't ever sit down to have coffee, but at least we've learned to tolerate each other. I suspect Brad might have given her an ultimatum, not that her reasons for being so pleasant are any of my business."

"I guess I can't complain too much either. I haven't seen a lot of my undistinguished neighbors since Michael and I gave our party in July."

"I'm not surprised. If you'd said to me what you said to them I'd stay out of your way, too."

"Listen, I wrote on everyone's invitations that no kids were invited. I still can't believe the way George and Gail Morton showed up saying they couldn't get a baby-sitter. From the way Gail had those kids dressed to the nines, it was obvious she expected me to say it was all right." Kim giggled. "I'll never forget the looks on their faces when I said I was afraid it just wouldn't work out, that we were entertaining poolside and weren't prepared to have little kids running around. George actually said, 'You mean we can't come in?' "

"That really was a nervy thing of them to do," Lisa said. "I mean, they could have called first and asked if it was all right."

"I agree. Of course, I still would have said no, but that's not the point. So naturally when Larry and Sondra's boys managed to get in when my back was turned, I told them the kids would have to leave because it wasn't fair to the other guests. They looked just as insulted as George and Gail had. I know they all think I'm a big snob, but I've had it with them."

"I don't blame you, Kim."

"Even Flo's been low key lately. The only thing she's done to annoy me lately was hold up the mailman."

"Hold him up?" Lisa repeated.

"Yeah, last Saturday. I was waiting for my bonus check to be delivered, but the mailman got tied up at her place. Maybe he had a package or something. Anyway, his truck is sitting outside her house, and he's nowhere in sight. He musta been in there ten minutes." Kim grunted. "Of course, if I know Flo, she gave him a tour of her house."

"Now, Kim, be nice."

"All right, all right. She and Ernie don't bother me anymore. I think they're too busy trying to make money to worry about what Michael and I are doing."

"What do you mean?"

Kim shrugged. "Well, a couple of months ago Ernie was home all day for about four or five weeks. They told us he was working on some writing project for his job. I think he was unemployed."

"Are you sure you're just not being suspicious, Kim? It's entirely possible he could have been doing what they said. A lot of people work at home nowadays."

"I guess. But they're both gone a lot of the time. I think they're moonlighting. Of course, Flo claims she got a promotion at work and has to put in more hours."

"That makes sense."

"And," Kim continued, "on top of all that, now they've got some college kid staying with them. They say he's the son of their 'dear friends' from Fernandina, but I've been to several of their parties and I've never met anyone who lives in Fernandina. I'll bet he's just somebody they rented a room to for money."

Lisa laughed. "Kim, you should have been a detective."

"Maybe I'm wrong and it's all a coincidence. But something tells me Flo wouldn't tone down her curiosity without a damn good reason."

Kenya and Gregory stood in a quiet corner of the room, well away from the other guests. "You look great in that dress," he said admiringly, staring her up and down in her simple but formfitting red knit.

She glanced around to make sure no one stood within earshot before whispering, "I look even better out of it."

"I know you do. I wish my parents weren't going to be home so much until after New Year's."

"No bowling over the holidays, huh?"

"Both their leagues are taking time off." Just because he fucked Kenya every chance he got didn't mean she had to know about his parents' financial difficulties. He liked Kenya. He'd be crazy not to. She knew more about sex than any girl he'd gone out with, and she would pull down her drawers and spread her legs at a moment's notice, even if they only had ten minutes before his parents were expected home. Sharif knew what was going on behind the closed doors of Gregory's bedroom, but he'd agreed when Gregory asked him not to mention it to his parents. Sharif was an all right guy. The way he looked at Kenya suggested he'd like a piece of her if he could get it, but Gregory wasn't in the mood to share. If Sharif wanted some, he'd have to wait till next year after he graduated and went to the university in Gainesville. Then he wouldn't care, not after he'd moved on to greener pastures.

"That's too bad," Kenya said. "I wish I could be with you that way right now." She couldn't wait for this vacation to be over. She hated how everything shut down for the holidays. She liked going to school, not so much for the lessons as for being known to all the kids as Gregory Hickman's girlfriend. It had opened up doors for her.

But her feelings for Gregory ran deeper than a mere boost to her ego. She cared for him like she had for no other boy she'd ever known. Lots of times people married their high school sweethearts. It could happen to them, too. Maybe they'd be together forever. . . .

Brad put an arm around Suzanne. "Do you think Bradley is safe upstairs, or should I go check on him?"

"I told him to be careful. His skin is going to be all marked up if he keeps falling down. But all the kids are dressed up tonight, and I'm sure they've all been told by their parents not to roughhouse. Paige and Devon are up there supervising the little ones, along with the other teenagers." She caught sight of Flo at the same time Brad did.

"She hasn't had much to say, has she?" he said.

"No, she sure hasn't. I don't know what the problem is. I don't think I did anything to alienate her."

"I wouldn't worry about it if I were you. Personally, I don't think she was ever really your friend in the first place." He turned at the sound of Ernie speaking much louder than he needed to. "Lord knows her husband could stand a personality change, not that I think it'll ever happen."

Suzanne looked at the uncomfortable expressions on the faces of the couple Ernie was talking to and tried not to laugh aloud. "Probably not," she agreed.

Brad looked around at the festive surroundings. "It's kind of nice, having Christmas at home. We haven't done it since before we bought the cabin. Do you think we ought to stay here for the actual day next year and fly up to Maine on the twenty-sixth?"

"No. The kids love spending Christmas Day up there, especially if there's snow. And . . . it'll just be us, if you know what I mean."

He nodded. If they stayed in Jacksonville, her family would join them. That in itself would be fine, except he knew they'd want to come over Christmas Eve and spend the night. Then he'd play hell trying to get them out of the house so they could catch their plane the next day. He'd become resigned to the fact that his in-laws would never be far, even if they were no longer in the house. It wasn't all bad. At least Arlene kept their landscaping pretty, and Matthew showed signs of a real desire for improvement, working the midnight shift at one of the hospitals, supervising the busy lunch shift at the Subway, and in January he would begin pursuit of a degree at ITT Technical Institute. He'd get something out of life, unlike Derrick, who would probably spend the next thirty years wheeling patients in and out of surgery, and Kenya, who just wanted to snag a well-off husband. Brad wondered if Gregory Hickman had noticed the stars in her eyes. His money said Gregory would forget about her the moment he went off to college.

Suzanne was right, he thought. Best to continue what they'd been doing all along, fly up to New England a few days before the holiday in order to buy and decorate their tree. "I was looking at all the decorations and got carried away, I guess," he said. Other than lighting on the outside of their house and the palm trees on the front lawn, they reserved holiday decorating for the vacation house.

She linked her arm through his affectionately. "I know our place looks kind of barren and cold compared to this cozy setting, but two days from now you can get carried away all you want. Just picture all of us taking a carriage ride through town, sipping hot cider with cinnamon sticks."

He closed his eyes for a few seconds and breathed deeply. "I can almost taste it. Funny how those little details make all the difference."

He looked into his glass cup. "Like nutmeg in eggnog. It doesn't taste the same without it."

"Here, give me your cup. I'll get some from the kitchen. I'm sure Teresita will know where it is."

Suzanne found her housekeeper in the Canfields' kitchen, and Lisa as well. "Can I get some more nutmeg for Brad's eggnog?"

"Of course, Miss Suzanne," Teresita replied. She offered Suzanne the shaker, and Suzanne sprinkled a liberal dose in the glass.

"I meant to put the shaker by the punch bowl in case anyone wanted extra," Lisa remarked.

"I'll do it, Miss Lisa," Teresita said. "Then I'll finish setting up the buffet."

"She's fabulous," Lisa said when she had left. "No wonder you sing her praises."

"I told you," Suzanne said with a smile.

"She's got everything under control. I guess I'd better get back out to the guests." Leaving the kitchen, they fell into step together, and Lisa said, "I meant to tell you, Suzanne, that's a fabulous outfit you're wearing."

"Oh, thank you." Suzanne fingered her black velvet jacket with red satin cuffs. "Our daughter picked it out."

The insinuation of them sharing Paige as a daughter startled Lisa, but she quickly recovered. After all, this was no different from her and Paula sharing motherhood of Devon, but this time she was the natural mother doing the sharing, not a stepmother who'd accepted her husband's child as her own. It made a huge difference. Even though Lisa felt reasonably certain that Suzanne was merely trying to be polite rather than having any real interest in claiming Paige as her own, she wondered if Paula found the idea of sharing Devon with her as distasteful as she did about sharing Paige with Suzanne.

A man Lisa recognized as the date of one of her single friends approached them. "I've been meaning to ask if you two are related."

Lisa and Suzanne looked at each other and laughed. "Technically, I suppose we are," Suzanne said.

"You know how some people are related by marriage?" Lisa said to her guest. When he nodded she said, "Well, this lady and I are related by divorce."

"We've been married to the same man," Suzanne explained to the bewildered man, who nodded in embarrassment. She looked up to see Brad beaming at her from across the room. He probably never expected to see her and Lisa laughing together. "Don't be embarrassed," she said to the man, patting the back of his hand. "It doesn't bother us, so don't let it bother you." Then she rushed across the room to join her waiting husband.

Lisa, too, moved on. Darrell came to meet her, his arms outstretched. "There you are. Everyone's been looking for you."

She happily went into his embrace. "This is the best party we've had yet," he said after kissing her lips lightly.

"I think so, too." She'd never felt so blessed. Their friends were happy, their family was well, Darrell had received a generous year-end bonus, and they were celebrating their first Christmas in the new house, along with the newest addition to their family: the twins' new Jack Russell terrier, Timmy, who had been a gift for their ninth birthday just two days before. Best of all, she and Suzanne had learned to do what Darrell and Brad had done all along: make the most of living next door to each other. Lisa would never envy Suzanne again. She didn't need to.

She had everything she wanted out of life.

She and Darrell slept, locked in a loving embrace, when they were awakened by the sound of the ringing doorbell. They looked at each other in puzzlement, instinctively knowing it was early morning. Lisa turned to look at the bedside clock. "It's seven A.M. Who could be ringing our bell so early on a Sunday morning?"

"I can't imagine, but I'll go see."

"I'm going with you."

He pulled on a T-shirt over his bare chest, and she reached for the matching wrapper to her nightgown. The bell rang again before they reached it, increasing Lisa's curiosity.

Darrell, wearing drawstring plaid flannel pants, peeked through the sheer panels that covered the narrow paned windows flanking the front door. "My God, it's Paula!" He quickly opened the door.

Paula stood there, looking like she hadn't slept in a week. Lisa didn't believe she'd ever seen Darrell's ex without makeup.

"My husband is divorcing me," Paula announced tonelessly. "I took emergency leave from my job, got in the car and just started driving. I drove eight hours before I even knew where I was headed."

"Paula, for God's sake, come in the house," Darrell said.

She crossed the threshold. "I drove all night," she said, so softly that Lisa had to strain to hear her. "Once I realized I was headed here I kept saying I should call ahead, but I kept putting it off. I guess I was afraid." She looked at Darrell first, then at Lisa. "I decided I need a fresh start, someplace to begin again. Nothing seemed better than where Devon is. I need to spend the rest of my life trying to make up for the awful way I treated her. I hope you guys will let me stay here with you for a few weeks until I get a place."

"I think the first thing you ought to do is go to sleep," Darrell said. "We can talk about the rest later."

"Come on, Paula," Lisa said. "You can sleep on the pull-out in the bonus room. Do you think you can make it up the stairs?"

"Sure."

Darrell brought Paula upstairs. Lisa stopped to get linens from the closet. It only took a minute, but that was long enough for Paula to stretch out across the sofa and fall asleep.

Darrell touched a finger to his lips. "Don't wake her," he said. "I've got a feeling she'll be knocked out for a long time. Let's go back to bed."

He fell asleep right away, but Lisa felt numb. How could this be? Had she actually just spent six months going at it with Suzanne, only to now be faced with Darrell's ex staying with them for a few weeks and then moving nearby?

She yawned, sleep overtaking her at last. Darrell, facing her, shifted and placed a hand on the curve of her hip. She slipped an arm beneath his armpit, her hand resting on his upper back. She closed her eyes, reminding herself how just hours ago she noted that she had everything she wanted. That hadn't changed, despite Paula's unexpected appearance. Paula would merely be another challenge to rise to. This time there'd be no catty remarks, no shouting matches, and no competition over Devon's affections. Any head butting would be strictly between Paula and Darrell, or perhaps between Paula and Ma Canfield. *She* was butting out.

Lisa's eyelids fluttered shut. Paula's stay with them would only be temporary, but she'd be part of their family forever, just like Suzanne and Brad next door. Family didn't mean what it used to.

Life wasn't easy, she thought as she drifted back to sleep in her husband's arms. But the rewards could be magnificent.

THE PEOPLE NEXT DOOR

BETTYE GRIFFIN

ABOUT THIS GUIDE

The suggested questions are intended to enhance
your group's reading of this book.

DISCUSSION QUESTIONS

1. Who was your favorite character in this story? Your least favorite? Why?

2. Do you think that Lisa and Brad's marital problems could have been resolved without divorce? Why?

3. Brad feels that he and Lisa would not have divorced if her career hadn't allowed her to support herself. He likes the fact that Suzanne is totally dependent upon him financially. What are your feelings about this?

4. Suzanne obviously treated Paige like the proverbial stepchild. But did Lisa make any differentiation between Paige, the child she gave birth to, and Devon, her stepdaughter?

5. Did Suzanne's strong dislike of Lisa seem rational to you? Why or why not?

6. Suzanne wished Paige didn't exist, that Brad's only children were the two she gave birth to. What do you suppose makes some second wives feel this way?

7. Darrell and Brad dealt with their unusual domestic situation rather well. Do you feel this is feasible? Do you blame Lisa for feeling uncomfortable with having her former husband next door?

8. Darrell was angered by what he perceived as Lisa's envy of Suzanne. Do you agree this existed?

9. Did you notice any similarities in the personalities of Lisa and Suzanne? If so, what were they?

10. Brad found the behavior of his in-laws to be occasionally embarrassing. Can you relate to this? Do you feel these feelings are common within families?

11. Ernie had a pressing need to know all about his neighbors' personal business. Have you ever met anyone like this? Did you regard them as harmless, dismiss them as pathetic, or did their questions anger you?

12. Lisa tried to get Brad to postpone buying a car for Paige until she and Darrell could get Devon a vehicle as well. Darrell was annoyed when he found out. Do you think she handled the situation well? If not, what would you recommend she should have done?

13. Paula's husband Andre was clearly concerned with what others thought about her age and fertility. While most people want to give favorable impressions, do you think Andre went too far? Where do you draw the line?

14. Darrell's mother, Esther, remarked how difficult it was to watch her son enter a marriage she felt certain would fail. Do you feel it's a parent's duty to advise their adult child that they feel he or she is making a mistake, or should the parent keep quiet?

15. Flo made desperate efforts to prove that she and Ernie could compete with anyone. Do you feel that the "Keepin' up with the Joneses" syndrome has become more prevalent with the rise of the African-American middle class?

16. Do you feel that divorce severs the extended family relationship, or does it continue? Under all circumstances? What are the exceptions?

17. Would you recommend this novel to your friends? Why or why not?